A SACRIFICE OF LIGHT

A PRACTICAL GUIDE TO SORCERY

AZALEA ELLIS

To Jared.
Your body was made of earth,
But your soul
Of stars.

CONTENTS

JOIN THE INNER CIRCLE**

Become part of the Inner Circle.
Instantly receive a free excerpt from Siobhan's illustrated grimoire.

https://www.azaleaellis.com/newsletter

I will send you new release updates, exclusive content like pre-release or deleted scenes, as well as news about giveaways or contests I'm doing (signed paperbacks, posters, etc.) and other cool stuff I think you might enjoy. Sometimes I tell weird stories about my life.

Plus, you get discounts on all products sold through my online shop, many of which you can't get on other retailers.

Support me on Patreon

https://www.patreon.com/azaleaellis

Read along chapter by chapter as I write the next book in the series, with early access chapters not available elsewhere, plus exclusive short stories/bonus chapters, and other goodies like various illustrated excerpts from Siobhan's grimoire.

NOTE TO READERS

The world-building for this story is extensive and can be quite complicated. If you find yourself forgetting terminology or wanting a little more detail about a term, the end of this book holds a Glossary of Magical Terms.

Thank you for reading!

Azalea

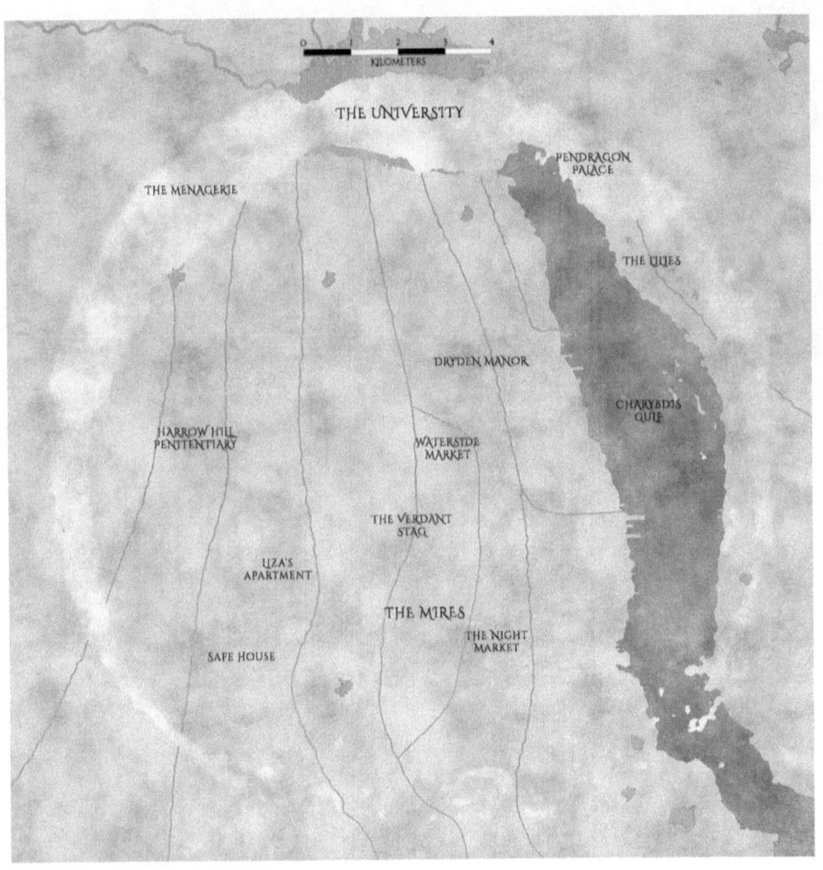

KILOMETERS
THE UNIVERSITY
PENDRAGON PALACE
THE MENAGERIE
THE LILIES
DRYDEN MANOR
CHARYBDIS GULF
HARROW HILL PENITENTIARY
WATERSIDE MARKET
THE VERDANT STAG
LIZA'S APARTMENT
THE MIRES
SAFE HOUSE
THE NIGHT MARKET

A PRACTICAL GUIDE TO SORCERY
RECAP

If you have not read the first two books in the Practical Guide to Sorcery series, spoilers lie ahead.

Previously, in *A Conjuring of Ravens*:

Siobhan Naught unwittingly becomes a wanted criminal when her father steals a mysterious book during their visit to the Thaumaturgic University. Her hopes of becoming a student dashed, she runs from the coppers with the book. Later, in danger from being caught by their ambush, she meets Oliver Dryden, who tries to help her escape.

When the coppers corner them, she accidentally activates a transformation amulet that had been hidden in the stolen book, turning herself into a young man who looks nothing like her original form. With this new body, she deceives the coppers and escapes arrest. To have a chance at entering the University under a new identity, she takes a huge loan—one thousand gold—from Oliver and Katerin at the Verdant Stag, the criminal organization they run.

Oliver helps her create a new identity for herself as Sebastien Siverling, but she makes a bad first impression on Damien Westbay and his group of Crown Family friends upon their first meeting.

When Siobhan learns the coppers caught her father Ennis, she and Oliver enlist the help of local illegal thaumaturge Liza, who helps Siobhan contact Ennis with a spelled raven messenger. To Siobhan's disappointment, Ennis has tried to sell her—and the stolen book—to the Gervin Family in marriage, in exchange for benefits for himself.

Much disillusioned, Siobhan studies for the University entrance exam and works for the Verdant Stag, who actually seem to serve and help the people within their community. When young Theo, Katerin's nephew, injures himself, Siobhan unthinkingly uses some harmless blood magic learned from her grandfather to heal the boy, earning both Katerin and Oliver's ire for the reckless use of illegal magic that could get her executed, and them implicated by association.

As Sebastien Siverling, she takes the University entrance exam, but her results are poorer than she hoped, and the panel of professors who administer the verbal portion of the exam plan to deny her entrance. In a fit of rage, she refuses to be dismissed, casting a hastily prepared spell to prove that she has the only thing that matters to a potential sorcerer—a strong Will.

Professor Thaddeus Lacer, a famous free-caster and Siobhan's childhood hero, takes an interest in her and overrides the panel of other professors, forcibly admitting Sebastien Siverling under special circumstances.

Sebastien falls into her University classes with glee, learning with feverish enthusiasm. She keeps to herself except for a budding new friendship with Anastasia Gervin, a Crown Family heiress, and Damien Westbay, who remembers their first meeting and finds Sebastien abrasive, nurturing the pseudo-rivalry between them. One of their student liaisons, Newton Moore, also extends an olive branch of friendship, believing her to—secretly—be a poor student just like him.

When she is not studying, Sebastien brews alchemical concoctions for the Verdant Stag to pay back the debt she owes them.

Oliver makes moves to expand the power of the Verdant Stags, but things backfire when the Morrows, a rival gang, attack one of his warehouses with the help of a mysterious sorceress. Oliver sets off Sebastien's alarms, waking her in the middle of the night to give emergency aid to his people.

Returning to her female form, Siobhan uses the minor spell exercises she's been practicing for Professor Lacer to sling balls of shattered glass at the Morrows. When the fighting is over, she tries to help the Verdant Stag warehouse workers, some of whom have been severely injured. Unable to do much, she patches up what she can before the coppers arrive.

Trying to give the others a better chance to escape, Siobhan uses a harmless esoteric spell that controls her shadow, molding it into a frightening creature of tattered darkness with a huge raven's beak. The coppers are successfully frightened, but one of them shoots a grasping spell at Siobhan, tripping her and cutting her hand.

She and Oliver escape to a safe house owned by one of Oliver's subjects, but the coppers found some of her blood left behind at the scene and use it to cast scrying magic on her. Siobhan's warding medallion, given by her grandfather, holds off the scrying attempt—at the cost of Siobhan's Conduit—and they go to Liza for a more permanent solution.

Liza creates a divination-diverting ward, anchored in five disks that she inserts underneath Siobhan's skin. The ward uses her blood for power, and can activate at low efficiency on its own or be further empowered by Siobhan's conscious efforts.

Thaddeus is called to the scene of the crime to consult on the investigation at Titus Westbay's request. Given the available evidence and witness accounts, they come to some erroneous conclusions. Siobhan Naught—codename Raven Queen—is a free-caster with some unknown, nefarious purpose that involves curses and blood magic.

She fascinates Thaddeus.

Siobhan, now without a Conduit, contacts Ennis in jail again, hoping to retrieve her mother's Conduit from him, but learns that he gave it to the Gervin Family as a bond for his word in the marriage agreement he gave on her behalf. Enraged and desperate, she spends most of her remaining funds to buy a dinky, overpriced replacement Conduit, then breaks down in tears.

But she isn't the same person who came to Gilbratha with Ennis those months ago. She's no longer under his—or anyone else's—control. She takes ownership of her life and her choices, pulls herself back together, and returns to the University.

In *A Binding of Blood*:

Sebastien does her best to keep her Will-strain concealed, but she remains concerned about future attacks from the Morrows. To better prepare, she experiments with ink-and-paper spell arrays with some success.

One day, while practicing slicing spells, Damien distracts her, causing her to accidentally injure him. She uses her flesh-mirroring spell to heal him, concealing the mechanics and the fact that it is technically blood magic. The effort re-strains her already fragile Will.

Feeling guilty and impressed, Damien resolves to befriend her.

Sebastien then begins to develop a sleep-proxy spell that will allow her to avoid her nightmares, as another sleeps on her behalf.

Professor Lacer sets up an in-class tournament for the sphere-spinning spell and becomes dissatisfied with her sandbagging against Damien, believing she does so to ingratiate herself with a powerful peer. Sebastien insists neither of them tell Professor Lacer the truth.

When the rogue magic sirens go off, the frightened students shelter in the library, and Sebastien discusses named Aberrants with Damien, asserting that they are more dangerous and less well-contained by the Red Guard than it might seem.

As classes continue, delving deeper into the details of both transmutation and transmogrification, Sebastien researches divination in the hopes of stealing or destroying the blood sample the coppers have been using to scry for her. When she manages to take advantage of a scrying attempt to trace her blood back to Eagle Tower on University grounds and only a short distance away, Damien stubbornly follows her.

Damien believes Sebastien is going on an "adventure," and is surprised and intrigued to learn he is spying on an attempt to find the Raven Queen, his imagination leading him to some dramatic conclusions.

Their student liaison, Tanya Canelo, interrupts the scrying attempt with an explosion just as Sebastien is becoming concerned. After talking about the situation with Oliver, Sebastien inducts Damien into a fake secret organization and together they hire their other student liaison, Newton, to help them keep tabs on Tanya.

While contemplating the foiled attempt on the Raven Queen, Thaddeus has an epiphany: When Sebastien refused to cast to her full ability, she had Will-strain. He interrogates Damien, who hints that Sebastien needs a better Conduit. Thaddeus wakes Sebastien in the middle of the night to lend her a Conduit and threaten her against similar recklessness.

After putting a tracker in Tanya's boot, Siobhan goes to a meeting with Lord Lynwood, leader of the Nightmare Pack gang, whom Oliver allied with. Lynwood and his prognos sister Gera give Siobhan a tribute of a black star sapphire, and request she help Millennium, Gera's cambion child who cannot sleep. As this happens to be Siobhan's area of expertise, she develops a spell to help the boy, leaving the Nightmare Pack leaders both fearful and in awe of her.

Later, following Tanya's suspicious activity, Siobhan discovers a secret organization of thaumaturges and joins. Her divination-diverting ward activates for the entrance interview, leaving the administrators convinced that she is the Raven Queen and frightened by her abilities.

Together with the Nightmare Pack, Oliver is planning an attack on the Morrows, who have become more aggressive toward people in the Verdant Stag's territory. He hires Siobhan as a healer's assistant for this.

In the meantime, Sebastien competes in the Practical Casting tournament and performs well, but sees the first classmate dead from Will-strain.

She knows they will not be the last.

The day of the battle arrives, and as Siobhan helps to heal the injured enforcers and civilians, Oliver attacks the Morrows' main warehouse and kills Lord Morrow, only to discover a storage room filled with beast cores and magical supplies all meant for the University.

Ana rushes home to comfort her little sister Natalia, who is being badly bullied by her adult cousin and uncles, as they hope to discredit Ana and her sister in their father's eyes, so that neither can become the Fourth Crown Family's heir.

Newton reveals that some of his family members were injured in the fighting and their house was lost. Desperate for coin to continue studying at the University, he accompanies Tanya to one of the secret meetings.

Siobhan is trailing them, keeping tabs on them with the tracker in Tanya's boot. Paranoid, Tanya realizes they are being followed and decides to attack.

Despite Newton's fear, the three of them are in a stand-off, but Tanya calls for backup from what few Morrows were not killed or captured in the earlier battle. When the Morrows come, they decide to capture all three of them, despite Tanya's protests, hoping to receive a ransom for them.

But when one of the Morrows sees Siobhan's face and recognizes her as the Raven Queen, fear causes them all to attack. In the confusion, Siobhan casts her shadow-familiar spell to draw attention and spell-fire away from herself.

Newton loses control of the spell he was casting and experiences a break event, turning into a string-based Aberrant. When the strings touch a human being, they unravel them alive.

Together with Tanya and the surviving Morrows, Siobhan works out how to pass somewhat safely through the strings and helps move them to safety.

But her bag is still with the Aberrant, and she decides to go back for it, as it could be used to find her, and she does not want to give up her place at the University to flee the law again. She manages to retrieve her bag and return to Sebastien's form, but the Red Guard has arrived and, when they notice strange divination readings, knock her unconscious.

Professor Lacer arrives to monitor her questioning and they are quickly joined by Gera, who misleads the investigation. As Professor Lacer takes Sebastien, cleared of suspicion, back to the University, she tells him her suspicions of Tanya and some of the other University faculty.

Not knowing Sebastien's fear of sleep, he then knocks her unconscious.

A Sacrifice of Light begins immediately after these events.

TRANSFER PAPERWORK

BENEATH HUNDREDS OF METERS OF WHITE STONE, IN A SMALL room carved into the most secret of places and illuminated only by light crystals, stood four people. To the left side of the doorway, a human woman sidled closer to her male companion. On the right, their boots still muddy, waited two men, one with ginger-orange hair and another with a pair of furry tails. All four wore the red shield symbol of their order and held a clipboard, the paperwork already filled out and reviewed.

Atop a wheeled dolly in front of the quartet sat two large rectangular iron cases. They were coffin-like, the source of an unnamed dread.

The woman cleared her throat. "These are the ones you're here for," she said unnecessarily, breaking the ominous silence.

The ginger-haired man looked the cases over, humming thoughtfully. "Two in such a short period. It must have been quite an eventful time for you, Agent Fike."

The woman sighed. "Well, you know how it is in a big city, Selby."

Her companion placed his fists on his hips and thrust his chest out. "Some sorceress calling herself the Raven Queen has been going around making trouble. I still think we need to do something about her." His voice was loud, echoing off the smooth walls of the small room. He didn't seem to notice his mistake until the others winced and turned toward one of the iron cases. Face paling, he took a large step back and eyed it warily.

When nothing happened, the twin-tailed man asked, "Blood magic?" His soft voice carried a faint accent that hinted at faraway lands.

The loud man nodded, then shook his head. "Well, yes, but nothing egregious. No slaughter rituals. No murders at all, actually. It's the strangeness of it, the rumors, the whispers."

"Nightmare-type?" the red-headed Agent Selby asked.

Agent Fike raised a hand to stop the loud one's response, giving him a long-suffering look. "No. Agent Berg here is just a little too susceptible to rumors. She's a flashy free-casting sorcerer who likes to play games of cat-and-mouse, and a fantastical, romantic figure to the commoners. The stories have been getting wild." Fike turned to Agent Berg, crossing her arms. "Not every frightening incident in the night is caused by an Aberrant."

Agent Berg frowned down at her. "Letting a potential threat go unchecked because of negligence could lead to unnecessary deaths, or even more Aberrants. We should be investigating and suppressing every danger to the future world, as we vowed."

Agent Selby let out a single sharp laugh, raising an eyebrow as he shared a look with his fluffy-tailed companion. "A bit of a fresh-oathed newbie, huh?"

Agent Berg's frown grew darker, but Selby waved a hand before he could retort. "Look, kid, that's a noble idea, but there aren't enough of us to go patrolling around every dark alley and responding to every peasant's report of evil creatures curdling their cow's milk in the teat. We have processes in place to catch the actual threats. Even if you only focus on those, they will be more than sufficient to keep you busy. And with that said, let's make this quick. Agent Marcurio and I have to get back to our base and then to a little village outside Paneth in less than a week."

"You can't tell me she didn't have something to do with that one," Agent Berg muttered, gesturing to the iron case they'd been so wary of earlier.

Fike rolled her eyes but didn't deign to respond aloud.

Agent Selby stepped up to the more benign case, flipping through the paperwork on his clipboard. "Scourge-type with a Nightmare-type sub effect?" He shook his head, muttering, "I don't know why we bother with that old classification system. It's too vague to be useful." Louder, he added, "I heard there were multiple requests for it."

Agent Berg shuddered. "To be honest, it disturbs me. Unnatural, for one of them to act like that. I'm looking forward to having it gone."

Agent Marcurio's lips twisted in a wry smile, his tails undulating in the air like fluffy snakes. "Its strangeness makes it all the more interesting, I'm sure."

Berg shuffled and looked away.

Selby reached out to touch the second case, then snatched his hand back, rubbing his fingertips together with morbid fascination. "This is the new one, the Blight-type?"

Safely tucked into the corner of the room, Agent Berg grinned, forgetting his earlier attempt at volume control as he boasted, "I handled the aftercare myself."

Agent Fike raised an unimpressed eyebrow. "His first time."

The other three snickered, but quickly sobered. "I heard your Captain—Goldfisch, was it?—applied to keep the Blight-type despite it being against policy," Selby said. "Too risky to keep them locally. Your base can requisition something similar and less likely to be recognized from elsewhere." He took the handle of the dolly and maneuvered it out of the room. As he pushed the two heavy iron cases down the hallway, the other three followed behind.

Agent Marcurio's eyebrows slowly rose higher until, after a couple of seconds, he could no longer restrain himself. "Captain Goldfisch? Is that really his name?" he asked, his tone thick with amusement.

"Don't joke about that in his presence if you want to live," Agent Fike warned.

"And don't mention anything about us being lucky to have Thaddeus Lacer stationed in the city, either," Agent Berg piped up, his voice echoing down the hallway with obvious resentment.

"Thaddeus Lacer?" Marcurio asked. "Is he here? Could I meet him?"

Agent Fike lifted a hand to curb the man's sudden enthusiasm. "He's not here. He's assigned to the Thaumaturgic University…and not particularly happy with our team at the moment. I wouldn't advise trying to get an autograph or anything during your visit. Even at the best of times, he can be disagreeable."

Berg let out a besotted sigh. "I know, he's brilliant."

Still pushing the dolly, Agent Selby sent Berg an incredulous look over his shoulder. "Is there enmity between Goldfisch and Lacer?" he asked, looking to Fike.

Marcurio also focused on her with avid interest, his fluffy tails swishing back and forth eagerly.

She shrugged. "They have a history, I guess. I'm not sure of the details, but the captain openly dislikes him. He's mentioned Lacer caring more about amassing knowledge than the methods he takes to obtain it. Then he likes to segue into a long denunciation of former Red Guard members who forgot or misinterpreted their oaths, and the disasters they caused in their pursuit of secrets and power better left alone."

Agent Berg's mouth drooped. "He goes on and *on*. One time I pretended to have diarrhea just so I could hide out in the bathroom to get away from him."

Agent Marcurio's tails wilted. "Ah. Goldfisch is one of *those*, huh?" He shared a commiserating glance with Selby.

Berg clapped Marcurio on the shoulder hard enough to make the man wince. "He is. But that's not the reason Special Agent Lacer is upset with our team at the moment. No, that's all Agent *Vernor's* fault. You see, Thaddeus Lacer has finally taken an apprentice."

"Really? But I heard he refused even the High Crown's heir a few years back! Who did he choose?"

Berg sighed wistfully, then began to rhapsodize. "I heard the boy has silver hair and looks like a little lordling. Supposedly, he's not even a noble, but..." Berg basked in the rapt attention of the visiting agents as he ran through his limited knowledge about the apprentice and moved on to the various fantastical stories he'd collected about Thaddeus Lacer's time at the University. Notably, how the irritable professor had almost stolen the powerful familiar of a visiting witch. Obviously, the creature found Lacer more appealing than its contracted master.

The agents lost their initial unease as they listened, the two iron cases all but forgotten as they loaded them into reinforced wagons to be transported away.

Confined within the first, which was as bright as daylight on the inside, huddled a twisted, ugly form. Its whimpers and hoarse, broken sobs were inaudible through the thick metal.

The being within the other case had been pruned like an overgrown bush or tenacious weed so that it would fit inside the container. Its iron coffin had been meticulously crafted and enchanted for better containment, so that not even a hair-thin seam remained. The thing inside still needed to breathe, so they had given it an air refreshing artifact, but that was all. The iron hummed softly, almost imperceptibly.

1

ON THE NATURE OF SHADOWS

Thaddeus
Month 1, Day 21, Thursday 7:30 a.m.

Thaddeus made his way through Harrow Hill Penitentiary's cafeteria, a squat, dark room that carried over the feeling of confinement from its cells. He took a small breakfast plate and coffee, adding a few drops of his own specially formulated wakefulness tincture into the liquid. He drank it black. Any added cream would curdle, and nothing could mask the taste.

Thaddeus grimaced as he gulped down the eye-watering liquid. He hated the combination of sludge in his mouth and the deep, dark smell that would rise from his stomach afterward, so that he could still half-taste it. His tincture was not as long-term a solution as Siverling's sleep offloading spell, but Thaddeus had no desire to give up his rest forever, even in exchange for gaining more productive hours. Studies had been done; powerful thaumaturges who structured rest into their lifestyle and indulged their mortal desires were much more likely to maintain their sanity. Work-life balance and hobbies, so to speak. Thaddeus's work was his life, and he had few hobbies that did not involve magic in some way. Thus, sleep remained one of his few indulgences. Besides, he had spent too many years going without it for long stretches at a time.

The thought of his provisional apprentice brought to mind the boy's foolishness. Young Siverling had tried to be secretive, but Thaddeus suspected the boy had been snooping into dangerous secrets...and perhaps hiding a few embarrassing ones of his own.

The clothes Siverling had been wearing the night of the latest Aberrant incident, in addition to those stuffed hastily into his bag, were evidence enough. The boy may indeed have been at the Silk Door, but he had been in a liaison with someone wearing men's clothing, while Siverling had worn a dress.

The boy must have needed to leave in quite a hurry when Newton Moore set off the alarm on that clever little linked bracelet, and ended up borrowing his paramour's clothing to do so. Siverling's normal clothes were of much higher quality than what he'd been wearing, and there was no other reason for a dress to be stuffed so thoughtlessly in his bag. If his paramour had been wearing the dress, he would have left it for her. It made the boy's obliviousness to—or perhaps thorough disinterest in—the girls who flirted with him around the University take on new meaning.

Thaddeus remained deeply disinterested in his apprentice's sex life or specific proclivities, but if the boy wanted to keep his activities a secret, he would really need to learn to be more discreet. Siverling was brazen in many ways, but not yet bold enough to do as he wished without fear of the whispers.

Not like the Raven Queen.

Both Morrows had refused to speak of her at first, not with complete silence like Canelo, but with a strange combination of belligerence toward the coppers and fear of the Raven Queen. However, their reticence eventually crumbled under pressure. As soon as they were cleared to move on from the quarantine zone, they had gone into separate interrogation cells at Harrow Hill. When the standard intimidation tactics and attempts to sow distrust failed, they resorted to mild torture—nothing that would leave them looking too pitiful in front of a potential audience—and that did the trick. Unfortunately, Harrow Hill employed no professional information extractors, so it took longer than Thaddeus would have liked for the coppers to break the two, and he had to wonder about the quality of the resulting statements. Pain was one of the less effective ways of extracting coherent, truthful information, after all.

The mysterious woman had made enough of an impact for them to endure through the pain where many would have broken. The young one had even started blubbering aloud, praying for her to save him, and then, when he could hold out no longer, for her to forgive him.

It was fascinating.

Investigator Kuchen stepped into the cafeteria, making a beeline for Thaddeus. If Kuchen and Titus were back from the temporary quarantine zone, which would take days or even weeks for the Red Guard to clear, it likely meant that Tanya Canelo would be arriving soon for questioning.

Kuchen confirmed as much, and Thaddeus rose from the table to follow.

Once in the relative privacy of the hallway, Kuchen announced, "I have been thinking about the Raven Queen's shadow companion."

Thaddeus remained silent, but Kuchen required no prompting to continue. "Could it be possible that she is a witch, and it is her familiar? She has been seen to cast without a normal Conduit on several occasions."

"I am unconvinced," Thaddeus replied dismissively. "She has used a celerium Conduit at other times. To support your theory, all instances when she supposedly did not would need a connecting theme—her familiar's particular aptitude. But it is possible, I suppose. What would the familiar be, then? A shade might cover nightmares, but not the blood magic or the healing. I believe there is a rare Eastern beast called an enenra that might match her companion's physical description, but they are said to be born from bonfires and only appear before those who are pure of heart and mind. That theme seems poorly matched to her."

"What if it is a devil from the Plane of Darkness?"

Thaddeus stopped walking to stare at Kuchen, who turned back when he realized. "Are you aware that the Plane of Darkness is entirely hypothetical?" Thaddeus asked.

"There has to be some counterpart to balance the Plane of Radiance, though. A devil would match the abilities she's displayed perfectly!"

"I have always found a pentagram to be quite balanced. Five elemental and one mundane plane do not *require* another. But even if the Plane of Darkness indeed exists, somehow defying all of our attempts to access it, you cannot know what characteristics an elemental would carry."

"Well, the opposite of radiance, naturally. Just like water is the opposite of fire and air is the opposite of earth. And what if Myrddin discovered the way to access it, and that was in the book she stole? Her shadow companion didn't make an appearance until after she got away with the book."

Thaddeus wanted to smack Kuchen in the skull with a blast of power, but knew from experience that this would knock no sense into him, nor shake loose any of the idiocy. He settled for glaring, allowing his contempt to shine through. "This devil would not be her first familiar. A neophyte in the craft would never have the strength or the Will to bind a sapient, humanoid familiar. So where is the evidence of any other familiar?"

"Maybe the devil ate them all as a requirement of the contract? You know the powerful ones don't like to share."

"And yet, before making this contract, she escaped from the University with wit and a few simple tricks—cast with a Conduit, might I remind you— and even at that point without evidence of a familiar? So, in addition to being a free-caster who goes to great lengths to display her spell arrays on the air, the Raven Queen has somehow contracted with a powerful familiar from a previously undiscovered Elemental Plane. Do you also believe that she is a creature from an ancient species of shapeshifters? Or that she can hear when her name is spoken, even from across the city?"

Kuchen seemed to realize Thaddeus's point. "It is just a theory," he muttered, turning to walk again.

"That is precisely my point. You are creating explanations for the unknown in the same way ancient peoples created stories about the sun and earth and moon to explain what they did not understand. Rather than hypothesize first and then try to mold all of your evidence to fit your narrative, simply admit that you do not understand and remain open to new evidence that will make things clear. We do not know what the shadow companion is, and there is certainly not enough evidence to support such an outlandish claim, especially when some of your supposed evidence contradicts the remainder."

Kuchen did not reply, though he walked faster so that his face was not visible, his grip white-knuckled around his clipboard.

Thaddeus supposed it was possible that the so-called Raven Queen really was a shapeshifter with an affinity for shadows and dreams…but it seemed more likely that someone had been deliberately working to exaggerate her reputation. The shadow-creature that appeared when she was threatened might be a construct, a rare familiar, or even an Aberrant that she had managed to control. But what was *important* was that she was a powerful free-caster and fully in control of her formidable faculties.

The Morrows had both told the same story, which lined up with the reports from the victims and young Siverling. Canelo's flare beacon had attracted them, but rather than follow her request to help detain an unremarkable and unassuming young woman, they grew greedy and hoped to extort all three—Canelo, Moore, and the Raven Queen. It was almost as if the woman had been luring them into a trap. How had two young students caught her in the first place?

Both men agreed that, when they realized her identity and panicked, the Raven Queen had stopped a fireball spell mid-air with her bare, empty hands, then deflected it to the side and into the wall behind her. Although extremely intriguing, Thaddeus knew that witness reports were notoriously unreliable, especially in times of stress.

After that, the Raven Queen had released the shadow-creature, which absorbed the battle spells from their contraband wands without seeming to take any damage. Thaddeus suspected it was only selectively corporeal, letting the spells pass right through its body. That it could absorb the energy from battle spells was not impossible, he supposed, but it was the kind of ability that could easily backfire if the caster became distracted or overwhelmed. His theory was reinforced, though not proved, by the state of the crime scene; if the Morrows had actually been hitting something, there should have been some evidence. Instead, the walls and furniture on the side of the room opposite the Aberrant were burnt, cut through, and blown apart, as if the men had been fighting an apparition. It might even have been an illusion.

When Moore's Will broke, the magical feedback put both Canelo and the Raven Queen on the floor. Surely, no matter how reckless the Raven Queen was, she would not put herself in such danger. There were better, safer ways to cause a break event.

Most confusing were the events that followed. The Raven Queen protected Canelo, healed one of the Morrows with blood magic—again seemingly declining to use a Conduit—and then perfectly copied the spell Moore had been using, having deduced on the spot that it would protect them from the Aberrant's effects. This was almost certainly evidence that she had prior experience with Aberrants and the theories behind their creation, or at least an interest in the topic.

Why had the Raven Queen been there at all? What had been her goal? He would have thought she had some interest in the Aberrant, but she could not have known that young Newton Moore would lose control and become one. Even if she had facilitated his break on purpose, there was no way to tell what exactly would happen. He could have died, wiped out the entire building with the magical backlash, or become an Aberrant with an entirely different anomalous effect.

No, the Aberrant had not been in her plans. The Morrows believed she had been there as part of a trap for them, and that Moore and Canelo had been working with her to lure them. But then why had she saved two gang members, her supposed enemies? If her original plan had been ruined by the Aberrant, it was possible she let them go free to serve as a warning to any other Morrows still acting from hiding, but something about that theory simply did not fit. For one, there were no *credible* reports of her being involved in the gang battle a few days prior, and that seemed incongruous if she were truly so interested in the Morrows.

But the real source of the niggling sensation of wrongness currently plaguing Thaddeus stemmed from the "blessing" she had given Siverling—an automatic, if weak, defense against divination, accompanied by some protection against being noticed by those nearby. With what Thaddeus had deduced of her, there was no way it was anything but a message. Before that night, Sebastien's only connection to the Raven Queen, as far as Thaddeus could deduce, was actually through Thaddeus himself, as he had consulted on her investigation on multiple occasions now. Did she know that? Was the message for *him*?

Thaddeus tried to avoid jumping to conclusions, but there was something about the idea that felt appropriate. She seemed to be playing a game with the University and the Crowns, leaving little hints for someone like him along the way, deliberately stimulating his intrigue. But if that was the case, what did she want from him? Simply someone with the intellect to match her in her maneuvers and machinations? Or might she be more interested in his particular skill set? Did she know about his research?

Thaddeus was, after all, rather famous—both to the masses and among those who mattered, though for different reasons. Or perhaps she was interested in the most recent Gilbrathan Aberrant, the one they had named Moonsable. Its anomalous effect was weak, but Moonsable was one of the rare mutations to retain some small measure of sapience and lucidity after the break event. If that was what had led the Raven Queen to him, perhaps she did have an interest in his research after all.

Thaddeus shook himself from these thoughts as they arrived at the dim viewing room, where a few coppers and a representative from the Red Guard were already waiting. Without any real facts to find purchase on, he was spiraling. That way led to unconscious biases that would later skew his deductive abilities toward the ideas he wanted to be true rather than bare reality. Like Kuchen. Thaddeus shuddered at the idea. He hoped to gain the missing pieces of information from Canelo's interview but had his suspicions it might not be that easy.

As soon as they learned which of their students were involved in the incident, a couple of University faculty members had rushed down to the quarantine zone with a healer. Rather than show concern for Siverling, a colleague's apprentice who had manifested an anomalous effect and been attacked by the Red Guard, their interest had focused entirely on the girl. The healer had insisted that Canelo's refusal to speak stemmed from trauma and that further mental or emotional strain could lead to long-term damage or even another Aberrant. They had demanded the girl be given a calming potion to allow her to sleep, and that she return to the University for a full wellness examination before being forced to answer questions.

The Red Guard had allowed it, ostensibly because, unlike his own apprentice, she gave off no anomalous readings, and the University held a lot of power in Gilbratha. Thaddeus wondered if there were not more to it, like bribes or blackmail. Despite their oaths, members of the Red Guard were not incorruptible.

Kuchen flipped through his sheaf of loose papers, murmuring to Titus. "You asked for someone to double-check that prognos woman's assessment of the crime scene. Preliminary reports haven't found any discrepancies, though there is some argument over the method and sequence of events during the fighting that caused Mr. Moore's break."

At least Titus wasn't an idiot, which was a large reason the man was one of the few Thaddeus might consider a friend. It had escaped neither of them that the prognos had interacted with a friendly Raven Queen, meaning her testimony could be compromised.

A copper and prognos pair led Canelo into the interrogation room, while a few University faculty members joined Thaddeus and the others. The viewing room had a large example of the newly developed half-silvered mirror, also known as a one-way window. It would allow them to watch the interrogation without being seen. As long as the interrogation room remained bright, while their viewing room remained dark, anyone in the interrogation room would think it was a simple mirror. Spell arrays embedded into the stone wall would send the sound from the interrogation room through to them while keeping their own conversation secure.

The questioning started off normally, with the girl answering baseline questions about her identity and background for the prognos to better divine the truth of her words. But as soon as the first real question about the night before came up, Canelo said, "I cannot speak of it."

Everyone in the viewing room shared confused looks with each other, except the newly joined University faculty members.

Thaddeus's eyes narrowed.

Further questions were met with the same exact answer. The girl was frustrated, rocking back and forth and biting her lip, but that seemed to be the only response she could give. The interrogating copper sighed, rubbing his tired eyes. "Miss Canelo, I understand that the events of last night were traumatizing, but we must have your testimony."

"I *cannot* speak of it."

The prognos focused intently. "She believes that."

Thaddeus turned to the only people in the room who seemed fully aware of what was going on. "Do you care to explain?" he asked.

The other professor, someone from the divination department, coughed self-importantly. "Miss Canelo regained her ability to speak when the sun rose, but any attempts to question her about the events of yesterday evening yield only this one answer. It's the same for any questions involving the Raven Queen. We believe the Raven Queen placed some sort of curse or geas on her. We were able to uncover Miss Canelo's diary from her room, and there are hints that she and Moore were interested in the bounty offered for information on the Raven Queen." The man pulled a small book from his satchel and handed it to Investigator Kuchen. "Perhaps you will find it useful. I can only hope so, as I doubt our unfortunate student will be much help to you at this point."

"A cursebreaker, perhaps," Kuchen suggested.

The man nodded quickly. "We have already sent word to a faculty member who teaches the subject to upper term students. If there is any solution to the problem, we will find it, I promise you."

Thaddeus almost snorted aloud. It was a shame that the ward against untruth did not extend into the viewing room. It might at least make the man hesitate before spouting such obvious drivel. He turned to Titus. "May we speak privately?"

Titus and Kuchen followed him into the hallway while the useless interview continued, the copper trying to find *any* relevant question that Canelo could answer.

Titus rubbed his face with one hand, his other clenching and unclenching at his side. "I want our own cursebreaker working on her," he said to Kuchen. "No University affiliation."

Kuchen nodded quickly, making a note of it in his small notebook.

Thaddeus remained more amused than frustrated. "I doubt that journal belongs to Canelo, or that the contents are legitimate. The girl knows something they would rather keep silent. If they did not place that curse themselves, then at the least they did not try very hard to save her from it. It has had time to settle in, now. Very *convenient*, that the only other living being able to testify about what happened last night is the Raven Queen herself. Canelo was involved in their faction's attempt to find the Raven Queen without the coppers or Crowns knowing, I suspect. If I remember correctly, she was also on the scene when the Eagle Tower divination array was destroyed? During the false rogue magic alarm?"

Kuchen's eyes widened. "Oh, well, yes, the name does sound familiar."

Thaddeus relayed his apprentice's suspicions about Canelo's collusion with someone at the University.

Titus was unsurprised. "I didn't know the details, but I did suspect. The blood sample we were using was conveniently corrupted. If we hadn't kept some of it behind in the Harrow Hill evidence vaults, we would have been out of luck. There's not much left, but our diviners are powerful and skilled enough to work with very little. It will simply make things more difficult—and more expensive."

"How long until Eagle Tower's repairs are completed?" Thaddeus asked.

"Six to eight weeks." Titus smiled wryly. "They aren't in as much of a hurry to repair it as one might hope."

Kuchen snorted.

"Is there no other divination array you can use in the meantime?"

"None that make the expense worth it, especially when they have so little chance of success."

Thaddeus doubted they would ever find her using divination if they had not succeeded yet, but he had no incentive to offer better options. "This Crown-opposing faction is being reactionary, rather than proactive. It is more evidence against them. The person who set off the false rogue magic alarms last time knew what was going on and what copper procedure is. Either it was someone at the University, or it was one of us—one of the coppers," he clarified, motioning to the three of them despite considering himself an outside party. "The last option is that one of our organizations has a leak that the Raven Queen is taking advantage of. While I certainly would not rule that out, the evidence makes it increasingly likely that someone at the University sabotaged the previous efforts. If they have a chance, they might act against us again."

"If so, the High Crown may feel even less favorable to them," Titus said. "They are playing a dangerous game."

"What was in the book, the one she stole?" Thaddeus asked. For the University to go to such lengths—thinly veiled treason—it had to have been more valuable than Thaddeus suspected.

Titus looked at him for a moment, then shook his head. "Something valuable enough that we *must* find Siobhan Naught first."

Kuchen opened his mouth to ask further questions, perhaps an attempt to confirm his ridiculous theory, but wisely closed it without speaking.

Titus continued. "I had considered requesting the Red Guard's assistance, despite my lord father's feelings on their involvement. Perhaps, if I could convince them she is the kind of threat that requires their intervention, their particular brand of resources would allow us to find and detain her. But Father has threatened to disinherit me if I disgrace the Westbays through such a failure. Beyond the embarrassment to the coppers, ceding authority to the Red Guard could affect our future funding." He gave a wry, bitter smile.

"You would think we should all be on the same side," Kuchen commiserated.

Thaddeus nodded absently, his mind elsewhere. The book must have been valuable indeed, if some faction of the University thought it was worth making an enemy of the Crowns over. They would rather allow the Raven Queen to go free than let the Crowns have it. He wondered how many of the administrators and professors were aware of what was happening under the surface.

Whichever side ended up with the book, it did not bode well for the ongoing stability of Gilbratha, or Lenore as a whole. As long as the upheaval did not impede his research, Thaddeus did not particularly care which side won, but he *was* becoming more interested in whatever that archaeological expedition had uncovered. Knowledge was power, and if he was any judge, this knowledge seemed capable of shifting the balance of power significantly in favor of whichever faction got hold of it.

And at that very moment, the Raven Queen had it. The Raven Queen who was, maybe, trying to get Thaddeus's attention. "I want to see Ennis Naught," he said.

2

THE SUN IS ALSO A STAR

Sebastien
Month 1, Day 21, Thursday 11:30 a.m.

Siobhan was struggling, desperate to escape but trapped in a body that wouldn't listen to her commands.

A bracing sting on her cheek provided a way out. She woke with a gluttonous gasp of air, bolting upright in a bed she didn't recognize—a room she didn't recognize—with someone holding her arms to her sides, restraining her!

She panicked for a good few seconds. Fighting against the shackling grip, she let out a low, panicked moan as she grasped around for her Conduit, which *wasn't there*—until Damien's familiar, if tired, face resolved into coherence in front of her.

He was forcibly keeping her from flailing her way off of a University infirmary bed. "Help! We need help over here!" he yelled, turning his head. "Sebastien, you're okay. You're safe," he said in a lower, soothing tone that did nothing to disguise the worry underneath.

The sound of her other name helped ground her, and she stopped struggling to escape, blinking rapidly at his reassuring grey eyes.

The healer bustled up. "Panic attack?"

"He was having a nightmare," Damien said. "I tried to wake him, but he wouldn't, so I tapped him—maybe a little too hard—on the cheek, and he woke up fighting and making these noises like he was hurt."

"'M fine," Sebastien mumbled, still panting, the crashing thump of her heart against her sternum slowing. She looked around, unable to help her paranoia, or the niggling sensation that she was seeing things that shouldn't exist out of the corner of her vision. In a way, the clear signs of panic were a relief. Her body was reliably responding to the stimuli sent by her mind, which had plenty of cause for hysteria.

"We gave him a strong calming potion along with the sedative—I'm surprised he still managed to have nightmares—but sedatives can make it harder to transition from sleeping to waking. Sometimes they cause sleep-walking and the like." The woman turned to Sebastien, pulling a vial out of the pocket of her apron "Mr. Siverling, everything is alright. You are safe in the University's infirmary. You've had a big shock, but nothing can harm you here. You need your rest to recover, so why don't I give you another calming potion, and once you're feeling better we can help you get back to sleep?"

"No!" Sebastien snapped. "No calming potions. No sedatives. Not now, not ever. Never again! I—I have a bad reaction." Professor Lacer must have transferred her to the infirmary after free-casting that sleep spell on her. With the sedatives keeping her from waking herself up, she'd been trapped inside her own mind. With her nightmares.

The woman seemed taken aback. "Oh, I'm very sorry, Mr. Siverling. It wasn't in your file. Are you allergic to any particular ingredient? The laughing poppy, perhaps? We do have alternate brews available—"

"No," Sebastien said again, more insistently. "Calming potions only with my permission, but *never* sedatives. *Nothing* that will force me to sleep."

There was an awkward pause before Damien spoke, his voice small, the tone almost childish in its hesitance. "Is that what the Aberrant did to you? Force you to sleep?"

The healer's eyes opened wide, a hand flying up to cover her mouth. "*Oh. Oh, I'm very sorry, Mr. Siverling. It was just standard procedure—*"

Sebastien ignored the woman, climbing off the bed and searching for her things. Someone had stripped her to her underclothes and dressed her in worn cotton pajamas—the standard garb for everyone admitted to the infir-mary overnight, apparently, as she saw others wearing the same on their own beds.

All the bruises she had accumulated the night before were gone, and someone had cleaned her with a spell. She had the dry, irritated skin to prove it, and her fingernails were clean of the blood that had been crusting their edges. Agent Vernor had noticed and taken a swab, but Sebastien had explained that she must have accidentally touched some of the blood on the floor. It wasn't nearly enough evidence to suspect her of being the one who'd healed Chief, or whatever the maimed Morrow man's name was.

Thaddeus Lacer being Sebastien's Master probably had a lot to do with how accommodating the Red Guard had been. Perhaps, without him, she would have found herself locked in a windowless cell in Harrow Hill for the investigation process, and overall much less likely to fool them.

Sebastien's belongings were tucked under the bed, and a quick perusal showed that nothing seemed to be missing. Her right boot still had the black star sapphire Conduit in it, though it had fallen into the toe. She didn't mention it, and could only hope that no one had noticed it when they were undressing her. "Leave," she ordered.

The healer, who had still been babbling about something, quieted, staring at her.

"I want to get dressed," Sebastien explained.

"You need to stay at least another twenty-four hours for observation," the woman argued. "Professor Lacer indicated you might be in danger of Will-strain from your...ordeal."

"I'm fine. Staying in *this place* certainly won't improve my mental health. I just want to leave."

The healer still hesitated, so Sebastien turned to Damien. "Please." As manipulations went, it was clumsy at best, but it had the desired effect.

Damien turned toward the healer and crossed his arms. "I'll handle any paperwork."

"But Professor Lacer—"

"Can talk to me if he has any complaints. Feel free to tell him I said so, if he asks. As Mr. Siverling here is an adult, you cannot by Crown law keep him against his will even under the *suggestion* of a professor, unless he is deemed likely to be a danger to others. I will ensure Sebastien gets the rest he needs in a place where he will be more comfortable. Really, sleeping in the open with only a curtain for privacy? And can you even call this slab a bed? Unacceptable."

As they left to handle the paperwork, Damien's complaints continuing on, Sebastien drew the curtains around her, using the privacy to do a more thorough check of her belongings as she got dressed. Even the thin, broken bracelets she had taken off Newton were still in her pocket. *'Thank the stars above no one decided to do a little snooping while I was insensate. I'll need to have a conversation with Professor Lacer about respecting my boundaries, no matter what he holds over my head. This* cannot *happen again.'*

Damien returned, standing outside the curtain while Sebastien struggled to fasten her many buttons with fingers that were slow and clumsy from the lingering sedative. "Professor Lacer got you a pass from class and homework that is good until this coming Wednesday, so you can take your time to recuperate."

A surprising wave of relief ran through Sebastien. "Okay. Good. I'm leaving." She stepped out, settling the strap of her satchel on her shoulder. Its weight made her want to give up and lie down again. The black sapphire Conduit was hidden again in her boot, and her borrowed celerium Conduit in an easily accessible pocket. Professor Lacer's jacket was folded on the bedside table, and after a moment of hesitation, she left it there.

"Leaving? From the infirmary?"

"From the University."

"For good?" Damien asked, aghast.

"No, of course not. Until Wednesday. You can give my pass to the professors, right?" A mere week seemed inadequate.

Damien's fingers flexed, as if he were trying to hold onto control of the situation. "Um, I'm not sure if you're allowed to just leave? Students are required to live in the dorms."

"I'm leaving," she repeated. "I will be back on Wednesday. The faculty will simply have to accept it, and if they feel like punishing me somehow upon my return, so be it." She couldn't stand the thought of being stuck in the dormitories, listening to the gossip, trying to rest in a tiny little room without a proper door or ceiling, surrounded by curious imbeciles.

Damien's bloodshot eyes tracked over her face. "If you want, you can stay at my house. The Westbay estate has plenty of servants to look after you, and an impressive library. I'm sure my brother won't mind, and my father is away, so you wouldn't have to worry about him."

Sebastien realized suddenly that Damien had either been up all night or had been crying sometime before she awoke. The puffy eyebags would indicate tears, but then again, he always looked like that, even after a full night's sleep. His nose wasn't red, and he wasn't sniffling or hoarse, but that only meant he'd stopped long enough ago for the symptoms to clear, or that he'd used a spell to hasten the process. Either way, she forced herself to relax a bit, unclenching her jaw and nodding at him. He was worried and only wanted to help her. There was no need to be rude. "Thank you, but no. I have a place to go."

Damien looked like he wanted to question her further, but he restrained himself. "If you're sure… You really would be very comfortable at Westbay Manor. You could be alone as much as you want. No idiots to irritate you, and you can even order the servants around."

One side of her mouth quirked up in a small smile, but she shook her head silently, striding toward the door.

Damien followed.

As they exited the infirmary, the cold hit Sebastien like a blow, and she hunched into herself, holding in an exhausted moan.

"When the rogue magic sirens went off, I asked for a carriage back to the University right away," Damien said. "Then my bracelet, the one you made for Newton to warn us, it got so cold. I kept waiting for the one linked to you to get cold, too, but it didn't. And I thought maybe that was a good sign, but when I got back, you were gone. I checked the dorms, the library, even the Menagerie. Tanya and Newton were both gone, too, so I knew something had happened. I didn't tell anyone to send help, because I didn't know if that would just make things worse. I went to the gates to watch for you, or for some sign of something wrong in the city, like the gang battle last time. They tried to send me back to bed, but I wouldn't listen. I actually got a demerit!"

Damien laughed wryly, then continued, speaking even faster. "I overheard a professor say a student had been involved with the Aberrant's break, and I tried to ask them for details, but they wouldn't tell me anything. Then Professor Lacer arrived, and he was floating your unconscious body in the air beside himself. I thought maybe you were dead."

Damien shuddered as he stared off into the distance. "You looked so pale. But he took you to the infirmary. You were just asleep, and he was worried about possible Will-strain..." Damien swallowed, looking at her. "He said you'd experienced a traumatizing event. But he still wouldn't tell me any details, even though he knows we're friends."

The dorms were thankfully empty, all the students away in class. Sebastien had left her own wool jacket at the Silk Door, along with the male outfit she'd been wearing, but she would have to retrieve that later. She began to bundle up in the warmest clothes she had remaining.

Damien watched her for a while, then continued updating her on what had happened in her absence. "They brought Tanya Canelo back, but they didn't keep her in the main infirmary room, so I didn't get a chance to talk with her. She looked...horrible. Worse than you, even. The coppers came and escorted her away this morning. And Newton didn't come back at all. Is he..."

Sebastien stilled, her scarf halfway wrapped around her neck. "Newton is dead," she said softly.

Damien rocked back on his heels, his eyes fluttering closed as if she had struck him. "What happened? Did Canelo..."

Sebastien shook her head, her throat tightening. Her shadow-familiar had been meant to draw away attention, but it had instead drawn *too much* attention. Too much *fear*. Perhaps, if not for her, Newton wouldn't have lost control and broken. There would have been no strings, no people dead...except for herself, fallen to the Morrows. Sebastien swallowed heavily past the lump in her throat, feeling dizzy. She lifted a hand to her forehead, closed her eyes, and took a deep breath.

When she opened her eyes, Damien had stepped closer, his hand raised halfway, ready to support her. "I am...*restricted* from speaking of the details." She gave him a significant look, hoping he would get the hint.

"You had to make a magical vow. To the Red Guard?"

Hesitantly, she nodded. Nothing stopped her from doing so, though she felt some resistance.

"Did the Aberrant kill Newton?"

She rubbed her dry lips together. "Not…exactly."

Damien let out a harsh, ragged breath. "Newton was the Aberrant?"

She nodded again, more shallowly because she could feel the magic of the vow restricting her. In the eyes of the spell, Damien must not know enough for her to communicate with him freely. And whatever that skull had done, this vow was based around compulsion, not the threat of punishment. *'I wonder how strong the compulsion is, how far I can push it?'* She hesitated before attempting to tell Damien everything, however. Partially because she worried the Red Guard might somehow learn of her unfaithfulness—she had no idea how that artifact worked, after all—and partially because she was simply too fatigued to make the effort. "I'm sorry. I'm really unable to talk about it. If you want details, Professor Lacer knows most of it, though not about the order of no name or our longer-running surveillance of Tanya. You might be able to get more information if you pester him."

"Are you…are *we* safe?"

"As far as I know, yes. But you'll want to avoid acting suspiciously. And give me the bracelet—the one Newton triggered." The one *she* had triggered while removing evidence from Newton's metamorphosed body.

Damien did as she asked, and she tucked it into her pocket with the others, trying to remember if there was anything else waiting to cause problems. She could think of nothing, though in her current state she wasn't entirely reassured by that.

"Did Newton die because of us?" Damien asked, visibly bracing himself for the answer. "Because we brought him in to watch Tanya?"

Sebastien hesitated. "We never lied to him," she said instead of answering. "If a copper dies on the job, is it the fault of the person who hired him? Even if he took the more dangerous mission voluntarily, when he didn't have to?"

Damien didn't look away from her gaze. "Maybe. If that person should never have been hired. If they weren't cut out for the job, and then didn't get proper training."

She nodded. "Then maybe." She turned to leave, but Damien stopped her with a hand on her arm.

"What do we do now?" he asked.

She hesitated. "You can get out—of the pact we made, of the secret group —if you want. Your oath of secrecy for anything that's passed would remain, but you wouldn't be involved in anything further." This could be a dangerous tipping point for him. If he withdrew, it might solve some of her problems, but she felt ambivalent about the idea. Without him, she would be even more alone in all this. She hadn't realized it, but his alliance—his friendship—had become a pillar of support, despite the potential trouble he represented.

Damien frowned at her. "No, I—that's not what I meant." He shook his head. "I'm not quitting the thirteen-pointed star. This is...horrible, but I'm not giving up or running away. I just want to know what our next step is, now that something like this has happened. Are we going to be sanctioned by the higher-ups? Do we keep watching Tanya? Do we get transferred to another mission? What is happening?"

"I don't know," she admitted. "I don't think we'll be disciplined." After all, aside perhaps from Oliver, their little organization didn't actually have any higher-ups to reprimand them. "I don't know if we'll keep watching Tanya or not. Whatever we do, it will be with more precautions now that everything's gone to shit. As for the rest, the generalities? We keep going." She pressed her fingers to her mouth, resisting the sudden and irrational urge to claw at her lips. She didn't want to be saying any of this, not the lies, and especially not any plans to keep going down the path that got Newton killed. "We get stronger, and smarter. More powerful. If you don't know what you need to solve your problems, Damien, seize power. True power can be converted into almost anything else." Her grandfather had told her that, long ago. She occasionally remembered the advice, usually when everything was going wrong. As always, it seemed truer than ever. If she'd been more powerful, perhaps she would've had other options last night.

"That's it? Just..." Damien trailed off, shaking his head. He looked like a lost child.

Sebastien softened. Gracelessly, she leaned over and wrapped her arms around him in what was probably the most awkward hug either of them had ever experienced. She didn't normally like to touch people, and he obviously hadn't been expecting it. "Sometimes we fail. That doesn't mean we were wrong to try." She fumbled for words, but pressed on. "Do you remember observing the night sky during the acceptance ritual? Sometimes it's too clouded to see the stars, but the sun is also a star, and its light reaches us through even the heaviest storm. We take responsibility for the things within our grasp, and we keep going. Otherwise what was it worth? What was it all for?"

She didn't know if what she was saying made any sense. She didn't even know if she believed it. But she pulled back and kept her gaze locked on Damien's, trying to imbue it with the sense of stability that she felt so little of.

He was trembling slightly, but he steeled himself, straightening. "Okay."

She hesitated, then said, "We can do something for Newton even if he's not here. He had a family. He cared about them a lot."

Damien pressed his lips together, his eyes growing glassy as he nodded quickly. "Yes."

She felt awkward about leaving Damien when he was so obviously emotionally compromised, but she wanted to stay in the dorms even less. She had to get away. "Maybe *you* should go home to Westbay Manor for a couple of days," she said.

Damien gave her a one-shouldered shrug.

With another uncomfortable squeeze of his shoulder, Sebastien walked away, leaving Damien standing alone in the dorms behind her. Her words of comfort to Damien rang hollow in her ears, and she hugged herself, pressing her fingers into her arms until her joints ached and the dull pain of a future bruise bloomed beneath her skin.

She took the tubes down the side of the white cliffs and hailed a carriage, heedless of the cost. "Take me to Dryden Manor," she told the driver.

3

———

SHE WHO BRINGS THE NIGHT

Thaddeus
Month 1, Day 21, Thursday 8:15 a.m.

Titus's eyebrows rose at Thaddeus's sudden request for access to the Raven Queen's father, but he waved his hand magnanimously. "Of course. We have gone through every method possible to find the holes in his story but have been unsuccessful thus far. Have you been inspired with a new angle we might try?"

"I need to see all the records on his questioning and the examination reports, from the beginning," Thaddeus said instead of answering.

"I am to report to the High Crown later today. Please let me know if you find anything of interest, Thaddeus. I would like to be able to give him at least *some* positive news."

Thaddeus agreed, and Titus assigned Kuchen to accompany him to the records room. Two hours later, Thaddeus had pored through every report in the Raven Queen's investigation file, which held little that he did not already know, or at least suspect. Ennis Naught was telling the truth, even if they didn't want to accept that.

The coppers had made no obvious mistakes or oversights, but some piece of the puzzle had to be missing. If Ennis Naught was telling the truth about his daughter, then she could not be the Raven Queen. They had searched for signs that the man's memory had been tampered with and found none, though that sort of thing could be subtle. Naught believed, and it seemed to be true, that he had a daughter, and that daughter was the same person who came to Gilbratha with him. He *believed* he had stolen the book on a whim, out of anger.

And yet, they had first-hand reports of the Raven Queen's exploits. Multiple acquaintances they had tracked down from her childhood confirmed that she matched Siobhan Naught's appearance. Except, of course, for the new reports of her growing red and black feathers and the Nightmare Pack's resident prognos insistence that she was an inhuman being.

From that, Thaddeus would normally assume that Siobhan Naught's identity had been stolen, and the real girl's bones were being picked bare by insects somewhere. To test this, the coppers had gotten permission to do a lineage test using some of Ennis Naught's hair, attempting to see if he had any living descendants. The divination spell, which took weeks to produce results, had shown several, though the results could be quite unreliable. Apparently, the man had impregnated multiple women across the country during his lifetime, though Siobhan was the only legitimate offspring, and the only one the elder Naught was aware of. The spell only suggested the existence of others bearing his bloodline; it did not allow the coppers to track down any of his children without clearer knowledge of who they were. A separate spell had been used on the drop of recovered blood to confirm that the Raven Queen was one of them.

While that would normally have been conclusive evidence, in this case Thaddeus still withheld judgment. Something felt off about the whole thing. Some pieces of evidence fit together using some theories, but with no theory did *all* the pieces fit together.

That the Raven Queen had contacted Ennis Naught *twice* since the theft and his subsequent incarceration only increased the ambiguity. Though the reasons Naught had reported for the visits were suspect, they hinted that the Raven Queen, whether or not she had ever truly been Siobhan Naught, felt some sort of connection to him. Thaddeus considered the possibility that her attempts to contact the man were more purposefully laid clues—or red herrings meant to send the investigators chasing their own tails—but was also conscious of the ever-present risk of over-attributing canniness and purpose to the Raven Queen, a bias too many had already proven susceptible to.

No, there was something they were missing. Thaddeus read the investigation note about Ennis Naught apparently having given an heirloom celerium ring to one of the Gervin Family's branch lines, as a bond for his daughter's...*marriage* into the Family—as long as she brought the stolen book along with her, of course.

Thaddeus almost laughed aloud at the Gervin Family's audacity. The Gervins had acted quickly, before the full extent of what they were dealing with had become clear, and, luckily for them, had not had a chance to follow through on the agreement. Even if the Raven Queen herself did not cow them, the High Crown might not look kindly upon what could be seen as subversion of a criminal investigation, or even a direct attempt to weaken his authority.

Still, Thaddeus made a note to tell Titus to keep an eye on them. Even if they were not planning to reach above their station, they might be a future target for the Raven Queen if she truly had an interest in that Conduit. Hells, she could have already stolen it without them realizing, if the rumors about her skills were even partially true.

He noted that the coppers who had been attacked by her shadow-creature companion were showing no lingering side effects except for the occasional nightmare, which could just as well have been caused by stress. The warehouse workers who had given her drops of their blood seemed healthy as of the last time they had been called to Harrow Hill for a follow-up.

Thaddeus also noted her amicable connections to both the Verdant Stag and the Nightmare Pack. The leader of the Verdant Stag was a metaphorical ghost, only ever appearing in a mask and leaving most of the operations to his underlings, but Lynwood of the Nightmare Pack was accessible. However, the reports stated that he simply refused to testify to the coppers, even when they brought him in to stay the night in a cell. The Nightmare Pack prognos had mentioned that the Raven Queen gave them a boon. What had she given, and what had she gotten in return? Was this the same method by which the Verdant Stag had become allied with her?

Having gleaned all he could from the reports, Thaddeus retrieved Kuchen, who was to give him access to Ennis Naught's cell. Thaddeus would rather have spoken to the prisoner alone, but he did not have the clearance, and records had to be kept.

Thaddeus wrinkled his nose as he stepped into the cell. Naught's chamber pot had not been emptied, and the cell smelled of acrid urine, feces, and a rancid buildup of sweat and grime from the unwashed man himself.

Naught huddled in a corner atop the thin cot, wrapped in his blanket. He looked nothing like his daughter. She was supposedly ochre-skinned with long dark hair, evidence of her heritage from the People, northern nomads who still practiced some of their old, esoteric magics. That was to say nothing of sprouting feathers or missing irises.

Thaddeus's eyes narrowed as they trailed over the man's pale skin, red hair and unkempt beard. Pale, watery eyes gave away the soft mind behind them. Thaddeus felt an idea stirring in the back of his mind, too immature to grasp yet.

"I'm not talking any more without food," Naught announced with hoarse petulance. "And none o' that porridge. I want meat, fresh bread, and cheese."

Thaddeus debated the effort it would require to threaten the man into compliance, but another waft of the unwashed stench coming off him made

Thaddeus decide on the easier route. He turned to Kuchen, who was holding his handkerchief over his face, but not coughing into it for once.

Kuchen nodded to one of the guards, who headed off toward the cafeteria.

"And an apple!" Naught called after him excitedly.

Thaddeus eyed the room's only chair with distaste. Pulling out his Conduit and one of the beast cores he always kept on his person, he cast a quick scouring spell on it. The wood splintered a little under the force, but the magic left it clean enough to sit on. He gestured toward the ceiling, and a small, bright ball of light appeared there, illuminating the room.

Naught squinted against the sudden brightness. "I suppose you're 'ere to ask more questions about that ungrateful girl?"

"Siobhan. Your daughter," Thaddeus corrected immediately, with an unexpected surge of irritation.

Naught merely squinted at him silently.

"She had some training as a sorcerer, yes? From her grandfather?" Thaddeus asked.

"The girl was apprenticed to 'im when she turned eleven. Taught 'er a few useful tricks before 'e died a couple years later. I came back for 'er—took me a while to find her—and then she lived with me for six years, on the road, making 'erself useful with 'er thaumaturgy before I brought 'er to Gilbratha so she could attend the University and become a real sorcerer like she always wanted. I've told you all this so many times. She wasn't acting strange, she was just excited, nervous. She didn't make me take that book, though I dearly wish she 'ad so you would just *let me go*. I don't know anything about this Raven Queen, but more'n likely the girl's just playing tricks on you, smoke and mirrors and the like. Maybe she made some powerful friends. She was on the road with me and picked up the bad with the good, you see."

"Her grandfather, did he have any connections to anyone suspicious?"

"Who knows? The man kept to 'imself, out in the woods near a small village. Didn't talk about 'is past. I didn't spend much time with 'im. We didn't get on, truth be told. Old Kal didn't much like me marrying 'is daughter —thought I wasn't good enough, not being a sorcerer. Made me take Miakoda's last name, marry into the People instead of 'er marrying out."

"Miakoda—your wife. What was this Kal's full name?" Thaddeus asked quickly.

"Raz Kalvidasan. Mean old piece o' jerky."

Thaddeus frowned, the name sparking a connection that he couldn't quite remember. He repeated it aloud. "Raz Kalvidasan," then again, with a slight accent. "Raaz Kalvidasan. He was a foreigner? Not one of the People?"

Ennis's eyebrows rose. "Yeah. 'e adopted my wife when she was young. 'ow did you know?"

Thaddeus turned to Kuchen. "The grandfather's name literally means 'secretive learned one,' or something like that. I was never fluent, and it has been years. You will want someone to look into him." It was interesting that a foreigner had held the bloodline of the People in such high regard. He turned back to Naught. "Tell me about the circumstances of this Raaz Kalvidasan's death."

"Oh, it was *bad*. Everyone in the village died. The Red Guard came in, I 'eard. Of course, I wasn't there at the time. I only got word of it later, and that's when I came back for Siobhan. The village was gone. Couldn't find the girl for weeks, maybe months."

Well, that was rather interesting.

Kuchen flipped through the papers on his clipboard. "You didn't tell us this! We have it that a plague wiped out the village where she lived as a child."

"I didna' say it was a plague. I said everyone died, and your interrogator didna' seem so interested," the man said, his brogue growing stronger with spite.

"You should have realized we would be interested in this! It could be valuable information." Kuchen's voice broke under the strain of his outrage, and he was reduced to yet another fit of wet coughing.

Did the coppers not pay the man enough to see a healer? Thaddeus dropped the light spell long enough to cast a cleansing spell through the air. He did not want to catch whatever the investigator had, being confined in a small area with all his germs.

Naught seemed temporarily cowed by the flicker of the light and the feel of sterilization magic rushing past him, but recovered quickly. "I've told you plenty I didn't 'ave to, and look where all that *cooperation's* gotten me." Naught turned his head and spat on the floor.

Disgusting.

Kuchen was coughing too hard to retort, but he sent his best glare over the top of his handkerchief.

"Continue with what you were saying," Thaddeus said, motioning impatiently at Naught.

"Hmph. Well, I finally picked Siobhan up in a village a couple days over. She was in the local gaol for stealing and beating the baker's son. Almost tied a knot in my tongue talking 'er out of that little fix. She was…different, for a long while. A real burden, truth be told, but she was too young to marry off, and who would 'ave a girl like that, even if she was pretty? Wouldna' talk, wouldna' practice magic, couldna' sleep."

Thaddeus leaned forward with interest.

Naught continued, his gaze going soft and vacant with memory. "I'm no monster, to just abandon my own daughter, so I took 'er around, looking for someone who could fix 'er. Took maybe two years. Drove me to poverty. She didn't start acting normal again until she learned there was a spell that could ward off nightmares. And just like that, she was back talking and running around, practicing all those little magic tricks until I had to beg 'er to stop. After that, though, she made 'erself useful wherever we went. Saved my bacon a couple times, truth be told. The girl never talks about those times, and I kinda got in the 'abit of avoiding those memories, too. But I'll tell you right now, the Raven Queen didna' replace my daughter when she was thirteen. I lived with the girl for six years after that. I watched 'er grow up. I would've noticed."

Thaddeus leaned forward with fascination. "Do you know any more about the reason the Red Guard was called in at that time? Was it an Aberrant?"

"No idea. The whole thing was cleared by the time I arrived. Village was empty. Only 'eard rumors from the surrounding villages, and of course the Red Guard was no 'elp. Told me my daughter was probably dead and burned. But I wouldna' believe them. And I was right. Took me a while, but I found 'er. Little scrapper, she was," Naught said with sudden fondness.

"We will request their records," Kuchen assured Thaddeus.

Thaddeus nodded absently, still staring at Naught. "What about the girl's mother? Your wife?"

Naught's face went slack with nostalgia. "Miakoda was the most beautiful woman I ever saw. Tall, shapely"—his hands drew an hourglass shape in the air—"and a tongue like a barbed whip. She was a witch with a demon familiar."

"A demon? A humanoid, sapient being from the Plane of Fire?" Thaddeus clarified. People often used the word incorrectly to refer to any creature from the Plane of Fire, and sometimes even the other Elemental Planes.

Naught nodded. "Yes. Named Paimon. Just a little guy, most of the time." He held his hand about a foot above the ground. "Powerful, though, and the funniest little tyke you ever saw. The creature was always getting into trouble or offending someone by making rude gestures or blowing smoke in their face. Liked to eat his food raw—cooked it in 'is mouth. 'E slept in the fireplace."

"Miakoda sounds like a powerful witch. She died when Siobhan was young, you said?"

Naught deflated, the humor fading from his face. "Yes. That's when Kal took little Siobhan in."

"How did it happen?"

"We were with a caravan, traveling down to Paneth for a show, and to pick up some supplies for Kal. There was a storm, a bad one, and we were looking for shelter." Naught swallowed heavily, going silent.

Kuchen looked up from his notes. "It was a roc, correct?"

Naught blew out a slow, rancid breath and nodded. "Blown our way by the storm. An angry, mean bastard, so big its wings blocked out the sky when it swooped down on us, like the sails of a death-ship. It picked up one of the wagons first, then flew up and dropped it on us. Killed a couple people and spooked the horses something 'orrible. That's when Miakoda and Paimon went to fight it. I tried to stop 'em. They couldn't stand up to the roc and the storm both. She was flinging the flames about, with Paimon as big as a giant. Little guy died protecting Miakoda and the rest of us...and she went crazy."

Naught's voice was low, haunted and compelling. "She screamed so loud, 'er voice all filled with magic, it blew the roc into the ground. Then she struck it with lightning. The light of it blinded me. When I could see again, she was walking away calm as you please, and the roc was smoking on the ground behind her, dead. She told me we 'ad to go back right away, that the trip was off. I thought she was just distraught at the loss of little Paimon, but something was wrong." Naught tapped his temple. "Wrong in here. She broke something. We got back to the village, and she went straight to Kal, but even 'e couldn't save 'er."

"Will-strain leading to death," Kuchen said, nodding. "Most likely an aneurism."

"No," Naught shook his head. "It was the magic. She killed herself with casting magic."

"That is how Will-strain occurs," Kuchen said slowly, as if talking to a child.

Thaddeus stood, tingles of electric excitement flushing through his fingertips. "Explain."

"It's why Kal didn't want her marrying me, isn't it?" Naught said with a shrug. "The pure Naught bloodline was too good for me, supposedly. But all it did was keep 'er alive a little longer after she lost Paimon. It couldn't save her from the sickness in her head. She just kept casting, even when she didn't need to, even when she knew what it would do to her, just for the *pleasure* of it. She didn't care about me or little Siobhan anymore, only the magic. I didn't see 'er when she died. Kal said it was a mercy. I wouldna' recognize 'er corpse, and..." Naught shuddered and fell silent. "Well. I left Siobhan with Kal, after that. But my girl knows better than to cast without her Conduit. I—I shouldn't 'ave given the ring to those Gervin Family people. She needs it, now, and what if something happens to 'er, like with Miakoda, because she doesn't 'ave it?" Naught buried his face in his knees, pulling the ratty blanket tighter around his shoulders.

Thaddeus was too busy with his own elation to pay attention to the man. Siobhan Naught. *Naught.* Perhaps a variant on "Null?" He had heard rumors, of course, about those who were born with the traits of a Null, yet still able to cast magic. How they could resist the madness that came with casting through their own flesh and blood. It was clear enough that they were more than children's tales, but he had thought all those with that particular mutation gone hundreds, if not thousands, of years before. Resistance was not complete negation, after all, and they were a powerful potential threat to enemy and ally alike.

Perhaps the Naughts had managed to slip through the cracks, the secrecy of the People keeping them out of modern records, maintaining their abilities through careful breeding, or even inbreeding.

Or, perhaps the Blood Emperor's experiments had not been so fruitless, after all.

This changed everything.

4

IN THE STILL OF THE MORNING

SEBASTIEN
    Month 1, Day 21, Thursday 1:15 p.m.

WHEN SEBASTIEN ARRIVED at Dryden Manor, Sharon took one look at her and bustled out of the kitchen to grab her arm as if afraid she was about to fall over. "Mr. Siverling! Oh, you look absolutely wretched! Thomas!" Sharon called to the servant who had opened the door for Sebastien, her voice loud despite them all standing within a few feet of each other. "Take Mr. Siverling's things up to his room," she commanded. "And you come into the kitchen, dear," she said to Sebastien more quietly. "I'll get you fed with something warm."

"No need. I was just going to have a nap. I've been granted leave from the University for a few days."

"Nonsense! How long has it been since you ate? And something good, not that University cafeteria slop." Before Sebastien could answer, Sharon was divesting her of her jacket and bags and dragging her into the kitchen by her arm.

Sebastien sat at the kitchen table, nursing the steaming cup of tea that had been thrust into her hands while Sharon bustled about, chattering. She set a loaded plate of food in front of Sebastien and sat across from her, suddenly silent. She sipped her own cup of tea and shot Sebastien subtle, inviting looks.

Sebastien ignored the encouragement toward conversation. She didn't want to talk. However, despite being sure she wasn't hungry, she ended up clearing the whole plate, and felt better afterward. The weight in her belly acted as a stabilizing anchor. Her fingers felt warm for the first time since...before.

With the feeling of weight and substance causing her to move even slower, Sebastien trudged up the stairs to her room, which was pleasantly toasty from the roaring fireplace. Her magical plants were in the window, a light crystal shining on the sempervivum apricus to give it more brightness, but neither looked healthy.

With a sigh drawn up from deep inside her like the last gasp of a dying man, Sebastien watered the wilting mandrake root, humming a half-remembered lullaby from her childhood to it while she tickled the leaves. Mandrakes appreciated music and being petted, according to the *Comprehensive Compendium of Components*. The sempervivum apricus, she took out of the window and set on a chair, settling light crystals pilfered from the various light fixtures in her room and the hallway atop the dirt. *'That is a ridiculous amount of secondhand sunlight. Hopefully enough to rejuvenate it.'* The pot was too bright to look at without squinting, so she covered the whole chair with a thick winter blanket, draping it over and around the pot to contain the light.

Having done what she could to keep her magical components alive, Sebastien finally took off her shoes and outer clothing. She touched a finger to the skin of her chest, wincing. There was a distinctly medallion-shaped freeze burn there, from when her grandfather's artifact had sucked up warmth to deflect the fireball the Morrow man had shot at her.

One of the infirmary healers had put a salve on it while she was unconscious, which made her frown with a renewed feeling of violation. It was their job, of course, and better they be too thorough than miss a dangerous wound for privacy's sake, but she didn't like the idea of someone manhandling and casting magic on her while she slept.

Sebastien dug through her school satchel for the basic supplies she always kept on hand, using some burn paste and a dab of thick juice squeezed from one of the sempervivum apricus's leaves on the skin. She would like to avoid a medallion-shaped scar.

With the strongest dreamless sleep spell she could manage and an alarm on her pocket watch to wake her up in a few hours, she crawled into bed.

Huddling underneath the blankets, she clasped her Conduit between her hands, fingers laced together. "I'm in control," she murmured to herself. "I'm in control." She repeated it until her eyelids grew heavy and her tongue clumsy.

She slept, woke, and slept again.

When the fire had long died out and the faint rays of dawn were painting the rolling fog outside her window in pastel hues, the mattress shifted under her. She blinked crusty eyes open, her hand gripping the Conduit, which had slipped under her pillow, in confusion and alarm.

Oliver looked down at her from where he had perched on the edge of her mattress, a glass of liquid in his hands. He looked almost as tired as she felt. "Hey," he said softly. "You've been sleeping for a while. I brought you something to stave off dehydration."

She pushed herself up, taking the glass from him. Honeyed water. She downed the whole thing, gasping for air as she handed it back to him, and then wiped the back of her arm against her mouth. "Thank you," she croaked.

"You're alright?"

"Fine. Just...tired."

"When you set off the alarm, Katerin and I happened to be in a meeting with Lynwood and his sister, Gera. It was very lucky. Gera used Katerin's bracelet to track you. I couldn't check for myself that you were okay without raising suspicion. I told Gera to let you know that if the coppers arrested you, as long as you could remain as Sebastien, I would find a way to get you free."

Sebastien shook her head. "Gera didn't get a chance to tell me. We weren't alone. But she did help deflect suspicion off me—with the Raven Queen as a scapegoat." She smiled wryly at the irony. "They now believe the Raven Queen can give blessings, one of which is some sort of anti-divination effect."

"Clever."

Sebastien let out a sputtering laugh. "Gera pulled so much stuff out of her ass, I almost couldn't believe what I was listening to. It was great. I mean, at this point even if someone met Siobhan Naught dancing naked in the street, they would think she's a little too *normal* to possibly be the Raven Queen."

Oliver didn't return her mirth, his voice remaining careful and soft. "She told me your friend died. Newton Moore? I recognized the name—you'd mentioned him to me before."

Sebastien's throat stiffened, her smile disintegrating. "I am restricted from talking about the details."

"I assumed. The Red Guard likes to keep their work out of the ears of the public. But I know what happened, broadly, and you can talk about how it affected you."

She stared at him silently for a while. "I don't know what you want me to say."

"Whatever you want. There's a reason you've been sleeping for the last sixteen hours, and as far as I know it's not because of lingering anomalous effects."

She closed her eyes. "I hate sleeping more than anything, Oliver. I'm just... too tired to do anything else. I have been trying so hard, for what feels like a really long time, and then this happened and... I just cannot keep going. I feel like I've been frantically juggling balls, and before I really got the hang of it another would drop out of the sky and I would have to add it to the rotation, throwing the balls higher and higher and moving faster and faster. But now I've dropped them all, and they've scattered everywhere. It seems like an impossible effort to find them and get them back up in the air again."

She opened her eyes to see him nodding slowly in the pre-dawn light. "That makes sense. What else?" he asked.

She hesitated again, but finally said, "This isn't the first time I've seen someone die, you know that. But this... When an Aberrant is created, it's the loosed magic itself that turns against you, that kills you and uses your body as fuel to create something else in your place. Magic...it is not our friend. It is a rabid beast that we leash to our wills, and it uses every mistake as a chance to kill its master and break free again."

"And you're a sorcerer. It could happen to you," he deduced.

"Or to one of my classmates, or to you, or to some random person walking down the street. And when it does, it could kill everyone around it in passing." She needed magic, she even loved it, but this was a visceral reminder that she feared it, too, and for good reason.

She had gotten lucky with Newton. He wasn't particularly strong before losing control, she had been intimately familiar with the spell he was casting, and the Aberrant happened to manifest in a way that didn't kill them all immediately *and* that could be defended against. It had been a confluence of fortunate coincidences. That wasn't always the case. "I just wonder how the world hasn't already fallen into ruin. It seems like we as a society are perpetually on the brink of a cataclysmic event. And if something worse happened, it's likely I wouldn't be able to do anything about it, or even save myself."

Oliver's hand moved, like he wanted to take hers, but in the end he only said, "Magic is dangerous. You don't have to worry about me losing control, but it is, in general, a valid fear. That's why we have the Red Guard, and they are very good at their job. The world was around for a long time before you were born, and yet somehow we survived until now." One side of his mouth twitched up in a tentative smile. "For the remainder of your concerns, I suppose you must do what you can to decrease your risk—like sleeping when you need it—and then ask yourself if the remaining danger of being a thaumaturge is worth it."

"It is," she said immediately. It had never been in question, really, but saying it aloud settled something inside her.

His smile grew larger. "Well then. Come down to breakfast."

Sebastien still wasn't hungry, but she didn't protest. After eating, which sapped what little energy she had gathered, she slept again for a few hours.

When she awoke, the streets below were busy, and the sun had burned off the fog of the early morning. For the first time in a while, she took out her grimoire, lightly running her fingers over its leather cover and slightly ragged pages. Her grandfather had helped her create it when she turned thirteen. It held a deceptive number of pages, was encrypted to allow access to only her, and held her accumulated knowledge of magic and sketches of the interesting places she'd been and things she'd seen.

She flipped through the pages from the beginning, chuckling at her younger self's awkward handwriting, occasional misspelling, and excitement at the basic fundamentals of sorcery. She had been so cute and innocent. She'd actually learned quite a lot over the years, despite lacking a formal teacher after her grandfather, but much of it was the type of thing that would be useful to small rural villages or while traveling. She knew many minor healing concoctions, spells to keep a chicken laying eggs, and how to ward off erlkings and bogles.

Sebastien had stopped updating her grimoire frequently just a few days into her stay at the University, as she got too busy to keep up with the rest of her work. Now, she took out her fountain pen, filled the internal cartridge with ink, and began to write. Her thoughts and many, many questions spilled out onto the page, along with some of the more interesting lessons she'd learned at the University. She didn't push this process, allowing herself breaks whenever her hand hurt or she grew bored.

It took days.

Her appetite returned, and as she sat at the window, watching the rhythms of the city in between bouts of writing in her grimoire, she slowly lost the overwhelming desire to sleep. The occasional spark of irrepressible excitement filled her as she explained the magic she'd learned to the grimoire, and she realized just how much she'd improved in the last few months.

Oliver was so busy she only saw him in passing a few times, but she didn't try to ask if he needed help. She hadn't replenished enough to spare even a fraction of herself.

She woke early Thursday morning, for the first time in the last week not feeling like she wanted to go directly back to sleep, and slipped down to the kitchen as the sun rose. When breakfast was ready, she imbued two cups of Oliver's expensive coffee with wakefulness intent and took a tray filled with food up to his office, where he was already working.

Oliver cleared a spot on his overflowing desk before grasping the cup of coffee from her like a man stranded in the desert might take a canteen of water. His clothes were rumpled, his hair slightly greasy, and his eyes ringed by dark circles. He still smiled in greeting, and it seemed genuine, though that might have been more for the *coffee* than for her.

"I'm going back to the University today. I wanted to talk with you a little before I left," Sebastien said.

Oliver nodded silently, his mouth busy with gulping down dark, steaming liquid.

"Did the…*incident* cause problems?"

He let out a deep sigh as he set down the empty mug. "The Aberrant was in Nightmare Pack territory, so despite the appearance of the Raven Queen, the coppers haven't had much to go on when questioning my people. There is increased scrutiny, however, and there have been attempts to insert an undercover agent into our operations. Nothing we cannot handle. I did have to make some concessions to Lynwood, both for the Pack's help obfuscating the issue and for causing such a significant disturbance in their territory."

Sebastien cringed. "What concessions?"

Oliver waved a hand indifferently, speaking around a bite of the omelet Sharon had cooked him. "Nothing critical. I don't hold you responsible. Sometimes things just go wrong… And sometimes things blow up and cause a shit tornado. It could have been worse. You kept some of the residents from dying, at least, and this whole incident has done more than a little to reduce resistance among those who weren't so pleased with our presence in the new territory. No one wants an angry visit from the Raven Queen."

Sebastien grimaced, then let out a resigned sigh. "That's something, I suppose. I'm not going to be able to keep track of Tanya like I did before. I screwed up. She knows the Raven Queen was following her. She and anyone she might meet with will be wary, and without Newton…" She stared unhappily into the steam rising from her coffee, unable to stop the faint trembles that sent ripples across its surface.

Oliver scratched at the stubble on his jaw, stuffing another bite into his mouth. "I wouldn't say it's the best outcome, since this is sure to put the University on their guard against us, but Tanya Canelo is no longer our only source of information on what's been happening. We have many captured former Morrows who know quite a lot. Long-term, we'll simply need to work with what we have. It's not worth putting you in further danger."

"The captured Morrows are actually part of what I wanted to discuss. Have there been any attempts to break those prisoners free?"

"No. Why?"

"Tanya was asking about their location and the Verdant Stag's security measures during the secret meeting. They must have been planning something, and this little incident probably won't deter them indefinitely."

"We'll increase our precautions. Thank you for the warning." It was Oliver's turn to sigh, and he hunched over his desk as if an invisible weight were trying to crush him into the mounds of paperwork. "Perhaps we can upgrade the alarm wards. All our enforcers have already been pulling double shifts for the last week, and it will take some time to increase our numbers with trustworthy people."

"The battle didn't go as smoothly as planned," she stated.

"That's true, unfortunately."

"Has the takeover of the new territory encountered much difficulty?"

"The Morrows may have managed their territory in a way I wouldn't, but they weren't completely foolish. They were more heavily armed and prepared than we had hoped or expected. It is difficult to conceal all signs of an operation with so many people and moving pieces. Nevertheless, it did not go as horribly as it could have. A few of our people died, more were severely injured. We managed to capture a large percentage of the Morrows. We mitigated the collateral damage as well as we could and are making basic aid available to those who need it—food, minor healing, and a place to sleep.

"It will take us some time to consolidate all our gains, but we immediately secured a large sum of coin, consumable resources like artifacts and components, and income producing businesses, both legal and illegal. Some of those businesses might not be as profitable under our control—I am unwilling to force anyone into prostitution or a fighting arena, for instance—but it should still help with our liquidity. I expect there to be a fairly long period of upheaval as we bring the new territory in line with the standards of the Verdant Stag. I'm hoping to turn several of the buildings into textile factories, but I'm waiting on Lord Gervin to officially accept my request for a textile sub-commission, since their Family legally has domain over the industry. Once I have that, I will be able to very quickly create jobs. And we already have a few new thaumaturges to help, including a whole alchemical workshop and the brewers, so there should be less pressure on you and the handful of others we were relying on."

"But I can still brew for the Verdant Stag, right?"

"Of course. We will always have some sort of work for a thaumaturge. There aren't nearly enough of you. Also..." he said, raising a finger and leaning to rummage in one of his desk drawers. "Here is a small bonus for your performance during the battle. The report I received stated that you fought and captured a handful of Morrows who were threatening the healing station, which was not part of your job description. It's a bounty, plus your fee for doing the Verdant Stag's purchasing at the previous underground meeting. I would have given it to you before, but..." He shrugged pointedly.

"Oh. Thank you." The small purse held fourteen gold. Four for the meeting, ten for the bounty.

Sebastien decided not to put the extra coin toward her debt. It would instead help her maintain a reasonable emergency fund. Taking a bracing breath, she said, "I'd like to give you my report on what happened that night now."

"Are you sure? You don't need to talk about it if you're not ready."

"I'm sure." She'd done her best to remember the glyphs carved into the skull artifact the Red Guard had used to bind her vow. She'd noted nothing that seemed like it would alert them if she broke her word, and she'd given them nothing of herself. Even so, she pressed her hand against her chest, where the black stone amulet hung under her shirt, and focused the barest wisp of Will on it.

That was all it took to return her to her original form. She shrank down a bit in her seat, her clothes growing suddenly baggy on her.

Oliver watched with interest. "That is as fascinating as ever."

"Speaking as Siobhan might help push past the Red Guard's compulsion," she explained. She took a moment to shift about, moving her face and limbs to settle into her transformed body. After reminding herself of her name in this form, the one that she had not given the vow under, she began to speak.

The vow still guided her away from sharing too many details, causing a growing tightness in her throat the longer she spoke. Still, she found that she didn't mind this terribly, as she had no desire to dredge up the irrelevant minutiae.

When she was finished, she returned to Sebastien's body and left Oliver to his huge pile of work. In the cheek-tingling cold outside, she turned north, to the University settled atop the white cliffs, as bright and proud as ever. She was out of time.

$$5$$

TEA AND COOKIES

Sebastien
Month 1, Day 28, Thursday 9:00 a.m.

Sebastien arrived at the University with barely enough time to make it to History of Magic. Although this class was with a different dormitory group than her others, and none of these students really knew her, Sebastien's entrance was greeted by a sudden hush followed by a resurgence of murmuring.

As Sebastien took her seat, the gazes that followed her made it obvious that her involvement in a rogue magic incident was widely known. She hoped that was all that was known.

To Sebastien's relief, Professor Ilma made no public display of concern for her, teaching as she would normally. "Your mid-terms have been graded," the woman announced without preamble, handing a stack of papers to her student aide to pass out. "Results and rankings have been posted on the announcement board in the library. We will not be discussing your test results during class time. There is too much content to get through. If you have questions, you may stay after class or come to my office hours."

Sebastien looked with slight pleasure at the grade atop her test paper. Ilma was a harsh taskmistress, but Sebastien had still managed to answer most of the questions to her satisfaction and received close to full marks. Some of the students near her peeked blatantly at her test, so she covered it with a glare that had them turning away, red-faced. *'The rudeness is already getting on my nerves. If the day continues like this, I might very well snap.'*

Ilma had only been lecturing for a few minutes when the door opened again.

Another student aide stepped in and murmured something to Professor Ilma, and then they both turned to look at her.

"Mr. Siverling, your presence is required elsewhere," Ilma said. "Feel free to see me later if you feel this undue interruption might negatively impact your studies."

The aide shuffled uncomfortably, but apparently whoever had called for Sebastien had enough clout to risk Ilma's dissatisfaction.

Sebastien followed the aide out into the hall. "Do you know what this is about?" she asked, adjusting the strap of her bag over her shoulder as she tried to keep the apprehension out of her voice.

The aide shook her head, walking quickly and not looking at Sebastien. "I do not."

"Who wants to see me?"

"The History Chair, Grandmaster Kiernan," the woman said succinctly.

Sebastien had never met the Chair of the History department before. *'Is Grandmaster Kiernan part of Munchworth and Tanya's faction? Munchworth is in the History department, too… Could they have suspicions about my presence at the scene?'* Possibilities ran rampant through her head, and she found herself reaching for her Conduit before she noticed and stopped herself. All too soon, before she had any kind of plan in place, they arrived at Kiernan's door.

The student aide opened it and waved her through with a shallow bow.

Swallowing, Sebastien lifted her chin and stepped into the room.

Grandmaster Kiernan, who was sitting behind an expensive desk, looked up with a smile when she entered. He did not remind her of Munchworth in the least. Kiernan had a polished, bald head and a short grey beard. His office was warm and filled with historical artifacts and relics. They sat on warded stands and display cases, filling the spaces between books on the shelves that lined the walls.

"Mr. Siverling! Thank you for coming. Take a seat, please," he offered, motioning to the plush couch next to a window instead of the chairs in front of his desk.

Slowly, she complied.

The low table in front of the couch already had a tea service tray atop it, and Kiernan sat on the cushion next to her and prepared a steaming cup for each of them. "I am Grandmaster Kiernan," he said, "but I prefer students just call me Professor Kiernan. Is it alright if I call you Sebastien?" he asked, his tone making it clear that he expected her to agree eagerly.

She nodded silently.

"One of my former students sent me this tea all the way from the Dragon Well area of Longjing, which is a small province in the East known for its tea." He motioned to the cream and sugar, but Sebastien shook her head, accepting a plain cup. "Cookie?" he offered. "I know you young people burn through calories as quickly as they hit your stomachs, and I hear the cafeteria food leaves something to be desired."

"No, thank you." She was always in need of caffeine, so she drank the tea, but only after he drank first. *'I doubt he would try to drug Thaddeus Lacer's apprentice, but one never knows.'*

"I understand you are in Ilma's class section. An interesting woman. How are you enjoying it?"

"She's a good teacher," Sebastien said cautiously. "She tries to make us think, not just regurgitate information."

Kiernan nodded. "So I hear. And your other classes? How are you finding the University so far?"

"I enjoy my classes," Sebastien said. She wasn't going to start complaining about Pecanty here.

"I'm not surprised. I hear you are a rather impressive student, despite your...unfortunate background. Your current guardian is Lord Dryden? It must be hard, without parents alive to guide you," Kiernan said searchingly.

Sebastien tried not to stiffen visibly. "Mr. Dryden has been very kind to me," she said noncommittally, though Oliver wasn't legally, or even informally, her guardian. *'What is Kiernan getting at? Why bring up my parents? Is he trying to hint that he knows my background doesn't stand up to scrutiny?'* The stress of the conversation was getting to her. She downed her tea and decided to cut through the inscrutable small talk. "Professor Kiernan, why am I here?"

He laughed, smacking a hand on her shoulder and did not seem to notice her flinch. "Oh, I like to chat with the students when I get a chance, keep abreast of how things are going in the 'real world,' as they say. But I did call you here for a specific reason."

Kiernan stood and grabbed a card-sized piece of paper from his desk. "We at the University wanted to thank you for what you did." He handed her the card. "At great risk to yourself, you acted to save those in danger during a rogue magic incident. Without you, several innocent civilians and one of our other University students might no longer be alive. Mr. Siverling, I hear that you successfully stunned the Aberrant, which may have bought time for the Red Guard and greatly affected the outcome of that night."

Sebastien Siverling had indeed stunned the Aberrant when she, supposedly crawled in the window to search for an unconscious Newton. She looked down at the card filled out with one hundred University contribution points. An exorbitant amount for a first term student. If converted to the equivalent in coin, this was worth about ten gold if she redeemed items for resale.

"You can upgrade your meal plan with that," Kiernan said jovially, slapping his knee and laughing.

"I don't understand," Sebastien said. *'Is what I supposedly did actually worth contribution points? Is this…a bribe? Carrot before the stick? Is he about to threaten me?'*

"You're a hero, Sebastien! A credit to our school. We wanted to make sure you understood you are appreciated, and also ensure that the stress and pressure from your experiences will not adversely affect you going forward. I know Professor Lacer was worried you would be in danger of Will-strain from the trauma."

"I'm fine."

Kiernan shook his head sympathetically, once again clapping her on the shoulder. "There's no need to put on a brave face, Sebastien. What you experienced would leave anyone with some mental or emotional strain. Sometimes it's best to talk about these things. Recounting your experiences with someone trustworthy can help to lessen any hold they might have on you, and if it turns out that you need any further help, a little leeway, I do have some pull with the other members of the University board…"

She blinked down at her empty cup.

Kiernan hurriedly poured more tea for her with a grandfatherly smile.

"You want me to tell you about what happened that night?"

"I think it would be best. Take your time, feel free to explore the details and how everything made you feel."

'So the contribution points are *a bribe. An excuse to question me in person.'* She sipped her tea and shook her head sadly. "I made a vow to the Red Guard. I'm unable to talk about anything that happened."

Kiernan froze for a second, then nodded. "Of course they would do that…" he murmured, but then perked up. "But surely they left leeway for you to speak with a mental health professional?"

She shrugged. "If that mental health professional works for the Red Guard, then yes."

Kiernan's eyebrows and mouth both collapsed downward, his grandfatherly kindness replaced by pointed frustration, as if he suspected she was being purposefully difficult. "How did the three of you, normally all good students, end up in such a situation?"

Sebastien sighed mournfully. "I'm not sure what happened before I got there. And obviously, by the time I arrived, Newton was already…" She trailed off with a small, pained sound like a wounded animal, and brought a hand to her tightening throat with an expression of distress. "I'm sorry. I'm really unable to talk about it. The vow makes my throat close up."

Kiernan patted her shoulder but continued his questions. "But you did encounter the Raven Queen. She was also there by the time you arrived, I'm told."

Sebastien grimaced. "I didn't know it was her at the time."

"I've heard that she gave you a blessing."

"There aren't any ongoing dangers, if that's what you're worried about," Sebastien assured him with an expression that was as sincere as she could make it. "The other students are safe to be around me. The Red Guard cleared me for release, and Professor Lacer was there, so you can ask him if you want confirmation."

"Oh, I believe you, my boy. I'm sure you wouldn't place your fellow students in danger. But I am curious, did the Raven Queen do anything... special? Anything to indicate why she was there, or what she's been up to, where she's been hiding?"

Sebastien shook her head silently, taking another sip of tea while she held Kiernan's gaze over the rim. He wasn't even being subtle with pumping her for information. The apprehension she'd felt upon being summoned was quickly turning into irritation.

"But she gave you a boon. You cannot tell me you didn't interact. How did it happen?"

"Seemingly by..." Sebastien lifted her hand to her throat again, frowning, and squeezed out, "coincidence." She took another sip of the tea as if to soothe her throat, making a mournful expression at her inability to expound further.

Kiernan scoffed angrily. "Apparently this entire situation, from the beginning, was by seeming 'coincidence.' Forgive me if I don't believe it."

Sebastien leaned over and patted Kiernan on the shoulder, like he had so presumptuously been doing to her. "I know the Raven Queen stole something from your department, but I'm sorry I can't be of more help. Grandmaster Thaddeus Lacer has taken me as his apprentice, which you probably know. He heard my report in full. If you'd like more information, you should talk to him, or perhaps the coppers. I'd rather not continue attempting to speak of it. Due to the restrictions the Red Guard placed on me, it's both difficult and stressful, which is counterproductive to any beneficial effects a counseling session with you might have. So, if there's nothing else... I'm very thankful for the contribution points, but I'm worried about falling behind in my classes, after having already been out for a week."

The man gritted his teeth for a moment, but then resumed his jovial pretense. "Oh, yes, yes, I don't want to disrupt your studies. Make sure to let one of the faculty know if you feel you need medical attention, either physical or mental." As she stood to leave, he said, "Are you sure you won't have some cookies? I don't need them myself. Don't want to pack on any extra winter padding around the middle!"

Sebastien smiled at him. "Oh, well in that case, perhaps I will share them with my friends. Thank you, that's very generous of you." She picked up the entire plate, and, without waiting for him to protest, walked out of the room with it. '*A little vindictive,*' she admitted to herself, '*but unlikely to have any consequences.*' She still didn't want to eat them herself, but perhaps she could give them to the members of Damien's little cohort—and keep watch for signs of lowered inhibitions or loosened tongues afterward.

6

———

PROSE AND POINTS

Sebastien
Month 1, Day 28, Thursday 9:40 a.m.

Professor Ilma didn't make a fuss when Sebastien slipped back into the room halfway through her lecture, despite the distraction she caused to the gossip-hungry students.

After the period was over, Sebastien hurried through the halls to Pecanty's Sympathetic Science classroom, not because she was eager for his class, but because she wanted to speak with both Damien and Ana.

Sebastien had apparently hurried too quickly, because neither was there when she arrived.

Some of the other students began working up the gumption to approach her as soon as she entered the room. She was unguarded, like a baby lamb separated from the flock.

Waverly Ascott, quiet as ever, moved her bag out of the seat next to her and waved Sebastien over with barely a glance.

Sebastien placed the plate of cookies pillaged from Kiernan on her desk.

Ascott kept her eyes trained on a thick book about witchcraft, but took one of the cookies and started nibbling.

Brinn Setterlund came up on Sebastien's other side, leaning against the desk and crossing his arms. He sent a weak glare out at nothing in particular, which Sebastien found supremely unthreatening, but was apparently enough to keep the other students from approaching.

'They're protecting me,' she realized with an uncomfortable moment of inner warmth.

Rhett Moncrieffe took a seat behind her with a cool nod. "Welcome back."

Alec Gervin also took a guard position, though he had to kick another student out of their place to do so, which reduced Sebastien's warm feelings.

Damien and Ana arrived shortly after and took the seats in front of her before immediately turning to face her. "Stars above, Sebastien, I'm so glad you're back. Things have been rather unpleasant here," Damien said.

She leaned forward. "I wanted to ask you two about that. What's happened while I was gone? What rumors have been circulating? Everyone seems to know I was involved." Damien might have information from his brother, since they seemed to communicate frequently and the elder Westbay wasn't particularly circumspect with what he revealed to his little brother. And Ana always seemed to know the latest gossip.

"It's been all anyone's talking about," Ana said. "What actually happened is still rather vague, but, as always, there are rumors that range from plausible to outrageous."

Damien nodded. "The coppers haven't come out with a statement, but everyone knows Newton is dead, and there was an Aberrant that got the Red Guard called in."

Ana, like Waverly, took one of the cookies from Sebastien's desk without even bothering to ask. "Delicious. Where did you get these, Sebastien?"

"Grandmaster Kiernan from the History department gave them to me when he called me to his office this morning," she said pointedly.

Damien's eyes widened before he controlled his expression, but the tension leaked through in his voice. "He's the department Chair, right? What could he want with you? Why did he give you cookies?"

Sebastien grimaced. "Kiernan gave me contribution points, but they were just an excuse to question me about what happened."

Ana nodded sagely. "He's probably worried about the University's reputation and what rumors you might spread. Canelo has been stripped of her student liaison position, you know. She was absent for a few days, perhaps being questioned by the coppers, but she's back now. It's bad press to have two of your student aides implicated in an incident like this. Especially when one turns up an Aberrant." Ana plucked at her clothes, smoothing imaginary wrinkles. "And on that note…what *actually* happened?"

Sebastien could feel the weight of attention from every remotely close-by student straining to hear her answer. She shook her head. "I had to make a vow with the Red Guard. I can't talk about it." She had a feeling she would be repeating that a lot in the near future.

Damien groaned in frustration, sending Ana a glare. "I told you guys not to bother him about that!"

Ana shrugged. "No harm in asking. I'm not ashamed to admit that I am quite curious. Perhaps I could relate some of the rumors to you, Sebastien, and you could simply tell me how close to the truth they are, on a scale of one to ten?"

Sebastien shrank down in her chair to get away from Ana's gleaming eyes. "No, thank you."

"Leave him alone, Ana," Alec said, scowling down at his desk. "Someone died."

Ana passed Alec a cookie and a sympathetic look, patting him on the hand. "Here. Eat something before you get any grumpier." She turned to Sebastien. "Newton Moore was his tutor, you know. It's a little frightening to think about."

Alec scowled but, with a surreptitious look at Sebastien, shoved the entire cookie into his mouth with an angry grunt.

Damien tossed his hair back. "I sympathize, Sebastien. Everyone keeps asking me for details since my Family runs the coppers. But I couldn't tell them anything even if I wanted to, because I don't know much. I sent a letter to Titus, but he's too busy with the investigation." Damien coughed awkwardly. "Also, it is confidential since the investigation is still ongoing, even if Titus isn't bound by the secrets of the Red Guard like someone in a lesser position might be."

Damien probably knew, or had extrapolated, more than he was letting on. Sebastien was grateful that he wasn't sharing with the others, as he likely would have before being inducted into their fake secret organization.

"What else has been happening?" she asked.

The others shared looks. "The coppers and some of the Red Guard came around to interview some people, but they didn't stay for long," Damien offered.

Ascott piped up. "There have been a lot of lectures about spell safety. There are sign-up sheets for counseling in the dorms. I'm not sure why they're making such a big deal of this, specifically. Didn't they give that lecture at the beginning of term about how one in fifteen of us would die or go insane before reaching Master level?"

"A lot less than one in fifteen people break and become an Aberrant," Alec muttered, accepting another cookie from Ana. The plate was rapidly emptying.

"Quite a few people are in the infirmary for Will-strain," Brinn added.

Moncrieffe nodded. "And Fekten has been more brutal than usual. He keeps going on about how we're all incompetent and will die at the first sign of danger. Tuesday we had to run five miles while he chased us and threw around stinging jinxes. I think he's trying to train our Wills through hardship."

"Oh!" Ana said. "All of us took turns making notes of what you missed during the lectures. I know how you obsess over being the best, Sebastien, so we thought you would want to avoid falling behind as much as possible." She pulled out a three-ring binder with clearly marked, color-coded sections. "Rhett did the organization. He loves that stuff."

Moncrieffe coughed awkwardly and looked away. "It was no big deal. I just copied what I do for my own notes."

Sebastien took the binder, suppressing the urge to argue that she did not obsess over being the best. She simply expected herself to perform at a level that wouldn't embarrass Professor Lacer. "Thank you," she said instead. Some notes were much clearer and more complete than others. Damien had even drawn little explanatory doodles in the margins of the lectures he covered, like he must have seen Sebastien doing on several occasions.

The group finished off the rest of the cookies, leaving Sebastien with a crumb-covered plate that she didn't know what to do with. They didn't exhibit any strange reactions, which meant that Kiernan probably hadn't been trying to drug her, just disarm her with gifts—and the unconscious desire to reciprocate his generosity. She didn't truly suspect they would be laced with anything, since that was the kind of crime that could get him in huge trouble. But people did stupid things all the time. She was a perfect example of that.

Professor Pecanty arrived shortly before the bell rang. He walked with an elaborately carved cane that looked as if he had chosen it specifically for the way it—combined with his vintage tweed jacket with the elbow patches—made him look like a wise old intellectual. He certainly didn't need it to help him walk.

Pecanty had their graded mid-term tests, but unlike Professor Ilma, he had apparently decided that their class time was best spent going over the test in detail. "We will start with some of the particularly bad answers and contrast them against much better examples," he announced, pulling out a few tests that had sections marked with clips. "Perhaps you will find some examples from your peers edifying."

Sebastien shrank down in her seat, holding back a groan. *'He's going to publicly shame me, I know it.'*

However, Pecanty didn't mention any of the students by name, only picking a question or two from each section to review while he wrote notes on the blackboard. "Here, you were asked to give synonyms and associated words for the keyword *'rain,'* and then use them in a sentence. One student provided three links. *'Storm,' 'cloud,'* and *'water.'* Uninspired, to say the least, as each of those words can quite literally be *combined* with *'rain'*: rainstorm, raincloud, and rainwater. The sentence provided was, 'The dark clouds broke with a rainstorm, filling the streets with water.'" He recited it quickly, with an unusual lack of lilting inflection, then looked up again, slapping the test down on his desk. "Boring and plain. I cannot imagine myself there, nor feel anything from that sentence."

He picked up a different test, flipping to the same section and reading aloud, this time with his usual cadence, as if reciting a piece of poetry. "'The dreary drizzle that had filled the morning turned, by evening, to a drenching squall, sheets of water crashing down from an oppressive, bruise-purple sky.' Keywords were '*drizzle,*' '*squall,*' '*crashing,*' and '*oppressive.*' I hope the difference is obvious, but if not, let me point out that none of these words can be directly joined to '*rain*' to form their own word. This example used both alliteration and metaphor, as well as evocative imagery."

He moved to yet another test, flipping to a new section. "You were asked to list the connotations associated with a certain component, and then relate those associations in a memory or scene highlighting the component. In this particular case, the component was daisy petals. This test-taker correctly enumerated daisy petals' connection to the ideas of new beginnings, hope, innocence, fun, affection, and purity. Most of you got that right, which shows that at least University students can memorize information from their textbooks." Pecanty paused for a scathing moment that *almost* reminded Sebastien of Professor Lacer. "The problem is here: 'The girl picks daisies in a field, plucking petals as she attempts to divine, "He loves me," or "He loves me not."' I am forced to wonder if the point of this assignment was clear, seeing as many of the answers were like this. Let me read you a proper response."

He cleared his throat. "'The daisy pushes through the earth, all green, wet with spring's morning dew. It reaches for the sun, drinking in the light and warmth, and unfurling a flower that opens itself to the embrace of the sky, allowing the buzzing honey-makers to drink from its cup. My mother plucks the daisy and tucks it behind my ear. I am not much taller than the swaying grasses, which smell of sweet earth and buckwheat, and the hem of my cloak is wet and itchy against my legs, but I laugh and pluck one for her in return. She kneels to allow me to tuck it clumsily into her hair.'"

Sebastien had frozen as soon as he began to speak. That was *her* answer. She had been following the advice of the upper-term student, going over the top with poetic description, mention of the senses, and had even made up a connection to her own past. In addition to writing with unnecessarily pretty handwriting.

"Notice the expression of new beginnings, innocence, and affection symbolized by the anthropomorphization of the daisy itself, and then the innocent exuberance of the child, who is fully grounded in the sensations of that moment," Pecanty said. "It's practically *bursting* with connections to all the meanings a daisy petal might hold. If time allowed, we could examine this answer alone for most of the class period."

'That is…utter bullshit.' Sebastien had to wonder if all the themes, subtext, and meaning Pecanty found in the books, poems, and plays they studied in class were as similarly nonexistent as this, unintentional on the author's part and attributed with layers of significance that the work did not, in fact, possess.

After a few more examples, Pecanty moved on to the theoretical spell section of the test. "You were asked to create a spell array and casting method for a spell that would help someone process their sorrow or grief, explaining your choices along the way. Some of you chose to use a pentagram, a safe but uninspired choice." He turned to copy out two spell arrays on the board. "This one, using a hexagram for the main symbol, for its connection to spiritual balance, guidance, and mental or emotional aid, is ideal. Especially with the inclusion of the tetragram, or four-pointed star, which in this case was added to turn the focus toward stability and the past. This will help anchor someone who might be more emotionally fragile."

He turned back to the tests. "Now, one student included mermaid tears as one of their primary components. I can only imagine this was because tears usually stem from sadness, and mermaids are known for their beautiful, mournful singing. However, this student seems to have been under a misconception." He spoke loudly, emphasizing his point. "Mermaids are a magical cephalopod. They lure prey by sticking tentacles above water and making them look like a human woman, and this false form lets out a haunting song and asks for help. When the victim gets too close, the 'mermaid' suddenly comes apart into a mass of tentacles that grab them and drag them into the water to be eaten. Mermaid tears do not exist, as mermaids do not have tear ducts and cannot cry."

A student gave themself away by groaning aloud.

Pecanty nodded at them. "Painful indeed. Blue poppy for its melancholy and sedative properties makes sense, but as this spell array is created, it seems like it might actually *induce* grief. That is, if it produced any effect at all, since the glyph used for *'feel'* is one for physical touch rather than emotion."

He gestured next to the hexagram spell array on the board, ignoring the students' snickers. "This student had a much better idea. Golden apples sprinkled with cinnamon for nostalgia, balanced against shade dust for a connection to the past, and condensed granules of etherwood smoke for calm contemplation. That last choice might be a bit too potent for certain types of trauma, and shade dust assumes that the grief cannot have a present-day, ongoing cause, but the addition of lotus bulbs for their connection to self-regeneration, cleansing, and enlightenment was a genius combination. In conjunction with the tetragram, it would add a fortifying element to support the target of the spell *through* their grief, to be reborn afresh on the other side."

Pecanty went on in this vein for most of the class period, finally stopping to give their graded papers back to them. "Sympathetic Science is all about connections," he said as he walked among the desks, placing each test paper in the students' hands personally. "Those connections must be rich and varied, a spiderweb filled with points that cause dozens of lightning-fast responses to bloom when there is a tug on any single node."

When he placed Sebastien's paper on her desk, he stopped to murmur, "Exemplary work, an admirable improvement over your past efforts. I knew you would come around, once you gave up your stubborn way of thinking."

Sebastien flipped over her test to see that Pecanty had attached a slip with five contribution points. She wasn't sure whether to be happy or outraged that the nonsense she had written was rewarded like this.

After class, Alec stopped Sebastien in the hallway with a hand on her arm.

She turned to him, already brewing a scowl, but his expression was uncomfortably earnest, throwing her off.

"So, I put together a care package for the Moore family. Damien and I wrote letters to them about what it was like being friends with Newton, and gathered up some of his stuff that was left in his room, plus some coin to help them get by. I heard their house was burnt down. Anyway, um, do you want to write a letter for them, too? I can put it in with the rest of the package."

Sebastien was taken aback, and remained silent for a long few seconds. She had not expected this, and especially not from Alec.

Alec shuffled, his eyebrows drawing down. "I know I'm not good with people like Ana, but care packages are something you do when a family goes through a traumatic event. It's too simple to mess up. Do you want to write a letter or not?" he asked, growing belligerent.

"I have Newton's Conduit. I'll send that along with a letter of my own."

He harrumphed. "Well, finish it by Monday. I'm not waiting on you if you don't."

They walked on to the cafeteria, where she stopped and scanned the large room from the entrance. Stopping Alec, she handed him the empty cookie plate. "Give this to the kitchen workers."

"Why can't you do it?" he asked.

She didn't reply, already leaving. To her surprise, Damien caught up with her a few moments later. "Where are you going?" he asked.

"To find Tanya Canelo. We were both *there*. I want to see what she has to say." Really, she wanted to know what Tanya had told the coppers and the Red Guard, to see if she could glean any clues about what their next move might be.

"I'll come, too," Damien offered immediately, adding in a murmur, "It might be dangerous to meet with her alone."

Tanya's personal room had been taken away and she now roomed in the fourth-term student dorms, but she wasn't there. Sebastien finally found her in a less-trafficked corner of the library. The blonde, square-jawed girl looked almost as exhausted as Sebastien felt.

Her mouth tightened when she saw Sebastien, but she nodded a sharp greeting. "Siverling. If you're here to talk about the rogue magic incident, I'm unable to speak of it."

Sebastien sat down across from her. "The Red Guard made me take a vow too, but I can talk with those who already know the details. I was there shortly before the Red Guard arrived. I saw you going upstairs with the others, from outside the window."

Tanya looked between the two of them, not relaxing. "So?"

"So… Does anyone know why the Raven Queen was there?"

Damien sucked in a breath.

"I cannot speak of it," Tanya repeated.

"Do you need Damien to leave?" Sebastien asked.

Damien scowled immediately. "I'm not leaving you alone with her, Sebastien." He glared at Tanya, making no secret of his distrust.

Tanya glared back at Damien, looking as if she might snap and attack him, but instead, her eyes welled up with tears.

They rolled down her cheeks like big fat diamonds, one after the other.

Damien stepped back, alarmed.

"I cannot speak of it!" Tanya squeezed out in a choked voice.

It was so far out of character, so different from what Sebastien had been expecting, that she stared at the crying young woman for a long few moments. *'Was this what that skull was supposed to do to me? If so, vowing under the incorrect name made a huge difference. Or maybe she gave a different vow, and I got preferential treatment.'*

When Tanya hunched over, sobbing, Sebastien regained her wits, laying an awkward hand across Tanya's shaking shoulder. "I know you didn't mean for this to happen. What happened to Newton…wasn't your fault."

Tanya let out a watery snort. "If only that were true." With an obvious effort of will, she got herself under control, straightening and looking at Sebastien with a gaze that reminded her of a suffocating fish, wide-eyed and desperate. "But I would take it back, if I could. Newton was my friend, too."

Damien shuffled awkwardly, but Sebastien said, "I know. I didn't realize the restrictions they placed on you were so harsh. We don't have to talk about it."

Tanya nodded, looking as if her head might fall and never rise again. "Could you leave me be? I have a lot of studying to do. My mid-term results weren't as good as someone in my position needs."

They complied, though Damien seemed unsatisfied as they walked away.

"Why aren't you angry with her? Did she really have nothing to do with how Newton ended up?"

Sebastien sighed. '*If I were going to be angry with* her, *what would I need to feel for* myself?' Aloud, she said, "I sympathize, I suppose. Who knows how she got into this, but at this point, she's trapped. She's in too deep to escape, even if she wants to."

The feeling was familiar.

7

BINI FROGS & EXISTENTIAL CRISES

Month 1, Day 28, Thursday 1:45 p.m.

After the unsatisfactory conversation with Tanya, Sebastien went to see the overall mid-term results openly posted on the library notifications board. She was accompanied by Damien, Ana, and the other Crown Family group members, who she didn't exactly want to call friends but seemed to be spending more and more time with.

As they entered, she noticed a group of upper-term students blocking off a lounge alcove near the entrance, their eyes darting around in obvious, nervous glee, occasionally using their hands to cover immature giggles.

Sebastien ignored whatever mischief they were up to, moving on to the notifications board. She was closer to the front of the rankings than she had feared, having gotten about ninety percent of the available points across her six classes. She had done quite well in Practical Casting, Natural Science, History, and Modern Magics, modestly well in Sympathetic Science, and about average in Defense. Out of the three thousand students who had started the term, they had already lost about a hundred. Sebastien was ranked in the low three hundreds, which Professor Lacer wouldn't find particularly impressive, but should satisfy his minimum requirements.

At the very least, it was a stronger performance than her entrance exams. As opposed to facing a comprehensive test of anything and everything the professors felt appropriate, the mid-terms had only covered what they'd already learned. Additionally, she'd been better prepared for how they would be graded, which had paid off especially well in Pecanty's class.

Sebastien threaded her way back out of the crowd teeming like minnows around the board, and the others joined her after a few minutes.

"I still beat your score, Sebastien!" Damien announced, preening like a little rooster. "I got rank one hundred twelve."

"Congratulations," she said, making sure not to seem frustrated. She *didn't* always have to be the very best. And besides, she'd had many other projects taking up time she might have otherwise spent on studying. Sure, Damien was taking one more class than her and had still managed, but surely she was busier than him?

"We are all in the top five hundred," Ana announced.

"Except for me," Alec said, giving the girl a look of mixed anger and shame, his hands stuffed deep in his pockets. "But I still did pretty good, compared to normal. My father won't have any reason to be angry. He doesn't expect much at this point, as long as I don't embarrass him. I guess all that tutoring with Newton actually did help." He rocked back and forth on his feet during the couple of awkward seconds that followed, looking at the floor.

"Sorry," Ana said with a reconciliatory smile.

Alec shrugged. "No harm done."

Ana slipped her arm through his, giving a little tug. "You worked hard. Cheer up, Alec. We're now all one-eighteenth done with our higher schooling."

Alec snorted. "So encouraging. One-eighteenth already?" He tightened his voice to give a high-pitched imitation of Ana. "Guys, that's basically nearing the end already!" He gave his nonexistent long hair a dramatic flip and fluttered his eyelashes.

Ana punched him in the arm, and he stumbled away from her, but both were grinning.

Sebastien was too aware of the people whispering about her to get drawn into the banter. At first, she thought the whispers were because of the incident with Newton, but when she scowled at a group of particularly obvious women, one returned Sebastien a bold, flirtatious smile.

Thrown off, Sebastien looked away. *'Either the attention has nothing to do with the rogue magic incident at all, or these women are somehow attracted to men who've recently had a close brush with death. How foolish can you get, that something like this could make me seem like a* more *viable partner.'* She wasn't sure if it was better than being a pariah, which at least would have been a more rational response from the other students.

"They're drawn to the idea of danger," Rhett said, as if reading Sebastien's mind. He clapped Sebastien on the shoulder and leaned in to murmur in her ear. "Apparently there are some extra benefits to being associated with you."

With a wink, he turned toward the girls with a sad look on his face. "My friend Sebastien is so brave… Have you heard what happened?"

The women cooed and simpered, drawing Rhett into their midst.

A quick flash of irritation that he would take advantage of her situation to flirt with vapid women bloomed inside Sebastien, but instead of slicing him to ribbons with her tongue, she turned to leave. *'It's not a big deal. I'm just on edge. I'll consider this his repayment for organizing my notes.'*

Brinn hurried to catch up with her. "Sorry about Rhett. He doesn't mean anything bad by it, that's just how he is. I can say something to him if it's bothering you."

Sebastien gave the taller boy a small, strained smile. "No, it's okay. I'm just feeling a little…off."

Brinn nodded easily. "Anyone would be. You can't expect to go right back to normal after such a traumatic event. Be kind to yourself."

Sebastien's smile relaxed and grew a little bigger. "Be kind to myself, huh?"

"Well, you can't count on anyone else to be."

She eyed Brinn for a moment, until he ducked his head shyly, a quick blush rising to his cheeks. *'He's the most likable of the entire group,'* she decided, *'except maybe for Ana. But Ana is likable to everyone, like a bright light. Brinn is like the last cookie in the jar, a little stale but still sweet—a surprise.'*

She wasn't stupid enough to say this out loud, because she'd learned that people didn't appreciate mixed compliments, but the whole thought was wiped from her mind when an unfamiliar alarm cut through the building, followed shortly by screaming.

Sebastien's blood chilled as she stumbled through the panicking crowd, looking for the source of danger, her fist tight around her Conduit.

Her mind went blank when she saw it, stuttering as she struggled to comprehend.

A sky kraken, so huge that even one of its eyeballs matched her in height, had descended upon the library building and was looking in through a window, its glistening, chameleon-like flesh rippling with every twitch of the giant eye. A tentacle pressed against the window, seeming to tap on it inquisitively.

Near the window, the upper-term students she'd seen earlier were standing frozen, staring up at the creature in awe and fear.

Sebastien's eyes narrowed. No. Not awe and fear. Excitement and poorly-suppressed glee? She had seen similar expressions on people playing cards with her father when they got a particularly good hand. *'Did they summon that creature?'*

Outrage flushed her with heat so suddenly she grew faint, the sensations of her body falling away. But then the kraken tapped again, its eye twitching.

The image blurred just a bit with its movement. "An illusion," she said aloud. Then even louder, "It's an illusion!"

Some of the students near her caught her words and calmed, inspecting the window more closely.

"There isn't even a window on that part of the wall," she said louder.

The whole prank dissolved at that point, with library and administration workers descending on the group of upper-term students who had cast the illusion like the hammer of judgment. The wall went back to normal, the pranksters were told off and assigned punishments, and Sebastien left; she had better things to do than stand around gawking.

She flexed her fingers, shook out her arms, and rubbed the back of her neck to release some of the painful tension her body had accumulated in those few initial moments of panic.

"That was amazing!" Damien yelled, running up behind her.

"It could have gotten someone trampled to death," she bit back.

His smile lost its exuberance. "But it was impressive, right? Even better than some of the illusion plays I've seen when the big troupes are in town. Very convincing."

Sebastien had to admit he was right, though she'd never seen a professional illusion play. "Even so," she grumbled, leaving Damien to roll his eyes.

The next day, Sebastien struggled to rise from her bed, feeling as if a great weight were pressing her down under the safety of her warm blankets, until Damien brought her some coffee from his morning study group. The concern on his face alone was enough to get her out into the harsh reality of morning without delay. *'The last thing I want is more questions about if I'm okay.'*

In Modern Magics, Sebastien's first of only two classes on Fridays, Professor Burberry followed up on their project of the week, a scouring bath alchemical concoction. Sebastien had missed most of the lessons on theory, as well as their preliminary introduction to brewing, but she would make the actual concoction today.

While Modern Magics was not the most difficult class, it gave students a good grounding in many of the basic thaumaturgic crafts, which was the point of a practical class. Still, at times Sebastien wished it were a bit more challenging.

This was not one of those times.

Sebastien stared blearily up at the board while Professor Burberry spoke.

"We have a special opportunity today," Burberry said. "We are going to be brewing this scouring bath with a more potent component than you might normally have access to. The University's Zoology section is providing us with a few dozen bini frogs in their male form, which have a corrosive skin. You will be killing them, dissecting them into their useful parts, and then using a couple of strips of their skin in your concoction. If you feel queasy or light-headed at the thought of killing and dissecting a frog, I have some anti-anxiety potions at my desk. See me for a dose."

As the student aides for the class passed out jars with the large, bubble-skinned frogs inside, Burberry introduced them. "The bini frog is a magical creature commonly found in northern peat bogs. What makes them interesting is that they are both mother *and* father to their offspring, not through asexual reproduction, but through a hormone change that allows them to lay eggs as a female and then fertilize them as a male. They're a good example of how hormones can affect and regulate gene expression, as only their male forms have the caustic skin. The same frog not only looks different, but also behaves differently, and has different magical properties."

Ana leaned over to Sebastien, murmuring, "Bini frogs are being used in some interesting research to allow same-sex couples to have children." She sighed. "I would love to invest in it, but it's beyond the Gervin Family's domain, and Father isn't interested."

Sebastien replied absentmindedly, a little worm of a thought wriggling distractingly in the back of her mind. "Can't you decide to invest on your own, separate from the Family? The law doesn't state that you can't, as long as the domain isn't controlled by another of the Crown Families that opposes your entrance, right? What you might consider small sums of pocket money could still be significant to the researchers."

Ana replied, but Sebastien couldn't concentrate on her answer, because the worm of a thought had crawled up and made itself known to her consciousness. *'Could the bini frog have been a component in whatever spell the amulet casts on me to create Sebastien?'* She had been researching how the brain worked for her developmental sleep-proxy spell, but for some reason, despite seeing how important hormones were over and over, she had never really applied that understanding to her own situation.

Hormones affected not just the body, but the brain.

Sebastien stood abruptly, cutting off Ana's words with a muttered, "Bathroom," before hurrying from the class.

A quick peek under the stalls showed they were all empty of feet, so she had her existential crisis in front of the mirror over the sinks, which pumped in fresh water at will, just another example of the wonders of modern invention.

'How much of someone's personality comes from their brain, and how much from their hormones?'

The question sent cold spider legs crawling down her back, and she stared into her own reflected eyes, trying to take comfort in the fact that those, at least, were the same in both of her bodies. *'Are my hormones the same as Sebastien and as Siobhan?'* That seemed impossible, simply because of the distinction in sex. Her brain itself might not even be the same. After all, everything else was different. '*But injuries transfer over. And my blood is traceable in either form. So what does that mean?*'

Unlike the frogs, she was not swapping between sexes—between different expressions of her own body. Which would have been mind-bending enough on its own. No, she was shifting into a different body entirely. '*How much needs to change before I'm someone else? Even my name is different.*'

She realized she was panting and leaned over to splash some cold water on her face. '*Have I been feeling differently,* thinking *differently?*' She hadn't noticed and wasn't sure she could tell. After all, she was not an objective, outside observer.

For a moment, the stream of water sounded like a calm, insistent humming, and she jerked her head back, staring at it in alarm. She turned the faucet off, then snapped her fingers next to her ears to disrupt the phantom memory of sound, taking comfort in the agitated pounding of her heart.

Discovering the truth of her fears would take more than just awareness and introspection. Understanding the effects of such magic would require extensive study, hundreds of subjects monitored by objective outside agents as they underwent the same transition she had. But this, of course, was impossible for more than one reason.

She had continually reassured herself that she was the same person, that a change of bodies meant nothing about who she was on the inside, and in fact had felt bizarrely comfortable in either body, after getting over the initial shock. That comfort might be a sign to the negative, however, since it could have been an effect of the spell itself, meant to mitigate the chance of a mental breakdown.

She wiped her frigid, wet hands over the back of her neck, taking a perverse thrill in the shiver that wracked her body. Water dripped from her blonde lashes. '*My consciousness is continuous between both forms. There's no interruption. My memories are the same. It's not as if I'm temporarily killing and later resurrecting either version of myself each time I switch. Even if the transformation is affecting my personality, I still consider me to be "myself" under the effects of alcohol or other substances. Why can't this be the same? My name might change, and my body, but there is something deeper than that, something that makes me* me, *which is constant.*' The words felt right, but still, she was unsure.

'*There is no evidence of a soul,*' she admitted to herself. '*And without that, what am I except for the consciousness created by my body? The consciousness which is* dependent upon *my body.*' When the Aberrant had taken control of her body, forcing her to calm, its effect had infected more than just her physical flesh. Her mind had begun to lose its grip, too. And what was *she,* if not her mind? '*If I do not run my own mind, what runs it? If I don't control my own thoughts, my own decisions, my own feelings, where is the barrier between "me" and "other?" Will I even notice if I cease to be myself?*'

Though she had been trying not to think of it, blood and fire flashed across her mind's eye. Squeezing her eyes closed, she pressed a knuckle into her temple until it hurt—until it felt like she would leave a bruise—but the pain pushed the memory away.

Her panic had grown too large to grasp entirely, and so, perversely, was settling into a dull dread instead. *'That all may be true, but does it actually matter?'* She was at school, away from the string Aberrant that was once Newton. It couldn't get her. And it was dead by now anyway, proper punishment for devouring Newton and killing those people. It couldn't control, or *consume*, anyone.

And as for her body, she couldn't be sure that she was feeling exactly the same as she would have, entertaining the exact thoughts she would be in her original form, but it *felt* authentic. If she had thought of these possibilities when she first discovered the effects of the amulet, she might have been more frightened at the implications, but she had been switching back and forth for months now and noticed no adverse effects. *'Perhaps now is not the time to have a mental breakdown. There is nothing I can do about it, after all. I won't give up the opportunities that Sebastien allows me, and I won't throw away my past as Siobhan. If some part of my mind is lost and replaced every time, which* isn't *necessarily the case—I don't know how the artifact works, after all—at least my magic seems to be constant.'*

When her fingers had stopped trembling, she wiped away the water, leaving her cheeks and nose red from the cold. She dug out a small jar of bruise balm from her bag and wiped it on her temple as a preemptive measure. Staring at her dark eyes in the mirror, she whispered, "I'm in control," and when she was sure they seemed confident in that statement, she returned to the classroom.

Burberry gave Sebastien a half-sympathetic, half-exasperated look, then offered her a dose of anti-anxiety potion. "I get a few dozen who don't have the stomach for dissection every term. It's nothing to be ashamed of," the woman said kindly.

Sebastien accepted the potion and returned to her desk, though her anxiety had nothing to do with the killing and dissecting of a magical frog.

"That was kind of her," Ana murmured with a small smile. "Very discreet."

Sebastien had no idea what Ana was talking about, too busy downing the potion in a single gulp. Its magic took effect quickly, but not before she had the sudden thought that this, too, was a mind-altering substance. Under the effects of the potion, she felt that she really had overreacted. The question of identity was a serious one with important implications, but it was not as though she was trapped in this body. If it really was affecting her mind, she should first decide if that was actually unacceptable rather than simply horrifying. If she found that it *was* unacceptable, she would eventually return to her original form for good. When she was ready.

To distract herself from her thoughts, Sebastien reached out for a topic of conversation. "Ana, with everything that's happened, I forgot to ask if your little sister was alright, after you had to leave in such a rush last week."

Ana, who was using a scalpel to remove the frog's tiny lungs, didn't reply for a few seconds. "She's okay. I got her another artifact to wear that she can use to alert me if any more situations like that arise. It was Damien's idea."

'*I wonder where he got that one,*' Sebastien thought wryly, thinking of the bracelets they both wore. "Does your Cousin Whoever do things like this often?"

"Cousin Robbie. His father encourages him. Both my uncles take every opportunity to discredit or make Nat and me seem weak—to make us seem unworthy as heirs to the Gervin Family. They encourage their children to do the same. Alec could have turned out much worse, really. He's nothing like Cousin Robbie. Uncle Malcolm and Randolph are hoping to convince my father to name one of them, or maybe their children, as heir."

"But he wouldn't actually do that, would he?"

Ana hesitated. "My father… Well, all three brothers have some antiquated views about the capabilities and 'proper place' of women."

Sebastien snorted. "Really? But you're a thaumaturge, same as the rest of them. Women might be physically weaker than men, but our—your magic is in no way inferior. Our magic is no different, nor our capability as leaders."

Ana shrugged. "The truth doesn't actually matter to a certain kind of person. 'Women—so emotional. Weak mind, weak Will,'" she said, obviously quoting someone unpleasant. She sighed. "Really, it's a remnant of our grandfather, and my mother doesn't help the situation. She married into the Family, and—" Ana cut off, shaking her head as she used small scissors to snip away the bini frog's intestines. "Well. In any case, my father has the option to choose his heir, and while he has made no actual declarations, I've seen the way things have been going over the last few years. I've tried to display my competence, but his brothers' opinions carry too much weight."

They were both silent for a few seconds, and then Sebastien asked, "Is that why you never wear skirts or dresses?"

Ana gave a short, sharp laugh. "I've been wearing pants at every opportunity since I first tried them as a child. Drove my mother spare, but eventually she gave up, except for special occasions. Perhaps it does have something to do with wanting to seem more capable, but really they're just so much more comfortable and practical. Do you know how cold skirts are in winter? And have you ever tried to run without flashing your thighs?"

Sebastien coughed into her fist. "Well, I've never worn skirts. But I believe you."

"My uncles have grown more aggressive with their campaign as I get older. I'm fine, I can handle it, but Nat… Now that I'm gone, she has no one to shield or comfort her. My mother tries, but she's afraid of conflict and stepping outside of acceptable social boundaries, so sometimes she can be almost as bad as the rest of them. I think she'd prefer it if I could just marry a nice man who would take over running the Family while I indulge in hobbies and run a charity or something." Ana got a little too violent with her frog, and its slippery kidney went shooting off onto the floor.

She hurried to retrieve the bean-sized organ before Burberry noticed, and when she returned she gave Sebastien a demure smile. "Everything's fine overall, I'm just...frustrated. I feel helpless."

Sebastien knew that smile was fake. She'd seen its overly sweet rays pointed at too many other people to believe it. Ana's real smile was slightly lopsided, edging on a smirk. "Assuming you don't want to be usurped by your uncles or one of your cousins, or to marry a man who will keep you as arm candy, you can't just let them go on like this. You're being passive, reactive. You need to be the aggressor if you want things to change."

Ana set down her dissection tools, turning to look at Sebastien more fully.

Sebastien continued, peeling the frog's skin off with careful slices of her scalpel. "You need a more permanent solution to your problem." It was something she might not normally have said, if she wasn't still shaken up—something honest.

Ana hesitated, then asked, "What kind of permanent solution?"

"Nothing that could backfire and harm you severely if it goes wrong. Nothing...illegal. Something that would cut off their source of power and influence at its roots. You know more about the situation and the people involved than me—you're the one who would know what might work best."

Ana was uncharacteristically silent for a while, before murmuring, "I would need help..."

"Mmm," Sebastien agreed absently, distracted with brewing the scouring concoction.

After turning in a single vial for grading, Sebastien carefully packaged and kept the leftover components, since no one seemed to keep track of those things, or care. Some students just threw away the remainder, not caring that they were basically throwing away coin. Sebastien had accumulated a handful of random components this way over the course of the term. As they were filing out of the classroom, Sebastien wondered if she might secretly replenish other supplies from the University's stock.

She was trying to calculate if the benefit was worth the risk when she heard someone say Newton's name in a scandalized tone. Her head pivoted toward the source as if pulled by a string.

8

PROPERTIES OF EXPLOSIVE MATERIALS

Sebastien
Month 1, Day 29, Friday 10:30 a.m.

Sebastien recognized one of the girls gossiping about Newton from Practical Casting. Some time ago, the young woman had tried to flirt with her, hinting that Sebastien should buy her a gift from the offerings in the Great Hall with her contribution points. Sebastien had forgotten her name.

"But Moore always seemed so nice!" one girl exclaimed in a scandalized tone, leaning further into the huddled group. They had either not realized Sebastien was standing nearby or were too oblivious to realize how rude they were being.

Another girl tittered. "Well, obviously he was involved in…*questionable* activities. The revelation might be sudden, but there's too much evidence to deny it. I mean, how else do you find yourself entangled in a battle with gang members and the *Raven Queen,* and then turn into an Aberrant?"

Sebastien's breath was coming fast. She curled her hands into white-knuckled fists, her short nails digging into her palms with a welcome sting.

"He must have corrupted his Will," said a third girl. "What kind of magic do you think he was dabbling in? And what about the other student liaison, that Canelo girl? I hear she's refusing to talk."

The girl Sebastien recognized from Practical Casting shook her head. "She was cursed to be unable to speak of it, from what I heard. As for Newton

Moore, he probably did it because he needed the coin. People will degrade themselves in a lot of ways when they need coin."

The first woman sneered. "He didn't fit in here, did he? If he was going to end up so desperate to stay that he let his Will be corrupted, perhaps he shouldn't have been admitted in the first place."

Perhaps cued by some change in Sebastien's bearing or expression, Ana reached out for her arm, but it was too late. Ana's fingers slipped off as Sebastien strode toward the group. Her breath came hard, her wide-eyed gaze tracking over the women's amused, scandalized expressions, taking in every nuance as if preparing for battle.

Sebastien's voice was deep with anger, and she could feel the rumble in her chest, but couldn't quite hear it past the rush of blood in her ears. "Newton Moore was worth more than the entire lot of you."

The women spun to face her, their expressions ranging from surprise to dismay. The girl from Practical Casting blushed, then paled.

Sebastien's slow, bitingly enunciated words came faster as she continued. "It is clear you have no idea what you are talking about, yet find some kind of sick, self-titillating pleasure in spewing vile opinions and allegations about others who aren't around to defend themselves. It speaks more about *you* than it does about Newton. I feel like I'm being made dirty just standing in your presence, but putting you in your place is a service to the entire world that everyone else in your lives has obviously neglected."

There was a short, stunned silence, and conversation began to die out around them as people turned to watch the altercation. "Excuse you? We were just *talking*!" one girl retorted.

Sebastien let out a sharp laugh. "I am also 'just talking.' The difference is that I do not pretend my words are harmless. My words are meant to slap you across the face in lieu of my hand."

The girl flinched back, looking at the fists balled at Sebastien's sides.

"I'm sorry, Sebastien, we shouldn't have…" The girl from Practical Casting trailed off, biting her lip.

"Do not sully my name by letting it pass your lips," Sebastien hissed. The crowd was growing thick with onlookers.

One of the women looked around as if for help, then burst into tears.

Ana stepped up behind Sebastien, laying a hand on her shoulder and murmuring into her ear. "That's enough. I understand, but if this goes on, you could be the one getting in trouble." Louder, she called out, "I'm sorry, he's been under a lot of stress with everything that happened, and I don't think anyone would have appreciated hearing people speak ill of their dead friend." There were sympathetic murmurs among the crowd. "Please let us pass. He needs some space."

Sebastien clenched her fists even harder, gritting her teeth, but had enough sense not to protest or continue her tirade, letting Ana usher her through to freedom.

When they were clear, Ana gave her an exasperated look. "Was that really necessary?"

Sebastien remained silent, unrepentant, her jaw lifted and clenched.

Ana sighed. "You may get away with that sort of thing now, under the circumstances and with your budding reputation, but one of these days your tongue is going to get you in trouble with the wrong person."

"I know," Sebastien admitted. "It's almost surprising that it hasn't happened already. But sometimes, I just—when I heard what they were saying —" She peeled back her lips in a silent, feral snarl and shook her head. "It's not in my nature to be silent," she finished in a softer voice.

Ana sighed, wrapping one arm around Sebastien's shoulder as they walked and pulling her in to her side for a half-embrace. "Oh, Sebastien," she murmured, shaking her head. Ana kept a hold of her for a few more moments, gaze firmly forward, then relented and released her.

By lunchtime, the remnants of Sebastien's rage had left her, like a glowing ember cooled to ash. Its passing left her so fatigued she could barely muster up the energy to eat. Normally, she was ravenous from the constant effort of working her brain and her Will to learn and channel magic. After forcing down food until she started to gag with every bite, she left the others at their cafeteria table and went outside, hoping the fresh winter air would invigorate her.

She huddled into her jacket, sitting on a bench below a crisp pine tree to watch her breath fog up in little clouds. The chill sank into her slowly, but not unpleasantly, and away from the noise and press of the other students, she didn't feel so jarringly out of sync. She closed her eyes and pulled up her scarf around her nose and ears, hibernating until it was time to go to Practical Casting. Her joints felt stiff and old, and even Professor Lacer's class wasn't enough to excite her.

When she entered, the classroom felt wrong, and she realized that its size had decreased once more, to accommodate the reduced number of students remaining. At this point, it was a similar size to many of her other classrooms, down from the beginning of term when it had been by far the largest.

Professor Lacer made his dramatic last-minute entrance as he often did, immediately quieting all conversation. The man looked tired, the lines at the sides of his eyes a little deeper.

Sebastien took a perverse pleasure in the evidence that other people were struggling in the same way she was.

"Some of your number have recognized their inability to proceed in this class and decided to give up, either for this term or forever," he announced at full volume, his deep voice easily carrying to all corners of the room. "If you are questioning your ability to handle the workload or the pressure, I urge you to follow in their footsteps. I have limited time and do not wish to waste it on doomed prospects."

With that, he turned to the blackboard, casting a spell with an absent wave of his hand. A stick of chalk jumped up and began to scratch out words and glyphs. "We will continue to work on your grasp of light as a Sacrifice. For those of you who may be interested in healing, proficiency with channeling and controlling light energy can give you a significant boost with spells that use components or energy from the Plane of Radiance. Of course, healing is not the only option for Radiant energy. I once saw a woman use a pocket-sized planar portal to channel a focused beam of energy that burnt cleanly through an entire group of enemies, and a few hundred meters into the mountainside behind them."

Sebastien was momentarily distracted wondering how that would be possible, since as far as she was aware, planar portals were specifically designed to contain and shield against uncontrolled spillover from the Elemental Plane they were accessing. People passed through the portal—each wearing a specially designed protective suit—gathered and secured components, and exited. Only wild, natural planar portals were unconstrained in a way that would allow immediate use of their energy. And she was pretty sure that direct planar warfare was against some treaty all the major and most of the minor countries had agreed to. The potential consequences were on par with loosing a high-level Aberrant.

Professor Lacer first lectured on various glyphs that were directly or tangentially associated with light-based spells, then set them to practice.

Sebastien had made significant progress on her illusion spell, but still hadn't caught up to Nunchkin's level. Normally, that would have bothered her, since she was still bitter that he had bested her in the class tournament, but at the moment she simply wanted to make it through the class period without drawing Professor Lacer's ire.

A few minutes before the end of class, Professor Lacer ended their practice. "With mid-terms over, it is now time to start considering the end of term exhibitions. In many classes, particularly in the upper terms, they will display the practical portion of the final exam as part of the exhibition. While *this* class is almost entirely practical, I do not include it in the exhibitions at lower levels, since none of you are advanced enough to do anything impressive. If you wish to prepare an individual presentation for those classes that are not automatically entered, you are free to do so—at risk of great personal embarrassment. However, I urge you not to attempt to free-cast in the exhibitions. While success would certainly be an impressive feat and gain you points, I have a clear understanding of your capabilities, and let me assure you that you are more likely to cause yourself Will-strain, or worse." He looked to Sebastien for a moment, and she nodded back quickly to assure him she had no plans for such foolishness.

It was a reminder that she was supposed to earn fifty points in the exhibitions. She hadn't forgotten, exactly, but she'd put it out of her mind as something that she wouldn't need to worry about until later.

Lacer continued, "If your goal is to earn points, especially in the first three terms where most students have no particularly impressive skills, I would suggest something more flamboyant or flashy." He let slip a grimace of distaste, which Sebastien thought was ironic considering his own penchant for the dramatic. "While, nominally, the point of the exhibitions is to demonstrate skill in various areas, *in practice,* you are statistically more likely to be rewarded with points if you provide an entertaining demonstration versus showcasing your skills in a way that does not stimulate the audience. After all, the University wants to show off to all the guests who come specifically to watch. And spend coin."

When the class was released, Sebastien turned to Damien. "I thought the point of the exhibitions was to showcase our talents for potential sponsors or employers. Can they, or the judges, not discern between skill and flash?"

Damien looked incredulously to Ana, who laughed and shook her head. "Sebastien, you seem to have misunderstood."

Damien nodded. "It's true, they *say* the exhibitions are for the sake of the students, but they seem more like a multi-day magical street fair. I attended every year as a child, and they were the highlight of my spring."

"It's not optimal for students who are trying to focus during that critical time," Ana added, "but the University has some token policies in place that are supposed to be for student benefit and maintain our learning environment. But they'll never restrict entrance to only potential employers or sponsors. It's too big a revenue source, as well as a great way to build and spread their reputation."

"So…I'm supposed to put on a show for who knows how many people, who might not even have any idea about how magic works, as part of a gigantic festival. And get fifty contribution points," Sebastien said, dragging her hand down her face in the way that she'd seen Oliver do when he was overwhelmed.

"You're not shy around crowds," Damien said. "Or around anyone," he added in a low mutter. "I'm sure you'll be fine as long as you prepare."

Ana smiled encouragingly. "I believe in you. But in case you're interested, there are records, both from the internal University publication and official reports, that detail what kinds of exhibitions received rewards. That should allow you to tailor your efforts to your audience."

"Thank you." Sebastien didn't want to research prior exhibitions, or start planning and developing a magical performance. She was struggling to *care*. But she recognized that trying to "wing" something at the last minute was a bad idea. If she failed to meet his demands, Professor Lacer might not allow her to remain at the University. Even though she was too tired to feel it at the moment, she knew her lifelong dream of learning magic wasn't something she could allow to slip through her grasp. When she had recovered from this malaise, whatever it was, she would regret inaction.

Damien seemed to notice a little of what she was feeling on her face. "Are you okay, Sebastien?"

"Tired," she replied simply.

"Really? I mean, is that it? I know you can't talk about what happened with us, but maybe you should go to the infirmary? They have mind-healers who've taken confidentiality vows. You seem…"

Sebastien rubbed her eyes. "I don't need a mind-healer, Damien. I just have a few too many things on my plate at once."

Damien was silent for a moment. He looked to see that Ana was distracted with talking to someone else, and far enough away not to hear, then said quietly, "Maybe I could help take a few 'things' off your plate? I can handle more responsibility."

Sebastien wanted to snap that his nosiness, his inclusion in her secrets, was one of her many problems. Instead, she gritted her teeth and announced abruptly, "Actually, I am going to go to the infirmary. Maybe they have something stronger than coffee to help keep me awake."

She could practically feel Damien's solicitous gaze on her back as she strode away.

Instead of the infirmary, though, she veered off and made for Professor Lacer's office, where he retreated as soon as possible after his classes. She knocked sharply, then opened the door and strode inside, stopping in front of Lacer's desk.

He looked up slowly from the scattered papers and books. Some held complicated spell arrays and what might even have been a half-finished ward plan for a residence. "How can I help you, Mr. Siverling?"

Sebastien clenched and unclenched her fists, let out a slow breath, and said, "Professor Lacer, I respect and admire you."

He raised an eyebrow.

"However, I have to insist that you respect my personal boundaries. It is unacceptable for you to cast magic on me against my will, without my consent. *Especially* magic that will force me to sleep. Or in any way affect my mental state. I would never have consented to it, and will not consent to the like in the future."

Thaddeus Lacer placed down his pen and leaned back in his seat. He met her gaze for a few long, agonizing seconds. "I understand. I will not do such a thing again, and will try to remember to ask your consent before casting any other magics that affect your person, unless I judge you are in immediate and severe danger without my interference."

Sebastien's shoulders loosened, but she lifted her chin, giving him a dignified nod. "Thank you. I'll leave you to your work." With a shallow bow, she turned and left the room without another word.

9

―――――

EXCESSIVE FORCE

Oliver
Month 1, Day 30, Saturday 3:30 p.m.

Through the curtained window of the discreet carriage Oliver had appropriated from Lord Morrow, which allowed him to look out but did not allow others to see in, Oliver noted an unusually large number of coppers patrolling his expanded territory. A pair of coppers had stopped a man on the side of the street and were shaking him by his elbow, drawing angry looks from all around.

"It's ironic that we break fewer laws than the Morrows ever did, and yet the coppers find us so much more offensive," Oliver said.

Huntley's ever-flickering gaze remained on their surroundings. "It's because we make it so much more obvious that the coppers aren't doing their jobs. It will die down."

Oliver wasn't sure it would. The coppers were harassing Katerin and anyone else who worked for the Verdant Stag, trying to bring Lord Stag and the Raven Queen in for questioning and arrest. Oliver doubted the coppers were getting much from those they harassed, but it was still a problem.

Oliver had managed to get most of his people released, but the fines and bribes were becoming prohibitive, and the coppers weren't showing any signs of slowing down. In a way, it was similar to what he was doing with the Morrows. They were holding his people ransom. The coppers needed to be seen doing something after the widespread fighting and collateral damage had made them seem so ineffectual, and they were getting their arrest numbers up.

Of course, not all the coppers were corrupt. Some of them actually wanted to help the community, and others were at least willing to do the right thing if it didn't significantly inconvenience them. Many of them had started the job with high ideals, but it was hard to stay clean when so many others were crooked, and the system itself seemed to subtly encourage that.

Oliver needed to find more coppers who still held to their principles, or would at least *prefer* to be bribed to look the other way by an organization more like the Verdant Stag than one like the Morrows.

Perhaps more easily, he could make harassing his people unappealing. He pressed his hand over his chest, where a black leather notebook sat in the inside pocket of his jacket. Before he had found the book and its key—having meticulously rifled through Lord Morrow's properties and belongings from top to bottom and broken all the wards and safeguards the man had put in place—Oliver's best idea had been to hire a team of solicitors specifically to make arrests more hassle than they were worth.

Lord Morrow had kept a team specifically for that type of thing. Instead of just paying the fines and the bribes to get his people out, Oliver could set solicitors to argue every case. It would be as tedious for him as it was for the coppers, and it would drag out the whole process and probably cost him even more, but it would make his people seem like a less appealing target.

He would still do that, but the notebook offered another type of solution. With one to two pages for every entry—some entries with only a few lines and others packed with neat, tiny writing—the book was filled with blackmail material. Blackmail on anyone remotely important, some who the Morrows had worked with, and some who Lord Morrow simply wanted to be prepared for in case of need.

There was even a page for Lord Stag, though there was nothing truly incriminating listed, just tidbits of knowledge about illegal activities he'd been involved with, as well as speculation and notes about failed attempts to find his civilian identity.

But there was plenty of information on local law enforcement, covering people who worked on every level, in all the different departments. When Oliver had realized what it contained, he'd been grateful for the featureless mask of Lord Stag, because the wild grin splitting his face from side to side was probably disturbing.

He'd gained more than just the little black notebook, though. The Morrows had been profitable. Very much so. And a large portion of their resources and businesses were now in Oliver's hands, ready for him to do with what he would. Attached to all that came the contracts, employees, and supply chains that kept all of it running, which was as much a blessing as it was a curse.

Lord Morrow had several properties filled with everything from overpriced furniture embroidered with actual gold thread, to a library of books he'd probably never read and only displayed for the aesthetic, to an old, abandoned printing press down in the basement surrounded by other knickknacks, non-working artifacts, and even some actual junk. The man may have been a hoarder. And it was all Oliver's.

Lord Morrow's widow had signed over almost everything she had legal control over, except for some properties outside Gilbratha and enough money to provide a modest stipend for her and the younger children for the remainder of her life. Which could be years yet, as long as she didn't try to go against the terms of the magical contract she had signed.

Oliver had questioned her extensively under illegal wards against untruth. The minor torture tactics he had okayed for the rest of the Morrows weren't even necessary to get her to talk. Then he had forced her, like her children and all the other captured Morrows who hadn't deserved execution, to take rather restrictive vows against retaliation. Those vows, along with the signed-over assets, were exchanged for her life and freedom.

It wasn't a perfect method, but legally, it was safer and less problematic than simply trying to steal the assets once owned by the various Morrows. Forcing people into contracts or vows under duress was illegal, and they could sue to regain what had been unlawfully taken from them, but the vows they had made also stated their admission of certain crimes.

Most of those who agreed outwardly but planned to betray him right away should have been caught by the prognos diviner he hired, and were, of course, denied release. Those who might change their minds once they were free, despite the vow's minor compulsion, would still think twice, both because betrayal would allow him to use their blood print to have someone place a curse on them, and because he could turn their admissions of guilt over to "his" coppers.

Without the resources they once had access to, the damage they could do to him would be reduced, but he was aware that the contacts and networks they'd built up over the years still existed, and he couldn't remove them entirely. By bankrupting rather than killing, he was hoping to avoid some of the retaliatory hatred. This way, even if they had powerful contacts or could call for aid from the few Morrows who avoided capture, they would be a drain on enemy resources instead of making themselves martyrs.

If people still tried to sue or otherwise cause him problems, then some high-profile assassinations would be in order as a warning.

He wasn't prepared to kill when it wasn't necessary, so this was the best solution he could come up with.

Oliver had only taken a moderate fine from those who hadn't committed any particularly serious crimes, while hiring the best—and least offensive—for the Verdant Stags.

He had been in a position where he needed to either expand or die, and he had expanded. Now he was consolidating, tightening his grip. He had dozens of good places to put the new resources to work, such as an alchemical workshop that had been creating addictive substances for the Morrows. Under Oliver, it was going to be turned toward a new—legal—enterprise making emergency response kits, household concoctions, and even cosmetics available to the common budget.

The income that would continue to come in from illegal substances while they transitioned would go towards a rehabilitation center, complete with healers and incentives, that he hoped would help fight against the addiction endemic among some of the worst off among his people. Rather than making the substances illegal, a change that would require ponderous enforcement, Oliver suspected that rehabilitation would prove a more successful—and cost effective—method of solving the epidemic. And if nothing else, it would make him *look good*.

Oliver watched as another pair of coppers swaggered out of the doorway of a shop that bore the bright green antlers of the Verdant Stag above their doorframe, the younger of the two smirking as he dropped a handful of coins into his pocket. Too much coin to be change for a purchase. They'd just extorted the shop owner.

They were losing all sense of moderation. They thought he was an easy victim.

"Stop the carriage," Oliver ordered, rapping on the roof to alert the driver, because the man wouldn't be able to hear him past the carriage's privacy wards, and he didn't want to lower them with a pair of coppers right there. The carriage was spelled to be both unremarkable and difficult to track, but all the wards were on the same system.

Huntley's gaze flicked around, through the windows in both doors, then searched Oliver for signs of illness or injury. "You're scheduled to go straight from the alchemy workshop to the Verdant Stag. What's wrong?"

"The coppers are harassing a shop owner under our protection." Oliver's instinct was to do something about it personally, but that would have been the worst possible decision, giving them exactly what they really wanted on a silver platter. "You should get out and dissuade them."

"Absolutely not," Huntley replied.

Oliver scowled at him. "It shouldn't be that difficult. It is our job to provide some measure of security for the people in our territory, Huntley. Otherwise they will lose faith in us, and that leads to attempted coups."

Huntley crossed his arms over his chest. "No. *My* job is to keep *you* safe.

Worst case scenario, I go out there and end up getting arrested, and then something happens to you."

"I'm not completely helpless without you, you know. I've handled myself against worse threats, and I'll stay hidden in the carriage the whole time."

Outside, the coppers had stopped beside a stall selling thin bowls of steaming soup run by a scowling middle-aged woman. The one who'd pocketed the coin swaggered up, saying something to the woman. Perhaps a threat, or perhaps just a request for a bowl of soup.

She sneered, crossing her arms over her chest as she retorted.

Oliver noted the subtle antlers painted clumsily on the corner of the wooden sign that hung from the stall.

The crowd outside grew thicker as people stopped to watch the commotion, scowling and muttering.

The older copper said something to his younger partner, gesturing for them to leave, but the young man ignored him, stepping around the stall to drag the woman out into the street by her arm.

"Just go out and act vaguely threatening, Huntley. They're going after a woman now. I'm worried things could go poorly." More passersby were now stopping to glare at the coppers, and the muttering was growing louder.

A thickly muscled man in a leather apron yelled out an angry remark that Oliver couldn't make out, but which roiled the crowd and drew hostile looks from both coppers. People were beginning to mill around the carriage, blocking the horses, so they couldn't leave anyway.

Huntley settled back, crossing his arms. "This isn't a negotiation. Even if I was inclined to abandon my duties, which I'm *not*, Katerin would kill me. The proprietress will be fine. At most, the coppers will mess the stall up a little and make her come in for questioning. That's half a day's earnings gone. If I go out there, all it gives us is a minor show of force against two beat coppers who don't much matter. Either I threaten them and they come back more angry, with a legitimate reason to arrest me, or I bribe them to go away and we still look weak."

"I think it could be worse for her—"

The woman spat in the copper's face.

Oliver's heart sank.

White-faced, the man shoved her to the ground, his hand going for the battle wand at his waist.

Oliver lunged for the door handle, but Huntley blocked him. "He'll kill her!" Oliver snapped.

Huntley hesitated, following Oliver's gaze out of the window.

While Huntley was distracted, Oliver slipped on his Lord Stag mask, letting its suction settle onto the skin of his face, and opened the carriage door. The angry clamor from the crowd flowed over him. He paused, because the copper hadn't used the battle wand to shoot a spell but had instead cracked the woman across the cheekbone with it.

The man raised his hand to repeat the action just as a skinny, dark-skinned young man stumbled his way out of the surrounding crowd, tripped, and went sprawling onto the cobblestones.

He was carrying a bulky device in both hands, which fell across a box of soup ingredients set next to the stall, and the sharp flash of blinding-white light from it was evidence enough of what had happened, even with the sound of the camera obscura's shutter being drowned out by the screams.

The copper stopped his second swing mid-way, turning toward the fallen young man with an expression of stunned alarm that quickly morphed into rage.

His older partner was obviously uneasy, and he stepped forward to put a restraining hand on the younger copper's arm.

Many of the crowd probably didn't know exactly what the artifact was, but they knew magic when they saw it, and the response of the coppers was enough to spread a hush through them.

Oliver heard it clearly when the young copper asked, "Did you just take a photograph of me?"

The dark-skinned young man scrambled clumsily upright, almost tripping over his own feet again as he did so, fumbling to get his wire-rimmed glasses to sit straight on his face. "No—I—it was an accident. I just need—" He cut off with a twisted, horrified expression.

A shockingly loud, stuttering grumble of flatulence tore through the crowd. The young man jerked, his hands twitching toward his backside as if he could hold the sound in—to no avail, as it ripped through him, the occasional squeak interrupting the rumble until it finally died out with a reluctant wheeze.

The silence in its absence was deafening. The boy's face was noticeably pale despite the dark tint of his skin, giving him a greenish pallor. "I'm sorry, that was an accident. I ate something bad, and I thought I was going to—at least it was only gas. Better out than in, my dad always says!" he added with a high-pitched, anxious laugh, his eyes darting around as if searching for an escape route.

The coppers were not amused.

"That's right, you tell 'em!" someone in the back of the crowd called, vibrating their tongue and lips together to create an exaggerated farting noise of their own. Someone else soon repeated the sound.

The boy paled even further, shaking his head desperately as the young copper stepped forward, swinging the baton once more, this time aimed at the young man.

The boy lifted a forearm to block the blow, and the copper punched him with his other hand, sending his glasses flying.

The boy cringed away, falling to his knees as he felt about frantically for the glasses.

The copper lunged forward as if to kick him in the side, but before he could do so, someone in the crowd threw a small stone, hitting the man in the back of the head.

The older partner spun around, lifting his wand and throwing up a shield spell. That only set off the crowd, and soon more projectiles were flying. Mud, stones, and even chunks of trash and old food.

"Don't you dare shoot at the crowd!" the older copper screamed over his shoulder at his young, foolish partner who had gotten them into this precarious situation.

Oliver's carriage driver had apparently had enough, and he tried to get them away, but the crowd was blocking the road and the horses quickly grew spooked. Oliver was worried that they might panic and trample someone.

When an angry citizen tipped a whole barrel full of coal out of the wagon a few meters in front of them, blocking the way with too little room for them to maneuver, even Huntley knew there would be no easy escape.

Both coppers were shielding now, standing back-to-back and preparing to try to ram their way through a thin section of the crowd before things escalated further. The older copper tossed out a couple of philtres of stench, the nausea-inducing clouds sending people coughing and retching to the ground.

Both the stall owner and the young artifact-toting boy had scrambled away in the confusion.

"Well, I suppose you've gotten your wish," Huntley said bitingly. "We have to get out and retreat on foot. We are *not* wading into the fray, sir. Keep your hood up and follow me." Without waiting for a response, he jumped down to the ground, his wand out with its own protective barrier springing from the tip. The man winced at that small exertion, lifting one hand to his side. The broken ribs and punctured lung he'd gotten in the fight against the Morrows were still healing.

Huntley yelled for their driver to take care of the horses, to cut them free from the carriage if necessary.

Oliver kept a firm grasp on his own wand, his cloak obscuring his mask as they wove through and among the crowd. Oliver was less worried about someone seeing Lord Stag out and about than recognizing Oliver Dryden and making an unfortunate connection. Perhaps one day he would be able to go around his territory as "Mr. Oliver" again, but at the moment the situation was too fraught, tensions too high.

Oliver and Huntley weren't the only ones escaping the fray, and other than a few jostles against elbows and shoulders, they managed without incident. As they turned the corner a block away, with Huntley angled to shield Oliver's back and side, someone coming around in the other direction slammed directly into Oliver with an audible "oof!"

The artifact-toting boy from earlier bounced off Oliver, so focused on protecting his camera obscura that he fell onto his bottom hard enough to force out a whimper of pain. He pushed up his glasses, one shattered lens obscuring a swelling black eye. He blinked up at Oliver, then immediately went wide-eyed and green with horror. Obviously, he had seen under Oliver's hood.

Oliver sighed regretfully, rubbing at the chin of his mask where the boy's forehead had clipped him, grateful for the unexpected protection it had afforded. His eyes narrowed as they caught on the camera obscura.

The boy stood up, scrambled backward, and bowed deeply to Oliver. "Sorry, so sorry!"

Huntley stepped forward, switching off the shield spell coming from his wand and pointing it threateningly at the boy, who looked to be a year or two younger than Siobhan.

"Oh, Myrddin's balls!" the boy babbled. "I'm really on a roll, first the coppers and now Lord Stag." He swallowed, smiling ingratiatingly at Oliver, his eyes flicking nervously to Huntley. "I don't suppose you'd let me go if I promise not to mention I saw you? I don't have any particular love for the coppers!" He pointed to his purpling eye.

Oliver shook his head slowly, and the boy quailed. "I mean you no harm," Oliver assured him. "However, I believe we have business to discuss." He gestured to the camera obscura. "I'm interested in purchasing that photograph you took earlier." With the little black journal, he had blackmail in the forefront of his mind, and had realized the potential uses of such a photograph. He thought back to the moment of the flash. He believed the angle of the artifact's lens was correct to have captured something interesting…if the photograph wasn't too blurred.

The boy's mouth opened and closed like a fish, and he looked down at the camera obscura, dumbfounded. "But it might not even *be* anything. The flash went off by accident. It probably wasn't pointed at anything except a couple of potatoes, and even if it was, surely everything's too blurred to make out…?"

"You will come with us," Oliver ordered. "You can find an appropriate spot at the Verdant Stag to check the photograph. Under supervision."

The boy shook his head. "That won't work. I can't just expose the photo negative to light to check it without first developing and 'fixing' the disk. It would ruin the captured image. And I don't have that processing artifact on me."

"Where is it?"

"Well, it's at home…"

Huntley nodded to Oliver. "I'll have someone escort him to fetch it."

After a painful moment where the boy looked constipated with the desire to argue, but didn't seem to know how to do so, he acquiesced, deflating.

They made their way through the city on foot for a few blocks, Huntley's eyes on a constant paranoid search for danger, though he put away his wand after a while so as not to draw extra attention to them.

The boy chattered nervously as they walked. "It's not a photograph inside, you know. This model has a magic crystal disk that captures a reverse image. It can capture three whole images before I need to replace the cartridge! Though it's not really a *reverse* image, it's just got the bright parts dark and the dark parts light. They call it a 'negative,' and it means that I can make as many photographs from the original disk as I want..."

Oliver tuned him out as they walked, vulnerable, toward the Verdant Stag. He knew this situation would never have happened if he were riding Elmira instead of inside a supposedly much safer carriage. An erythrean wouldn't have been so spooked by the crowd or commotion, and she was sure-footed enough to have maneuvered through, over, or around almost any kind of blockage in her way. Of course, he'd also been ambushed before while riding her, since a man riding a horse—even a completely common-looking one like her—stood out in some of the poorer parts of town.

Oliver mused about getting her a saddle with the same kind of wards the carriage had. Huntley might not agree to let him ride her even then, however, since it was a lot harder to protect a man riding a horse than one inside the shielding walls of a carriage.

A few blocks away from the incident, Huntley flagged down a hackney with the Verdant Stag antlers painted discreetly on its side. The man took a bright green badge from an inside pocket and flashed it at the driver, who gave a deep bow of the head and motioned for them to hop on.

Oliver looked on in surprise. Katerin had been using the Stag funds to kit out the enforcers in more ways than just their equipment, it seemed.

The young man, sitting squeezed between Oliver and Huntley, hugged his camera obscura to his chest.

"What is your name?" Oliver said, breaking the tense silence.

"Percival Irving. Well met, Lord—um—Mr...." He threw an awkward glance toward the driver, who was studiously not paying them any attention.

Oliver's wry smile was hidden under his mask, but he nodded graciously. "Well met."

As the carriage passed by the Verdant Stag, he saw Siobhan. She stood out from the crowd. Although she was wearing a cloak with a hood that disguised most of her physical features, she carried herself with the regality of a queen. Yes, he was sure it was her.

Oliver hummed to himself, feeling ambiguous as he watched her enter the inn-cum-entertainment hall. He had grown closer to her than he planned. He was one to take on "projects," obviously, and though he'd hoped she would grow to be truly useful—which had happened even sooner than he could have guessed, though not in the way he expected—he hadn't thought it would be more than that. Yet, now he was worried for her, pleased to see her, and disappointed that he couldn't stop the carriage on the street and call for her to jump in so that they could talk.

The driver took them around to the Verdant Stag's back yard where there was a locked entrance with a route to the upper floor where Oliver kept his office.

Huntley gave the man, who was sensible enough a driver to not even peek under Oliver's hood as he got out of the carriage, a large tip, then took Percival off to the enforcer office.

While Oliver waited for someone to escort the boy back home and return, he called Siobhan up to visit him, and they had a pleasant chat that erased most of the tension from his morning, sharing troubles and ideas for solutions. She looked haggard and a little too thin, but her company was as compelling as ever. When she left, Oliver put his mask back on regretfully.

Percival entered shortly after, holding a sealed cartridge that Oliver supposed contained the negative image.

The boy cleared his throat. "The camera obscura did actually capture a good image of that copper. Very…impactful."

Oliver waved the boy forward. He opened the cartridge, pulling out the first disk and examining it. It contained a miniature black and white image, with the dark and light reversed, of the copper beating the woman shop owner in the street. The copper's arm was blurred with motion, and both of their faces were clear enough, vibrant with emotion. Oliver gave a satisfied smile. "I will purchase it from you. Seven gold. If you're interested, I can also hire you to develop an actual photograph from the negative."

Percival's fingers tightened around the cartridge. "Seven gold?" He swallowed. "That sounds good. Wait, no, I want at least nine gold."

Oliver raised an amused eyebrow, though it wasn't visible beneath the mask, "Eight gold, then. That's my final offer."

"And…I also have another negative I think you might want to purchase. One of the Raven Queen. It's impactful, too."

10

———

CHARITABLE PERFORMANCE

Siobhan
Month 1, Day 30, Saturday 4:30 p.m.

People were packed into the ground floor of the Verdant Stag like pickled cucumbers stuffed into a jar. It wasn't until Siobhan got further into the room that some space cleared up and she was able to get away from the stifling crush. The heat from all the bodies made her warm clothing unnecessary, but she caught sight of a pair of uniformed coppers at one of the tables and decided not to take off her hooded cloak. Sure, she was Silvia, a civilian who, at most, helped at a healing station during the fighting, and had the identity papers to prove it, but if they took her to Harrow Hill, papers might not save her.

'*Why are they here?*' she wondered.

Everyone seemed to have come for the people on stage at the other end of the room, who she thought must be putting on some sort of play at first, but when she actually listened, it was a rather strange monologue.

"After the earlier testimony of both the accused and the accusers, which was verified through prognos divination and wards against untruth, Eric Hanna, Morrow member, has been found guilty by the Verdant Stag of the following crimes: public nudity, blackmail, three counts of mugging, twenty-two counts of extortion, and six counts of assault, one of which caused grievous and permanent injury. By order of Lord Stag, he has been relieved of the fruits of his crimes, and restitution is due to those he has harmed."

The cheers were immediate and deafening as people clapped, slammed their tankards of ale and beer on the tabletops, and stomped their feet.

When the noise died down, the second person atop the stage stepped forward. "As the executor of a trust held at Citrus Bank, and in no way associated with the Verdant Stag, or other criminal activity," he added, with a dark glare toward the two coppers, "I have been charged to publicly convey the beneficiaries of this trust and the amount they are receiving."

Siobhan noticed then the banner above the stage that introduced the "charitable performance."

The trust executor listed off names, accompanied by varying monetary amounts that ranged from a few silver to a few gold. It wasn't even close to what the coppers would have fined for those same crimes, and was certainly less than what Oliver had extorted out of the accused Morrows, but the audience didn't seem to care.

Siobhan sidled closer to a particularly enthusiastic woman. "What's going on?" she asked, her voice almost drowned out by another wave of cheers as the executor announced the next person to receive restitution.

The woman gave her a huge, slightly drunken grin that revealed a couple of missing teeth. "Something's actually being done about the injustices we all been subjec—subjd—" She stopped to hiccup, then finished, "the injustices we went through."

"And they're really paying? How do you get chosen for restitution?"

The woman nodded dramatically. "Yes, Lord Stag is really paying out. If your name is called, you go down to Citrus Bank with identification, and their people there take out the money from that trust account he was mentioning—coin straight into your hand! And it's easy to get considered for restitution, just go note what the Morrows did to you, and which've 'em did it. You've gotta give testimony under some kind of spell that keeps you from lying, and once the trial is over it's too late to submit a claim. Not everyone gets the restitution, if there's not enough proof of what was done, or who did it, or if who did it doesn't have any coin for the Verdant Stag to take back for you. Still, a damn sight better than anyone else would do for us." She looked over to the table that housed the coppers and yelled, "A damn sight better than the coppers ever did for us!"

Siobhan tugged at the corner of her hood to make sure her face was hidden, trying to do so as naturally as possible so she didn't seem suspicious. "Have you gotten any restitution?"

The woman grinned toothily again, holding up her mug in a toasting motion. "Three silver!" she announced proudly. Judging by her level of drunkenness, as well as the crumbs on the empty plate in front of her, she'd already spent at least that much, the coin going right back to the Verdant Stag.

'Maybe Oliver isn't so crazy.'

Siobhan watched the proceedings for a few more minutes, until someone sidled through the crowd, reaching out to touch her shoulder.

Siobhan jerked away, whipping around with her hands held up defensively, which she immediately decided was rather foolish, because she had little skill as a hand-to-hand combatant.

A young man raised his own hands, empty palms facing outward to convey his harmlessness. With a glance at the coppers, he reached down to his jacket, pulling one side open far enough that she could see the bright green antlers of the Stags embossed on a badge tucked into his shirt pocket. "Apologies, ma'am. I didn't mean to startle you. Your presence has been requested upstairs."

"By whom?"

He didn't answer, instead giving her a significant look. "Mr. Huntley told me to pass the message along."

She vaguely recognized the name as belonging to one of the Stags' lead enforcers. Most likely, either Katerin or Oliver had called for her. Siobhan lowered her hands, nodding for the young man to lead the way. As they climbed the stairs at the edge of the room, the bottom of which was guarded by another enforcer, she asked, "I noticed the coppers are just sitting there. Have they been causing trouble?"

The young man laughed, as if the question was ironic. "Oh, plenty of it. But they can't stop us. They don't know where the Morrows are being held, and the two men on stage are a licensed actor and a lawyer who was hired to enforce the Citrus Bank trust independently. They're not actually involved with the Verdant Stag or the trials or anything, they were just hired to talk on stage in a clearly labeled performance for charity. I'm not totally sure how that all works, but it's not illegal. The coppers have still been arresting them, of course. This is the fourth or fifth set of performer and lawyer." He grinned as if that was hilarious. "But they just stay down at Harrow Hill for a day or two for questioning while someone else takes their place on stage. None of them actually know anything, so Harrow Hill has to release them within three days. Those two coppers down below are just there for appearances. They haven't tried anything."

Siobhan hummed. "It still seems like they could arrest people on charges of collusion or something?"

"They'll arrest people on charges of almost anything, but it's not sticking. You go in, you take a few sleepless nights and shitty food and maybe a few bruises, but as long as you don't talk, you come out again when either the laws or the bribes say so. Everyone got lessons on what to do, and we even got to practice against one of those lying wards."

That seemed...dangerous. All it would take would be for someone higher up, like Titus Westbay, to notice and care that Oliver's people were bribing their way out of charges, and suddenly an arrest might not be such a simple matter. And it would only take one person with the right information to give the coppers what they needed to make other charges stick. Oliver's people might not be as bad as the Morrows, but they'd all committed crimes in the eyes of the Thirteen Crown Families.

If they arrested Oliver, Katerin, or someone else with actual knowledge and power, things would become much more dangerous. She wasn't sure a bribe would be enough to cover them. And of course, the coppers would remember that the Raven Queen had been associated with the Verdant Stag, too.

The whole situation made her uncomfortable.

The enforcer led Siobhan to Oliver's office, which she had never been in before. It was significantly more ostentatious than Katerin's office, all dark woods and plush furniture, with a layout that suggested the chair behind Oliver's desk was instead a throne, and all who entered must supplicate before him. It would have been more impressive if his desk wasn't covered with a mess of ledgers, binders, and loose paper.

Oliver looked up from a small leather notebook, the kind with a lock, and gave her an excited smile as she entered. He quickly closed the book and set it aside, then, deciphering her expression, said, "Yes, this office is generally only used for meeting with people. I'm considering moving the administrative headquarters to another building. Somewhere more discreet. We've got quite a few former Morrow properties whose rights were signed over." He stood from the desk, moving to one of the plush chairs nearer the fire and gesturing for her to join him. Someone had left a coffee tray, and he offered her a cup of dark liquid brewed so strongly the sugar spoon almost stood up straight.

"Is there a plan to deal with the coppers, other than antagonizing them with public shows meant to undermine their authority?" she asked.

Oliver sipped his own coffee, giving her a nettled look over the rim. "Feeling prickly, are we?"

Siobhan grimaced. "Sorry, that came out slightly harsher than I intended."

"Only slightly?" Before she could respond, he said, "I do have a plan. And a rather good one. It includes a whole flock of solicitors who will make the coppers bleed for every unwarranted arrest, and a heaping dollop of blackmail on top. Those who are corrupt will soon see that my territory isn't worth it, and those who genuinely care about their jobs will realize their efforts are better spent elsewhere, in the places that need them. This whole thing, believe it or not, is a lot more reserved than I originally intended. I wanted to do public executions for the worst of the Morrows, if you remember, but Katerin and some of the others talked me out of it. I'll still make sure they get what they deserve, but it won't be directly by our hand, and thus won't make the Crowns look like they've lost control."

"How are you going to handle them instead?"

"They'll be handling it—the coppers, that is. I'm just going to make sure everyone involved has extra incentive to follow the law, no matter how influential the accused men once were." He grinned like a child with a stolen cookie. "In fact, I've got quite a few things in the works. I think you'll be impressed."

Siobhan hummed and raised one of her eyebrows, but couldn't help the corners of her lips twitching up, his enthusiasm spreading infectious energy to her.

They were both silent for a moment, drinking their coffee at the perfect almost-scalding temperature. Finally, Oliver said, "You seem tired."

"I'm sleeping more than I have been for the past five or six years," she said wryly.

"And hating every second, no doubt."

She let out a short, surprised laugh. "Well, yes." That was the main reason she was here, but since she had Oliver at her disposal, she brought up another issue. "I don't want to take up too much of your time since you're so busy, but I wonder if I might get some of your particular brand of insight on a possible problem?"

He tensed a little but nodded. "Titan's balls, let it be a problem I can actually fix."

"Damien Westbay is going to become a problem, and perhaps even more so now that it's not safe to spy on Tanya Canelo anymore. He's too curious, too eager for action. I've been trying to shut him down, but he doesn't stay down for long. You're the one who's good with the social things, getting people to do what you want."

Oliver settled back in his chair with his booted feet closer to the fire. "Tell me more. And give details. I need to understand how his mind works."

Siobhan spoke while Oliver asked probing questions, almost all of which she answered in detail. She knew Damien well, even better than she'd realized.

Finally, Oliver seemed satisfied, steepling his fingers together in front of his chest like some kind of stereotypical evil genius. "You need a little more carrot to go along with your stick. Don't keep trying to shut him down. When Westbay wants more, give him more, but dangle that carrot in the direction that's most convenient to have him run. Ideally, *away* from anything you're hoping to keep secret. Once he's busy enough, even he won't have time to indulge his curiosity."

"So I need to come up with some project for him to throw himself into? Ideally something that won't require me to put in even more work."

"Yes. You can take some time to consider what you might like him pointed toward, or you can even see if he has any ideas for a 'mission' that you wouldn't mind allowing. That might be dangerous, if he's the type to become fixated on ideas once he has them, but it would give you an idea where the danger lies."

"I understand. I'll think about it. Thanks."

"When you get time, feel free to stop by the manor and do some more brewing for the Verdant Stag. With all the new territory, we're running through concoctions faster than we can stock them. Particularly healing concoctions, and some little fireplace-in-a-bottle things that one of our other alchemists has been supplying."

"You have a lot of homeless and injured people, then?" she guessed.

"Too many. But let's not talk about that."

"How about the people downstairs?" She laughed as another set of cheers and stomping rattled the entire building, only mostly muffled by the two floors between them. "They *love* the free coin, especially when it's paired with 'justice.' How much are you earning off all this?"

Oliver's grin looked more than a little evil. "Oh, a *lot*."

They chatted for a while longer, until a check of her pocket watch revealed that it would get dark soon. She didn't want to be trudging around the city in the frigid night, so took her leave.

Oliver sounded disappointed to have to get back to work, and his dramatic sigh followed her out the door as she left.

With her cloak back up, Siobhan's peripheral vision was impaired, and she bumped into someone at the edge of the narrow back stairway that led to Oliver's office.

She'd knocked a small cartridge out of his grip, and as he fumbled to catch it, he tilted precariously backward. Just as he regained control of the cartridge, his foot slipped off the top step, and if not for her grabbing him by the waistcoat and yanking with all her strength, he would have tumbled down the stairs.

He fell to one knee beside her, but seemed rather unscathed by the whole thing, laughing awkwardly. "Oh, thank you. Bit clumsy of me, are you alright?"

"I should be asking you that," Siobhan said. "I apologize, I didn't see you."

"To be honest, it's probably not your fault. My luck has been atrocious today!" the boy said, laughing as if at some inside joke as he rose to his feet. He was about her height, with skin much darker than hers, but the deep purple bruise around his swollen eye, shielded by the shattered lens of his glasses, was still conspicuous.

"If you need a bruise salve, they sell them here," she said, grimacing. "There's a little apothecary on the other side of the building, to the left of the main staircase. They're quite a bit cheaper than what you can find elsewhere, and good quality."

"Can just anyone buy from them? I don't work for—well, I'm trying to sell something to Lord Stag, but I don't work for them, and I'm pretty sure I live outside the gang's territory."

Siobhan shrugged. "It shouldn't be a problem, but I can't be sure. Are you going up to see, er, Lord Stag? You could ask him."

The boy's grip tightened noticeably. "Oh, umm, do you really think I should? He's so… Isn't there someone else I could ask?"

Siobhan let out a quiet laugh. "I know the mask can be intimidating, but Lord Stag really isn't that frightening. He's quite friendly, and he actually enjoys helping people."

"Is that so?" the boy asked, looking extremely skeptical.

"It is," Siobhan asserted.

"Well…thank you." The boy reached out to shake her hand. "Percival, but you can call me Percy. Do you work around here?"

"Well met, Percy." She hesitated only a moment before introducing herself as Silvia. "I do some contract work when it's necessary."

"Do you have any advice for me? I'm trying to sell him something a little… sensitive. I'm pretty nervous about it." Percy shuffled his feet, seeming not to notice how close to the edge of the stairs he still was.

Siobhan raised an eyebrow, reaching out to nudge him away from danger. "Well…don't take his first offer, I suppose. And don't be too nervous. The worst he can do is say no."

Percy looked down at the cartridge, muttering, "I don't think that's the worst he can do," but then gave her a bright smile, wincing as the expression squished the swollen flesh around his black eye. "I'd better get in there. Thanks, Silvia!" With a wave of his hand, he stepped past her, taking a fortifying breath before knocking on the door to Oliver's office.

Siobhan shook her head, a little bemused, then made for the apothecary tucked away on the other side of the building, the hallway guarded by yet another Verdant Stag enforcer.

Within, she found the main purpose of her trip, and the reason she had risked coming to the Verdant Stag—a triangular vial of what looked rather like slug poop. The substance within was a grey-brown, porous sludge, nothing like some of the more interesting-looking potions that came in bright colors, glowed, or roiled within their containers. Still, Siobhan had to suppress a huge grin as she picked it up, despite the three-gold price tag.

Katerin's assistant, Alice, was running the shop, and fixed Siobhan with a gimlet eye when she tried to buy it. "I need a prescription from a healer to sell this to you," she said.

Siobhan suppressed a frustrated groan. "I don't have a healer's note, but I'm an alchemist, and well aware of the tincture's usage and requirements."

"Beamshell tincture is addictive, and leaves an energy debt. People who abuse it will keep pushing until they collapse, malnourished and dehydrated, and for thaumaturges, with a significantly increased chance of Will-strain. If you have narcolepsy, or insomnia, or some other legitimate reason to need this, I'm happy to sell it to you once you bring me proof."

Briefly, Siobhan considered asking Oliver or Katerin to come down and vouch for her, or even coming back the next day with a forged healer's prescription—but no, that was ridiculous. She leaned forward and said in a low voice, "I encountered an Aberrant that caused a severe sedative effect. You probably heard about the incident." Aberrants were the kind of thing that was hard to argue against and likely to engender an emotional response. In this case, hopefully sympathy, and a hesitance to ask too many questions. "I don't have narcolepsy, I just need a little help staying sharp when I'm awake. I assure you, I have no plans to abuse the concoction. I brew a good number of the potions you stock here," she added.

What Siobhan said was more or less true, except for her fatigue being caused directly by lingering anomalous effects of the Aberrant. She just needed something a little stronger than coffee to give her energy while she was awake. She couldn't continue to drag her way through her days, barely scraping by. She wasn't stupid enough to abuse the beamshell tincture until she got herself addicted.

Alice still hesitated, drawing a weary sigh from Siobhan. "I can get Katerin to vouch for me, if she's here." Bringing in Oliver would be a little too much, probably.

Alice finally conceded. "If you need a second vial, I'll require that healer's note." She rattled off a series of dosage and use instructions that Siobhan had already memorized, and Siobhan walked out three gold lighter, with a vial of bottled energy burning a hole in one of her inner jacket pockets.

The excitement of potential relief got her all the way to the Silk Door without feeling the nip of the cold.

Within her closet-sized backroom, she changed into her male form, then picked up Sebastien's clothes, which she'd left there the night of the incident before everything went so wrong.

She'd also brought back the Raven Queen's dress, which she would stash there until she had a chance to take it to a used clothing shop for sale. There was a small chance the outfit might be recognized or otherwise used to connect her to the scene of the crime.

She picked up the pile of red and black fabric, intending to cast the shedding-destroyer spell on it, but her finger brushed up against what felt like a metal wire.

She jerked back, tossing the clothes to the floor as if she'd been burned. Her skin rippled with goosebumps as her hindbrain seemed to realize what she'd touched before her conscious mind made the connection. "Oh..." she whispered.

Siobhan stepped forward cautiously, pinching one corner of the fabric and lifting until the wire revealed itself.

Only it wasn't a wire. It was a piece of the flesh-and-bone string that Newton's Aberrant had been formed from, and which had infected and subsumed anyone it touched, woven through the fabric. The sharp edge suggested that a slicing spell had severed it at some point.

It didn't move, even when she clicked her tongue experimentally to see if it reacted to the noise.

There was also no smell or evidence of decay. *'It might not actually be made out of flesh, come to think of it. Just because it's the same color means nothing. This is a piece of an Aberrant. How did the Red Guard not notice this?'*

That they hadn't perversely reassured her. *'If the string was dangerous, surely they would have found it with one of their scanning artifacts?'*

Horrified and fascinated, Siobhan used the edge of her cloak to protect her skin as she pulled the string out from where it had woven itself into the hem, almost invisibly. It was a couple of inches long, as thin as a hair, and rigid. She stared at it for a long time, watching for any signs of life.

When she finally got back to the dorms, any excitement regarding the beamshell tincture was long forgotten.

She closed the curtains around her cubicle, then pulled a glass vial from her pocket, checking on the single Aberrant string she'd placed within. She assured herself that it was still unmoving, definitely dead, and safe. Even so, she melted some wax around the thread-screw top of the vial, put the whole thing in a leather pouch, and hid it safe at the bottom of her school trunk.

Sebastien rifled through her encrypted grimoire until she found the notes she'd made about the blood-print vow, then reviewed the information about the warding aspect that would incinerate the blood if someone tried to access it or use it for sympathetic magic. The principle could be repurposed to secure other things that she would rather destroy than lose or have used against her.

Using the paper spell array for stone disintegration—one of the spells she had learned in Practical Casting—Sebastien carved the lines of the warding spell deep into the stone floor where the trunk at the foot of her bed usually sat. She blew gently to clear out the lines and collected the dust in a small pile, then cast the ward spell, pouring power into what was technically a simple artifact with only two parameters. It would store the energy until it needed to be used against an attack, or when the trickle of natural loss ran it dry.

Then, she used another paper spell array to cast the stone-forming spell on the saved dust, but slightly modified the output to create a flat section of stone rather than a sphere. She formed a thin facade of stone over the warding spell, which was still active but now almost undetectable.

Finally, she moved the school trunk, with the Aberrant string at the bottom, back into its normal spot over the ward.

She lay down on the thin bed, a sheen of sweat on her forehead. Imagining the thread secretly growing in the dark, she shuddered, wondering if she'd just made a mistake. She could have given it to the Red Guard, or Professor Lacer, or even simply tried to burn it up with a fire.

But she wanted it. Perhaps it was irrational, but she wanted to keep it, this last piece of Newton. The Red Guard had taken the rest of him, along with the others who had died, and probably destroyed it all. Since she certainly wasn't going to place the vial on her bedside table or the windowsill, like some kind of paperweight bauble, this was the compromise.

The string would stay hidden, and she would check on it periodically, to make sure it wasn't growing.

11

THE PRESS

Oliver
   Month 1, Day 30, Saturday 5:30 p.m.

Oliver froze, deliberately keeping himself from visibly reacting to Percival's revelation. "You have a photograph of the Raven Queen," he repeated.

Percival nodded, clutching at his left wrist as he stepped closer. "I got it that night a few months ago, when she fought against the Morrows from that old bell tower. That time was an accident, too, actually. My camera confused the lightning for a flash and triggered on its own."

"What exactly does the photograph show?"

Percival grimaced. "It's the view from a building a few blocks away, looking up at the Raven Queen across the street. She's free-casting, with the spell array glowing above her hand, her cloak whipping around in the wind, and the afterimage of a lightning bolt behind her. My camera obscura has the latest cutting-edge technology. It only takes about a second to capture the image, so it's feasible to take photographs of more than just still objects. She's barely blurred!"

Oliver's voice remained tightly controlled. "Is her face identifiable?"

"Well…no. It's from quite far away, the lighting conditions are sub-optimal, and the spell array is between her face and the camera. But it's her!"

Some of Oliver's tension departed. "I will need to examine the image. Have you shown it to anyone else?"

Percival fiddled with his glasses, shaking his head. "I was too afraid. I thought she, or you, might retaliate against me if I talked. They say the Raven Queen holds grudges, and the rumors about what she does to those she doesn't like..." He shuddered visibly. "I do not want to anger her. Or you. This isn't some insane threat that I'll sell the photograph to the coppers or the newspaper. But since I have it...I thought you might be interested in buying the negative as a package deal with the one I took today."

Oliver leaned back in his chair despite his desire to get up and snatch the cartridge from the boy's hand. "How is it you find yourself in these situations, Percival Irving? Are you searching them out? Were you following the Raven Queen? Or actively trying to make contact with me today?"

Some of Oliver's emotion leaked into his tone, and Percival was at least smart enough to recognize the danger, flinching and waving his hands frantically in denial. "No, no! It was all a coincidence," he insisted, then hesitated. "Well, perhaps not totally a coincidence, because I have...peculiar luck. Things tend to go wrong for me, all at once, in cascading, *interesting* ways." The word "interesting" had the tone of a particularly vile curse word, and Percival's lip drew up in a grimace of loathing. "I periodically find myself in the middle of events that I never intended to be involved in and am not prepared to handle."

Oliver was silent, staring at him through the shadow-black eye holes of his mask.

"I'm not just saying that!" Percival assured him. "I had a run-in with a hag, and there seems to be some luck magic involved."

"*Luck* magic?"

"Whatever you want to call it—luck, probability manipulation, or just some force influencing my decisions or the events around me in seemingly random ways that are actually calculated and deliberate—I don't know. Call it what you will, strange things happen around me. I'm really, really not searching out danger."

Oliver steepled his fingers together, watching the frustrated boy return his gaze. "And these coincidences lead to you taking photographs of important people and events?"

"Among other things, but yes. I've witnessed or been involved in six incidents that could have gotten me injured or even killed in the last few months alone, and which made me witness to multiple serious crimes. Seven events if you count today, I suppose. When interesting things happen, it's like a magnet draws me in against my will."

Oliver might have brushed the claim off as ridiculous, but he'd spent years traveling the settled areas of the world, and had experienced enough to hesitate before discounting a tale such as Percival's. "Tell me more."

The boy did, in a rambling, passionate account that lasted almost twenty minutes and proved to be quite entertaining. Several times Oliver nearly burst into riotous guffaws at the ridiculous situations Percival got himself into, only holding back so that he didn't seem too eager. The boy even rolled up his sleeve to show Oliver the mysterious tattoo that had started it all.

Finally, Oliver admitted, "If what you tell me is true, it does seem that you've experienced a strange number of coincidences. Even more surprising were the ways you managed to get through them." Anecdotal evidence was useless, of course, and the boy could be either misguided or an excellent liar, but Oliver was intrigued nonetheless. Although the truth wasn't verifiable, he made a note to keep Percival as far from Siobhán as possible. The last thing he needed was the boy dragging her into his orbit of misfortune. She got into enough "interesting" situations without extra help. "I will buy both originals. Did you bring the other with you?"

Percival reached into his pants pocket, pulling out some lint, a couple of coins, and a wad of thick, dark paper, which Percival had used to cover the negative disk in lieu of a cartridge.

After verifying that it was safe to do so, Oliver unwrapped and inspected it. The image had been captured from quite far away, and was indistinct but still dramatic. He could make out his own form beside Siobhán, his mask a white spot against the darkness, battle wand outstretched, with the blurred streak of a glowing spell shooting toward the silhouetted forms on the street below. "Sixteen gold for both, then?" he asked, already putting the negative back in its protective wrapping and moving both it and the cartridge into one of his desk drawers.

"Umm, that works, but I actually need the cartridge from today back? It's got two other negatives in it that I took earlier today. Nothing you'd be interested in. I saved up for the camera for a long time, but I didn't realize how expensive negative disks and development would be. I've been trying to cover the cost by taking portraits of people. That's what I was originally doing in the market today."

Oliver pulled out the cartridge, then carefully examined the other two disks to ensure they were really as innocuous as stated.

"I guess this camera really is paying for itself!" Percival babbled nervously as he accepted the disks from Oliver's outstretched hand. "I sent a couple of my photographs—normal ones, nothing like this—to the newspaper, but they weren't interested in purchasing them without a story to go along with the photo. The only stories I have are the kind I can't sell for fear of retaliation, or that the newspaper wouldn't *buy* for fear of retaliation!" He laughed at his own joke.

The mention of the newspaper brought to mind the old printing press Oliver had found in Lord Morrow's basement, covered in junk, dust and cobwebs. He stilled, making connections and sparking upon an idea that had been half-formed until that moment.

With some soap, lubricating oil, and maybe a bit of magic, he was sure they could repair the press and get it working again—certainly for much less than it would cost to buy a similar artifact. In fact, it might be possible to drive such an old model with manpower alone, without the need for a thaumaturge on staff. "Are you a decent writer, Percival?"

"I can read and write as well as anyone! My mom taught all us kids," the boy said proudly.

"I don't mean just technically. Are you engaging? Can you tell a decent story in text form, the same way you just told me all those stories about your misfortunes?"

"I haven't written them down or tried to get them published, if that's what this is about?" Percival said, tilting his head to the side with a frown, looking like a one-eyed owl.

Oliver leaned forward. "How would you like a job as the main investigative journalist of a brand-new publication, dedicated to the needs of the people and telling the truth? That artifact of yours will come in handy. And I can give you your first interview right now."

12

———————

GAME PLAN

Sebastien
Month 1, Day 31, Sunday 9:00 a.m.

Sebastien took her first dose of the beamshell tincture immediately after her morning meal on Sunday. She had eaten every bit of her food even though she wasn't hungry and had even started to gag. This ongoing lack of hunger was foreign to her, since, despite the cafeteria food's lack of flavor, her normal appetite usually left her feeling only semi-full.

Sebastien went into the bathroom, then, and following the usage instructions very carefully, she used a toothpick to measure out approximately one tenth of a gram and mixed the crumb-sized piece of paste into a cup of warm water, which she chugged. A decigram wasn't even a full dose, but she was being cautious.

She clamped her mouth shut around the renewed desire to vomit. As her stomach settled, it began to tingle, as if the tincture inside her were crackling with lightning. This electric energy quickly spread outward, rushing up to her head and down to her toes, filling her with a flush of warmth and vibrancy.

Sebastien suppressed a giddy laugh.

With the new energy fizzing inside her, she headed to the library to fix her life.

One unoccupied table caught some spillover light from the shimmering spelled glass that made up the library's domed ceiling. She sat down and paused, basking in the brightness for a moment. The tincture had left her feeling buzzy and flighty, but she forced herself to stillness, considering her goal.

'It's time to take control and figure out my problem. I need a real plan, and a schedule to implement the plan.' When she felt composed and calm, she opened her eyes and pulled out some note-taking supplies.

'I will list all of the problems first before trying to come up with solutions to them.' She scribbled a list of bullet points.

'The coppers can still use my blood to scry for me, unless it was destroyed in the explosion.'

'I still owe the Verdant Stag almost eight hundred gold crowns of the original one thousand debt. Interest is a devil.'

'I'm feeling awake at the moment, but this will do nothing to stop the nightmares, which are the real problem.'

'Damien needs a sense of purpose, focused on something that has less chance of getting me caught.'

'I've got to maintain good academic standing in general, while also completing Professor Lacer's auxiliary exercises, and to prepare something that will earn at least fifty contribution points in the end of term exhibitions.'

She paused, staring at the list, then continued.

'It's also possible that there could be incoming repercussions from Tanya's University faction, or from the coppers, for my involvement in the Aberrant incident, even in my Sebastien Siverling identity.'

She hesitated, wondering if she'd covered everything. *'If I solved these problems, would my life be fixed?'* She considered Ennis for a moment, but decided that she did not, in fact, care to do anything about his imprisonment, and would be fine even if he was sentenced to work in the celerium mines for the rest of his life.

Finally, she added one last bullet point.

'Do something about the Raven Queen's reputation, and/or clear Siobhan Naught's name?'

That would be ideal, but how she might go about doing that remained nebulous.

She mulled over the problems, trying to find issues she hadn't dredged up, but finally decided that if she could deal with the whole list, it would be enough. Be that as it may, neither the list's size nor severity were trifling.

'First, the danger of repercussions from the University or the coppers.' She wasn't sure what she could do to mitigate such an indefinite threat. She would keep her eyes open and gather any relevant information, but her power here was limited. Oliver had plenty of contacts in law enforcement, and she had Damien, so there was a non-trivial chance that she would learn of danger to either identity before it became critical. Beyond that, she had to hope that the important people believed what she had told them about her—Sebastien's—

involvement and thought her harmless. The coppers' investigation was still ongoing, but if they found something to implicate her, she would have to deal with that when it happened.

Sebastien could, however, anticipate that the things that could go wrong, *would* go wrong, and attempt to prepare for that eventuality. She might need to run, hide, or even fight. She needed contingencies in place for the worst possible outcome. If she had done this before, *actually* taking the safety of herself and those around her with deadly seriousness, and planned accordingly, maybe Newton would still be alive.

Her grandfather had told her once that it was hard for people to imagine experiencing the kind of catastrophe that had never affected them before. People in flood or storm zones only wanted to pay for wards strong enough to protect them from the strongest disaster in their own memory, not the strongest that could realistically affect them. People read about accidents, illnesses, and crimes in the newspapers, but didn't believe those things would touch *them* or those they cared for. If they did, every house that could afford it would have anti-fire wards, and people would carry defensive artifacts when they left their homes, and would go to the healer at the first worrying sign of illness. Children thought they were immortal, because they'd never experienced death firsthand.

But she... *She* should have known better. Her life with Ennis might have been relatively safe and mundane compared to her current circumstances. She might have gotten used to not being *able* to prepare for everything due to lack of knowledge, funds, or most often both. But *she* knew how dangerous, how horrific, how absolutely devastating life could really be. She should have tried harder to be ready for it, taken the danger of what they were doing more seriously, rather than assuming things would somehow just work out.

Sebastien had known better, intellectually, but she could see now that she hadn't *believed* things could really go so wrong. If she had, she would have been much more cautious. And maybe, even now, even if she did everything right, there was something she couldn't see waiting to destroy this new, precarious life she had built. There was not even an ounce of fairness in the world, she knew that well enough. Catastrophe could and would fall on those that did not deserve it, and it could come with all the power and shock of a meteor fallen from the heavens. It was up to her to decrease the chances of such an event as much as possible, and that meant preparation of the kind that didn't come naturally to a human brain. Preparation for the things that *could* go wrong, not just things that had already gone wrong.

She added more bullet points to the list.

'*Make preparations for if I am caught.*'

'*Imagine various doomsday events and ways that I might avoid or navigate them. Run drills?*'

'*Train myself to be less foolish.*'

The thought spurred a horrible realization, one that might have been hiding in the back of her mind for some time now, waiting for her to acknowledge it. '*I shouldn't have gone back downstairs for my bag. There is nothing in it so valuable that I should have willingly faced the Aberrant.*'

Her grip on her pen tightened at the thought. '*If I had left the bag, the worst possible thing that could have happened was them realizing that Siobhan Naught and Sebastien Siverling are the same person. Perhaps, if things escalated, I would have had to escape Gilbratha. But the worst-case scenario leading from my decision to go back and retrieve it is that I could have died—or become a second Aberrant.*'

She let the pen drop to the table as a full-body shudder rolled through her. She understood the concept behind calculating worthwhile risks. It was based on a simple formula of desirability vs. likelihood.

Dying or becoming an Aberrant were the worst possible outcomes, with a value of negative ninety-nine and negative one hundred, respectively. Getting caught and giving up her schooling would be horrible, but if she were alive, she at least had a chance to overcome somehow, so that outcome had a value of negative seventy. At the time, getting kicked out of school had seemed totally *unacceptable*, but when compared to the threat of dying, it was immediately obvious that school wasn't nearly as important as her life.

Then, to pick which option she should have gone with, she only needed to multiply the likelihood of each event with its desirability value. If the coppers had found her bag and the bracelets on Newton's arms, she guessed that Sebastien Siverling had a seventy percent chance to get caught, making the overall utility value of that choice negative forty-nine. It would have been smartest to just give the whole ruse up as a lost cause and escape preemptively, but there was still a chance she could have continued on if she played everything right.

Going down there to confront the Aberrant face-to-face had *almost* killed her. If not for the flash of a waking nightmare, it would have. In truth, she was ridiculously lucky to be alive to have this realization right now. And the decision had *still* almost gotten her caught. If she'd been just a little slower, instead of finding Sebastien escaping, the Red Guard would have found the Raven Queen, insensate and basically captured for them.

With a ninety-five percent chance of a break event or death, with an additional chance of capture even if she avoided the first two, the value of that choice was negative ninety-five, at least.

Her calculated utility values could be off, because factors in the real world didn't come in discrete, whole numbers, and there were many variables and potential outcomes that she couldn't anticipate. But there was almost *no way* that facing down the Aberrant had been the correct choice.

"Why am I so stupid?" she whispered to herself as tears pooled in her eyes, burning like acid. Before they could fall, she tilted her head back, opening her eyes wide and staring at the ceiling until they subsided. Perhaps the Aberrant's hums really had been affecting her judgment, as she had claimed to Professor Lacer and the Red Guard. She almost hoped that was the case, because the alternative was that something was deeply wrong with her judgment. Though she didn't believe she was suicidal, her actions suggested differently.

Sebastien took a few deep breaths and swallowed her shame. "I just have to do better. I can do better," she said to the ceiling.

When her fingers could hold the pen again, she made a list of sub-points with all the things she needed to do to prepare for the possibility of a fight or flight situation. This list was even longer than her original list of problems, but at least each point was something she could accomplish. Tentatively, she marked which items were the most critical, knowing there would be more to come and that no matter how much she might wish it, she couldn't do everything at once.

Next, she considered the blood sample the coppers had. Eagle Tower was in the process of being repaired, and unless the coppers had lost her blood, or it was damaged in the explosion, which she couldn't count on, they would be trying again. The next time, Tanya's little trick wouldn't work.

She'd considered the problem before and had a few different ideas about how she could get rid of the blood. Most of them were unfeasible, requiring either a very powerful thaumaturge, or a group of them, to channel enough power. The coppers weren't entirely incompetent. Evidence was well-protected. *'Liza offered to solve the problem for eight hundred gold crowns. Is there any way I could afford to hire her?'* Looking at the next point on her list of problems, which was her overwhelming debt, Sebastien set that idea aside.

Her best bet was still working out how to combine the reverse-scry spell with a curse, which meant she would need to research and practice sympathetic curses.

This extracurricular project was one she wouldn't be requesting Professor Lacer's help on. He might be willing to overlook something like the sleep-proxy spell, and maybe even research into curses, but he was too sharp for Sebastien to give him any hints about her identity. That could end up going very badly for her.

However, maybe Liza would be willing to *consult* for a much-reduced price, with some wheedling or extra incentive. Of Sebastien's contacts, Liza was the most knowledgeable about divination, and maybe could suggest some better ideas about how to handle the situation. If Sebastien could afford it.

Which brought Sebastien to her next issue. Funds.

Beyond her debt to the Verdant Stag, it seemed like all other types of problems were easiest to solve when one had coin to throw at them. It reminded her of a joke she'd heard once: "If a fireball spell can't solve your problem, you need a bigger fireball." With enough gold, Sebastien could make other problems into money problems. She could hire competent help or bribe important people to do what she wanted. Of course, that level of wealth was well beyond her reach. Sebastien was now at the point that an entire weekend spent brewing for the Stags until she reached exhaustion would cover about two weeks of interest, plus a little left over. That was huge, compared to where she'd started.

She thought back to the concoctions she'd seen in the Verdant Stag's little apothecary. She had taken no particular note of the prices, but her mind was a steel trap. She closed her eyes, trying to recreate her experience as she walked through the shelves. Even after a couple of minutes of effort, however, the details wouldn't come to the clarity she was used to. *'Perhaps my memory was impaired by how fatigued I was at the time.'*

Still, she had the initial list Katerin had given her of what concoctions they were willing to buy, and a good idea of what the shop's new offerings cost. Many of those she had no experience with. She chose a couple for their usefulness to her, some for the practice they would give with a particular type of magic, and some for their effect. All-purpose battle magic, like potions of night vision, feather-fall, and fleetfoot, would pay well, and she wanted at least one or two of each to keep for herself anyway. If she could conceal herself, see where the coppers couldn't, and move where they could not follow, she would have a significant advantage.

With more estimation than she would have liked, she calculated what other items would get her the best return on investment for her time and effort. Impotence relief potions, for instance, were very lucrative, but she discarded that option because they were best brewed by a man—a man in a full state of arousal. She technically might have been able to meet that requirement, but she wasn't interested in doing so in Oliver's office, not for any amount of coin.

If she were to work as an alchemist for the Verdant Stag full time, producing a reasonable amount every weekday instead of pushing herself to exhaustion, she could earn about one thousand seven hundred gold a year, significantly more than the average Apprentice's wages, and more than enough to pay off her debt. With their expanded client base, they could probably move sufficient product to make it possible.

Sebastien stared at that number on the paper before her, reconsidering her conception of the Stags' generosity. They could have, fairly, offered her much less. Of course, it helped that they didn't pay the thirty percent magic tax, they had no Master thaumaturge trying to get rich off the backs of their lessers, and they didn't spend extra money on a fancy storefront, decoration, or any marketing besides word-of-mouth referrals. Even their potion vials were the cheapest versions.

Still. A low-wage laborer might earn about five silver per day, or one hundred thirty gold per year, skewing slightly higher for men and lower for women. In many common families, everyone contributed what they could, even the elderly and children. A huge chunk of a low-income family's wages would go toward basic food and lodging, with the rest going toward clothing and healthcare. Taxes took what little might be leftover. One emergency could leave the poorest families homeless, or someone dead for lack of healthcare, because so many lived forever on the knife-edge of poverty.

In contrast, an Apprentice-certified thaumaturge, even though they could only legally practice magic under the supervision of a Master or for their own personal use, not sell items or services directly to others, could make up to forty gold a month. Almost four times as much as a low-wage laborer. It was enough to support a family, frugally, and if they budgeted well, they *might* even have enough left over to save for emergencies.

But despite the generous sum Sebastien made from alchemy, she only had ten weeks before the next term started, when she would need to pay for more classes. She had slightly over fifty gold to her name, if she didn't count the dozen coins sewn into her clothing, which she wouldn't, because that was hidden away for exactly the kind of emergency she was trying to be better prepared for.

'If I spent every weekend until next term brewing, and then the whole of Sowing Break, and didn't put any of the earnings toward the loan, I could maybe eke out three hundred extra gold. Altogether, I could barely afford the fee for six classes. Realistically, with my other expenses, that's five classes, not six.' The thought pained her, but dropping a class wasn't the worst thing that could happen to her. She could learn a lot through self-study in the library, after all. And at the moment, the extra free time sounded heavenly.

Still, unless she dropped a class, she would have zero coin left over for any other endeavors, including her new preparations. It also left her no time for taking a break. Alchemy alone wouldn't be enough.

Even if Sebastien had cared only about coin, dropping out of the University to spend all her time brewing wasn't an option. The Verdant Stag had given her that loan as an investment, and they were expecting greater things from her than low-level alchemy. Beyond the knowledge and skill the University could impart to her, the access to higher-level magic would become invaluable.

A thaumaturge needed variety and new magic to grow. Simply increasing the power channeled through the spells they were already familiar with was insufficient. Even if she could brew a batch of twenty, fifty, or even a hundred regeneration potions, eventually the homogeny would lead to stagnation of her Will's growth. Thaumaturges who became Archmages moved on from simple spells to complex ones that bent the world in new and interesting ways, their skills constantly building upon the foundation they created until they reached heights of understanding and skill that the average professional thaumaturge couldn't even imagine. There were no Archmages who were *only* alchemists, or *only* diviners, or *only* skilled with any single craft of magic.

Sebastien was willing to take requests from the Stag for other favors, as long as they were lucrative and relatively safe, but she couldn't control if or when they would have work for her, or what kind of work it would be.

Tutoring was another option, but it was high-effort and low-reward, unless she could somehow fill up an entire classroom with people willing to pay multiple silvers each for a single lecture. Sebastien simply didn't know anything people would pay that much to learn. Nothing legal, anyway. And imagining a gaggle of gossiping, intrusive classmates showing up with the idea that they could ask personal questions of her made her shudder.

Prostitution, while it could be lucrative, was also not an option she was willing to consider.

With great caution, she could make coin from the underground thaumaturge meetings. The University knew the Raven Queen either attended personally or had a contact who did so, but despite that, the meetings were too useful a resource to give up.

Sebastien created a list of sub-points to make attending safer. Many of these tasks were duplicates from the fight-or-flight preparation, but some were new. The first step would be reporting the issue to the group's administration so they could increase security.

And maybe, now that she didn't have to trail Tanya, Sebastien could convince Liza that they should travel to the meeting together, which would make at least half of the trip significantly safer. Anyone foolish enough to accost Liza would regret it the same way they would regret slipping their foot into a boot that a brown recluse spider had commandeered. Siobhan could just hide behind Liza while the woman dealt with any threats.

The final option to earn coin was accepting requests as the Raven Queen, as she had done with Lord Lynwood. Even if she couldn't answer people's questions or solve their problems, they would have to give something of value just for the chance to meet with her. It seemed likely to backfire, with as high of a downside as the potential upside, but she could consider it if she got desperate.

Contribution points could also be exchanged for items of value or used to offset tuition directly, but at about one silver each, even a couple hundred would barely make a dent.

Sebastien continued noting down useful preparations and solutions until her mind ran dry, then ranked them by priority. Many of her problems would require more thought, and perhaps some discussion with Oliver, and quite a few of her possible solutions were temporarily beyond her reach, either because she couldn't afford them or wasn't strong enough to implement them.

When she finished, she stared at the ink-heavy pages in front of her to memorize them, then took them into the nearest bathroom, which wasn't warded to set off an alarm from simple magic use like the library was, and burnt all the evidence to ash. She poured the ash into one of the self-cleaning chamber pots and watched as it disappeared.

Then she found the back catalogue of newspapers and began her research on the exhibitions. Professor Lacer had been right. Lower term students had earned the most contribution points for things like a water molding spell that took the shape of a magical creature; a pair of shoes that let the wearer walk about a foot above the ground; and there had even been a witch with a phoenix familiar that did some sort of *fire dance* that, as far as Sebastien could tell, didn't require any magical skill, but showed "impressive control of her bound companion."

'I should do something with light,' she mused. That alone would be moderately impressive for a first term student, because light was a more difficult energy source to use, and a delicate spell output to control. It was also flashy by nature.

Sebastien scribbled down ideas of things that might seem more impressive than they actually were to a layman, modeled off of what would be popular in a traveling circus. *'Ideally, whatever I come up with will use the same principles from the Practical Casting exercises. I need over a hundred more hours of practice on those by the end of term, anyway.'* Combining the two was clearly prudent.

Hopefully, by the end of term her Will would have continued to grow at the recent explosive rate. With all the practice she was getting with new, difficult magic, it seemed an inevitability. It had been a big disappointment to learn that, while her sleep-proxy spell might be viable, it wasn't within her grasp as a thaumaturge, and she was looking forward to rectifying that.

Sebastien straightened. *'I know someone who could easily cast that spell. Liza might be expensive to hire...but what if I could obtain her help* without *pay?'* The idea felt shocking, almost subversive, but Liza had proved she was interested in new, useful magic. Enough to pay *Sebastien* for it, if it was fascinating enough.

Sebastien stood. She still had problems to solve and potential disasters that she didn't know how to evade, but she would need more time to think them over. In the meantime, she'd recognized an opportunity to work on the one project that would lighten the constant, bone-crushing weight of all her other obligations.

13

———

FIRST MOVES

Sebastien
Month 1, Day 31, Sunday 12:00 p.m.

As the first step in implementing solutions to her problems, Sebastien returned to the unused second floor classroom where she'd practiced her divination.

While she set up the spell array and components for the mapping spell, Sebastien kept thinking. *'If I could get the coppers off my back entirely, I might not even need to worry about them having my blood. Perhaps I could make it more costly to keep pursuing me than what they would gain by catching me, or give them something they want even more than the Raven Queen…'* She sighed, shaking her head. Even if she could keep them from charging her with treason and blood magic, some of the other things she'd done in the meantime would probably still be considered a crime, and she was unwilling to go to jail for any length of time.

This wasn't a problem she could fix through entirely legal means, not at this point, and not when she had so little power. Illegal means, such as black-mail or bribery, might still be on the table. If she had some way to be sure she could trust the coppers not to arrest and execute her, she could make a deal to give back the book in exchange for her freedom. But making that kind of deal would require some extra leverage to ensure they wouldn't go back on their word whenever it became convenient for them.

Still, it was worth keeping in mind that there might be other solutions to her problems, visible if she came at them from a different angle.

If she could decrypt the book, perhaps that would give her a better idea of the best options, or the leverage she would need to keep the University and the coppers sufficiently wary of her retaliation.

And yet, she wasn't sure she was willing to give up the identity of Sebastien Siverling. Not unless the same opportunities she had as Sebastien could be afforded to Siobhan, which seemed…unlikely. At the very least, her Crown Family schoolmates would probably feel betrayed by her duplicity. '*And would Professor Lacer be willing to take Siobhan Naught as an apprentice?*' But these problems were pointless to consider at the moment, and so she set that line of thought aside as she moved on to the actual casting of the divination spell.

Mixing a couple shavings of the bone disk with the mercury for the mapped divination spell—rather than her blood—didn't increase the difficulty of casting, and Sebastien soon found Tanya's location, tucked away in the library. With this, she didn't need to follow Tanya to know where she was, though the downside was the increased difficulty compared to the compass spell.

'*That's one small step of many complete. Now for the things that can be completed with a handful of coin.*'

The morning gloom had burned off by the time Sebastien arrived at Waterside Market, but despite the winter sun shining down with all the strength it could muster, the residue of the inter-gang battle lived on in more than the faint smell of smoke. The crowds were sparse, and people moved faster, trying to finish their shopping and get home without lingering. Coppers patrolled around the market or stood glaring near the more expensive shops.

Sebastien bought an eclectic variety of items, stocking up on extras of her most-used components and supplies as well as a few dozen small vials, jars, and pouches for organization. Despite the nearby law enforcement, she was able to get what she required with nothing more than a flash of her student token.

After becoming Siobhan at the Silk Door, she took a roundabout way to Liza's house. The streets grew busier the farther south she went, with people huddled by braziers of fire in the alleys and curled up in doorways to escape the icy wind.

But not as many people as she had feared. The fires caused by the fighting had been put out before they could ravage the whole of the Mires, and both the Church of the Radiant Maiden and the Stewards of Intention had taken in refugees. If she knew Oliver at all, she was sure the Verdant Stag was doing the same.

Siobhan's path took her past some of the damage. There must have been areas worse affected, but it wasn't as bad as she'd been expecting. A few destroyed walls let in the elements. The cobblestone street had shattered in places from excessive force. Scorch marks from overpowered spells lingered, accompanied by barriers of poured stone that no one had gotten around to dissolving.

Siobhan rapped on Liza's door with the lion door-knocker, avoiding its teeth. After a few moments, it apparently decided she was safe, and the lock opened with an audible "click." Siobhan walked in and waited in the dining area attached to the kitchen.

Liza arrived a long few minutes later with a steaming mug of dark tea in her hands, sleep-grit in her bloodshot eyes, and a scowl on her face.

'*She's tired. Perfect,*' Siobhan thought.

"What do you want? Be quick about it. I've barely gotten any sleep for the past two weeks dealing with all this *shit,* and I am running low on fucks to give." Liza didn't even bother to glare at Siobhan, staring wearily into the mid-distance and gulping down her steaming tea.

Siobhan replied without preamble. "I have a newly developed spell in the testing stages that can allow you to give up sleep without side effects."

Liza's expression was blank for a whole second of continued bleariness, and then she turned to Siobhan with sudden hawklike focus, her Will tightening the air between them. "Continue."

"The spell array and theory have been reviewed and approved by an extremely accomplished sorcerer, but I haven't attempted to cast it yet. It works on sympathetic binding principles. Technically blood magic, but it only requires a raven. I assumed you would have no qualms with that."

"No side effects? No sleep debt? No decrease in mental or physical function? How long does it last?" Liza asked, rapid-fire.

Siobhan held back her smile and answered confidently. "It's still in the testing phase, but it's based on restricted experiments carried out during the Third Empire. No side effects for the person giving up sleep. There would probably be some minor sleep debt if you push the duration of the spell to its limits, but nothing like what you would normally experience. I'm not sure of the specifics when not using another human as part of the spell. I'd estimate you could spend one to three days awake in a row. You'll likely still experience some fatigue, and any serious injuries or extended stressors would require you to rest outside of the bounds of the spell…but the benefits are obvious, I think. These last two weeks could have left you feeling as tired as you might after a long day of work, rather than as if you'd been pushing yourself without a break for days straight."

Liza stared at Siobhan like a dog staring at a juicy steak. She tried to take a drink from her cup but realized it was empty. "Give me a moment." She retreated to the kitchen, returning a few minutes later with two cups full of tea. She seemed slightly less eager as she handed one cup to Siobhan.

Siobhan took it with thanks but only blew on the steaming liquid, not taking a sip. It wasn't that she thought Liza would drug her…but the other woman hadn't hidden her greed well enough. *'There are spells that keep people from paying attention to what they're signing, so why not a couple drops of a tincture that can make someone a little too compliant while negotiating?'*

"You have my attention," Liza said. "I'm skeptical about these claims, especially since you say it's merely in the theoretical stage right now, but I would be willing to test it for you. I assume the components are expensive?"

Siobhan almost snorted at the blatant attempt to swindle her. "The details of the spell are proprietary information. I'm willing to give you the information, but it certainly won't be for free. The components aren't cheap, but I was able to get my hands on them, so I don't need your help with that."

"What *do* you want?"

Siobhan hadn't expected Liza to be this interested. She'd simply hoped to avoid paying to cast the spell while also keeping everything set up at Liza's house. But she wasn't one to let opportunity go to waste. *'Liza was willing to knock sixty-five gold off her fee to study the warding medallion Grandfather made me. This isn't as magically impressive as that…but obviously Liza could make great use of it. She might be able to develop a similar spell herself, but without access to the University library resources…maybe not.'* "One hundred fifty gold," Siobhan tried.

Liza scoffed. "Ridiculous! I haven't even seen this spell in action, and you admittedly haven't cast it yourself. Everything you're telling me is hearsay. Twenty gold, and I'll help you test it. I have protective wards built into the casting room below that should help keep us safe against violent spell reactions, and my Will is almost certainly necessary for a spell that does what you say. Without me, you would be risking your sanity and your life. Hells, something like this could easily trigger a break event."

That was an undeniably persuasive argument, especially considering Siobhan's recent experience, but she would not give in just like that. Liza had actually offered to *pay* her! For a spell that Siobhan developed herself! "It's not quite as demanding as you think. I wouldn't turn down your help, but with some effort, I can cast it myself. I'm not worried about serious reactions. As I said, another sorcerer has already reviewed it. One I trust. This is the kind of spell that could change your life. An extra eight hours a day? How much is your time worth, Liza?"

Liza narrowed her eyes. "Eighty gold."

"One hundred twenty gold, and the ongoing use of your casting room downstairs."

"One hundred gold, the use of my casting room, and I'll assist in the development and testing of this spell. But if the spell is totally unviable, I'll want my coin returned."

Siobhan almost agreed, but hesitated. "You'll sign a blood print vow of secrecy. And I want ten percent of the income if you ever use this spell or its principles for anyone else or otherwise earn coin from the knowledge." She didn't want Liza able to pass on the information to others for money or favors, but casting the spell directly should be fine. With Liza's prices, even a small percentage could fatten Siobhan's purse significantly.

Liza smirked. "Not bad, girl. Five percent."

"Agreed."

Once they had worked out the details of the vow, which protected each of them in both word and intent, and completed it, Liza waved at Siobhan impatiently. "Well, let's see it. You brought the spell information, I hope? I won't be able to devote any significant time to the project for the next couple of weeks while I finish up my current commitments, but I can take a look."

Siobhan pulled the wrinkled sheaf of papers from the bottom of her bag. Women's fashion made carrying all the necessary items so difficult. "While I'm here, I was wondering if you could take a quick look at my warding medallion. It experienced some strain," she said, pulling it from underneath her shirt while remaining careful to leave the transformation amulet hidden.

Liza waved her over to a desk covered in bits of metal and tools, turned on an extremely bright lamp, and settled a multi-lensed monocle device on her head. She set the medallion under the light and peered down at it. "Which spell saw use?"

"Umm, energy-deflecting?"

"Hmm. It seems fine. No melting like the anti-scrying function. That one is probably on the edge of breaking, but my divination-diverting ward should protect it as long as it remains on your person." She flipped the medallion over, inspecting it with an absent smile for a while longer. "Still one of the most impressive artifacts I've ever seen. It protects against most dangers someone might face, both magical and mundane."

Siobhan took it back, rubbing her thumb over the cooling metal. "What are all the functions, exactly? I've looked up all the glyphs on the surface, so I know the gist of it, but I've never had the chance to examine what's woven through the inside layers."

Liza pulled off the monocle and considered her for a few seconds in silence. "It wards against scrying, of course. In addition to that, it tries to divert or counteract specific energy, temperature, and force parameters. Those will help to protect you against the worst of the most common battle spells. It's got a list of common minor curses, too. It acts to discourage its own theft, or being noticed unless attention is specifically drawn to it. It will protect you, once, against a fall greater than ten meters, and can filter out an air bubble from the water around itself if you start to drown. And it should stop a small projectile like an arrow—anything moving faster than thirty meters per second."

That was…more thorough than Siobhan had realized. Grandfather had thought of almost anything, even if he hadn't gotten to finish the medallion before she took it. '*Thank you,*' she thought, though she knew nothing of him was left to hear her.

"I'll be back in a couple of days with the most important supplies," Siobhan said as she stood to leave. "I was thinking we could start testing with mice. Try to get some sleep in the meantime."

She was halfway through the door when she paused, almost tripping over the doorjamb with the sudden idea that had halted her. "I need to get a simple battle wand, and some kind of remote-triggered artifact that would allow me to destroy evidence—a bag, for example, or footlocker—in a radius of a few feet without causing additional destruction. Can you give me a referral to someone in the Night Market that does good, *affordable* work?"

Liza glared as if Siobhan were a flesh-eating slug that had crawled up her boot, nearly pushing her out the door, but not before giving Siobhan the location of a shop, as well as permission to say that Liza had sent her. "*I* certainly don't have time to dance to this girl's crazy whims," Liza muttered to herself before slamming the door behind Siobhan.

Siobhan grinned. Liza loved her.

She stopped by the shop that she'd sold Ennis's belongings to, where she picked up a handful of different outfits for both women and men, each with a distinctly different look, just nice enough to be unmemorable. She purchased those plus a few canvas satchels and backpacks in various states of wear.

Siobhan felt the pain in her purse-strings as she paid, a good seventeen gold poorer. Clothing was so expensive. She hadn't even bought shoes! It would have been even more expensive if not for her trading in her old Raven Queen outfit—which she'd cast a color-changing spell on to avoid recognition.

After that, she went to the Night Market. The sun was setting by that time, but the Night Market had been aptly named, and the street and shops within maintained their inviting lights. She was surprised at first to see scattered shoppers, and even a couple of shopkeepers, wearing masks, but realized it made sense that some people would not want to be seen doing business there.

The shop Liza had recommended had an empty stunning wand on sale, and the artificer on staff absorbed her order for a remote-triggered destruction device with extended, dubious silence. Finally, he said, "I think I have a land mine from the Haze War that could be modified to do what you want. That would be cheaper than a booby trap meant for a safe, which would be your other immediate option. The purpose is destroying *evidence*, yes, not for use on your enemies?" he asked, giving her a hard stare.

"Yes," Siobhan assured him, trying to look trustworthy. "And I need the triggering mechanism to be discreet, something I can hide."

"How soon do you need it?"

"As soon as possible?"

He gave her another judgmental look. "An extra gold for the rush job. I can have it ready in an hour."

Siobhan reluctantly agreed.

While she was browsing, waiting for them to charge up the wand and modify the land mine in the workshop at the back of the store, she found the perfect artifact to solve another of her problems.

She almost missed it, because it sat on a corner shelf among a jumble of less dazzling items that most people would have little use for. She wouldn't have even known what it was if not for the little card attached to it by a string. The artifact was composed of two glass-and-copper spheres. The large sphere contained a clear liquid, within which a tapered iron needle floated, suspended in the center. The second sphere, attached to the top, was much smaller and opened up to allow the user to place something inside it.

It was a dowsing artifact, meant for miners, spelunkers, or wild herb gatherers. One simply placed a sample of what they were hoping to find within the little sphere at the top, closed and twisted it to activate the divination, and then followed the compass needle, which could rotate in the four cardinal directions and also adjust up and down.

Some of the glass between the embedded copper braces had obviously cracked and been repaired, and the card said the divination only reached out about ten meters from the artifact, but it was perfect for Siobhan. When the shop's artificer came back out, she bought it for only three gold after haggling him down due to the obvious damage.

The stunning wand, which now had twenty-one fresh copies of the standard stunning spell, cost seventeen gold. The remote-triggered mine, which had been retooled to cast a single, powerful disintegration spell, cost another twelve gold, and could be triggered by pressing a discreet, compressible button. Altogether, it was more expensive than she had been expecting, and she wondered if she was being charged extra because her purchases were so obviously illegal.

On the whole, she had spent over fifty gold on her shopping excursion, almost every coin she'd had to her name before the agreement with Liza. To potentially buy herself safety, it was a bargain.

Now she only needed to find the most optimal places to set up her own safe houses, places she could escape to, pick up a stash of emergency supplies, and change her appearance.

The Silk Door could probably operate as one. *'Other than that, I could do either Dryden Manor or the Verdant Stag, but it would be prudent to have the emergency stashes somewhere completely unrelated to the Verdant Stag. If I can get to Oliver's house or the Verdant Stag, I'm likely to be okay. I need contingencies for when I can't go to them for some reason.'*

Siobhan returned to the Silk Door, looking around the little closet for a place to keep a secret stash. Although the room was reserved only for her, others might still enter while she wasn't there, and she didn't want to chance her valuable stash being stolen.

Eventually, she used an idea she'd originally come up with as a better hiding spot for the stolen book currently embedded in a mattress at Oliver's house. At the time, she hadn't had a clean way to cut into and control the manor's marble floor. But now, she knew a very handy, simple spell that allowed her to create extremely precise incisions. Using the stone-disintegration spell she had been practicing for Practical Casting, she carved out a circle of the floor and lifted it up from the rest. *I need to practice a version of this spell for wood, something that will allow me to hollow out part of a tree or take apart wooden floorboards without the damage being noticeable.* There were plenty of places throughout the city where she could create a similar stash.

She divided up some of the basic components she'd bought into the vials and pouches, then made copies of her most useful spells on some new seaweed paper, keeping the arrays small and portable. Into a single emergency getaway bag went one spare outfit for both her male and female form, a basic set of spell-casting supplies—including a small, adjustable-flame oil lantern—and an assortment of coin totaling ten gold. She only had enough clothes for two full kits, but enough of the other supplies remained for a few more stashes.

She placed one of the prepared bags and all the extra supplies in a hollow space between supporting floorboards, underneath the stone veneer. Before she sealed the stash up again, she drew a complete spell array for the stone-disintegration and reformation spell on the underside of the veneer. That way, if she arrived in a hurry, she wouldn't need to take time writing it out again. She could cast with the spell array whether or not she could see it, as long as she remembered where it was. *I should add some dried food rations and a canteen of water,* she realized as she stood, rubbing her aching knees. Best to be prepared for anything, even fleeing into the wilderness. If she had the coin, another battle wand would be an optimal addition.

Her new stunning wand and the disintegration mine both went into her bulky school bag, though she had to use her cutting and mending spells along with some scrap leather to create a discreet, additional secret pouch for the mine inside. With it, there would be no need for another scenario where she had to place herself in danger to retrieve the bag and items within it. She could simply destroy it all from a distance, leaving no evidence leading back to her.

She hesitated over where to put the disintegration mine's compressible button, which needed to be pressed three times in quick succession to activate the artifact, and was useless if she was over two kilometers away from the mine.

Eventually, she decided that she currently didn't have any good spaces for the button and decided to follow up on another idea she'd had, using the last of her leather mending scraps to create a kind of holster that she could wear around her waist. It held her black sapphire Conduit and the beast core Tanya had given her flush against the skin of her left side, over her ribs and in a position where her arm would shield it. A much smaller pouch contained the mine's activation button, surrounded by stiff enough leather that it would be difficult to trigger by accident.

She moved around while watching herself in the small mirror to test the holster out. It was much more comfortable than keeping the sapphire tucked inside her boot, where it always dug into the skin of her calf. The holster's design required a few tweaks and a color-changing spell to look more like skin, but when she was finished, it was invisible from the outside. Even if someone pressed up against her, the leather was angled and tapered such that they might feel something strange but wouldn't immediately realize she was keeping something stone-shaped under her clothes. She even added some notches that would allow her to adjust it based on the current size of her torso when she switched between forms.

Lastly, she copied the hidden pockets for the mine and wand into the bag she used as Siobhan.

She took the second filled emergency getaway bag with her as she left, mulling over a good location for it as she walked through the darkening streets. Eventually, she found a nice alehouse in the northern part of the city, located between the University and the nearest exit through Gilbratha's white cliffs. It had a public bathroom for customers, which had a window large enough for her to crawl through. She locked the bathroom door, then worked quickly to cut out a portion of the floor in the back corner and dig out a hollow space below it, where she placed the second getaway bag. She cleared away the evidence, packing some of the stone and dirt into the side pocket of her school satchel to dump out later, and left the alehouse with no one the wiser.

She grinned to herself, feeling rather clever and, if she were to admit it, like a child playing at being a spy. She had always had a fondness for hidden pockets and compartments. It felt like she had made real progress with the day's work. While she hoped these arrangements were never again necessary, knowing that they existed gave her some measure of comfort. It was a start.

On the way back to the University, Sebastien made sure to pass by a very specific shop window. She noted the folded paper decorations sitting in it. The next secret meeting of thaumaturges was twelve days away.

That was plenty of time to prepare, as long as she stayed on top of her schedule and managed her time. She needed to be more efficient, perhaps getting a few minutes of homework and study in during the breaks between classes, when other students were ambling through the halls and chatting with each other.

Above all, however, she needed to avoid adding anything more to her plate. She couldn't afford another project, or another problem.

14

ILLUSION CHAMBER

SEBASTIEN
Month 2, Day 3, Wednesday 10:40 a.m.

THAT WEDNESDAY, Sebastien arrived at the Natural Science classroom a few minutes early, hoping to squeeze in some of her History reading before class started. She had a new schedule to optimize her productivity. It wasn't much different from the old one, just more rigid and regimented, with less room for breaks, side projects, or aimlessness. It—along with the beamshell tincture—was allowing her to keep up with all her classes and projects, but afforded her barely any leeway. She hoped that a few stolen moments of extra work here and there would allow her to get enough ahead that she could occasionally take an hour or two to herself.

Ironically, despite her underlying fatigue, the hardest part of the plan was making herself get a full eight hours of sleep every night, in two four-hour chunks with only an hour of homework slipped between them. She had to force herself to cast her dreamless sleep spell and actually attempt to rest.

Sebastien stopped before the closed door to Professor Gnorrish's classroom, frowning at the paper stuck to the door. "CLASS MOVED TO LIBRARY TUNNEL," it read in big block letters. With a quick check of her pocket watch and a put-upon sigh, Sebastien spun around and hurried to the northern edge of the Citadel.

The crystalline tunnel between the Citadel and the library was dark, letting none of the outside light through with its normal shattered rainbows of color. A couple people at either end of the tunnel had opened a part of the wall that she'd never noticed before and were messing with something inside. Sebastien stepped into the tunnel warily, letting her eyes adjust to the gloom.

Gnorrish stood in discussion with a handful of other men and women at the center of the tunnel, though beyond the glint of a faculty token, it was too dim to make most of them out.

Sebastien sat cross-legged against the wall, imitating the handful of other students who had arrived before her. Her eyes slowly adjusted, but it was far too dim to read, so she tried to let her mind relax. She was still buzzing with energy from her morning dose of beamshell tincture, which tended to give her a feeling of bottled-up energy that needed to be released somewhere.

One of the men who had been talking with Gnorrish turned in her direction, his familiar silhouette attracting her attention.

"What are *you* doing here?" Sebastien blurted out to Professor Lacer, drawing the attention of the other professors and students.

He sent her a scathing look, and she ducked her head in an apologetic bow. "I meant, I'm surprised to see you, Professor Lacer," she amended in a much softer tone.

"I am here to do a favor for a fellow professor, and, not incidentally, for my apprentice as well," he drawled.

She wondered what kind of favor would require so many of the faculty.

Reading the curiosity on her face, Lacer simply said, "You will see," and moved to stand nearby, his expression clearly stating that the conversation was over and anyone who disturbed him with idle chitchat would feel his wrath.

The other professors split up as well, at equidistant points along the length of the tunnel.

When Damien and Ana arrived, they looked around with curiosity. "What are we doing here?" Damien asked, the question aimed toward no one in particular.

"The whole tunnel is a simulation chamber focused on visual illusions," Ana said. "I imagine there will be some sort of demonstration."

Gnorrish loudly instructed the students to arrange themselves into groups and join a professor. A handful of other random students quickly joined Sebastien's trio.

Sebastien rapidly tapped her fingers against her knee, letting Damien and Ana's light chatter flow over her head.

Gnorrish walked slowly between the groups of students along the length of the tunnel, a ball of light floating above his head. His booming voice carried easily. "The next few weeks of this class will be an exploration of light. Or, more correctly, an exploration of the electromagnetic spectrum that includes visible light. It is an important research area in modern natural science for multiple reasons. Not only is light a freely available energy source for your spells—in some cases even more abundant or useful than heat—it is both versatile and powerful. I believe it has the potential to do so much more, and as it is considered one of the more difficult energy sources to channel, we will be spending extra time learning about it."

Sebastien tracked Gnorrish's slow pace with her eyes, unblinking, as if she could suck the knowledge out of the man with her eagerness alone. *'The more I understand the subject through the concepts of natural science, the better control I'll have with all magical applications that use light.'*

Lifting his hands to the sky, Gnorrish paused, and then, with a dramatic flourish like a conductor before an orchestra, he dropped them.

An illusion sprang to life in front of each student group, not unlike what they were learning to do in Practical Casting, but somehow, perhaps because of the surrounding darkness, seeming more tangible. "Behold! One of the many utilizations of light magic," Gnorrish trumpeted, throwing his arms wide with a grin.

The illusion spell displayed a stack of waving lines. They all seemed to move, flowing from left to right, with the ones at the top at such a gentle slope they barely rose or fell at all, and the ones at the bottom in a zig-zagging frenzy.

Sebastien peeked toward Professor Lacer, who had one hand pressed against a section of the tunnel wall and the other curled around his Conduit, his focus on the illusion hanging in the air before them. The other professors seemed to be doing the same, and, though the image in front of each group was almost identical, Sebastien thought theirs seemed more *tangible* than most. As if she would feel the lines if she reached out to touch them.

"Light is a form of energy, and it travels in waves like these," Gnorrish said. "We can tell how much energy an electromagnetic wave has by the frequency—how many waves, from peak to trough, pass through a point in a set period of time. As long as light isn't passing through substances with different densities, that means light with a shorter wavelength has more energy, while light with a longer wavelength has less. Light doesn't have mass, so it's not like water, but water can still be a good analogy. Imagine you're in a boat on the ocean. Your boat is anchored, a single immobile point, while the water moves under and around you." The illusion changed to show the side view of a cute little boat, floating atop deep water. "The peaks and troughs of each wave are always the same height. If each wave is so far apart that you rise and fall over them so gently it's barely noticeable, with one wave passing underneath your ship every minute, you might say the waves were low-energy.

Now, suddenly the waves get closer together, and as they pass under you, *ten* every minute, your boat pitches and sways so steeply you need to grab onto something to keep from being thrown off the side." Gnorrish mimed a wild scramble for purchase against the pitching deck of a boat, to the laughter of many of his students. "Those are high-energy."

Gnorrish stopped his wild flailing, grinning at their response. Professor Lacer switched the illusion from a boat back to the stack of waving lines, and Gnorrish pointed to a very small section of light waves in the middle of the nearest group's illusion, which took on the appearance of a section of a rainbow. "Our eyes and brains are adapted to perceive this particular range of wavelengths, which we call 'light.' Can anyone tell me what's special about light?"

Students shifted uncomfortably as his eyes roved over them, but no one spoke.

He looked to Sebastien. "Mr. Siverling! What do you think?"

She was confused for a moment, then realized it was a trick question. "The only thing special about it is that we can all see it, and we gave it a label called 'light.'"

Gnorrish lifted his hands, bobbing them back and forth as if weighing something on an invisible scale. "That's not entirely wrong, but not entirely right, either. The leading theory is that we see this part of the spectrum because it's the most *relevant* for us. The majority of our sun's radiation happens to fall within this range, and it manages to pass through our atmosphere without being absorbed or scattered. It could also be because visible light is the only set of electromagnetic radiation that propagates well in water, where it is theorized all the mortal species rose from. Yet *another* theory is that radiation in that part of the spectrum is easily stopped by matter. If we had evolved to 'see' using super-long wavelength radiation, for instance, which can pass *through* matter, we'd be bumping into trees and falling into holes because they'd be invisible to us! Or perhaps we wouldn't be able to see at all, because the radiation would pass right through our eyes and out the back of our skulls."

With another conductor's wave, Gnorrish changed the illusion to show a tree standing before a huge eyeball, which was sliced in half so they could see its pieces and what was happening inside it. "Thousands of years ago, people thought that sight came from our eyeballs sending out tiny little information-gathering probes, which returned with the images we see." The eyeball shot out little birds, which landed on the tree, and then returned, flying back through the pupil. "Of course, we know today that sight comes from *light* entering our eyes, passing through our pupil, and hitting the retina, which lines the back of our eyeballs and contains two types of photoreceptors."

He went on to explain how rods allowed humans to see in greyscale in low lights. In brighter light, the red, green, and blue cones allowed the perception of seven distinct colors, with some ten million distinctions between individual shades and hues. "Did you know that human infants only perceive black, white, and grey?" Sebastien reached out, letting the tips of her fingers trail over the gigantic slice of eyeball, and almost jumped when it rotated away from her finger as if she'd actually touched it. She snatched her hand back, rubbing the tips of her fingers—which hadn't felt anything—and looked at Professor Lacer. She wasn't sure if she was imagining his almost imperceptible expression of smugness, but her attention was soon drawn back to the lecture.

"It's not until about five months of age when we begin to see all the colors. Prognos children, however, see all colors from birth." Gnorrish's hand sketched out a wide arc, and the illusions morphed into bright light passing through a prism, splitting into the full spectrum of color. The rainbow beam stood out starkly against the relative darkness, revealing fine particles of dust in the air.

"This is what it looks like when you separate light into its different wave-lengths, which is easy to do using a prism. Right on the edge, below violet, there is *another* color." He paused dramatically. "Ultraviolet. Interestingly, it can be used for sterilization of bacteria and the newly discovered 'viruses' in lieu of sterilization potions, once thought to be working against 'bad humors.' Prognos, who have an extra two photoreceptors, as well as special oil droplets in their photoreceptor cells, can see ultraviolet, as well as distinguish between colors much more accurately than us. They live in a world of color that most of the other species cannot even imagine." He paused wistfully for a moment, staring at the rainbow of scattered light. "Other creatures can see further on the spectrum in the other direction, known as infrared, which allows them to identify heat sources even in relative darkness, making them wonderful predators."

As if reading Sebastien's mind, Gnorrish answered her immediate ques-tion. "Attempts have been made to create spells that allow people to temporarily see beyond our normal visible spectrum, but they haven't made it into general use, even among adventurers and the military, who would seem to particularly benefit from additional sensory abilities. Why?" He didn't pause long enough for anyone to attempt an answer. "Basically, these spells have too many side effects, including synesthesia, where the brain confuses one sensory pathway with another and you begin to feel, taste, or smell colors. Other side effects are confusion, disorientation, and pain—in some cases, to the point of causing mental trauma. And in a few unfortunate instances, people have experienced rupturing of the vessels of the eye or brain due to incompatibility and overstimulation. Please do not experiment with this."

He paused to let that warning sink in, meeting students' gazes again to impress his seriousness upon them. "There are some potions that work safely, particularly for the infrared wavelengths, but they require an ongoing regimen over several months to adapt the brain to the expanded sense, and then continued upkeep to maintain that adaptation, which is very expensive and hasslesome, especially in the beginning."

He turned back to the illusion, which morphed several times to show different examples as he walked them through the mechanics of refraction and reflection. As she took in the detailed visual examples, Sebastien felt her grasp on the concepts deepening beyond the surface-level understanding she'd once thought was all she needed. The illusion chamber made learning these somewhat abstract concepts significantly easier.

"Let us pause and think. How is this knowledge useful? What could you do with it?" Gnorrish asked.

"Invisibility spells," a young woman piped up immediately. "You could just bend light around yourself so people see whatever's behind you."

A young man lifted his hand. "That works for illusions, too, making people think something is there when it really isn't."

Gnorrish nodded, pointing at the man as he replied. "That effect is encountered in nature through mirages, including the superior mirage known as the Fata Morgana, which have created illusions of floating islands that lure sailors to their deaths. It's also why, in the morning, you can see the edge of the sun before it has geometrically risen above the horizon. Continue."

Several others had their own ideas of varying obviousness.

"Shared perception spells, like you were saying."

"The eagle vision potion and spell."

"Dark-vision magic!"

"Some magical beasts are really attracted to the color red," another young man piped up without waiting to be called on. "Maybe it's the only color they can see? That's important to know if you want to survive in the wilds."

"Image-capturing artifacts," Ana murmured.

Damien leaned forward. "Hidden messages! If you can tune a spell's output to create a specific wavelength, you can have a receiver spell set up to recognize that exact wavelength—ideally one of the invisible ones—and you can use it to send pre-set signals. There's a new communication device the coppers are using that probably works on those principles. It must!"

'A temporary blindness hex,' Sebastien thought. '*You could interrupt someone's sight without permanently damaging them just by keeping light from hitting their retina.*'

A witch with a clear, jelly-like eel from the Plane of Water winding around her damp shoulder said, "Healing spells to mend or replace eyeballs. Or augmenting spells to improve the distance or ocular precision, even. Eagle vision could be permanent, if you did it right."

'*It's probably also applicable to wards against certain kinds of divination or revealing spells,'* Sebastien thought. *'Reflect or redirect the magical waves. I wonder if my divination-diverting ward uses any of these principles?'*

Damien raised his hand, speaking before Gnorrish had a chance to point at him. "There's a shield spell that looks like a super-smooth silver mirror and reflects all kinds of energy attacks. Aberford Thorndyke used it to survive being thrown into a pool of lava. And maybe you could make a spell that turns infrared radiation into red light, to help illuminate the dark!"

Some of the students laughed, but Gnorrish only grinned wider. "Indeed, both very creative applications of the principle we've discussed."

'Sundered zones,' Sebastien thought. She only realized she must have said this aloud when Damien's head snapped around to look at her. She shrugged. "They're obviously reflecting all light, to be that perfectly white, and magical effects can't pass through them." Supposedly. And yet an Aberrant like Red Sage managed to affect the world through its prophecies, despite containment.

Though Professor Lacer seemed uniformly unimpressed with the students' offerings, Gnorrish was pleased. "All good ideas!" Gnorrish continued lecturing, explaining how refraction worked in mirages, rainbows, sunsets and sunrises, and various different lens shapes, with illusory illustrations for all of them, with ridiculous jokes peppered throughout the lecture to help them remember the mechanical details. He even used a couple of equations to explain things for the more mathematically inclined.

Then he let their groups play with the illusions directly, setting them various tasks with light sources, lenses, and different substances. Sebastien took charge, allowing no dissent, using hand motions and the occasional verbal request to Professor Lacer to change brightness, angles, and shapes. This interactive capability was the true feature of the illusion chamber. If only it didn't require other professors to collaborate, putting forth their personal time and effort, perhaps it would be used more often.

Under Sebastien's guidance, her group created their own simple eyeball, then both a telescope and a microscope, and some fun-house mirrors that morphed their reflections in various ways. They simulated infrared vision in one of the mirrors, and, at her request, Professor Lacer attempted to make a ball of light give off ultraviolet radiation, which was very strange. As Gnorrish had said, none of them could see it, except for a single half-prognos student in one of the other groups, but it caused normally invisible smears and splatters on their clothes and surroundings to stand out with a peculiar glow as the substances absorbed the ultraviolet and converted it back into visible light.

By the time class ended, her group was trying to produce their own miniature Fata Morgana mirage of a floating island in the sky, though they had some trouble with the delicate balance of the required conditions.

Sebastien had lost herself in it like a gleeful child playing with a fascinating toy and couldn't help but be slightly disappointed when the illusion dispersed and the walls of the tunnel lightened, allowing the weak sunlight to come through in blinding rainbow-colored sprays and sparkles.

All the professors looked exhausted. Professor Gnorrish didn't even have the energy to raise his voice or wave his arms about as he dismissed them. Even Professor Lacer had a faint sheen of sweat on his brow, but when he met Sebastien's gaze and incandescent smile, the corners of his lips twitched up faintly in response.

15

A FIT OF PIQUE

Sebastien
Month 2, Day 3, Wednesday 2:00 p.m.

The excitement over the simulation chamber lasted through the lunch period, which Sebastien rushed through to focus on homework. However, as she settled into her usual spot near the front of the Practical Casting classroom and waited for Professor Lacer to appear, her thoughts turned back to the weight of her problems.

Specifically, that she was wanted by the coppers and would never have a chance to live and openly practice magic in her real identity.

When a copper crown appeared on her desk and slid forward under the force of Damien's finger, her gaze trailed up his arm and met his own.

She raised an eyebrow.

"Copper for your thoughts?" he asked, his somewhat embarrassed grin revealing that he understood how banal the joke was.

She snatched up the coin and tucked it away. "My thoughts are worth at least twice that much, but I suppose I'll give you a discount." She leaned in to make sure they weren't overheard. Eyes brightening with excitement, Damien did the same. "I'm wondering about what the Raven Queen stole," she murmured.

Damien initially looked surprised, but he focused as she continued.

"That book was just one item out of the whole haul from an archaeological expedition, right? Why exactly is it, specifically, so valuable? All of this interest and effort seems a little much for a simple antique, right?"

Damien looked around to make sure no one was listening in. "I read an Aberford Thorndyke story where someone stole an old painting worth ten *million* gold crowns. If it was old and rare enough, maybe something pre-Cataclysm, some people would be willing to pay a ridiculous amount for it."

She hadn't considered that the book could be pre-Cataclysm. She suddenly remembered that she'd cut the leather apart to examine the inside more thoroughly, and then used a mending spell to put it all back together. *'Surely I didn't rip apart a prehistoric antique worth ten million gold crowns...right?'* She suppressed a shudder.

Sebastien hesitated, tapping her forefinger nervously against the desk. "What if that's not it, though?" she asked, her voice even lower. "Because... why wouldn't they just say so? The fact that it's all so shrouded in mystery makes me suspicious."

Damien frowned, humming thoughtfully. "What if she didn't actually steal a book at all, but they don't want to reveal what she really took? Maybe she kidnapped someone important and is holding them hostage, but they don't want to tell the public because..." He trailed off, then shook his head. "Well, I can't think of a reason why they wouldn't want to tell anyone about a kidnapping. At least not that doesn't sound too silly to be real."

He didn't notice Sebastien's deadpan look, continuing with increasing enthusiasm. "Or what if they're trying to capture her because she has some blackmail on someone important, and they can't afford to give her what she wants? And they don't want to *kill* her because she's set a dead man's switch to release the blackmail. Oh! Or maybe she's cursed someone powerful and rich with a slow death, and they're trying to find her so she can lift the curse, but don't want anyone to know. Or—"

Damien stopped, his mouth still open but the excitement draining from his face. He turned to meet her unimpressed gaze. "Sebastien, what if she stole something really, I mean *extremely* dangerous? Something the University shouldn't have had in the first place and doesn't want to admit they lost? They wouldn't want to tell anyone what it was because they wouldn't want to panic the masses with the truth. And that would explain why the High Crown is putting so much pressure on Titus. It would even make sense why she's so bold, because she knows they're probably wary about pushing her to the point of desperation. But..." He shook his head, taking a relieved breath. "If that were the case, Titus would have definitely called in the Red Guard. That's the kind of thing they exist to handle, after all. And, I forgot, but I'm pretty sure it really is a book, because I eavesdropped on—well, I *overheard*—Titus talking about it with one of his investigators some months ago, and he mentioned how the University hadn't been able to decipher anything useful from the remaining books."

Before Sebastien could reply, Professor Lacer arrived. After a few minutes showing them variations of fully fleshed-out light-molding spell arrays, he set them to continue their practice with the minimalist arrays allowed.

The understanding she'd gained from Natural Science made the illusion spell easier. Though the placebo effect was a real thing—which Gnorrish had vehemently cautioned them about when trying to teach them how to do experiments—she didn't think it was just her imagination. The detailed understanding had improved the clarity of her Will, and so she required less sheer force to achieve superior results. It was as if the light wanted to follow her instructions, rather than being forced to do so.

When class ended, Professor Lacer stopped her as she walked by his desk. "Mr. Siverling. Please come to my office Saturday morning. Free up a couple of hours."

"Why?" she blurted. When he raised his eyebrows, as unimpressed as he had been when she was similarly rude earlier that morning, she cleared her throat and amended, "I mean, I will, but what is the purpose of the meeting? So I can be prepared."

Lacer stepped slightly closer, palmed his Conduit with one hand, and made a grasping motion with his other.

The air was suddenly so still it almost seemed like a liquid, pressing against the small hairs on her skin with every minute movement. *'It's that sound-muffling spell. To anyone trying to eavesdrop, we must seem as if we're under water.'* She recognized it from when he'd woken her up in the middle of the night to berate her for casting with Will-strain.

"I want to do some tests on that boon you received," he said, privacy ensured.

Her heart gave a single desperate clench, then started pounding. "What kind of tests?"

"Do not worry. I have no reason to suspect that you or those around you are in danger from it, as I said previously," he assured her, obviously noting her sudden anxiety and attributing a different reason to it. He paused, then added, "These tests will not invade your privacy or take away your autonomy. I simply wish to learn more about the magic in play and see what clues it might give about the mindset of the caster. I do not believe she acted on a whim, and if it was deliberate, I want to understand why."

"Oh. Okay," Sebastien croaked past numb lips before realizing that she should have protested. *'But what reason could I give?'* she wondered desperately.

"Head along then," Professor Lacer said, dropping the sound-muffling spell as easily as he'd cast it.

Sebastien tried to control her expression as she left, pressing her hands to her flushed cheeks, lamenting the pale skin that showed her physical responses so easily, but she stopped mid-step and turned back to Lacer. She had some questions that he seemed like the only person who might be able and willing to answer, and perhaps a limited amount of time in which to ask them. *'He took me as an apprentice, gave me his old Conduit, and even came out in the middle of the night to save me from the Red Guard. Surely he won't be upset if I just ask? If he doesn't want to answer, he's not the type that will be reluctant to say so.'*

She walked back toward him, clearing her throat uncomfortably.

"What is wrong?" he asked immediately, throwing up the sound-muffling ward once more. "Do you need to go to the infirmary?"

"I'm fine. I just had some questions, and I don't know who else to ask."

He stared at her assessingly for a moment. "Proceed."

"The Raven Queen... What did she actually steal?"

Professor Lacer adjusted his grip on his Conduit. "I understand your curiosity." She thought for a moment that he would refuse to tell her more, but he continued. "It was a book, as you have probably heard. As to the exact contents, I am unaware. However, I do know something about the expedition that retrieved it."

Sebastien's grip tightened around the strap of her satchel, and she tried not to look too desperately interested.

"I applied to join the expedition but was denied. At the time I considered it to be petty infighting and politics, and thought little of it, but now..." He trailed off, leaving the rest to her imagination. "The expedition went into the Black Wastes." He nodded at her raised eyebrows. "Yes. All who went were aware of the risks, and they were extremely well supplied. They judged the possible rewards to be worth it. Supposedly, some powerful diviners had found the location of Myrddin's hermitage, where he spent much of his time in solitude toward the end of his life."

Sebastien couldn't help but suck in a sharp breath of air.

"Of course," Professor Lacer continued, "people have been claiming to have found Myrddin's hermitage every couple of decades since he died, so I am rather skeptical. However, it is obvious they did find something of historical significance, and perhaps of great worth. The rumors of Myrddin's lost inventions and discoveries are, frankly, overblown and ridiculous. The man, while impressive, lived over a thousand years ago. We have made many advancements in sorcery—in thaumaturgy as a whole—since then, and to think that he may have made breakthroughs we struggle to comprehend today is extremely unlikely. It is a particular failing of character to long constantly for the 'better days' of the imagined past when really, the best days are *now*, with even better to come tomorrow."

He let out a deep breath, his dark blue eyes growing distant as he looked past her. "That being said, there are obviously mysteries in this world which we do not yet understand, and I suspect many of them come from the pre-Cataclysm eras, which I do not long *for*, but long to *understand*. Perhaps Myrddin made some discovery along that vein and spent his later years trying to decipher it."

Lacer's attention returned to Sebastien. "In that case, if they really did find his hermitage, the things they retrieved *could* be of value. The Raven Queen's interest in the items points increasing weight toward that possibility, in my opinion. The University still retains possession of the remainder of the expedition's haul, but a select number of people in the History department have exclusive access while they inspect the items. The theft has made their paranoia about security seem more reasonable, but they have reported no significant findings yet, and I believe people will eventually begin to grow impatient with the secrecy and apply pressure for open access. Knowledge, like any other resource, can only be kept for oneself so long as one has both the skill and the power to ward off others."

Sebastien couldn't help but feel that was a warning about her own secret, though she knew he hadn't meant it that way.

"That is all I know," he said, "and keep in mind that much of it is speculation."

"I understand. Thank you," she responded, giving him a shallow bow as she turned to leave, her mind already spinning with this partial confirmation of what she had speculated herself.

She'd passed halfway through the bubble of the sound-muffling spell when she paused yet again. "I'm not sure if you were aware, but Grandmaster Kiernan called me into his office last week, ostensibly to give me contribution points and make sure I was doing alright, but really to pump me for information about what happened. I told him to talk to you."

Professor Lacer's eyes narrowed. "I was not aware. I will discuss this with him."

This time, Sebastien really did leave. Most of the students had already moved on by the time she exited the classroom, but she tried to keep herself from being visibly uneasy. She wanted to find the nearest bathroom stall and lock herself inside it until her fingers stopped trembling and the tension in the muscles of her neck and back stopped sending electric arcs of pain up into her skull.

'Professor Lacer might be skeptical of Myrddin's accomplishments, but I have proof that whoever made the transformation amulet did things I've never heard of before. So I stole Myrddin's journal or something. Stars above, no wonder they're all so desperate to catch me.' She shuddered, wondering again if there were some way to get rid of it, to just give it back, without endangering herself.

'But more immediately pressing, Professor Lacer wants to examine my ward, or at least how its magic works. It makes sense, since they are under the impression that the

divination-diverting ward Liza created for me is actually some mysterious boon given by the Raven Queen. Is there a chance that he finds something dangerous? No matter my desire for control or privacy, the possible danger involved in a spell cast by the Raven Queen is arguably more important than my comfort. There's no way I can just refuse a checkup. Should I contact Oliver, or maybe Liza, to warn them? How risky is this? Do I need to give up my identity as Sebastien and leave the University in advance?'

"Sebastien!" Ana's voice called.

Sebastien's head jerked up, the movement sending another spike of pain up through the back of her neck. One of her eyelids twitched.

Ana was leaning against the wall in the hallway outside Lacer's classroom. She tucked away the pink leather notebook artifact that allowed her to communicate with her little sister, smiling. "Accompany me?" she asked.

Sebastien hesitated, her mind stumbling a little as she struggled to focus on anything but her pervasive anxiety, but nodded, hoping whatever Ana needed wouldn't take too long.

Ana slipped her arm through the crook of Sebastien's elbow and led her off.

"Where are we going?" Sebastien asked.

"I have something important to discuss with you. I'd rather not do it where random passersby can eavesdrop."

Sebastien hoped it wasn't some juicy piece of gossip or the like. Ana was much more socially attentive than Sebastien, and tended to care about things that could create social leverage, whereas Sebastien just wanted to focus on the magic. Someday, she would leave all this behind, and knowing all the latest gossip would be useless.

Even though the hallways were mostly empty of students, Ana pulled Sebastien into an unoccupied classroom, closing the door behind them.

Normally, this level of intrigue would have raised Sebastien's interest, but at that moment, it was all she could do to keep herself from vibrating apart. She suppressed another shudder at the unfortunate wording of her thoughts.

Ana ran her fingertips lightly over the smooth knit of her scarf, her face alight with some emotion Sebastien couldn't place. "You mentioned that I needed to deal with my uncles in a more effective and permanent way, do you remember? Well, I've figured out how to do it. I'm going to discredit them and, hopefully, have them removed from the Gervin Family line of succession. My father has the ability to do that, if there's just cause. I simply need to convince him it is necessary."

"Great," Sebastien said. She realized her fingers were tapping impatiently against the side of her thigh and stilled them. "Did you need feedback on your plan, then? I'm not particularly versed with social manipulation, and I don't know your father at all, so I'm not sure I'll be much help, but I'm happy to listen."

"Actually, I was hoping you could help me implement the plan. I know my uncles have done things that could be used to blackmail them. There's almost certainly proof in Uncle Malcolm's office, probably in his vault. If I could access that, I could use it to knock them down and put myself in a position of power."

Sebastien stared at Ana. "You want me to break into your uncle's office and go through his vault?"

"Well, maybe," Ana said, biting her lip anxiously. "I'm open to suggestions about the details of how we'd implement all this. It shouldn't be that dangerous; I've a plan to make sure Uncle Malcolm is preoccupied at the time, and I know how his security system works."

Sebastien let out a short, sharp laugh as a sudden surge of outrage rose up in her stomach and through her throat, spilling out into the world as cutting words. "I'm happy you've figured out a solution to your problems, but I really don't have the time or the wherewithal to get involved in this kind of dangerous scheme. Why don't you commandeer someone who has more time on their hands, like the rest of your Crown Family friends? Or hire someone to help you who would be willing to place their safety at risk for some coin. I'm sure you can afford it."

Ana went pale, and in the silence that followed, Sebastien knew she'd made a mistake. She didn't want to take on a new project—she could barely handle her current workload—and she was wound up like a coiled spring with stress. Even so, she hadn't meant to snap at the other girl like that. She should have turned her down more gently.

Ana gave her a wide, bright smile that looked almost feral, her eyes glittering with the sheen of unspent tears. "Sebastien Siverling, do you think you're the only *real person* in the world? You act like your goals and interests are the only important ones, like your ideas are the only ones that hold value."

Sebastien tried to interject, but Ana's voice only grew louder. "If someone disagrees with you, thinks differently than you, or just acts in some way that you don't like, they must either be stupid, ignorant, or otherwise unworthy of your attention—perhaps because they're a noble and thus somehow worthless? The Crown Families might be elitists, but you're a reverse snob, which is really no different than a normal snob. You need to open your eyes and realize that in the real world, you don't stand atop some pinnacle of worthiness alone. You're just like the rest of us, down here mucking about in the shit, blind to the wider reality." Ana growled the last sentence, spun on her heel, and stalked out of the room.

She slammed the door behind her, leaving Sebastien alone with the echo of Ana's bitterness off the stone walls.

16

UNCOMFORTABLE SCRUTINY

Sebastien
Month 2, Day 6, Saturday 10:00 a.m.

Sebastien didn't flinch from the needle-like stabs of the artifact disks in her back as they sucked up her blood. *'I wonder if I will bruise if they keep activating again and again under these tests.'*

She stood in the middle of Professor Lacer's office, where he had drawn a divination spell array on the floor in a hard wax that resisted melting even with the power he pushed through it. It had only been a week since she came up with her plan to fix everything, which included a more stringent schedule, but already she was off course, accommodating him instead of brewing for the Verdant Stag.

She had skipped dinner on Wednesday to bring Liza the sleep-proxy spell components, and while she was there, asked the ward's creator about the danger of it coming under scrutiny, vaguely describing the situation.

Liza had stared at Siobhan for a good thirty seconds of silence, clearly exasperated by the way Siobhan always seemed to get into trouble. "I don't understand how this situation came to be in the first place, but I gather that someone who doesn't know you're the Raven Queen somehow found out about the ward, and for some unfathomable reason you're going to let them examine you. Either that, or you plan to encounter a hostile situation where someone rapidly tries successive, creative ideas to break the ward, rather than simply overpower it."

Siobhan had clasped her hands together tightly, sighing with acknowledgement of how foolish and precarious the whole thing sounded. "The former is partially correct. I just want to make sure they won't find some sort of loophole in the ward, or something besides its particular effects that links me to the Raven Queen. If it seems too risky, I can avoid the examination, but there's a lot at stake, and that's an option of last resort."

"Do not undress and let whoever is casting scan you for heat fluctuations," Liza had warned. "It's possible the five disks could cool the skin of your back enough to stand out, and if someone found them and extracted them... Well, it wouldn't lead back to *me*. And I expect *you* won't do anything to lead them back to me, either," she said firmly. "Remember that I still have my copy of our blood print vow, and I assure you, that ward will not protect you from me if I find I have been wronged."

Liza took a slow sip of her tea, letting that threat sink in. "Other than that, I didn't knowingly design a ward with loopholes, and I am an expert in the field. It will protect itself from examination just like it protects you, but it can be overpowered. Your examiner will find that the ward is extremely well-designed and has no obvious source. That is suspicious in and of itself."

"I don't think that will be a problem, exactly. Is there anything else I should worry about?"

"If you can, I would appreciate an update on the results of these tests," Liza said, seeming rather unconcerned.

Oliver had been more apprehensive than Liza, perhaps because he knew the details of the situation and had more at stake. "They already think the Raven Queen created the ward. It makes sense if it's suspicious and mysterious. Even if Thaddeus Lacer does find the disks, that doesn't unquestioningly implicate Sebastien Siverling. She could still have done that to you without you realizing or remembering, though it stretches belief in a completely different way than her free-casting such a powerful, ongoing effect. However, if he finds them, it will surely lead to additional invasive tests. Everything gets a lot trickier to explain away if their original blood sample points right to Sebastien Siverling. Even if they didn't believe you were her, I can't see you avoiding the inside of a cell 'for your own protection' while they ran more tests."

Oliver had rubbed his hands roughly down his face, taking a few moments to think. "I'm not sure the risk is worth it."

Hesitantly, Sebastien revealed the conversation she'd had with Professor Lacer in the carriage, where he had thought she might be the Raven Queen in disguise. "Unexpectedly, if he did find out, he might not turn me in right away. It's possible he would listen."

"You can't depend on that!"

"Of course not. I'm merely saying things might not be as bad as they seem. Even the worst-case scenario has a *chance* of working out."

"You need to get out of it, Sebastien," Oliver had insisted.

Sebastien tried. On Thursday, she'd gone to Professor Lacer and told him she remained uncomfortable with the idea of him casting spells on her and asked if it was absolutely necessary.

"I think you should rather *I* do it than someone from the infirmary or the Red Guard, Mr. Siverling," he'd replied, unmoved. "I will only be casting some divination spells to examine the nuances of how the boon works. If it makes you feel more comfortable, I can explain each spell beforehand so that you know what's being done."

"But I still don't understand what you're hoping to find. Do you think this boon will somehow lead back to *her*?"

"That would be a pleasant surprise, but I very much doubt it. No, I am looking to decipher more about how she thinks. Magic always carries the signature of the caster, and even more so of its creator. Perhaps I will discern something about her background based on the things she thought to ward against, and the ways she implemented those defenses. I could find hints about where she was trained as a sorcerer, or the culture she grew up in, or even just how her mind works. Does she prefer misdirection or complex traps? Does she lean toward punishing aggression directly or circling around to attack from behind? Did she leave any strange loopholes or responses in this boon that are meant to hint at her purpose more directly, to the right person?"

This was a significant relief, though Sebastien was disappointed that her mentor's willingness to respect her boundaries only extended to this point. After all, he didn't seem to believe that Sebastien was in danger from the ward, and yet he still insisted on something he knew she didn't want.

She'd gone back to Oliver.

He reluctantly agreed that taking a risk to remain at the University was worth it, if they were prepared. If Professor Lacer tried to have her arrested, Oliver would have a team standing by to rescue her on the way to Harrow Hill. No one Oliver could hire was a match for Thaddeus Lacer, but they could probably overcome a team of coppers. If that failed, he would have someone impersonate the Raven Queen while Sebastien was confined to help keep her identities separate. She'd even practiced acting believably innocent in front of a mirror while trying to come up with some reasonable lies.

She wore even more alarm bracelets and a toe ring, each connected to Oliver and with a particular meaning. Her hidden stunning wand and disintegration artifact, as well as a range of paper spell arrays, were neatly filed in her bag and ready to go. She'd arranged useful potions and philtres in individual bands, their locations thoroughly memorized as she practiced retrieving the correct one using touch alone. She had Professor Lacer's Conduit attached to her pocket watch and the black sapphire in her hidden holster. If Professor Lacer asked her to take off her clothes, she would refuse, and was even prepared to fake a panic attack. Surely that would be enough to stop him.

Even if Professor Lacer noticed anything incriminating while examining the divination diverting ward, he might not immediately realize the full implications or become hostile, which gave her the element of surprise. Even if all that failed, which was unfortunately likely when going up against a man as powerful, insightful, and starkly intelligent as Thaddeus Lacer, he might still be reasoned with.

Now, halfway through Professor Lacer's examination, Sebastien felt that all their preparation and worrying had been mostly unnecessary. The whole process was quite anticlimactic. He had explained all the spells he was planning to use when she arrived that morning, and there were none she thought would be dangerous—just various forms of divination, some with a twist on the standard application.

"Do you feel anything?" the man asked her, frowning down at the crystal ball in front of him, which was as cloudy as ever.

"Uncomfortable," she admitted. "It's as if cold fingers are trailing down my back, or like when you think you see someone watching you through the window from the corner of your eye, but when you turn, there's no one there. I...instinctively want to cringe away."

He hummed, muttering to himself. "Fascinating. I wonder if the sensory connection somehow increases the spell's ability to help you avoid notice. Magic feeding off emotion..." He trailed off, scribbling notes by hand because he couldn't guide the pen to write on its own while also casting the divination spell. He turned his gaze back to the crystal ball, frowning slightly.

Sebastien cried out at a sudden spike of power. Whatever was allowing her to metaphorically slip to the side, deflecting the tendrils of magical attention, simply *broke*, and suddenly she was bare, naked before Professor Lacer's divination magic. She shuddered with the sense of vulnerability, but resisted further empowering her ward to fight back, if that was still possible now that he'd succeeded. Thaddeus Lacer was a Grandmaster. This close, he could overpower even her best efforts, and with him already *knowing* where she was, there was no point in resisting.

He didn't seem to notice her discomfort, dropping the spell after a couple more scribbled notes, and then moving onto the next. "How does this one feel?"

Her eyebrows rose. "Slightly different. Like I'm being painted into a corner, the safe space getting smaller and smaller, until it will be too small for me to fit," she said, her surprise almost overpowering her discomfort.

He looked up, giving her a smile. "*Very* interesting. The woman who cast this on you is quite skilled." He dropped that spell, too, not bothering to channel power into it until he broke past her defenses. "Tell me about her again. Describe her in detail, everything you can remember. If your memory is fading, I have a small ritual that can boost recall of a specific event. It's rather unpleasant, but quite safe."

Sebastien swallowed hard. "No need for that. My memory is superb."

"Stressful situations can often result in impaired recall, or even completely fabricated memories. There is no shame in that. It is simply how the human brain works." When she didn't reply, he looked up at her, but she just stared back, which seemed to satisfy his doubts. "Go ahead, then."

"She was…tall, for a woman. Wearing a hood, so I couldn't really see her features. Umm, it looked like she was growing feathers mixed in with her hair." Sebastien hesitated, then added, "She did not look particularly evil, not like the wanted posters. And she was protecting those people. Why do you think she did that?" She watched him carefully, trying to gauge his response. *'Is he hostile to the Raven Queen? As far as I can tell, he's only displayed curiosity. If I could make him an ally…'*

He met her gaze, perhaps sensing the importance of the question from some clue in her voice. "I do not know. But I would like to."

"Is there any news about the investigation? What are the coppers and the Red Guard doing?" Now that she was peripherally involved, it didn't seem strange for her to be interested in things she was probably not supposed to know.

"The Red Guard have done their part, securing and clearing the site for continued habitation. Titus Westbay is considering calling them in to assist in the ongoing investigation to capture Siobhan Naught."

"Is that…likely?"

"We will see. It is not the kind of thing the Red Guard usually involves themselves in. They are here to deal with existential threats, not every blood sorcerer that evades the coppers. Additionally, I happen to know that Lord Westbay the elder holds a particular dislike for the Red Guard, and while Titus is nominally in charge of the coppers and the investigation, his father still holds quite a bit of weight in this type of decision. There is no proof of the kind of threat the Red Guard is sworn to shield against. Miss Naught has not even killed anyone, unless you count Mr. Moore, which I do not, as one cannot predict a break event. Her major crime is stealing something very valuable and then being *embarrassingly* good at getting away with it. In the end, I suspect it will be up to the High Crown. The Red Guard might take the case if he feels the Raven Queen is making the coppers, and thus the Crowns, look too incompetent."

"If they do take over, will they be able to capture her?"

Professor Lacer gave a small shrug, one side of his mouth drawing up in a subtle smirk. "Who knows? They are very competent, but she is obviously both powerful and cunning."

Sebastien let out a deep breath as he dropped the latest divination attempt. "Are *you* trying to find her?"

"Yes."

Her heart sank, but he continued.

"But not for any reward, or to turn her in."

Shock and relief coursed through her in equal measure, despite the hints to that effect that he'd already dropped so freely. '*That is a very dangerous thing to admit to anyone. Almost treasonous,*' she realized. "Why do you want to find her, and…why are you admitting this to me?" When he didn't answer at first, she feared he might grow impatient and cut off the line of questioning.

Professor Lacer cast a different divination spell, this time standing up and walking around her with a contemplative expression. "The spillover effect is rather fascinating. Entirely in line with her ability to make mischief in plain sight, yet remain uncaptured—unnoticed—until she wishes it otherwise. I wonder if this part of the boon might be some sort of 'tag,' or signature, a way for Miss Naught to leave a special mark on her work."

He stopped in front of Sebastien, just on the edge of the Circle, meeting her dark eyes unflinchingly, undeterred by the dissuading effects of her ward. Finally, he answered her question. "I am honest with you despite the danger, Mr. Siverling, because you are my apprentice. While you have shown a penchant for certain types of foolishness, you have displayed no *insurmountable* stupidity, and I chose you both for your display of Will and the signs that you were not yet trained into the mindsets that lead to hopeless mediocrity, unlike most of those who would call themselves your peers. If you prove yourself worthy, it will be my job to guide you in the Way of true power."

She could hear the capitalization of "the Way" in his emphasis. She stared back at him, trying to catalogue the strange jumble of emotion in her chest.

"No one's opinion of you matters more than my own, and you know this. Beyond that, I do not worry about your betrayal, because you do not have the power to harm me, even if I am mistaken and you are foolish enough to repeat my words to the wrong ears. But also, as your mentor, I know that you need to hear sources telling the truth rather than the things that are acceptable to say in polite society if you are ever to distinguish truth for yourself, which is the heart of the Way, and paramount for any thaumaturge that wishes to grasp *true power.*"

Her heart beat harder, not out of fear, but from half-understood excitement. What did she wish for but true power? And the acknowledgment of Thaddeus Lacer was nice, too. She stood even straighter, unblinking.

"Burning curiosity is the first virtue of a thaumaturge, Sebastien." It was the first time he'd ever used her given name, rather than her last. His voice was loud, the pressure in his dark gaze trying to force her to look away. "And the ability to distinguish truth is of paramount importance. It is not just curiosity for curiosity's sake, but curiosity for usefulness's sake. The curiosity may be general and widespread, because a wise thaumaturge knows that *all* knowledge is useful, and that with enough broad areas of learning, each topic meets the others and coalesces to form a picture of the greater whole...and the secrets hidden at the center."

She could feel his Will in the air, not just pressing on her ward, but coiling around the room like a giant snake ready to squeeze, holding everything within its mercy. Tentatively, she brought her own Will to bear, focusing on remaining strong and upright, on maintaining her defiant gaze. '*I am weaker than you, Thaddeus Lacer, but I am not lesser. I am not cowed.*'

He smiled as if he could read her mind. Perhaps he could read her expression, or he had just noticed her clenched fists. "Defiance is good. Sometimes it hurts to see the truth, but how else will you rise above your limits?" He spoke more softly, then. "Knowledge of the truth is power. And I am intensely curious about the Raven Queen."

He stepped away, releasing his Will along with the divination spell as he returned to his desk to write more notes.

Sebastien was panting and small beads of sweat dotted her temples, even though she had done nothing but get into a staring contest with her mentor while he lectured. '*My mentor, who says he will teach me the way of true power.*' It was a giddy thought. '*As long as I don't mess it up.*' She wasn't so overwhelmed as to admit anything about her connection to the Raven Queen, however. Professor Lacer might not intend to turn her other identity in to the coppers, but she couldn't assume it was safe, either. Would he be impressed if he knew, or would he find her multiple brushes with disaster proof that perhaps she wasn't quite as worthy as he thought?

As Lacer tried more variations on divination spells against her ward, she fell into thought. '*Sometimes it hurts to see the truth,*' she repeated silently to herself. It brought up another problem that she'd been avoiding the last few days, focused as she was on preparing for this examination. '*Was Ana right about me? Am I a reverse-snob who treats the people around me like they don't matter?*' She instinctively wanted to deny the accusation, but the little twinge of unease inside stopped her.

'*If I really thought her words had no merit, would I keep thinking about it so much?*' She considered Ana a friend, though not a close one that she could confide all her secrets to. It hurt that the other girl had been so angry with Sebastien and was now avoiding her. Others had noticed and asked about it, but Sebastien had refused to explain. Some of the other women in Sebastien's classes had tried to take the opportunity to sit with her, but they had been blocked by Brinn Setterlund, who took Ana's regular seat on whichever side Damien wasn't stationed.

'I did treat her poorly. She might have made assumptions about receiving my help, but isn't that normal between friends? Would I have been so snappish if I were in my original body—in Siobhan's form? Was it only bad timing and circumstance, or am I more irritable as Sebastien?' Men had different hormones than women, after all, and were often more aggressive.

She was aware of the amulet against the skin of her chest, resting next to the warding medallion and the fading scar of the cold burn it had given her. She wondered if anyone who used it would turn into Sebastien Siverling, or if someone else would end up as a completely new person. *'And what would happen if a man used it?'*

She could have answers if Katerin or Oliver were willing to try it, but even the idea made her frightened and uncomfortable and had her hunching her shoulders forward protectively. The amulet was hers. She needed it. If something went wrong, if it were to stop working, she would be trapped without it.

'Besides,' she comforted herself, *'neither Katerin nor Oliver are likely to agree just to sate my curiosity.'*

Professor Lacer dropped his latest spell and tried a new one, snapping her out of her spiraling thoughts.

She massaged her jaw muscles, which she had been unconsciously clenching until her molars ached. *'It doesn't really matter if I have a tendency to be more aggressive or self-centered as Sebastien. Which might not even be a factor, so it is doubly no excuse! I know right and wrong, and I still have a duty to take ownership of my actions. I make my own choices no matter what body I'm in, or what influences might make one path or another easier.'*

Sebastien cleared her throat awkwardly, then said, "How do you deal with a question that's uncomfortable? One you don't really want to ask, because it hurts?"

Again, Lacer didn't answer her right away, dropping the latest divination and then writing out his notes first. Finally, he said, "There are a lot of facets to both finding and accepting truth. It is a mental discipline that is an ever-ongoing struggle. I cannot answer that question succinctly, but I do have an exercise, a small trick, if you will, that I have found useful in similar situations."

He leaned back in his chair, steepling his fingers together. "Simply take your dreaded question, this possible state of reality that you do not believe is true, that you do not *wish* to be true, and imagine if it were. Take your time on this, and delve deep. Model an entire world, and yourself within that world, existing within the framework of that uncomfortable question. 'Is my wife really cheating on me?' 'Am I as intelligent as I always thought I was?' 'Is there any meaning to life?' That kind of thing. When you can model that imaginary world while still leaving yourself a line of retreat, in the idea that it is only "imagination," you can trick yourself into accepting and coming to grips with these uncomfortable truths, and from there act on them in the most optimal way."

He squinted at her for a few seconds, then said, "I am pleased you asked this question, Mr. Siverling. It is of special importance to lean into the uncomfortable truths, to twist the knife of inquiry in the places that hurt worst, *because* they hurt worst. You must keep going until you have released yourself from the prison of your own mind. Even if you are frightened."

She wondered if he thought her question related to the Raven Queen instead of something so mundane as an argument between friends.

Professor Lacer stood and moved over to Sebastien, making the first adjustment to the rudimentary array drawn around her. All the previous variations of the spell had been based on its broad, sturdy foundation, with the nuances of the Word held in his own mind. "This anti-divination magic has proved impressively robust, even to what clever workarounds and tricks I have been able to devise."

He stepped back, palming his Conduit again, and this time the pressure on her ward felt stranger than ever—vague, almost, as if the divination was one step removed from her.

She shook her head like a dog trying to get water out of its ears.

He dropped the spell, smiling down at the spell array. "I cannot even model what I know of you to find someone that matches my hypothetical construct. I thought for sure that one would work. I suppose it is best not to push it. Divination is dangerous, even for someone like myself. Secrets do not enjoy being cracked open," he added with wry amusement. "They struggle."

That kind of spellcasting was beyond her, both in power and in theory, but Sebastien wondered if perhaps that kind of trick couldn't work because he didn't actually understand her, and thus the parameters of his hypothetical construct were all wrong.

"What I am most curious about is how this boon even works," he said. "It is not impossible to scry you, it simply takes enough effort and power to break the effect. Is she actively protecting you from a distance? Did she cast some kind of binding spell so that you would instinctively draw on that aspect of her power? I almost wonder that she did not do some powerful human transmogrification and adjust your very properties. That would be incredibly illegal, of course, and so, *so*, dangerous, but you seem to be fine, and the whole thing is rather a puzzle." He looked up, seemingly realizing the alarming nature of his musing. "Whatever the truth is, it does no good to deny it. It is true whether you know it to be or not. And you do seem fine," he reiterated encouragingly.

Sebastien nodded silently. *'It's actually kind of funny that he's so bad at comforting others.'*

He made a few more notes, then leaned against the edge of his desk with his legs crossed, staring absently at his Conduit for a while.

"Is that everything you wanted from me?" Sebastien asked, finally.

"It is." He hesitated, then said, "You may remain for a few minutes, if you like, if you have something non-disruptive to work on. Or if you have any questions or concerns…" He scratched the side of his short-cut beard with uncharacteristic discomfort. "I am available," he concluded.

Sebastien blinked at him twice, then suppressed a giddy smile. The chance to pick Thaddeus Lacer's brain was invaluable. Questions flitted through her mind faster than she could register them, about everything from her spellwork to stories about his past. Knowing him, however, he would grow impatient and cut her off after one or two answers, and even faster if she asked something boring or invasive.

In the end, she decided to ask something she had little chance of finding an answer to elsewhere. She bit her lip, considering how to word it. "If you want to…transplant a person, or replace their body, with their knowledge and personality intact, how would you go about doing that?" Once started, the words spilled out of her. "Does it require the exact same brain, or could you create a new one? Would the person experience personality changes due to the effects of the body transplant?"

Professor Lacer's eyebrows rose. "I admit, that is not the sort of thing I expected you to ask. Your interest in subverting the limitations of the human body continues, I see." He chuckled briefly, crossing his arms. "Across the eras, there have been many experiments that attempted to keep someone alive artificially, since even among thaumaturges no one has been able to halt the effects of aging entirely. None of these experiments or attempts have been successful. Those who lived—if you can use that term for a mind trapped in a barely functioning body—still experienced horrible side effects such as immune responses that attack the body and brain. Most attempts simply resulted in painful and unpleasant deaths. A better way to increase a creature's lifespan is to Sacrifice a similar creature's vitality. Of course, unless such a thing was classified as a powerful healing spell, that would fall into the category of blood magic, since it would certainly kill the Sacrificed creature. Those spells also produce rapidly diminishing effects. If you are worried about death, I would suggest investing in some robust warding artifacts and then channeling enough magic to extend your lifespan as long as possible, rather than experimenting with forbidden magics. You are much too young—and inexperienced—for such things."

He thought she wanted to know how to extend her lifespan. She hesitated to correct his assumption with a more direct question, because it could be too easily connected to the transformation amulet if someone else discovered what it did. It would be a clue to her involvement. "I understand," she said. "I was just curious, not planning to do anything reckless."

He gave her a gimlet stare of suspicion for a few seconds, then seemed to accept her words.

Before he could grow tired of her presence, she blurted out another question she might not find answers for elsewhere. "What happens when a thaumaturge breaks? I mean, I experienced…something." She couldn't remember exactly what she'd felt, the same way people talked about incoherent dreams slipping away upon waking. "I was still a few blocks away at the time," she hastened to add, realizing that she might give her lie away through discrepancies in her stated timeline if she wasn't careful. "But I'm pretty sure I felt it when it happened. I don't really have the words to explain it, but it was like reality fell apart, or my brain got temporarily scrambled like an egg. I fell to the ground. It…took me some time to regain my wits, and by the time I arrived, it was already much too late."

"Another interesting question," he said. "No one truly understands how Aberrants are created. The break event is named such because it seems to follow when the Will is strained to the point of breaking, for whatever reason, but also because of the phenomenon you experienced. Thaumaturges can sense when a break event happens, and those with developed Wills experience it more powerfully. Some theorize that what we feel is the soul of the caster shattering, destroyed utterly and never to pass on to the afterlife. Others think some kind of malevolent sentience reaches through, possibly from the spirit world, and takes over the weak-minded, citing as evidence the fact that chain break events are possible, where one causes another in a nearby caster. Some think that we somehow sense the fabric of magic itself experiencing localized damage, which mends back together *incorrectly*, thus creating the Aberrant."

"What do you believe?" she whispered.

"I do not know the answer, but if I were to choose an option that seemed most likely, it would be the last." The bell rang to mark the hour, and he turned back to his notes. "If that is all, run along to lunch."

She gathered up her bag and jacket, still thinking about what she'd learned.

Just as she reached for the door handle, he said, "If you happen to encounter the Raven Queen once more, please tell her that I have noticed her interest and would be willing to meet with her."

"Um." Sebastien swallowed with a suddenly dry throat, her grip tight around the cold metal door handle. "Okay." Without turning to look back, she stepped into the hallway, closed the door behind her, and leaned against it, her legs shaky from the sudden rush of adrenaline.

Pushing back her sleeve, she looked through the many wood and pewter bracelets that ran up her forearm, picked the correct one from the color and placement of the thread wrapped around it, and broke it to let Oliver know everything was okay.

17

———

WITCHCRAFT

Sebastien
Month 2, Day 6, Saturday 12:00 p.m.

'*I believe other people are real*,' Sebastien thought as she walked back to the dorms. '*I know they have real emotions, desires, and their own stories about how they got to the place they're in. But I have very little confidence in them, other than that.*'

Using Professor Lacer's thought exercise, Sebastien tried to imagine that the things Ana had said about her were true. Sebastien was sharp-tongued and rude. She'd known that for a long time. People didn't enjoy having the unpleasant truth pointed out to them. Or at least, that was how Sebastien had justified things. But could she have been lying to herself? Was she the kind of person who treated people poorly just because she couldn't be bothered to care about them? Or worse, because somewhere deep inside, she *enjoyed* hurting others?

She remembered her tirade against the group of girls that had been gossiping about Newton. She had to admit that, sometimes, she did enjoy it. The rage behind her words to those girls was rare, however. More often, she made offhand cutting remarks to those who simply annoyed her, like Alec and even Damien. Ana hadn't often been on the receiving end of those before, but Sebastien could remember several times that Ana had laughed behind her hand at one of Sebastien's more scathing observations. While Sebastien was rude to people's faces, Ana made snide comments behind their back.

Sebastien groaned aloud, drawing some strange looks from a couple of students sitting on a bench beside the cobblestone pathway. She ignored them, scowling as she continued to mull over the issue.

She could admit that she had been dismissive of many of her classmates, particularly the Crown Family nobles. It wasn't the wealth itself that bothered her, but that they felt entitled to it and thought that they were somehow better than those they ruled over. *'As if it were anything they'd done to win the genetic lottery of birth parents.'* They were oblivious to what it was like to live in the real world that the remaining ninety-nine percent of the population inhabited, where things were difficult and unfair and someone could do everything right and *still fail.* It grated on her that they should have such opportunity and not even appreciate its worth, while she struggled for every scrap of knowledge and power.

Sebastien recognized she was working herself into a righteous anger and tried to let it go. While they hadn't done anything special to deserve it, the Crown Family members and other wealthy, connected students also hadn't done anything *wrong* by being born into privilege. Sure, they were ignorant and rude sometimes, but…wasn't this whole situation caused by Sebastien's own rudeness? And ignorance could be corrected. Some of the Crown Family students weren't as bad as she had expected, once she got to know them. She could imagine someone like Damien genuinely caring if he were forced to truly understand what life was like for the common people.

If she were being fair, she wouldn't hold their prejudice and immaturity against them any more than she would despise a poor commoner for not being able to read or understand the vast world of books they were missing out on. *'Just because there are many equally as deserving as them who don't get the opportunity doesn't mean the nobles are less deserving.'*

'So,' Sebastien concluded, *'maybe I am a snob.'* She still couldn't help but scorn many of her classmates' ignorance, but if she was going to acknowledge that ignorance was correctable, shouldn't she try to do something to correct it? That was a monumental job, better suited for someone more like Oliver than Sebastien. She simply didn't have the patience or the time. And didn't each individual have some responsibility to correct their own ignorance? Why should that be her job?

Feeling like she'd made little progress on figuring anything out, Sebastien found Brinn and Waverly in the dorms, notes and components laid out over the girl's rumpled bedspread.

Brinn waved Sebastien over, and she tried to force a more pleasant expression onto her face as she joined them. "What's this for?" she asked.

Waverly took the initiative to speak, which was rare for the small girl. "I'm going to the Menagerie to make an offering! I'm pretty sure I saw a gremian in there the other day, and they're a great option to practice making a short-term contract with, if we can get it inside a Circle."

"Do you want to come, Sebastien?" Brinn asked.

She hesitated. Really, she would prefer to try to talk to Ana, or maybe Damien, who knew the other girl well enough that he might be able to give Sebastien advice about how to handle the situation. "Are Damien or Ana around? I haven't seen them today."

"Both of them are visiting their homes." Brinn tilted his head to the side. "They mentioned it several times over the last few days."

"Oh," Sebastien said. She...hadn't been paying attention. She sighed, using a finger to try to smooth out the crease of frustration between her eyebrows. "Thank you. Um, I suppose I will come along, then, if you don't mind?" she asked Waverly. These two had been nothing but kind to her, after all, and she was interested in the chance to see some witchcraft in action. She didn't have the mental capacity to do her homework or practice spells at the moment, anyway.

The trio gathered up all of Waverly's preparations and walked to the Menagerie, making their way along the winding paths until Waverly pointed out a tree housing what looked like a particularly large bird's nest. When Sebastien commented on it, Waverly grinned, exposing small, pearly-white teeth. "That's not a bird's nest."

"A gremian, then?" Sebastien asked, repeating the word Waverly had used earlier. "I don't think I've ever seen one."

"Oh, they're wonderful!" Waverly gushed, the most high-pitched and enthusiastic that Sebastien had ever seen her. "So cute, and *trainable*. They're not sapient, and they can't talk, but they're clever enough, and willing to perform tricks and favors if you know what to offer."

Inside a Circle scratched into the snow with a stick, Waverly set up feathers, a chicken egg, and a small drawing of a bird in flight. They were an an offering meant to entice a gremian into the Circle's bounds. If it accepted the offering, that would be considered consent, and the gremian would be forced to enter into negotiations with her. Of course, if it didn't like the terms she put forward, or just didn't like *her*, it could refuse to make a further contract, but it wouldn't be able to leave until she'd at least made the attempt.

"What would happen to the creature if you didn't offer any terms? Would it be indefinitely trapped, perhaps to the point of starvation?" If so, that didn't seem fair, since agreement under duress wasn't exactly agreement.

Waverly laughed as they drew far enough back from the Circle that they wouldn't spook the creature from approaching. "Oh, there are Circles like that, but they're exceedingly foolish on the part of the caster. The creature, or elemental, that you bind isn't forced to be loyal, only to follow the exact wording of the contract. Even if it tries to engender loyalty, that's very dependent upon interpretation and intent. There are a ton of stories about witches binding powerful, unwilling familiars through trickery or blackmail, and it *always* goes badly. It would be like trying to cast with a celerium Conduit that had a mind of its own and didn't like you. This Circle will release the creature within an hour if no deal is made, and anyways, I'm not trying to make a familiar contract, only—"

She stopped, lifting a forefinger to her mouth to signal the need for silence as she stared up at the sloppy nest molded from twigs, strips of fabric, and daubs of mud.

At first, Sebastien thought that some of the twigs were rising, but then she saw the bulging black eyes and realized that the twigs were actually brown spikes sprouting from the creature's head.

The gremian looked at the offering below its tree, then at them, and then back at the offering. Apparently unable to resist, it crawled out of the nest and down the trunk. It was a small humanoid creature with spikes running from its head down to its butt, large bug-like eyes, and small, razor-sharp claws. It had attached feathers to its arms with precariously tied bits of old string, and strange flakes of dried fluid covered its thin, bony form, crumbling off when it moved too violently. Altogether, Sebastien imagined it was the kind of thing children might have nightmares about.

"Oh, isn't it cute!" Waverly squealed, bouncing up and down with her hands clasped under her chin.

Sebastien and Brinn shared a dubious look over the girl's head.

The gremian snatched up the offerings, not seeming to either notice or care as the binding activated, trapping it inside. After almost a minute of staring lovingly at the drawing of a bird in flight, while Waverly took tiny, slow steps closer, the gremian turned its attention to the chicken egg, which was half as big as its head.

The source of the flakes covering its body became obvious as it crushed the egg over its head, smearing the viscous liquid all over itself until it glistened.

"Gremians want to fly more than anything," Waverly explained in a calm, soothing voice. "Some believe that they branched off from homunculi that were attacked with some kind of ancestral curse thousands of years ago, and eventually devolved into what you see now. They collect feathers, steal eggs, and live in nests—all futile attempts to reach the skies."

Sebastien watched with interest as Waverly knelt in front of the Circle to bargain with the creature. She pulled out a contraption made of bamboo and waxed fabric, showing it off as she murmured, occasionally miming something to get her point across.

Eventually, the gremian agreed to whatever deal she had put forth. They both spat in their palms, shook hands—which looked rather ridiculous considering the difference in size, and the creature scampered off.

Waverly turned, grinning back at Brinn and Sebastien. "It worked. He agreed!"

"To what, exactly?" Sebastien asked.

"Well, a short-term contract, wherein he retrieves something for me and in return I give him this," she said, holding up the bamboo and cloth contraption. "Really, the deal was pretty irresistible."

While they waited for the creature to return, there wasn't much to do, and Sebastien fell back into thought.

"I'm not sure what happened between you and Ana, but if you want to reconcile with her, you should be the one to make the first move," Brinn said, catching Sebastien by surprise. "She's not very good at reaching out, even if she wants to."

Sebastien turned to search his gaze, but Brinn wasn't looking at her, instead watching as Waverly molded a knee-high snowman a few yards away. "I'm not sure she does want to," she said after a moment of consideration. "She asked me for a favor, and I...I was frazzled and the last thing on my mind was taking on a new project. I turned her down quite rudely, and she gave me a thorough verbal thrashing and hasn't spoken to me since. She said some things that made me think she might not actually like me very much."

Brinn blew on his bare fingers, which had turned red from the cold. "I doubt that very much. Ana can be quite fierce, but I think it's more likely she lashed out in an attempt to hurt you rather than out of real dislike. She gets angry in the moment, says things she regrets, and then is too embarrassed and stubborn to take them back. Once, she told me I was an overly tall sad-sack who—well, I won't get into that. Suffice it to say, she's like the opposite of you, in a way. You're casually rude, but once people get to know you, no one takes it seriously. It's almost like a test, to tell apart those who have the fortitude to be your friends from the rest of the rabble. Ana wants to be everyone's friend, but she only says cruel things to those she cares about enough that they managed to hurt her."

"But she's put up with my sniping and grumbling until now. Sure, most of it wasn't turned toward her, but..."

"Have you considered that it wasn't so much your exact words, but the emotion behind them? Generally, you speak without malice, Sebastien. But this time, you were frustrated. Maybe you wanted to put her in her place, just a bit? She's quite sensitive to intent, the meaning beneath the sweet exterior."

Sebastien knew that her words *had* been offensive, but now that Brinn had pointed it out, it seemed clear that her tone had been meant to wound. There was little Sebastien could have said with the frustration and derision filling her voice that wouldn't have sounded like an insult, an attack, and Ana had responded in kind. That didn't mean the other girl's accusations had been pulled out of nowhere, however.

Sebastien crouched down, hugging her knees to her chest. "I am *so* bad at all this 'people' stuff."

"Ehh." Brinn shook his hand back and forth in a "so-so" motion. "That's not incorrect, but you have a certain charm, despite that."

She puffed out a surprised laugh, but they were both distracted as the gremian returned, a few mushrooms in its clawed fingers.

Waverly exchanged them for the contraption, which she carefully showed the excited gremian how to use.

Sebastien's eyes widened as she understood what was going on. "I have an idea!" she said. After explaining, the three of them drew a scattering of gust spell arrays around the gremian's tree, making sure to dig past the layer of snow and into the ground.

The creature clambered up to its nest with the contraption, which was almost bigger than it was, and then, tucking itself inside the frame as Waverly had demonstrated, it jumped off.

Sebastien activated her gust spell, throwing snow and a rush of air straight upward. It caught the wings of the gremian's makeshift glider, and the little creature screeched in ear-piercing excitement as it began to fly.

This lasted for about fifteen seconds until it hit a tree and tumbled to the ground, dazed, but despite Waverly's worry, the gremian seemed unharmed, and immediately scrambled back to its nest.

Sebastien laughed aloud the second time it jumped into flight, as Waverly and Brinn activated their own gust spells, trying to keep the little creature aloft. They played at this until one of the glider's wings broke in a particularly nasty crash.

The gremian keened over it as if it had lost a family member or one of its own limbs, enough emotion in its scratchy, high-pitched wails that Sebastien felt genuine sympathy for it. She approached it slowly and, explaining her intentions in a soothing tone, though she wasn't sure it could understand, reached for the miniature glider.

It was reluctant to let go at first, baring its teeth, but Sebastien managed to get the glider free without being scratched or bitten. Using a random twig as a component, she cast one of the many variations on her mending spell, fusing the broken wing of the bamboo frame back together.

The gremian didn't thank her as it snatched the glider back and scampered off with it.

By that time, Waverly and Brinn were both getting hungry, and so they left the creature to its doomed flights, heading toward the cafeteria.

The two of them got lost in chatting about Waverly's outstanding success and her plans for her next contract attempt while Sebastien trailed a few feet behind, sinking back into her thoughts.

Something Brinn had said stuck with her, the part about having a certain charm. *'Professor Lacer is sharp-tongued. He often makes rude, even scathing comments.*

He makes people cry. But...I like him that way,' she recognized with a strange sense of surprise. '*I'm rude, too. Do I actually want to change?*'

She tried to be brutally honest with herself. '*No,*' she admitted. '*I wouldn't change if there weren't consequences. I haven't changed, despite past consequences. But I do want people, specific people like Ana, to like me.*' To that effect, she could try to be more charitable toward those around her. Not some ever-smiling, gregarious butterfly. The very idea made her shudder. But at least she could try to be kind when it mattered—to those who had shown her goodwill. To those who deserved it.

18

—————

NEGOTIATIONS BY PROXY

Oliver

Month 2, Day 6, Saturday 4:15 p.m.

The team of enforcers currently doing their best to stand at attention in front of Oliver was comprised of fifty percent new hires, all as green as the antlers that now graced their jackets like a badge. He sighed, spinning on his heels. "Mr. Gerard, if you would take command of this operation?"

The second of his two lead enforcers nodded, slipping on a pair of leather gloves and grabbing some battle equipment off the rack on the wall.

"Make an example of them," Oliver said clearly.

The man paused, but nodded again, meeting the eye holes of Oliver's mask to show he understood.

One of the new enforcers gave an audible gulp in the silence that followed, but when Gerard led the way out of one of the Verdant Stag's side entrances, they all fell in behind him.

Oliver turned to the woman sitting in a chair near the door.

She wore a cloak clutched tight over a low-cut dress that clung to her body, obviously meant to look enticing rather than ward off the cold. She met his gaze with a belligerence that reminded him of Siobhan, one eye partially obscured by the swollen, purple bruise blooming across it. Her lip was split, dried blood crusted in her nostrils, and her makeup had run and smeared, a painting of violent colors spread across the canvas of her face.

The woman probably wasn't particularly pretty, even without her injuries, nor was she particularly young or innocent. But that didn't reduce his anger. His mouth tightened.

She raised an eyebrow, uncowed by his mask. "What's to be done with me, then, my lord?" she asked, her tone jaded and tired. She had been skeptical when she arrived with the enforcer who had helped her escape from the Verdant Stag's newly acquired brothel, formerly owned by the Morrows. Her chin high and her eyes skeptical, she had watched to see what he and his people would do. Now, she gave him the tiniest quirk of a smile.

Though he knew the expression held no real joy, Oliver could respect her resilience. "You'll stay here, at least for the evening. Longer, if needed." He turned to the enforcer that had helped her. "Take her up to Alice in the apothecary, and then find her an empty bed for the night."

When they had gone, Oliver let out a weary sigh, allowing his shoulders to sag. The brothel's manager and some of the patrons hadn't been following his new rules about acceptable treatment of their employees. Perhaps they had thought the regulations about health and safety weren't in earnest. They had made a fatal error. The workers might have chosen to be prostitutes, as much as such a thing really was a choice in a place like the Mires, but they had not chosen to be mistreated while doing their job. Thankfully, this woman hadn't accepted it in silence, so now they could do something about it—swiftly and brutally.

If he could set a good enough example here, perhaps it would cow some of the other troublemakers that plagued this takeover into ducking their heads.

Another young enforcer stepped into the room, leaning close to murmur to Oliver. "A Tanya Canelo is here to see you. She says she has an appointment to 'be guided to your location.'"

Oliver squared his shoulders again and checked his pocket watch. "She's late." She had requested this meeting a few days before, a move he had been anticipating since he first heard that she'd been asking questions about the Raven Queen. Oliver was curious to learn if the request for contact was on her own initiative or done at the behest of the University. Either way, it was an opportunity for him. "Take her to the processing room, then bring her up to my office once she's been searched and questioned." He was tired and hungry, but there wouldn't be time to eat or rest.

Oliver took a small outer hallway and the attached stairs back up to his office on the third floor. The room was less than pristine since he'd been spending quite a bit of his time working there rather than using it only for meetings. He organized the desk, putting away papers and tossing out a half-eaten sandwich he'd been unable to finish before he was called away.

When he was younger, his sister had mashed together her own quote taken from Oppenheimer and Golden: "Having a clear mind and a clear space allows you to think and act with purpose. A mind troubled by doubt cannot focus on the course to victory." She had many misquoted sayings like that, and would adjust them on the fly to fit the situation or win an argument. It had driven him crazy. He remembered sputtering with outrage at the age of nine. "You can't just break the rules like that!" he'd told her.

Now, he would give a lot to have her here, misquoting at him. And he was more of a rule-breaker than she had ever been.

So Oliver sat, going through a much smaller stack of papers while he waited for Canelo. He stopped on a receipt of payment for an exorbitant sum to a workshop in Osham. Despite the price, he smiled. He had signed off on the purchase of several devices that would make producing low-quality cloth easier and faster, with no magic necessary. He had multiple suitable warehouses waiting to be turned into textile factories, and was only waiting on acceptance of the contract he'd sent to Lord Gervin to get started.

Seeing proof of his plans in motion relieved some of his fatigue, and he leaned back in his throne-like chair, massaging his temples. He could do this. Soon, everything would settle down, and he would finally have the resources and clout to make more substantial improvements within his territory.

A knock on the door had him sitting upright again. "Enter," he called, speaking loud enough to be heard past the sound-dampening magic embedded into the walls and floor.

The girl, dirty blonde hair cut just past her jawline in a style similar to Sebastien's, though not nearly so striking, looked around in surprise, her gaze freezing when it landed on Oliver—or more precisely, on his mask. She was alone. She swallowed, then said, "After all the security precautions, I was expecting to be blindfolded and led to a separate location."

He smiled wryly under the mask, which was beginning to irritate his skin after wearing it for so long. "That is part of the precautions. You will still be escorted to a different location and go through the motions of a secret meeting there, in case anyone is following or tracking you."

Her hands tightened around the handle of the hardened leather suitcase she carried. "Okay."

"What have you brought?" he asked, gesturing to it.

She came forward, setting the suitcase on the edge of his desk. She opened it to show the large, complicated device inside. "This is a phonograph, a recently developed artifact that records sound and can play it back. My employers would like me to store this conversation so they can listen to your words directly." An inch-wide strip of glittering black paper was wound between cylindrical spell arrays, but nothing moved or glowed, and the device let off no heat, a sign that it wasn't active. "Your people already looked it over for hidden tricks."

Of course they had. He trusted the device was safe enough, but it still piqued his ire. He let out a scoffing laugh. "This seems rather rude, especially when your employers can't be bothered to meet with me themselves. I cannot imagine you are foolish enough to have come up with this idea on your own," he added, a small test of her attitude.

She gave his shadow-backed mask a strained smile. "I apologize for the presumptuousness. I believe they want the phonograph recording as…insurance. The Raven Queen is known to bestow both boons and curses."

"Is that why they sent you alone? They're afraid she might attack them?"

Canelo shrugged. "I already met with the Raven Queen and lived, even after foolishly threatening her. I think they are hoping she has a…*soft spot* for me, and if not, then they wouldn't lose anyone too important. If I die doing something suspicious, or simply disappear, it wouldn't be particularly surprising to anyone at this point."

That was an unexpected level of honesty, and Oliver suspected that Canelo was weaponizing her vulnerability, attempting to lower his guard and take advantage of any softheartedness. "They consider you a liability," he stated. It was an educated guess, based on what he'd learned from both his contacts within the coppers and Sebastien.

Her lips almost disappeared as she pressed them together in a thin line. "This is a chance for me to prove my value. Things haven't gone exactly as planned, lately. I'm meeting with you in good faith to negotiate, hoping to repair the situation."

He stared back at her for a few long seconds, then nodded. "You won't use this," he stated, gesturing to the phonograph. He didn't know what else was recorded on the thing before their meeting, or what might be recorded afterward. Even if he spoke with Canelo in vagaries that couldn't be used as evidence of any crimes, it was still stupidly risky. They could try to use it as blackmail, or even just to cast divination spells to suss out his secrets. "If the exact wordings of our conversation were so necessary, they should have sent the people who needed to know. *This* is an insult. Place it outside the door."

Canelo complied quickly and without argument, her movements stiff, a sign that she was forcing herself not to betray her genuine emotions through sloppy body language. An inexperienced negotiator, but not incompetent. Returning, she sat tentatively in a chair before his looming desk and clasped her hands together in her lap. "I sincerely hope that we can still come to a mutually beneficial agreement."

"I hope the same," he replied truthfully, though he suspected his ideas about what that could entail might be broader than hers. "I believe there are many ways in which our interests could align. What, specifically, did your employers send you to discuss?"

"My *unnamed* employers had an agreement with the Morrows to provide supplies and the occasional favor. This was extremely lucrative for the Morrows, and offered them opportunities they might not have otherwise come by so easily." Canelo spoke confidently, and he suspected that she had rehearsed this. "It seems your agreement with the Nightmare Pack allowed you to take over the majority of the Morrows' hold on the smuggling industry. Are you interested in continuing the arrangement with my employers? Without them, you will struggle to find buyers for all those goods."

"With the Crowns' tariffs and restrictions making certain products unusually rare or prohibitively expensive, I'm sure I could unload everything eventually, and there are plenty of other things I could import that don't require the University's purchasing ability. I actually have quite a few ideas."

Canelo's knuckles whitened briefly. "My employers had already provided payment for the previous shipment of supplies that you seized."

"Yes. I have extensive records of all the Morrows' transactions. I believe thirty percent was paid up front, with the rest due upon delivery. I would be willing to honor that." It was both a warning not to try and cheat him and a threat that he had blackmail material on their illegal doings that might be used if they moved against him. Some of the University's supply orders were quite incriminating, such as the sudden request for beast cores in bulk. "To be clear, I *am* interested in working with the University, even if only to avoid the hassle of pivoting the business so soon, but further cooperation will need to be negotiated. As for providing the occasional favor, I'm open to that on a case-by-case basis, with proper compensation." Having the University on his side in the Verdant Stag's power struggle against the Crowns might prove quite useful.

"There are other operators who could provide what the University needs," Canelo said, apparently giving up on maintaining plausible deniability about who her employers were.

Oliver leaned back in his throne-like chair. "Sure. *Eventually*. But none of them are so perfectly positioned to provide as the Verdant Stag. I'm not an unreasonable man, Miss Canelo. But I will neither be bullied nor taken advantage of. If the University wants to deal with me, they are welcome to do so in good faith."

She leaned forward, swallowing heavily. "I agree that we should deal with each other in good faith. The potential upside is too great, for both parties, to sully it with schemes and ruses. As a show of their commitment to this alliance, my employers are prepared to offer you significant aid in cementing your control of your new territory. Wards, artifacts, or even a large, no-interest loan. My personal services are also available to you, should you have need of them."

"And in return?"

Canelo hesitated. She seemed to realize the display of anxiety she was putting on, unclasping her white-knuckled hands and laying them flat on her knees. She looked around, to the corners of the room and the window, then back to him. "I want to make it clear, I do not mean to offend you...or *her*. I'm just carrying out my duties as an intermediary."

Oliver's eyebrows rose with interest, and he sat forward, leaning his elbows on the desk and steepling his fingers together. "Go ahead, say what they have instructed you to. I will not blame you."

Canelo's eyes narrowed. "And her?"

"Well, I do not control her. But she is not here to listen, and even if she learns whatever you fear passing on, I doubt her anger would be aimed at *you*."

Canelo seemed to find this reassurance enough, nodding absently to herself. "They want to know where the book is. The one the Raven Queen stole."

"I do not know where it is, nor how to find it," he lied easily. "I'm unable to help with that. Surely they don't think I'm able to succeed where both they and the coppers have failed? And even if I could, I'm not sure that the risk would be worth it."

"And the Raven Queen herself? D-do you know her location?" the young woman pressed on, her voice breaking.

Emotionally, Oliver rejected the idea of betraying Siobhan immediately, but he still stopped to consider it. No, he was bound too closely to her to sell her out. She was privy to too many of his vulnerabilities, and neither the University nor the Crowns could be allowed to gain that knowledge. Besides, she was *his* asset, and he didn't want to trade her away, no matter what they offered. The Verdant Stag didn't need them anyway. He and his people would rise on their own. "If you are suggesting that I should betray her, that's impossible. Or rather, I'm unwilling. It's a very bad idea, for *both* of us."

Canelo nodded, letting out a slow, shaky breath. The girl wasn't doing a very good job of pretending loyalty to her employers, which had to be at least partially on purpose. Perhaps she hoped to keep from being blamed for their decisions, or perhaps it was a subtle hint that she could be turned, given the right incentive. "Would you be willing to facilitate contact with her? I've tried previously but met...roadblocks."

Oliver suppressed the urge to smile. He'd heard of Lord Lynwood's order that none of his people even speak her name to outsiders, after Oliver had relayed Siobhan's request that Lynwood suppress gossip about her from the Nightmare Pack's enforcers. That, along with the rumors that she could hear when her name was spoken, no matter where she was, had led to some interesting results. "I can pass along your request, but I cannot guarantee anything. If she agrees, you will want to have a suitable tribute prepared as payment for her presence. Perhaps there is some way she and the University can come to an agreement." That would be ideal, and it sparked excitement within him. A true alliance with them could push forward his plans by years.

"I understand. Please let me know as soon as possible," she said.

"Should we discuss the details of our future cooperation, independent of the Raven Queen?" Oliver suggested. "Perhaps you aren't able to sign off on agreements or make vows on their behalf, but it would save time if you could leave here today with a reasonable proposal. And if they are amenable, I have some ideas about how we could collaborate in other ways."

Canelo seemed relieved by the change in subject, and after some negotiation that left the Verdant Stag in a slightly better position than the Morrows had accepted, she stood and gave him a deep bow. "If that is all, I will take my leave. Thank you for your time, Lord Stag."

"Actually, there is one more thing," he said, rising and moving around the imposing desk to lean against its front edge.

She remained standing, her eyes flicking to his empty hands as if searching for potential danger. "Yes, my lord?"

"I would like you to consider working for me in a more immediate capacity. I'm not sure what led you to your current position, or how they are compensating you, but I also have both power and influence, and am in need of competent employees with…specialized access. I'm willing to work around whatever restrictions you may be under, or even attempt to break them entirely."

Her eyes widened, her lashes fluttering in shock. "You believe there will be future enmity with my employers, then?"

He shrugged, slipping his hands into his pockets. "*I* am not planning on it, but it is always good to be prepared. I'm sure they will attempt something similar with my own people. They don't seem to trust me very much, after all," he said, allowing himself a wry smile, even if she couldn't see it. "Unfortunately for them, I treat my people much better than they treat you."

"I…" She swallowed. "It's too dangerous."

"More dangerous than the alternative? I would not consider you expendable. And if your employers make foolish choices, the Raven Queen would know not to lay that upon your head." It was as much a threat as it was persuasion, but he kept his voice gentle.

"I have no wish to anger you or *her*, but my employers… They have taken measures against betrayal, and the consequences would be severe. Also, I need what they're offering me."

Oliver almost kept pushing, but thought better of it. "Well, keep my offer in mind. There are ways around all kinds of restrictions, and perhaps they are not the only ones who can provide you what you need." Better to let doubt and discontent slowly fester in Canelo's mind than be seen as desperate. And after all, he wanted to hire someone who didn't *immediately* jump to betrayal when an opportunity revealed itself. "My men will take you to an undisclosed location to hold your official 'meeting' with me. You'll be expected to stay in that location with my proxy for at least half an hour before returning to the University. Just in case you're being followed."

Before she left, Canelo stopped. "I didn't tell anyone that the Raven Queen herself was attending the secret meeting. They know that you probably have an agent that attends to make purchases for you, and that she found me on my way back, but that's it. So if she wishes to continue attending as if nothing happened..." The young woman trailed off meaningfully, gave him a deep nod, and left before he could reply.

Oliver's empty stomach gurgled audibly. He considered having food brought up from the kitchen below, but he had other engagements that required him to be Oliver Dryden that evening, not Lord Stag. Slipping on his jacket, he opened the door and nodded to Huntley, who was standing guard in the hallway outside.

With all the precautions against being followed or recognized, it took longer to arrive at Dryden Manor than he would have liked.

Sharon, his cook, was on her way out the door when he arrived, but she took one look at him and went straight back into the house, taking his jacket and shooing him up to his office. "Dinner's a nice stew, still lukewarm. I'll heat it up and serve it to you within minutes, Mr. Dryden!" she called.

Oliver stoked the embers in the fireplace, adding more wood, then poured himself a tumbler of whisky and took a sip, relishing the burn as it settled into his stomach.

This subversive University faction had the resources to keep a large smuggling operation afloat, and having influence in the educational sphere would be a valuable long-term investment. It was yet to be seen if their end-game goals could coexist, as the University was part of the entrenched authority that he wanted to rip open so that its metaphorical guts could spill out and feed the people. It was obvious, too, that they didn't consider the Verdant Stag an equal, sending only a lackey with a recording device to meet with him. The lack of respect was worrying, especially when paired with the fear he believed they felt toward the Raven Queen.

Some fresh correspondence waited at the edge of Oliver's desk. For a moment he wished he could ignore it, but then he noticed Lord Gervin's signature on the envelope the servants had placed at the top of the stack.

Eagerly, Oliver broke the seal. He had been waiting on approval for a sub-commission to produce low-quality textiles en masse for a while. The envelope was a little thinner than he had expected, but perhaps the contract itself wasn't included. He might have to go to the Edictum Council Hall to sign the paperwork.

He read the hasty but still elegant penmanship of Lord Gervin's secretary, then the Fourth Crown's signature at the bottom. Oliver's stomach clenched around a sudden, nauseating ball of ice, despite the liquor that had been warming him only seconds before.

"Denied?" he whispered. Oliver's request for a sub-contract from the Family that, by law, controlled the textile industry had been turned down almost perfunctorily. Lord Edward Gervin had taken an erythrean horse as a gift and still denied him. The man hadn't even bothered to write the note himself. It was a significant slight.

Oliver absently registered a knock on his office door, but he was too busy reading the note once more, as if hoping its contents would change, to answer.

He had already earmarked the warehouses, already ordered the machines from Osham, already planned for the jobs and income this would provide.

The door opened as Oliver set the note down. He picked up his whiskey, took another sip, and, as his shock turned into sudden, overwhelming rage, he screamed and hurled the half-full glass against the wall.

Sharon screamed in response, jumping so hard she spilled his dinner all over the floor. "Mr. Dryden," she started, breathless and shocked.

"Get out!" he bellowed, not even looking at her.

She jumped again, but didn't stop to pick up the bowl of spilled stew off the ground, holding the dinner tray like a shield as she fumbled her way backward through the door and closed it.

He heard her heavy footsteps hurrying down the stairs soon after.

Oliver pressed both palms flat to the desk, breathing hard. This was a significant problem. He realized now that he shouldn't have been so hasty in implementing plans. Lord Gervin had seemed so amenable when they discussed his intentions, and with the bribe, Oliver had thought it a sure thing, only waiting on the slow bureaucratic process to hash out the details and sign the contracts.

"Calm down," he told himself. "This is not the end of the world. Perhaps something happened. If I can just speak to Lord Gervin in person..." If that didn't work, he *could* try to continue in secret, running the business entirely under the Verdant Stag rather than through his legal persona. That was risky —the kind of thing that brought the harsh fist of the law down upon people, like a hammer on the head of a nail. It could allow the Crowns to seize all the Verdant Stag's holdings.

Alternatively, he could find a different path entirely. If he canceled the machine order now, he might be able to recoup most of his costs.

He brought his hands up, roughly rubbing his face with his palms. He let out a deep sigh, his shoulders sagging. He headed toward the door, stepping over the steaming stew spilled over the floor and rug. He could clean that up later. More importantly, he hoped that he could catch Sharon before she got too far. Oliver needed to apologize to the poor woman.

19

PEACE TALKS

Sebastien
Month 2, Day 6, Saturday 4:15 p.m.

After a late lunch, Sebastien saw Brinn and Waverly off to the supervised casting rooms, while she stopped by the dorms to pick up some overdue library books. She checked in on the Aberrant string she'd bottled, which was as inert as ever within its sealed vial. She returned it to its hiding spot with care. After all her plans about being prepared for the worst, she had viewed her decision to keep a piece of an Aberrant more critically. It had been an impulsive decision, and though she wasn't sure exactly how things might go wrong despite the precautions she'd taken, that didn't mean it was a safe choice.

Still, she couldn't bear to destroy it or give it to the Red Guard. She was irrationally covetous of it. Having it within her possession, under her control, so obviously dead and helpless against her... She *would not* give it up. Even if she was being foolish, her mental and emotional health also had worth, and this was helping her.

Sebastien drew open her curtains to leave, then froze.

Ana was sitting at the small desk in the cubicle across from her, leaning over an essay. It had been a short visit home, apparently.

Sebastien stared at the other girl's turned back, then took a deep breath and strode forward. She stopped in front of the door to Ana's cubicle. "Can we speak in private?"

Ana didn't smile, but nodded. "Lead the way."

Sebastien hesitated, trying to think of a place where they wouldn't be overheard. There would be no open private rooms in the library on a weekend afternoon, and the grounds were scattered with students despite the cold. In the end, she settled on the classroom that Damien's little study group used to practice in the morning. When they arrived, she closed the door gently, steeling herself to speak.

Before she could, Ana said, "I have another offer for you. Your guardian, Lord Dryden, recently attempted to get a sub-commission from my father. He was denied."

Sebastien blinked, taken aback.

Ana continued, standing stiffly beside the large table at the center of the room. "If you'll help with my uncles, I will use my influence to change that decision."

Sebastien tilted her head to the side. "Is that something you can actually do?"

Ana lifted her chin with a small smirk. "My father is not as shrewd and observant as he thinks, or my uncles wouldn't get away with half of what they do. I will attempt to persuade him first, but even if he doesn't agree, I will have little trouble slipping the paperwork right under his nose."

Oliver had probably been hoping to break into the industry as part of his plans for strengthening the Verdant Stag and providing opportunities for the people in his territory. Sebastien imagined it could be quite a lucrative opportunity. *'I might be able to get Oliver to pay me for that. It certainly counts as a favor to the Verdant Stag. But Ana doesn't know that.'* She narrowed her eyes. "That's certainly an interesting offer for Lord Dryden, but how does that benefit me?"

"That's up to you to negotiate. He's sponsoring you through the University, is he not?"

Sebastien's eyes widened, but Ana shook her hand as if waving away a fly. "That's not so hard to deduce, Sebastien. Who else would be doing it? The Siverlings certainly aren't a wealthy, influential family anymore, and you've been staying at Dryden Manor when you're not here. Lord Dryden was interested enough in the sub-commission that he gave up an erythrean gelding to my father. Do you know how much those horses are worth?"

Sebastien didn't, but she understood the general idea. "I'm interested. But I want to be involved in the planning, and I reserve the right to veto any proposals that are too dangerous. You'll cover any expenses."

Ana's face broke into a wide smile. "Agreed."

Sebastien stepped away from the closed door. "Actually, I wanted to talk to you so that I could apologize."

"I know."

Sebastien pushed on. "I was rude when we previously spoke, and I ask your forgiveness."

"And I was presumptuous, and didn't tailor my offer to your personality. I'm sorry, too. I shouldn't have been so...pushy." Ana shrugged uncomfortably. "I can see that you've been under a lot of stress, and perhaps I didn't choose the best time to talk. I wasn't paying attention to the signs you were putting out because I was so excited to have figured out the plan, and I was impatient to move forward. I thought you...would be excited, too. I wasn't angry so much that you refused me, but the way you went about it. I do realize that you're under no obligation to take on this kind of campaign, whether we're friends or not."

Sebastien crossed her arms. "That's why you came back with a sweeter deal."

Ana's smile dimmed, and she stepped forward, clapping Sebastien on the shoulder and leading her back toward the doorway. "Indeed. But, Sebastien, I must tell you. For someone who is so inclined to see the world and relationships as transaction-based, you really should learn to negotiate better. I would have been willing to concede or offer other things to obtain your help."

"What other things?"

"Well, you'll never know, now. You already agreed." Ana gave her a crooked grin.

Sebastien chuckled, adjusting the strap of her satchel over her shoulder with one arm and offering the other elbow to Ana. "I'll keep that in mind," she said. And she would. "Are you pulling the rest of your friends into this, too?"

"Damien, but not the others."

"Why not?"

"It's illegal, underhanded, and they're not suited for it like you and Damien. Brinn is too kind and anxious. He would do it, if I asked him and explained why it was necessary, but he's terrible at lying, and the whole thing would leave him a nervous wreck. Waverly wouldn't be interested. She doesn't get excited about anything but witchcraft. Alec... Well, Uncle Malcolm is his father. He probably hates the man enough to go against him, but..." Ana grimaced.

"He's too volatile and loud-mouthed to trust with anything delicate," Sebastien completed.

Ana shrugged one shoulder, sighing. "Maybe. He's grown up some over the last couple of years. Alec might know some of his father's secrets, which could be invaluable. And we might be able to use another pair of hands. But this is about Nat's safety. It's not worth the risk. If I were him, I wouldn't agree to help depose my own father, no matter how much I hated the man.

Not unless I could be sure of severing our relationship and securing my own standing and freedom."

Sebastien hummed. "And Rhett?"

"He could probably be persuaded, if we found a task that played to his strengths. If we need an attractive woman distracted and seduced, or someone defeated in a duel, we could call on him. But he's not interested in these kinds of political games or intrigue. He might think less of me, if he knew."

Sebastien thought perhaps Ana was being paranoid, but the other girl knew Rhett better than she, and had a better sense for how people worked, with all their foibles and inconsistencies. "So just us three. Has Damien already agreed to help?"

"I haven't spoken to him yet. I wanted your agreement, first. Damien is reliable in his way—he'd jump to help me with anything I really needed—but sometimes he doesn't fully grasp the gravity of the situation. I don't want the plan to be jeopardized because he's having a little too much *fun* with the whole thing."

Sebastien completely understood, though she didn't say so aloud. "We can start planning on Monday, then, after classes."

That gave Sebastien plenty of time to talk to Oliver first. She had brewing to do, according to her tightly-scheduled plan, but this new opportunity might make her finance problems less pressing. *'Perhaps it would be best to prepare before seeing Oliver. Just like with Liza, a little haggling could make a huge difference. And I don't like the idea that I allow myself to be taken advantage of in negotiations. If I make ten extra gold due to preparing, I've exceeded what I could accomplish laboring over a cauldron for the rest of the day.'*

She and Ana split up when they reached the library, Ana going to study with a group of random female friends and Sebastien searching through the stacks alone. She wasn't sure that everything with the other girl was truly settled, but since they had both apologized, perhaps all that was needed now was time. Sebastien felt like she didn't really *understand* Ana—like she had seen only a couple facets of something larger and darker. In a way, it made her more comfortable. Or, if not more comfortable, exactly, it felt more familiar.

20

HARD BARGAINS

SEBASTIEN
Month 2, Day 6, Saturday 5:15 p.m.

FINDING a reference book for basic negotiation tactics in the library was easy. The more Sebastien read of it, however, the more she realized how right Ana was. She shouldn't have accepted fifty percent interest on the loan Katerin gave her. That was just ridiculous, but Sebastien had felt like she had no other options. And look where it had gotten her.

She probably could have gotten more than seventy percent of the price of the offerings the Nightmare Pack gave her for their meeting, but she hadn't leveraged her own value. Without her, Oliver would have had no chance at the star sapphire or the pixie eggs at all. Subconsciously, perhaps, she had let her amiable relationship with Oliver affect her judgment. He certainly hadn't been doing the same, even if he made it seem like he was being generous.

There were other, smaller incidents, but they added up.

Realizing how much coin she'd lost herself made it hard to sleep that evening, and on Sunday morning, Sebastien looked up the cost of a well-bred erythrean horse before heading out for Dryden Manor. She needed to know how valuable he found the textile industry sub-commission.

Knowing that Oliver's schedule had been hectic in the wake of the Morrow takeover, Sebastien arrived at his home early. She found him coming out of the kitchen with a breakfast tray.

Sharon caught sight of Sebastien and tried to coax her to sit at the table with the other servants and take breakfast, but Sebastien begged off. "I have some business to discuss. If you'll save me a little, I'll be back down to pick it up in a few minutes."

"Oh, nonsense, Mr. Siverling." Sharon said, waving a rag at her. "I'll bring it right up post-haste. Knowing you, you'll be holed up there all day over a steaming cauldron, half-starved. You're much too skinny."

Oliver, who had paused at the base of the stairs to wait for Sebastien, grumbled something unintelligible under his breath, glaring at his own breakfast tray, which he was carrying himself.

Remembering her commitment to take better care of those who showed her kindness, Sebastien reached out and gripped Sharon's hand within her own. "Thank you. You're the best, Sharon. My favorite auntie." The words felt uncomfortable coming out of her mouth, but Sharon didn't seem to notice.

The woman blushed scarlet and shooed Sebastien away in a fluster while the other servants snickered into their food. Sebastien felt comfortable around the working class in a way that she didn't around the Crown Family crew. They lived in the same world as her, one she understood.

Oliver glowered sleepily at Sebastien as she followed him up the stairs. "Sweet-talking my servants, are you?"

Sebastien shrugged. "Like you don't do the same. You treat everyone you've ever met like they're the most interesting person in the world. To their faces, anyway. I'm just trying to return a little of the kindness people show me. To those who are deserving. I've realized I can be…just a tiny bit rude, sometimes. More rude than necessary, that is."

Oliver snorted, but the amusement quickly slipped from his face. As they entered his office, he sighed, "Perhaps I, too, have been slipping in that regard lately. I may have been too caught up in the big picture and forgotten the importance of the basics, the foundation."

"People are power?" she said, quoting something he'd told her shortly after she met him.

"They are. An angry cook can make your life quite miserable," he said, sounding as if he were imparting great wisdom.

"While I still prefer the power of magic, I cannot deny that a network of well-placed connections can be supremely valuable." She sat down at a chair to the side of his desk, resting her elbows on the armrests and steepling her fingers together under her chin. "That's what I'm here to discuss, actually."

Oliver raised an eyebrow, taking a sip of pitch-black coffee. He pulled it away with a grimace, wiping chunky coffee grounds from his lips. "Oh? I thought you were here to get a head start on your brewing, since you missed yesterday."

"Well, I'll do a little of that, too, but I need to stop by the market for the components for some new concoctions. No, I'm here because I heard that you got turned down for a Gervin textile commission."

Oliver set down his coffee. "You heard about that already? I barely got the notice yesterday evening."

"I'm friends with Anastasia Gervin, heir to the Gervin Family, and she visited home yesterday. I heard about it from her. Would it be right to assume the loss is a rather large deal for the Verdant Stag?"

"Well, yes," he admitted. "It won't entirely devastate my efforts, but it is a great blow. I'm hoping to appeal the decision, but if that doesn't work, many of my plans will need to pivot. It's possible I could try to legitimize some of the smuggling operations I've taken over through a commission from the Emberlin Family. I'm also working on a large-scale project to bring more alchemical products into the common citizen's life, which, outside of healing applications, doesn't need the approval of any Crown members. The problem is, as reports from Osham are already showing, with some machinery, the textile industry has the opportunity to employ a large number of non-thaumaturges while also providing a much-needed product to those who can't afford the luxury market anyway. I would prefer not to abandon this path."

Oliver ran a hand down his face, the stubble on his jaw creating an audible scratching sound. "I wonder if Lord Gervin realized that. Perhaps he, or someone he would prefer to work with, wanted to take advantage of the opportunity once I showed it to him. It all seemed to be going so well, and then, out of nowhere, a rejection. I don't understand what changed, but I'm hoping this is still salvageable." He lowered his head, taking a bite of his slightly burnt, unbuttered toast.

"I have a solution," Sebastien said.

Oliver looked up, crumbs on the edge of his mouth. He forced himself to swallow. "What?"

"As I said, I'm friends with the Gervin Family heir. She has access to her father's paperwork, and has assured me she could approve a sub-commission without her father's input. Once it's been filed through the Edictum Council, it won't matter what Lord Gervin's plans are, he won't be able to go back on his legal word. I might even get you more favorable terms. Of course, I have to do a favor for her in return."

"What kind of favor?"

"I'm going to help her depose her uncles, who are a little too power-hungry."

Oliver nodded thoughtfully, his expression slowly brightening. "Keeping a valuable ally in a position of power is worthwhile. But how do you plan to depose the uncles? Do you need the Verdant Stag's help?"

"Ana has a preliminary plan. We'll be refining it before going forward with anything. I might find a bit of aid useful, but I'm not sure yet. I'll let you know. However, while my favor to her is quite set in stone, hers in return is unfixed. Anastasia Gervin could do a lot for me personally. Something of equal value to her Family's sub-commission."

Oliver seemed surprised, but only for a moment. One side of his mouth turned down in a wry twist. "And you want me to make it equally worth your while."

"I do."

"Did you forget that you are vow-bound to pay off your debt with either gold or favors to the Verdant Stag? You cannot simply refuse unless you find our request morally objectionable."

Sebastien lifted her chin, anger kindling in her at this proof of his willingness to take advantage of her. "This was not your request. *I* brought this opportunity to *you*. And I must say, I find it morally objectionable to be asked to perform favors without *proper* recompense. That's extortion, in a way, isn't it? I don't think the vow will stop me from walking away on this one."

Oliver grimaced, leaning back and waving a hand at her. "I wouldn't actually force you to do anything you don't want to, you know. Go on, then. What is it you want from me?"

According to the information Sebastien had looked up that morning, erythrean horses, being magical and so hard to breed properly, sold for between one to two thousand gold, depending on quality and if they had been gelded. Of course, not all of that would be profit, but she estimated that Oliver had given away seven to fifteen hundred gold, net, with that bribe to Lord Gervin. She was hoping for somewhere over eight hundred gold, to pay off her debt and have enough left over for other things. "For salvaging the opportunity to take a chunk of the textile industry for the Verdant Stag, with a favorable, long-term sub-commission from the Gervin Family, I want five thousand gold."

Oliver's eyes widened as he straightened. "Five *thousand*!? Are you insane?"

Sebastien knew it was an outrageous amount. That was why she'd said it. By "anchoring" the conversation at such a high value, he would be less likely to offer her something like fifty or a hundred gold. The negotiation would hopefully settle much higher than it otherwise might, with her real goal seeming, in comparison, more reasonable. "I assure you, I am moored quite firmly to reality. Five thousand would be enough to pay off my debt and get me through the next few terms at University. I'm sure you would earn considerably more than that over the next few years, if the deal goes through."

"You do realize that not all the income from a business is profit, right? I'm already pouring money into the infrastructure, the employees, and the supplies to make the cloth. I have no proof that the business model will be successful here." He threw up his hands in exasperation. "I could be losing money for a *long* time on the whole endeavor. I would be willing to pay five hundred gold for your help. That's an actually reasonable sum, and still *quite* generous."

His seeming irritation did not cow Sebastien. Though she had made an excessive initial demand, his counteroffer was unreasonably low, and for once she held the position of power in this negotiation. "You could be losing out on a lot more than five hundred gold if you don't accept my offer. How about four thousand?"

His eyes narrowed. "Out of the question. In fact, I might be able to salvage the contract on my own. In that case, I wouldn't need you at all."

She shrugged. "If you can do that, fine. You've already failed once, and you might just end up making it more difficult for Ana to push the contract through without her father noticing. But if you want to go that route, I'll just extract a different payment from Ana. Some small percentage stake in her Family's income, once she becomes the head, perhaps. I would probably make a lot more going with that option. I'd just need to wait a few years for the coin to start rolling in."

"Sebastien," Oliver said, placing his hands flat on the desk and leaning forward, as if to impress the importance of his words on her. "Funds that go to you are funds that can't go into building up our territory, or into the pockets of the poor who really need them. It would be irresponsible of me to pay you that much, even if I wanted to. And you don't actually need that kind of coin. How about I waive your debt to the Verdant Stag and give you a stake in the earnings this fabric and clothing business provides? That's about eight hundred gold immediately, and…a one percent cut of all profits, after expenses?"

"It's not my responsibility to get paid *less* so that others can be paid more, nor is it my responsibility to keep the Verdant Stag afloat. Do you think that just because I'm familiar with being poor that I can be convinced to work for less? After all, you 'gifted' Lord Gervin an erythrean horse while you were in negotiations, and all he would have had to do is sign some documents. I'll be putting in actual work here, and perhaps putting myself in danger to go against two Crown Family members. And as for a stake in the business…" Sebastien's smile didn't reach her eyes. "Didn't you just tell me you could be running that business at a loss for *years*? One percent of the profit doesn't seem so enticing. How about three thousand gold upon completion, and a ten percent stake in the total revenue, *before* expenses?"

Oliver's expression darkened, not with anger, but an internal settling of some sort that Sebastien couldn't read. "Twelve hundred gold upon completion, and a three percent stake of the profit, or a minimum yearly payment of four hundred gold paid in quarterly allocations, whichever is more."

Sebastien's heart was pounding, and she hoped the flush in her cheeks wasn't noticeable. "Fifteen hundred gold, and a five percent stake in the profit. The minimum payment is fine."

"A four percent stake, and if you require aid to complete your mission, you'll hire someone from the Verdant Stag to assist you…and pay at the standard rate."

Sebastien hesitated. Earning fifteen hundred gold was near the upper end of her initial hopes, and she hadn't even considered getting a stipend. She almost agreed immediately, but stopped herself, narrowing her eyes. "I'll hire Stags only if their skills fit my needs and they are reasonably priced. I won't pay more for services than they're worth. If I do end up needing help, payment will be taken out of my eventual earnings rather than required upfront. And I won't be liable for payment if the mission fails. I won't be going into any more debt to you, Oliver."

He gave her a small smile. "Not to me. To the Verdant Stag."

She snorted.

"Agreed," he said. "I'll let Katerin know. She's in charge of the Verdant Stag's funds and all our contracts, even if technically this will be running through my civilian name. You can go down to her office to seal the vow whenever is convenient."

Sebastien let some of the tension flow out of her shoulders. She would be doing that as soon as possible, just to ensure nothing changed.

Oliver shook his head ruefully, standing and moving to the shelves on the wall nearest his desk, where a large object sat. He opened its lid to reveal a strange, bulky artifact, with a strip of paper running across the front, underneath what looked like a blocky fountain pen suspended by a wire framework. Oliver pulled a lever on the side, which brought the pen down into contact with the strip of paper. Carefully, he wrote out a message, using a crank on the bottom to move the strip of paper sideways when he ran out of space. When he finished, he moved the lever back up, tore off the strip of used paper, and filed it in a binder to the side.

Sebastien watched the whole thing with fascination. "Is that a messaging artifact?"

"Yes. Recently developed by a University graduate, in fact. They're quite hard to obtain, but I have some contacts that managed to get me a set. Katerin has the other. You use the tuning knobs to choose a particular band—a small area from a wide range of possibilities. Any of the devices tuned to that same band will receive the message. It allows much more detailed messages than other long-distance communication artifacts, while maintaining moderate security. They're calling it a distagram."

Sebastien stepped forward to examine it closer. "If you had a whole group, say one in each major city, could you send the same message to all of them?"

"If the distagram was powerful enough. They are magically cheap—efficient—but my set only covers a twenty kilometer diameter. I believe the Gilbrathan coppers are adopting them, though the Red Guard and the army had the initial monopoly on all production. That's a large part of why it's so difficult to get one as a civilian, but I believe they will quickly become widespread as production increases. I'm trying to get a sub-contract to produce them from the Cyr Family, now that they're coming into the civilian luxury domain. Having more of these would certainly make Verdant Stag operations simpler."

"But anyone on the same band could intercept the messages, right?" She wondered if it was working off the invisible light frequencies. It seemed plausible that this was the artifact Damien had mentioned. Rather than creating the more magically intensive sympathetic link between two artifacts, if the distagram instead sent and received the message through a particular frequency of electromagnetic waves, it could be feasible at much longer distances.

Oliver moved away, taking his breakfast tray around to the table in front of the couch facing the fireplace. "Messages can be intercepted, which is why you send only innocuous information, or communicate in code, and change the shared band at a regular interval."

"Still, that's amazing. Think of how convenient it could be!"

He grinned back at her. "And how cheap. Affordable enough for commoners to use. I also think it could be useful for long-distance merchant caravans and ships. They could have a common channel and use it to warn others of dangers in their area. If you had a relay of them at equidistant, strategic points, you could get critical messages all the way across the continent in just a few minutes."

"Magic is amazing," she sighed dreamily.

His smile shrunk, and he turned back to his breakfast. "Yes. Even better if it can benefit everyone. Well, why don't you go pick up your food from the kitchen and rejoin me? We have something else to discuss."

Regaining some of her tension, Sebastien moved to leave, but Oliver stepped closer as she passed by him, clearing his throat. "As much as your new penchant for vicious haggling has hurt my pocketbook, I must say that was well done. You're coming into your own, Sebastien. I'm happy to see it happen."

Sebastien tilted her head to the side. "You're not upset, then?"

"I actually prefer it this way. Otherwise it feels like I'm taking advantage of you," he said solemnly.

She raised an eyebrow. "You were *trying* to take advantage of me. You would have if I'd let you."

He grinned. "Exactly."

Sebastien felt a sudden rush of outrage rising up through her chest, but what burst out instead was a single, breathy laugh that surprised her.

Oliver laughed, too, and gave her a surprisingly warm look. "You're always interesting."

She snorted. "Some might take that as an insult."

"I assure you I did not mean it as one. To be clear, Sebastien, I've never tried to get you to agree to anything I thought you wouldn't be able to get out of eventually. I don't believe you should bind people with a collar they have no chance to escape. There always has to be a reasonable way out, or I've become a problem. And when people lose hope, they start looking for *other* ways to solve their problems."

"Like assassinating you?" she asked, tilting her head to the side.

He winced. "Well, among other things. And beyond the utility of it, it just makes me feel bad if I think I've ruined an innocent person's life. I prefer feeling good about my impact on the world."

"Is that why you do all this?" Sebastien asked, feeling she'd had a sudden insight. "It makes you feel good?"

"Well, that is one of the reasons," he admitted. "Maybe even the main one, if I'm being honest. People will go to extreme lengths to feel pleasure, happiness, satisfaction."

"Yes, your methods of entertainment are quite...moderate, considering," she said mockingly. "Just a little criminal world takeover with the purpose of revolution. Some people try exercise, or taking up a new hobby like painting, I've heard."

Sharon knocked then, bringing in another breakfast tray, this one loaded up much higher than Oliver's—including unburnt, buttered toast, and a full cup of properly filtered coffee.

Oliver seemed suddenly awkward, taking an absent sip of coffee which he immediately choked on. Apparently, he had forgotten it was filled with loose coffee grounds.

Sharon gave him a few hard slaps on the back, cooed at Sebastien to ring the bell if she needed anything else, and left without looking back as Oliver heaved for breath, his eyes watering.

He almost went to take another sip of the offending coffee to soothe his throat, but Sebastien stopped him in time, pressing a hand to the mug to keep him from lifting it.

Exasperated, Oliver pressed his hands together in a pleading motion. "Ask Sharon for an extra cup of coffee. But don't tell her it's for me!"

2 1

―――――

HIDDEN DAGGERS

Sebastien
Month 2, Day 7, Sunday 12:00 p.m.

When Sebastien returned from the kitchen with a second cup of coffee—properly filtered—she joined Oliver on the couch. "So, what is this other thing we need to discuss?"

Oliver took a deep drink from the steaming mug, then let out an exaggerated sigh of relief. "I met with Tanya Canelo yesterday. She was sent to negotiate on behalf of Munchworth and his associates."

Sebastien paused halfway through a bite of her toast. "What happened?"

"We agreed that the Verdant Stag would continue supplying them in place of the Morrows, but the important part is that she asked about the stolen book, and about you."

She swallowed heavily. "And what did you tell her?"

Oliver placed a hand on Sebastien's shoulder, his skin warm through her shirt. "Don't look so worried! I told her I wouldn't even entertain the idea of betrayal. But then Miss Canelo suggested something that might be worth consideration. The University wants to set up a meeting with you—well, with the Raven Queen. They're willing to pay for your presence with a tribute, just like Lord Lynwood did."

A sour ball of anxiety formed in Sebastien's stomach. "What for? Do you think they can be trusted?"

"I imagine they're hoping to negotiate with her for the book. But no, I don't think they can be trusted. Setting up the meeting was the *secondary* suggestion, after all. But if we could ensure your safety while still acquiring the tribute, it might be worth it for the chance that you can gain something while losing nothing. It would also make me seem more influential and amenable. Though I would caution you against giving up the book, no matter what they offer. Without it, you have very little leverage against more severe retaliation, and it's possible they could use it against you, even in your identity as Sebastien Siverling. We don't know what's inside it, after all."

"I've had similar thoughts," she admitted. "I would be willing to give back the book if doing so could really clear my name, but I don't see how that's possible. Even if it was, the University couldn't make me that promise. It would have to be the coppers. The High Crown, maybe."

"It is possible, but I would be more cautious of him than the University."

She hummed in idle agreement, wondering if the danger of a meeting was even worth it in exchange for the value of their tribute. If everything with the Gervin uncles went well, Sebastien wouldn't be so destitute that the promise of coin could yank her around like a dog on a leash. Still, she'd never had a chance to *talk* to the University faction before. "I at least want to hear what they have to offer. Perhaps there are paths that I haven't considered."

"I can prepare a location, hire security that won't be associated with the Verdant Stag, and set up an intermediary to meet with them. A raven, perhaps?" Oliver asked with a mischievous smile.

Sebastien laughed. "We'll need wards. Protections. Plans to neutralize anything they might come up with."

"I'll hire Liza."

"I'm not paying for that."

"I will handle it out of my thirty percent cut of the tribute's value."

She narrowed her eyes, but that seemed reasonable with the level of expenses he would be incurring. He might actually lose money. "That's acceptable. *This time.*"

"Oh, Sebastien. So jaded." Oliver sighed dramatically, staring toward the ceiling.

They discussed the plan while finishing breakfast, and Sebastien couldn't help but feel...optimistic. She tried to tell herself not to get too excited, but this meeting felt like the kind of thing that might make a real difference. Maybe it could be like the arrangement with Ana, and they would surprise her.

While she daydreamed about being free, no longer a wanted criminal, Oliver sprang up. "I almost forgot! I have something for you. A surprise." He hurried out of the room with a boyish grin on his face, returning with a ribbon-tied box. "I had them specially made."

He handed Sebastien the box, then sat down across from her, watching her unblinkingly, as if to absorb every movement and reaction.

"Is this for any particular occasion?" Ennis had given her gifts on her birthday, when he didn't forget, but they were often last-minute, re-gifted items.

"No particular occasion. I thought these would be useful, and the kind of thing you might not think to buy for yourself."

She tugged at the ribbon, feeling strange. She hoped she wasn't blushing. "Umm, thank you."

"You don't even know what it is yet. Open it."

She did, finding a pair of leather boots, a brown so dark they were almost black, lying beside a small, slim dagger in a holster with straps.

Oliver leaned forward with excitement. "You see how the dagger is so flat? That's so it will be comfortable and easy to disguise. It's got a fish-hooked edge, which I thought could be good for cutting through rope or other bindings, and is also a great way to do really severe damage if you manage to stab someone somewhere soft. It's meant to be hidden against your shin, so the handle rests just at the edge of the boot collar. If you prefer, the holster can be adjusted for your forearm instead."

She unsheathed the dagger, admiring the complete lack of sheen on the dark, matte metal. "No reflection to draw the eye and give away my position." She didn't dare to run her finger over the razor-sharp edge. The whole blade was about the length of her palm, with a flat metal hilt that had finger holes to both decrease the weight and give her a sturdy grip on the weapon.

"If you're ever in a position where magic isn't feasible, either because you have no supplies or your Will is shot, a good knife has many different uses, including self-defense," Oliver said. "It's also a lot faster than setting up a spell."

"Thank you," she said again, more sincerely. This was the second thoughtful, personalized gift Oliver had given her, just because he wanted to.

Oliver's grin widened, curling a little too far into his cheeks with excitement. He held up a hand to cover his face. "That isn't even the best part. Take a moment to examine those boots."

Sebastien did. They were nondescript, perhaps slightly androgynous in style, not fancy enough to wear to some noble party but sturdy enough for every day, and with a tread that would handle rough or slippery terrain well. "I won't have any trouble running in these."

"Anything else?" He was still covering the lower half of his face, but she could see the glee in his eyes.

"You're too excited for these to be normal boots." She looked them over again. "Are they an artifact?" Her eyes caught on an almost-invisible seam in the heel's tread. "Wait...is there something hidden in there?"

"You gave me the idea, when I heard how you were tracking Miss Canelo."

Oliver leaned forward, taking one of the boots to show her how it worked. He grabbed a part of the tread and twisted it, then flipped up a section of the heel to reveal an even tinier blade nestled securely within. It was shaped like a teardrop with a hole for a single finger to slip through as the grip. "I had them custom made. This edge here"—he pointed to a black tab at the back of the slot where the finger-dagger would hide—"is flint. You can scrape it with the blade to start a fire in an emergency. For warmth, or cooking food, or casting magic." He pried the blade out, then struck it quickly against the flint, creating a small spray of sparks.

"That's amazing."

"That's not all. They're size-adjusting." He opened a small decorative flap of leather on the side of the ankle, then pushed a small switch. The boot *unfolded* at the seams. Oliver stretched it a little bit with his hand, and within a few seconds, the boot looked exactly the same, just slightly larger. "The cordwainer was very confused about why I wanted the boots to be able to shrink back down after expanding, but he managed to make it work." Oliver flipped that same switch, and the edges folded back into themselves again, leaving the boots slightly thicker at places, but otherwise indistinguishable. "This way, you can use them no matter what body you're wearing."

"Oliver...this is..." She shook her head, speechless for once. *'How much did this cost?'* she wondered. It was by no means a trivial gift.

"I'm glad you like them. I've noticed that thaumaturges can be somewhat single-minded in looking to magic to solve all their problems, so I wanted to make sure you had a more mundane, creative option for protection. Something no enemy would be expecting." He put the finger dagger back into its hiding place, then closed the heel of the boot again. "Even if someone searches you, once they find the shin dagger, they're unlikely to keep searching for blades."

At his urging, Sebastien tried them on, switching them out for her other boots and settling the dagger on her shin. They fit well and gave her an additional sense of security. *'One more option to deal with disaster when a metaphorical meteor strikes my life.'* Suddenly, she felt bad that she'd bargained so viciously with him earlier.

She shook off the feeling. The book on negotiation tactics had mentioned gift-giving as a way to disarm the other party and make them instinctively feel the need to repay you. It helped make someone more malleable to terms or favors they might have otherwise denied, and she wasn't going to fall into that mental trap. But it would be nice to do something kind for Oliver in return, so she didn't feel so awkwardly grateful and beholden. But what did one do or buy for the wealthy, powerful lord of an illegal organization, who could purchase anything he wanted for himself, and whose main goal was overthrowing the current regime and revolutionizing the country? She blinked, shaking her mind away from that potential rabbit-hole. She cleared her throat. "I'm very grateful. This is a wonderful gift. Thank you."

"No need to thank me again and again. I'm happy that you're happy. I hope you never need to use them. Will you be staying the rest of the day to brew, then?" he asked expectantly.

Sebastien looked at the alchemy tables set against the wall, but with food in her stomach, the difficult conversations out of the way, and her new boots on her feet, she was growing tired again. The idea of spending the remainder of the day toiling over the cauldron made her want to cry, just a little bit, wiping away most of the positive emotions she'd been feeling. The sudden mood swing surprised and worried her. She could remedy her fatigue with a dose of the beamshell tincture…but she didn't want to. *'I've just negotiated a huge payment. Probably more than one. Perhaps just one day to myself is warranted? If this works, the grueling work schedule part of my plan might become optional.'*

Aloud she said, "No. I won't be brewing today." The relief that accompanied those words was almost tangible. She could visit Waterside Market and purchase the necessary components for upcoming concoctions. However, instead of spending the remainder of the day chopping, grinding, and channeling magic until her eyes crossed, she would stop by the Verdant Stag to get her new contract signed and vow completed. And then she would just…take a break.

The thought crossed her mind that it would be a good chance to visit Newton's family, but she immediately shied away from the idea, the sudden surge of fear, guilt, and aversion so strong it made her physically cringe.

"Can I take a look at a map of the city, actually?" she blurted, turning her body physically toward Oliver, just as she wrenched her mind from the painful thoughts. "And do you have a comprehensive list of safe-houses around that would be okay for me to use in an emergency?"

He tilted his head slightly, scrutinizing her reaction. "Sure. I don't have the safe houses written down anywhere here, but we can go over their locations and access protocols together."

While Oliver cleared his desk and brought out a detailed map, Sebastien tried to settle her mind, pushing a bit of Will into the effort when deep breaths didn't seem effective enough. *'It's time to learn. This is important and requires your total focus. This knowledge will be power,'* she told herself. She joined Oliver, standing by his desk and looking at the impressively detailed map filled with streets, canals, and tiny circles and rectangles for the buildings, so dense they looked like mold growing upon a petri dish. Unlike most maps she'd seen, it even stretched into the slums, though with less detail. The paper took up almost his whole desk, and Sebastien was struck again by the size of Gilbratha, and the number of people that lived there.

"This is Mrs. Branwen's house," Oliver said, pointing to an area of the slums. "You hid there with me before." He moved his finger. "We also have a safe house here, just off Waterside Market, with a second exit in case you need to throw off someone following you. The password is..." Over the course of the next half hour, Oliver took her through almost a dozen emergency options. She was pleased and impressed by the extent of the preparations. As he spoke, she focused like she was trying to cast magic, letting the rest of the world fall away. She repeated each bit of information mentally, tying it into her memory with different connective threads and doing her best to imagine the streets and buildings around her as if she were walking them, instead of looking down from above.

When he finished speaking, he asked, "Do you want to go over any of that again? I know it was a lot of information all at once."

She shook her head. "No, I memorized it all."

"All of it? From only hearing it once?"

"Yes." She pulled the map a little closer to herself, pointing to location after location and repeating the key information in truncated form. She was a lot more familiar with the city than she'd been when they first met, but she still sometimes had trouble navigating areas she wasn't familiar with. "I really need to memorize the whole city and come up with some optimal routes to various destinations. That will be the hard part."

"The hard part," he repeated, sounding a little odd.

She nodded absently, picking up the map and making her way back to one of the plush chairs near the fire. "I'm going to spend a little time looking this over, if you don't mind. I'll let you get back to your work. I know you're busy."

He said something, but she was already too immersed in absorbing the information in front of her to listen.

She covered the map section by section, memorizing street names and landmarks while trying to simulate the experience of walking through the city in her mind. She took note of several buildings and businesses that the Verdant Stag now owned, including a couple of interesting shops and a rather nice hotel in the business district. This method, merely absorbing a map, wasn't error-proof. Theoretical information was too likely to fail her in the dead of night, or with panic muddling her senses and her recall. She would be best served by traveling the streets herself, on foot. But that was too large a project to complete quickly, and would have to wait.

She studied until her brain started to protest against the strain of absorbing new information, well before she'd actually finished memorizing the whole map. She sat back with a sigh of disappointment to rub her temples. "I think that's all I can do today."

She tidied up the dirty breakfast dishes that had been left out, stacking them on a tray to take back down to the kitchen. "If this whole thing with the Gervin side branches does work, isn't it actually rather dangerous for you to get the commission?" she asked, looking at Oliver. "If it's known that the Stags are running the textile industry that you agreed on, can't that lead the coppers back to Oliver Dryden's identity?"

Oliver shrugged, standing to help her stack the dishes. "Sure, but that was always going to happen eventually. I'll put buffers between my two identities, just like I have been. Even if someone becomes suspicious, I have some readily available counterarguments and excuses. There's no reason to believe I didn't hire people in the Mires simply because they're cheap labor and also the potential main source of my clientele. I'm well known to be a philanthropist, and the higher wages I plan to pay might be seen as naive, or bad business, but certainly not out of character. And if the Stags were attracted by those benefits and money and have somehow gotten their tentacles into my business, charging the workshops and stores for protection and getting a lot of people from their own territory hired? Well, there's not much I can do about that. The Stags do the same to a lot of other businesses that Oliver Dryden has nothing to do with, after all. It's very sad, but they're insidious," he said, shaking his head with an overdone morose expression. "I suppose, if criminal organizations can't be eradicated, I would rather be plagued by the Verdant Stag than some of the other options."

Sebastien was still chuckling as she left, tucking a stuffed meat bun that Sharon had pressed on her into a pocket, the box that now held her old boots under her free arm.

22

CUNNING AND CRAFT

Month 2, Day 8, Monday 10:30 a.m.

DAMIEN RETURNED from a wonderful weekend visit to Westbay Manor—wonderful mostly because his father had been away, leaving just Titus and the servants—barely in time to make it to his Monday morning class. He brought back with him three things: news about the latest developments on the Raven Queen's case, delicious treats, and a terrible secret.

As they went through their classes, Damien watched Sebastien with more care than normal, trying not to be obvious about his revived scrutiny. Despite the shock of the knowledge Damien now bore, he reassured himself that the secret was only new to *him*. Sebastien had been dealing with it all along, unable to talk about it, but his emotional state seemed to be improving, if anything. His stint of working every spare moment to try and bury the pain of what had happened to Newton seemed to have passed, and he and Ana had worked out their argument while Damien was gone. Sebastien was still jittery, though—probably drinking too much wakefulness brew to combat his chronic sleep deprivation.

Damien had tried to tell Ana that she should give Sebastien some slack because it was normal for someone to be a little emotionally unstable after a traumatic experience. But though Ana had seemed subdued by this reminder, she had remained too stubborn to reach out.

Damien waved for his friends to linger as Introduction to Modern Magics let out, dispensing the desserts wrapped in wax paper. He gave an extra to Sebastien, hoping they would spark his appetite, and then was forced to give an extra to all his other friends as well when they complained at his unfair treatment. "I have news," Damien told them in a hushed tone, his excitement somewhat exaggerated to cover up his anxiety.

Ana leaned in with interest, Sebastien's gaze sharpened, and Alec grinned, but Waverly was more focused on her dessert, Brinn just gave Damien an indulgent smile, and Rhett was busy making googly eyes at some girl across the room.

"Do you remember the Raven Queen's accomplice, Ennis Naught?" Damien asked.

Sebastien wasn't fast enough to keep the flicker of expression from his face, but Damien couldn't quite tell what emotion had caused it. Anger, or maybe fear?

"His sentencing has been scheduled, and it's going to be public," Damien continued.

This time, Sebastien's expression didn't slip, remaining mildly curious. "Is that normal?" he asked. "And don't you have to hold a trial before sentencing?"

"It is somewhat uncommon, though not quite as rare as a public execution," Ana said, taking a delicate bite of her pastry. "Usually they hold a public sentencing for the more high-profile cases, to remind everyone that the hammer of Crown law is still as powerful as ever. I would guess the trial is either ongoing or scheduled to complete before the sentencing. What did they charge him with, exactly?" With a distracted, indulgent smile, she handed off her second dessert to Waverly, who had already finished both of hers.

"Eat, Sebastien," Damien reminded. He waited for Sebastien to take a big, scowling bite before he continued. "They charged Mr. Naught with felony theft, conspiracy to commit treason, and being an accomplice to illegal magical practices. Plus some other things, like resisting arrest." He waved a hand glibly. "There's also a whole list of minor crimes he committed over the years and confessed to while in Harrow Hill. I didn't memorize it."

"When is the sentencing?" Sebastien asked.

"A couple of months from now."

Ana brightened. "Oh? We'll be free from the University for Sowing Break, then. Maybe we can attend! I imagine quite a lot of people will be there."

Alec shrugged. "That just means it will be uncomfortably crowded. Plus, I'm not really that interested in seeing some poor sod get told the rest of his life is ruined."

Sebastien flinched, and Damien gave Alec a look of irritation. "Poor sod? He's the Raven Queen's accomplice and a career criminal. The whole of Lenore will be better off without him."

"Ehh." Alec didn't bother to argue with him, probably because he lacked good justifications for his opinion but didn't want to admit he was wrong, either.

As their little huddle dispersed and they walked toward the next class, Damien fell back from the group, tugging on Sebastien's sleeve. "This is a ploy to try and trap the Raven Queen," Damien murmured.

"*Obviously*," Sebastien said. "They're not even being subtle about it."

"Do you think she'll show up?"

Sebastien's lips were pressed together in a thin line. "Not if she's smart. And if she did, I'd like to see their plan to keep the audience from panicking. Have you ever seen someone stomped to death by a crowd, Damien?"

Damien stared at Sebastien. "No."

"It doesn't even take that many people. Just a small enough space and enough panic."

"Maybe they'll restrict the number of attendees? And increase the security, of course. Titus probably has some clever plan to catch her as soon as she gets near, before she has a chance to do any damage."

"Either that or someone decided the danger was worth it," Sebastien said darkly.

Damien fell silent, trying to figure out how to bring up the more important thing he had learned from Titus, but they arrived too quickly at the Natural Science classroom, and the discussion had to be postponed.

Professor Gnorrish had arrayed a strange assortment of things on their desks, from candles to ugly-looking mushrooms, and when all the students were seated, he dimmed the lights. Some of the items revealed a glow.

"There are many sources of light energy," Professor Gnorrish began, his loud voice cutting harshly through the wonder of the glow. "The most obvious source of light is the sun, followed by flames. These are 'incandescent' sources of energy, and are rather inefficient, because most of the actual energy goes into producing heat, with very little left over for light. Less than one percent of incandescent energy is expressed as light, even for the hottest flames from the heaviest fuel.

"Light is also created through electric discharge, which you've all surely experienced through lightning. You can create an arc lamp using two charcoal strips as electrical conductors and a slow-release artifact array filled with electrical energy—lightning-aspected energy, as it was once called. If any of you wish to experiment with this, I recommend you do some research on limiting current and voltage to avoid a catastrophic discharge. See me after class if you want a list of good resources." He looked pointedly at one student, who Damien vaguely remembered had caused some sort of explosion in the dorm a few weeks back.

"After electric discharge come phosphorescence and fluorescence. Some materials can absorb energy from another source, often ultraviolet light, store it, and then emit visible light gradually, at a longer wavelength and reduced brightness. This is rare, and happens naturally in minerals like barite, as well as a few magical species such as fey-flowers and glow-slimes. If the light disappears immediately, it's fluorescence. If it lingers, it's phosphorescence."

Gnorrish let his eyes rove discouragingly over the students, some of whom seemed a little too interested in their rocks and mushrooms. "If you come across something glowing eerily in the dark, do not eat it."

Damien thought it was probably not a good idea to eat random things you found lying around in the dark, in general.

"Finally, we have chemiluminescence and bioluminescence. Chemiluminescence is when chemical energy is converted to light with little to no change in the temperature, unlike incandescence. This process occurs naturally, and when it does, it is called bioluminescence. You may be familiar with fireflies, jellyfish, and the moondew drosera, which is a magical carnivorous plant."

Gnorrish went on for a while longer, but they spent most of the class period practicing casting with different sources of light as Sacrifice.

Damien found the exercises difficult, though he performed better than most of their classmates.

Sebastien attacked the task with a single-minded ferociousness, outperforming everyone else as if his life were on the line, and when the bell rang, announced with satisfaction, "I think that helped a lot! I could feel my grasp getting stronger, by the end. Maybe in a few more weeks, with a *lot* of practice, I'll at least be competent."

Damien realized he was scowling and had to force the muscles in his face and brow to relax. He consoled himself that, while he might not be a prodigy like Sebastien, he was *not* incompetent. Sebastien just didn't see the world from a realistic point of view. For someone so obviously intelligent, Sebastien could be amazingly oblivious. He was so self-centered he didn't seem to notice that many of the other students didn't come close to his skill with light.

This made Damien feel no better, so he decided to try and get up a half hour earlier so that he could work on Professor Lacer's light-based exercises during his study group, which Sebastien still only rarely attended. Damien refused to be left behind. He'd already written to Titus requesting private tutors for the spring's Sowing Break. He might not be able to keep pace neck-and-neck with Sebastien, but he would keep him in sight, at least.

Damien again tried to talk to Sebastien after classes ended, but Ana chose that moment to draw both of them aside, fidgeting with her clothes as she was prone to do when overexcited. "We need somewhere we can speak privately. Somewhere we won't be overheard."

Sebastien nodded thoughtfully, as if he already knew what was going on. "Not the Menagerie. It's too open. We would need wards or a spell to ensure privacy, and I don't know any. The best option is probably an empty class-room. Or a storage room with a lock. I should be able to open it as long as it's not too complex."

Damien stared back and forth between the two of them. "What's going on?" Was Sebastien bringing Ana in on their secret order of the thirteen-pointed star? Damien wasn't sure how he felt about that. It would be great to have his other best friend in on all their secrets, but at the same time...the secret order had been something special, something that only Damien was worthy enough for.

He wasn't sure if Sebastien guessed what he was thinking, but Sebastien shook his head, pushing back his hair without regard to neatness or the way it looked. "Ana has something she needs our help with," he explained. "Something sensitive."

"Can you bypass a lock, then, Sebastien?" Ana asked, intrigued.

"I've been practicing."

"Already? You're more dedicated to this than I had expected. I'm impressed."

Sebastien rolled his eyes.

"What is going on?" Damien asked again.

"You'll find out soon enough," Sebastien said, callous to Damien's painful curiosity. "Can we just use the study group room? There's no one in there right now. We have permission to be there, and a ready-made excuse for what we're doing if anyone happens to pry. Maybe we can even get some practice in while we discuss."

Ana and Damien shared a look of fond exasperation at Sebastien's obses-sion. Ana said, "I suppose that would work, and I doubt any of the others will feel sad to be left out of this extra study session."

Damien hurried to lead the way, as the sooner they arrived, the sooner he could be brought in on the secret his two best friends shared without him. "If anyone asks, we can just tell them Sebastien thought we were embarrassing Professor Lacer with our *incompetence*." He sent Sebastien a peevish glare but received only a bewildered expression in return. Damien sighed. "Never mind, I suppose."

"Practicing is how you strengthen your Will," Sebastien mumbled stub-bornly. "Don't you want to be free-casters?"

Ana shook her hand from side to side in "so-so" motion. "I wouldn't mind, but that is not my main goal in life."

"I do want to," Damien said. "I just don't understand how you can stand to practice a handful of basic spells over and over again for hours at a time. Don't you get bored?"

"It's not boring. I don't just cast them by rote again and again. I'm always trying to improve some facet of my Will—my clarity, or explosiveness, or endurance—or I'm testing out different ways to think about how the spell effect is achieved, or competing against myself to stretch the limits by changing the parameters of the exercise in different ways. I don't just do the exact same thing a million times in a row. That *would* be boring."

Ana's eyes had glazed over, but Damien found this interesting and would have pumped Sebastien for more ideas of things to try during his own practice, but they had arrived at the classroom, and Ana was having none of it.

She closed the door behind them, looked around with an unnecessary amount of caution to ensure the room was empty, then announced in a whisper, "I have a plan to overthrow my uncles and solidify my power and status as heir to the Gervin Family. Sebastien has already agreed to help, but some of the details might be slightly...illegal. Are you interested in joining us, Damien?"

Damien blinked. He mentally repeated what she had just said, trying to absorb the shock. Slowly, a grin stretched across his face. "Are we going to make those bastards as miserable as possible while seating you on the throne?"

Ana crossed her arms, cocking one hip out. "Of course."

"I'm in."

Sebastien waved them over to the main table, where he was already setting up Professor Lacer's illusion spell exercise. "I have yet to hear the details of this plan, and I warn you, I'll be the one to decide if it's viable."

Ana and Damien sat across from him, and Ana pulled some notes out of her bag, setting them on the table. "The plan is actually quite simple," she said. "I want to erode not only my lord father's trust in them, but also his *faith*. To do that, we only need to break into Uncle Malcolm's vault."

Sebastien looked incredulous. "I can get past a simple lock, not crack a Crown Family vault, Ana."

"That's the beauty of it," Ana said, her smile widening and taking on a malicious tilt. "We don't need to crack it because I know how his security system works. We only need him to be in the right place at the right time, and I've thought of a way to get him there. While I do that, you and Damien can access the vault's contents and plant the evidence."

Damien's heart gave an extra-hard thump, and a thrilling rush of energy pounded through his veins. "Plant the evidence?" he repeated. "Ana, what exactly is the plan?"

"I know my uncles have committed...indiscretions. They've embezzled from some of the Gervin Family businesses they manage, my Uncle Randolph was racing his horse while drunk and crippled someone, and I'm pretty sure my Uncle Malcolm murdered a prostitute two years back."

"I...I didn't know all of that," Damien said, leaning back so that the chair could help support his suddenly watery spine. "Why didn't you tell me, Ana?"

She waved a nonchalant hand, not meeting his eyes. "It wouldn't have changed anything if you knew."

"Titus runs the coppers! We could have done something!"

Ana gave him a wry smile. "Do you think no coppers have ever come sniffing around? My uncles paid off the coppers, Damien. Maybe not your brother specifically, but..." She shook her head, tugging at the wrist of her sleeves and adjusting her cufflinks. "How often do you think members of the Crown Families, especially high-ranking members, are arrested and convicted?" She didn't wait for him to give the answer. "And please don't tell me you think it doesn't happen because they don't commit crimes."

Sebastien nodded as if this was obvious, common knowledge.

Damien smoothed back his hair, this idea settling into his mind like stones thrown into a pond, disturbing everything with ripples as they sank to the depths. Before he was really settled, he said, "I take your point." He needed time to think, not to continue arguing.

Ana was gracious enough to move on, but Damien's mood was effectively dampened. "I'm sure that Uncle Malcolm will have evidence of at least some of these misdeeds in the vault he keeps in his office. I want that evidence," she said.

"What will you do with it?" Sebastien asked. "Blackmail? Or give it to your father?"

"Both." Ana's vicious grin was back. "And that's not the whole of it. I want to plant evidence that they are planning to overthrow and kill my father once he has removed myself and Natalia from the line of direct inheritance."

Damien let out a slow breath. "Do you think he'd buy it?"

"Maybe he wouldn't normally, but I think we can make it more credible. I want to blackmail them with whatever real evidence of misdeeds we find inside, then document their response—proof that they feel the information is legitimate enough to respond to. Once I bring it all to my father's attention in the most embarrassing way possible, they might deny what exactly they were being blackmailed about, but with the real evidence mixed with the false, they'll have damned themselves. Proof of any of it acts as proof of all of it. Plans to overthrow Lord Gervin or even kill him won't seem so unrealistic." Ana's cheeks were flushed pink, her eyes bright. "Their corruption and incompetence will erode his trust in them. Getting blackmailed for wrongdoing might actually be *worse* in his eyes than the original crime. And their planned betrayal will erode his faith. They won't be able to continue undermining my authority and trying to tear my rightful birthright out from under me."

Sebastien fiddled with the Conduit attached to his pocket-watch's fob, frowning into the distance. "That might work, if you play everything just right. But there are some pivot points where everything could break apart. First, even if we can get into Malcolm Gervin's vault, do we *know* that we'll find reliable blackmail within? Secondly, this plan hinges on them responding to the blackmail attempt the way we want, in a way we're able to document. And finally, how are you going to ensure that all the evidence comes to light at the right time, in the right way? If we're blackmailing your uncles, we can't plant the false evidence at the same time we break into the vault. They'll definitely check to make sure nothing's missing. How do you plan to control the outcome? That's not to mention all the details of how to pull this off that we've yet to discuss. There could be pivot points there, too. The more variables, the more chances there are for things to go wrong. Real life isn't like a story—inevitably, things go awry, often most horribly at the worst possible moment. Rather than a complicated plan with a lot of excitement and moving pieces, an exceedingly simple plan that can be adjusted as needed is preferable."

Ana was undeterred. "Okay, well, that's what we're here for. We'll work out all the kinks and come up with backup plans or less dangerous ways to do things."

"Let's run through it from beginning to end, solving problems as we go," Sebastien said. "Do you have the blueprints for your uncle's house? I need to know the details of the layout, the security, and you can't overlook the servants, even if they walk around acting like they're invisible."

Ana didn't have the blueprints but ran off to grab a sheet of paper large enough to sketch out the mansion and grounds from her memory.

When they were alone, Sebastien turned to Damien. "I need you to tell Ana that the Gervins have a betrothal contract with the Raven Queen. It's with one of the branch line men, and I'm not sure of the details, but it was likely negotiated by one of her uncles. Ana didn't mention it, and it seems like it would be perfect blackmail material. Hypothetically...we could gather evidence that makes it seem like they're colluding with the Raven Queen."

Damien's mouth dropped before he could suppress the uncouth expression. "Wait, how do you know this? Titus never mentioned anything about this to me."

"There's no good explanation—not one I can give Ana—for why I know that," Sebastien said, not exactly answering the question. "But *you* have a plausible source. The coppers know about this. But like Ana said, it must not have been a big enough issue for them to go after someone from a Crown Family, since the deal wasn't made with the Raven Queen directly."

"Wait, what?"

"The Gervins have a Conduit set in a ring that they took from Ennis Naught when they negotiated the deal. It seems like the kind of thing they would keep in a vault. I'm thinking, if possible, we could use that to blackmail them. We won't steal it, but perhaps we could take a photo to help make a drawing of it, to prove what we know. This mission isn't just for Ana, Damien. It's been approved by *our* bosses."

Suddenly, it made sense why Sebastien knew these things. He must have learned it from another member of their secret order, or from his investigations into the Raven Queen. Damien swallowed, trying to suppress the resurgence of giddiness. "Do they have any special missions for us?"

"You just need to keep two unworthy men from coming into greater power. If there *were* any secret missions, I would be the one tasked to complete them."

Damien pursed his lips unhappily, but then realized it looked like he was pouting and straightened his expression. "I'll tell Ana," Damien agreed. "And we'll frame them for *treason*. Oh, this is perfect!" He threw back his head and let out a cackle.

"It is...interesting," Sebastien said. He didn't seem nearly as enthused as Damien, but his frown of worry was matched by a small curve of his lips. "Dangerous, but interesting. This is the kind of thing where so many things could go horribly wrong. *If* we're going to do this, we'll need to be truly and properly prepared. I think the reward could be worth the risk, though, with the proper plans in place."

Damien sobered abruptly as he remembered something less pleasant, feeling almost dizzy from his own mood swings. He checked his pocket watch. They still had plenty of time until Ana should return. "I heard something else from Titus, Sebastien. I didn't want to mention it in front of the others."

Sebastien's frown returned in full force. "Tell me."

Damien hesitated. "I suppose you couldn't mention it to me...because of the vow to the Red Guard. But I heard the Raven Queen cast something on you when you went to try and save Newton from whatever Tanya dragged him into." Damien swallowed past the growing lump in his throat, watching carefully as Sebastien shifted uncomfortably, looking away. "Sebastien...what did she do to you? Are you okay?"

"It's nothing."

"It's not nothing!" Damien said, his voice rising. "It's not nothing," he repeated more quietly.

Sebastien's scowl grew harsher. "The Red Guard and Professor Lacer examined me extensively. I'm safe, and no one around me is in danger, either."

"But that doesn't mean you're *okay*."

Sebastien sighed, rubbing away the wrinkles between his eyebrows, then smiled, finally meeting Damien's gaze. "I'm okay, Damien. Really. The Raven Queen, she...wasn't acting maliciously."

That seemed implausible to Damien. "Can you tell me what she did?"

Sebastien hesitated before speaking, and when he did each word was slow and carefully considered. "It wards off divination, with some minor knock-on effects. I can't really talk about it, but please believe me, I'm being honest when I say it's fine. If it wasn't, I wouldn't be here talking with you right now."

"Why would she do something like that to you?"

"Professor Lacer thinks it didn't have much to do with me at all. She was just trying to get his attention, taking advantage of an unexpected opportunity. She...maybe wants to meet with him." Sebastien's lip quivered, but instead of the tears Damien half expected, Sebastien burst out laughing. He was obviously more stressed out about the whole thing than he admitted, if he was breaking into insane laughter.

Damien stared at him, bemused, and even though he didn't really think it was so funny, he couldn't help but start laughing too, letting his jumbled-up feelings pour out as mirth.

Ana returned to find them bent over in hilarity, wiping tears from their cheeks. When she asked what was so funny, they just shook their heads silently. "You had to be there," Damien said smugly, tossing his head to flip back a lock of displaced hair.

"Fine!" She sniffed. "Keep your little jokes between boys. But I expect your full attention on the plan."

Damien reached into his pocket, running his fingers over the thirteen-pointed star disk hidden within, which would shine a light onto the world when activated. "I remembered something important, Ana. It's the perfect blackmail material."

23

MYTHS AND LEGENDS

Sebastien
Month 2, Day 11, Thursday 10:30 a.m.

"I want to learn more about Myrddin," Sebastien told Professor Ilma, standing next to the lectern as the rest of the students filtered out after the end of class. "I checked the library, but there are so many books about him, I don't have any idea where to start. I was hoping you could give me some recommendations?"

"Are you hoping to focus on any particular aspect of Myrddin's life, or are you looking for general information?" Ilma asked.

"I'm hoping to learn historically *accurate* information about him in general, but I do have a particular interest in his inventions and discoveries."

"Hmm." Ilma took a few moments to gather up her things, then checked her pocket watch. "I believe I have just the thing, Mr. Siverling. If you will follow me? This shouldn't take long."

Wondering where they were going, Sebastien trailed alongside the blue-tinted woman.

"Did you ever solve your problems?" Ilma asked. When Sebastien didn't immediately answer, Ilma clarified. "I'm referencing whatever had you so foiled when we met in the library some time back, that I offered unsolicited advice about. I believe you said, and I quote, 'My life is falling apart.'"

Sebastien flushed at the reminder of her own dramatics. "You told me humans are like cockroaches," she remembered. "Versatile, incredibly resilient, and we breed quickly. I do seem to keep going somehow, no matter what happens."

"That does not exactly answer my question."

Sebastien considered the question for a long moment. "I'm working on it," she finally said. "I found a different way to approach solving some of my piled-up problems, and I'm trying to make sure that my current issues don't create a further avalanche of problems by destabilizing the precarious balance that makes up the rest of my life. It was good advice. To be honest, however, I had a hard time figuring out how to implement it. One of my friends actually offered the current solution I'm working toward."

"Giving advice is easy. Taking it is harder, and implementing it hardest of all. It is not so simple to really *change*. It requires us to go against all the rivers of habit and mental conditioning that have been worn deep into our bodies and minds throughout our lifetimes. Diverting those rivers requires dams and digging new pathways and a ridiculous amount of work. At least you were receptive enough to take your friend's guidance when offered. Being willing to grasp opportunities is important."

The last few days, since working out her agreement with Ana and Oliver, had shown Sebastien how foolish she was being when she tried to design a plan to solve all her problems. Instead of working herself to the bone, she'd been doing only the minimum required to keep up with her school assignments, and it had been absolutely wonderful. Her only side project had been planning and preparing for "Operation Defenestration," as Damien had insisted on calling it. That was more than enough to keep her busy outside of schoolwork, but she wasn't alone in the project, and she'd found, with a pleasant feeling like a surprise sunrise, that she could delegate a lot of the work to her two very motivated partners.

Sebastien was still tired in a bone-deep way that had nothing to do with lack of sleep, but she had actually woken up with a few sparks of energy that morning, even without the beamshell tincture. Not enough to get through the day, but it was a sign that, whatever was wrong with her, she was recovering.

Some of her ideas to fix things had been good, but her overall solution would have only made things worse in the long run. She had tried, but hadn't successfully taken Ilma's advice to come at her problems from a sufficiently different angle, or to be ruthless with discarding problems that couldn't—or shouldn't—be solved, and she hadn't focused enough on pulling in new resources that would give her more options.

Sebastien had kept trying to solve everything the same way she always did —more work, more personal responsibility. She knew she wasn't capable of living fully in the moment when there were problems on the horizon, and that kind of lackadaisical lifestyle seemed eminently foolish and undesirable anyway, but she'd been forgetting to *live*. She needed to grasp the opportunities she was being afforded and enjoy them while she still could. After all, as Newton had proved, her world could abruptly and conclusively end at any time.

It's not as if she hadn't been able to recognize the problem, the unsustain-ability of all her obligations, but when it came down to it, she hadn't been able to break herself out of that pattern of behavior. When she was on the edge of breaking down, she somehow returned to trying to fix the world, and herself, with *more work*. Like an addict.

Now Sebastien had a viable path in front of her that didn't require her to spend every spare moment of her days practicing and casting, and meant she didn't need to brew from sunup to sundown both days of the weekend. She could take time to chat with her friends, or take a walk in the Menagerie, or even just read a book that wasn't critical to her immediate advancement.

Even if Ana's plan fell apart completely, Sebastien would still try to avoid falling back into the same grind. Hard work was one thing. Causing herself a nervous breakdown, or Will-strain, was another entirely.

Sebastien was jostled from her thoughts as Ilma stopped, unlocked a door, and waved Sebastien inside.

"Welcome to my office," Ilma said.

It reminded Sebastien a little of Kiernan's office, with all the books and strange knickknacks, except much more cluttered and less expensive looking.

Ilma went straight to one of the shelves that lined the walls and pulled down two books. She handed them to Sebastien. "I recommend these two references."

Sebastien took them, scanning the titles quickly. Both were thick, leather-bound books. The first, *Myrddin: An Investigative Chronicle of the Legend*, seemed like just the thing she was looking for. The second, *Enough Yarn to Last the Night: A Collection of Myths from the Life of a Man with Many Names*, was covered in a faded gold filigree and, as far as she could tell, contained a multitude of hand-painted illustrated children's tales, fantastical and anything but histori-cally accurate.

Perhaps reading the doubt on her face, Ilma said, "It is best to absorb opposing views and different sources of information when approaching contentious topics. Broadening your horizons is valuable and allows you to see things that others cannot. Do not discount the worth of these tales gath-ered from and written by the people who lived during Myrddin's time. Under-standing the culture, the biases, and the things everyone of the time thought were 'obvious,' will give you perspective. Also, there are some notes within these books that you might find relevant."

Sebastien held them carefully, aware of how valuable they probably were. "Thank you. I will read them both," she promised, suddenly worried that she was leaving sweaty fingerprints on their covers.

"You are welcome. Bring them back to me when you are finished, preferably by the end of next term, before the summer break," Ilma said, turning away. "You had best hurry to your next class. You only have a few minutes."

Sebastien thanked her again and turned to leave.

"Also, please tell Professor Lacer that he still has my book on pre-Cataclysm information storage artifacts. He promised he would return it to me a month ago. I won't have him 'accidentally' adding my rare texts to his personal collection."

"Er, I'll remind him," Sebastien said.

During their next class together, Sebastien borrowed a square silk scarf from Damien and carefully wrapped both texts, fearful that they would accidentally be scratched or have ink spilled on them, or something equally horrifying, while stored in her school satchel.

That evening, after running through a couple hours of Professor Lacer's spell exercises and taking a half hour to carefully transfer the gold coins sewn into the lining of her old boots to her new pair, she pulled the books out for a bit of reading while she procrastinated going to sleep.

She examined *Myrddin: An Investigative Chronicle of the Legend* first. The book was heavy in names, dates, and constant mentions of cross-references and corroborating information, but still managed to be engaging.

Little was known about Myrddin's early life, and while rumors had abounded and speculation continued long after his death, none had any support beyond hearsay. The author speculated that Myrddin may have been low-born, or, more likely, the illegitimate child of a minor noble. Even his original name was somehow in question, as various records from around the known lands referred to him by different monikers. In different countries and cultures, he was known as Emrys, Ambrosius, Merzhin, and in the central plains that became Lenore—Myrddin.

Myrddin began to make a name for himself around twelve-fifty BCE, when he was already an adult. The roving sorcerer's exact age was unknown, but he was fairly powerful by that time, and supported himself by taking difficult to solve contracts from villages and towns that could afford his help, slowly working his way up to more and more prestigious—and difficult—projects.

Myrddin's fame truly began to explode when he agreed to a duel with a wealthy noble scion from a country to the south that no longer existed. Different accounts gave different reasons for the duel: Myrddin wanted the noble to free an abused griffin, or gift Myrddin his manor, or vouch for Myrddin to enter a secret society of elites.

But the duel, along with its terms, was widely popularized and well attended by the wealthy and literate, resulting in extensive anecdotal records of the event. Myrddin would cast only one spell, a shield, and if the noble scion could get past it through any means of cleverness or brute force, without violating the standard terms of a duel—which required both parties to stay within their allotted spots on the field—Myrddin would admit defeat. The nobleman was allotted from sunup to sundown to complete this.

Myrddin spent over an hour before the sun rose setting up the spell array, which had not been documented and was unfortunately lost to time. Despite the work that went into casting it, his shield spell seemed innocuous, even laughable, at first. It manifested as a small black disk hanging in the air between Myrddin and his opponent.

The noble mocked Myrddin loudly, boasting that such a tiny shield would not be able to protect him. Then he attacked. Some said the noble's first spell had been a fireball, others a flaming arrow, and others some kind of flashy fire-bird construct.

All agreed that the black disk had absorbed it. Myrddin stood unharmed, and the shield grew larger.

Each time the nobleman attacked, whether in the form of energy-based spells or using the environment to shoot physical projectiles, Myrddin's spell absorbed it, moving to do so if necessary. The small black disk grew with each attempt, as if feeding on the energy of his enemy's attacks. Even when the nobleman tried a pincer attack, Myrddin only had to take one step to the side to avoid it while the shield flitted back and forth.

Some accounts from the audience said that the disk began to create its own cold wind, with a rim of frost around the edges, and that as the blackness grew larger it began to curve around into a giant dome to cover Myrddin, still expanding.

The nobleman cast more and more frantically, trying to overwhelm the shield, to find a loophole, or to slip past its defenses with subterfuge.

Nothing worked, and the shield only continued to grow.

By midday, when the sun was highest in the sky, Myrddin's opponent had exhausted himself. He sat down on the ground to rest and contemplate his next move.

Myrddin stood behind his shield. Some of the records said he was silent, eminently self-confident, while others claimed that he mocked the nobleman.

When an hour had passed, the nobleman stood and admitted his defeat. He knew that he did not have the energy to continue to cast indefinitely, and worried what would happen when the black dome grew so large that it reached him, fearing that it would eat him just as it had eaten every one of his attempts to harm Myrddin.

The author mentioned that there was some speculation among historians about the function of Myrddin's spell, suggesting it to be more mundane than popularized by these anecdotes, and its ability to absorb attacks was just smoke and mirrors to make it seem more intimidating. It could have had matter disintegration and energy dispersal functions, with Myrddin manually controlling its size after each attack as a way to play up his prowess and psychologically dominate his opponent.

Sebastien didn't believe it. After all, the transformation artifact was no illusion. She imagined casting such a shield herself. No longer needing to worry about the dodging and footwork that Professor Fekten was trying to carve into his students would be amazing, since she was, frankly, terrible at that kind of thing.

Myrddin's spell may have been lost to time, but surely she could recreate it, and others just as impressive, once she became an Archmage. Even better if she could free-cast such a wonder. She spent a few minutes imagining herself as powerful as Myrddin, preeminent above all others. It felt a bit childish, but at the same time, what was her goal if not to be the best?

If she never stagnated, never stopped improving, what other outcome could there be? She would live a long, long life of ever-increasing power, until she had unraveled the secrets of the world, unraveled the secrets of magic itself.

A note at the bottom of the page, written in Ilma's sloping hand, drew Sebastien out of her juvenile daydreams. It referenced an entry in the other borrowed book.

Curious, Sebastien opened *Enough Yarn to Last the Night: A Collection of Myths from the Life of a Man with Many Names*, being even more careful as she turned the lovingly-painted pages.

The first section contained stories about Myrddin's childhood, each more fantastical and unlikely than the next. One told of how Myrddin's mother had been barren, and after a long search, was able to find a friendly Titan that fed her a drop of its blood that grew into Myrddin in her womb. Considering the last of the titans had died or disappeared around eight thousand BCE, this was exceedingly unlikely.

Another recounted how Myrddin was found as an infant, cupped inside the flower of a gigantic water lotus from which he had grown—sprouted, to be more accurate. Sebastien actually snorted aloud.

Yet another talked of how he was half-fey and had grown up much-abused in their secret realm before escaping as a young man and entering the world of humans. Still ridiculous, seeing as someone would have been able to discern the signs of his parentage, just as she had done with Millennium, but at least the war that wiped out the fey had only occurred a few hundred years before Myrddin lived. It was more believable than him being molded from a drop of Titan blood, but that's about all she could say for the theory.

Sebastien flipped to the story that the note had referenced in the first book. It told of how Myrddin, as a young, willowy sprout of a man, had looked up at the sky and yearned. So he rode upon a cold northern wind, up, and up, and up. He spoke to the moon, but she would not help him. He flew farther and spoke to the stars, but they were too fickle. Finally, he flew even farther, into the darkness beyond the edge of heaven, and spoke to Night herself.

She thought him brave and charming, though his life was just a twinkle, a blink of an eye, to one such as herself. Saddened by the future she knew would come, she agreed to grant him a boon.

Myrddin asked for an unbreakable shield that could not be bypassed and would protect him from even Death itself.

Night told him that nothing could protect such a bright spark from Death, but she gave him a piece of herself to shield him from all else, should he use it correctly.

With a piece of Night in his hand, Myrddin fell back down to the earth.

Sebastien saw why the note-taker—probably Ilma—had made the connection. Both stories were talking about the absorbent shield, though one was based in reality and the other in the fantastical imaginings that people without education, who had been raised on stories and lore and superstition to explain their world, might use to explain such a thing.

'It is somewhat interesting, I suppose, but I'm not sure if it's actually valuable,' Sebastien thought. Perhaps one of the later stories would provide the insight Ilma seemed to be hinting at.

Too much time had passed while Sebastien was reading, so she cast her dreamless sleep spell and forced herself to close her eyes, thinking only of the phantom swirls of random color that swam across the inside of her eyelids and not of all the work she needed to do.

In the morning, she returned to the abandoned art supply room on the second floor of the Citadel to practice casting something she didn't want anyone to see. It was part of her general decision to be more prepared, but also a bit of a break from all the planning and groundwork for Operation Defenestration.

Taking a jar of dead beetles, crickets, and even a couple of cockroaches from her satchel, she broke several into pieces. Some of the pieces she scattered around the edges of the room, keeping the rest for herself.

Using her folding slate table, she drew out a relatively simple spell array based on the same principles of the shedding-disintegration spell she used to get rid of any stray pieces of herself that might otherwise be lying around. Except this new spell worked not just on the area inside the Circle, but on the sympathetic connections of her target.

She calmed her mind, taking out the beast core she'd taken from Tanya in case her lantern wouldn't provide enough instant power, and began to cast.

With a surge of Will and power, the beetle within her Circle turned grey and fell apart into a small heap of dust and a waft of almost-invisible smoke. The tiny pile of dust seemed smaller than the section of beetle had been.

The magic hadn't fought her like she had been prepared for, which meant that even though she had created this little curse herself, it wasn't new magic. Someone, probably multiple someones, had used either this exact spell or a variation of it enough times that the spell had flowed easily. Which made sense.

Sebastien stood and moved to the other side of the room, where a matching tiny pile of ultra-fine dust sat, dispersing in a puff with the accidental air current her approach caused.

With a grim smile of satisfaction, Sebastien returned to her spell array to repeat the process. She would be ready if the time ever came that she needed to combine this spell with the reverse-scrying function. She only needed to find a way to protect herself from disintegrating like the rest of her pieces, but she had some ideas for that. If the coppers still had her blood, they would receive a nasty surprise the next time they tried to use it against her.

Plus, being well-practiced with sympathetic curses seemed like a useful thing in general.

24

HEED MY PRAYER

Siobhan

Month 2, Day 12, Friday 6:30 p.m.

Siobhan felt surprisingly secure as she walked through the darkened streets of the Mires. Her new dowsing artifact was active, trying to find her through a piece of thread she'd pulled off her scarf. The attempted divination activated her ward, which simultaneously blocked the dowsing and hid her from more mundane methods of observation. The eyes of those she passed slid off her, their minds turning to other things when they might have wondered about her. If anyone tried to follow her, the ward, along with her evasive maneuvers and circuitous route, would make things exceedingly difficult. Even if someone did manage to follow her, she had her stunning wand, her warding medallion, and even her hidden knives.

She might not be a dangerous free-caster yet, but she was well prepared for either fight or flight. Hopefully better prepared than any potential enemies.

Siobhan had used the map-based divination to check Tanya's location before leaving, then stopped once along the way to check it again to make sure she didn't run into the other young woman. Regardless of what Tanya was up to, Siobhan could no longer involve herself. She merely needed to be careful not to walk into any ambushes.

Rather than head straight to the underground thaumaturge meeting, Siobhan was on her way to Liza's in the hope that they could travel together.

She would take all the protection she could get, even if only for a portion of her evening.

At that moment, Damien was back at the University working on Operation Defenestration, while Ana was meeting with a shaman who was supposed to help her magically remember the exact moment she'd seen the combination to Malcolm Gervin's vault.

There had been some talk of kicking off the plan this weekend, but Sebastien had insisted they wait, both so that they could be better prepared in general, and so that she could finish creating a fake version of her heirloom Conduit ring. If the original was in Malcolm Gervin's vault, she was going to take it back and replace it with a fake.

The forgery was rather slow-going, as she wanted it to be as indistinguish-able from the original as possible, and it required a lot of delicate control with the various modifications of the stone-creating exercise they had learned in Professor Lacer's class. She had bought some quartz, which she was molding and faceting into the fake Conduit, and some silver for the setting and ring itself. She was even doing her best to embed a fake chameleon spell array, which wouldn't *work*, but would seem to have simply run out of power unless it was examined by an artificer. After that, the ring would need to be properly scratched and tarnished.

As she walked, Siobhan reviewed the map of Gilbratha she had memo-rized, but found some sections of the city foggy, as if her brain just skipped over that section of data when she reached for the information, unable to make a connection. She frowned. *'What? My memory is fantastic, and it's only been a week.'* But if her mind was a vast ocean, that knowledge had settled to the dark, cluttered depths, improperly categorized and lacking the interconnected links that would normally allow her to access it. *'Maybe I was trying to cram too much at once,'* she reasoned. But it was unpleasant to be unable to remember something she felt she should. She relied so much on the strength of her mind that its failure made her uneasy.

When a woman's angry scream pierced the air from a nearby alley, Siobhan flinched out of her contemplation. Her first instinct was to duck out of the way and take cover in an unlit doorway, but she realized the scream didn't have anything to do with her.

The woman's scream was followed by a man's, and then a loud slap followed by obvious sounds of a struggle. The woman screamed again, much weaker this time, almost despairing.

The streets weren't yet completely empty, but Siobhan watched as the few others still out ducked their heads and hurried away even faster instead of going to investigate or trying to help. Siobhan looked toward the nearest street corner, but this part of the city was apparently outside of Verdant Stag territory. There was no green flag to pull for help.

Siobhan hesitated. *'This could be some sort of trap. But is that more likely than someone actually needing help? I've got my stunning wand, my ward active, and all my utility spells on paper. I'm in a better position to do something about an incident than almost anyone else here. If I duck my head and scurry on, just like the rest...'* Some time ago, Siobhan had resolved that she would try to avoid making choices she would regret, and if she just left, she knew she would always wonder.

So Siobhan walked over to the alley, stepping gingerly to try and reduce the noise of her boots against the ground, and peeked around the corner.

A woman was lying on her back, desperately clinging to a satchel, while a man knelt over her, yanking at it, and another man stood a few feet away, apparently acting as a lookout. The three were silhouetted by light shining through the alley from the street on the other side, but Siobhan couldn't make out many details.

"I curse you!" the woman wailed. "I will sacrifice to the Raven Queen tonight, that she may listen to my prayer!"

Siobhan's eyebrows rose.

"May the Raven Queen cast down a curse upon you! May you never sleep in peace again!" the woman continued.

The man kneeling over her gave her another harsh slap, finally yanking the satchel away from her suddenly weak fingers. He tossed it to the lookout, who began to rifle through it. Then the first man started fumbling around the woman's waist. Siobhan didn't know if he was trying to search her pockets or strip off her pants for something worse, but she had seen enough.

The woman's curse had given her the perfect idea to deal with the situation without having to endanger herself. She hesitated for a moment as she held her hands to her mouth in a cupped Circle, remembering the last time she'd cast this spell. But the people in the alley weren't casting anything to be distracted from, nor were they on the edge of a mental breakdown from terror. *'The spell itself is harmless,'* she reminded herself, knowing she was being foolish but unable to push away her deep dread. Hearing a faint sob from the woman, Siobhan steeled herself and began to cast, channeling power through the Conduit strapped to her torso. With a thrice-repeated chant, her shadow rose up from the ground, stretching around the corner into the alley and looming over the men.

She molded it into the form that was quickly becoming familiar, a hooded figure with a huge beak, tattered cloak billowing in an intangible wind. There wasn't much light for her shadow to absorb, so the warmth of her breath through the Circle of her cupped hands made up the difference in power, and Siobhan winced at the biting cold in her fingers.

She couldn't see what was happening, but there were no screams or sudden sounds of fleeing footsteps, even after she waited a few seconds.

Hoping her divination-diverting ward would keep them from noticing, she peeked around the corner.

The woman was staring at the shadow-familiar's form, wide-eyed and silent, but the men both had their backs to it and hadn't noticed.

Grimacing at the cold in her fingers that was beginning to become a bone-deep ache, Siobhan adjusted her shadow's form, letting it reach out with one void-black, spindly appendage with too-long fingers. Those fingers reached around as if to grasp the skull of the man who had, at this point, pulled the woman's pockets inside-out and fumbled open her belt.

He noticed immediately as the inhuman fingers passed in front of his face, absorbing the light of the far street. He screamed, high-pitched and hoarse, jerking back and falling onto his backside.

His eyes bulged wide open as they followed the fingers back to the arm, back to the floating figure.

Siobhan turned its hooded head, as if following the man's movement.

His partner with the stolen satchel had turned to see the cause of the disturbance, but froze in place, silent. The sound of trickling water against the ground gave away his loss of control over his bladder.

The man on the ground scrambled backward like a crab until his back hit the wall, started to scream again, but cut off the sound halfway by clamping his hand over his mouth.

Siobhan waited for them to run away, but they just stood there. The shadow-familiar spell couldn't control sound, and if she spoke, she might give away her position peeking around the corner. With an uneasy sigh, she stepped into the mouth of the alley. "Leave her be," she said through her cupped hands. "Go home."

It wasn't the most dramatic thing to say, but it worked to wake the men from their stupor. They scrambled to run away, the one who'd urinated himself still holding the woman's satchel.

Siobhan sighed, and then, with some effort, sent her shadow to the other end of the alley to block their way.

The men skidded to a stop at its sudden movement, so quick it seemed to almost fly. "No, no, no!" the man who had hit the woman muttered between ragged sobs.

The distance made maintaining control of her shadow more difficult, as it was only connected to her by a thin string running along the length of the alley, but the increase in absorbed light helped to mitigate the strain.

Her shadow reached for the satchel.

The man flinched away before realizing its purpose, but then tossed the satchel toward her shadow's hand like it was a live coal. "Take it, take it!" The satchel moved through the shadow and fell to the ground.

That was enough for Siobhan. She let her shadow sink back to the ground, flattening and rushing toward her at a speed too fast for the naked eye to capture.

The men sprinted away without a single glance backward.

Siobhan tucked her hands under her armpits, trying to regain some of the heat the frigid air had sucked away from them. "Do you need healing?" she asked the woman.

The woman had been looking toward the other end of the alley, and at Siobhan's question, her head turned back around with almost comical slowness. She swallowed, wide-eyed. "Queen of Ravens?" she asked, her voice cracking. She scrambled to her hands and knees, bowing until her forehead touched the ground. "I beg your forgiveness! I should not have used your name in my curse, I—"

The woman stopped speaking as Siobhan sighed and took a step forward. "I am not angry at you," she said. "Stand up, if you can."

Hesitantly, the woman raised her head, then crawled to her feet, refastening her belt and smoothing down her clothes with trembling hands. "Thank you for saving me, um, your majesty."

Siobhan almost groaned aloud. "I have no need for such titles."

"My apologies, Queen of Ravens," the woman said, immediately bowing again.

"Do you need a healer?" Siobhan asked again.

"No, no, I'll be fine. Just a couple bruises and scrapes, thanks to you."

"Do you need help getting home?"

"...No?" The woman was wringing her hands, looking everywhere but directly at Siobhan.

'Perhaps I am frightening her, only making things worse,' Siobhan realized. "I will take my leave, then. Be careful."

She turned to go, but the woman called out, "Wait! I will sacrifice to you tonight, as I promised, Queen of Ravens. Do you have any requirements for your altar? What do you prefer to receive?"

Siobhan gave the woman an incredulous stare. No one in modern times actually believed you could sacrifice to some higher power on an altar in exchange for their blessings. She realized that if she simply left the woman, the rumors about her could get truly out of control. She needed to set the record straight if she didn't want people burning up dead ravens, or food they should have kept to eat themselves in the hope that Siobhan could somehow improve their lives. "I do not take sacrifices made upon an altar," she said, her voice slow and firm as she tried to impress the words upon the woman. "It is also of little use praying to me. I am not all-powerful. I happened to be near and able to do something tonight, but you cannot count on that happening again."

"I understand, my queen," the woman said. "But...I do not have anything worthy of repaying you for this boon. I have heard about your requirements—a tribute upon meeting, something of value, both worthy and interesting. I could give you the contents of my bag, but—"

Siobhan lifted her hand to stop her. "No need. This was a simple enough thing, and though I do take tribute of valuable items, that is only from those who have the wealth to afford it."

The woman's handwringing grew more violent. "What will you take from me, then?" she whispered.

Remembering how the Morrow goon, Chief, had asked if he owed her the life of his first-born child after she patched up the stump of his arm, Siobhan suspected something similar was going through the woman's mind. Doubting she could disabuse her of these superstitious notions entirely, Siobhan decided on a different approach. "I will take from you a favor," she said. "One day, you will have a chance to repay my aid, either to myself or to one under my protection, one like you were tonight. When the moment comes, you will take it, even at some small risk to yourself."

The woman's handwringing stopped. "Yes, Lady Raven Queen. How will I know the moment when it arrives, or what I am to do?"

"You will know it by the feeling," Siobhan said. This way, the woman could choose to help anyone, in any way, whenever she had the opportunity, and feel reassured that she had repaid her debt.

The woman bowed yet again, and Siobhan took the opportunity to further empower her anti-divination ward and walk away.

She checked the time on her pocket-watch and grimaced. There wasn't enough leeway remaining for her to get to Liza's house and then on to the secret meeting before things started, and she needed to arrive early enough to talk to the organizers.

With a surreptitious check to ensure she still wasn't being followed, Siobhan hurried on. She put on her mask and feathered hair ornaments outside, then walked up and gave the passphrase. "I need to speak to the person in charge of security," she told the door guard.

He eyed her dubiously, but told her to wait in one of the side rooms down the hallway, similar to the one where they'd held her initial interview. Soon after, a couple of masked people entered, one a prognos. Siobhan suspected this was the same woman she'd spoken to previously, who had conducted Siobhan's entrance interview. The prognos nodded to the other administrator. "I am at your service, honored guest," she said to Siobhan.

Siobhan explained that their members might be under additional scrutiny, or even in danger of people attempting to track them home. "I hope you can put some measures in place to mitigate the risk."

"Is this...because of the incident that happened a couple of weeks ago with the Morrows?" the prognos woman asked.

"It's an effect of that altercation," Siobhan said. "Your meetings here have at least one member that works for the University. While they are quite interested in finding me, I doubt they care as much about following your rules. They may cause harm to others in their desperation. I suggest you increase your security, particularly with measures to keep the members from being followed or ambushed. I would also suggest that you put particular care toward vetting any new applicants."

The prognos woman and the masked man shared a sour look. After a few moments of severe silence, the woman bowed deeply to Siobhan. "We take this information extremely seriously, and I assure you we will take immediate measures to mitigate the danger. Thank you for bringing this to our attention."

Siobhan nodded. "I'm sure." A secret organization like this wouldn't survive if the members couldn't feel secure about attending meetings. Before returning to the main room, Siobhan discreetly removed her feathered hair ornaments and slipped on gloves to make sure that every inch of her skin was covered before finally turning off the dowsing artifact. Keeping it active might have drawn more attention than it diverted, if people noticed difficulty focusing on her.

She paused at the entrance, scrutinizing everything and everyone. Liza didn't seem to be present, though Siobhan couldn't be sure. Tanya was there, again recognizable from her shoes.

Siobhan, too, was still wearing the same pair of new boots that Oliver had bought her, but she'd cast a color-changing charm on them while at the Silk Door. In addition to their size change, the change in color was more than enough to keep them from being recognizable. Compared to her, Tanya was sloppy.

Siobhan tried to guess if there was anyone new attending the meeting, perhaps planted by the University. Oliver had passed on Tanya's message that they didn't know about the Raven Queen's participation, but Siobhan didn't trust that assurance of safety. She couldn't tell if there were new members or not, especially since not every member might attend every meeting, and the majority of members didn't have any particularly distinguishing features that she could recognize past their masks. At the very least, that anonymity worked in her favor as well.

Siobhan entered and took a random chair.

Tanya didn't seem to notice Siobhan, her gaze unmoving from her own clasped hands.

Siobhan outwardly ignored her in return, though in truth she kept a watchful eye on all the members, not relaxing for a moment.

Tanya shifted uncomfortably every time a woman spoke, but kept her head down.

In the first part of the meeting, Siobhan tried to make her voice sound a little deeper without being obvious, offering up three decryption and unlocking spells she'd learned while attempting to decipher the stolen book.

She ended up selling spell information to several different members, some of them taking all the spells and others only choosing one, for an astounding total of one hundred ten gold. *'Spells that can be used for illegal, or at least questionable purposes, seem to sell quite well. Perhaps some of these people want to know the spell so they can guard against it, but more likely, this kind of information is harder to find through legitimate means. And, of course, the people that come to these meetings are less likely to care about legality.'*

When it was time to make requests, she spoke up again. "I'm willing to purchase more powerful or unconventional decryption spells. I have some foundation in these types of spells, so I am interested in new methods. I'm already familiar with symmetric decryption against one and two-block independent encryptions. I'm interested in spells that can break two-block encryptions that have gone through multiple rounds of encryption processes. I will pay in gold."

Symmetric encryption had been around for a long time and was one of the simplest methods, allowing decryption with the very same key that had been used to encrypt in the first place. If the first letter was encrypted with a move of six letters down the alphabet, which would turn the letter "A" into "G," then the decryption would simply reverse the process, moving the "G" six letters back up the alphabet. One needed only thirteen guesses on average to break such an encryption, and simple divination spells could run through that many variations in a minute or two, depending on the power supplied.

To make symmetric encryption more complex, an alphabet table could be used, representing possible mappings from one letter to another as a matrix, with a short key repeating over and over to shift enciphered letters at different points, and thus disguise letter frequency. Though the invention of this method was credited to Grandmaster Bellaso during the reign of the Blood Empire, about a thousand years after Myrddin lived, Siobhan knew that Myrddin had made discoveries people of her time still hadn't recreated. The flaw was that language had a lot of repetition, and once a duplicated segment was found, one could use the distance between them to figure out how many characters the key had. It got even easier if the encrypted text was long enough, because it would inevitably contain more repeated text segments. Finding the exact key took a divination spell more time and power to brute force all the possibilities, or some moderately complex mathematics to speed things up.

Block encryptions took the message and split it into pieces, applied encryption separately on each part, then combined them again for the encrypted result. This allowed a shorter key to be used for longer messages, like a book.

The most powerful encryptions, ones she'd only read about and that required more mathematics than she was comfortable with even for brute-force decryption, took each block through several rounds of encryption, each of which needed to be worked through backward. For instance, a first letter "A" from one block would turn into "G," but only if the key contained a letter after "M" as the sixth letter, otherwise it would become an "F." And then after every letter was changed, the key was rotated, and it would all happen again with slightly different rules.

Siobhan turned down some offers, either because she already knew a spell based on the same principles, or because the requirements were unmanageable, but there were a couple of offers that drew her attention.

A man raised his hand. "I have a method. It requires a lot of power, but it's very effective. It is best joint-cast with another person, but I have an adapted method that allows you to set up and charge one side as a slow-release artifact and then move your attention to the other. I would not recommend this method for any security that needs to be cracked in less than an hour. Three thousand thaum minimum capacity, and it will work on encryptions that have gone through up to five rounds of processing. The set-up is quite complicated, and I don't have it memorized, but I could bring it to the next meeting, for one hundred fifty gold."

The spell sounded well beyond her, but she had realized while creating the sleep-proxy spell that if you were willing to be creative and spend a *lot* more time on casting, many spells could be recreated at a lower capacity requirement. Decryption should be equally viable cast over a long period as a short one, unless of course the passkey was actively changing. An actively-changing passkey seemed like just the kind of trick her book would be based around, even if no one had openly invented spells based on that principle yet. Still, she couldn't turn down the chance. If she couldn't use the spell, she still might be able to sell the information on it at some point and recoup her costs. "That might be of some use to me," she admitted. "But the restrictions are rather inconvenient. Seventy gold."

"This knowledge is quite rare. One hundred twenty gold."

"Rare only means it is more likely to be unoptimized, and dangerous to cast from its newness. Eighty-five gold."

"That's a risk that most higher magics will carry, especially these kinds. It seems you've tried other options and haven't had success. One hundred ten is my final offer."

Siobhan waited.

During the pause, another man on the opposite side of the circle of seats tentatively raised his hand. "Um, I have an option you might consider, depending on what you're trying to crack. It's not decryption, exactly. It's a divination that helps to reveal hints about the passkey. It works best if the encryption, or lock, or whatever has been opened many times. Basically, it picks up on echoes of what previous people have done."

The man who'd made the first offer crossed his arms with irritation at the interjection.

"Do the echoes need to be recent?" Siobhan asked.

"Well, it does help. The divination is picking up clues in the environment, and those will be fainter with more time passed. But as long as there is a strong enough impression, or the traces have remained undisturbed, even if a lot of time has passed it can still work. It's based off similar principles to the spells coppers use to investigate a crime scene."

Siobhan doubted much trace evidence would remain on the book after all this time, especially after the lengths she'd gone to trying to find clues. "I'm not sure that would be useful for this particular application, but I am interested. Twenty gold?"

"Thirty?" he asked hesitantly.

"Twenty-five. That seems more than fair, especially as I happen to have another contact that I believe has access to that same spell." That wasn't exactly true, but it was *possible* Damien could access the spell the coppers used, and she could theoretically find some excuse to get him to teach her.

"Deal," the man agreed.

Siobhan turned her gaze back to the man who'd made the first offer. "It's possible that I will no longer need your spell by next week. I'm willing to offer you ninety-five gold today."

He hesitated, tapping his foot on the floor. "I would require assurances that you wouldn't spread this information around. For such a low price, I need the information to remain limited and valuable to others who might be interested."

"That's acceptable."

"Then we have a deal, I suppose."

Siobhan looked to the arbiter, and he nodded, noting it down. In the end, counting what she'd earned and what she'd spent, she had gained two new spells that she would have had trouble accessing elsewhere for only a net loss of ten gold. A bargain.

As the meeting moved on from sales to a free exchange of information, Siobhan listened curiously. People offered up warnings about areas where crimes had been committed, places to find limited-time deals on certain components, and the latest news about the Morrows, Nightmare Pack, and the Verdant Stag, which devolved into arguing until the arbiter brought the discussion back into line.

There were even a couple of rumors about sightings of the Raven Queen, but she knew none of them were actually her.

It was during this time that the arbiters began to take small groups of people aside, bringing them through the hallway into the back room. Siobhan noted this with interest and wondered if it had anything to do with the warning she had given them.

When the meeting ended, she completed what transactions she'd agreed to settle that day, giving out coin and sheets of paper with carefully-transcribed spell instructions. For the decryption spells, neither seller had them memorized or written down, and so she would have to wait for the next meeting to receive them.

When that was done, the familiar prognos woman took Siobhan aside, alone. "We are ensuring that none of our members have ill will toward the Raven Queen, nor any intention to betray the rules otherwise. None will leave until we are confident in them, and any who do not pass under scrutiny will not return. The next meeting will not be held here," she said, giving Siobhan a slip of paper with an address. "Your passphrase will stay the same. I hope this is all to your satisfaction?"

Siobhan memorized the address and handed the slip back. "You are moving to act on this even quicker than I had hoped." And, in truth, much more thoroughly as well. "I am reluctantly impressed," she admitted.

The woman let out a relieved sigh, and Siobhan could hear the smile in her voice as she said, "Please feel free to leave now, through one of our secret exits if you wish. We have no need to question you, and no wish to waste your valuable time."

There should still be time for Siobhan to work on forging the ring that evening, but she had big plans for the weekend. Only Sunday would be spent in an exhausting all-day slog of alchemical brewing. Saturday would instead be spent on a visit to Liza's to follow up on their agreement. Siobhan was so excited she doubted she would be able to sleep properly.

She slipped back out into the night, her exit watched by a guard with a harsh scowl and glowing eyes that tracked through every shadow and flicked to every hint of movement with suspicion. *'It is quite nice to be taken so seriously,'* she reflected. *'Perhaps there are some positives to this Raven Queen identity to go along with all the danger.'*

25

TINTINNABULATION

Gera
Month 2, Day 12, Friday 8:00 p.m.

Gera stood in the doorway to her son's bedroom as Millennium sat cross-legged in front of a large hourglass filled with euphonic sand, his hands on his knees and his eyes closed. She kept her breathing light and her body still so as not to unduly disturb his meditation, the ever-present divination that she cast allowing her to sense him as well as her ruined eye ever could have.

Every couple of minutes, he let out a soft, musical hum, imitating one of the notes that she couldn't hear as the sand rang and tinkled against the other grains. As the merchant who sold it to them had boasted, to Miles's delight, the sand let off "a wee tintinnabulation, faint as sprite bells," and was the perfect thing for her son to safely strengthen his mind, as the Raven Queen had instructed.

In a few months, when he had built up more strength and his health had stabilized along with his sleep schedule, Gera would allow him to start basic magical exercises as well.

As the last of the sand fell into the base of the hourglass, Miles opened his eyes, looking straight at her as if he'd known she was there all along. Her heart ached with happiness to see the peaceful, confident expression on his face. His eyes, which no longer radiated the melancholic greyness of a child slowly fading into shadow and nothingness, focused on her without trouble, and he did not sway with fatigue. He hadn't had any episodes of extreme emotion since the day after the Raven Queen granted her boon, when he had woken in the morning and started laughing aloud, then quickly devolved into sobbing from sheer relief.

"Is that...what it feels like?" he had asked, barely coherent, his whole body heaving in her arms from the force of his emotion, his words interrupted by shuddering gasps. "That's how...everyone else feels...when they sleep? I felt so..." He shook his head, unable to find the words. "It was so quiet, so nice."

Gera had cried, too, the tears streaming out around her ruined eye. "That's how it will always feel for you from now on, my love," she had assured him. It was a vow as much to herself as to him. If this method ever stopped working, they would call upon the Raven Queen's aid once more, no matter the cost. No matter how disturbing Gera found the woman—if a creature such as her could even be considered a woman at all.

Gera smiled at her son. "Are you ready for sleep? The sorcerers are on their way."

"Yes!" he exclaimed with excitement, jumping onto the bed in the center of the room and arranging his pillows just so, so that they propped up his back and curled around under each arm. Holding him—just as the Raven Queen had held him that night.

Gera moved to the bedside table and took the small vial of herbal oil that Millennium had so carefully mixed with her brother's help, discarding mixture after mixture until they got it right. She stared at the vial for a minute, suppressing a pang of mixed jealousy and unease, then handed it to her son.

He took a small dab and placed it on the pillow behind his head, then settled in with a contented sigh. He took a deep breath and began to hum, so deep and soft as to be almost inaudible, a sound that she felt a child his size shouldn't be able to make.

After the Raven Queen's visit, Millennium had asked Gera to cradle him and help him relax like the Raven Queen had. But Gera's humming only left Miles frustrated and on the edge of tears. "It's not right!" he'd insisted. "It does not feel the same. When she did it...it was the most wonderful thing ever. I could hear nothing past her humming, and I heard it *everywhere*. It was in my ears, but also in my body, all the way down into my bones and organs. It felt like my heartbeat was blending with it, like two instruments in harmony. When she hummed, it wasn't trying to tell me anything, except that I was safe. Do it like that."

"I cannot do what she can," Gera had said, trying to suppress the emotions fulminating inside her like a cauldron of lightning. "I do not know that there is anyone else who can do what she can."

Miles had sighed with unhappy acceptance, and after that started working on formulating the Raven Queen's exact smell so that it could help lull him to sleep in Gera's stead. His hums were not magical like the Raven Queen's, but they were another form of meditation that prepared him for sleep.

As the three sorcerers she had summoned entered the room, Gera stepped aside to supervise as they set up the necessary components within the spell array she'd had carved into the floor under and around Millennium's bed. All three had heavy bags under their eyes, tired enough that their blinks were heavy but not so tired that their hands shook—not so tired that they would be a danger. The Raven Queen's methods, while harsh, were effective. Lynwood had promised them that, when each of them was able to hold the spell to keep Miles asleep and dreamless throughout the night on their own, they could sleep whenever they wished.

They were improving rapidly.

As they began to cast, one of the servants poked her head into the room and waved for Gera. When she slipped out, the servant said, "The delivery woman you sent out earlier is back, and she says she has critical news for you. She requests to speak to you urgently."

Her mouth tightening, Gera gave a single, silent nod to the servant and strode down to the drawing room. As had become an unwelcome habit, she searched the corners of the room for any unassuming shadows. Gera's divination did not reveal light and dark, and she could walk through the wilderness on a moonless night without trouble. If there were shadows, that meant there were blank spots—voids.

The woman she had sent out earlier that evening awaited her, fidgeting in front of the fire.

"Mrs. Dotts," Gera said. "What is the issue? Were you able to complete the delivery?"

The woman spun to face her, a strange, wavering expression on her face. "I completed it. There was trouble, and I almost didn't make it, but then..." She took a deep breath, eyes wide. "Then I called on the Raven Queen for help... and she appeared."

Gera sucked in a sharp breath. "Tell me everything."

"Well, everything started off fine. I had the goods in my bag, under the false bottom. Then I was attacked by two heavy-handed cretins. I don't know if someone tipped them off about the drop or if they just wanted a few easy coins and I was unlucky, but they got the drop on me," she admitted, shame-faced. "I was down before I could manage to get the wand out of my calf holster."

Gera made a rolling motion with her fingers, urging the woman to continue on to the important part.

"They roughed me up a bit and took the bag, and...well, I cursed them in the name of the Raven Queen, that"—her voice grew quiet, her eyes searching the room, looking everywhere except Gera—"they would never sleep peacefully again."

Gera almost choked on her own spit. "You did *what*?" she asked hoarsely. "Do you know how dangerous that was?"

Mrs. Dotts ducked her head. "It was foolish of me, I know. I thought maybe I would go home and burn some incense while saying a prayer. I never expected…"

"What happened? Was she angry?"

"She wasn't, or at least not at me. I didn't even see her at first. Her… companion, the bird creature made of darkness, arrived first. It rose up out of the shadows on the dark side of the alley. The two mooks didn't notice it at first, and it just stood there looking at us. Then it moved forward and…" She shuddered. "I think it cursed one of the men. It grabbed his head with these long, bony claws. He tried to dodge, but its thumb sank right in through his skull like it wasn't even there. I was expecting him to die, but…there wasn't any wound. I think maybe…maybe it was depositing the nightmares inside, just like I threatened that I would pray for her to do."

Gera shuddered as phantom fingers of cold trailed down her back.

"They stopped attacking, but it was like they were frozen. And suddenly the Raven Queen was there, in the same spot the shadow being had risen before. I didn't notice her arrive. She might have even been there all along, because even when I knew she was there my eyes wanted to look away."

"Quite possible," Gera agreed, remembering the Raven Queen's disconcerting presence all too well.

"So she told them to leave me be and go home. They turned to run right away, but one was still holding my bag, and her shadow companion…it moved to cut off their escape, moving so fast I could barely see it. Faster than a horse at full gallop, faster than a flying bird. It actually blurred. They had no chance of escape. It made them drop the bag, and I think it was satisfied then because it sank back into the ground and disappeared. I checked the bag afterward, and everything seemed normal, but I'm pretty sure the creature touched the package. I hope that won't be a problem?"

"You delivered it, so it's out of our hands now. What happened after the shadow being disappeared?"

"The Raven Queen asked me if I was alright, and…I think she offered to walk me home? She told me that I shouldn't expect her to respond to my prayers every time because she's not all-powerful, but she just happened to be in the area when I was in need. I thought she would be angry, but she wasn't." Mrs. Dotts' brows shot up as she remembered something. "Oh, and she doesn't accept offerings, only tributes."

"What did you give her?" Gera asked gravely.

Mrs. Dotts shook her head. "I owe her a favor now. She said I would know what I needed to do when the moment came, and that there might be some 'small risk' involved."

"That's it? A small risk specifically?"

"Yes."

"Are you *sure*?"

"She told me she only takes valuable, interesting tributes from those who can afford them. She knew I couldn't, so she took a favor instead. And then suddenly, when I looked away for a moment, she disappeared."

Gera was silent as she contemplated Mrs. Dotts' story. The Raven Queen had taken their tribute and given them a boon—proper rest for Millennium. An equal exchange. But her actions tonight seemed…charitable. That could be taken two ways. Either this debt was much more ominous than the Raven Queen had suggested, or it was only a token repayment to ease Mrs. Dotts' mind. Because, after all, Gera had done a favor for the Raven Queen.

Gera had been worried when she followed that little bracelet from Katerin's assistant into the middle of an active rogue magic incident with the coppers and Red Guard crawling around.

Oliver had warned her, but when she walked into the tent and sensed a familiar empty spot in the world, in a new shape, with the voice of a young man, she had been terrified.

She'd quickly calculated the situation and done her best to deflect suspicion from the boy, getting quite close to lying at times, saying things that were distantly plausible, or that she didn't know to be *untrue*, instead of revealing her true suspicions. She had been worried that giving away information about the woman would draw her ire, but the boy had seemed satisfied enough with her testimony. She had waited for some kind of message from the Raven Queen afterward, but none came.

Gera still wasn't sure how the boy had been connected to the Raven Queen, or if he was perhaps the Raven Queen in another form. The woman was capricious enough to play with the Red Guard in such a way, pretending to be a victim or a bystander for her own twisted amusement.

She could only be relieved that the Raven Queen had some kind of honor. The creature pretending to be a woman was malicious, but only to those who had wronged her. Perhaps tonight had been her way to repay Gera, in a roundabout way.

Gera's musing was interrupted by movement in the doorway. "Millennium!" she said. "You're supposed to be asleep, young man." She turned around to face him, crossing her arms.

"I heard her coming in, so agitated," Miles said, nodding to Mrs. Dotts, "and there was a whisper about the Raven Queen. I wanted to hear the news. Do you think she will come visit me if I pray to her?"

"You are *forbidden* from doing such a thing!" Gera said, raising her voice more than she had intended in her sudden fear.

Miles frowned back at her, uncowed. "She is not actually that scary at all, you know. Maybe she could teach me some real magic!"

Gera placed a hand on her forehead, trying to press back her budding headache. "Go back to bed immediately, child. Why did your sleep team even let you leave? Are they just lazing about in your room?"

"Well, I told them I had to go to the bathroom..."

Gera shooed him back upstairs, but found, to her surprise, that she was a little relieved. Surely, the Raven Queen would return his innocent goodwill, just as she returned Gera's favor, and just as she rained down terror upon her enemies sevenfold.

That did not mean Gera felt comfortable with her son's veneration toward such a creature. He had spent all of a few hours with that woman. Gera had raised him his whole life.

2 6

EXPERIMENTING ON MICE

Siobhan
Month 2, Day 13, Saturday 8:00 a.m.

Siobhan had to knock at Liza's door a second time after the first yielded no results. When the lion door-knocker tried to bite her, she yanked her fingers away and glared at it.

There was a sharp *thud* followed by copious swearing from within, and when Liza finally opened the door, she was favoring one foot slightly. She scowled at Siobhan, her dark brown curls springing out from her head every-which-way, not so unlike a lion's mane of her own. "The sun is barely risen. If this is not a matter of life-and-death urgency…"

"Er, didn't we plan to test the sleep surrogate spell today?"

Liza's scowl grew darker. "I have had four hours of sleep, and you are here while the *sun is literally still rising.*"

Siobhan nodded in a way that she hoped looked sympathetic. "I under-stand. But on the bright side, that will no longer be a problem for you once this spell is ready. If you let me in, I can start getting the spell array set up while you sleep a little longer."

Liza stared at her inscrutably for a moment, then sighed, moving aside so Siobhan could enter her home. She shuffled into the kitchen, muttering some-thing about an "inconsiderate, willfully-oblivious child."

Siobhan ignored Liza's grumbling, cheerfully requesting a cup of tea for herself. Liza was like one of those dogs that barked a lot, even at people they knew and liked, but who would begrudgingly allow themselves to be petted anyway. Making progress on this spell couldn't wait, and would likely take the majority of the day. After ensuring she wouldn't get struck by a lightning ward or a stupidity curse or the like, Siobhan made her way through the closet at the back of the apartment into the secret side of the building where Liza kept her books and components.

The few dozen mice Siobhan had bought were held in a multi-leveled terrarium in the corner, scampering happily around a bed of sawdust.

The sempervivum apricus, which she had brought over along with the mandrake from Dryden Manor, was looking a bit better after a couple of weeks under bright light, but its soil was growing drier than even such an arid climate plant preferred, and the mandrake was no longer dehydrated, but its leaves were still drooping. Siobhan found a watering can, and after peering into it suspiciously and giving it a few sniffs, she watered the mandrake, caressing its leaves and humming to it as best she could. Then, she took a small jar of water imbued with energy from the Plane of Radiance that she had bought from an expensive alchemy shop, mixed a few drops with the remaining water from the can, and poured it onto the sempervivum apricus.

The little motes of light beneath the succulent flesh brightened noticeably and began to travel through its system more quickly.

Siobhan had never been the best at horticulture, with more skill at harvesting plant components than keeping them alive. It hadn't ever made sense to start a component garden since she had to move every few months, but she took some small pleasure in keeping these two plants alive.

Liza came into the room with two cups of tea, looking slightly more alert. She chugged her tea immediately, ignoring the heat, but when Siobhan stretched her hand out to receive the other, Liza pulled back and started drinking from that one, too. "Rude girls who make me take care of six dozen mice and show up unannounced to cause me problems do not get tea."

"I'm not tired, anyway," Siobhan mumbled, unperturbed. She had taken the beamshell stimulant that morning, and for once had been sleeping enough that she wasn't physically exhausted.

Liza's supercilious smile fell away, replaced by another frustrated scowl. "Are you *attempting* to irritate me?"

Siobhan paused to consider. "No?"

"You are not paying me enough to put up with this. Perhaps I should raise my fee."

Siobhan opened her mouth to remind Liza that it was actually Siobhan who was being paid, but the other woman's scowl was warning enough. She closed her mouth silently.

Liza gave a satisfied "hmph" before taking another sip out of her second teacup, and then gestured to a pile of large sheets of paper atop one of the tables. "Since I found myself with more time than I had expected while I waited on the remaining supplies, I did a little research and made some modifications to the spell theory that I think will improve the efficiency when the subjects are separated by a greater distance. You seem to have referenced the Lino-Wharton messenger spell, but the process behind its function is not entirely in alignment with what you intend for this new spell."

Siobhan eagerly looked over the modifications. Liza had made more adjustments to the method of binding, which Siobhan hadn't been able to find much solid information on. Many binding spells were either not robust enough to handle this kind of powerful spell, considered blood magic, or too complicated to be held on the library's first floor. Liza had tweaked other small things across all the steps of the spell and added a note that a docility spell cast on their animal subjects beforehand would make the whole process easier. "This is fantastic," Siobhan said. It would have taken her months of research to come up with the refinements Liza had been able to do in a week.

Liza dropped a stack of books on the table beside Siobhan, each with several strips of paper peeking out between the pages to mark places of interest. "You can read up on the theory while I get the spell array inscribed. With a delicate spell like this, it is very important that we both have the same understanding of how it works so that we can exert our Wills toward the same goal. Struggling against each other even subtly could lead to catastrophe."

Siobhan nodded absently, already tuning out the world as she fell into the spell theory. Professor Lacer had encouraged her to take further developments back to him for approval, but she didn't feel it was necessary, considering Liza's credentials.

Over an hour later, she was drawn from her studying as Liza came back up.

From one of the supply closets, Liza pulled out a large metal ring that looked something like a bear trap, with smaller disks and adjustable legs shooting off it. She cleared a table to use the device while Siobhan watched curiously. "It is a medical diagnostic artifact. An old one that I have upgraded and recharged. It's meant for humans, but it will still return *something* for the mice, and it is not as if I will be attempting to heal them based on the diagnostics," the woman explained.

Siobhan understood instantly. "We'll be able to accurately measure the changes in their health from beginning to end. It could be valuable data, even if we have to do some translating to mouse and eventually raven biology." It was a serious improvement over the basic diagnostic spells Siobhan had found in the library.

"Exactly."

They placed the mice within the metal ring one after the other, tagging them with little identifying labels around their hind legs. They used a notebook to record the meanings of the complex color and shape readings the artifact gave, which they needed a separate scroll with the key to understand. Siobhan was sure that modern diagnostic artifacts had been upgraded to output more easily decipherable words or numbers, because it was a trying process that had both her and Liza scowling and cursing with frustration by the time they finished.

Finally, they moved to one of the warded spellcasting rooms below.

The bounding circle Liza had drawn covered nearly the entire floor. The sleep-proxy spell would be cast in multiple stages, and rather than having to redo the spell array for each stage, Liza had set up different sub-arrays around the main central array so they could simply move the mice from one step in the spell to the next in a circular path. Finally, the mice would be bound to each other in the final, central step.

Each subordinate spell array was written in a different medium. Plain chalk was enough for the easiest steps. Thick lines of glittering wax—the sparkle coming from a mix of powdered quartz, amethyst, and moonstone—were used for one of the more powerful sub-arrays. Another was composed of carefully deposited lines of black salt, bound to itself and the floor with honey and nightshade oil. Most of the components were already set in their places, just waiting.

Siobhan scrutinized Liza's work, checking for mistakes, a giddy feeling bubbling up in her chest the whole time. She felt like, if she jumped, she might just float away. *'It's finally happening. This is the answer, and it's almost ready. I must ensure nothing goes wrong, so close to success.'* The last thought sobered her a bit, but nothing could have subdued her at this moment.

When Siobhan had reviewed the setup and deemed it correct, Liza stepped carefully around the edge of the room, scooping the mice into a large bowl, deep enough that they couldn't crawl out of it. She set the bowl in the center of the complex subordinate spell array nearest Siobhan. "Have at it. This one should be simple enough for you to handle on your own." Their agreement to collaborate included allowing Siobhan to gain skill casting the necessary magic, otherwise Liza probably would have handled everything by herself.

The forceful calming spell used a small drop of laudanum to sedate and a snake's tongue to make the mice more suggestible to commands. Siobhan had never cast it before, but she'd seen Liza do so more than once. It was a stretch to spread the magic through the whole squirming pile of mice, but after a few minutes their struggles eased.

Siobhan dropped the spell and picked up one of the small creatures, which sat in her hand pliantly. Trustingly. "Sorry about this," she murmured, picking up another and moving them both to the next subordinate spell array.

For this spell, she needed Liza's help.

Using transmogrification to enhance a creature through the Sacrifice of another was blood magic, of course, especially since the Sacrificed mouse would be alive for the process. The Third Empire had done a lot of experimentation with transmogrificational enhancements under the rule of the Blood Emperor, some of them notoriously gruesome, but rarely successful.

"Remember not to bind their lives together," Liza said.

Under Liza's guidance, they drew on the vitality and brain function of one mouse, creating a sympathetic connection between its required properties and those of the other mouse. The Sacrifice squeaked shrilly, writhing in sudden pain, but it was soon over. The small creature lay dead next to its companion, a thin ribbon of blood running from its whiskered nose. Siobhan cringed, realizing they would need to do this at least a dozen more times that day. "Couldn't we at least sedate them more thoroughly, or do something to numb their pain?"

Liza gave Siobhan an unimpressed look. "It's a *mouse*."

"And?"

Liza let out a scoffing sigh.

The mouse in the center regained some vigor as the initial steps of the spell worked to make it more robust. Its trust turned to alarm at the fate of its counterpart, but it didn't break through the docility Siobhan had forced on it.

Overcoming her distaste, Siobhan used her silver athame to open the dead mouse's skull and scoop out the brains, along with cutting away a small chunk of each of the organs, muscle, and even a tiny bit of bone. She moved to the next subordinate array, setting the tiny brain in one of the component Circles, and other bits of meat and organs in the others. They had taken a bit of everything because they didn't know what hidden processes might be carried out while sleeping, or what organs besides the brain might create necessary hormones. This step required more power, for which Liza had provided a dull orange beast core the size of a grape. It would be plenty, for such a small creature.

The pieces of the Sacrifice had already been linked to the still-living mouse in the previous step, and now they would imbue it with their properties. "Spells like this are always a bit wild," Liza warned. "Remember, we care about the brain, any hormones that facilitate rest and sleep, and the immune system. If we do this well, little number one here will improve by about thirty percent."

"Only that much?"

"Without me, you could not hope to reach even fifteen percent. One-third improvement from a single Sacrifice is quite outstanding. Reaching fifty percent without Sacrificing a specimen that is significantly superior to the creature you are boosting is nigh impossible, even if you are willing to spend ten lives to improve one."

"What a waste," Siobhan said softly, looking at the small carcass she'd set in a bowl to the side, ready to be disposed of.

"Indeed. But you cannot gain something for nothing, and in any transformation there is always loss." They turned back to the spell, and with Siobhan's command to "Eat," the mouse traveled around the Circle, swallowing the chunks of bloody meat from each of the component Circles. She could almost sense the magic weave itself into the mouse as it went, occasionally stuttering until Liza and Siobhan's Wills forced it to smooth through the fabric of the creature's being, irrevocably changing it.

The power expenditure was frankly ridiculous, and Siobhan knew that without Liza, a spell that they completed within twenty minutes would have taken her an hour, and had her approaching Will-strain, too.

The next step was kinder—on the creature, at least. It was the linchpin of the whole plan, and if it failed, everything would be for naught. *'No pun intended,'* she thought.

This sub-array was drawn in black salt, carefully poured into the shapes of symbols and glyphs using a funnel. In the final spell, they would use a preserved raven's egg to strengthen the connection, but binding only two mice together didn't require that, so the main components were only the mandrake root, still in its large pot, and a knot formed of wood, not carved but woven in on itself and forced to grow that way until it hardened. The knobby, vaguely human-shaped vegetable beneath the dirt would provide its surrogate-concept properties to the spell.

They took a moment to make sure they were both in the correct mindset, maintaining clarity over a strong desire for wakefulness, relief that someone else would take the burden, and Siobhan's own inherent fear of sleep. That last bit had garnered only a silent look and a nod from Liza, no questions, for which Siobhan was thankful. She could not turn that emotion off, so Liza would have to adjust her own focus to match Siobhan's.

They used a small needle to prick the enhanced mouse along with the one that would be wakeful, taking a tiny speck of blood from both. They mixed that with a pinch of elcan iris pollen in a small metal bowl. Siobhan held a flame beneath the metal bowl until the mixture began to smoke, a pink-tinged incense that they avoided breathing in lest it make them sleepy.

Liza carefully guided Siobhan through dragging that incense into the shape of six glyphs, including those for *"exchange," "sleep,"* and *"binding,"* while whispering a chant to help solidify the Word.

"Share the crimson blood of oaths, little griefs soon to be soothed."

"Breathe the stinging wind of sleep, brief regrets soon to be forgotten."

"Weep for the blissful shadow mists, stygian dreams soon to be gifted."

"Awake to the burning midnight sun, scattered hours soon to be harvested."

Siobhan could feel the magic in their words, in the way the sound undulated and deepened with the passage of power.

This wasn't Siobhan's area of expertise, but it seemed a better method of binding than what she'd come up with on her own. Still, it was enough of a strain, even with mice as the subject, that she was relieved Professor Lacer had insisted on the testing. The magic was almost tangibly wild, pushing against the confines of the spell array and their Wills—untamed. She couldn't have done this with any more difficult test subjects, and certainly not on herself.

Despite the difficulty, it was the quickest part of the process. After drawing the glyphs and speaking the chant, they waved the blood and pollen smoke in a circle around the two mice. As soon as the creatures inhaled, it was done.

The inhalation was a form of consumption, a symbol of their willing acceptance of the other's blood. That bound them to each other, with the mandrake allowing one to be a proxy for the other, and the pollen helping tune that binding specifically to the domain of sleep.

Liza waved the smoke away, and some of the wards on the walls shimmered as they worked to clear the air, which Siobhan thought was a rather clever setup.

Siobhan peered curiously at the mice. They both seemed fine. A little drowsy, perhaps, but still unquestionably alive. The enhanced mouse, which was bearing the load of sleep for both creatures, didn't seem visibly more affected than the other one, either. "The extra fatigue isn't instant," Siobhan said. "I thought it wouldn't be, but since I had to design the spell myself, I wasn't sure..."

Similar to Siobhan's latest iteration of her dreamless sleep spell, the rejuvenating spell was halfway to being an artifact. It had no trigger and no way to stop the release of magic after the initial spell was cast, but the spell array would trap the magical energy to be released over time. The magic wouldn't have a consistent output, but would trickle more and more slowly until the rejuvenating spell broke entirely and needed to be recast.

Liza probably could have made an actual artifact to cast the rejuvenating spell on the mice, but it would have been prohibitively expensive while being less efficient, with the way the binding spell was set up. It was the same reason they weren't using a rejuvenating potion.

Instead of cutting pieces from the sempervivum apricus or even using up the whole plant to power a real artifact or potion, drawing on the plant over time—while it still lived—allowed it to steadily replenish its own healing properties without needing to recover from trauma. It also fit better into the symmetry of the spell, the sleeping mouse drawing on the healing properties of a living object over time, the same way the wakeful mouse drew on the sleeping mouse's healing properties.

Liza placed a second, empty terrarium within the inner Circle of the final array. The main components for this bit were the sempervivum apricus plant and a handful of moonseed berries.

This part of the spell took the longest to cast, but didn't strain against Siobhan's limits so harshly. Liza was providing most of the power, and the magic felt much more tame. Still, when they were finished, Siobhan was breathing heavily from the effort. "At least we don't have to do that part every time." The spell would heal all the mice within its inner Circle, so they would just be leaving the second terrarium there with all the sleeper mice in it, while the wakeful mice would go back into the main terrarium upstairs.

Liza took a note of which mouse was bound to which, and then they started the process from the beginning with a new trio of mice. Though Liza had grumbled about it, she gave the Sacrifice a drop of pain-numbing solution that wouldn't impair the vitality transfer too much. It was easier when Siobhan knew the creature wasn't terrified and in pain.

They were able to get through a good handful of mice over the next few hours, as the casting times were much reduced when working on such simple creatures. When they finally cast it on a human, it would take longer and require even more power.

They took a sorely-needed break for the lunch hour, eating in exhausted silence until Siobhan asked, "What kind of terms could a second-term University student expect, if they wanted to borrow approximately five hundred gold?"

Liza didn't even look up from her plate. "I am not lending some random University student—or you—five hundred gold."

"I'm not asking you to lend me anything. I just want to know realistic terms that someone who does lend money would offer. Do you think a second-term University student could do better than fifty percent interest, compounded yearly?"

"Are you trying to break into the loan shark business?"

Siobhan lamented the fact that Liza seemed to have such a low opinion of her. "I'm asking for a friend."

Liza stared at her. "Right." Her tone said that she didn't believe Siobhan whatsoever. Even so, after a dramatically weary sigh, she answered. "If your friend is lending to someone that can prove they've passed at least one term, I'd say twenty to twenty-five percent interest is reasonable. If the borrower has proof of above-average grades, or has something valuable to put down as collateral, your friend could probably reduce that to fifteen percent. Most certified banks don't do that kind of lending because of the regulations and the need for a certified thaumaturge co-signer, so the numbers I'm quoting are from more...questionable organizations. You cannot reasonably charge someone fifty percent interest, Siobhan. If they have even the slightest bit of sense, they will go elsewhere. If they, for some reason, have *no* other options besides you, I would advise you to think twice about lending to them. To people who are truly desperate—reckless—even a blood-print vow may not allow you to recoup your investment."

Siobhan absorbed this information with dismay. Apparently, she didn't have even the slightest bit of sense. Though, she supposed she *was* a particularly high-risk borrower, what with being actively wanted for treason and blood magic. "I understand. And let me reiterate that I'm not trying to become a loan shark."

Liza grunted dubiously.

Siobhan mentally tucked away this information. Her current loan was soon to be covered by the Gervin textile commission, but she would need more, both for the next term and to spend on experiments like this one. Having other, better options would be useful as a bargaining chip if she needed to negotiate with Katerin and Oliver.

There was *no way* she would be duped into another fifty-percent-interest loan.

Even if Ana's plan fell through, and thus Siobhan didn't get paid for it, she might still reach out to a more reasonably priced loan shark, get a lower interest rate loan, and use that to pay back the Verdant Stag. It would save her a lot of coin in the long term.

She would even bet that, if future loans were necessary, Oliver would be willing to beat anyone else's terms to keep her employed and doing ongoing, random favors for the Verdant Stag.

"Were there any results from your mysterious examination that I should know about?" Liza asked.

Siobhan, who had almost forgotten about Professor Lacer's tests already, grinned. "Nothing. You do impressive work."

Liza harrumphed. "Of course I do."

When she and Liza had rested enough to regain some mental vigor, they returned downstairs. By the end of the day they had completed casting the sleep-proxy spell on over a dozen sets of mice. Siobhan was in no state to concentrate after that, so Liza handled the second set of diagnostic records. The first sleeper mouse was already resting, while its counterpart was zooming around with the other wakeful mice, playing exuberantly. Liza would continue casting the spell on more mice over the next few days, until their sample size was at a reasonable number. It wasn't as if she really needed Siobhan's help, after all.

According to Liza, there were no immediately concerning signs in either the wakeful or sleeping mice. Siobhan didn't even try to suppress her ridiculous grin.

Liza gave her a small smile in return. "You're not nearly as abysmal at this as I feared. Oliver must have been working you hard."

Siobhan shrugged noncommittally. "I keep busy."

"It's the only way to avoid stagnating." Liza gave her a slice of melted cheese between two thick pieces of bread, then shooed her out of her house. "Come back soon, and we'll look over the results. The spell should last for at least ten days, just covering those tiny little mice. I'm hoping for a full two weeks." Without waiting for a response, Liza shut the door in her face.

27

———

OPERATION DEFENESTRATION

Sebastien
   Month 2, Day 20, Saturday 8:00 p.m.

One week after her day of spellcasting with Liza, Sebastien huddled outside in the biting cold of the evening, shivering her ass off for Operation Defenestration. She was less "euphorically excited" and more "stomach-churningly anxious." No matter how much preparation they had done, it didn't feel like nearly enough. She would have pushed the operation off further if Ana wasn't so insistent and Damien wasn't so foolishly confident. Even if she felt sick about it, Sebastien had to admit that it really did seem like they would be able to pull this off.

Sebastien consciously avoided muttering anything like, "If nothing goes wrong…" or making any optimistic plans for what they would do when they succeeded. She didn't want to tempt the gods of irony. She'd learned from her experiences with Ennis that as soon as someone made a comment about how things "couldn't get any worse," or how, "I told you, my plan would go *perfectly*," inevitably it would start raining, or the only candle would blow out, or someone Ennis had stolen from three months before would suddenly spot him on the street and try to get him arrested.

Damien and she were hidden in a dark corner on the side of the Gervin branch-Family manor, where each uncle had a wing for their families. They didn't reside at the branch manor all the time, but the whole Gervin Family was there tonight for Randolph's wife's birthday.

Sebastien and Damien had gotten past the warded manor gate with Anastasia and her cute little sister Natalia. It had been the only way they could figure out to bypass the wards embedded in the wall to keep out intruders. Damien had suggested they somehow ride underneath the carriage, which at first Sebastien had vetoed as completely unrealistic, but in the end she couldn't figure out a better way to get inside without being noticed, either.

It was Ana who came up with the idea for them to simply ride inside the carriage with her and her younger sister. "They aren't going to check inside my Family-crested carriage for intruders. My driver is extremely trustworthy. I'll just have to come up with some reason for Nat and me to ride separately from my parents."

The three of them had brought Ana's younger sister in on the plan as soon as they realized they needed another agent on the inside—one who would attract less attention than Ana, and could get away with doing things that weren't strictly acceptable for an adult. Ana had vouched for her, and so far it seemed she had been right to do so.

Past the gate but only halfway along the driveway to the mansion, Nat had started screaming for the carriage to stop. "We ran over a bunny!" she had howled, so high-pitched and piercing that Sebastien, sitting nervously across from Damien, had physically flinched.

As soon as the carriage stopped, Sebastien and Damien both took a couple of quick swigs from liter-sized bottles of Enkennad's draught of shadowed concealment, brewed by Sebastien the Sunday before. It was her first time making the potion, but she was meticulous as always and had learned a lot from Natural Science that made the process easier.

The effect was powerful enough to let them slip out of the carriage's other door unseen while Ana and Nat made a commotion, looking around on the path behind them with a bright light for a nonexistent rabbit corpse.

Sebastien and Damien had been waiting in the shadow of the mansion for over an hour, silent and shivering, hoping that no one noticed them and that nothing went wrong with Ana or Nat's role on the inside.

As they waited, Sebastien's thoughts wandered. The exploration of how light worked had also given her some ideas about her philtre of darkness, which she hoped not to use tonight, but remained one of the most useful items in her emergency stashes. The particles of that philtre, when expanded, were catching, and perhaps absorbing, all the visible light that entered their dark clouds. But an opponent might be able to circumvent that with a spell that allowed them to see a slightly broader spectrum. She had tried making a batch that could catch even non-visible radiation, to ward against someone with an otherwise clever counter-spell, and halfway through the process realized that rather than creating complete and indiscriminate blindness, *selective* clouds of darkness could be even more useful. *'If I could find a spell, or better yet, a potion, that would allow me to see through the philtre of darkness while others remained blinded...'* She let out a devious chuckle at the thought, rubbing her gloved hands together.

Giving her a strange look, Damien held up the coin they had spelled to grow warm when Ana gave the signal, pulling Sebastien from her thoughts. "Right on time. We're lucky Malcolm Gervin is so anal retentive," he said. He tucked away the magically warmed coin, and they ran one last check of their supplies. Damien, despite being shorter than Sebastien, was stronger, so he was in charge of carrying the camera obscura artifact that would allow them to quickly record visual evidence. It even had a special shutter-muffling enchantment that Ana had ordered.

Sebastien tugged at the edges of the black balaclavas Damien had bought for them, making sure no stray skin or blonde hair was visible. When presenting the balaclavas, Damien had boasted proudly about being "concealed in comfort," as the merino wool wouldn't irritate their skin and would even keep them warm while they waited in the darkness and the cold.

He'd also bought their climbing equipment, which, after downing a second full swallow of the shadowed concealment potion, they used to begin scaling the side of the manor, making their slow way toward the upper window that looked out from Malcolm Gervin's office.

Sebastien couldn't help but think back to a much more precarious climb she'd made up the wall of an inn, back when she only had one identity, when all of this had just started. She was still a little traumatized from that fall from the window and the subsequent breathless sprint from the coppers, battle spells shooting after her. She had suggested that they hire someone else—a professional—for this part of the plan, but she had no way to safely offer that they source someone through her contacts at the Verdant Stag.

Ana vetoed the idea. Malcolm Gervin had let it be widely known that if someone were hired to act against him, he would pay double to anyone who defected to his side instead. "Anyone who can be hired to commit a crime like this isn't someone I can trust with that kind of temptation. If word got out about what we're planning, it would be disastrous. Whatever restraint Uncle Malcolm has been showing until now, in deference to the fact that Nat and I are family, would disappear." Ana had shuddered at the thought. "If I thought I could trust hired thugs, I would not have pulled you two into this in the first place."

Sebastien took comfort in knowing that, despite their precarious positions, she and Damien were as prepared as possible. Yesterday evening, they had practiced climbing a similar wall at Westbay manor, accidentally scaring one of the maids out of her wits. They had worked out the kinks and knew their limits.

When the two of them reached the window of Malcolm Gervin's office,

Sebastien's heart sank. It was still closed. She pressed on it and suppressed a frustrated curse. *'Did we get the wrong one? Maybe something happened to Nat before she could get up here. I could try one of my unlocking spells…'* She had drawn up a few on seaweed paper specifically for this mission, just in case, but there was a reason the plan had called for the window to be opened from the inside; there was a good chance that using an unlocking spell would trigger the security wards.

She pressed on the window again, harder.

It popped open with a reluctant shudder.

Sebastien sighed with relief. Natalia had done her job, slipping away from the rest of the family to open the way for them. The eleven-year-old girl seemed, if possible, even more motivated than Ana to depose her uncles, and had taken to the whole operation with almost comical seriousness.

Muscles burning, Sebastien clambered through the window as quietly as possible, then helped Damien through behind her before closing the window again. *'Someone becoming suspicious due to a cold draft would be an amateur mistake.'*

"There it is," Damien whispered, nodding his head at what looked like a large metal coffin standing on its end against the wall near the door. He moved as if to walk toward it, but Sebastien stopped him, slowly examining the entire room for traps or other nasty surprises.

The office was meticulously clean, not a single pen out of place or book spine out of alignment. She suspected that one could eat off the floor without worry. "Be very careful not to disturb anything," she breathed. "He will notice."

"He'll just think one of the servants did it."

"And have them beaten for the error?"

Damien grimaced. "Point taken. We'll be careful. Do you remember the lock combination?"

"Of course."

"You'll need to move quickly once he comes up. Are your fingers warmed up properly?"

"Let's hope so." She moved to stand in front of the vault, examining its code-protected locking mechanism, which would require her to input a matching sequence of letters and glyphs.

Damien quickly pulled a folding strap of leather from his own pack and laid it out at the bottom of the door to block any light or moving shadows from being visible through the space between the door and the floor. For good measure, he locked the door as well. If things went poorly, the barrier might give them an extra minute or so to escape.

Then he took out the camera artifact from its case on his back, uncapped its lens, and unfolded its portable tripod stand in front of a clear area on the floor. When this was done, he checked over everything from the beginning with nervous energy. "If this doesn't work…"

Neither of them needed to finish the thought.

Soon after, the first shouts from down below filtered up to them, too muffled to make out the details. Quickly, the screams grew louder, and were followed by the sound of shattering glass. The faint music from the string quartet that had been playing at the birthday dinner petered out as the sounds of an altercation grew louder.

"That sounds…way worse than I expected. I thought she was just going to dump some gravy on him, or throw a pie or something," Damien whispered, staring at the floor as if he could see through it. He fumbled in his vest pocket for a wax pastel, quickly drawing out his enhanced hearing spell on one palm, which he held up to his ear and angled downward. "I can't make it out. It's too far, and too jumbled. Everyone's yelling over each other."

"The girls will be fine," Sebastien assured him, though she wasn't entirely sure it was true. "They've been dealing with the rest of their family their whole lives. And even in the worst-case scenario, they won't be injured so badly that a healer can't fix it in a couple of days."

Damien gave Sebastien a long look that she couldn't quite decipher past the shadows obscuring his face, but he didn't reply.

Soon enough, quick footsteps sounded against the stairwell, and Damien hurried over to Sebastien's side, pulling out a familiar coaster with a star-burst-shaped light crystal embedded in its surface. With a twist of the arti-fact's base, a gentle light shone on the locking mechanism.

As soon as the footsteps neared, Sebastien began to input the combination she had memorized, using both hands at once for speed. The footsteps had already passed by the time she finished, as Malcolm Gervin slammed into the washroom next to his office. If everything went to plan, Ana had insulted and dirtied him, and his obsessive-compulsive nature meant that he would be meticulously bathing himself for the next twenty to thirty minutes.

She wrapped her fingers around the vault door's handle and slowly, care-fully, twisted down while pulling outward. Both she and Damien held their breath.

The handle came to a stop with a dull clank halfway through the arc.

Heart sinking, she tugged. The door remained closed. "It's still locked," she whispered.

"How? Did you enter the combination correctly?"

"I did. His ring must not have gotten close enough as he passed by. Or maybe he was just walking too quickly to enter the whole thing while it was in range. Or maybe he changed the passkey since the time when Ana saw it. It has been years, after all."

Damien reached out for the handle, trying to open the vault door himself, as if that would change something. "What do we do?" he asked, voice tight and cracking with tension.

Sebastien was silent for a moment as her mind raced. *'We could abort the mission,'* she thought. She considered that option seriously for a moment, looking to the window they had just crawled through. They had failed the most critical step of the entire operation, and dawdling any longer than necessary could get them caught. They had plans in place to flee, and even plans for if they really did get caught, but Sebastien would be in far more danger than either Damien or the Gervin sisters, lacking the inherent protection against any punishment that their bloodline offered them.

'But giving up here would mean whatever Ana and Nat just went through was for nothing. We would have to come up with an entirely new plan from scratch, and maybe I won't end up getting the textile commission, which means none of my debt will be paid off.' She tried to take a mental step backward, calculating the possible value of either option. Getting caught would be horrible, but not as bad as getting caught as Siobhan. The chances of being discovered if they stayed were... moderate. If they left now, they faced a lot less potential danger, and, while losing the textile commission was huge, they would still have a chance to try again, though it would be much harder. She was afraid, but it seemed like such a waste to abort things already. They still had a good window of time before the danger of discovery increased.

'If we stay, how likely is it that we actually succeed? That's an important considera-tion, too. There must be some way to make this work. Assuming the combination is correct, we just need to be in close proximity to the ring for long enough for me to enter it.' She briefly considered trying to use her divination-diverting ward's spillover effects to sneak into the adjoining washroom, where she could hear the sound of a bath running. If Malcolm Gervin had taken off the ring to bathe, she might be able to steal it without him noticing.

Sebastien quickly vetoed that idea as not only ridiculously dangerous, but almost impossible to pull off. Even if he'd taken off the ring, just entering the room would send a puff of cold air his way and draw his attention. Without somewhere she could hide, even her ward combined with yet another dose of Enkennad's draught of shadowed concealment would still get her caught immediately.

'But perhaps there is another option.' She looked to the far wall that adjoined the washroom, where Malcolm Gervin—and the ring that was keyed to the vault—were stationed. There was a clear spot against the wall, large enough for the vault to fit. "Damien, what's your thaumic capacity right now? Best guess."

"Umm, I think I should be somewhere north of two hundred fifty thaums. I've been practicing a lot all term," he whispered with obvious pride. "Why do you ask?"

Sebastien herself should be somewhere around three hundred fifty thaums based on the amount of practice she'd been doing since she used the Henrik-Thompson capacity test with Professor Lacer. "Combined, we're at about six hundred thaums. Maybe a little more." Using her fingers, she did some quick calculation. "That's enough to lift sixty thousand grams one meter per second. Or…one hundred thirty-two pounds."

Damien caught on immediately. "That vault weighs much more than one hundred thirty-two pounds."

"Sure. But we don't need to lift it an entire meter, and it doesn't need to happen rapidly. A couple of inches would be plenty, just enough space for us to move it. At only a couple inches per second instead of an entire meter, we should be able to lift over a ton. Twenty-five hundred pounds, give or take."

"Move it *where*? We can't steal the vault, Sebastien. For one thing, it wouldn't fit through the window—" Damien cut off, looking toward the bath-room-adjoining wall as his brain caught up with his mouth. "Oh. Well, that might work. But even if we only need to lift it a couple inches, how do we get it to move? We'd have to re-draw the spell array over and over, all the way across the floor. And I'm not sure I can *sustain* that much weight once it's in the air, either. In fact, I'm positive I can't. I'm only an Apprentice thau-maturge, Sebastien! You can't expect me to hold up half a ton with my Will alone!" Damien's voice had grown tight and a little too loud, and his fingers fluttered over his balaclava in place of smoothing back his hair.

She shushed him with a motion, keeping her own voice calm and low. "I brought a large piece of flame-retardant paper. We'll draw the spell array on that and just slide it across the floor, *very carefully*. I think it should be able to handle six hundred thaums if we make the lines of the array thick enough. As for holding the vault up, you're thinking about it all wrong. Magic doesn't work like a human body, Damien," Sebastien whispered, already dropping to her knees as she rifled through her bag for the biggest piece of seaweed paper and began to unfold it onto the floor. The paper already had a different spell array on one side, but the back was clear.

She didn't have any ink brushes with her, but she did have an inkwell. Removing her glove, she dipped her finger into the ink to paint out a simple, if somewhat sloppy, spell array. "The float spell was the first one I ever learned. Well, actually it's not exactly a float spell. My gr—my master at the time explained to me that, if you can wrap your mind around it, magic can perform the same task in many different ways. You can lift something by expelling air from the bottom to create force, or by creating a magical buoy to make it float by increasing the surface area to mass ratio, or by creating an artificial hand that lifts it up and holds it in the air. All these different ways have varying effi-ciencies and drawbacks, but they are far from the only methods."

She finished the spell array and paused to blow on it to try and dry the ink faster, making sure to keep her blackened forefinger from touching anything else as she slipped her glove back on. This spell had been one of her first introductions to real magic, and she'd had more than a bit of trouble wrapping her mind around the concept. Her grandfather had taken her through several lessons and various examples and experiments to get the concept across. "You don't have to imagine that something floating is being *held* above the ground. Instead, it can *rest* there, like an apple resting above the ground by lying on a table."

Damien crouched down beside her. "I don't understand. Are you saying I need to compress the air into the shape of a table instead of trying to lift the vault directly?"

"Not exactly. Normally, when something stays aloft in nature, it uses air displacement or an artificially lowered density to do so. That's how most spells of this nature work, too, but this one is different. Imagine this: a bee lying on a table isn't going to fall through, right? The wood is solid enough to compress only negligibly under its weight."

Damien nodded. "Okay?"

"Air is much less dense than the ground, and it doesn't push back hard enough. It just slips away with a touch, which is why a bee has to keep flapping its wings to stay aloft—it needs to access *more* air to reach the same equivalent density as what it would find on the ground to be able to keep that much compressive force between itself and the ground. If the air were as solid as the earth, a bee would float without issue, kind of like how you can float by lying on your back in a still pond. The water is dense enough that it pushes back against you and keeps you from slipping through to the bottom."

"I don't understand what you're getting at."

"Just listen. I'm covering the normal applications so you can understand how *not* to think. Trying to do this the wrong way could scramble your brain like an egg."

Damien nodded solemnly. "I prefer my brain unscrambled."

"When you lift an apple off the ground and hold it still, you know that it takes continued energy to keep that apple up, so it seems like a spell would require continued effort, too. But really, all the necessary work was done during the initial lifting. Gravity isn't continuing to leech more energy out of you for every moment you hold the apple. All the energy you're losing is because of the chemical reactions within your own body, and your muscle fibers rubbing against each other and converting that energy into heat. If you were able to become completely, absolutely motionless—to turn into a statue —you wouldn't get any more tired at all by holding up that apple, because you wouldn't be doing any more work. Just like a table isn't doing any extra work to hold up an apple, because the table is solid enough that it compresses only negligibly under the apple's weight."

Damien still seemed confused, so she tried again. "Okay, how about this? Imagine lying on your back on the ground. You lift up that apple from beside you. That takes energy. Then, you put the apple on your forehead. Does it take any more energy to keep the apple 'floating' above the ground at the height of your forehead?"

He frowned. "It doesn't."

"If the apple doesn't float, but instead *rests*, then you only need to pay the price against gravity once. Here is the key point, Damien—our magic isn't holding anything aloft, or making it float, it's *creating a repulsive force* against the floor that matches the same compressive strength of the floor. If you can wrap your head around that, you only need to lift the vault once, and the repulsive force handles the rest for very little extra power." Her thoughts sparked with the light of a previously unmade connection. "Kind of like a strong magnet with a really exact edge to its repulsive field!"

The last bit seemed to unlock Damien's confusion. "Oh. Why didn't you just say it like that from the beginning? Magnetism is a *force*, but it exerts no *energy*. That's why thaumaturges can't use a single magnet as an energy-source Sacrifice. Everybody knows that." He huffed irritably. "You always make everything so much more complicated than it needs to be."

Sebastien rolled her eyes before shuffling over to the vault to slide the paper spell array under the space where its peg legs met the floor, thanking the unknown designer. If the vault had been flat-bottomed, resting flush against the floor, her idea might not have been viable, unless they could tunnel in underneath the vault somehow, or cast the float spell through the ceiling of the floor below.

While she placed the components, Damien pulled a clear blue beast core about three centimeters across that must have cost about fifty gold from one of his vest pockets and slipped it onto the spot for the Sacrifice. "I can do this," he whispered, seemingly trying to reassure himself as much as Sebastien.

The two of them knelt on either side of the vault, Conduits in hand. "Lift by one centimeter on three," Sebastien instructed. "One, two, three." She brought her Will to bear, and the glow of the spell array beneath the vault spilled out as she and Damien combined their efforts, clumsily at first, but well enough to lift the huge metal vault.

"We did it!" Damien whispered. The glow brightened.

"Stabilize your mind," she said. "Efficiency is key. We don't want to burn a hole in the spell array." She knew from experience that it was possible, and it would be disastrous. Joint-casting was considered hazardous for a reason, and she didn't want to deal with the magic under both of their control lashing out like an angry, maddened snake if it managed to get free of the spell array. Keeping the spell up wasn't entirely without further energy expenditure, despite their little trick with the implementation. As with all magic, there was loss somewhere along the conversion process from Sacrifice to effect, some of it being lost to heat, some to the glow, and some disappearing into the ether in a manner no one could explain. While their capacities weren't being strained to maintain the repulsion between the vault and the spell array, both the force and stability of their Wills was constantly tested.

When the glow had subsided a bit, she warned Damien, then reached down and began to slide the spell array with her free hand. The paper resisted movement, almost as if the weight of the vault were pressing directly on it, but with a small adjustment of her Will—which she again warned Damien of first—she managed to get it to slide.

The glow brightened alarmingly, and she felt heat coming off the paper.

Damien pushed on the back of the vault as she moved the spell array, and ever so slowly, having to pause and stabilize their control quite often, they moved the vault over to the wall.

There, she entered in the passkey combination once more, sweat beading on her forehead.

This time, the vault opened.

With no time to waste, they pulled out the folders of documents, ignoring the pile of "high crown" bars—each worth a hundred normal gold crowns—as well as the other jewels and artifacts. They weren't there to steal, no matter how much such a fortune could do for Sebastien.

Her mother's ring sat on a velvet display bed right at the front, in a place of honor. Damien lifted the display out of the vault. "Is this the Raven Queen's ring?" he whispered, his voice almost inaudible with awe. He reached out as if to touch it with his finger, then thought better of it. "It might be cursed," he warned.

"That's it," she said. *'My mother's ring.'*

Keeping his fingers at the base of the velvet box, Damien set it on the floor and worked the camera, and though the sound of the shutter was muffled, they both jumped like scared rabbits at the brightness of the flash. They hadn't thought of *everything*, apparently.

Sebastien hurried over to the window and pulled the curtains, just in case. When she returned, she picked up the ring box and put it back in the vault while Damien scanned through the first folder of documents. With his back turned to her, she quickly switched out the ring for the forgery she'd spent the last couple of weeks getting as close to perfect as possible. It wouldn't hold up to scrutiny, but hopefully by the time anyone noticed, that wouldn't matter. She tucked the real ring carefully away, then turned back to their task.

Sebastien scanned through the documents with the light of Damien's coaster. Those that covered the topics or keywords that Ana had thought might be suspicious were laid out on the floor for photographing. The big find, apart from the ring itself and the binding agreement that said Siobhan Naught was supposed to marry either Alec or Randolph's son Robbie, were two books—ledgers filled with financial information. They covered the revenue from the Gervin Family businesses that Malcolm and Randolph handled together, and were outwardly identical. Except one showed different numbers than the other. One official ledger, and one for Malcolm Gervin to keep track of what they were embezzling, not only from their older brother, but from the High Crown in the form of avoided taxes.

Damien and Sebastien finished their job in a few minutes, with well over a dozen photos—enough that Damien needed to switch out the artifact's storage cartridge multiple times. They hurried to pack everything up, trying to maintain the same level of neatness and perfection that Malcolm Gervin had kept everything in before their intrusion. Ana would go over their haul, gleaning what relevant information she could from their photos. They didn't have to perfectly compile irrefutable evidence of the Gervin uncles' crimes. That was what the blackmail was for.

The sounds in the washroom seemed to indicate that Malcolm Gervin was done cleaning himself and would soon be leaving, so they hurried to place the vault back in its original location, moving quickly enough that the paper holding their spell array let out a few thin trickles of smoke near the end. *'Hopefully not enough to be noticeable.'* Unused to such effort, Damien panted and winced, putting a hand to his temple.

They took away the strip blocking light from the doorway, unlocked it, and hurried back to the window.

Damien crawled out first, while Sebastien stopped to make sure nothing was out of place. They had retrieved the spell paper from under the safe, everything had been returned just as they'd found it, and the smoke had already dissipated. Satisfied, she climbed out the window and used one of her other paper spell arrays to cast a locking spell from outside the window, erasing the last evidence of their presence.

28

BABYSITTING

Sebastien
    Month 2, Day 20, Saturday 8:40 p.m.

Sebastien's muscles were shaking with exertion and adrenaline by the time she and Damien reached the ground again. They raced across the manicured property and scrambled over the stone wall that bordered the manor, their forms magically obscured by the darkness. Ana knew from the servants' chatter that the wards didn't detect people leaving, only coming, so their departure hadn't required any elaborate plan.

Sebastien stopped to look back while hanging over the far side of the wall, just to make sure no one had seen them. While they might not get arrested, being spotted at this point could make things worse for Ana.

Assured of their success, they jogged into the night, following the road but staying well away from its light.

To Sebastien's surprise, a familiar carriage stood at the side of the road a few blocks down, motionless.

"That's Ana," Damien said. "Do you think something went wrong?"

Sebastien ran her tongue over the back of her teeth in silent thought. "Take off your balaclava and go up to the carriage."

"What? Why me?"

"Because you're a Westbay. You live in the Lilies, and, even if it's strange that you're running around at night all in black, no one will report you to the coppers for it."

Damien handed off his balaclava and the camera obscura to Sebastien and approached the carriage.

He only got three quarters of the way there, just stepping into the edge of the light, when the door swung open. Natalia poked her head out, waving for him to approach as she scanned the darkness beyond for Sebastien. She had been crying, leaving her eyes puffy and her skin blotchy and red.

Damien spoke to her for a few seconds, then turned and waved for Sebastien to follow.

Sebastien hesitated, but complied. When she got close enough to see Ana within the shadows of the carriage, her jaw clenched compulsively.

Ana's left eye was purple and already swelling shut, and blood crusted the edges of her nostrils where she hadn't completely cleaned it up. "My driver is trustworthy," Ana assured Sebastien. "He won't say anything about the two of you. I wanted to stop and let you catch up because I'm not sending Nat back home tonight. Father is too angry, Mother is too useless, and I don't want to leave Nat alone. I'm going to a hotel in the city proper, and we wouldn't mind some company if the two of you would be willing to join us."

"Of course I'm not leaving you alone," Damien said, puffing out his chest like a little rooster, though his grey eyes were stormy with a heavier emotion. "I would offer for everyone to stay at Westbay Manor for the evening, but my father is there."

Ana smiled humorlessly. "I know. That's why I suggested a hotel."

Sebastien glanced up at the driver, who was looking studiously ahead as if he had no idea what was going on, then climbed into the carriage. *'I suppose one night away from the University couldn't hurt.'*

Natalia kept her shoulders hunched and head down as Damien and Sebastien sat.

"Did your father do that to you?" Damien asked Ana, his tone dark and controlled.

"It was Uncle Malcolm. I insulted him and threw a boat of cranberry preserves on him. I'm not sure if Father was more angry at him or at me. Mother actually screamed at Uncle Malcolm, too. It wasn't lady-like at all." One side of Ana's mouth lifted up in a tiny, wry smirk. "I'm fine. This is nothing that a healer won't be able to fix before classes on Monday. Did everything go alright on your end?"

Damien hesitated, but after a glance at Nat, who had started to sniffle again, he launched into a dramatic retelling of their night. His version of events seemed much more theatrical than Sebastien remembered, with exciting highs, worrying lows, and even occasional comedic moments. In the retelling, Damien saved them from possible capture at least twice, while story-Sebastien rambled on about complex magical theory and used dramatic, powerful spells to bind the very forces of nature to his Will.

Natalia was captivated, her tears forgotten, and even Ana found it amusing, though she suppressed several snorts of disbelief.

When Damien had finished, Nat turned to Sebastien. "Is that really what happened, Sebastien?"

Sebastien shifted in her seat uncomfortably as both Damien and Ana gave her piercing looks of warning. "Well...it happened more or less like that." Less rather than more, but the end result was the same, she supposed. "We left everything as close to the way we found it as possible. Hopefully Malcolm won't even notice that anyone was there."

Damien crossed his arms smugly. "And we didn't even have to use any of the twelve emergency plans that Sebastien made us come up with."

Sebastien raised her eyebrow at him. "And yet the plan almost failed catastrophically at least three times, if not for *your* timely intervention, like you just explained so thoughtfully for Ana and Nat. Perhaps I should have insisted we plan *more* thoroughly, so that less improvisation and cleverness would have been required of you."

Damien deflated, but Nat laughed with delight.

The four of them arrived at a nice hotel within half an hour, and Ana gave her driver some coin to board the horses and find a room for himself while Damien booked two adjacent suites for them. The hotel was clean, bright, and decorated with fresh flowers. When they found their rooms, Damien looked around and shrugged. "Not particularly luxurious, but I suppose it will do. It's better than the spartan conditions at the University, at least. I swear that place treats us like prisoners to try and make us desperate for contribution points."

Sebastien, who had slept in plenty of rural inns but never a high-class hotel, thought it was by far the nicest room she had ever slept in, comparable only to her room at Dryden Manor, where perhaps the sheets were a bit nicer and the floor was made of stone rather than wood.

Ana and Nat were in the adjacent suite, which was joined by a door in the wall that locked from both sides—probably meant for families whose parents wanted a separate space from their children.

Damien opened the attaching door, allowing Ana and Nat to join them in their suite. Ana had washed her face to remove the remaining blood, but the bruising and swelling was only becoming more prominent.

"I have some minor healing items in my satchel," Sebastien offered. "It's best to get the process started right away, before the damage has time to settle in."

"Alright," Ana agreed. She sat on the edge of one of the beds, with Natalia perching next to her, while Sebastien rifled through her satchel, pulling out the necessary supplies.

Sebastien handed Ana a regeneration-boosting potion first, and then used a bit of wound-cleansing potion on the part of Ana's eyelid that had split, dabbing it gently onto the raw flesh.

"Did you stock all of these healing supplies for the mission?" Nat asked, leaning forward to watch curiously.

"I carry healing supplies everywhere. You never know when you might need them. But I did stock some special things for the mission, like this draught of shadowed concealment," Sebastien replied, pointing to the half-empty bottle of dark liquid.

"That's what Damien was talking about earlier! Oh, do you think I could try some?" Nat begged, her hands clasped under her chin and her eyes open wide. For good measure, the girl batted her lashes a couple of times.

Ana hesitated. "Is it dangerous, Sebastien?"

"I brewed it myself, and Damien and I can both vouch that there aren't any side effects."

Nat hopped down from the bed to pick up the bottle. "Are you an alchemist, then? I thought you were more of the free-casting type? Damien told me you were apprenticed to Thaddeus Lacer."

"I wouldn't call myself an alchemist. I can follow instructions and a recipe as well as anyone, and I do a little brewing on the side as a hobby, that's all."

Damien helped Nat open the lid. "Don't listen to Sebastien, Nat. If he says he dabbles in something as a hobby, what he really means is that he's on his way to mastering the craft. If he says he's 'almost competent,' that means he's in the top five percent of the population."

Nat turned to Sebastien, eyes gleaming with respect. "Can you brew all sorts of amazing things, then? Like, potions to make someone fly, or a cream to make people beautiful, or a philtre that creates tornados?"

Sebastien snorted, pulling out her bruise cream and warming a good dollop of it in her palm before she began to apply it generously around Ana's eye and nose. "Damien is the one you cannot believe. Being in the top five percent of the population is actually quite unimpressive, since the majority of the population will be totally unskilled at whatever random subject you choose. I mean, think about it. Less than five percent of the population can cast magic at all."

"That's not what I meant, obviously," Damien rebutted. "You can't just go around counting people who aren't even part of the equation. I meant top five percent of thaumaturges."

"But that's not what you said. And I'm not even in the top five percent of students in our *term*, which you might remember from our mid-term results that came out recently. I'm closer to the top ten percent. That leaves me far below being in the top five percent of the entire thaumaturgic population."

Damien threw up his hands in exasperation. "Test results aren't every-thing, Sebastien! I've *seen* what you can do, remember? And suddenly going from your spot in the entrance exams all the way to the top ten percent of students in the term is *actually* pretty amazing. For Myrddin's sake, you're Thaddeus Lacer's apprentice!"

"Provisional apprentice. Hopefully I'll become an official apprentice next term, if I can prove myself. It's nice of you to try and make me look more impressive in front of Nat, but you can just be honest, Damien. I do plan to be truly exceptional one day, but I'm still very far away from real skill at anything important. I am willing to put in the work where others will not, I have the determination and drive that others do not, and I am talented enough, but there is just so very much to learn. Compared to someone like Professor Lacer, I am but a child still."

Nat's head had been bouncing between them as she followed their conversation, but when Damien didn't deign to reply to this final argument—instead tugging at the sides of his hair like he wanted to pull it out—Nat sneakily tipped back the bottle of Enkennad's draught of shadowed concealment and took a swallow so large it made her cheeks bulge and her eyes water.

Damien took a few deep breaths, then let out a sigh so loud and deep he seemed to deflate as it left him.

Sebastien shot him a look, letting him know how overblown she thought he was acting. Perhaps he was still keyed up from all the adrenaline and didn't know how to let the energy out appropriately.

Damien tossed his head and turned away from Sebastien with a vehement snort, stomping around to turn off some of the lights in the room.

Nat lifted the bottle to her mouth again, trying to sneak another swallow, but Ana gave her a gimlet stare, and the girl put the bottle back with a cute blush.

Damien took Nat into the attached washroom so that she could see herself and the effects of the alchemical draught, only to discover that there was no mirror affixed to the wall as he had expected.

The other suite's bathroom was also without mirror.

Damien huffed. "This is outrageous! Paying for a room with no mirror? I'm going to go down to the desk and complain."

Nat pouted as Damien left, but was quickly enchanted by the draught's effects, even without a mirror to watch herself in. She blended into the shadows like an incompetent chameleon. Finding this absolutely fascinating, she ran around the room to different semi-shadowed spots to observe the effect, sporadically letting out a maniacal giggle.

When Sebastien was done administering aid to Ana's face, Nat's concealment was beginning to wear off, and Damien had not yet returned.

Nat pouted at Ana and Sebastien until Ana allowed her to take a second swig, but Sebastien had an idea.

"Wait," she said, taking out a stick of soft chalk and moving over to the far wall. She took a minute to draw out a spell array with a huge central Circle, setting her beast core on the floor within the range of the only component Circle.

Nat took an even bigger swallow than before, emptying the bottle before Ana could stop her. "What spell are you going to cast?"

In lieu of answering, Sebastien bore down with her Will. When a surface was too dense for light to propagate within, instead of refracting, it reflected. Glass, water, and other semi-transparent substances only reflected a small percentage of the overall light that hit them, but because they could have such smooth surfaces, it allowed that mirror-like reflection. For a true mirror, one needed a smooth substance that reflected more light. Or, in this case, they needed to catch all light that hit a certain arbitrary plane and bounce it back.

Just a millimeter away from the wall, a wavering reflection appeared, and then solidified and settled, as perfect as the most expensive true mirror, except around the circular edge, which wavered, mirage-like.

Nat gasped in delight. The mirror was larger than any Sebastien had ever seen, and more than adequate to capture Nat's antics as the girl stalked around the room with delight, pretending to be a spy, or maybe an assassin.

Ana watched with an indulgent, slightly crooked smile that seemed more real, somehow, than her normal sweet expressions.

Damien returned just as the effects were wearing off for the second time. "Some thaumaturge cast a glass-breaking spell on the whole building after being offended by one of the employees. There aren't any mirrors to be had, and there won't be until—" He stared at the wall for a moment, his eyes then flicking to Nat before finally settling on Sebastien. "Oh. Brilliant."

"Is there any more?" Nat asked, staring down at her arms, which were no longer blending into the shadows in the corner.

"You drank the last of it?" Damien asked with dismay. "I barely got to watch."

Nat shifted awkwardly. "Um, sorry? Maybe Sebastien has other interesting potions?"

While that was technically true, Sebastien did not want to waste her emergency supplies on entertainment, and so quickly thought up a distraction.

She let the mirror spell drop, stepped forward to add some instructions to the spell array, and then brought the mirror up again. This time, though, she concentrated not only on reflecting the light, but adding extra brightness in a particular shape.

She had to step back a few more steps to get a better idea of what the others were seeing, trying to make the glowing shape of wings that she had attached to Nat's image in the mirror seem realistically placed. It was difficult at first, but she quickly settled her grasp on the idea, a kind of opposite to how she used to do shadow-puppet plays on the wall with her shadow-familiar spell.

Sebastien found she had to anchor the wings to the light bouncing off Nat so that they appeared in the right place no matter where in the room they were viewed from. Adding a glow to the reflection of the girl herself helped them to seem less unnatural. Sebastien didn't quite manage to make the wings look solid or three-dimensional, but Nat was not a particularly discerning audience.

"Oh, I look like an angel!" She tried to pet her wings, watching as her hands passed through them in the reflection, and then turning to peer behind herself as if suspicious that she might, indeed, have grown another pair of appendages.

Ana held a hand to her mouth to hold in her delighted laughter. "Oh, Damien, are there any more storage cartridges for the camera obscura? I must capture this moment."

"Will it work on this?"

"If we can see it, the artifact can," Ana explained. "It works on a similar principle to the retina, but instead of sending signals to the brain, the light affects the photo disk, changing its shade according to the level of energy in the capture light. It creates a black-and-white version that has exactly the opposite values of darkness and light from reality, which allows the *correct-*value image to be transferred to photo paper with the help of some alchemical solutions. I think there is a huge potential market for the device. I even invested some of my personal funds in a local camera shop."

Damien hadn't stopped to listen to the entire explanation, too busy getting the artifact out of its case, popping in a new cartridge, and setting it up on its tripod stand.

Nat turned to pose prettily, but Sebastien dropped the mirror spell before Damien could capture anything.

Everyone turned to Sebastien with varying expressions of surprise and irritation. She held up a hand to forestall their arguments. "It will be better to take a photo of a direct illusion, rather than a reflection. It would be rather gauche, to have the artifact and Damien both in the photograph as well, would it not?"

This was a mistake, as Sebastien quickly learned. It seemed fine, at first, as Nat posed artistically, seated on a cushion in the middle of the floor with bright wings stretching out to either side. Sebastien made them as realistic as possible with the full force of her concentration and a white feather added as a spell component to copy details from. It was good practice, and everyone seemed to enjoy it.

But then Damien insisted that Sebastien create varying illusions for him and Nat to pose with, nitpicking every detail while Ana adjusted the artifact's location to get the perfect angle. He grew more demanding with each successful idea, even going so far as to force Sebastien to add false backgrounds.

First, he wanted a tiny dragon perched on his shoulder breathing fire. Then, Nat riding a unicorn, in a meadow. Then himself standing dramatically on the top edge of a volcano, with Nat as his small, half-bear companion, complete with round ears, fangs, and paw pads.

Sebastien pushed through the best she could, though with more things to focus on, the details began to suffer. The whole thing was only tenable because the camera would blur out some of the details that weren't precisely in focus. She could never have done it with a three-dimensional or moving illusion.

Unlike Sebastien's practice in class, these illusions did not suffer from seeming thin and ephemeral. Instead, they were solid, but let off a telltale glow that gave away their deceit. She deduced that it had something to do with using a beast core as a power source, thus having more power at her disposal. It was surprisingly hard to tamp down on the excess glow without making the illusion transparent.

When Damien dictated an elaborate crime scene, complete with a fake corpse and Aberford Thorndyke standing beside Damien as they both contemplated the mysterious murder, Sebastien reached the end of her patience, a headache beginning to pound in her right temple. "I am not adjusting Aberford Thorndyke's cheekbones or nose any more, Damien. He is a fictional character and he looks fine. Capture the image or walk away."

Damien then requested a shot of himself riding a sky kraken into battle, which Sebastien flat-out denied. There wasn't even enough space in the room for such a thing.

They had run out of empty storage cartridges at that point, anyway. Damien stored these new cartridges separately from the others, with Sebastien's warning that he would need to use two different photograph development shops as a precaution.

Ana clapped her hands to put an end to the play and ordered up food to the room, since they had missed dinner due to the whole fracas. The four of them ate while sitting on one of the beds, eschewing good manners for comfort and camaraderie. Nat had entirely forgotten her earlier tears and began to nod off halfway through her meal.

Ana tucked her into one of the beds in the adjacent room, and then told them what had happened that night in more detail, speaking in a low voice. By the time they all went to sleep, the signs that Malcolm Gervin's violence had left on Ana's face had faded but not disappeared.

In the morning, the swelling was gone, but some green and yellow bruising remained around her eye, a little too prominent to cover up completely with makeup.

"I want to take Ana to a healer," Damien said. "You can watch over Nat while we're gone, right, Sebastien?"

Sebastien looked at the small girl. "Are you okay with that?"

Nat's face had gone bright pink to match her dress, but she nodded emphatically.

And so, Nat and Sebastien ate breakfast down in the inn's common room below, where Nat showed off impeccable table manners and had several people cooing over the "brother and sister" pair, though Nat muttered under her breath, "He's not my brother. We're *friends*," the third time this happened.

After that, somewhat at a loss of what to do to keep a young girl entertained, and hoping not to get pulled back into creating illusions, Sebastien suggested they take a walk to Waterside Market, where there were usually some street shows on the weekend.

Nat slipped her hand into Sebastien's as they walked, looking away shyly.

Waterside Market was quite busy, but they easily found the street shows, with scores of people crowded around the most interesting. As they tried to get close enough to actually see one of the street performers, Nat huddled closer to Sebastien, probably unused to mingling with the crowd like this.

Just as Sebastien was about to suggest they try somewhere else, an oblivious man knocked into Natalia and pushed her down.

Sebastien shoved her shoulder into the man, pushing him back to create space for the small girl to rise to her feet. She ignored the man's curses as she pulled Nat back out of the crowd, where she kneeled down to examine the young girl's knee on the side of the road. When Nat fell, she had landed on a raised cobblestone, ripping a small hole in her dress and scraping the skin raw. "Good thing I keep healing supplies on hand, huh?" Sebastien asked, smiling at Nat, who was doing her best to hold back tears. "This is going to burn a little. Take a deep breath, and then make a hissing sound when the pain hits."

Nat hissed loudly as Sebastien rubbed a drop of wound cleanser over her bloodied knee, continuing until she ran out of air.

Sebastien followed that up with a smear of skin-knitting salve, which began to work right away. "Pain, pain, go away," she said, blowing gently on the girl's knee, something she vaguely remembered her own mother doing for her. "Good job. That wasn't so bad, was it?"

Nat didn't reply aloud, and when Sebastien looked up to check that she wasn't crying, she saw that the girl's face was as red as a cherry tomato. Nat quickly lowered the fabric of her dress back over her knees, clearing her throat. "It was bearable, I suppose."

"Do you want me to carry you on my shoulders? You'll be able to see over the crowd and won't have to worry about anyone knocking you over."

"On your shoulders?" Nat asked, eyeing them dubiously.

"I won't drop you, I promise."

Nat acquiesced, so Sebastien knelt by the sidewalk and allowed the smaller girl to climb aboard. She straightened slowly, keeping a firm grip on Nat's calves.

Nat let out a squeal. "Oh, I'm so high up! This is wonderful. Get closer, Sebastien."

They watched the show and then wandered around the market for a while longer like that, until Sebastien's back grew tired and they returned to the inn.

Ana and Damien were already there waiting for them. Ana's face was back to normal, with only an almost-invisible scar where her eyelid had split to prove what had happened. "How was your outing with Sebastien, Nat?" Ana asked.

"Oh, it was *wonderful*! We had breakfast together in the common room, and everyone kept commenting on how fine we looked together. And then we went to Waterside Market, where there are *sooo* many people just milling about, so close they actually touch each other when they all squeeze in together, and some commoner *accosted* me! But Sebastien defended me, and used some of his amazing alchemical concoctions to heal me right up." She lifted her dress delicately to show Ana her knee as proof, not pausing the tumbling stream of words. "And then I actually *rode upon Sebastien's shoulders*, but I wasn't embarrassed at all, it was actually wonderful. I could see everything, as tall as a giant, and I was totally safe." She patted Ana's hand reassuringly. "Don't worry, my reputation wasn't tarnished. It was only commoners around to see me, anyway. And I saw a street performer..."

Sebastien tuned the girl out as her rambling continued, musing that, while Nat was much shyer than Theo to start out, her excited dramatics once she felt comfortable were much the same.

Damien sidled over to Sebastien and murmured, "I think you have an admirer."

"I'm not the best role model for a child, so I hope she doesn't pick up my bad decision-making. But maybe it's already too late? We've already drawn her into a coup at the age of eleven."

"That's not the kind of admirer I—" Damien cut off with a sigh. "Never mind."

2 9

WAVE-PARTICLE DUALITY

Sebastien
Month 2, Day 21, Sunday 5:00 p.m.

It took some time for the trio to return to the University, as Nat had been afraid to return home, and Ana took some time getting her settled.

To Sebastien's surprise, they found Alec sitting on a bench not far from the transport tubes, his head hanging while one knee bounced rapidly. As they drew close, he looked up, his face slackening with relief. He hopped up and hurried over, his eyes searching Ana's face as he fumbled in his school satchel. He paused in front of them, only then seeming to realize Ana was not alone. "They know?" he asked.

She nodded silently.

He pulled out an awkward handful of small, half-full jars. "I was worried about you. I can't tell if you've already seen a healer or if that's just a really good glamour, but I wanted to give you some of the stuff I keep on hand." He thrust the jars at her, which she had to cradle awkwardly in her arms when they were too much to hold in her smaller hands. "I took off the labels, sorry about that. This one helps a lot with bone fractures, but you'll want to use it first because it irritates the skin and it'll show if you use it last. This one is good for healing cuts without leaving any scars. Just leave it on until there's no trace. This one is good for the really deep bruises, and this one for the surface level bruises, to remove the traces of blood from underneath the skin and heal up your burst capillaries. Oh, and this one is a burn salve. I don't think you need that one so I'll just take it back."

'He's used those himself. Often.' The words resounded hollowly in Sebastien's head.

Ana remained silent for a few moments, staring down at the jars. "Thank you. I did already get healed, but I appreciate it." She put them in her own bag as Alec shuffled awkwardly.

"How bad was it? I can't believe you finally snapped. I almost had a heart attack when you insulted Father and threw cranberry sauce on him, Ana. You're so slender and—I mean—your bones must be delicate. I had this horrible thought that your eye socket would shatter and your eyeball would fall out, just hanging by a string. I saw that once, on one of Father's hunting dogs. He had to put it down."

Ana reached out and grabbed Alec's hand where it had been fiddling with the strap of his satchel. She held it between both of her own. "Thank you."

Alec settled, closing his eyes as he took a single deep breath. "It's best not to provoke him, Ana."

"It's too late to stop now," she murmured. "Someone needs to stand up to him for once."

Damien moved forward, clapping a hand on Alec's shoulder. "You should stop visiting home for the next little while, Alec. He's probably going to get worse."

Alec's shoulders started to hunch for just a moment before he straightened them again. "He wouldn't like that. He likes me to make a report every other weekend, at the very least. Like I said, it's best not to provoke him. He can hold a grudge."

"So cut ties entirely," Sebastien said, the words spilling out without her conscious control.

Alec's caterpillar eyebrows drew together. "But that's impossible. He's my father."

"That means nothing." She swallowed hard. "You have options. Listen to me. You don't have to go see him. You don't have to follow his orders. If he comes after you, you have friends. You never have to be alone with him again. If you're willing to go scorched-earth, threaten to give an expose on his treatment to one of the local newspapers. Or one of his rivals. Not a bluff. A threat."

"But..." Alec shook his head.

"What do you really have to lose? Does he provide any benefits that you can't afford to be without or find elsewhere? You are not obligated to obey him or to love—"

Sebastien cut herself off, looking away as she cleared the lump in her throat. She had kept going back to Ennis. She'd felt like she should, or that she had to, but why?

Damien was nodding along. "Sebastien's right. You're his only legitimate child. For various reasons, he's unlikely to disinherit you."

Alec pulled his hand back from Ana's. "He might. Just to spite me. If he withdrew his donations, I could lose my place at the University," he admitted, looking at the ground.

Sebastien shrugged. "Even if he did, as long as you place high enough by the end of term, you won't be expelled. And after that, you don't *need* him to pay your way. There are other options."

He scowled at her. "I'm not interested in leeching off my friends. I don't need charity."

"You wouldn't need to. You can get legitimate loans from quite a few different places and pay your own way."

"And then what? Get a job working for one of the other Crown Families?" he scoffed. "Try and run a shop or something?"

"Perhaps. You have time. There is no reason you have to remain incompetent."

Alec opened his mouth as if to retort angrily, but then slowly closed it again. "Is that what you did? Cut ties with your family?"

Sebastien's lips tightened. "Does it matter?"

"It matters if you're giving me advice you have no idea about."

"I have no more family," she said, not exactly answering the question. "And no need of them. You don't, either."

Damien stepped forward, pulling on Alec's shoulder to turn him around and walk onwards. "*All* of us can relate, I think."

Ana reached out to give Sebastien's hand a squeeze, and she looked over at the young woman in surprise.

Ana smiled softly, crookedly. "That was nice of you," she murmured as the other two walked ahead.

"I literally did almost nothing, except insult him."

"I think he needed that. I wasn't being harsh enough. He doesn't like to feel weak. Coming from you, it seemed more legitimate. A challenge rather than a defeat."

Sebastien raised one dubious eyebrow. "Are you sure?"

Ana shrugged, smiling mysteriously. "We'll see." She wrapped her arm through Sebastien's and they followed Damien and Alec.

After a lingering silence, Alec said, "I could join the army, maybe. They don't require you to be a really great thaumaturge, as long as you're competent. I'm not good enough for them to sponsor me, but they would probably pay enough to get by once I got my certification. And it's respectable enough, serving the country." He sounded doubtful, but his posture straightened.

The next few days passed uneventfully, and by Wednesday, Sebastien felt she was really beginning to get a grasp on working with light. She had been practicing with Professor Lacer's exercises, both creating illusions as well as the auxiliary exercise that required her to change the color, brightness, and shape of a candle flame. She had even been playing with a lens-based fire starter and a couple of spells she had learned as a child, such as the glow and light-show spells.

She'd also been secretly practicing with her shadow-familiar, repeated castings easing the lingering trauma and trepidation she had felt toward it since the incident with Newton. She played around with shadow-puppet shows and made random objects sparkle with an intensity that she hadn't shown since she was a child with the untiring obsession of learning a new trick.

Some of Sebastien's deeply depleted well of internal energy was returning, though she had good days and bad days, and had already consumed half of the little vial of beamshell tincture. Soon, she hoped, she wouldn't need it any longer.

As Ana and Damien joined her outside the Natural Science classroom, Sebastien lifted an inquiring eyebrow.

Ana looked around the mostly empty hallway, then murmured, "Nat wrote that everything is fine. Father has been grumpy, but mostly everyone is just leaving her alone. Uncle Malcolm visited him this morning and they seem to have gotten over their anger at each other. If Malcolm suspects anything, he's not making it obvious."

Ana had been called home to the Gervin manor for a visit on Monday evening, reamed out by her father, and stripped of her allowance and further visitation rights with her little sister for the remainder of the semester. Luckily, Lord Gervin didn't know about the sympathetically connected journals the two girls shared, and he didn't respect Ana enough to be truly wary of her.

"When can we move forward with the second phase of the plan?" Damien asked.

"I'm still compiling the blackmail note. Are you finished with the sketch of the ring, Sebastien?"

"I am, but I think we should give it some time before contacting Malcolm. Better to let the incident on Saturday evening fade from his memory a little. It will make him less likely to draw connections. Perhaps you can send the first contact next week. That would also give you a chance to find some corroborating evidence for the other crimes, like embezzlement, before he's wary enough to try and clean up any crumbs that might still be lying around." What Sebastien didn't say was that she wanted to postpone the next phase of Operation Defenestration because Oliver had set up a meeting of sorts between the Raven Queen and the University that Friday, and she didn't want to try and split her attention between the two high-stress undertakings.

She was trying not to be too hopeful about the outcome of their meeting, but she couldn't help the anticipation building in her gut. She didn't know what they might be able to offer her, but they were powerful and had political influence. And if they could be reasoned with, perhaps the coppers could be reasoned with, too. *'Would the High Crown be willing to meet with the Raven Queen? He has the power to give me a blanket pardon. Working with the coppers might anger the University, since they want the book, but it could be more beneficial for me.'* She resolved to keep her eyes and her mind open. Perhaps they could even work out some kind of deal like she had with Ana, where Sebastien got what she needed not directly through the University, but tangentially, cooperation with them giving her another bargaining piece.

The bell to mark the start of class interrupted Sebastien's thoughts, and the trio hurried in to take a seat.

Professor Gnorrish's assistant was handing out components to every desk, mainly consisting of a ring on a stand, a few petri dishes, and a small, clear glass bead. "Today marks the end of our study of light," Gnorrish announced. "You will be using what you have grasped to create your own lens spell, which you will use to observe and sketch a likeness of some cells and microorganisms. I have provided various slides of plant and animal cells, as well as some relatively harmless bacteria. To pass this segment, you must be able to refract light well enough to observe the animal cells, but I have contribution points for anyone who is also able to clearly observe the bacteria, which will require much finer control. I expect developing and refining this spell will take many of you some time, so you had best get started. Also, as a reminder, spells to view microscopic organisms are not new magic, but if any of you develop something particularly innovative and feel that the magic is struggling against you, please err on the side of caution and call me over to review your attempt rather than risking your safety."

The students immediately got to work, drawing out their spell arrays on their desks, which had a perfect Circle already carved into the surfaces.

Sebastien chose the triangle as her base symbol, because light was a form of energy without mass, and she would be using only transmutation to achieve the effect. She brought her Will to bear, lightly and idly pressing it into the chalk lines as she mused over the best way to get the desired results.

She took longer than many of the other students to complete the spell array, pausing to stare at it silently multiple times as she considered the best placement for glyphs and the best way to clearly explain what she wanted to happen. When it was complete, she moved one of the bacteria petri dishes to the center, below the metal ring she would be using as a viewing range, but she still didn't start casting.

Instead, she mentally reviewed everything she knew about light that could be useful for this particular application, trying to grasp it all at once like her mind was a fist stuffed full of wriggling worms. A wave of dizziness overtook her, sending her swaying in her seat. Concentration broken, she shook her head and took a few deep breaths, squinting against her sudden headache. It was as if the weight of the knowledge had knocked her off balance. Perhaps she was just hungry. She'd had little appetite, and might not have eaten enough at breakfast. She rubbed on some minty headache-relieving salve and tried again. She remembered how they had played with light in the crystal tunnel illusion chamber, how it had reacted to their meddling. She imagined her eye and mentally tracked the path of how the human body processed visual input. When she felt that she had meticulously examined all of her relevant knowledge, she finally began to cast.

Her spell created an additional light source beneath the petri dish and used multiple concurrent lenses. The one nearest her, hanging within the metal ring, magnified things a little, perhaps thirty times. But below that she had a second lens effect that was smaller and stronger, and below that, another that hung just above the petri dish, even stronger.

It was a strain to hold all three lenses at once as part of a single spell, but not beyond her capabilities.

At first, the spell showed her only a vague blur when she looked into the ocular lens, but she was able to calibrate the output with a few adjustments of her Will. Soon enough, she was able to focus on the strange little organisms that she had seen before only in drawings. Even her best efforts left things a little blurry and hazy, as it seemed like the light was shining right *through* the bacteria, their edges and details undefined. Even the slightest jostle of the table or the petri dish sent the field of view wildly off course, and holding the spell was quickly worsening her headache. She had been feeling a little off-kilter lately. *'Has something changed? I'm tired, but I'm always tired.'*

She could spare little attention from the casting, though, and set her thoughts aside to sketch out what she saw as quickly as possible, trying to get through the most difficult part of the assignment before moving on to the cell slides, but before she could do so, a looming presence beside her table, wafting off heat, made her look up from the spell.

"May I?" Professor Gnorrish asked, gesturing to the ocular lens.

Holding the magic in a vice grip, Sebastien nodded, stepping back.

Gnorrish made some interested, excited humming noises as he looked through the lens, then to the sketches she had made, and finally examined her spell array in greater detail. Finally, he straightened, and Sebastien released the magic with a small wince of mental fatigue.

"Fantastic!" he said, his voice less booming than normal in consideration of the other students who were busy casting and who might make a mistake if they were suddenly startled. "You have a strong understanding, which has led to strong spellcasting, and Will that shows both force, stability, and clarity.

This is one of the best attempts of this exercise by a first term student that I have seen in the last ten years. Come by my desk at the end of class to pick up your contribution points." Gnorrish spun around and lumbered off on a slow round through the classroom, occasionally stopping to give praise or helpful tips to other students.

By the time Gnorrish called a halt to the exercise, less than fifteen minutes remained to the class period, but he seemed more enthusiastic than ever. "While this has been a quick review of the topic, we've barely scratched the surface of understanding what light is, how it affects the world around us, and what we can learn from it. With light, as in all aspects of natural science, everything goes deeper. I don't fully understand light, and I suspect even the researchers focused on the study of electromagnetic radiation don't, either. Let's take these last few minutes of class to discuss some topics on the cutting edge of natural science, currently being unraveled by the best and brightest of us. A group of my former students have recently submitted the results of their experiments for peer review. It seems they have disproved our current model of the atom, and they have reason to believe that the negatively charged electrons orbit a positively charged, much larger nucleus. Like moons orbiting a planet, rather than floating through a 'soup.' The new model shows an 'electron cloud' with specific orbit rings at different distances, upon which the electrons can step up or down as they gain or lose extremely specific amounts of energy."

He lowered his head and took a deep breath. "I have reviewed their findings myself, and I believe them to be valid. Some may argue that because we have been wrong in the past, and have accordingly updated our models—or 'changed our minds'—that our theories cannot be trusted. But I say, that is the *point* of our endeavor! Because we actively work to disprove our theories rather than defend them, our knowledge changes, always moving closer to the truth. We are not dogmatic. Our god is not being right. It is acknowledging how little we know, and freely admitting that there are a thousand—a million —more steps upon the path. We have lost nothing to acknowledge we were wrong about how atoms were built. We *succeed* every time we update our beliefs. That is why natural science is so special, and why it will eventually take us beyond even the farthest horizon we can now imagine."

Sebastien hurriedly took out her new binder of notes and a fountain pen. More difficult topics that showed deeper understanding were the things Gnorrish loved to use for extra credit questions on his weekly tests.

"Let us combine this with another recent discovery. A 'quantum' is the term coined for the smallest measurement of energy. An indivisible, single tiny packet.'

Sebastien frowned, scribbling quickly to try and get the new definitions down.

"This is important because, by understanding that energy can only be absorbed or released in these tiny, differential, discrete packets, we can account for certain objects changing color when heated, as the electrons within their atoms gain or lose discrete amounts of energy in the form of light. Just as a blacksmith can judge the temperature of metal by the color of its glow, so can we judge the heat of a star."

Sebastien knew what electrons were. Their existence had been confirmed and defined by one of Gnorrish's contemporaries only a few years ago. But she didn't know anything about electrons' ability to absorb or lose energy within that structure.

For once, Gnorrish wasn't waving his hands around or pacing, his voice loud but measured as he spoke from the front of the classroom. "All matter can absorb electromagnetic radiation, and all matter at a temperature above absolute zero will emit electromagnetic radiation, even if it's too little for your eyes to pick up. With a light-sensing artifact thousands of times more sensitive than the human eye, we would be able to distinguish not only temperature, but the exact makeup of other celestial objects. The amount of energy given off by a hydrogen atom, when its electrons lose a very specific amount of discrete energy packets, is *different* than the amount of energy given off by a helium or calcium atom. These differences in energy correspond to minute differences in the color of light that escapes as they lose energy. We will soon be able to look at Ares, Nibiru, passing asteroids, and even planets from the next solar system, many light-years away, and calculate what they are made of."

Sebastien's hand began to cramp as she wrote even faster. Gnorrish was blowing past words and ideas that she'd never encountered before. '*What is this about electrons emitting light?*' She needed to stop and think about it to let her mind wrap around the ideas, but Gnorrish wasn't pausing.

He turned back to the blackboard, where he used a quick spell array to create an illusion of a small sphere of white light floating within darkness. "I believe light can tell us more about the universe we live in than even that."

When he launched into an explanation of how light sometimes acted as a wave, and sometimes like a particle, and the different experiments that gave confusing results, Sebastien gave up taking notes, staring at Professor Gnorrish with dismay as she flexed her aching fingers.

His eyes roved over the students slowly. "As one researcher said, 'It seems as though we must use sometimes the one theory and sometimes the other, while at times we may use either. We are faced with a new kind of difficulty. We have two contradictory pictures of reality; separately neither of them fully explains the phenomena of light, but together they do.'" He paused dramatically. "Light is like *nothing else* that we are accustomed to dealing with. If we could understand this seeming duality, it might be the key to unraveling more of the inner workings of the universe."

He pointed to the illusion of a sphere of light floating in darkness. "Perhaps, one or more layers of understanding deeper, we could begin to understand the fundamental principles of existence, and even how magic itself works."

Sebastien's eyes widened. *'Is it really that significant?'*

Professor Gnorrish continued trying to explain "wave-particle duality," "quantums," and how it all interacted with electrons and stuff, but Sebastien was rather…lost.

She looked around. Some of the other students were also showing expressions of confusion, a few were staring blankly, having obviously given up, but some were diligently taking notes without concern. *'I'm lacking some sort of fundamental understanding. I'm not grasping these definitions, the underlying mechanics and properties of discrete quanta, or what electrons really are, or maybe even what radiation really is. Without that, I certainly can't understand how these things fit together into a greater explanation of the mechanics of the universe. I know keywords and I've memorized where to insert those keywords into patterns and sentences, like "light is neither a particle nor a wave, but some combination of both," but I actually don't understand what that means.'*

She was surprised by the sudden surge of keening distress that rose up in her chest like sour wine, and she tried to tamp it down. *'I don't understand,'* she admitted to herself. She was normally quite confident in her own intelligence, but she felt so out of her depth she might as well have been a floundering child who had never before even seen the ocean.

'Are some of my classmates actually understanding this? Perhaps they have a much better educational background than me.'

At the desk to her right, Damien was frowning, and a quick peek at his notes showed that he'd written several question marks in the margins. Surely, Damien Westbay, second in line to become the Family head, would have had the best possible education.

'Or perhaps those who seem unconcerned have fallen into the trap of memorizing keywords and answer-patterns, and don't realize that they, too, don't understand.'

But Ana was one of those taking nonchalant notes, her chin resting on her hand and her elbow on her desk as she listened to Gnorrish.

When the bell clanged to signify the end of class, Sebastien packed her things in a daze. "Did you understand what Professor Gnorrish was talking about, at the end? About the waves and particles and quantum?"

Ana shrugged. "I understood well enough."

Damien and Sebastien shared a look of dismay.

"Not in the way that Gnorrish talks about understanding!" Ana added quickly. "I don't grasp it so completely I could recreate it from nothing, but is that really necessary? He said it was on the cutting edge of natural science, and, what, a primordial particle?"

"Elementary particle," Sebastien corrected automatically.

Ana rolled her eyes, ignoring Sebastien's interjection. "If I actually understood that, I'd be an Archmage already. I have no ambition to start casting spells that unravel the universe or whatever. Grasping the general concept is enough for me."

Damien nodded, his shoulders falling. "I suppose we are only first term students."

Sebastien couldn't relate to Ana's sentiment at all. The idea that someone could know something was wrong, *deficient*, in their understanding, and know that there was a way to at least somewhat fix that deficiency, but deliberately decide not to... It was alien to her. Especially—specifically—when that knowledge would affect her facility with casting an entire branch of spells.

As the other students filtered out, Sebastien stayed behind to pick up her contribution points. Ten of them, which was a rather large amount for someone like Gnorrish, who often gave out fractions of points so as to be able to give them more often. "Thank you. Are there any references that could explain what light is and how it works on a fundamental level more...simply?" she asked. "Maybe with illustrations to help me imagine how it works? I couldn't really grasp much from the last bit of class, and I feel like I'm missing something foundational."

Gnorrish laughed. "I commend your curiosity, Mr. Siverling. The true secrets of light are a bit beyond the purview of this class. If you wish deeper understanding, self-study is indeed your best option." He gave her a small list of books, as well as a larger list of specific research articles that would help with the more recent theoretical advancements. "The articles can be quite dry and...impenetrable. And generally, there are no illustrations, except for a few graphs and tables, perhaps. I hope you don't get too discouraged, nevertheless. Even I wouldn't confidently state that I fully understand how light works, and I've been at this for far longer than you. Light is only energy, after all, and energy is one of, if not *the* elementary building block of the universe."

Thanking him again, Sebastien took Professor Gnorrish's list to the library. The articles were indeed "impenetrable," written using long, convoluted sentences filled with jargon. She couldn't even check them out because many did not have duplicate copies yet, and thus the research and knowledge contained in them was rather valuable.

'Perhaps I won't come to understand the mechanics underpinning the universe, but this should at least help me make my end of term exhibition more likely to impress...and maybe give me the edge I need to beat Nunchkin in Practical Casting.'

30

A GILDED CAGE

Siobhan
Month 2, Day 26, Friday 9:00 p.m.

Wearing all the accoutrements and the blue-black iridescent hair of the Raven Queen, Siobhan rode in a nondescript carriage through the night streets of Gilbratha, accompanied by Oliver and a couple of the Verdant Stag's most trusted enforcers. They were on their way to a meeting with a handful of University representatives.

"We gave them the location at the last minute," Oliver assured her, perhaps picking up on the anxiety that she had tried to keep hidden. Or perhaps he just knew her well enough by now to guess at it. "So they won't have had a chance to lay any traps, and we already know they won't be calling in the coppers. With the additional layer of distance that Liza agreed to help with, you'll be even more secure. We've scouted out both locations ahead of time, and you have three different escape routes and plenty of backup if necessary."

 "I know," she assured him. She wouldn't even be in the same room, or the same city block, as the University representatives. She was more anxious about the possibility that, just maybe, this meeting could lead to a solution to her status as a wanted criminal, and not just be a way for her to scam something valuable out of Munchworth's faction.

The carriage, which had taken a circuitous route to avoid any tails, soon stopped in front of a high-class restaurant with no direct connection to the

Verdant Stag, which sported an open floor plan and stairs on either side that led up to a loft area.

Liza was waiting on the ground floor. She had already cleared an area of tables and set up the Lino-Wharton messenger spell array on the floor. She was halfway through casting already, and waved Siobhan forward to complete the latter half of the binding.

She handed Siobhan a pouch of dead bird pieces, which Siobhan hung around her neck, then attached a string around Siobhan's arm. She noted that it was much longer than the ones Liza had used when Siobhan was paying her, which meant she would have control of the raven over a greater distance. This was all on Oliver's bill and would be taken out of his cut of whatever tribute the University representatives brought, so she didn't care that it must have cost extra.

"Due to all of your shenanigans, I've had to order a whole new batch of raven chicks. I can't keep up with the demand, and even if buying random ones from live component shops can make up the numbers, it's best if they're from the same brood for this kind of thing. Do you know how much hassle it is to raise a batch of raven chicks?" Liza grumbled. "I need an assistant, but of course it's impossible to find someone who is competent, trustworthy enough to allow into my home, and also palatable enough to spend time with. Plus, they should be attractive. A nice, muscular man with good teeth to do my bidding around the house, that's what I need…"

Siobhan had been sympathetic at first, but as Liza's muttering went on, she let out a snort.

The woman's glare snapped over to Siobhan. "You think I'm joking? You try running a black-market business for damn fool clients, all by yourself, and see if you don't long for a competent helper."

"But does he need to be an attractive, muscular man with good teeth?"

"As a grown woman, having visually pleasant surroundings is an important factor in improving my workplace environment, and accordingly, improving my mood." Liza cast the last step of the spell, and as the string burned up, fast enough to singe but not injure her, the connection was formed. Liza handed Siobhan the raven and shooed her away.

Siobhan realized that their little conversation had significantly calmed her anxiety and wondered if, perhaps, Liza had done it on purpose. She carried the raven up to the loft, where an open window was waiting for her. Taking a moment to review the directions from this building to the meeting point, she tossed the raven out of the window, letting its flight instincts take over as she guided it using the mental tether between them.

The raven arrived in only a few minutes, flying into a warehouse, that was in no way associated with the Verdant Stag, through an open window. How convenient it was to have wings.

The building was lit with a few lanterns set about. In the middle of the room, placed upon a crate for height, rested a large bird cage decorated with metal filigree. With her human eyes Siobhan guided the raven down to it, pulling the door closed with the raven's beak. The lock latched automatically and she swore the raven could feel the magic wash over its feathers in an uncomfortable prickle.

The room's single occupant, a Verdant Stag enforcer, nearly jumped out of his skin at the noise, staring wide-eyed and breathless for several long seconds before bowing deeply.

She had the raven bow to him in return, then asked, "Are they on their way?" with the squawky bird's voice.

The enforcer gulped, looking as if he wanted to be anywhere else. "Yes, my lady. They should arrive in a few minutes at most. Can I... Do you need anything in the meantime?"

She squawked out a laugh. "Are you offering me refreshments?"

"Umm..."

She felt a little bad about the way his wide eyes darted about frantically. "Do not worry, I was only humoring myself. I need nothing."

It didn't take long for the University cohort to arrive, three men and two women led by yet another Verdant Stag enforcer.

Siobhan recognized Grandmaster Kiernan immediately. Somehow, she wasn't surprised by his involvement. There were a couple other professors she recognized as well, also from the History department. Munchworth wasn't there. *'Perhaps they are displeased with his performance, or maybe he just doesn't rank high enough to be involved in a meeting like this.'* She did her best to memorize the remaining faces.

Kiernan looked around the warehouse, then narrowed in on the raven with a piercing stare. "Where is she?" he asked, eyeing the raven with some suspicion.

"I am here," she said through the bird. In her real body, she opened her eyes and looked around with paranoia, despite knowing how unlikely it was that she could be discovered there.

"We were under the impression that you would meet with us in person," Kiernan snapped. "I like to look my conversation partner in the eye."

"And I like to maintain a healthy distance from people who wish me ill," she replied, letting the raven nonchalantly groom a couple of feathers on its shoulder with its beak. "I agreed to this meeting when your request was most humbly brought to me by Lord Stag, but even he cannot convince me to do anything I do not wish to." At Oliver's request, Siobhan was trying to reinforce their idea that she and the Verdant Stag were separate, and that no amount of pressure on them would equate to pressure on her.

After a long moment, during which she was pretty sure she heard him grinding his teeth, he said, "I am Grandmaster Kiernan."

"I believe there is no need to introduce myself in return. What tribute have you brought me?" If it was something worthless, she might just fly away and make them try again with something better. She couldn't let them think that she could be bullied or pushed around.

Kiernan stepped aside, and the woman behind him brought forward the wooden box she was carrying. The woman knelt, then pulled a somewhat smaller case out of the box, which she opened to reveal a bejeweled gold bowl engraved with intricate designs, and a lid covered in holes. "This censer was used by shaman-king Deon, who ruled in Qusnia, which is a country to the southeast that has long been lost to the sands of time. It was gifted to him by his wife upon their first meeting, and is valued at one thousand to fifteen hundred gold. All authentication documents are included."

That was much more expensive than Siobhan had expected, and it made the danger of this meeting worth it for the tribute alone. But it was also quite inconvenient, since it wasn't the kind of thing one could sell easily on the open market. They would have to find a wealthy collector, or perhaps give it to an auction house on consignment. *'I'm sure they did that on purpose, just to be a nuisance.'*

"It is acceptable," she said after a long moment of consideration. She turned to the enforcer beside her, giving him a nod.

The man picked up the case, put it back in the box, and then took it to the front door of the warehouse, where a delivery runner was just arriving. The runner didn't work for the Verdant Stag and had no idea what was going on, other than the need for a standard vow of discretion. He took the box, bowed quickly to the enforcer, and ran away with it. He would take it to another secure location, where Oliver's people would examine the tribute for tricks, repackage it to avoid any sabotage or tracking spells, and from there store it somewhere safe.

The University cohort watched the runner disappear with consternation. There were a few long moments of awkward silence as no one spoke. A couple of Kiernan's companions shuffled uneasily, looking between her and the shadows at the edges of the warehouse.

When the silence continued past the point of awkwardness, Siobhan wondered. *'Is this a negotiation tactic? Is Kiernan trying to make me uneasy and force me to speak first?'* If so, she was displeased to admit that it was working. The Lino-Wharton raven messenger spell would only last so long. If the meeting dragged out too long, the raven might just suddenly die in the middle of their conversation, and that wasn't the message of confidence and authority she wanted to portray at all. So she guided the raven to speak. "Do not waste my time. You have come to ask a boon of me, so do so."

Kiernan cleared his throat. "The book. Do you still have it?"

Siobhan paused, then asked carefully, "Myrddin's book?"

Kiernan nodded, confirming her suspicions. In her real body, Siobhan turned from the window, pacing back and forth for a few steps as the reality of her situation settled in her mind. She turned her attention back to the ephemeral tether controlling the raven. A little too much time had passed, and everyone was staring at the creature with expressions that ranged from fear to suspicion.

"I do have it."

Almost as one, the entire University group relaxed, failing to suppress gusting sighs and letting their relief show plain on their faces. Kiernan smiled, but his expression quickly grew cautious again. "Have you decrypted it?"

Siobhan considered lying, but that was too dangerous. After all, the University had everything else from Myrddin's hermitage—enough to recognize if she had no idea what she was talking about. "I have not." She hesitated, but added, "My purpose for it was different. While I am sure whatever lies within is fascinating and of great historical significance, I have no immediate need for it."

"Then why did you steal it in the first place?" one of Kiernan's companions demanded.

Kiernan shot the man a glare, but still turned back to the raven in expectation of an answer.

"The theft was...incidental. It was never my goal, in truth. You could consider it a coincidence." She doubted even a skilled diviner would be able to discern whether a raven was lying without actively casting a divination spell on it, but she was trying to show sincerity. Lying about this would just make everything more complicated.

The man who had interrupted previously gave an angry huff. "You don't expect us to actually *believe* that?"

Siobhan wished the raven had eyebrows that she could raise individually. "I find it amusing that you believe your security so unbreakable, so *competent*, that there must be some grand conspiracy behind my acquisition of the book. I assure you, that is not the case. This line of conversation is becoming tedious. Let us get to the point. You would like the book returned."

"Yes," Kiernan said.

"I am amenable to that, but I will require something in exchange. Something that cannot so easily be bought with coin."

Kiernan frowned, tilting his head to the side. "The censer...was it not sufficient?"

The raven let out a sharp, squawking laugh that made the enforcer standing next to it jump. "That was a tribute, given for the honor of my presence alone. It was not *payment*."

Kiernan scowled, but said, "Fine. What is it that you wish?"

"I wish to stop being hunted for the theft. And for any other crimes I may or may not have committed in the meantime," she said simply. "I would like a legal pardon."

Everyone in the room stared at her as if she had just grown a second head, or as if she had suggested that she and Kiernan go into a back room and do something lewd. "A legal pardon," Kiernan repeated.

"I find it tedious to be so harassed. Having returned the book, and done no real harm to those who do not deserve it, it seems reasonable that I should be free of reprisal as well, does it not?" She was aware that wasn't really how the law worked at all, but she was also aware that the law was not enforced equally and impartially. "This is what I want. However, I have doubts about whether you can realistically promise me this. Do you have the authority, or the *influence*, to grant me a pardon? Or perhaps some other way to ensure I can walk the streets in peace? I am open to…*creative* solutions."

There was a long silence, and she had the raven open its beak again to say, "You are not the only ones who want this book. Perhaps someone else would even count it as a positive that I kept it out of your grip. Someone like the High—"

Siobhan reeled backward, cringing as she tried to protect her head with her arms. She stumbled into the railing at the edge of the loft, and if not for its protection, she might have fallen right off and dashed herself onto the floor below like a too-ripe peach fallen from the tree. She crouched down, and only when she felt large hands on her shoulders, gripping her roughly, did she realize she was keening aloud.

She quieted herself, taking quick, deep breaths, her eyes wide and staring out over her knees.

"What happened? What did they do? Siobhan, talk to me!" Oliver demanded, giving her a little shake as he examined her for damage.

She raised her gaze to his, noting the tight lines of strain around his eyes. "The raven died," she whispered hoarsely. Saying it aloud helped somehow. It was the raven that had died, not Siobhan. "The cage activated and killed the raven with a superheated fireball. Very…" She swallowed. This had been very different from times before, when she ended the spell on purpose. She had been fully immersed in its senses, and some of the raven's own emotions might have rippled back to her through their connection before it was imme- diately and forcibly severed. "It was very melodramatic." She rolled her shoul- ders back to release some tension, and straightened her clothes in a way she suddenly realized she'd picked up from Ana.

"They tried to bypass the wards, then?" Oliver asked.

"A free-cast divination spell, I'm guessing. It couldn't have been an artifact unless one slipped past the search. I think I felt my ward start to activate for a moment," she said, rising back to her feet with Oliver's steadying hand on her elbow. "I'm fine," she assured him. "But they were probably trying to find me."

He looked around suspiciously, already moving, his hand on her shoulder as he guided her down the stairs, like he was afraid she would trip and fall. "We're leaving. Mr. Huntley, any signs of hostile activity or observation?"

The enforcer shook his head. "Negative, Lord Stag. We are safe for extraction."

As they rode away in the carriage, on their way to another of Oliver's warehouses where she could change back into Sebastien, Siobhan tried not to let the disappointment settle in her bones. It wasn't so surprising that they would betray her, really. She hadn't been expecting it at that particular moment simply because she hadn't considered that one of them might be a free-caster, allowing them to move against her without any outward sign. She knew free-casters existed, obviously. She was trying to become one, after all. But they were rare. Rare enough that she'd made assumptions, at least subconsciously.

The warded cage had detected that something was trying to access the raven utilizing similar principles to what the blood-print vow used to protect the blood thumbprints. Such wards weren't infallible, but they could detect divination tendrils—or rays, or waves, whatever divination used to gather information—as well as sudden transfers of various types of energy. False positives were possible, of course, but Siobhan was certain this hadn't been a false positive. They had been trying to find her. That was why Kiernan was upset that she hadn't met with them in person. "They never planned to negotiate with me in good faith," she said dully.

Oliver grimaced. "Maybe. Or maybe one of them just got a little too bold. In any case, you won't be taking such a risk again." His hand was still on her elbow, and he took his gaze away from the carriage window to look her over again for damage. "I'm sorry. I never should have agreed to set up a meeting with the Raven Queen."

She let out a low sigh. "It's alright. It's not like we're any worse off than we were beforehand. If their words can be believed, we now have a censer worth at least a thousand gold. I...overreacted. To the raven getting disintegrated, I mean. It just took me by surprise."

Oliver was silent for a moment, and then his hand slid down from her elbow, gripping her smaller hand in his and squeezing. "I'm going to have quite a lot to say to them as Lord Stag. If the Raven Queen really was a wild creature of vengeance, that little stunt they pulled could have put me and the whole of the Verdant Stag in danger. The University has a lot of power and resources. I thought it would be truly advantageous if we could be allies."

"To avoid being beset by enemies on all sides," Siobhan deduced. "Since they're already rivals with the Thirteen Crowns."

"Yes. But...tonight has made me warier."

"What are you going to do?"

He turned back to look out the window, and a few seconds passed before he answered. "I don't know. In the short term, at least, I have to bide my time and consolidate the Verdant Stag's power. We're not strong enough to afford direct confrontation."

She let the conversation die, taking some comfort in the anchor of Oliver's hand against hers. When the carriage finally slowed to a stop in front of a small house, she asked, "What do you think happened to the enforcers who were in the warehouse with the raven?"

"I don't know," Oliver said grimly, but it went unspoken between them that there was a good chance fighting had broken out, and against University professors with at least one free-caster, the Verdant Stag enforcers, competent and well-equipped as they were, might not have come out ahead.

31

CARNAGORE

Sᴇʙᴀꜱᴛɪᴇɴ
Month 2, Day 26, Friday 10:00 p.m.

Aꜰᴛᴇʀ ᴛʜᴇ ᴅɪꜱᴀꜱᴛʀᴏᴜꜱ ᴍᴇᴇᴛɪɴɢ, she changed back into Sebastien's body at the safe house. Oliver insisted on her coming back with him to Dryden Manor, just in case. She doubted there would be any suspicion brought by a student being gone from the dorms on a weekend night.

"Don't worry about doing any more investigating on your own. No following Miss Canelo, or snooping around Grandmaster Kiernan's office," Oliver said, his tone more warning than reassuring. "Sebastien Siverling getting tangled up in some trouble is the last thing we need now."

Sebastien felt vaguely offended. "We have that map-based divination spell that I linked to her boot. I wouldn't need to track her directly."

"That's fine, as long as you don't get caught." Oliver's fingers tapped the edge of the carriage seat for a moment. "Honestly, what we really need isn't someone to spy on her. It's for her to work for us. The target for any espionage should be Kiernan and his more direct lackeys like Munchworth, not a second-tier lackey just running errands."

Sebastien still passed along the names of those she had recognized, adding, "I can find out the names of the others without drawing attention to myself. I'll send you an anonymous, encrypted letter with the details."

Oliver seemed skeptical, but didn't protest.

That night, Sebastien slept uneasily, an anxious sense deep down telling her that she had gone wrong somewhere along the way, maybe some time long ago, like a tree that twisted and grew grotesquely around some restraint it could not overcome.

She woke early on Saturday, took a bit of the remaining beamshell tincture in her morning coffee, and slipped away to the Silk Door. She had more supplies for her emergency stash there, adding some disguise items—hair dye, a weak second-hand pair of glasses that wouldn't affect her vision too much, and a couple of makeup products. She also added a small canteen of water and a sealed pouch full of dried fruit, totally hardened bread rolls, and some dried meats. She had learned a simple dehydration spell and created them herself. Everything except the dried fruit would probably taste quite horrible, but it was cheaper than buying proper rations. '*I suspect this dehydration spell could be turned into a desiccation curse with some minor adjustments,*' she mused, sealing up the floor over her emergency stash once more.

Water was more important than food, and the canteen was too small to last even an entire day, but water could be gathered from the air with a relatively simple spell, while it was much harder to access calories on the run.

She had already added the same extra items to her other stash. '*It's a start, but two locations isn't enough.*' She put the task from her mind for the moment, reassumed Siobhan's form, and headed off to Liza's, where she helped with a second round of sleep-proxy tests on more mice. The whole bottom level of Liza's apartments was filled with the experiments, the air warm to the point of stifling despite the chill outside.

Before leaving that evening, Siobhan borrowed Liza's diagnostic artifact, hoping it would help her to answer some of her many unanswered questions about Myrddin's transformation amulet. When she got to the Silk Door, Siobhan attempted to use the diagnostic artifact on herself...only for it to slide away against the barrier of her divination-diverting ward. She groaned aloud. "Of course. How else would it work?" There was no way to stop the ward's automatic activation, and the diagnostic artifact wasn't strong enough to overcome even that level of resistance, so it was useless.

She still timed the transformation process, and though she'd been keeping track for a while now, the variation between transformations was tiny, perhaps having more to do with her inability to measure with total exactness at such small intervals than any actual variance in the amulet's speed.

Because she needed to return the diagnostic artifact in the morning, she went back to Dryden Manor instead of returning to the University, having settled in Sebastien's form.

Oliver was either gone or already asleep by the time she arrived, and she shuffled through a dark, silent house to the upstairs bedroom set aside for her. Her sleep was restful, as it could only be with her dreamless sleep spell, but short. She awoke with a start in the wee hours of the morning, well before the sun had even begun to edge in pastel colors toward the eastern horizon.

A restless anxiety was filling her again, and she decided to get up and make herself useful instead of forcing herself back to sleep. She walked in sock-covered feet to Oliver's office. Locking the door behind her, she turned on the light crystals and turned toward the alchemy table, where supplies were waiting for her. She hadn't been brewing as much lately, her weekends taken up by other, more pressing matters, but this was a good opportunity to perform a test while also making some coin and strengthening her magical facility. Plus, she needed another bottle of moonlight sizzle for herself, as her own had spent a lot of time shaking around in her bag and glowing futilely within, and thus was starting to dim prematurely.

Taking extra care to be aware of both her mental state and the effect and qualities of her Will, she brewed a large batch of moonlight sizzle in the huge soup pot that had never made its way back to the kitchen after she originally commandeered it months ago. The pot required her to adjust the direction of her Will a little, since it didn't have the fat, spherical stomach of a standard cauldron, but the potion within would be little affected as long as she stirred it properly.

After her first batch was completed and bottled, she made sure the curtains were drawn over the windows and the door was locked properly, and then switched back into Siobhan's body.

Then, she brewed another batch of moonlight sizzle, again with extra awareness of her mind and her Will.

Halfway through this batch, a knock on the door made her jump, though she was proud of the fact that her grasp on the magic she was imbuing into the concoction didn't slip, despite her surprise. "Who is it?" she called, deepening her voice in the hope of approximating Sebastien's normal tone.

"It is I, the owner of this house, attempting to get into my own study?" Oliver replied through the door, his tone rising at the end in bemusement.

Siobhan hurried to the door, staying out of sight of the hallways as she unlocked and opened it just enough to let him through. She closed it and locked it behind him, then turned to find his eyes trailing slowly over her form. Sebastien's clothes were too tight in some places and too loose in others, and she had rolled up the hems of the pants and sleeves so they didn't drag.

Oliver raised his gaze to meet hers without a hint of apology, giving her a questioning look.

"I'm doing some tests on the transformation," she explained. "I thought I might as well make myself useful while I'm at it."

"You're lucky I didn't immediately assume you were a burglar and kick down the door. If I hadn't smelled your brewing from the hallway, I might have."

She rubbed the back of her head awkwardly, fingers tangling in her long hair and forcing her to tug them free with a wince. "Oops? I hope you don't mind that I spent the night again?"

His expression flickered too fast for her to track, some unknown emotion or automatic response quickly suppressed. He hesitated slightly too long, just staring at her, then said, "Not at all."

She raised one eyebrow.

He gave her a slightly lopsided smile. "You should know you're welcome to spend the night any time you like."

Siobhan blinked once, and then the possible double entendre filled her with horrid, belated embarrassment. She hurried around him and back to the alchemy station to continue her work, thankful that her darker skin would not show a blush like Sebastien's. It took a few moments for her to regain full focus on the magic, but she managed, and the next time she looked away from the soup pot, Oliver was at his desk writing a letter, seeming to have forgotten her presence entirely.

She completed the second batch of moonlight sizzle and used up the remainder of the potion vials she had on hand. She had believed that her magic was the same, her Will just as forceful and clear in either body, but testing it so purposefully had confirmed that, which left her relieved. The downside to this relief was that what tests she could perform left her as clueless as ever about the function of the amulet, and frustrated that she had made no progress decrypting the stolen book. She had some hope for the spells she'd ordered at the last secret meeting, whose instructions she would receive at the next meeting in about a week.

The sun had risen and the streets grown busy by that time, and Oliver spared her yet another trip to the Silk Door and back to Liza's house by hiring a runner to return the diagnostic artifact for her. When she asked about his progress with Kiernan's faction, he said, "I have made more than a few moves in response to what happened, gathering information and preparing for the worst. I am meeting with him later today. I plan to make my stance extremely clear, and we will see how they respond. Their next move will determine everything going forward, but so far, my experience with them has not led me to optimism."

Siobhan let out a small breath.

He twirled the pen in his fingers, which somehow didn't spew ink everywhere. "It's not all bad news. We're going to put the censer in an auction being held in Paneth the end of next month. I had it appraised, and it's genuine. If things go well, you and I will split almost a thousand gold."

She paused for a while to let that sink in. It wasn't so long ago that such a number, when Katerin offered it as a loan, had seemed astronomical. She knew such an amount was pocket change to Oliver, but to her it meant freedom. "If that's accurate, it'll be almost enough to pay off my remaining debt." Then, her earnings from the textile commission would be mostly profit. She would be…rich.

Oliver chuckled at her sparkly-eyed look of anticipation. "I hope you'll still stop by to brew for me every now and again, even if you don't need to?"

She turned back to Sebastien as Oliver watched. "Well, it is good practice, and I'll need to restock and expand my own potion supply anyway."

He smiled ruefully as she left, shaking his head.

She took a carriage back to the University and used one of the lift tubes instead of walking up the steep winding path cut into the white cliffs, looking out over the city as she rose. The sight was invigorating. What waited for her at the University was slightly less so. "Homework."

Sebastien filched some of Damien's coffee to invigorate herself, and was joined in her ink-smeared labor over the next few hours by varying members of the Crown Family group. When her most critical homework was discharged more quickly than she had anticipated, Sebastien considered going to the supervised spellcasting rooms, or even to the abandoned classroom to work on her sympathetic curses, but instead she pulled out the history books Professor Ilma had lent her.

Remembering the various professors who had accompanied Kiernan to the meeting with the Raven Queen, most of whom she believed were directly part of or tangentially related to the History department, Sebastien wondered if Professor Ilma was involved with them at all. It was hard to imagine such a thoughtful woman who valued critical thinking so dearly joining up to the same cause as Munchworth, but either way Sebastien supposed it didn't really matter. The knowledge Ilma offered was still valid and valuable.

Sebastien had been reading *Myrddin: An Investigative Chronicle of the Legend* in small chunks when she had time, but had only managed to get a few chapters into the book, which all covered Myrddin's earlier deeds, often with handwritten notes pointing to similar myths from the other book. She continued from where she had left off.

Around the time when Myrddin was rising to prominence, he and a few of his contemporaries demonstrated the first known self-charging complex artifacts. Some of these were operated to great effect and some to great disaster when things went wrong. There was contention even at the time about who was the first to achieve such a landmark advancement in the craft of artificery, but the back-and-forth struggle for supremacy certainly sped up growth in the field.

At various times, Myrddin displayed several artifacts believed to be self-charging. Sebastien found one anecdote particularly amusing. During Myrddin's travels through the Tataroc Desert with one of the local clans, he was said to have developed a box-like device that gathered water from the air, using the heat within to both create balls of ice as well as play sensual, soothing music—which of course he composed himself, because Myrddin was the consummate polymath. This ice-making music box, the ultimate desert climate luxury, had a great appeal to the young men and women of the clan, who vied to be the ones to share iced drinks with Myrddin each day.

But Myrddin's most famous self-charging artifact was his horse. Like him, the creature had several names, depending on the region and time period, but the most commonly used was Carnagore, which might have had roots in the words "hooves of dawn," but in the current language sounded rather blood-thirsty.

When Carnagore, a great beast made of white metal, made his first appearances, many had assumed Myrddin was doing fell experiments on a living subject. This wasn't illegal at the time, being well before the atrocities and stigma of the Blood Empire, but even then the idea of turning a horse's skin to malleable metal, replacing its eyeballs with spherical stone artifacts, and replacing its teeth with multiple rows of shark-like fangs was frowned upon for its brutality.

Several journals, letters, and even one autobiography from a contemporary agree that Myrddin eventually made a statement that Carnagore was not a modified creature of flesh, but an artifact that he had created, and which was —most notably—charged by a beast core. His huge mount was said to sprint twice as fast as a normal horse and could gallop tirelessly for a full day and night without breaks, a feat that would have killed a flesh-and-blood animal several times over. It did not spook or shy, could climb mountainsides like a goat, and was a vicious, bright-shining, glowing-eyed beacon of terror in battle.

Over time, Myrddin continued to add to Carnagore's abilities, giving it a range of auxiliary spells that could be activated when necessary. Some speculated that he even managed to give Carnagore some semblance of a sentient mind, either created from whole cloth or taken from a living animal and inserted into the artificial beast. Evidence of this included the times that Myrddin was said to have given his horse instructions and left it to carry them out autonomously, or instances where Carnagore acted to protect Myrddin from threats even the man was not aware of. However, the rumors and hearsay about Carnagore were at times even more outlandish than those about Myrddin himself, so many of the creature's reported abilities could not be corroborated.

This entry in *An Investigative Chronicle of the Legend* led Sebastien once again to the less academically rigorous book, *Enough Yarn to Last the Night*.

Myrddin was said to have gone deep into the Forest of Nod, a land untouched by man, and in the very center crawled into a well. He crawled down for three days and three nights, and when he finally reached the dry bottom, he rested. When he awoke, the sun shining down from directly overhead for but a moment as it reached the perfect alignment with this round tunnel into the depths of the earth, Myrddin found that he was not alone, but accompanied by a palm-sized, chimerical beast.

Its features shifted, the head of a lion and the tail of a scorpion at one moment, and then the wings of an eagle and body of a turtle the next. The beast had been sealed for eons and was very weak, and so it entered into a pact with Myrddin. It would serve him, and he would take it out of the well and strengthen it.

It hungered and thirsted greatly, and each time it feasted, it grew stronger. Myrddin rode it into battle against an adze—the insectoid, vampiric source of misfortune, not the woodworking tool—and Myrddin's beast companion drank its blood. They killed a skolex worm, and the beast ate its teeth. They hunted a mammoth, and the chimeric beast ate every inch of its fur and skin, from snout to tail. They hunted a dragon, and Myrddin's beast ate its bones. With each defeat of an enemy, it consumed a piece of them, growing larger and more powerful, taking on their strength and discarding its own weaknesses.

They traveled together for many years, and the creature was loyal, acting as Myrddin's mount, his shield, and his sword as needed, its shape-changing abilities allowing it to be always the perfect companion. Finally, they hunted a human, and the creature ate the brain, and thus grew to understand the loves and hates of man.

It remained loyal, becoming a sworn brother to Myrddin, but its hunger could not be sated. Eventually, no prey in the world could slake its ravenous hunger or increase its strength, and its gluttony turned to Myrddin himself. It longed to kill and devour the man, from the hair on his head to the marrow in his bones. It knew the evil of this deed and wept bitterly, but could not resist its nature. It would kill and consume Myrddin, and then it would devour the world itself.

And so they fought, again for three days and three nights. Myrddin struck it down endlessly, carving off its wings, peeling off its skin, pulling its teeth, and chopping off its limbs. It grew smaller and weaker with each defeat, and when it again fit within the palm of his hand, he returned it to the well in the Forest of Nod, leaving it sealed once more, but not without giving it one last gift.

He dropped seven tears into the well, so that the creature could drink them and know sorrow.

The myth ended there, leaving Sebastien somewhat bemused about the connection between it and Myrddin's creation of Carnagore. Both were mounts with expanding abilities, and both were said to have developed some greater intelligence over time. Technically, both would also have used the power of defeated beasts for sustenance. Rather than blood and fur and bone, that sustenance probably came from the beast cores of slain magical beasts, and it made sense that such a powerful artifact as Carnagore would have needed powerful beast cores as well. *'Hells, the cost of running Carnagore might have been what spurred Myrddin to slay all those magical beasts,'* Sebastien mused, snorting to herself.

What interested her, however, were the times when Carnagore seemed to act on its own, while Myrddin was otherwise occupied with something else. It was certainly possible that Myrddin had either given it true reasoning capabilities or just such complex instructions that it simulated a sapient mind, but she wondered if some of those rumors could have stemmed from him creating artifacts that could be operated with an application of Will alone. Just as her amulet needed no physical switch or verbal command, Carnagore, a much more complex creation, could have acted based on Myrddin's Will, a puppet of sorts.

Corroborating her theory was the fact that Myrddin had once left Carnagore at the top of a mountain for several months—perhaps he'd run out of beast cores—and witnesses said the horse became as cold and still as stone, its eyes dark and lifeless. It did not move even when birds perched atop its body, finally only returning to life when its master returned. Perhaps there had been some energy remaining to sustain an organic mind in a hibernating state, or perhaps the creature really was just created with enough complex commands to simulate the ability to reason, thus allowing it to be turned on and off at will. *'But isn't it also possible that Carnagore is evidence of an entirely different innovation?'*

Sebastien was lost in her musing, staring at an illustration of Myrddin slaying his chimeric companion, which at that point had taken the form of a human with tentacle arms, when her eyes caught a small note written in the margin. It read only "B.K.?" Sebastien wondered what the initials might stand for, and almost instantly a possibility came to her.

The Beast King was sleeping, deep below the ground, and had been for the entirety of living memory. No one knew what he looked like or what his capabilities were, but powerful diviners consistently predicted when asked that if he woke from his long sleep, calamity would follow. However, the Beast King was sleeping somewhere in Silva Erde, not the semi-mythical Forest of Nod, whose location was lost to humankind, if it had ever existed.

Some of the details seemed to fit, but if Professor Ilma had been correct to link the legend of Carnagore to this myth, then it would mean that Myrddin's horse was buried in Silva Erde, and was the potential harbinger of great destruction. Sebastien's preferred theory was that the Beast King was a powerful Aberrant, on the level of Metanite or Cinder Stag, horribly dangerous but ultimately harmless if managed properly and not provoked.

Perhaps the initials weren't even referring to the Beast King. Like many of the entries in the books, Sebastien felt they held a peculiar weight of significance, but if any deeper meaning or epiphany existed, it remained opaque. Perhaps she was only assigning meaning where none existed, swayed by the weight of the amulet around her neck and her long-stymied desire to understand.

32

———

THE DAILY SUN

Sebastien
Month 3, Day 1, Monday 7:25 a.m.

Sebastien arrived to breakfast a few minutes late, joining her friend group—because they were her friends, and if she was being honest and less of an asshole, she should admit that—at the table. She took out a pouch of mixed nuts and dried fruit from her pocket, sprinkling it atop the steaming slop, then looked up to see Ana watching her over the morning newspaper with an expression of concern, her mouth tight as if holding back words.

"Extra calories and some flavor. I picked this up from the market. Just because the University won't sell us firsties proper food doesn't mean we can't bring it in ourselves, as long as we're discreet." Sebastien smiled, shaking the pouch invitingly. "I'm willing to share?"

Ana just stared at her, swallowing hard, then looked away, her eyes flicking around the room.

Sensing that something was wrong, Sebastien followed Ana's gaze. Those with their own newspaper subscriptions were buried within the flimsy, ink-stamped pages, reading avidly. "Did something happen?"

Rhett lowered his own newspaper. "The coppers released their report into..." He paused, looking at Ana, and then to Damien, who was reading the other half of Ana's newspaper, the part with the comics and stories instead of the serious news.

Ana cleared her throat. "Into the Aberrant incident," she finished for Rhett. "With Newton."

The whole table looked up at once. Sebastien's blood ran cold.

Damien reached over and ripped the paper out of Ana's hand, his eyes flickering over the words and widening with horror.

Sebastien wished she, too, could grab the paper for herself, but Damien was too far away. "What does it say?" she demanded.

Damien's eyes stopped racing back and forth over the words. He closed them for a few achingly drawn-out heartbeats and reached up with trembling fingers to smooth back his hair.

Sebastien stood up, reached over the table, and took Rhett's paper, ignoring Damien as he began to read the article aloud for the others, her eyes flicking over the words faster than he could speak.

Corrupted Magics Led to Rafton Street Aberrant Incident, Seven Dead

Readers may remember the rogue magic incident of six weeks prior, many being woken from their sleep to the disquieting sirens. While speculation and rumors surrounding the events of that evening on Rafton Street have abounded, the investigation carried out by the coppers and the Red Guard has now been completed and their report released. You are reading it first, here in *The Daily Sun*.

On that foggy evening, seven people died, including one copper, two civilians, and the University student whose self-destruction caused most of the damage. Photographs of the site and victims have been restricted, but according to the investigation report and eyewitness accounts from the family whose home was broken into and destroyed, those deaths were appalling and brutal. "My husband unraveled like a spool of thread," Molly Harper said, sobbing as she struggled to get through her interview with this reporter.

Local copper Willy Brodson, who was first on the scene and witness to his partner's death, said, "This job is dangerous, and you know that, but you never quite expect that your next patrol will be your last. He didn't even know what hit him. To die like that...I can only pray to the Radiant Maiden that his soul will be able to rest in peace."

The night's horrific events were hosted by an eclectic cast. According to the investigation report, a group of local gang members, the Morrows—who were one of the main forces involved in the fighting that caused so much destruction to the city not long prior—arrived at the Harpers' business and residence late at night, having captured three people they believed to be unexceptional. The scoundrels planned to rob and perhaps ransom or blackmail their captives. Unknown to them, one of the seemingly innocuous victims was none other than the Raven Queen herself in disguise.

Though the Raven Queen needs no introduction to the locals, this reporter will remind you that she has been involved in several violent incidents, and is wanted for treason, the practice of blood magic, and numerous other crimes. For more details, see previous Daily Sun issues, listed at the end.

The other two stars of the evening were a pair of third-term University students, both student liaisons and respected among the faculty and their peers. How this eclectic trio came to meet, this reporter does not know, and, alas, those who might tell either will not or cannot. We can speculate that perhaps the students, both being from impoverished backgrounds, hoped to gain the bounty for the Raven Queen's capture. Or, perhaps, the Morrows captured them while they were dealing *with* her in some more nefarious capacity. It is even possible that the whole incident was planned to draw out and kill the Morrows.

In any case, once the hooligans had broken into the Harpers' shop, which is on the ground floor beneath their home, fighting broke out. While the Raven Queen and her shadow companion were terrorizing the astonished Morrow members, University student Newton Moore tried to cast a dangerous spell. It was at that point that everything went horribly wrong.

As readers may know, those who cast immoral magics—and blood magic specifically—are more likely to corrupt their Wills and become Aberrants when the strain of their evil magics becomes too much. The exact nature of Moore's attempted spell is unknown, but Elden Preem, a local expert on rogue magic events, speculates that it may have been some sort of mass mind-control spell meant to take control of the fighters for his own benefit.

It does cause one to wonder, could mind-controlling spells or other under-handed tactics have played any role in Moore's admittance to the University? Master Patham, a University faculty member, assured this reporter that, "The entrance procedures are properly safeguarded against any kind of exploitation or malicious influence. Newton Moore may have become misguided out of despera-tion, but he entered the University legitimately and earned his position as a student liaison."

Inquiries revealed that Moore's family lost their home in the recent gang violence, with some of his family members being injured and in danger of even-tual destitution. Friends of his say that it was around this time that he began to act differently, becoming more secretive and showing signs of mental and emotional strain. He began to fall in with a bad crowd and likely experimented with corrupting magics as an answer to his problems, not knowing what the consequences would be. It is even possible that he was out for revenge on the Morrows, who he could have held responsible for his situation.

One anonymous friend who was close to Mr. Moore before he fell to his darker impulses stated, "Newton was always a little desperate, you know? He really needed his place here. At first, that just made him a hard worker, and he seemed like a really nice guy. But after his family hit hard times, I started seeing a hint of something darker in his eyes. He started acting strange and slipping away to do secretive stuff at odd times. I distanced myself from him at that point, but I never imagined he could actually be doing blood magic or whatever. It just goes to show, you can't trust everyone."

Whatever the reason, Mr. Moore dragged many victims down with him. There has been some valid speculation about whether this includes his fellow student liaison and friend, young Tanya Canelo, or if she was complicit in these events from the beginning. In either case, she no doubt regrets her involvement, as the girl who experienced the whole event was hit by a powerful curse that will affect her until her dying day. What she saw that night, she may never speak of. "It's very tragic," one University faculty member who declined to be named stated. "The curse is unbreakable, and the poor girl cannot even undergo counseling to soothe the burden these memories must place on her mind. So betrayed by one she thought a friend. I know she had nothing to do with Moore's degeneracy. He probably called upon her for help that night, just like that Siverling boy, and she had no idea what she was getting into. I'm sure she would have reported him to the faculty if she knew what was going on."

And Moore did, indeed, call upon another innocent for help—young Sebastien Siverling, first-term apprentice to Grandmaster Thaddeus Lacer and friend to a number of Crown Family youths, including the Gervin heiress and the younger Westbay. Sources say the courageous but somewhat hapless boy was contacted via artifact, arriving to find the Aberrant already in the midst of its murderous rampage. Gullibly believing that Moore needed his help, Mr. Siverling entered the scene and, apparently, was forced to do battle with the Aberrant itself. Though the exact nature of his duel with the evil creature remains undisclosed, the young man, widely known as a prodigy among his classmates, managed to subdue it long enough for the Red Guard to arrive!

"It's no surprise to me at all," one anonymous fellow student commented. "I mean, there must have been a reason for Thaddeus Lacer, a war hero, to take him as an apprentice. Sebastien is so intense, you can just tell he's got hidden, complex depths, like a tortured hero."

Several students agreed that, aside from his small group of friends, Mr. Siverling keeps to himself and focuses on his studies. Somewhat appropriately, considering who he is apprenticed to, he has gained a certain reputation for a sharp tongue. "I've never met someone so impolite and tactless. It's almost like he's *trying* to create enemies, too stupid to realize he doesn't have the foundation to bear the consequences of his actions."

However, other students argue with this interpretation of his personality. "Sebastien might come off gruff, but that's just because he has really high standards. He's actually kind of nice. I've seen him helping other students with their spellwork—even ones who aren't part of his group of friends, and he's nice to anyone who doesn't waste his time. And—this is kind of a secret, but [a fellow student who declined to be named] told us she saw him making a nest for some sprites when winter hit, so they wouldn't die. We've all been taking turns feeding them since then. It's a little secret pet project that Sebastien and a small group of us are in on. He doesn't have the patience for people who are lazy or rude to others, and he doesn't care if you're rich or connected or not. People who don't like him…well, they're the people who gave him a reason to comment on their misbehavior."

And so it seems that Mr. Siverling has a history of pitting himself against what he considers to be injustice, even at risk to himself and without ever asking for reward.

As Agent Vernor of the Red Guard stated about his actions that night, "Courageous is just another word for stupid, in this case. Both the Raven Queen and an Aberrant were on-site. It's only through luck that he managed to walk away from that night alive. But not unscathed…" Agent Vernor refused to comment further, but this reporter cannot help but speculate.

It is believed that Miss Canelo was cursed by the Raven Queen herself, and Mr. Siverling may have been subjected to a similar misfortune. Could he have required treatment for injuries, either physical or mental? The Raven Queen is known to be vindictive.

Mr. Siverling spent several days away from the University after his battle against the Aberrant. Student Bayo Oswin claims to have seen the aftermath, as Grandmaster Lacer brought Mr. Siverling back to the University for healing in the wake of his ordeal. "[Siverling] looked like a corpse. It was too dark to see if there was blood, but Professor Lacer was floating him in the air because he'd passed out from some kind of injury. Professor Lacer got him straight to the infirmary."

University healers have refused to comment on Mr. Siverling's admittance, citing confidentiality vows. Healer Prium announced, "That boy is a hero, and I'll thank all you vultures to leave him alone! Bad enough what he went through. Thank him by giving him the peace he so obviously wants and deserves!"

Grandmaster Lacer and Mr. Siverling were both unavailable for comment.

The biggest mystery of the evening surrounds the presence of the Raven Queen. Why was she there? What was her purpose in cursing young children? Was she the one who drew foolish Mr. Moore into the darker aspects of the thaumaturgic arts? Despite her known vendetta against the Morrow gang and her spiteful acts against the two living University students, eyewitness reports from both the surviving Morrows and the Harpers say that the Raven Queen protected them against the Aberrant, using unknown and powerful magics. It seems even such a bold criminal can unite with others to do good when faced with such horrific evil.

The mysterious villain then slipped away before the coppers arrived through some unknown means, seen by none. This reporter doubts the veracity of the rumors but has heard from multiple sources that it is well known among the southern areas of the city, where she has been most active, that the Raven Queen can travel through the shadows and has the ability to disappear as long as no watchful eye is upon her.

Despite the tragedy and mystery surrounding the event, the Red Guard arrived promptly and managed to secure the scene and kill the Aberrant, valiantly preventing any further deaths. After having conducted a thorough investigation, they assure the citizens that the area is safe, and that no anomalous effects linger either in the building or in the survivors. They once again caution against blood magic and other immoral undertakings, and they urge all citizens who have knowledge of possible practitioners of corrupting magic to report them. If you see something, say something.

Together, we can help create a safer Gilbratha.

WHEN SHE FINISHED, Sebastien started reading again from the top more carefully, reaching the end for a second time as Damien finished his recital.

"What. The. Fuck?" Alec said, punctuating the silence that followed.

"My sentiments exactly," Sebastien said, feeling perfectly attuned with Alec for once. Shock was quickly giving way to rage, and she could feel the tingle that signified her cheeks flushing. The things written about her were profoundly uncomfortable, but the things about Newton sent ripples of fury through her skin, the emotion seeming too large for her body to contain.

Damien laid the newspaper down, his clenched fingers wrinkling and tearing the delicate paper. "It's a hack piece. Newton fell in with a 'bad crowd?' He was casting corrupted magic? Bullshit! And the stuff about Sebastien? Who are all these people giving anonymous statements, acting like they know him!?"

"Newton wasn't like that," Alec said firmly, staring down at the table. "He was a nice person. He never got impatient with me, even when he was obviously tired and I couldn't grasp what he was trying to teach me. He never said an unkind word about anyone, even when people were rude to him. And there's *no way* he was doing blood magic, no matter how poor his family is. He wouldn't. This writer doesn't know what they're talking about. Who are the supposed 'friends' that said these things about him?"

"It's sensationalized," Ana said softly. "You've all seen this a thousand times, don't be surprised now. They just want to sell more copies, and the whole story makes for very interesting reading. But all interesting stories need a hero and a villain."

"I would have thought the Raven Queen would take the role of villain," Sebastien said.

Ana shrugged. "But she helped protect civilians against the Aberrant this time, and it's hard to make that fit. It's possible other newspapers will have different takes on the whole thing, though. And Sebastien, if I were you, I would be on the watch for a sudden influx of interest from the rest of the student body. Please don't snap and start cursing anyone. They're going to be stupid either way, and that'll just draw even more attention toward you."

Sebastien looked around, and as Ana had predicted, found dozens of people watching her from around the room, some clearly gossiping as they whispered back and forth.

"Did the reporters even bother to ask you for a statement?" Damien demanded. "No one talked to *me*."

Sebastien shook her head. "No. I didn't even know this was happening." In the corner of the room nearest the door, Tanya stood up, threw away her food uneaten, and hurried out, escaping the stares and whispers directed her way.

"I bet she was messing around with that same dangerous shit that turned the other guy into an Aberrant," someone said loudly in her wake, his voice carrying over the hushed murmuring.

Before anyone else could respond, Alec stood up, so abruptly that his chair skidded back and fell over. The cafeteria quieted so quickly that the clatter of the fallen chair was the only sound. "Shut up!" Alec yelled, turning to face the direction of the speaker.

Before he could continue, Ana grabbed him by the arm. "They're like a pack of rabid dogs right now," she hissed. "They'll tear you to pieces if you start siding with an Aberrant." When Alec looked as if he was going to protest, his thick bushy brows drawn down low like two bristling caterpillars, his eyes glinting with what might have been the first signs of tears, Ana hauled him physically out of the room.

Rhett watched them go, then leaned in over the table, resting his jaw on his palm. "It's social suicide to argue that a guy who turned into an Aberrant and killed six other people—in a way so horrendous that even the Raven Queen stepped up to save people—was actually a nice, innocent person," he drawled. "That's why his supposed friends turned on him."

Damien stood. "But the reporters should have some integrity, at least. This whole thing is outrageous. I'm going to write Titus about *The Daily Sun's* libel." He turned to Sebastien. "They'd never do such shoddy reporting without hard evidence about someone who could afford to sue them, don't you think? Maybe they'll change their tune when they realize Newton had real friends with enough power to make them sorry. I'm going now."

Sebastien's lips turned down wryly at the thought that this was the first time Damien was truly acknowledging the effects of the class divide. "I'll come with you," she said. "But eat first. You'll be dead on your feet by lunchtime without the calories." She never wasted food, no matter how upset she was, and it wasn't as if she could take the bowl of oatmeal with her to eat later. Her hands trembled as she brought the spoon to her mouth, and she was unable to taste the oatmeal or the treats she'd added to it. She had planned to take a half-dose of the beamshell tincture, but there was no way she could add that electric energy onto the wash of anxiety and anger that was burning like acid through her body.

Damien huffed, but when he couldn't convince her, he sat back down and shoveled his food away without even bothering to chew.

They left the cafeteria together, both wearing imposing scowls that were enough to keep the other students away, for the moment. Sebastien remained silent as Damien muttered angrily to himself about all the threats he would make to *The Daily Sun*, and how he wanted to make the people who'd given negative testimony about Newton sign a written apology. "If the Sun doesn't agree, I'll send Titus after their owner. I'm pretty sure they're run by a lesser branch of the Rouse Family..." Damien trailed off as they spotted Professor Lacer striding briskly down one of the nearby pathways. "We should talk to him about this!"

"Do you think he could do anything?"

Damien scoffed. "He's *Thaddeus Lacer*, he's a professor here, and this involves the reputation of a good student and the University itself. I'm sure he'd be willing if both of us asked him to do something."

They ran to catch up with Professor Lacer, and under the man's questioning, arched eyebrow, Damien spewed out the whole situation in a single breath, somehow remaining coherent as he did so.

Professor Lacer scowled. "The reporters refrained from harassing you, I hope, Mr. Siverling? I warned them *meticulously*..."

That explained why Sebastien hadn't been approached. Either the reporters had been discreet when questioning the other students, or she had simply failed to notice them.

"That's not the point!" Damien insisted. "It's everything else they wrote."

"I see," Professor Lacer drawled. "And what do you expect me to do about this?"

Damien was taken aback. "You don't...care?"

"About the reputation of a foolish student who I never met, that endangered my provisional apprentice's life while trying to take on the Raven Queen and doing a horrible job of it? I cannot say that I do. But that is not the point, child. Do you really believe that the University was ignorant of what would be printed? Yes, much of what you say was written is a lie, but that lie is beneficial to many parties. *Think.*"

"I don't understand. What good does it do anyone to tell people that Newton was a bad person?" Damien asked, his voice strained.

Professor Lacer sighed. "Not that he was a 'bad person.' That he corrupted his Will through morally repulsive magics." He turned to Sebastien, looking at her expectantly.

Frowning, she thought as quickly as she could. "It's bad publicity for model University students to have break events. Or any connection with the Raven Queen. But they couldn't blame it all on her because she fought against the Aberrant after Newton died...?"

"Partially," Lacer said, seeming disappointed in her response. "The University does not want it to seem like the Raven Queen has a particular vendetta against the institution, nor that she might make it a point to endanger innocent students simply for attending. Not when she's proven so difficult to catch, and fear and awe for her is growing so out of control. The University wishes to be considered as safe as possible, considering it's an institution that hosts young thaumaturges, and especially because the end of term exhibitions are coming up, which is a big source of revenue."

"So something needs to separate Newton from the rest," Sebastien mused.

"Indeed. Otherwise, people might start getting uncomfortable. What else?"

Damien still seemed confused, but Sebastien understood. "It's not just people worrying about the University being safe from the Raven Queen. It's about people feeling safe from thaumaturges in general, isn't it? Because if a nice boy like Newton could break, never having dabbled in anything corrupt, and end up horrifically murdering six other completely unsuspecting and innocent people...then no one is safe. And if no one is safe, that's evidence that the Crown Families don't have as much control as people think."

Professor Lacer smiled. "Very good."

Damien blinked, looking between them with dismay. "But what about Newton? And his family? They don't *deserve* this. Even Sebastien is getting pulled in!"

"Mr. Moore's family has surely been compensated for the dishonor. Generally, in a situation like this, the Red Guard would offer them something like a replacement house and to cover all their medical expenses. And if they like, they will have been moved out of Gilbratha to a place where none of the neighbors will know what happened. Despite your outrage, there is little to be done and, if you will take some advice from me, even less that you *should* do. As for Mr. Siverling's involvement, I am afraid that is an unavoidable consequence that he brought upon himself. I have done what I can, but even I cannot keep people from gossiping. Now off to class with you. I am busy." He walked away without another glance to them.

"See you in class," Damien mumbled after Professor Lacer's back. After a few moments, he turned to Sebastien. "So I can't make them retract the article?"

"Maybe you can, but it won't be the only article. And if even his family has been paid off to agree with what they're saying…" She looked down, kneading at the muscles in the back of her neck to try and stave off a headache. "This is very disappointing, and somewhat disillusioning."

Damien let out a scoffing laugh. "Understatement of the century."

"That's hyperbole. You've just been too gullible all your life," Sebastien retorted without any of the usual humor that would have accompanied their bickering. "I actually should have guessed something like this would happen."

Damien looked around to see if anyone was watching, glared harshly at those he caught looking, and then whispered, "Is there anything *they* can do? Our people? Newton was working for them, by proxy, I mean."

"I doubt it," she replied shortly. She wasn't prepared to put everything at risk just to fight a war of public opinion. "At least Newton isn't around to know about this."

"That is *not* a silver lining, Sebastien!" Damien snapped, then spun on his heel and stomped off to class.

Sebastien followed him, her mind playing over the memory of Professor Lacer's completely unsurprised face as Damien explained the situation. *'They reported on what happened, but they were duplicitous about the details. What else might be false like that? How many of the newspaper reports I've read about other Aberrants were partially falsified or purposefully misleading? Does the Red Guard keep real records of the break events? They must.'*

She remembered Liza scoffing at the idea of blood magic corrupting the Will. *'Is it possible…that they've been lying all along about what creates an Aberrant? I mean, the Will breaking and losing control of the magic is real, but what about the rest?'*

33

PRACTICAL TRANSMOGRIFICATION

Professor Lacer glared out over his classroom. "While you may feel compelled to distraction, you all would do well to give me, and this class, your full attention. Anyone who fails to do so will face…consequences." Some of the students had failed to immediately quiet when he entered the room, drawing his ire, but none were foolish enough to question what exactly he meant by "consequences."

Sebastien was grateful for the temporary cessation of stares and whispers, at least for the ninety minutes this class period would occupy.

"We are moving on to the final exercise of the term," Professor Lacer announced, "but we will start with one last opportunity for you to display your progress on the previous exercise. For those of you who are failing this class, you had better pray that you improved over the weekend. Begin casting your illusion spells. I will walk among you and take note."

Sebastien hurriedly chalked out the glyphs of her minimalist spell array on her desk. Many of the other students placed a component which they would use as a reference. Sebastien did not, the information for every detail she would manifest held in her mind.

Closing her eyes, she took a few calming breaths and began to bring her Will to bear as she reviewed the spell processes, taking light from the Sacrifice Circle and molding it to her Will within the inner Circle. She focused on the illusion she wanted to create, trying to solidify each detail with extreme clarity, until the image in her mind was as solid as reality.

She opened her eyes and cast the spell, her Will like a vice, squeezing every drop of power and control out of the Sacrifice Circle, which was suddenly nothing more than a black dome of nothingness. If her brain had been a muscle, it would have been trembling from the strain of the load it carried, just on the edge of her capabilities.

In the main Circle, a small fish appeared in the air, shiny-scaled and sleek. She had spent quite some time practicing this spell in the Menagerie, crouched next to one of the guld fish ponds until she had memorized their small flitting forms. Their bodies, which seemed to be formed of precious metals polished to a high sheen and looked nothing like their mundane carp cousins, were a great subject to show a solid grasp of reflection. She moved her head a little to see the fish from different angles, ensuring that it looked correct from all sides. The fish flickered and dimmed a little as even that slight bit of movement interfered with her concentration.

She sat back, holding the illusion until the strain settled a bit and her mental grip firmed up. Then, slowly, she guided the fish to move, swimming in slow motion through the air. She had sunk so deep into concentration that she didn't even realize when Professor Lacer stopped by her side.

"You lack a setting or backdrop to ground the illusory creature in reality," he murmured, his voice soft.

The fish flickered and dimmed again, and she scowled, sweat beading at her temples and her breath growing labored as she brought the illusion back into clarity.

"Your shadows are imperfect, too flat, and the reflection off of the scales is contrived. But the translucency of the fins is a nice touch, and the image does *approach* realism. I have seen enough."

With a shudder, she dropped the spell, releasing the fist that was clenched around her borrowed Conduit and looking up at him.

He gave her the barest hint of a smile. "A remarkable improvement from your first attempts, and impressive work from a first term student. A feat worthy of my apprentice."

She felt like a miniature sun had bloomed within her chest, warming her as it seared away her fatigue and frustration, and there was no way to hold back the huge smile she gave in return.

"As promised, for a passable three-dimensional image from imagination, I am awarding you five contribution points. For the addition of movement, another ten. See me after class." Before she could respond, he had moved on.

From the desk beside her, Damien scowled at his own illusion, which struggled to remain three-dimensional and solid-seeming but still earned him two contribution points. When Professor Lacer had moved on, Damien grimaced, tossing Sebastien a reluctant thumbs-up.

Ana hadn't even tried for the more difficult versions of the exercise, but her three-dimensional copy of a reference pinecone was without fault, and still received a nod from Professor Lacer.

When he had traversed the whole classroom, Professor Lacer returned to the front, where his pen had independently been scribbling all the necessary notes, and leaned against his desk. "This final exercise is the one students generally have the most trouble with. As we can anticipate the upcoming distraction of the end of term exams and exhibitions, I advise you all to put in the time and effort for this one as early as possible. We have previously dipped into transmutation, as well as the places where transmutation and transmogrification can meet and meld. Today and through the end of term, this class will be focusing solely on familiarizing all of you with *practical* transmogrification."

He turned to pull a box from one of his desk drawers. In response to a small motion of his hand, a black wax stick floated free of the box. He guided it to draw a thick Circle on the stone floor with a couple of component Circles attached, but as always, no written Word of any type. He placed a beast core in one of the component Circles and a jar of bright blue butterfly wings in another. "When you think of transmogrification, and especially free-cast transmogrification spells, awe-inspiring and dramatic visual effects might come to mind." A miniature snowstorm came to life within the Circle, the clouds writhing with ever-changing faces contorted with anger and fear. With a gust of wind, the snow blew out of the Circle and dusted the first few rows of students, including Sebastien.

She stared at one of the flakes as it melted against the skin of her forearm, the melting ice creating a screaming face that stared back up at her pleadingly.

Professor Lacer dropped the snowstorm spell and replaced the jar of butterfly wings with a bright purple plum, its skin shiny and inviting, with a bright green leaf still attached to the stem. "You think of the amazing things thaumaturges are able to do with magical components, or components imbued with the energy of one of the Elemental Planes." A ribbon of golden light grew out of the plum, singing with a voice that was part choral and part string instrument, but all enchantment.

For a few moments, Sebastien wanted nothing more than to consume that sound and the plum that had borne it. She had enough sense and self-control to restrain herself even under the effects of the music, but some of the other students stood from their desks and moved forward before Professor Lacer dropped the spell.

He scowled at them, and, shamefaced, they hurried to return to their seats. He returned the plum to the box and pulled out a large conch seashell in the light pink and deep orange of a sunset. "But magical components can become a crutch, a bad habit like inefficiency in your casting or relying only on fire and beast cores as power sources. For a powerful, properly educated, and mentally nimble thaumaturge, even mundane components can give you access to a variety of magical effects."

He waved nonchalantly toward the blackboard, where a piece of chalk rose up and drew out a pentagon. "You may have heard it said that ideas, or concepts, are like drops of dew on a spiderweb. Triggering one can lead to vibrations that trigger another, or a dozen others, in a way that may seem random but is in fact based on the complex logic of associations."

Sebastien had seen a lot of simple transmogrification spells in Pecanty's Sympathetic Science class, as he demonstrated things associated with whatever poem or play they were studying that day. She had also performed a few herself for Modern Magics, such as color-changing, locking a door using a leather knot as a component, and most recently a sharpness spell, which took the sharpness of a component to give a temporary edge to a dull knife. Despite her general consternation and confusion with the subject as taught by Pecanty, she was excited to delve deeper. Transmogrification could do things that transmutation couldn't yet, and with enough skill it was the craft most capable of further developing the dreamless sleep and sleep-proxy spells.

"First order associations are the most obvious, and often the easiest to use in transmogrification. Let us explore the options that this mundane seashell can grant, to the right mind and the right Will." Professor Lacer held up the conch for them to see, then placed it in the component Circle, and finally tossed a length of white cloth into the center Circle. "I could use transmogrification to take the exact gradient of color from the shell, for example, and apply it to a beautiful ballgown."

The cloth immediately showed a beautiful wash of sunset pink to orange, and Professor Lacer picked it up to display it to the class. He set it aside before pulling out a large jar of dirt and setting that in the center instead. "Or we could use the shell, which is created from almost pure calcium carbonate excretions, to adjust the properties of this dirt. As both of these spells use duplicative transmogrification to copy the *physical* properties—a feat that could be performed with transmutation as well—these effects do not necessarily wear off as soon as the caster loses focus." He picked up the jar of dirt, which was now a pale white color. "And so, this calcium carbonate can be used in soaps, or burned and mixed with other substances to create cement."

He turned to the board behind him. Inside the pentagon was written, "Conch shell," and each of the five corners grew an attached note of simple spell effects that could be drawn from it.

"Duplicative transmogrifications aren't the only first order effects. If this were a nautilus shell, with the ever-expanding spiral, the reference to the Fibonacci sequence can be useful in complex divinations dealing in certain kinds of prediction. If the crab, snail, or mollusk that lived in a shell is still alive and recently removed, one might use the shell in a divination to find the creature. The shell might even be useful as a simple representation of the sea itself, in combination with other components."

He put the length of colored cloth back into the Circle. "Second order associations are slightly more conceptual, less concrete. The shell could be used to give a beautiful ball gown an enchantment that makes its skirt undulate like the waves of the sea on the beach." The cloth rippled suggestively, but fell still as Professor Lacer dropped the spell and removed it again. "Without anchoring this enchantment to the cloth with embroidered spell arrays, the effect will not last without my Will, as this spell changes no physical property, only imbues the target with a concept. That concept has not been intrinsically bound to the cloth through a ritual to change the cloth's magical nature, simply attached temporarily through an actively cast spell."

The jar of calcium carbonate made a reappearance, this time poured out into the Circle. "The conch shell is used as a trumpet, and if you hold it against your ear, folk tales say you can hear the rush of the sea from which it was born, making it a passable component for spells to send or even store messages. Other second order associations would be a shield, armor, or shelter. A home." The particulate matter began to move, flowing first into a dome shape that vaguely resembled the conch shell, where it settled for a moment. "Here, we have an emergency shelter that is closely associated with the source component," Professor Lacer said. The material of the white dome flowed again, gaining four walls, a domed roof with a chimney stack, and a door. The material settled, turning vaguely pearlescent, like the inside of a shell. "And one less closely associated, but still a shelter. Now, you could do something similar with transmutation alone, if you have the knowledge and the power, but it would be more difficult to maintain both structural stability and such thinness of the walls, which allows a caster to create a larger structure with less power. This use of transmogrification is superior in other hypothetical situations as well. Consider a situation where you do not have an abundance of building material, or environmental forces require quick work."

Sebastien had seen a similar spell cast by an upper term student earlier that year, with which they used a model house as a component to mold snow. That had been interesting, but this was even more captivating.

The house rippled and flowed into a small canoe-like shape, and Professor Lacer continued. "Using transmutation to solidify particulate matter in the middle of the open ocean would be much more difficult, as the water seeks to turn your dirt to mud and wash it away. Transmogrification allows you to increase the speed of casting, and, using the shell as a template, negates the need to concentrate on and mold a molecular structure that is impervious to water." The boat fell apart, shrinking back into a pile of white dust that then floated up and returned to the jar on its own.

Professor Lacer turned to the blackboard once more, and lines extended from the pentagon, creating a second layer of spell effects. The web was beginning to take shape. "Now, for third order associations. These are even more conceptually vague, less anchored to the reality of the shell and more to the *ideas* of the shell."

His voice grew softer, more sibilant, as if caressing the words as they passed through his lips. "The creation of a shell is a *cumulative effort* of small steps that build into something greater over time. In this way, the shell is useful to stabilize magical projects that cannot be completed all at once but require a strong foundation that future advancements will rest upon.

"The shell is *protection* to its inhabitant, but also a *burden* that they must carry with them always, weighing them down. It has been used in spells that allow a protector or benefactor to share a curse—and thus weaken it—with those under their care. As the benefactor adds some important value to the beneficiary's life, ideally some level of protection, the beneficiary can take on part of the burden in order to continue to receive protection from the cursed individual.

"The shell is a barrier for a vulnerable creature. Ground down, they are used in talismans to protect babies and toddlers against harm. Some mind-healers suggest they might be useful in spells to soothe those who are overly receptive to stimuli. And finally, as they hold the supposed echo of the sea, they can be used in divination, to grasp an echo of things that once were, or even the echo of things to come."

Sebastien shuddered as goosebumps traveled down her back and arms at the sound of those words in Professor Lacer's voice. He understood the all-encompassing allure of powerful magic, and there was a hunger in his voice that reverberated against an answering ravenousness deep inside her. One day, she would grasp all this knowledge, this power, and more.

Professor Lacer's gaze drew inward with concentration, and as he swept his arm in a wide motion toward the class, she thought she caught a slight twitch of brightness from the Circle and beast core.

The shell disintegrated, but even as she was frowning, trying to figure out what had just happened, she realized that it would be better to do so from outside.

Damien reached over and grasped her arm. "It's not safe. We need to leave," he said urgently.

"Class is over already?" Ana murmured, picking up her bag and moving to pack away her note taking materials.

Some students were already on their way out the door, without even bothering to take their belongings.

Sebastien frowned harder, looking around in confusion. She definitely needed to leave, but...why? She looked to Professor Lacer, instinctively seeking support in his presence, and found him wearing a deep scowl of concentration, strain clear in the tight muscles of his jaw and flared nostrils. He was casting something.

'*A spell to protect us?*' she wondered. Instinctively, she knew that was not true. As more students left the room and Damien tugged impatiently on her arm again, she understood. '*No. Something to make us leave.*'

As soon as she understood, she brought her Will to bear as if casting a counter-spell, mentally circulating the ephemeral force through her body and mind, grasping her thoughts and emotions, and shining the light of scrutiny on them. "Sit back down," she ordered Damien and Ana. Her voice was hard and commanding, brooking no argument, just as her Will did not allow the reality of the world to argue against its commands.

They hesitated, though Damien half-lowered as if to obey her, his face screwed up with confusion.

"We don't need to leave," Sebastien continued. "Professor Lacer is casting some kind of compulsion spell using the seashell." She met both of their eyes. "It would be very embarrassing to be so weak-Willed that we left the room, don't you think?"

Both sat back down, and Ana stubbornly unpacked her things again, clenching her jaw and glaring at each item as if it had personally offended her.

They weren't the only ones to resist the compulsion, and Sebastien noted that Nunchkin barely seemed inconvenienced, leaning back comfortably with his arms crossed over his chest.

Finally, when about half the students had made their way into the hallway, where they seemed to be milling about in confusion, Professor Lacer dropped the spell. "An empty shell is an abandoned home," he pronounced loudly and sharply, so that all the students could hear him. "And can be used in both a hex and curse meant to remove people from their abode. The hex temporarily, and the curse permanently, and often maliciously."

As the students filed back in and retook their places, sheepish under Professor Lacer's judgmental stare, he continued. "A shell such as this can even be used as one component in a more nefarious curse. Just as the flesh of the inhabitant has left the shell, so might one force the soul to leave the body, and in so doing create a mysterious death."

Damien leaned toward Sebastien, covering his mouth to whisper. "I read about that! Aberford Thorndyke solves a mysterious murder by a lighthouse captain who was doing blood magic!"

Sebastien's thoughts caught on the reference to blood magic. '*Don't compulsion spells fall under that category? Professor Lacer just removed the free will of a classroom full of sapient beings.*'

She wasn't the only one to make that connection, apparently, as a girl on the other side of the room raised her hand and asked that exact question, her tone prim and more than a little disapproving.

"There are exceptions to every rule," Professor Lacer said. "Some of the milder spells that may technically fall under the broad categories that encompass blood magic remain legal due to their harmlessness or utility. Additionally, members of certain professions may receive licenses to cast necessary spells or groups of spells, just as one would procure a license to allow them to carry a battle artifact outside the army or employment by the coppers. This particular spell is often used to evacuate buildings on short notice, in case of fire or other danger. It is mild, has no lingering effects, and is non-traumatic. I assure you, I am licensed to cast it." He gave the girl a cutting look, slightly irritated, slightly contemptuous, and she shrank in her seat. Sebastien didn't really need more evidence that Professor Lacer had once been part of the Red Guard, not after the way he had interacted with them in front of her, but she imagined that it could be a useful spell for evacuating people during rogue magic events, too. Just the kind of thing they would have a reason to use.

He turned back to the blackboard, adding a third and final rung to the pentagonal web. "Fourth order associations are dangerous, even for me, and beyond the purview of this class," Professor Lacer said, dismissing the interjection. "Now, for the exercise you will be performing. Unlike previous exercises this term, where each of you may have cast slight variations on the spells or attempted advanced versions, each student will be casting their own unique spell. But all of you will be using the same component: one fallen autumn leaf. I have a collection in the box on my desk. First, you will take fifteen minutes to brainstorm a list of every transmogrification-based spell you could cast using an autumn leaf as the sole component, ranked by closeness of association. These lists will be turned in to me for grading. After this, you will choose one spell from an assortment of prepared spell arrays, which I have confirmed are all safe to cast from." Professor Lacer returned to his desk, where he pulled out a stack of papers, each with a spell array and instructions. "Begin."

Sebastien hurried to label a paper with three columns. The first order associations were the most obvious, and she scribbled out a half dozen easily. But the second and especially third order associations quickly became more difficult, and sometimes she had trouble knowing which category a certain spell would fall under.

When she asked about this, Ana said, "I don't believe there is a clear delineation between rungs. A lot about transmogrification isn't clearly defined."

"Go with your gut," Damien agreed, too busy scribbling to look up from his paper.

By the end of the fifteen minutes, Professor Lacer had pinned up almost a hundred spell arrays to the walls at the front of the classroom, and Sebastien had written down less than three dozen possible spells, each idea coming slower than the last. Thinking of Professor Pecanty's class, she had been able to come up with a couple of extra third order associations based on myths and stories where leaves featured prominently, but obviously she was missing a huge number of possible correlations. She didn't even come up with as many options as Damien and Ana. Her only consolation was that Nunchkin, too, seemed to have trouble with the assignment.

They turned in their papers and then moved on to browse the spell arrays on the wall.

When Professor Lacer spoke, his voice carried over the noise of their shuffle and scattered murmurings. "You will choose one exercise, which you will practice through the end of the term. Your goal will be to take the original spell array, and through practice and mastery, pare it down as far as possible while maintaining the most robust effect possible. I would advise you all to choose a spell that falls within your capabilities, considering your skill level and how much time you will have to devote to this exercise through the end of term. Ambition is a virtue for thaumaturges, but so is self-awareness."

Browsing through the spell arrays while she did her best to avoid bumping into the other crowding students, Sebastien saw that many were subtle variations on others, even ideas that she'd had herself. Autumn leaves could work in spells based on the premise of connection to the cold air of coming winter, transformation and metamorphosis, and decay. Some, however, were novel and surprising, like the third order spell that worked on the premise that leaves were to trees like feathers were to a bird. She could tell immediately that such a spell wasn't a good choice for her, because that concept didn't settle easily in her thoughts, like a puzzle piece not quite finding its spot.

She knew almost immediately when she had found the exercise she would work on, taking it down from the wall to claim it for her own. It was a third order concept, and would hopefully tie in with all the other work she had been doing to prepare for the end of term exhibition. An autumn leaf had stored all the light that went into its creation through photosynthesis. With the right mindset, that light could be released again.

There was still some time remaining until the end of class, so after browsing through the spell arrays remaining on the wall to try and see where her imagination had fallen short, Sebastien grabbed a random leaf from Professor Lacer's box, returned to her desk, and meticulously copied down the complex, detailed spell array from the paper to the carved Circle in the desk's surface. Using her little shielded lantern as a power source—which she kept closed so that she couldn't see the light of the flame and accidentally draw on that instead—she settled her mind and attempted to cast the spell.

The magic wasn't exactly wild, but it was in no way docile, either, and it felt like she was trying to blow a bubble out of room temperature tar as she channeled power through the array and tried to draw the stored light from the brownish-orange, slightly wrinkled leaf. She paused, settled her thoughts and tried to improve the clarity of her Will, then tried again. By the end of class, she thought she almost had a glow from the leaf, but it was more of a flicker, and before she could be sure, the bell rang to signify the end of class.

As Professor Lacer had requested, Sebastien stopped by his desk before leaving to pick up her contribution points slip. He attended to the other students who had earned points first, then turned to her. He leaned back against his desk, his gaze evaluating her, tracking from her fingers to her clothes, to the bags under her eyes and the tension at their corners. "Are you finding your classes a strain, with all of the recent events?"

'*Is that a trick question?*' she wondered. But she said only, "No, not any more than usual."

"How have you been progressing with the auxiliary exercises I assigned you at the beginning of term?"

She tensed. "I've been keeping up with them. I haven't started the final exercise yet, but I've been advancing through them at the same pace we do in class."

He nodded inscrutably. "I believe the instructions I left say that you are to develop a transmogrification spell yourself, but if you like, you can pick another spell that utilizes the leaf in a different way and use that as the final auxiliary exercise instead. This would allow you slightly more free time."

"Okay...?" Was she showing signs that she was having trouble keeping up with the workload?

His lips quirked up at her obvious confusion, subtle enough that some might not have noticed. "That extra time could be used taking an additional private lesson from me. Despite your questionable decision-making capabilities and general semi-competence at life, you've shown an acceptable work ethic, admirable curiosity, and an adroit grasp of concepts and control of your Will."

Sebastien reeled.

"Your other professors have given me positive reports of your performance in their classes as well, though Master Fekten laments your ineptitude with complex footwork." His smile grew slightly larger. "If you wish, and if you have the time and energy to handle it, I believe you may be ready for one of the preparatory exercises in spell augmentation that can be a useful foundation from which to approach free-casting."

Sebastien blinked twice, his words exploding in her brain like a flash of lightning and leaving her momentarily speechless. She was too surprised to be happy for only a few seconds, and then elation shivered through her, so strong she thought her eyes might start tingling with tears. She took a deep breath, only then realizing that she'd stopped breathing for a long moment, and then released it again, flexing her fingers and squaring her shoulders as she forcibly suppressed the roiling surge of emotion. "I would be interested in that. I'm sure I can make time."

"Spend the week practicing the transmogrification exercises. If you feel you can handle it, you may drop by my office on Sunday morning around nine."

Sebastien's voice broke when she tried to speak, and she had to swallow and clear her throat. "I—I'll be there."

"I look forward to it. That is all." He dismissed her with a nod.

Sebastien wasn't exactly sure how she got out of the classroom, and it wasn't until she ran into Damien and Ana, who had been waiting for her by the Citadel doors closest to the library, that she came back to reality.

When she explained what Professor Lacer had said, Damien turned a bright cherry red and drew himself up like a rooster. "Private tutoring!? I've been doing the extra exercises, just like you! Why didn't he mention anything about this to me? Is he trying to exclude me? I may not be the second coming of Myrddin, but I'm sure I can keep up with an extra spell or two to practice. I'm at least a one-in-a-hundred genius!"

Ana snorted out a laugh. "One in a hundred? That doesn't seem very impressive..."

Damien, if possible, grew even redder, then without saying another word, he stalked off in the direction Sebastien had come from, ready to have a pointed talk with their professor.

Sebastien and Ana went on to the library, where Sebastien spent some time frantically researching photosynthesis to try to improve her facility in the transmogrification exercise.

Damien never showed up.

"He must be sulking," Ana said wisely. "If he'd gotten his way, he'd be here crowing about it."

Ana seemed to feel that Damien was being foolish, but Sebastien could sympathize. If Damien were the one getting private lessons on free-casting from Thaddeus Lacer, she would be viciously jealous. Of course, she would have done whatever it took to get Damien to pass along what he learned to her, even if Professor Lacer refused to tutor her personally.

It wasn't until the middle of the night, when the ward she'd placed on her watch had buzzed to wake her up from her first sleep session before the night-mares could take hold, that she decided to try to cast the transmogrification spell again with her mind fresh from sleep.

On a whim, she took out her mother's ring—and Conduit—that she had hidden next to the piece of Aberrant string in the warded alcove beneath the floor. Something felt strange as she channeled the magic, the spell feeling rebelliously stiff and slow. In the dim light cast by her lamp, it was easier to see the faint shimmer of light that coalesced on the leaf as she began to have success.

And then, the clear Conduit set within her mother's ring shattered.

The magic reacted wildly, twisting and bucking like a wild horse, nearly wrenching free from Sebastien's control.

Sucking in a hissing breath, Sebastien reacted on pure instinct, transferring the pressure and energy flow to the black sapphire Conduit pressing against the skin of her side. Though she had to force herself to concentrate through the shock dulling her conscious mind, she maintained the magic for several long, tense heart beats.

Then, gently, afraid to injure her Will, she released the spell.

Her held breath shuddered out between tight lips, and her hands began to tremble as she stared down at the clear shards in her hand.

34

AN HONORABLE BURIAL

Sebastien
  Month 3, Day 2, Tuesday 6:45 a.m.

Early on Tuesday morning, Sebastien woke. She was still groggy, but the lingering sour-acid ache of anxiety made it impossible to sleep more than fitfully. She sat up in her bed for a few moments, staring out the window. The shards of the Conduit she'd broken the night before lay in a small pouch in her bedside drawer. She took it out, shaking them into her palm. They glittered with a kind of inner luminescence, distant lamplight scattering off the sharp edges and new facets.

She clenched her fist around them until they dug into her skin, just on the edge of slicing into her. With a sigh, she unclenched her hand. Injuring herself —drawing blood—would be foolish and do nothing to change the situation for the better.

Shaking the shards back into the pouch, she stood and got dressed, then went for a walk through the crisp gloom to the eastern edge of the white cliffs. Once there, she looked out over Gilbratha and the Charybdis Gulf. Fog stretched over the land below like a blanket, heavy and thick.

When her mother's ring had shattered, she had almost lost control of the spell and suffered backlash. If not for her paranoid preparations with the holster and its backup Conduit, she would have.

She had been horrified by its failure, thinking that she'd carelessly destroyed this last remnant of her mother. But subsequent examination had revealed something she never would have suspected: like the ring she had put into Malcolm Gervin's vault, the one she had stolen was a forgery. Or at least the gem was. She couldn't tell for the silver band, which was realistically worn and contained the same chameleon and anti-awareness field as the original.

The forgery was well done, to be sure, even better than her own, but the celerium had been replaced by a thaumaturge-created diamond—one with a fault that made it unusable as a Conduit. The diamond had fallen apart along clear-cut lines, almost as if someone had purposefully created it to shatter as soon as any attempt was made to channel magic. When she knew what to look for, she found proof. The celerium of the real ring had contained a small blemish, while the diamond did not.

'Did Malcolm Gervin have the foresight to keep a fake in his vault?' Perhaps they were antagonizing someone much more dangerous than even Ana assumed. Sebastien might be able to tell both for sure, when they completed the second stage of Operation Defenestration that weekend, but the possibility made her nervous.

At first, as she stared down at the broken ring after having just stabilized the spell, her thoughts had whirled like debris in a hurricane, the shock quickly giving way to panic. But there was a single thought that calmed them all.

'Celerium is worth a lot. Perhaps it was for more than sentiment and vanity that Ennis insisted he would wear the ring, not me. Me, who was the thaumaturge and rightful owner of the Naught family's heirloom.' She suspected that Ennis had sold the real ring, or at least the celerium within its silver setting, some time ago. He would have known how absolutely enraged this would leave her, so it made sense that he had hidden the truth.

After first coming to this realization, she had broken down and wept at the loss of this last link to her mother. Despite how much she denied it, how foolish she knew it was to care, there had been some lingering affection for her father, too. He had made life difficult, but he'd also given her sporadic affection that occasionally shone genuine. He had kept her fed, taken her to healers when she needed it, and never hit her. Ennis had been a precarious anchor when things were at their worst, when she had lost everything else. Now, the thought of him only filled her with rage. She screamed out over the silent city below until her voice cracked, and then descended into a violent coughing fit.

When she finally regained her breath, streams of tears once again cutting down her cheeks, she snarled out at the squat building of Harrow Hill Penitentiary, barely visible toward the western edge of Gilbratha. "May you receive exactly what you deserve, Ennis No-Name," she growled, her voice hoarse. "Once of my blood, but no more. I commend your blood and body to the earth, and your soul to the Plane of Darkness."

Sebastien stood there panting, but after a moment, began to feel rather foolish for the dramatics. At least no one had been around to see her. The horizon was brightening, and, in no mood to watch a cleansing sunrise, she turned back.

As she trudged toward the dorms to pick up her things, feeling sorry for herself, she noticed Tanya's familiar form standing to the side of the cobble-stone path near the door, looking down at something.

As Sebastien drew nearer, she realized the other woman was looking at a carcass. It was a raven, its neck broken and one side of its head bashed in. It was still too cold for ants or flies to be active, so the carcass was unmolested otherwise.

Tanya's face was pale, verging on green, her lips chapped and cracked, and she didn't shift or even blink as she stared down at the dead bird.

Sebastien slowed to a stop beside her. "Someone was playing with a sling-shot and using this poor guy as target practice, it looks like," she murmured.

Tanya jumped as if she hadn't noticed Sebastien's approach, but then relaxed when she saw who it was. "It's a girl," she said. She swallowed. "A female raven."

"Oh?"

"Yes. She's a little smaller than the males, and her throat feathers are shorter and neater."

Sebastien examined the creature dubiously. "They all look the same to me."

"It's a female. I know it. Of course it would be a female. Just lying here, dead and waiting for me to stumble upon as soon as I left the building. It's still warm, you know?"

Sebastien realized suddenly why Tanya was so petrified. *'She thinks this is some kind of message from the Raven Queen—maybe in response to that disastrous meeting with Kiernan and Munchworth's faction. She's terrified of retaliation.'* There was little Sebastien could do to reassure Tanya, especially without incrimi-nating herself for having too much information. She tentatively patted Tanya's shoulder. "Why don't we bury it," she suggested, "and then go to the library and get some studying done? If you want, we can steal some of Damien's coffee, too. I know where he keeps it."

"Yes, a respectful, honorable burial," Tanya muttered, nodding to herself. "Right away, let's do that right away."

While Tanya rushed to go get a "burial shroud," Sebastien used a stick to dig a hole at the base of one of the many trees, a difficult task with the ground so cold and hard.

Tanya returned with full pockets and a large silk handkerchief, fine enough to be worth a good handful of silver, in which she wrapped the dead raven. They buried it under the tree, and then Tanya pulled out incense, a few pieces of quartz, a polished silver coin, and a few vials of herbal oils from her pockets. She pressed the quartz and silver into the dirt, muttering something that could have been a chant for esoteric magic, or perhaps a prayer. After sprinkling the herbal oils around the whole area, she lit the incense stick, which she pushed into the soil so that it would stay upright as it burned down. "May I be forgiven in my ignorance," she murmured fervently, clenching her eyes shut. "And may the soul of this creature find peace."

Finally, Tanya let out a deep sigh of relief and turned to Sebastien, who had watched most of this process in tolerant bemusement. "Thank you. This was a great idea. Man, you're really useful, huh?" she added with a sharp chuckle.

Sebastien grimaced. The bell rang the hour, and students began to trickle toward the cafeteria.

Tanya rose, giving Sebastien a hesitant look. "Do you...want to eat together?"

"Go ahead without me," Sebastien said. "I need to get some things from the dorm first." She lingered, making sure that Tanya was going to the cafeteria, then hurried back to the dorms. She put on a pair of gloves, then stole a pen left on the desk of a random dorm mate. Thus protected, she wrote a quick note, hesitated before signing it, and eventually just drew a little doodle at the bottom. As Tanya was no longer a student liaison with a room of her own, Sebastien went in search of her new upper floor cubicle. It was bigger than the firstie cubicles, with a nicer bed and more furniture, but still only guarded by a curtain. She placed the note atop Tanya's pillow.

No one saw Sebastien enter or exit, but as she was walking to the cafeteria, Tanya came hurrying up the path in the opposite direction, her face tense and her eyes wary and darting. She wouldn't have had time to finish eating already, which meant that something had happened.

"What's wrong?" Sebastien asked, turning to follow when Tanya didn't stop for her.

"Someone broke the ward line around my bed."

Sebastien went cold. *'Of course she would have a ward placed.'* Sebastien herself had one, after all. "Do you know who it was?" she asked.

"Hopefully just one of my snooping dorm mates. Hopefully..." Tanya repeated, on the edge of breaking into a run.

Sebastien followed her into the building and up the stairs, keeping a couple of meters back as Tanya ripped open the curtain of her cubicle with wild eyes. She froze, then stepped toward her bed with trepidation.

Sebastien moved closer so that she could watch Tanya's face. What Tanya did next would hint at her true loyalties.

Tanya stared at the note for a few long moments, her eyes flicking back over the short message several times, then placed it on the ground and activated the spark-shooting spell array Sebastien had drawn around the message. She watched as the note burned to ash.

"What was that?" Sebastien asked.

Tanya lifted her head toward the ceiling, took a huge breath, and released an exhale so protracted it seemed like she might collapse in on herself like an emptied rubber balloon. "It was a reprieve," she replied cryptically, her voice soft and mellifluous. Then, with an awkward smile, perhaps realizing how strange this would seem to an outsider, she continued. "Nothing bad or dangerous. It was…a nice note. I burned it because some people might not like it that I'm not being completely ostracized, after what happened with Newton."

Sebastien didn't inquire further, though Tanya's explanation was sloppy. She had left the note, despite the danger, because Tanya had been so incredibly anxious and exhausted, wound taut like a string about to snap.

Sebastien remembered what had happened to Newton when he was that stressed.

It had contained a simple message. *"I do not blame you, but for your own protection, I advise you find other wings to shelter under."* This simple act might mitigate a similar future for the other woman. She wanted to be proactive enough to stop having such huge regrets. As an additional bonus, this was proof that Tanya was not completely loyal to Munchworth, or to Kiernan's faction, as she had used the spark-shooting array for its implied function without hesitation.

As they walked back to the cafeteria together, Tanya seemed to be thinking deeply. "Other wings…" she murmured. Suddenly, her eyes lit up, and she turned to Sebastien. "What are your plans for the future?"

Sebastien blinked. "Um, I'm going to become a free-caster."

Tanya nodded. "And what will you do then? Work for one of the Crown Families? Do research? Get a position at the University?"

"I'll…" Sebastien suddenly realized that she had no concrete goals for a profession. She perhaps normally wouldn't have said it, but her feelings about the ring, and Ennis, were still simmering in the back of her mind, making her reckless and truthful. "I will be powerful. And with that power, I will seize control of all that dares threaten me. I will bend this world to my Will and strip away all its secrets." As soon as she said it, she regretted it.

To Sebastien's surprise, Tanya laughed aloud, throwing her head back and looking at Sebastien with sparkling eyes. "Somehow I'm not surprised. Such a goal suits you."

Sebastien shifted the strap of her bag on her shoulder, looking away. *'Maybe I would enjoy a job as a researcher, as long as I got to pick the direction.'*

"Perhaps you will need allies to achieve such a future," Tanya said, her tone weighty. She gave Sebastien a small, innocuous smile that belied the meaning of her words. "I would be useful. I may have hit rough waters at the moment, but I am resourceful, and one might find that I have surprisingly few qualms. This all assumes, of course, that you are just as vehement in protecting your allies and subordinates as you are of protecting yourself."

Sebastien stared at her for a long moment. "Are you looking to secure a job, post-graduation?" she asked, offering the most mundane interpretation she could think of.

"A job? Perhaps. If my employer were powerful enough. You do seem to have a lot of connections."

There was no way that could be misconstrued. Tanya was trying to make herself useful to Sebastien in exchange for some sort of favor. She ran her tongue over the back of her teeth, considering, and then said slowly, "What do you need, and what can you offer me?"

Tanya quickly hid her smile, shrugging. "I'm not offering anything specific. If you need something that other people can't help with, or that you would rather be kept discreet, as I said, I'm resourceful. As for what I need... You have an aura around you, Sebastien. It draws attention. I just want to stay close enough that I'm illuminated by that light, so that I can't be dismissed as insignificant or disposable."

Sebastien narrowed her eyes, trying to parse Tanya's meaning. While it could have been simple social maneuvering, trying to get closer to the Crown Family members that Sebastien found herself spending time with, Sebastien thought Tanya's true goal was to give Kiernan and Munchworth a reason to hesitate before sending her on any more suicide missions—or simply killing her off as insurance.

But Sebastien wasn't sure that she trusted Tanya, and she didn't want to get this identity further embroiled in the whole intrigue surrounding the Raven Queen. It would have been easier if Tanya made this offer to someone like Oliver, who could actually use her. "I'll think about it, but I don't really need anything, and I think you've overestimated my influence."

"Do think about it," Tanya agreed, unperturbed.

Sebastien couldn't help but wonder if Tanya had any suspicions about her real identity, but she didn't think that was the case. There could, in fact, have been a much simpler explanation for Tanya's sudden interest. *'Does she think that her proximity to me at the time of receiving the message was some sort of sign? It's obvious from the whole thing with the raven burial that she's superstitious. Well, I can't see the harm in it, as long as I don't encourage her. Myrddin knows I don't need another Damien. Can't I just have a single week where nothing goes wrong?'* The thought registered in Sebastien's mind with an ominous echo, and she stopped in her tracks. "Go on without me," she said to Tanya. "I just realized I forgot something in the dorms."

Before the other woman could reply, Sebastien spun back around and hurried off. *'I'm not paranoid,'* she thought. *'Well, maybe I am. But that kind of irony-tempting thought is often a sign that something horrible is about to happen. Just in case, just in case…'*

She scurried into her empty dorm room and rushed through the steps to uncover the sealed vial with the string of an Aberrant within. Holding it up to the light, she peered at it intently, turning the vial around to look at the wire-like, blood-and-bone colored string from every angle. Finally, she let out a sigh of relief. It had not changed. Tentatively, she let out a deep hum, just to make sure. It didn't react.

Chuckling ruefully at herself, she put it away again. But she still made a quick check of all her other preparations and supplies, and did a mental review of her pre-planned escape routes and responses to various disastrous scenarios. *'As Master Heller said so famously, "Just because you're paranoid doesn't mean they aren't after you." After all, a concern for one's safety in the face of dangers that are real and immediate is the process of a rational mind.'*

35

THE ARCHITECTS OF KHRONOS

OLIVER

Month 3, Day 3, Wednesday 9:10 p.m.

OLIVER SAT IN A DIM, smoky bar, a location quickly becoming all too familiar, and sipped at an amber-colored fruit juice that was nearly as expensive as liquor. He was, yet again, waiting for a meeting with Gilbratha's premier information broker. The last few days had been less than pleasant as he pried around the edges of the truth about Siobhan's meeting with Grandmaster Kiernan's people and their, perhaps not-so-sudden, attack.

Kiernan's faction didn't take Oliver seriously, and the proof was that they hadn't been cautious enough in their aggression. Recently, Oliver had been increasingly impressed with the utility of Lord Morrow's little black book, and was thinking of ways to create similar leverage for himself. Really, his success was partially Kiernan's fault. That first meeting, when they had sent Miss Canelo with the phonograph, had given him the idea.

Kiernan's group had been so focused on the Raven Queen that they hadn't considered what other dangers might lurk in the warehouse where they met. And so, after their attack—which had left his enforcers thankfully alive, though injured and unconscious—they had spoken freely.

Oliver had hidden three phonographs throughout the room, and after the meeting went so disastrously south, he retrieved them. Their sound-capturing membranes had been shredded by the sudden explosions of spell-fire, leaving the captured sound indistinct and marred with crackles and hisses. With three copies at his disposal, however, an assistant was able to piece together a coherent recording of Kiernan's conversation.

It had been quite illuminating.

"They were prepared," Kiernan had said, once the sounds of battle against the Verdant Stag guards had settled, "but not enough to overcome us. But you moved too soon. We could have gleaned more clues about her real motivations and plans."

"She had no intention of negotiating with us," his female companion had replied. "I think that was obvious."

Someone else interjected. "Do you think she knows about our plans?"

"She is clever," Kiernan had admitted, "and I cannot figure out her game. But if she truly planned to go to the High Crown, why has she not done so already?"

Someone else laughed derisively. "Does she expect Lord Pendragon to first pay tribute to meet with her, I wonder?"

There was a pause, during which Oliver assumed looks were being traded, and then Kiernan continued. "What was this meeting about for her, really? If she knows of us, she must know the Architects of Khronos will not be thwarted by this setback she engineered. We will have what we need. Our hand will write the chronicle of history."

As far as Oliver had been able to dig up, the name "Khronos" belonged to a Titan with some kind of destructive, time-based powers. Details were hard to assemble, as Khronos either went by various names, such as Hyperion, Cronus, and Mylinos, or he was often confused with several of his contemporaries whose powers encouraged similar interpretations. So many thousands of years later, it was difficult to uncover the truth. But Oliver didn't need to be a history expert to understand the hubris and greed of the name they had given themselves.

On Sunday, just over a day and a half after they triggered the wards on the raven messenger's cage, Grandmaster Kiernan—ostensibly the leader of this faction—had agreed to meet with Oliver, bringing some subordinates and guards with him.

As Lord Stag, Oliver had made his position and the trouble they'd caused for him clear. Kiernan had seemed deeply frustrated by the failure of negotiations with the Raven Queen, blaming his female subordinate for going against his orders. After dumping the fault on her shoulders, he had waved the woman forward like a mother with a shy young child.

She'd bowed at a ninety-degree angle before Oliver and apologized profusely for her incendiary actions, her cheeks red and eyes glittering with shame and frustration.

As if to patch over the damage, Kiernan had pressed forward with an attempt to deepen their relationship with the Verdant Stag, offering high-level magical favors and submitting another order for all the same things they'd been buying from the Morrows.

"Speaking of the Morrows," Oliver had said. "As you know, the majority, especially in the higher echelons, were captured alive."

Kiernan had smiled with soulless joviality. "Yes, we've heard about your little 'trials' and the coin you've been throwing around in the name of restitution. Perhaps not what I would have done, but an interesting choice that has certainly yielded results for your reputation."

"Well, we are in the process of extracting everything of value from them, from assets to...knowledge. I do not believe in waste." Oliver had been satisfied to see the understanding in Kiernan's eyes, and even more satisfied to see the tension that understanding caused. Oliver knew about the Architects of Khronos, as well as their treasonous activities and preparations. If they made an enemy of him, there would be consequences.

"When I finish with them," Oliver had continued, "I will pass those who have signed nonaggression vows along to the coppers, but I would like to assure you that their tongues will be sealed from wagging about...particular topics. Those that might affect our interests, similar to what was done to one Tanya Canelo."

This time, Kiernan hadn't flinched at the proof of Oliver's knowledge, but he took a few moments too long to respond, and Oliver's peripheral vision caught a couple of Kiernan's underlings sharing a look behind his back.

Kiernan had cleared his throat. "I very much appreciate the...*honor* of a man who does not kill his enemies but instead uses them. However, I would be much more comfortable if my people could assist in the sealing process. I'm sure you understand how much a man like me values his peace of mind." He boomed out a sharp, jolly laugh. "Why, at my age, lost sleep leads to growing haggard and frail!"

Oliver agreed that they could help, if they wished, but Kiernan had more to say. "What of those who do not vow their harmlessness?" he asked. "I assume some of those in higher positions retain either loyalty or pride, despite your best efforts. And surely some you cannot trust, no matter what they vow?"

"Yes. And while I respect such dedication, they may not retain loyalty and pride in addition to their lives," Oliver replied simply.

Kiernan had coughed, bringing a fist to his mouth. "Hmm. Perhaps we could assist with those. Do not be too hasty to throw away their lives before all avenues have been explored. I assure you, we have means that the average torturer cannot match."

Oliver had agreed to that as well, feeling that he was beginning to grasp the edges of their goals.

And so, after more planning and promises, Kiernan and his "Architects of

Khronos" had left Oliver's office, leaving him to dig into a fresh pile of work, as unavoidable and unpleasant as a huge shit left in the middle of his bed.

He had told Kiernan, after the man continued to pry for information, that he planned to move the prisoners on the twenty-fifth of the month. He would be putting out false rumors of a plan to move them on the twentieth—bait to suss out any possible dissenters or enemies—but really, neither plan was legitimate. If things went well, he hoped to move the prisoners on the twelfth, well before the Architects of Khronos would be prepared to intervene.

It was his last test to see if their desire to cooperate was sincere.

And of course, almost immediately after returning to the University on Sunday afternoon, Grandmaster Kiernan had left again to meet with someone else. Oliver knew this—though not much more—because of his operatives within the University.

Oliver swirled the juice in his glass with a wry smile, taking an awkward sip through the piece of glass straw the bartender had inserted when he saw Oliver's mask. Perhaps "operatives" was too extreme a word. But he was slowly building a network of informants, made up mostly of student aides and upper-term students from common backgrounds. He was gathering promising young people in administrative or assistant positions, those who needed sponsors to be able to continue their schooling, so long as they orbited the people he was *really* interested in.

Siobhan had been a wonderful lesson in the possible benefits of such an arrangement, though none of the handful of people in this budding network had brought him anywhere near the same level of advantages—or trouble—that she did.

Oliver covered the cost of the minimum four classes for them, as long as they agreed to work exclusively for him for at least ten years after graduation, and would provide bonuses if they sent him any particularly juicy information. He was circumspect with his recruitment, but confident in the potential of such a network. It was obvious from how the faculty treated young Miss Canelo that they did not respect people like her, and thus would fail to be properly wary. People with power often dismissed the presence of "the help."

And so, the scattered reports he'd gotten from his handful of informants had led him to the Bitter Phoenix, with the cloying smoke in the air now filtered by the featureless mask of Lord Stag, and two of his most battle-capable enforcers sitting at a nearby table and watching for danger.

Before Oliver had finished the drink—with each sip requiring a careful balancing act of prying the bottom half of his mask away from his face while he sucked the liquid up through the glass straw—the doorman to the back room gave the bartender a nod.

At that cue, the man gave the current password to the information broker and waved Oliver on.

His bodyguards followed closely behind as Oliver moved into the large room beyond the tavern. The room was filled with even more smoke, and the people displayed a strange mix of unnatural conditions. Some were languid and mellow, some strangely joyful, but most were filled with the frenzied focus that signaled quintessence of quicksilver. He wondered how much of the information broker's knowledge came from extrapolating particulars about his own clients. Perhaps some of these people were not addicts—or not just addicts—but working for the well-informed man.

And perhaps some of them would go to the rehabilitation center that Oliver had built from Lord Morrow's former mansion in the city center to get help. Oliver made a note to tell his one and only journalist, young Mr. Irving, to do an article about it. He couldn't force anyone to admit themselves, but he could make sure they knew about the opportunity to take back control of their lives.

He passed through into the smokeless hallway beyond, and then into the information broker's room, where a secretary used a device to scan Oliver for weapons, then waved him onward to where his enforcers could not follow.

The information broker's bald head shone like a crystal ball in the light of the lamp on his desk. He looked up with a smile from a desk even more cluttered than Oliver's, taking off his thick spectacles. "Always good to see one of my favorite customers. I received your payment in advance. Eager, are we?"

"I think you can understand my concern."

"Oh, well, indeed. You came to me for knowledge, and as ever, I can deliver. Though I cannot say for sure what the goal is, your suspicions of movement were correct. Someone who very much wishes to remain hidden has put out offers to some powerful mercenaries in the last few days. If you suspect them to be your enemies, now is the time to prepare."

36

BLACKMAIL

Damien

Month 3, Day 6, Saturday 5:30 a.m.

A week after exposing Professor Lacer's favoritism and, despite Damien's best arguments to the contrary, being forbidden from attending Sebastien's private tutoring session, Damien was still fuming. According to Professor Lacer, he "had neither the requisite experience nor control." Apparently, whatever lesson he was going to teach would normally be restricted to students in their third term or higher. Damien had redoubled his efforts at the auxiliary exercises and even experimented with some variations to test his Will as Sebastien did, determined to have a firm grasp on all of them by the end of the term. He would prove to Professor Lacer that he could keep up!

For the moment, as Sebastien and he walked through the still-dark, early morning streets of Gilbratha, Damien set aside his ire. Not because he was too tired to care. To the contrary, Damien's every cell was alive with excitement.

Everything was ready, and they were about to carry out the penultimate step in Operation Defenestration. If this went well, Ana's uncles would be deposed, her power as the heir would be assured, and maybe Sebastien would even report Damien's contribution to the higher-ups in the thirteen-pointed star—the placeholder name he had given their secret organization—and they would finally make him a full member!

Sebastien was leading, and he took them on a winding route through the city, eyes flicking around with constant watchfulness in a way that kept Damien on edge, until they finally arrived at the hotel. From there, Damien stepped forward, nodding haughtily at the night shift clerk as he set down the luggage case with all of their supplies. "I would like to purchase a room. Full bathing facilities are required."

The clerk looked lazily between Damien and Sebastien, whose hood was still pulled down far enough to conceal his features, then smirked and said, "Of course. The honeymoon suite is available, if you would like?"

Sebastien froze, turning to stare at the clerk.

Damien felt his face flush horribly red. "No!" he snapped. He cleared his throat, amending in a more reasonable tone, "No. I misspoke. Two rooms. I wish to purchase *two* adjacent rooms, each with their own bathing facilities."

As the clerk complied, moving so slowly that it had to be on purpose, Damien avoided peeking at Sebastien's face, wishing for his own to cool down faster. He refused help carrying up their bags, and together they hurried up the stairs and to their rooms, only one of which was actually necessary.

Entering together, Sebastien immediately took off his cloak and jacket and moved to the dining table where Damien laid the luggage case.

After Ana had convinced them to go through with the costume, they had argued about who exactly was going to impersonate the Raven Queen. Sebastien won. He was taller, and thus more imposing. Damien had been miffed about this, but as he watched Sebastien emerge from the bathroom in the Raven Queen costume, he had to admit that he was impressed.

Sebastien wore a wig of long black hair that they had dyed themselves, and a long, lacy black dress under an oversized hooded cloak that concealed his lack of feminine curves. The clothes were tattered and wispy at the hems, artfully torn by Ana with her eye for fashionable dramatism, and they had sewn in black feathers here and there. The outfit was both authentic and intimidating. But what was most impressive was how Sebastien moved with a natural feminine grace—a hip sway that wasn't overdone, an alluring tilt of the jaw, and simultaneously elegant and arrogant gestures with his arms and wrists.

Damien stepped closer, examining what little skin would be visible through the tattered clothes. They had used a generous amount of Ana's bronzing lotion over Sebastien's skin, which made the pale boy a little too orange, but still much closer to the Raven Queen's supposed skin tone. "Not bad," Damien allowed. "Sit down, and I'll do your face."

With a long-suffering sigh, Sebastien sat by the table and tilted his head up for Damien's ministrations.

Wielding the makeup palette that Ana had bought and taught him how to use, Damien carefully dusted and painted until Sebastien's eyes were dark gems staring out of smoky blackness and his lips were a deep wine color, even darker than blood. Damien did his best to keep his hands steady, too aware of the warmth of Sebastien's breath for comfort. When he stepped back to admire his work, he had to admit that Sebastien made an undeniably striking woman. "Are you frightened?" he asked.

Sebastien raised an eyebrow. "No."

"Your hands are shaking," Damien pointed out.

Sebastien looked down to them with surprise. "I'm not frightened. Not excessively so," he amended. "I must not have eaten enough for breakfast. Or maybe I've had too much…coffee. But don't worry, I can handle my part." Sebastien stood and pulled up his hood. He posed with unnatural stillness, his head tilted as he stared at Damien from the darkness beneath the fabric, black hair and feathers obscuring most of his features while the makeup distorted the rest.

Damien shuddered, pretty sure he could feel Sebastien's Will roiling out like the hungry waves of a dark ocean, sinister and prepared to consume whatever it could drag into its depths. "That's *perfect*," he whispered, then added more loudly, "You should definitely activate your Will when we meet them. Oh, this is going to be spectacular."

"If everything goes well, that is," Sebastien said.

Damien rolled his eyes. "We've planned for literally everything that could possibly go wrong." He opened his jacket to display the rows of healing and battle potions within as evidence. "We have backup, and we're going to search Malcolm and Randolph for any nasty surprises when they arrive. It's going to go perfectly."

"Don't tempt the gods of irony," Sebastien admonished. "No plan survives contact with the enemy."

Damien just sighed, putting on his own disguise, which was much simpler. New clothes bought off the rack instead of tailored to him, a mask bought from a street stall—instead of a costume shop, on Sebastien's recommendation—and a cloak with an equally deep hood. All black and appropriately dramatic.

The coolest part of his disguise was the collar he wore around his neck, hidden by the high neckline of his shirt, which pressed into his voice box and would magically alter the sound when he spoke. They were great for costume parties, and the artifact had come from a joke shop. Rather than a collar that would make him sound like a little girl, which Ana had suggested, Damien had chosen one that would make his voice artificially deep with a strange reverberation. He hoped it would set the uncles' knees to trembling.

Still, he had been warned to speak as little as possible, just in case they somehow recognized the cadence of his voice, if not the sound.

Sebastien put on a second cloak, less tattered and more nondescript, to cover his Raven Queen costume, and together they left the hotel through a back entrance, still with plenty of time before sunrise. They wanted to travel while the streets were still empty, and hopefully arrive well before the two they were supposed to meet, in time to do one last safety check of the area.

Sebastien was still wary of tails, but he was impressively subtle in searching for them, and even their winding route would have seemed natural to anyone not specifically following them. He moved as if he belonged among the increasingly run-down buildings and streets lined by trash and frozen feces. Sebastien barely took note of these things; he didn't even seem nervous. It was as if he went undercover for high-stakes meetings all the time.

And maybe he did.

Damien did his best to imitate him, acting as if he belonged with absolute confidence. As they entered the parts of the city that had been involved in the gang fights earlier that term, the cleanliness actually improved, but there were still damaged buildings. Their destination was one such building, an old stone construct covered with dead crawling vines, the roof of which had crumbled away some time ago, if the interior was any indication.

Snow had piled up and mostly melted away, leaving a lumpy sheen of compacted ice in the middle of the room, with dead and dormant plants sprouting out of the ground in several places where the planks of the old wooden floor had either rotted away or been forcefully removed, perhaps for firewood. Tattered bedding and barrels full of trash and ash made it obvious that homeless people had been sheltering there to escape the elements, but Sebastien and Damien were alone in the building at the moment, as Sebastien had sent some local contact to clear the transitory residents away the night before.

After a quick search of the area, an examination of the surrounding buildings, and confirmation of the signals that meant both their backup and the private investigator Ana had hired were in place and ready for the upcoming meeting, Sebastien and Damien stood in wait, covered by the deeper shadow of the remaining roof, up against a load-bearing wall. "They will come, right?" Damien murmured.

"They should," Sebastien said, but his tone held a tension born from uncertainty. Ana had sent a blackmail note to her uncles the night before, threatening them with the information they had uncovered—the proverbial stick—and offering to trade the book for the Raven Queen's ring—the carrot. She had enclosed a black feather with the letter as a signature.

Damien had wanted to cut and paste letters from many different newspapers to send an untraceable and intimidating message, but Ana thought that wasn't "classy" enough for someone like the Raven Queen, and thus didn't seem believable.

Despite their initial worry, as the sun began to rise, their two victims arrived, scurrying nervously through the street with their heads on a paranoid swivel. It seemed they had done as the note demanded, coming alone.

Sebastien slipped his hand through an ingenious slit Ana had sewn in his skirts to the hidden pouch underneath, which held a small vial filled with a dark, roiling concoction. He uncorked it, allowing the contents to spew from the glass container. Smoke billowed out from beneath his dress, an ominous and translucent grey that sometimes flashed purple. Apparently, it was a modified philtre of smoke, meant more for theatrical effect than obscuration. The long-lasting cumulus clouds stayed low to the ground, roiling balefully as they spread.

Malcolm and Randolph arrived with perfect timing, just as the smoke reached the edge of the shadow that Sebastien and Damien had sequestered themselves within.

Both men stiffened and froze as the smoke attracted their gaze to Sebastien. Malcolm recovered first, tightening his grip around the ornate head of his cane and stepping fully into the room. Randolph—father of the infamous "cousin Robbie"—was less bold, though the tremor in his hands as he followed his older brother inside was just as likely the aftereffect of an overindulgence in alcohol, or some other less savory substance, as it was a physical symptom of his obvious fear.

Damien and Sebastien stepped forward in turn, with Sebastien leading and Damien trailing a few respectful feet behind. Damien shuddered as he felt Sebastien's Will roil out into the slow-moving smoke, riding on it with malevolent intent.

Both Malcolm and Randolph Gervin seemed to feel it too, as Malcolm stiffened and swallowed heavily, while Randolph sidled a little more directly behind his brother, as if to use him as a shield.

At this angle, with the roof and part of the wall gone, the four of them were fully visible from a window on the upper floor of a nearby building, where the private investigator was waiting with a camera obscura. Damien believed this would be the perfect moment to take a couple shots, but he kept his eyes from straying in that direction and hoped the flash of light wouldn't give their plan away too early.

Malcolm Gervin cleared his throat. "We came alone, as required, and have brought the ring. Did you bring the book?"

Sebastien turned his concealed face toward Damien in wordless command.

Damien stepped forward. "I need to search you for weapons or any other items that would constitute a betrayal," he said, his voice coming out like a rock giant gargling pebbles.

Malcolm's mouth tightened, but he nodded.

Damien came around behind them, searching Randolph first, and then Malcolm, being as thorough as possible as he ran through a mental list of all the ways people had ever hidden something on their person in an Aberford Thorndyke story. He found several pieces of contraband, including multiple battle wands, a philtre of liquid fire, a bracelet that Randolph insisted was just a valuable piece of jewelry, and an actual hidden breastplate underneath Malcolm's shirt. He took them all, including both men's coin purses and Malcolm's cane, which Damien knew held a hidden knife, and placed them in a pile beside Sebastien's feet. The man didn't need the cane to walk, after all, though Malcolm tried to protest that he did. Damien found the Raven Queen's ring, too, but Malcolm refused to let him take it until they had exchanged it for the book.

Through it all, Sebastien remained silent, communicating only by small twitches of his arms or head, which was more unnerving than being screamed at might have been.

Finally, Damien returned to his place at Sebastien's side. "We have the book," he confirmed. "And the proof of your other activities."

"How do we know you have made no copies, and that you will not betray us after getting what you want?" Malcolm asked.

Sebastien laughed, a low, eerie sound that genuinely made Damien uncomfortable.

He recovered quickly, saying, "If the Raven Queen planned to harm you, there would be little you could do to stop her. But she is honorable. You came to have what is hers through honest means, and though you may be of reprehensible character, so long as you do not make an enemy of her, she will have no reason to retaliate."

Sebastien nodded, reaching into the inner pocket of his cloak. First, he pulled out a folder stuffed with papers and photographs of evidence, and then a large volume, its leather binding tattered, its pages smelling of smoke and rancid, spiced sausage.

Damien allowed himself a smile of pride beneath his mask. He was the one who'd designed and put together the book, with a little help from Ana, and it was a perfect base for the skill with illusions that had cemented Sebastien's role as the Raven Queen in this little play.

The inside of the front cover held a spell array that Sebastien used to create the illusion of a strange, shifting glyph on the front, half-disguised by a streaked, bloody handprint, as if someone had died as it was pried out of their grasp. The pages glowed so slightly it was only visible in contrast to the relative gloom of their surroundings, but the light was a dark, sinister color that wasn't quite purple—blacklight, just on the edge of human perception. As the book's faint light passed over Sebastien's costume, the honey they had splattered and streaked over the fabric in violent patterns became briefly visible, like a dream clawing into the waking world.

Both of the Gervins' attention locked onto the book like it was a glass of water and they were parched and dying men—as if it were the most important thing in the room. "A worthy trade," Malcolm said, holding up the small jewelry box and opening it to reveal the ring within. "With this returned, and your silence about the rest, the bond made with your father—or at least the man who calls himself such—will be nullified, Queen of Ravens."

Sebastien stepped forward, leaning in to examine the ring with false curiosity.

When Malcolm moved closer to make the exchange, a huge fireball shot out from the roof of that same building where the private investigator was hiding.

The spell headed straight for Sebastien, who ducked just in time. It splashed against the ground a few feet away, the edges of the flame licking at the smoke and the hem of his tattered costume.

Malcolm and Randolph both stumbled back, each reaching for an artifact only to find it missing, taken by Damien during his search.

Sebastien stood, looking from the scorch mark on the ground to the roof where the fireball had come from.

Yet another black-cloaked form stood there proudly, pointing a battle wand down at them. Before anyone could respond, they shot again.

Sebastien and Damien moved back to evade it, and the spell landed between them and the Gervins.

"Betrayal!" Sebastien snarled, his voice almost unrecognizable with authentic-sounding rage.

Again, Damien couldn't help but flinch, a visceral reaction to the sound. Sebastien was, apparently, an amazing actor who could have made a name for himself in the University theatre club. The smoke beneath the Raven Queen costume began to billow more strongly as Sebastien activated the gust spell array they had scratched into the inner side of one of Sebastien's boots.

Putting a spell array in such a place was both dangerous and absolutely ingenious, but the effect was spectacular, sending his costume fluttering with imagined power and pushing the smoke out in waves of grey and purple.

"No, no, we didn't!" Randolph screamed.

"We are not allied with them, I swear it," Malcolm called. "We came alone, and in good faith!"

But it was too late, because another wand-wielding attacker walked up the street, and a third appeared atop one of the other nearby roofs. Both shot spells toward Sebastien and Damien, ignoring the Gervins.

And that was Damien's cue. In one smooth flourish, he pulled the wand from his own hidden wrist holder, throwing up the shield spell contained within. It blocked both the fireball spell—which was carefully calibrated to be more light than heat or force—as well as pieces of stone that a concussive blast spell had sent hurtling in their direction.

Then he switched to the second setting, which normally held a standard stunning spell. He had a license for the battle wand, but it was hard to get approved for anything more lethal on the grounds of "protection." Still, Sebastien had somehow come through again, taking the wand and returning with a different variation on the stunning spell charged within. It acted in almost the same way, but instead of the standard bright red, the spell that shot out, crackling faintly with arcs of electricity and glowing dust, was a sickly green that reminded Damien of puke.

Malcolm literally threw himself to the ground to avoid it, expressions of outrage and terror fighting for dominance on his face. "Stop! We're on your side!"

"You betrayed us!" Damien yelled. "You're going to *wish* you were dead." Adrenaline was coursing through his veins, and his voice cracked, but he was pretty sure, judging by the expressions on Malcolm's and Randolph's faces, that he was totally pulling off the charade.

Malcolm's expression hardened, and as he crawled back to his feet, he reached into his mouth. With one finger, he popped something out from between his jaw and his cheek and clenched it in his hand hard enough that his knuckles turned white.

Immediately, a dome shimmered around him, and a second later the man had disappeared. Only the faint disturbance of the smoke floating along the ground revealed his position as, shielded and invisible, he ran out the door.

Randolph fumbled to do the same, but dropped whatever artifact contained such an impressive spell. He went scrambling for it on the ground among the trash and rubble, his face turning puce with terror before he was able to retrieve and activate it.

The trio of attackers surrounding the decrepit building continued to attack Damien and Sebastien, though their spells were either seemingly mis-aimed, poorly timed, or just didn't manage to do any damage past Damien's shield.

Sebastien strode into full view in the middle of the room, head hanging low as he slowly raised his arms, hands peeking out from within his long, tattered sleeves. He turned his head toward their first attacker and reached out to them, pointing a finger and then making a crushing motion with his fist. Half a second later, something exploded with a rumble of thunder and the soundless eruption of a true philtre of darkness.

Sebastien did this twice more, once for each of the other two hired actors that his contacts among the secret organization had allowed him to procure, to the same sensational result.

With their "attackers" thus subdued, having each set off a philtre of darkness and a single-shot firecracker at their own feet at Sebastien's motion, he and Damien were quick to leave, rushing along their designated escape route to the safe house Sebastien had insisted on.

The coppers would be drawn by the noise, and they wanted as few sightings of the Raven Queen as possible. This whole thing was supposed to be a big production, but Damien shuddered to think of what might happen if the real Raven Queen heard about their impersonation and took offense.

They sprinted through back alleys and run-down buildings, with so many twists and turns that, if not for Sebastien to lead him, Damien thought he might have gotten himself lost. Then they turned abruptly into a little cottage's side door, where they changed their appearance. Sebastien took off the wig, carefully removed all of the makeup and skin toner, and stripped off the dress. With his white-blonde hair pulled back at the base of his neck in the same style Professor Lacer often wore and a different cloak over simple clothing, he looked completely different. Damien took off his mask and flipped over the reversible cloak he wore to display the inner forest green instead of the black.

They exited the cottage from a different door as nonchalantly as possible and found Ana's carriage waiting nearby. After they hopped in, the driver clicked his tongue to the horses, sending them off toward the nice part of the city and the hotel rooms Damien had booked.

"So, do you think it worked?" Ana asked.

"Definitely," Damien said, feeling like he was about to vibrate out of his seat. "Oh, Ana, it was amazing. You should have seen your uncles. So cowed. They fell for it completely. And Sebastien! Best impersonation of the Raven Queen I've ever imagined. He missed his calling as a stage actor." As they rode through the streets, Damien recounted the whole sequence of events to Ana, ignoring Sebastien's frequent snorts of disagreement and incredulous expressions.

"That's really exactly how it all happened, Ana. Sebastien likes to downplay things, you know," Damien insisted.

"And he's so jaded," Ana agreed, nodding wisely.

Sebastien ignored them both. "How do you think the coppers will take this?" he asked.

"I don't know, but isn't that irrelevant as long as they don't find out who was really involved?" Damien asked.

Sebastien did not seem mollified by this argument.

They had to duck out of the way of early-rising inhabitants a couple of times as they attempted to sneak back into their rooms, and Damien was relieved when the door finally closed behind them. "What's going to happen to all their things?" he asked, leaning against the inside of the door. "We just left them behind. Will the coppers be able to identify their owners, do you think?"

Sebastien gave him the first real grin of the night. "Our allies out there this morning should pick them up before the coppers arrive. Partial payment for their services, I suppose. There might even be some coin left over for us."

Neither Damien nor Ana had the same gleeful response to the promise of loot, until Sebastien added, "I was thinking, maybe we could set up an education fund for Newton's family. He has younger sisters, I think. If the family even wants more of their children learning the same magic that killed their son, that is."

That immediately sobered the mood, but they all agreed it was a good idea. Damien and Sebastien both retreated to the bathrooms to wipe off any evidence of their adventure, and then they all made their way back to the carriage to return to the University.

No one would even realize they had left.

As they were riding up one of the transport tubes, watching the sun as it rose high enough in the sky to cut through the morning fog, Damien turned to Sebastien, smirk displayed in full force. "I told you the plan would work perfectly."

37

———

OUTPUT CIRCLE

Month 3, Day 7, Sunday 9:00 a.m.

Sebastien arrived at Professor Lacer's office Sunday morning right at nine. There had been no need for the beamshell tincture to boost her energy levels that morning, such was her excitement for the chance to take another step toward learning to free-cast.

He waved her in, closing and locking the door behind her. "I do not want you distracted at a critical moment if some buffoon decides to burst in without knocking," he explained. He turned to his desk, where a coffee tray rested, and poured himself a mug. He looked to her with a questioning eyebrow.

"Yes, please," she agreed, more for the chance to share a morning coffee with Thaddeus Lacer than out of a desire for caffeine.

He reached for the trench coat draped over his desk chair, pulled a flask from the inner pocket, and poured some of the liquid within into his coffee. "I am not an alcoholic, if you were wondering," he said. "This is a special wakefulness concoction that I developed myself. Useful for when emergencies allow me no time to sleep. I would offer you some, but the taste is extremely unpleasant, and if you were so exhausted as to need it, that would be a sign that we should postpone this lesson."

Sebastien nodded, then shook her head. "I don't—need it, that is. I'm awake."

Professor Lacer handed her a steaming mug, into which he had added neither sugar nor cream, then took a reluctant gulp of his own brew. His exaggerated grimace and the little involuntary shudder that ran through him was...almost cute.

Sebastien turned her attention to her own coffee. '*I must be sleep deprived if my mind could make a connection between the word "cute" and Thaddeus Lacer,*' she thought. '*There has never been a man who matched that descriptor less.*' Aloud, she said, "So what am I going to be learning today? You said it would help prepare me for free-casting?"

Professor Lacer stepped back around his desk toward the center of his office, where the furniture had been pushed out of the way to provide space. "Thaumaturges, like all people, can become set in their ways, their brains wearing down comfortable pathways of frequent travel. This happens with the Will as well, and the more those comfortable pathways are traveled, the more difficult it can be to climb one's way out of the valleys created. This is why, for example, I assigned first term students an exercise using light as both Sacrifice and output. Climbing out of that rut is the point behind what you will attempt today."

He pulled a wrapped piece of chalk from his vest pocket, drawing a simple and yet somehow perfect Circle on the floor without any guidelines. Then he exchanged the chalk for his Conduit and a beast core. "Spells learned by fledgling thaumaturges like yourself are almost always bound by the confines of the central Circle of your spell array. The output effect is contained and controlled within. This is fine—and safe—to start out with, but one who hopes to become a free-caster should not settle too comfortably into this habit." A glowing sphere, a simple light spell, appeared inside of the chalk Circle. "Tell me what you know about spells whose output is actualized outside of the Circle."

Sebastien quickly organized her thoughts. "The easiest example of such spells still kind of work by controlling the area bounded by the Circle. Like a spell that creates cold in the area surrounding the Circle by gathering all the heat inside it, or the gust spell, which just expels air from the Circle in a specific direction. But there are plenty of spells with more complex directional effects. They still originate within the Circle of the spell array, but then travel outside it. You talked about this in the first lesson at the beginning of the term," she remembered.

Professor Lacer turned to watch her as she continued to speak, his gaze inscrutable as the words tumbled from her more quickly, her excitement building the longer she spoke.

"Examples are fireball spells, which shoot an actual ball of fire at the target, revealing spells, which shoot vibrations and unseen waves, and even the stunning spell, which shoots a low-current electrical charge along with the powdered saliva of a Kuthian frog, all contained within a field of force that dissipates on contact with the target. You said the commonality between these kinds of spells is that they shoot something that exists in nature, just bound in a compact form that decoheres with distance and time. *But*, with enough power and control, one should be able to shoot transmogrificational long-range spells by shooting both the Circle and the Word at its target, which is supposed to be incredibly difficult." She paused, then added, "I can shoot a directional slicing spell that works by compressing air. And the gust spell. And, of course, Newton Moore's spell that uses the Circle of the hands, but the effects of which travel throughout the caster's physical body."

Professor Lacer nodded, turning back to the spell resting on the floor. Suddenly, the area *outside* the Circle glowed with diffuse light, and then, after a few seconds, the light gathered in a wedge-shaped beam on one side. "These directional applications still depend upon the center Circle. As do projectile applications." The light coalesced back into a sphere in the middle, then suddenly shot out, expanding and dimming slightly before impacting against the far wall, where it burst and immediately dissipated. "These parameters of direction, velocity, and even containment force are generally written into the spell array."

"Are you going to teach me how to bypass those limitations? Remove those parameters from the spell array, maybe?" It seemed like the logical next step to her.

"That is not an unreasonable guess, but based on my observations, that is not something you should need my help with. If you practice slightly modifying those output parameters beyond the exact limitations of the spell array, you should be able to work up to removing them entirely. There is another parameter which we will be focusing on today." He glanced back at the Circle on the floor, but the sphere of light instead appeared floating between the two of them at head height. It had not originated within the Circle.

Sebastien stared into the light with admiration, and then turned to meet Professor Lacer's dark blue eyes with open avarice. "I'm ready."

His lips twitched with somewhat mocking amusement. "I am aware. This exercise is difficult, and for those with an undeveloped Will, can be dangerous. You have the requisite experience and control, as evidenced by the Henrik-Thompson capacity test I supervised a couple of months ago, as well as your recent performance with the illusion spell. One might expect to see the equiv-alent in a *third-term* student, one who entered the University having never cast a spell before," he said pointedly, though she knew he didn't actually care for the rules and laws restricting magic. "Most importantly, however, and unlike our young Mr. Westbay, I know you are prepared to learn this because you have done it before."

She looked at the ball of light hanging in the air and then back to him.

"What? When... Ah!" She thought she knew what he was referencing. "During the entrance exam. When I threw that...temper tantrum with the blue flame spell," she said, rubbing the back of her neck and looking away.

"Indeed. And when you accomplished this, the spell array certainly did not contain a coherent Word describing the parameters of an output generated outside of the Circle. You brought that flame to life in the air with Will alone. At the time, I remember being surprised you had not killed yourself in the attempt, but I am quite sure you at least approached Will strain, if not stepped directly into it. Today, you will learn to do this with the proper spell array."

Professor Lacer gestured to the chalk Circle on the floor, and a purposeful gust of wind originated at their feet, cleared away the dust, and deposited it in the wastebasket beside his desk. "Let us have a quick lesson on how to read and adjust the output parameters, and then you will attempt the exercise yourself."

He turned to one of his bookcases, pushing on the edge. It slid to the side, apparently resting on tracks rather than the floor, and revealed a blackboard that had been concealed on the wall behind it. Then, writing out multiple example spell arrays for her, he gave a thirty-minute lecture on the concept, which she absorbed like a dry sponge.

Finally, he said, "Now, put this principle into practice. You will start with an output on the ground approximately one meter away from your spell array. Once you've mastered that, you can try for longer distances, then lifting the output vertically, and then a combination of the two. More advanced applications will have you further increasing distance or trying to cast with a denser substance than air between you and the target location. I would request that you only attempt this under my supervision until I say otherwise. And, as a warning against your proclivity for reckless stupidity, do not attempt to do this with, say, a person or a crowd of people between you and your target. You are likely to face resistance due to the inherent magical barrier of their bodies creating an impassable obstacle. Also, you should be aware that most household wards will act as a shield against this by blocking the energy transfer."

Sebastien's eyes narrowed thoughtfully as she considered how one might get around such wards, but she didn't spend much effort contemplating it. Moving to the center of the room, she crouched to draw out her own spell array with a wax crayon, which was less likely to smear catastrophically as she walked around. Unlike Professor Lacer, she wrote out the full Word with detailed instructions inside her spell array, taking the beast core he tossed her way as a convenient source of power. She left out only the anchored location parameters.

As she palmed the Conduit Professor Lacer had lent her, attached by a chain to her pocket watch, she stilled, staring down into its crystalline depths. Despite her excitement for the lesson, her mind wandered to her mother's conduit. Malcolm Gervin had indeed brought the forgery that she had placed in the vault to their meeting. Either he was being disingenuous, or he had no idea that the one he had was a fake, which only confirmed her suspicions that Ennis had sold the original celerium at some point. The thought once more filled her with rage. She was almost looking forward to his trial, when he would finally see some consequences for all the harm he had done.

Sebastien forced her mind back to the present moment. The magic required her focus. Drawing on the beast core, she first created a small ball of light within the spell array's main Circle, both to warm up her mind and make sure she had no trouble with the spell effect itself. She had never drawn on a beast core for light before, after all.

Then she dropped the spell and prepared to cast it again, this time adding the final parameters. She brought her Will to bear, staring at a spot exactly one meter away from the center of the Circle and…nothing happened. Power had been drawn through her Conduit and was circling through the wax lines of the spell array, but no light had appeared where she intended.

No glowing sphere had appeared at all. It felt as if the magic had sputtered against her Will at the last moment, like a candle flame about to go out, struggling feebly for its life, and then…nothing.

She tried again, to the same result. And again. Frowning with consternation, she reviewed the spell array, then took a few moments to go over the concept in her mind once more, focusing on the mental image of a ball of light appearing where she had instructed. This would improve the clarity of her Will.

This time, she leaned into the spell, baring her teeth and driving her Will against the reluctant fabric of reality. 'Light. *Light!*' This time the magic didn't simply sputter, it bucked against her. It didn't feel exactly like the wildness of new magic that hadn't yet been broken in, but more as if she was trying to play the child's game of hoop-rolling, but her wheel kept getting stuck in unforeseen ruts in the road and being drawn off course.

Cold anxiety settled in her gut. *'Is my mind already so congealed in its ways, my Will so intractable, that I cannot adapt?'*

"This is expected to be difficult," Professor Lacer said. "Even I had trouble with it, on my first attempts. Do not grow discouraged. You must simply keep trying until you crack open the new paradigm. You may stay in my office until noon. There are plenty of protective wards, and I will not let anything happen to you. Schedules allowing, you may come back to practice again next weekend, and the one after that, and so forth until you succeed. Periodically, I will give other lectures on topics that may provide you…inspiration. For now, you may be best served by grasping the full measure of the problem. The better your understanding of your current limitations, the more use you will get out of related information."

She didn't respond, still scowling down at the floor with enough ire that her expression could have scoured the stone away.

When she failed to respond, he added, "Do not allow your frustration to make you careless. A mistake here could be very dangerous, with the magic outside the bounds of the spell array and thus unrestricted."

Sebastien stood, rolling her Conduit between her fingers and pacing back and forth. "I don't understand what I'm doing wrong. Like you said, I've *done this before* successfully. I—" Sebastien broke off as her eyes caught on the cover of the book Professor Lacer was reading. '*A History and Guidebook of those who Call Themselves the People: Nomadic Tribes of the Northern Islands,*' the title read. A shock of mixed alarm and curiosity shook her from her thoughts. Her mother had been of the People. That book was about her own ancestry.

Perhaps seeing the curiosity on her face, Professor Lacer said, "The indigenous peoples of the northern islands are quite fascinating. I recently became interested in them in relationship to the Raven Queen. Half of her supposed civilian identity comes from those who call themselves the People."

"How do you know that?" she asked, trying to seem innocently curious.

"I am a friend of Titus Westbay, who runs the local coppers. Occasionally I am called in to consult on particularly difficult or interesting cases. I was not always a teacher, you know," he added with a wry twist of his mouth, almost self-deprecating. "You may find it interesting to know why a group of insular, nomadic minorities are called that, even by outsiders, when it seems more likely we would come up with some other designation for them. It is an example of some of the most widespread, impressive transmogrification I have seen, a curse whose details have been lost to time and can only be speculated at. The Church of the Radiant Maiden was leading their crusade about four thousand B.C.E., expanding their grasp toward the scattered nations on the outskirts of the western continent, and had begun to persecute the People. You've heard the history, I'm sure. Many atrocities, dehumanization, slavery and forced familiar contracts of sentient beings, etcetera." He waved his hand nonchalantly.

"The People could not stand up to the weight of the Church's sheer scale, but they had other specialties. They forced all outsiders to call them "people" in their own language, a curse whose remnants last to this day. The closest guess we have about their method, pieced together from battle reports, is that they used a large ritual sacrifice of their enemies. When I say large, I mean a ritual that spanned tens of kilometers, coordinated by smoke signals and light shone on the clouds, performed on a day of importance and with the cooperation of every single member of the scattered tribes. Curses may all have their keys, but this one was never broken. Though the compulsion itself has faded, the power of even that much energy consumed by the eons, the naming habit persists. Impressive, is it not? These are the Raven Queen's ancestors."

Sebastien nodded silently, running her tongue over the back of her teeth for a moment. Her grandfather had told that story many times, though the details were slightly different. Hesitantly, she asked, "So, do you know anything else about the Raven Queen?"

He smiled with a strange, dark delight that made Sebastien's hair stand on end. "She had a very interesting childhood."

"What do you mean?"

"I only know as much as the coppers have been able to glean, but the Red Guard has records of an Aberrant incident, and some of those closest to her had very interesting backgrounds. I will not share the details, so snuff out that burning curiosity, child."

Sebastien took a moment to digest this, then decided to pry at the information she had originally wanted more directly. "I heard rumors that she made another appearance recently?"

Lacer snorted disdainfully. "Despite how much those currently investigating her might want to believe otherwise, that was not the Raven Queen."

Sebastien's throat went dry. "What do you mean?"

"Too many discrepancies. Supposedly, the Raven Queen and a companion were meeting with an unknown party and was either betrayed by them or ambushed by a third group. There is a surprising lack of testimony. However, examination of the crime scene has revealed that some of the attacks were underpowered, almost as if they were not meant to kill. There was some residue left from the Raven Queen's clothing, including a couple of black feathers. However, they were not raven feathers, but crow feathers, and had been sewn and glued onto the fabric." He gave her a pointed look.

"Crow feathers..." she murmured. "I suppose they look quite similar, to a layperson."

"Additionally, eyewitnesses say she and her companion ran away from the scene in a very mundane manner, which is certainly possible, but somewhat implausible, given that multiple previous reports have noted that she has some stealth-based ability to slip away or disappear, possibly with the aid of shadows. Even if for some reason that was not possible in this instance, we have the final discrepancy. The one unreliable eyewitness who saw the tail end of the actual incident insists that the Raven Queen was free-casting some kind of darkness spell on her attackers, and killed them all with little more than a wave of the hand. In reality, while there are signs of multiple different philtres of darkness and even some modified firecrackers, all the attackers seem to have escaped on their own, with no signs of injury. Given all this evidence, what would be your conclusion?"

Sebastien tried to smile, though it felt awkward on her face. "Someone was impersonating the Raven Queen?"

"Indeed. A clever impersonation, to be sure, but no match for the investigative power of Crown-funded law enforcement. If it really was her, then she is playing a game several levels deep, too many even for me to comprehend. But despite all this, and all the confusion this incident has created, some of the coppers are intent on labeling it a Raven Queen sighting. Apparently the hope of progress and having something to report to the High Crown is enough of a reason to ignore the facts."

"But that's entirely counterproductive," she said, noting the irony that if they found the Raven Queen impersonators or the Raven Queen herself, *she* would be caught either way.

Professor Lacer slid a marker into his book to hold his place, and then reached for the remaining coffee and poured himself a second cup, which he reheated simply by sliding the tip of his finger around the rim of the mug. "You would think that any rational person would understand that. When playing against someone as painfully clever, dangerous, and powerful as the Raven Queen, their halfhearted efforts will never be enough to catch her. Some of them are more interested in *seeming* as if they are doing their jobs than producing results. There is a difference between showing that you've tried and *actually trying*."

"But surely some of them are putting in the work?"

He took a sip, this time forgoing the splash of something extra. "Some of them. But you might be surprised by how common a failing this is, Mr. Siverling. The majority, alas, have not trained themselves to latch onto confusion like they should. *Confusion* is the difference between what your models of how the world works *predict*, and reality. The first virtue of a thaumaturge is curiosity, but the second virtue is relinquishment—the ability to let go of incorrect beliefs when they are leading you to incorrect answers. The ability to change your mind."

Lacer stood abruptly, verve flowing through him and animating him the same way it often did when he gave a dramatic lecture at the front of the classroom. "Sebastien, when you are confused, that is a sign. A huge red warning sign that, if you have trained yourself properly, you should realize is the equivalent of a rogue magic siren going off right next to you. But most people feel instead a slight uncertainty, or a sense of sneaking suspicion, there for only half a moment before they roll over and bury it with justifications and tightly held beliefs that are too precious to be challenged."

He moved around his desk and began to pace, gesturing with the hand not occupied with a coffee mug. "A man who has never seen the sky before may believe that it is purple. When he finally crawls out of his cave and sees an expanse of blue above him, he will be confused. His model of the world conflicts with reality. Rather than justifying that what he sees cannot be the sky, he should update his predictive models—his beliefs—and understand that the sky is blue.

"If a woman believes that her partner is faithful to her, but her partner is acting secretive and staying out late, she may become suspicious. Rather than rationalizing away these behaviors, since they are evidence against the believed faithfulness of her partner, she should investigate. Doubt's purpose is to erase itself, one way or the other. If your models of reality seem to conflict with actual reality, the ability to be curious, and the ability to relinquish your beliefs, will allow you to determine actual reality, and thus whether your models should be kept, discarded, or updated."

Sebastien couldn't help but absorb some of Lacer's passion for the subject, the rightness of his words settling somewhere deep inside of her. Their message seemed obvious, but she knew from experience that nominally understanding something and actually living by its principles was not the same thing. "You've mentioned the virtues of a thaumaturge before. Curiosity, and now relinquishment. Are there more?"

He stopped pacing and turned to face her. "There are twelve virtues in the Way."

She leaned forward. "The Way of true power? You mentioned that before, too."

"The Way of true power. The Way of victory. It has no formal name, but in simplified terms, it is simply the art of not being stupid." He sipped his coffee, staring at the floor with a mirthless severity. "A surprising amount of the time, you will find that winning is about not being stupid. Which is harder than it might sound, because these meat suits we wear, our brains, are built to take shortcuts that save energy, and to encourage behaviors that would keep us alive in a primitive environment. They are not built to be always *right*. One of the greatest frustrations of my life," he added in a low murmur.

"What are the other virtues?" Sebastien asked.

Lacer observed her for a few long moments during which she was careful not to fidget, meeting his challenging gaze unflinchingly. "No, I do not think I will tell you," he mused. She wanted to protest, but he continued. "Listing them out for you to memorize will not do you any good. At worst, it will make you *think* you understand and adhere to them. It is best if you search them out for yourself, internalizing their lessons as you learn and grow." His tone gentled. "This is the effort of a lifetime, child. You will have time."

"You'll still teach me about them, though, right?" she asked.

"When appropriate. Now, back to work with you," he said, waving his hand at her in a clipped shooing motion as he summoned the book he had been reading and moved to sit in one of the plush chairs resting against the wall.

She hesitated, looking from the spell array on the floor to the book in his hands. Grabbing her Conduit for what she vaguely recognized was the sense of comfort and safety it gave her, she narrowed her eyes. "I have a *sneaking suspicion* that you're reading that book out of more than simple curiosity. You're looking to gain knowledge towards a purpose," she said boldly, despite the little voice of anxiety inside that wanted her to shrink back and be silent for fear of exposing herself to danger. "Have you learned something new?"

He glanced at her over the top of the book. "Already putting my lessons into practice, Mr. Siverling?"

Sebastien nodded. "I always do."

Lacer actually smiled at that, filling her with a quick flush of pride, but he immediately returned to reading. "Might I suggest that if you have more questions that would distract from your spellcasting, you try to find out the answers yourself through applying your mind to the problem?"

"But I don't have access to the amount or quality of information that you do," she protested.

He quirked up one eyebrow. "An astute observation. Perhaps that is a sign that you, a first-term University student who has displayed a proclivity for questionable judgment and jumping into danger, are not qualified to deal with the issue and thus should not recklessly poke your head into it."

She didn't know what to say to that.

After a short pause, he lifted his head again, shifting slightly. "I understand that you are interested in the Raven Queen because of the 'blessing' she imparted upon you. But I assure you, she is not particularly interested in you. She was using you as a tool to communicate indirectly. You need not fear that she has some vendetta against you. If you *do* find yourself in contact with her once more, mention of my name might do well as a talisman of protection. There is no need to worry or obsess over her."

Sebastien wanted to protest that she was not obsessed with the Raven Queen, but instead asked, "Why do you think she's interested in you? You seem awfully sure."

Professor Lacer acted as if he hadn't heard her, but the sharp tapping of one impatient forefinger against the arm of his chair was enough indication that he had run through whatever limited pool of indulgence he allowed her.

She returned to the wax spell array, kneeling on the stone floor before it. The difference between her attempts now and her success during the entrance exam was that at that time, she had been desperate, terrified, and enraged. Her Will had been undeniably imbued with that ephemeral property, forcefulness.

Now, Sebastien tried to grasp hold of that again. '*I want this. I must make it work. If I fail here, my dreams are shattered. This is the step that will take me beyond my mediocre, helpless existence. Without this, I will not reach true power.*' She allowed herself to wallow in bad memories, something she so often avoided, until tears prickled at her closed eyes and goosebumps rose on her arms and back. With trembling fingers and a racing heart, she tightened her fist around her Conduit, opened her eyes, and reached over to draw an ephemeral Circle around the empty spot on the floor where the light should appear, hoping that the act would somehow bridge the gap in her mind.

And in doing so, she realized that perhaps she'd been going about this all wrong. Not only had she cast a similar spell during the entrance exam, but she frequently cast a spell whose output location she controlled at will: her shadow-familiar.

She sat back on her heels, rolling that thought over in her mind. Her shadow-familiar had the advantage of being formed of her shadow, which inherently belonged to her in a way that some random spot on the floor a meter away from her spell array did not. But perhaps she could borrow some principles from it. Namely, the fact that, as long as it was connected to her by a single thread of shadow, a tether, where it went and what shape it took mattered not.

She held her hand out over the Circle, far enough away to be outside of its bounds, allowing her shadow to fall within it. She imagined a band of control spreading from the center of the Circle out to the spot where the spell effect should be generated, a channel through which power and her Will could both flow.

'*Light*,' she snarled mentally, staring at that empty spot. She would not accept failure. She could not even conceive of failure, such was her determination.

A small glowing sphere bloomed on the floor a meter away, surrounded by nothing and wavering translucently. Her spell array glowed at first with inefficiency, but quickly dimmed as if cowed by her glare.

She was concentrating too hard to be elated as she brought the ball of light into greater resolution and stability. She held it until the trembling subsided from her fingers and her racing heart slowed, until the dread riding on her shoulders dissipated. Then, finally, she released the spell.

Sebastien turned to Professor Lacer only to find him already watching her, his book set aside and forgotten.

38

A MONSTER EGG

THADDEUS
Month 3, Day 7, Sunday 10:00 a.m.

THADDEUS SET DOWN his book and stared at his apprentice, who had just managed to detach the output of his spell from the central Circle after only an hour of focused effort. He had estimated that the boy, due to a combination of talent, work ethic, and sheer stubbornness, would succeed in two to six months, practicing for a few hours every weekend, wearing down those mental ruts as Thaddeus slowly helped him grasp the necessary concepts.

Thaddeus himself had taken almost a week of practice when he gained this same ability many years ago. He knew people that struggled with it for a year or more, and many more never managed to overcome their over-reliance on the spell array and, specifically, the bounding Circle.

Perhaps young Siverling's previous success under emotional duress had been more impactful than Thaddeus estimated. Or perhaps the boy had already been working toward this even before Thaddeus deemed him ready to make the attempt.

The boy released the light spell with a hiss of air, breathing heavily from the exertion.

"Do it again," Thaddeus ordered, moving to examine the exact mechanism his apprentice was using more clearly.

Siverling struggled with the attempt for a minute or so but managed the feat once more.

Thaddeus's eyes narrowed as he examined the spell array, and he cast a minor divination spell that was meant to aid perception, highlighting the signs of magic that were too subtle for human senses to parse. "Again, in the opposite direction."

Siverling adjusted his spell array, and once more created the light sphere outside of the Circle. Sweat began to bead on his temples.

"Hmm." Thaddeus leaned closer, examining the space between the output and the central Circle. He could see the energy flowing along the stone floor in a single band, not quite enough to let off a visible glow, but obvious enough with the aid of his perception spell tuned to exactly such a thing. "Rather than physically create a connecting line, you have extended your spell array with an effort of pure Will. In a way, this is impressive, and speaks to your future as a free-caster, but it is not the result I require."

The boy slumped with dismay, but quickly firmed up his spine again. "I don't understand."

"This is the most common method for displacing the output, but your understanding is still bounded by your previous experiences, and I think you will find this method to have certain limitations. Still, you have taken a firm step toward true detachment and are wearing away at the edges of familiarity."

Siverling's expression grew grim. "Am I?" he murmured. "What is the eventual goal, then? What do you mean by true detachment?"

"Better if you come to understand more organically. We can continue as planned, though the timeline has accelerated somewhat. You will explore the limits of your current abilities, and I will offer you knowledge that you may form into a solution. After all, following exactly in someone else's footsteps is its own kind of rut. Can you continue?"

Siverling nodded adamantly.

"Then let us begin. First, we expand the distance."

What followed forced Thaddeus to reconsider his opinion of his apprentice's talent. The boy was a monster.

Thaddeus, too, was a monster, but he had grown accustomed to being alone in that, outpacing the talented and crushing those with bright futures under the weight of their inferiority. He had thought Siverling talented, special—hungry—but for the first time, Thaddeus began to see that the boy was just an egg, still developing his potential. Given the right nutrients and guidance, when he hatched, his growth could be explosive.

This realization further fanned the flames of greed within Thaddeus, for what the boy could be to him. It did not exactly mirror his interest in the Raven Queen, but there was a special kind of pleasure in nurturing a seed—when the seed was worthy of the effort, something so elusive that Thaddeus had never before taken an apprentice.

Siverling seemed to have absolutely no trouble extending the displacement of the spell the entire length of Thaddeus's office, either finding the stretch no more difficult, or simply improving so quickly that the added strain only set him back to the baseline effort.

Thaddeus then had the boy close his eyes before casting once again, as many thaumaturges were over-reliant on their vision to guide their Wills. Siverling's brow furrowed, and his breathing deepened, but he managed after only a couple more minutes. "Wow, that was significantly harder," he exclaimed despite his almost instant success.

They adjusted the spell array's output parameters once more, to allow the light to hang in the air over Thaddeus's desk, and this time Thaddeus had his apprentice turn his back on the spell array and location of the output.

The boy gripped his Conduit tightly, his other hand clasped around his fist, his eyes closed and head bowed in concentration.

Thaddeus was fairly confident the increased difficulty here would stymie the boy, if not for several months, at least for a session or two.

Siverling's jaw grew tight, his brow furrowed, and despite his admirable control keeping his breaths deep and even, his temples grew wet with sweat. But then, he lifted his head proudly, opened his eyes, and rolled back his shoulders, and the light flickered into being over Thaddeus's desk.

Wisely, Siverling dropped the spell after only a moment to confirm that it had succeeded, the pride and command melting out of his posture as he did so. Without prompting, he moved to one of the chairs shoved over to the wall and plopped down to rest.

For the first time, Thaddeus became curious about the boy's background. To achieve this, he must have had a solid foundation, with a particular focus on his Will's forcefulness and clarity. Whoever had taught the boy had served him well. If it had been Thaddeus, though, he was sure Siverling's capacity could have been pushed much higher.

After allowing Siverling time to recover, they continued searching for a progression of the exercise that would finally stymie him. When he discovered one, he was unsure if he was pleased or dissatisfied. Siverling's Will-modified spell array could stretch around corners but could not pass through a solid barrier. It also could not navigate an area the boy had not seen before on its own, even to reach a theorized destination within that area.

It was obvious Siverling was tiring by this point, so Thaddeus allowed him to rest. "The method you are currently using is useful, but it has weaknesses, as you can see. You should consider it a crutch, at best. While it would be dangerous to demonstrate at the moment, based on what I have seen I believe your displacement method would be weak against shielding spells and general wards. It has no penetrative power. But, perhaps much more dangerous, it is likely vulnerable to severing spells and other disruptions. If you encountered that, there is a reasonable chance your spell would fail and you, as well as those around you, would have to deal with the backlash. Let me stress again, this is not a party trick to play around with and should not be practiced without supervision."

The boy nodded tiredly, barely able to focus his eyes. "I understand. I won't do anything foolish."

"Hmph. We shall see."

Siverling pressed his lips together and wisely did not argue. Instead, after a few moments, he simply said, "Thank you."

Thaddeus turned back toward his desk. "You are welcome. That concludes this weekend's session. If you have time, feel free to come back next Saturday to practice, though I will not be giving a lecture or more guidance just yet."

Siverling sat for a while longer, staring up at the ceiling, but eventually pried himself out of the chair and shuffled for the door. He paused before leaving, turning to Thaddeus with uncharacteristic hesitation.

"What is it?" Thaddeus asked.

Something resolved in his apprentice's eyes. "I'm not sure if you're aware, but I'm friends with Anastasia Gervin and acquainted with her cousin Alec. Alec went home to visit yesterday...and all was not well. His father and his other uncle were acting...agitated. Unusually so. Alec came home early to insulate himself from the tension. I was curious...and confused," Siverling emphasized.

Thaddeus raised an eyebrow. "I see. Anything else?"

"No. I only have suspicions, and I can't say they entirely make sense, especially if the latest incident wasn't truly the Raven Queen. But...perhaps it's something to keep an eye on, and I know you've helped with the investigation in the past. You're friends with Titus Westbay, right? Unfounded suspicion would sound better coming from you than troublemaking students like Damien or me. And I also don't want Alec to have to deal with the pressure of being questioned about his father. The man already has a tight grip of fear over him. I...am worried for Alec, as unpleasant a personality as he may be. I just hope that if there is something going on, if there is further evidence, it won't be overlooked." Sebastien closed his eyes for a moment, letting out a slow breath and some tension along with it.

"Thank you for telling me."

Siverling gave him a small, wry smile, a slight nod, and closed the door gently behind himself when he left.

Thaddeus set aside his reading, picked up his jacket, and made his own way out of the Citadel, walking toward the northwest. He was aware of the trust the boy placed in him. Such faith was foolish, perhaps, but he could not deny that it was perfectly designed to create mirroring feelings of warmth within himself.

Thaddeus, as well as the coppers, had already been aware of some non-inheriting members of the Gervin line attempting to treat with Ennis Naught, and by association, the Raven Queen, of course. But that had been early in the investigation, before she gained her current reputation. If those two had continued attempting to do so even now, acting without the oversight of the investigation, it would be considered an attempt to subvert the High Crown's justice. That they had not actually met with her did not matter, only that they had *attempted* to do so. There would be punishment.

He chuckled to himself as he walked into the trees, considering the irony of those two brothers treating with a fraudulent Raven Queen. Because Thaddeus was well aware of what they must have been attempting, and the whole thing was rather amusing. They had been lucky not to have met the real woman.

After a moment to consider all the factors, Thaddeus decided that he would, in fact, pass this suspicion along to Titus.

As Thaddeus exited the trees before Eagle Tower, looking up at the repaired edifice, so close to being finished, his smile widened. The real Raven Queen had been quiet lately. He wondered if the coppers would grow desperate enough to try something more than divination with what little of her blood remained to them.

But most of all, he wondered how she would respond this time.

39

RAVEN SUMMONING SPELL

Month 3, Day 8, Monday 10:15 p.m.

GRUMBLING internally about inconvenient meeting times and locations, Siobhan walked out of the secret meeting of underground thaumaturges. Tanya had not been at the new, appropriately *underground* venue this time, and Siobhan suspected that she, along with some of the other missing members, were no longer welcome after the security crackdown.

It hadn't subdued the trading, and Siobhan found herself leaving with more than she had planned. She had a box full of potions, a couple of scrolls containing the instructions for her new decryption spells, and a slightly heavier coin purse after selling a few pieces of her own information and fencing off the Gervins' confiscated belongings.

In addition to these planned purchases and sales, she found herself carrying a new enchanted satchel, large enough—due to a minor space-bending spell—to fit Siobhan's old, more feminine satchel inside. It even sat light on her shoulder due to a lightness spell. Also, there was a third scroll tucked away in her inner jacket pocket: the instructions for a spell to summon the Raven Queen.

The spell had been offered during the previous meeting but was, rightfully, met with general skepticism, both because of the high price and because summoning spells were so deeply unreliable, had potentially long payoff times, and even then the "results" were open to interpretation.

Summoning spells were supposed to create a weak attraction to something that met your defined requirements, subtly nudging the world so that the caster came into contact with the object of their search parameters over some vague upcoming period of time. The more undefined the parameters, or more distant the target in space or time, the weaker this force of attraction became. A few more scientifically minded thaumaturges had even posited that this whole subset of divination was a scam, with people succumbing to the placebo effect or seeing "signs" that matched their target. With a vague enough target and enough mental contortion, anything could meet the criteria. Even the fact that general summoning spells were still legal pointed toward their lack of efficacy.

In any case, this spell was supposed to allow someone to meet the Raven Queen. The seller even claimed to have tested it successfully, meeting and requesting a boon from her. An obvious lie. Even if the summoning spell had worked, forcing her to cross paths with the caster, they would have no way of knowing the innocuous person passing them in the street was really the Raven Queen. Only one person had been foolish enough to purchase it, and tonight they had come back, irate at the spell's failure, demanding a refund. Apparently, rather than allowing them to meet the Raven Queen, the spell had summoned a flock of corvids. The caster dropped the spell, but by the time the effects had dissipated, they were covered in small wounds and bird shit.

The arbiter had settled the dispute, but Siobhan found the whole thing hilarious and bought the spell instructions for a pittance, since it seemed like the kind of thing that might come in handy at some point. It almost didn't seem like the standard summoning spell at all, rather some sort of area-effect compulsion, much more direct in both execution and effect than the little she knew of such spells.

Stopping in a dark alley, Siobhan took off her feathers and turned her cloak inside-out to change the color, then flagged down a carriage that bore a small painted rendition of the Verdant Stag's green antlers on its side. The box of supplies was too heavy to carry all the way, and though she had traveled to the meeting with Liza, she was on her own now and felt safer within the obscuring walls.

She had bought some potions that she'd never made before, and sold the recipe for the fever reducing potion, which she had brewed several times for the Verdant Stag. Now, someone else could do the same, or just supply the people who would have otherwise bought from the Verdant Stag, still indirectly putting her out of a job. This was why spell information was often so tightly held, as having a monopoly on anything useful had obvious benefits. But that restrictive and selfish mindset seemed silly to Siobhan. *'Magic is better spread as far and wide as possible. If there's no longer demand for this concoction, it won't matter to me, because I'm always growing and learning and will be able to make something new that people want to buy. Additionally, the best thaumaturges will make the best potions, and their reputations can keep them selling even in a saturated market. And if that places a strain on the supply of magical components, then there should be more jobs in sustainably sourcing components, or research into viable alternatives.'*

Her mental tangent ended as she arrived at the Verdant Stag, going around to one of the back entrances, where an enforcer let her in. He immediately returned to reading a flimsy pamphlet, ostentatiously labeled *The People's Voice*, apparently one of the first editions of a newspaper run by the Verdant Stag. Oliver truly was the boy with a finger in every pie.

Siobhan dropped off the box at the apothecary, then made her way to Katerin's office. When she knocked on the door, a familiar, distinctly non-Katerin-like voice called, "Enter."

Inside, Katerin's chair was facing away from the door, seemingly empty. Then a small foot reached out for purchase on the side of the desk, and the chair swiveled slowly around. Theo was sitting there, his copper hair mussed and what looked to be homework sprawled out over the dark wooden desk. He had steepled his fingertips together and was glaring over them in a parody of a powerful businessman. When he saw Siobhan, he perked up, forgetting his little act. "It's you! I haven't seen you in so long! Why're you in your Raven Queen body? Didja go after one of your enemies tonight? Didja do something super awesome and nightmarishly horrible to them? Do you have any other bodies you can change into? Can you really travel through the shadows, and if so, can you take someone small with you, maybe? 'Cause I was thinking, that would be really awesome to try, and I promise I wouldn't be any bother—" He cut off the rapid-fire questions suddenly, having inhaled and choked on some of his own saliva.

Siobhan waited patiently for him to recover.

After some dramatic hacking, bent over the desk, Theo looked up at her, red-faced, watery-eyed, and suspicious. "Did you just hex me to shut me up?"

Siobhan rolled her eyes. "No. And if I did, it would have been a jinx, not a hex. Making you choke on your own spit is more of a prank than anything malicious. Isn't it a little late? I'm pretty sure Katerin wants you in bed by this hour. And are you still working on your homework?"

Theo quickly slammed shut his textbooks and shuffled all his papers into a haphazard stack, slipping the whole mess into one of Katerin's desk drawers. "That's not important, and Katerin isn't here right now. Now that all the trials and stuff are over, she's getting ready for transferring all the rest of those bad guys to the coppers for official sentencing and jail and stuff. Do you know how long it takes to earn enough money to buy a utility wand? I've been working on it for *months* now, and I'm still only maybe halfway there. Maybe you could talk to Katerin about increasing my wages?"

Siobhan raised an eyebrow at the non-sequitur, noting that he hadn't answered her questions. "Your wages for what?"

"Homework and stuff."

"The same homework that you haven't completed and just shoved in a drawer?"

Theo gave her a hard stare, his expression asking if she was *really* pointing that out. "Et tu, Brute?" he muttered, hopping down from Katerin's chair.

Siobhan wondered if he even knew what that meant or was just parroting something he'd heard others say.

"Well, to make up for it, you can take me with you when you go shadow-walking," Theo offered magnanimously, coming around the desk to stand in front of Siobhan.

"That's a rumor based on zero facts."

Theo's mouth dropped open in stunned dismay, but then his eyes narrowed suspiciously. "*Zero*? Really? Even if you can't shadow walk, you've gotta have something interesting that you can show me. I mean, you always have something interesting. Last time, it was all those totally awesome stories about the Black Wastes. Mr. Mawson totally *hated* that, but I cited all those sources you told me about and he *had* to give me a good grade. Katerin kept saying I was going to have nightmares, but I didn't have any at all, so you don't have to worry about treating me like a little kid." He reached out boldly to take her hand in both of his, staring up at her with big watery eyes.

Siobhan hesitated, but she was trying to be kinder to herself, as well as to others, and some childish play might be just the thing. As the end of term was approaching in just a few more weeks, the stress among her classmates had grown palpable. When she woke in the middle of the night now, several other students were likely to be awake as well, light coming from their curtained cubicles as they tried to cram a whole term's knowledge into their skulls. It was like the stress was infectious.

She herself wasn't worried about the general exams, because it was clear she wasn't in the bottom ten percent of her student group and thus in no danger of being held back, but the end of term exhibitions were looming ominously, and she was struggling to get as much power from Professor Lacer's transmogrification exercises as the spells should have provided at her capacity.

"Please?" Theo wheedled.

"Fine," she acquiesced. She had a few more spell arrays drawn on paper now, and she easily found the simple illusion spell. She placed the paper near the light on Katerin's desk, so that she would have more to draw from, and created an image of a cute little dog on the page, wriggling around with excitement as it looked at Theo.

The boy watched with wide eyes, smart enough to stop himself from reaching out to touch it, despite his obvious desire.

But soon enough, he frowned. "This is neat and all, but it's not very 'Raven Queen,' is it?"

She morphed the dog into a tiny black, fire-breathing dragon, which drew Theo's interest more strongly, but he still wasn't satisfied. "But it's just an illusion. There isn't a cool story to go along with it, and it's not even leaving the page. Don't you have anything more...dangerous? Or at least more impressive?"

Siobhan let the spell drop, staring down at the top of Theo's curly copper head with exasperation. "Fine. But we'll need a place open to the air, though preferably not exposed to widespread observation."

"Of course," Theo agreed, already tugging at her hand. "We can use one of the rooms with a balcony hanging over the back courtyard!"

Siobhan took a few minutes to more thoroughly examine the spell instructions and imprint the process into her mind, then got to work out on the chilly balcony, setting up the spell array on her portable slate table rather than wrestling with getting an unbroken Circle across the wooden boards beneath her.

It was a bit cramped to fit the three raven feathers—which she had double checked to ensure they weren't crow feathers after learning of Ana's mistake with the Raven Queen costume—plus the shade dust, an offering of something shiny and valuable, and a lump of iron. The spell called for a raven eyeball as well, but Siobhan didn't have one. Considering what the spell did and that she already had raven feathers, she was confident the eye wasn't necessary. She also didn't have a lodestone, which she had substituted with a normal piece of iron. Siobhan might have been able to forcibly magnetize her little lump of iron, but it seemed foolish to try without research and safety measures, especially for something so trivial. For the final component, she placed down a polished gold crown.

When she was ready, she set the slate table on the balcony deck, added her lantern for power, and stood over it with her hands raised dramatically as Theo watched avidly from the side. Siobhan was trying to take a lesson in spellcasting theatrics from Professor Lacer, who always looked so impressive. In a low, deep voice she said, "Oh raven of the night. With hunger I seek you, persevering. To the earth I draw you, a beacon. With luster I entice you, worthy."

The chant seemed obviously cobbled together, and the magic wobbled unsteadily under the grip of her Will, new and wild, but she refused to let it slip from her grasp.

She imagined the effects of the spell spreading out just like the tendrils of a divination, seeking a matching target and enticing it to approach.

As with any summoning spell, Siobhan knew there was a chance of failure. Despite the spell's previous "success" for the other caster, it might not be powerful enough to wake any birds from their sleep, for example, or reach far enough to draw a large flock. Still, for the next quarter hour, they sat on the corner of the balcony and waited, their legs dangling off the edge. Siobhan concentrated on the spell with one part of her mind while using the other to chat with an increasingly impatient little boy.

"Are you sure it's working?" Theo asked.

As if on cue, the first raven arrived.

It landed not on the balcony or the center of the spell array, but on Siobhan's shoulder.

Theo gasped, staring up at the creature in awe.

Unlike the account the previous purchaser of this spell had given, the raven seemed entirely docile, maybe even friendly—or at least curious. It watched them with its little black eyes, then pecked at Siobhan's hair, pulling gently in a motion that felt like grooming.

Tentatively, Theo reached up to pet it, pausing for a moment before his fingers came into contact with its feathers, giving it time to react.

The raven remained still, and when Theo finally touched it, gently sliding his fingertips over its dark, shimmering feathers, the boy sighed dreamily. "You're so pretty," he told it. "And smart."

The raven bobbed its head up and down, then nibbled gently on his fingers, making him giggle with delight.

"Oh, I should have brought some food for you," he lamented, suddenly heartbroken by this oversight.

"I have some," Siobhan offered, carefully moving to pull out the same pouch of dried fruits and nuts that she secretly took with her to breakfast.

Theo held up the bits of food in his palm, and the raven hopped over to his shoulder instead. He petted its feathers, murmuring constant and ever more hyperbolic praise as it nibbled away with its sharp beak, careful not to accidentally hurt him. "Oh, you're the most genius bird in Gilbratha. And the most beautiful. Your feathers probably look like a black rainbow in the sunlight. You're a mighty hunter. And a cunning thief. And all the other ravens are jealous of you..." He continued in this vein for a while.

Siobhan watched with satisfaction, feeling a warmth at his childish enthusiasm and instant adoration. But after another quarter hour, the second raven arrived, and there was an immediate tussle over who had rights to the food.

Theo struggled to mediate. "Be nice. There's enough for both of you. I've got a whole pouch, see?" he said, shaking the food Siobhan had bought for herself without a care to leave any for her. "No, Blacky," he said to the smaller one, "be nice to Empress Regal. She was here first. Why don't you ask her if you can have some of the raisins, too?" He turned a hard stare on the first raven. It hesitated, but then grudgingly nudged one single raisin toward Blacky.

The ravens seemed to start some sort of argument, hopping on Theo's lap and tugging at his hair and clothes while squawking belligerently and batting each other with angry wings.

Theo had to resort to threats to get them to stop. And then the third and fourth raven arrived, each taking one of Siobhan's shoulders. They cawed loudly right in her ears and eyed each other with distrust, and then all four started hopping and flapping around in some kind of territorial dance that she was worried might accidentally disrupt the spell array.

Siobhan dropped the spell, because she wasn't a complete fool, and drawing a flock of ravens, even in a discreet place at night, seemed like a great way to attract unnecessary attention.

Three more ravens arrived after that, flying around the balcony in confusion. After a minute or so they left, followed by the others.

Theo's raven was the last to depart, but not before finishing the last of the snacks. It gave Theo's bright copper hair a friendly tug, then swooped down and picked up the gold piece Siobhan had laid out as a component before flying off into the night.

"Hey!" she called after it angrily. "Bring that back!"

Its mocking caw soon faded into the distance.

Suddenly, the whole thing didn't seem worth it after all. A whole gold piece was a steep price to pay for less than an hour of fun for a little boy. With a sigh, she packed up the spell components and her lantern, shooing Theo off to bed before Katerin could return and get angry with the both of them.

After returning to the Silk Door and Sebastien's form, she checked her pocket watch, noting the late hour and vacillating for a moment over what to do next. Responsibly, she should return to the University and go to sleep. But the decryption spells she had been waiting for so long were calling to her from the inside pocket of her jacket, whispering of the mysteries they could uncover and the power of knowledge.

So instead, knowing she would likely regret it in the morning, Sebastien headed to Dryden Manor. She had the beamshell tincture if she really needed it, after all.

Oliver was there when she arrived, but seeing that she was busy and distracted, he said only, "Have breakfast with me in the morning before you head back. There's some upcoming work I want to talk to you about."

With a murmured agreement, Sebastien headed up to her room and took out the spell instructions, as well as the books on more complex math that she had borrowed from the University library in anticipation of this moment.

Spreading out her books and papers over the floor and plopping down cross-legged on a cushion, she delved into the theoretical information. As she had worried, the spell was complex, the math slightly beyond her, and the power requirements entirely beyond her. But those were only roadblocks, and with enough tenacity, they could all be overcome.

She worked well into the night, deciphering the math and turning the formulas into graphs and charts that took up a lot more space but were easier for her to grasp. She wrote notes that explained how the spell worked in more detail so she could stabilize the Word, and calculated out how to modify the spell to stretch out its casting time such that she could handle it on her own.

She got lost within the work, so focused on wrenching apart the puzzle pieces and forcing them back together that she didn't retire to bed until the early hours of the morning. Thinking of the raven stealing her coin, a giggle burst out of her. It probably had a whole cache of stolen loot. She drifted off to sleep imagining other people being victim to similar thefts, but superstitiously believing that the ravens were demanding tribute on behalf of their queen, tittering woozily to herself all the while.

40

SEALING OF TONGUES

Sebastien
   Month 3, Day 9, Tuesday 6:00 a.m.

Sharon had to pull Sebastien out of bed in the morning, chattering to herself as she cleaned up the papers scattered everywhere, daintily avoiding the writing Siobhan had done directly on the floor. The saintly woman didn't so much as give Sebastien a dirty look for the extra work.

Fifteen minutes later, Sebastien entered Oliver's office carrying an over-filled breakfast tray. "You have a job for me?" she asked without preamble.

His knee bounced rapidly for a moment before he stood from his desk, moving to pace in front of the fireplace. "As you know, I still have the worst of the Morrows, including the majority of those who held more influential positions, incarcerated in our secret jail. After what happened with the University, I started digging a little deeper into their activities. I believe they never intended to work sincerely with either of us. Why they are so determined against the Verdant Stag, I do not know, but there are signs that someone is putting together an assault force. It's possible that I am being paranoid, but I suspect they plan to try to stop me from sending the Morrows to Harrow Hill."

Sebastien set the tray down, her mind struggling out of its fugue as the seconds passed in silence. "I assume you have a plan to deal with this? How does it involve me?" she asked, her shoulders tensing as she prepared to argue.

"This Friday night—early Saturday morning—we'll be turning over the remaining Morrow prisoners to Harrow Hill for sentencing. I have a group of coppers in my pocket now, and we've arranged for everyone necessary to be on the midnight shift. As secretly as possible, we're going to deliver the Morrows to Harrow Hill directly, along with their confessions, witness accusations, and what evidence of their crimes we've collected, well before anyone suspects. By morning they'll all be booked, with evidence of their crimes on file. No matter how corrupt some of the coppers are, there will be no way to reverse the situation. It's the last step, and I want to make sure it goes perfectly."

"And you need me for this?"

He waved his hand. "Oh, no! I need you for what comes before. Nothing dangerous. As you might imagine, there is quite a lot the Morrows could potentially talk about under questioning, not only about their own activities, but also about Kiernan's faction—these University thaumaturges calling themselves the Architects of Khronos—and about the Stags. Some of them know things I don't want getting out, or that I'd like to hold in reserve rather than going full fireball spell, metaphorically. Keeping testimony about the Architects of Khronos in reserve could effectively hold them hostage. And so, inspired by Tanya Canelo, I've hired a cursemaster to handle placing a conditional lock on their speech."

Sebastien frowned. The whole thing seemed rather complicated, but she supposed that when you were in opposition to the established regime, didn't want to kill your enemies, and didn't have the resources to run a long-term prison or work camp, things got convoluted. "You...want me to assist the cursemaster?"

"I want you, as Silvia Nakai, to assist Healer Nidson. The whole process is a little dangerous, and I'd rather not have any of them be permanently damaged or die by accident."

She noted the use of the words "by accident." Perhaps if it was on purpose, permanent damage and even death would be acceptable to him.

"Healer Nidson requested you specifically. Apparently, he was impressed by your performance the last time you worked together. I do have others with healer training, but none that I trust as much as you. Information security is paramount. As much as possible, I want to surprise everyone not directly involved. It would be a few hours of late-night work, you would get to experience some very rare magic up close, and I don't expect you to put yourself in any danger. If anything were to go wrong, there is a back exit that you can take immediately."

She hesitated. "I can literally just run away if things go wrong?"

"Yes. Use your judgment to decide if that's necessary. The guards will be numerous and heavily armed. Even if we do meet obstacles, we should be able to blast right through them."

"But there is an enemy that specifically wants to stop you from succeeding. You cannot assume they are foolish or weak. And it seems like something always goes wrong with these dangerous missions. I don't want to be involved in things that could get me killed, Oliver."

Oliver's fingers kneaded at the muscles of his neck. "I am making every reasonable preparation, Sebastien," he said tiredly. "And we don't even know that something will go wrong. You've participated in plenty of missions for me that haven't resulted in combat. Most of the secret meetings, putting up the emergency response flags, and even this recent work against the Gervins. When things have been a little more dangerous, you've still acquitted yourself admirably. We're in this together, or haven't you realized? When the Morrows are safely locked away, you'll be safer, too. Why are you so resistant to the idea?"

'*Because things can only go horribly wrong so many times before I fail to stumble my way to unlikely safety. I'm deathly sick of my situation continually going from bad to worse,*' she thought wearily.

Oliver shook his head, then finally stopped pacing and really looked at her. "I'm sorry. I know you're struggling too, but I don't have a lot of options. And I think what I'm asking is reasonable. Do I need to remind you of the debt you owe? The Gervin sub-commission has yet to land on my desk."

She glared at him for a few long seconds. "I'll need to prepare. *We* need to prepare. If I'm going to be involved, I need to be sure things are done right. It's going to be difficult on such short notice. Stars above, I don't have *time* for this."

Taking a deep breath to fortify herself, she squared her shoulders, lifted her jaw, and said, "Let us discuss the payment first." She might not be able to get out of this, to be just a University student, but she could make Oliver's wallet hurt for the offense.

They spoke for over an hour as she questioned his preparations and suggested a few additions. When there was no more time, she hurried back to the University, mulling over all the necessary preparations and adjustments to her plans.

She took the beamshell tincture with the cafeteria breakfast, and then spent the rest of the day on the go, trying to squeeze every last drop of value from each spare minute. In the evening, she made a series of eclectic purchases inspired by Ana and Damien's ingenious contributions to Operation Defenestration.

The remainder of her week was spent in preparation, readying new emergency stash locations and disaster plans while struggling to recover from the sleep deprivation that single late night of spell research had caused.

When Ana and Damien had worked on the planning and preparation for Operation Defenestration, they had opened Siobhan's eyes to how much someone's image could change from just a bit of makeup and the right clothes, as well as the sheer extent of what some of the nobles would do to change their appearance, and thus the *market* for such things.

And so, she'd availed herself of some darkening cream for her skin, to turn her smooth ochre tint into a slightly more blue-based brown, a prosthetic nose with thicker nostrils and a bit of a bump in the middle, and some color-changing lenses made of reinforced glass that turned her dark eyes into a light blue.

The lenses were the most difficult part of the whole transformation, as she'd had a lot of trouble getting them into her eyes and, once there, to settle properly over her watering eyeballs. They didn't exactly make her eyes unre-markable, as the bright blue stood out starkly against the deep dark brown beneath, giving her a striking, piercing gaze, but they did help to make her look nothing like herself.

Along with a pair of horn-rimmed glasses, some artful grey streaks in her hair, and a little bit of transparent tightening paste she'd dabbed at the corner of her eyes while squinting to give herself wrinkles, she truly appeared to have transformed into someone else. Perhaps an aunt, or an older cousin.

Siobhan had wondered if she should start trying to think of herself as Silvia when she was in her new and improved disguise. Ultimately, she decided against it; incorporating more than two distinct self-identities seemed like both too much work and the kind of thing that could lead to dissociation of her base identity. She'd already had some trouble with that.

She arrived at the Verdant Stag's secret jail, an unassuming, rectangular brick building, the most interesting feature of which was the strategic posi-tioning of small windows that looked more like arrow-slits on the second floor. Apparently, some clever enforcer had started calling it Knave Knoll, a witticism based on Harrow Hill, and the name had stuck. It was a couple of hours before midnight on Friday, and she had slipped by the late-night revelers braving the barely-above-freezing temperatures without notice.

Each of the fifteen wagons waiting in a nearby warehouse would carry pris-oners to Harrow Hill, leaving in sets of three at slightly different times and taking random routes that some dice would decide at the last minute. The convoys would be escorted by dozens of enforcers, the most trusted from both the Nightmare Pack and the Verdant Stag. If everything was running on sched-ule, the enforcers would have already been questioned and searched, just to be sure, and they would currently be receiving their full kit of battle artifacts and potions. This, in addition to horses for each, had cost Oliver a fortune, but they were prepared for almost anything. And if all went well, they would have no reason to use any of it.

After going through the strict security process, she found Oliver inside, waiting with Healer Nidson. The man made no comment on her disguise, simply nodding in greeting, and she assumed Oliver or Katerin had informed him of her updated appearance. Her need for anonymity was a hint at her true identity, but there was little she could do about that at this point. Oliver seemed sure that Healer Nidson was trustworthy, and it was true he didn't seem inclined to ask questions.

Oliver was visibly tense, his muscles tight and prone to flinching. When he saw her, he made an obvious effort to relax.

Healer Nidson asked, "You're sure none of these people are going to somehow be let off or 'accidentally' escape Harrow Hill?"

"The shift manager made sure I would have all the right people there tonight, and none of the wrong. Once everything is on file, it would take someone very bold to try and tamper with the evidence. There is not that much leeway in the conviction process. When the right people are in the right jobs, Crown law isn't actually that horrible. These people are going to be executed or heavily fined and sent to work off their debt in the celerium mines. Even I wouldn't be willing to risk a mass breakout from Harrow Hill. The High Crown might call in the army to exact retribution and stomp down with the firm boot of the law."

'*So all we have to do is get them there,*' Siobhan reassured herself. '*And all I have to do is follow along behind Healer Nidson and do what he says.*' She didn't say it aloud, though; far better to be superstitious than stupid, and she wasn't about to tempt fate.

As soon as the cursemaster arrived, escorted by Enforcer Gerard, the five of them moved from the lobby area into Knave Knoll proper. The building had obviously been modified, and she suspected that, before the second floor was added, it had been a stable for exotic, dangerous animals. The steel troughs stacked in one corner and the ventilation tubes running through each of the stall-sized cells gave it away, as did the lingering smell of manure, distinctly different from human stench.

Gerard led them to a small infirmary room, where a prisoner was already waiting on the single narrow medical bed within, set in the far corner of the room. The guard who had been with him bowed and left in a hurry.

Within the infirmary, the cursemaster lowered the deep hood of his worn leather cloak to reveal sallow, sickly features. His cheeks still held the faint white lines of old scars, and his thin lips were shiny with spit.

Siobhan found him immediately distasteful. '*Is he deliberately trying to look the part of the evil cursemaster? The leather of his cloak is even discolored and patched, like it was made from pieces of human skin sewn together.*' She shuddered at the thought, glad they weren't doing this in a cell, where she would be forced to squeeze in close enough to smell him.

The Morrow man looked Enforcer Gerard and the cursemaster up and down. "Here to brand your insurance into me, huh? But if you're worried about us breaking the vow, what's to say we don't break a curse, too?"

"I am an expert," the cursemaster said simply, his voice dry and raspy, as if his throat had been slit at some point and the healer hadn't put it back together quite right. He wasted no time getting to work.

He pulled a jar from one of the many pockets inside his dank cloak and began to write on the floor with the dark-brown, congealed substance within, which shimmered green in the light of the wall lamp. A whiff of it hit Siobhan's nose, and from the salty-sweet, coppery tang, she identified blood as one of the major ingredients. He was creating a spell array, but she didn't recognize at least half of the glyphs, and the use of numerological symbols was… strange. He drew two different versions of a heptagram, one even and broad, and the other lopsided and spiky. Other lines branched off of this combined symbol, connecting particular glyphs and even a few other small symbols at the edges. In the center, he drew a filled-in circle the size of his fist.

When he finished that, the cursemaster took out a leather wrap and unrolled it to reveal over a hundred slender needles, some long and some short. He dipped a few dozen in the jar of blood, then set them aside. Next, he pulled out two small scrolls, one tied with a green ribbon, and the other with a red. "You understand the contents of the seal I will be placing on you?" he asked, waving them at the prisoner. "You may read them again, to familiarize yourself, if necessary."

Siobhan's attention caught on the word "seal," and her interest deepened. *'Was something like this done to me?'* she wondered.

The prisoner waved a hand, his jaw clenched tight as he stared with futile unwillingness at the cursemaster.

"Very well." He produced a milky-white potion, into which he dipped a tiny brush and wrote something indistinguishable around the edges of both scrolls. When he finally unrolled them, he used a polished bone athame to draw a thin slice across the Morrow man's hand and forced him to create a large blood print on both of the scrolls, which he then burned up. The prisoner reluctantly ate the ashes, and then the real work began.

The cursemaster brought out a strange lump of clay—no, not clay. Siobhan had thought it was clay because of the way it squished in his hand. But the surface was pink and smoothly textured, and the lines of his fingers left no prints in its surface as he began to mold it. It was a little ball of *flesh*.

The prisoner almost gagged, and she sympathized. The cursemaster worked with frightening speed, molding the ball of flesh into a surprisingly realistic doll-like form. "A hair," he demanded, holding his hand out. When he received it, fresh plucked from the man's head, he stuck it into the scalp of the doll, which absorbed it like someone hungrily sucking up a noodle. The doll's features clarified, and Siobhan watched in horror as it grew to resemble the prisoner almost exactly over the course of a handful of seconds.

The cursemaster produced a small wooden box, which looked rather like a miniature coffin, and set the tiny simulacrum inside, where it rested peacefully.

The Morrow prisoner was breathing hard, staring at the box with bulging eyes, and when the cursemaster reached for him, he jerked back. "No, no, don't touch me!"

"It is much too late for that," the cursemaster said. "Hold still. I will complete the task I was assigned with your cooperation or without it. But my employer would prefer it if I leave you undamaged. Excessive struggling will make things…dangerous. The brain is a delicate thing, after all."

When he picked up two of the longer needles, the prisoner started to hyperventilate and scrambled back into the corner. "Please, don't do this! I promise I won't talk!" Seeing the cursemaster unmoved, the man's eyes turned toward Healer Nidson and Siobhan. "Help me! Help!" He began to sob.

Siobhan turned to Healer Nidson.

His expression was grim, his lips pressed together tight and compassion in his eyes. "If you would like, I can give you a minor sedative to help keep you calm, and something to keep you from accidentally moving. I would recommend the latter, at least. Even a small flinch could do damage."

After a long moment of horrible disillusionment, the prisoner accepted both. Healer Nidson didn't need Siobhan's help to provide a couple of potion doses, and soon enough the cursemaster got back to work. The prisoner was moved into the center of the spell array, his head resting over the central dot.

The cursemaster inserted both long needles, tipped in that strange blood concoction, directly through the man's skull and into his brain, seeming to encounter no resistance as he did so.

The Morrow prisoner's eyes were open, leaking silent tears.

Humming under his breath, the cursemaster opened his subject's mouth, pulled out his tongue, and began to insert the shorter needles into the soft flesh. It quickly became apparent that he was building a particular pattern, though Siobhan couldn't be sure if it matched the spell array underneath or was something new altogether.

The cursemaster released the man's tongue to draw back into his mouth with the needles still in it, then stood up, patting his hands on his knees where he'd gotten a little dusty from kneeling. He pulled out the larger needles from the man's skull, cleaned them thoroughly, then picked up the little box with the simulacrum. Very casually, he wiped his finger across the lips to erase them, leaving a blank swath where the mouth had been. Then he closed the lid and handed the box to Gerard. "This one is finished."

Siobhan stared at the silently crying man as a couple of enforcers arrived to carry him away, wondering if this was what the Architects of Khronos had done to Tanya—if there were still needles in the other young woman's tongue, hidden within the soft pink flesh. At least this criminal had deserved punishment, either directly or through being complicit in the crimes of his organization and underlings. Still, the whole thing left the palms of her hands sweaty and an unpleasant dizziness in her stomach.

She watched an almost identical process play out a few more times with impressive speed, and finally mustered up the courage to speak about an hour later, while they were waiting for the next prisoner. "I noticed you used some principles of binding magic. But it wasn't an equivalent exchange, right? Which is why it's considered a curse. Does the seal only work on speech? Could you seal someone's ability to cast certain magic, or think of certain things, or…" She trailed off as Healer Nidson shook his head at her.

The cursemaster didn't respond to her questions. He didn't even look her way.

In the hallway outside, visible through the open doorway, the guards were beginning to lead away some of the less-important prisoners, those who did not require such powerful magical coercion, for loading into the wagon convoys. Some struggled, some were crying, and some looked numb. While none bore the signs of physical torture, she looked at some of their eyes and realized that did not preclude more subtle forms of persuasion.

One guard sneered at a woman who was sobbing and grabbing onto his shirt. He pried her fingers off him, then examined both of her empty hands as if suspecting that she had tried to pickpocket him. "If you didn't want to pay the price, you shouldn't have committed so many crimes," he said.

She scoffed through her tears. "We paid for our crimes, quite literally, and now we're being turned over to the coppers to pay again? You may pretend to be righteous, but in truth you're maggots, stripping every last ounce of flesh off our rotting carcasses!"

Enforcer Gerard turned to Siobhan. "That woman was a child trafficker. I'm sure you've heard the stories about what happens to stolen young children. Oliver found some of them in the basement of a Morrow lieutenant's house after two days of questioning her. Three were already dead, and one of the little girls was pregnant." He spoke loudly enough to be heard by those passing by.

Siobhan blanched, her stomach rolling over inside her as sudden tears prickled at her wide eyes. She knew too well what could happen. She pushed the thoughts away with a physical shudder.

"They were going to die anyway!" the woman screeched. "Their parents couldn't afford to feed them. You don't know where they came from. Some of them ended up with better lives, because of me!"

One of her companions, a too-thin man with pale skin, closed his eyes to her words. "Shut up!" he whined, half weak cry, half prayer, and Siobhan suddenly knew that he had been aware of the child trafficking. He felt badly about it now, but not enough to have done anything at the time.

The sympathy she'd had for the cursemaster's victims died a little inside her. If she ever found out that Oliver was doing something so heinous, he would immediately and forever become her enemy. That these Morrows had willingly worked with an organization where such things were acceptable made them complicit. Regardless of their reasons for joining, the people who were still here, being taken to Harrow Hill, *deserved* their punishment.

Her respect for Healer Nidson increased when one of the cursemaster's subjects began to convulse as he inserted the needles into her brain.

Healer Nidson immediately stopped the cursemaster, and with Siobhan's help, stabilized the woman so she didn't do any further damage to herself. Then he used a complicated healing spell with several components from the Plane of Radiance, catching the tail end of her seizure and soothing her into a deep sleep. The light was bright and pure, harsh and cleansing, and from the spillover alone, Siobhan could feel how light could be used in transmogrification to such great effect.

Undeterred, the cursemaster finished the seal and once again motioned for the next prisoner to be brought in. But before they could arrive, one of the guards hurried up with a whispered message for Enforcer Gerard.

The man's expression didn't shift, but his muscular shoulders drew forward like a bear preparing to run toward the enemy. Siobhan caught some of his murmured reply. "Only two more prisoners to go. Don't start loading the final convoy yet. Give us twenty minutes." As the guard ran away to carry the message, Gerard said to the rest of them, "Nothing for you to worry about, just some precautions."

Siobhan was intensely curious, but couldn't ask for more details when acting as Silvia and in front of the other two.

Halfway through the final seal, the hallway lights shut down. They flickered back on, shining a deep red, then off again, and then were replaced by blue lights. The sequence repeated with ponderous ominousness. In the sudden silence that followed, Siobhan could hear a low, moaning alarm, not screeching like the city-wide rogue magic alarms, but nevertheless disquieting. She recognized the sequence as one of the many preparations she had made for this evening, but Enforcer Gerard spoke first.

"Stop all prisoner transports and activate security measures," he recited.

"We're being attacked," Siobhan predicted with numb lips.

41

PRISONER CONVOY ATTACK

Oliver
   Month 3, Day 13, Saturday 1:30 a.m.

Oliver had been apprehensive about this final step of the Stags' takeover for a while. He still hoped that the rumors of clandestine preparation for violence had nothing to do with him, or at least that it had nothing to do with the Architects of Khronos. It could be that some member or affiliate of the Morrows, one of the few they had failed to capture or kill in the beginning, had hired mercenaries. Or perhaps one of the other gangs from the more affluent parts of the city had some stake in keeping the Morrows out of jail. It was even hypothetically possible that one of the previously released Morrows had somehow broken or sidestepped the vow of nonaggression Oliver had required.

Riding his intelligent erythrean horse Elmira, Oliver headed out with one of the convoys that contained a large percentage of the more important Morrows, just as Liza and Lord Lynwood had done before him. The most experienced and loyal enforcers from the Verdant Stag and Nightmare Pack accompanied them. Other than some useless struggling by some of the Morrows, his group had met no trouble so far, and Oliver knew that little could stand in the way of such a group, but he couldn't help but look around for potential danger, tensing every time they passed anyone still awake and about so late in the night. The sky was moonless, and the only illumination came from the sporadic streetlamps or windows spilling dirty light out into the street, which made every shadow more sinister.

He was just beginning to relax, having made it several minutes out from Knave Knoll, when a runner sprinted up behind their small convoy waving a slip of paper frantically in the air.

Heart sinking, Oliver turned Elmira back to meet him.

The young man was too out of breath to talk after sprinting such a distance, but the slip of paper said all that was necessary. *"Terrier heading directly to the egg. ETA 10mins."* It was printed on a familiar strip of paper, from the extra distagram he'd managed to buy for Knave Knoll's administration office. Of course, the message was in code in case anyone was tuned into the same band, but the message was clear to Oliver. Tanya Canelo was heading right to Knave Knoll and moving quick.

"How long ago did you receive this?" Oliver asked.

"Three...minutes," the young man gasped.

Oliver called for the convoy to halt, his thoughts racing as he considered the implications of this news. Canelo was not supposed to know anything about Knave Knoll, nor should she have any information about the night's events or the path his convoy was taking. It was exceedingly unlikely her movement was a simple coincidence. It was also quite possible she was part of a larger group heading to intercept them.

If they pushed forward, they might be able to reach Harrow Hill before anyone could catch them, and he doubted even the Architects of Khronos would be willing to start a fight directly in front of the coppers. Alternatively, they could fall back to Knave Knoll, which was heavily fortified and could withstand anything their convoy's guards couldn't.

The preparations that Oliver and Siobhan had taken over the last few days decided the matter for him. He couldn't imagine many scenarios that they were unprepared to handle, and so he ordered the convoy onward, urging them to increase the pace.

It took less than a minute for him to start doubting his decision.

The enforcers at the head of the convoy saw the enemy first, sounding the alarm.

"Ambush," Enforcer Huntley murmured, even before the forms hidden in the alleys on either side made themselves known, shining lensed lanterns at the convoy like spotlights.

Their attackers were riding horses of their own, and though it was difficult to make them out with the bright lights shining their way, Oliver counted more than a dozen.

"Stop!" called one of the men in front of them, arm straight and pointing a battle wand their way.

Oliver slowly reached under his jacket and fiddled with the artifact there.

"Reinforcements will be here as soon as possible," he murmured, drawing his hand back out with a battle wand of his own clasped securely in his palm.

"Give up the prisoners, and you may leave unharmed," the leader of their ambushers called. "If you resist, or attempt to attack, we will annihilate you all." There were no obvious signs of who these people were, and many wore hoods or masks to cover their features. Oliver didn't want to jump to conclusions. His enemy would remain unnamed until he was sure.

Huntley cursed, low and vicious, one arm tugging on the reins of his horse to move between Oliver and the enemy, the other already securely clutching his own battle wand.

"I must have been cursed to live a life of adventure," Oliver said wryly. Either someone had betrayed his plans at the last minute, even after all the precautions he took not to be predicted...or whoever objected so strenuously to their transfer of the Morrows was powerful enough that they didn't *need* to be tipped off. A last-minute divination, perhaps.

Eyeing their ambushers, the shadows behind the eye holes of his mask helping to dampen the harsh lights pointed at him, Oliver considered trying to just smash straight through. They would likely get into a running fight, but as long as they could make it to Harrow Hill, their opponents wouldn't be able to stop the arrests.

But that was dangerous. Their attackers were on horses of their own, and his people wouldn't be able to outrun them with the wagons. Getting the prisoners to Harrow Hill wasn't so high priority as to be more important than the lives of his enforcers, or those of his allies.

"Circle up and retreat to the base!" he yelled. "Move left!" The streets were too narrow to allow for the wagons to turn around directly, so they would need to move sideways before turning once again to return the way they'd come.

In the wagon beside Oliver, one of the bound Morrows, head covered with a sack, let out a crowing laugh. "You upstart pillocks think we don't have friends? When we're all free, we're gonna drag your men naked through the streets while those people you think love you throw stones."

Elmira shifted sideways and gave a threatening snap of her teeth toward the speaker, who flinched at the unseen clacking sound so near his face and wisely decided to return to silence.

Their attackers hesitated no longer, raising hollow tubes Oliver recognized as military-issue grenade launchers to their shoulders.

"Fire!" the leader yelled, the domed fog of a concussive blast spell shooting for the head of their convoy from his own battle wand.

"Take cover!" Oliver screamed in response. There wasn't much space to maneuver, nor cover to take, but his people scattered or ducked behind the wagons as best they could.

The grenade launchers released their payload with a sound that was half *pop* and half *crack* of thunder, shooting the clay spheres of true battle philtres in an arc toward Oliver's convoy and startling some of the more skittish horses.

None of his people were hit directly, but the spheres broke on impact with the ground and the wagons, bursting with the sick yellow-green of philtres of stench and the brown-red heat shimmer of pepper bombs.

Both were meant to incapacitate, not kill. It could have been much worse. Their enemies were taking the safety of the Morrow prisoners seriously, which could work to Oliver's advantage.

Oliver's people moved with alacrity, trying to stay as far away from the smoke as possible while still guarding the wagons. The wind blew the smoke back toward their attackers, which gave his people time to put on the single-use, clear-faced masks that would filter the air to protect their eyes and respiratory system. "Advance to the left!" Oliver urged again, sending back a few battle spells of his own, as did many of his people. Most missed or were absorbed by magical shields.

Beside him, Huntley was less trigger-happy, but took an opportune shot, perfectly placed to take out one of their opponents. Unfortunately, a shimmering, four-cornered translucent shield suddenly expanded outward from a much smaller shield carried by one of their ambushers, protecting the wielder and the men several feet on either side of him from Huntley's spell.

That their enemy had access to military equipment and powerful artifacts was worrisome, but Oliver's side had the greater numbers, and didn't need to worry about avoiding lethal shots to the Morrows.

The prisoners were beginning to cough and gag despite the protection of the sacks on their head, which was silencing some of their screams. Some of Oliver's people hadn't yet managed to get their masks on, too busy dodging or firing attacks from atop their panicking horses. Oliver was once again grateful for Elmira, because erythreans weren't nearly so skittish in the face of danger.

Thankfully, the man who had been outfitted for just such a situation remembered his orders and hurriedly pulled out an artifact from his saddlebags. When activated, it sent out a pulse of power that muted the panic as well as the senses of the horses in a dozen-meter radius. The magic was light enough that it wouldn't stop any particularly panicked horse from breaking free, and was tuned specifically to their species, but everyone within the area of effect felt some of the spillover.

The calm was useful. The dampened senses were not. But it was worth it to maintain their group's mobility and control over the wagons.

An enemy man raised his hands, not in surrender, but in a motion of power and control.

As if they were all in the eye of a hurricane, the wind stilled. The air turned thick and soup-like for a moment, enough for Oliver to feel the press of its antithetical solidity against his skin. It was hard to breathe.

The smoke from the battle philtres hung in place, the spewing gasses building up into a thick roil. And then it swirled outward, moving toward Oliver's people like a great python slithering toward prey, eager to encircle and constrict. It focused first on those who had not yet managed to put on their masks, but quickly attacked the rest. The protective masks could only handle so much. If they were rendered ineffective...

Shocked, Oliver looked back toward the man who had his hands raised. Either he was a free-caster, or a witch with a powerful—and invisible— familiar from the Plane of Air. One was, of course, worse than the other, but in both cases, his response was the same. Oliver's estimation of the danger his people were in rose sharply, and he screamed, "Go, go, *go*! Break through!"

His words were muffled within the strangely static air, but they still traveled well enough for his people to hear and try to comply. Oliver deftly switched his wand's output to a piercing spell, firing in rapid succession at the spellcaster.

Despite his people's attempts to cover their faces or hold their breath, many had begun to cough and gag as the air of the philtres followed them unnaturally.

"Damp masks over your mouth and nose!" a Nightmare Pack woman barked to those closest to her, using a canteen to wet a bright yellow bandanna and tie it over her mask as a second line of defense, clumsily controlling her horse with her knees alone. She was almost hit by a concussive spell, but one of the other enforcers got between her and the enemy to throw up a personal shield spell with their battle wand.

The Nightmare Pack woman nudged her horse closer to Oliver's. "I think I can give that air witch some trouble."

"It's definitely an air witch, not a free-caster?" Oliver called, directing Elmira to dodge a concussive blast with the barest twitch of the reins.

"No Conduit!" the woman replied distractedly to his question. "If he were a general free-caster, he would still be using a Conduit. That he's not means he's channeling through his familiar. We can hope air spells are the only thing he has this kind of control over. Besides," she added with a predatory crinkle of the skin around her eyes, "I am an air witch, and my familiar can feel his."

Currents of air gathered around and rushed out from her hand, which rippled under the effects of a mirage. She aimed the narrow gust of wind at the battle philtres in a sweeping motion, pushing their spewing fog away from their people and back toward the enemy, disrupting the snake-like currents that had been focused on the other enforcers.

The enemy witch responded immediately to this attempt at resistance, curling a larger portion of the smoke around to circle Oliver and the woman, trying to press in on them.

The expanding shield adjusted again as its wielder moved to stand slightly in front of and to the side of the spellcaster. Though Oliver experimented against its defenses, targeting different edges in the hope of overwhelming it, and even coordinated one overwhelming assault that had the man behind the shield grimacing with fear, in the end all attacks splashed harmlessly against the shimmering barrier.

But, despite the difficulty, they had managed to retreat into a cross-street, and then turn again to make their way back toward Knave Knoll, the enemy harrying them at every step. Another barrage of battle philtres landed in front of them, creating a yellow and red mix of clouds across the street, too thick to see through. Again, the cloud gathered itself up and moved to direct the effects toward the most vulnerable. At this point, his people were all wearing their masks, but they were down a couple of men.

"That shield spell is being actively-cast!" Huntley shouted loud enough to make Oliver flinch, despite the stillness of the air. "I can see his concentration straining. He must have a spell array embedded in the shield."

Oliver quickly snapped orders for several of the men to peel off from the main group with the express mission of taking down that shield. He ducked to avoid a shimmering orange curse that almost clipped the top of his head, then sent back a piercing curse to one of the enemies not covered by the giant magical barrier.

The woman wasn't quick enough to throw up a personal barrier or dodge, and took the spell to the side of her neck, ripping off a chunk of flesh half the size of Oliver's fist and sending her reeling backward with a lethal spray of arterial blood.

Huntley and three others went after the shielder, fighting their way past the answering concentration of enemy fire. One man took a flying jump off his horse as the creature went down under a nasty rupturing spell, its innards spilling out in a steaming mess from the gaping wound in its belly.

Spell-fire concentrated on the Nightmare pack witch and Oliver, and he was hard-pressed to block it all. He was thankful for Elmira's nimbleness, as the horse sidestepped several attacks that would have left them incapacitated or even dead. Soon, under the pressure of the more powerful enemy witch, there was no clean air to draw on.

The woman could have pulled her familiar back to protect herself, but stubbornly refused to do so. Even with all the protection against the battle philtres, her eyes began to swell and stream from irritation. She scowled stubbornly, her pressure on the magic unrelenting despite the distraction.

The attack team had managed to get a Verdant Stag enforcer into position. She had circled around from the rear, climbed a few meters up the wall of mismatched stone, and now took her shot. Her slicing spell cut through from the enemy's flank, behind the line of the shield barrier, perfectly targeting the wielder's back.

He was armored, but the spell was enough to break his concentration. His barrier spell broke like the bone of a Titan, sending an explosion of slicing force out in a vertical circle, cutting through the air and the ground but unfortunately not injuring any of their enemies.

But it was enough to distract the enemy witch, and the smoke of the philtres flushed out under the force of the Nightmare Pack woman's spell. She sucked in a desperate breath, then started coughing raggedly, but wind continued to gush out from her hands.

Before any of the enemy's number could respond to the fallen shield, the enforcer hanging from the wall followed her carefully aimed slicing spell with a concussive blast. It slammed the discombobulated shield wielder forward, sending him tumbling toward the convoy like a rag doll. The shield clattered into the street between their two groups.

A Nightmare Pack enforcer rushed forward into a struggle over control of the shield with an enemy man that had lunged to retrieve it.

Oliver's people took out two more of the enemy, and suddenly the advantage shifted. Even against such powerful thaumaturges, they were winning.

The Verdant Stag sniper aimed next for the air witch, but it was too late.

A violent slashing motion of the witch's arm across his chest—a single motion from right to left, filled with command—was followed a second later by a howl of wind. It knocked her off the side of the building, spinning her upside down and slamming her into the wall of the opposite building with so much force that she was pinned there for a moment. Finally, she slid to the ground head first, collapsing bonelessly into a heap at the edge of the street.

Oliver winced. The woman had been brave, and perhaps even turned the tide of battle for them, but she was unlikely to survive that. If she was still alive, they needed to retrieve her and get her to Healer Nidson as quickly as possible, which would be difficult considering the enemies between them.

She had also angered the witch, and after taking her out, the man turned toward the rest of them. Having given up total air control of the battlefield, he now resorted to individual attacks, waves of wind targeting those covering the rest of the convoy's escape.

The guards had been doing well, taking down a couple more enemies positioned at the flanks. But a few blows from the enemy air witch sent people sprawling, not nearly as forcefully as the attack against the sniper, but more than enough to disrupt their formations and put them back on the defense, halting any progress and giving their enemies the upper hand once more.

Their own witch was much too weak to match him, and one particularly harsh blow sent her reeling off her horse. Huntley caught her, but her eyes had lost focus, and the shimmer of her familiar was missing.

But they had made progress, and the canal bridge just before Knave Knoll was in sight at the end of the street. If they could get past it, not only would the reinforced building be a fortified position, but they could block off the bridge itself with liquid stone or some of the wagons and temporarily slow the enemy's advance.

As if sensing his intentions, the enemy leader, his own personal shield artifacts still fully active, called out instructions to his men. Within twenty seconds, several of the horses were dead, and at least two of the wagons were missing wheels.

Oliver gritted his teeth. He hated to compliment the enemy, but their leader was obviously insightful and decisive. Oliver could retreat, but not without a huge struggle to keep the prisoners.

Elmira whinnied in distress as he slipped down from her back, moving to put the single intact wagon between them and the enemy. Oliver patted her neck absently, his stomach hurting for the death of such innocent creatures.

A few guards rushed out from Knave Knoll to come to their aid, which was against protocol, but Oliver was grateful for it anyway. With them, the numbers would be even more in their favor, and perhaps it would give them the leeway to move some of their wounded back for treatment.

If they could just take down the air witch, the tide of the battle would turn completely in their favor.

He looked down to check his pocket watch, having lost track of the passage of time in the heat of battle. They needed the prepared reinforcements he had called for earlier to arrive soon.

A concussive blast spell ripped through the wagon right beside him, obliterating both wheels as it passed through the wood and continued on toward his legs. In a blur of confusion, Oliver belatedly attempted to leap up and over the foggy force and wave of wooden shrapnel. The blast clipped his shins painfully, sending him twisting through the air. As the world seemed to turn around him, the side of the wagon rushed up to meet his face, and Elmira screamed in pain.

4 2

———

REFRACTION

Under the ominous flashing of lights and the low moan of the alarm, Knave Knoll's guards rushed into action, ensuring all the remaining prisoners were locked away and then jogging to defensive positions.

Enforcer Gerard grabbed a young guard as she passed. "Take over here," he ordered. "When they're finished, escort the prisoner back to their cell."

He moved to leave, but the cursemaster called out, spittle flying off his shiny lips as he protested. "Just what is going on!? I was assured of my safety when I took this job. Surely, you cannot be leaving my protection to this woman and a couple of *healers*. I insist that you escort me away from this place if there is danger!"

Gerard turned back, his expression still as calm and impassive as ever. "Knave Knoll is the safest place you could be. When things have settled down, I promise we will escort you back to your lodgings. In the meantime, please complete the assignment." He jerked his chin toward the prisoner halfway through receiving their seal, then left, ignoring the cursemaster's sputtered protests.

Healer Nidson, by contrast, seemed entirely unperturbed. "Shall we continue?" he asked mildly.

The cursemaster gave him a curdling glare, but turned back to the unfortunate prisoner.

Siobhan had to shake her limbs to rid herself of the cold stillness that had settled over her when the alarm started. Per her agreement with Oliver, she could leave if she thought herself to be in danger. But whatever the problem was, she couldn't hear any sounds of fighting.

The prisoner and cursemaster were both agitated, which made this final seal more dangerous. She might be needed if Healer Nidson had to fight against another seizure. Plus, if she left now, it would be on her own, which might actually be more dangerous than staying put, surrounded as she was by well-stocked and trained enforcers who were ready to handle the danger for her.

'The situation is dangerous, but it doesn't yet seem to be a disaster, and doesn't call for panic or rash decisions. I need more information.'

The cursemaster moved faster than ever, and, with a nervous bow, the guard escorted the prisoner out of the infirmary as soon as it was done. She met no resistance from the Morrow man, who was probably relieved to get away from them.

This left Siobhan, Healer Nidson, and the cursemaster alone in the infirmary.

"We should find out what's going on," Siobhan said.

"Yes!" the cursemaster agreed. "I require a safer location, with guards, while the situation is ongoing. Somewhere I can set up wards…"

"I will clean up here," Healer Nidson said, already moving to arrange the room to his liking. "I have a sense that my service will be necessary. Miss Nakai, please go along to let them know that I will be prepared to assist with injuries as soon as possible, and report the situation back to me."

With the cursemaster tagging along, superciliously muttering to himself about the lack of respect and professionalism, Siobhan left to find Enforcer Gerard, or whoever was in charge of the security measures.

As she passed one of the small windows on the second floor, where a guard had lowered the glass and activated some kind of hidden mechanism that was probably a ward inlaid into the wall, she paused, peeking out over the man's shoulder.

To the west, less than a couple of blocks away and moving slowly in their direction, spells lit up the night. And suddenly she could hear the sounds of fighting. It was hard to make out the details, but she saw three wagons retreating along with the first of two separate groups of people. "One of the convoys was attacked," she whispered.

"If they can make it back, it will be fine," the guard replied.

Siobhan turned away, hurrying on to the administrative office in the upper corner of the building. *'This isn't the low-key mass arrest we planned,'* she thought. *'This is going to bring the coppers down on us, too. No matter what deal Oliver made with them, there's no way the Crowns will overlook a secret, independent jail run by a local gang.'*

When Siobhan and the cursemaster entered the already crowded room, Enforcer Gerard looked up from a distagram artifact just like the one Oliver had in his home office. The normally stoic man's expression had grown grim under the weight of the problem.

The cursemaster immediately and loudly complained about his treatment. "I am a man of particular means, and I never forget an enemy," he added with a yellow-toothed smile that was meant to be intimidating—and it was, but it also made Siobhan have the sudden urge to kill him and thus remove him as a threat.

Enforcer Gerard was more circumspect, sending two of the guards to set the cursemaster up in one of the solitary confinement rooms on the ground floor, where he would be "insulated" from any trouble.

When the distasteful man had left, Siobhan relayed Healer Nidson's message, sidling closer to the crowded window to see out.

Reinforcements from Knave Knoll had gone out to the convoy's aid, but the enemy had crippled two of the three wagons, and several dead or dying horses lay across the ground. And then, in the light of one of the bright lamps the enemy was shining to keep the guards half-blinded, Siobhan caught sight of Oliver's mask as he turned his head to look back. She felt like their eyes met for a moment, and then the bottom half of the wagon he was standing behind exploded.

Oliver went down with it.

His horse fell with him, screaming with a pain and terror that seemed all too human. The sound cut through the noise of the battle for an instant. And then the sounds dampened entirely, as if they'd gone underwater.

Siobhan frowned in confusion as the spell-fire from their side faltered and people began to claw at their faces and throats.

"Up to the roof!" Gerard snapped.

One of the guards hesitated. "But they're still out of range, we can't accurately—"

"I don't care!" Gerard screamed, his clipped voice reminding Siobhan of Professor Fekten for a moment. "Get up there, take your stations, and distract the enemy, or our people are going to die!" As three-quarters of the guards scrambled to do as he said, Gerard moved to the weapons cabinet against the far wall, picking up a machete and strapping it to his waist, then adding a thick vest with a rigid collar that came up to protect his neck and the back of his head. "I'm going down there. Someone needs to take out that thaumaturge before he suffocates the whole group to death," he announced. "Roberts, you're in charge in my absence. You know the protocol."

"But that's a suicide mission!" Roberts protested.

As she listened, Siobhan's skin had grown alternately hot and cold. Now, without thinking, she blurted, "I can help."

Gerard didn't stop to argue with Roberts, just waved for Siobhan to follow as he jogged down the hall to the stairwell. "I know you are…capable," he said, giving her a piercing look. "Can you remove the thaumaturge who is choking the air out of them? I estimate we have less than two minutes before the tides of battle turn irretrievably against us. I've seen this tactic before."

'I am not *getting into a one-on-one against a powerful thaumaturge!'* she yelled silently, the words echoing inside of her skull. Out loud, she blurted, "I can make you invisible. For a little while. Enough to get behind the enemy line and make a single blow."

"A powerful boon. I accept. What is required of me?" he asked without hesitation.

"I need you to remain in my line of sight. I'll go up to the roof. Pour some of this on your back so I can keep track of you," she said, her fingers adroitly pulling out a bottle of moonlight sizzle without needing to look. "The invisibility will only activate from the front. From the back, you'll glow as bright as a beacon."

Gerard took the sealed bottle and smashed it against the wall. From the broken spout, he poured the cool glow of the liquid over the back of his armored vest, still jogging toward the back exit.

Siobhan turned around and sprinted for all she was worth toward the entrance to the roof, thankful that she'd taken the time to look over the building plans beforehand. As she ran, she pulled at the knowledge and mindset she would need to cast an invisibility spell, her thoughts splitting and wrestling all the disparate pieces together at once with the inexorable dexterity of a kraken's tentacles. Central symbol, a triangle. She had enough time for three glyphs, maybe—just enough to stabilize the intent. The output-adjusting parameters. Some she had practiced, some she had only learned of during Professor Lacer's private lecture.

And most importantly, the actual application—the natural science of such a phenomenon.

"Get out of my way!" Siobhan shrieked at the guards blocking the pull-down staircase, scrambling up it so fast she had to use both her hands and her feet to stabilize herself.

All a half-sphere of invisibility required was tightly-controlled refraction. Professor Gnorrish had explained it during one of his recent lectures. She pulled at the memory, and for a quarter second of horror, worried that it would refuse to come.

But then it was there in its totality.

They were in the illusion tunnel between the Citadel and the library. Professor Gnorrish paused for a moment, using a handkerchief to wipe away the sweat on his forehead and take a few deep breaths. "Now, you've all heard of refraction, and seen examples of it. Refraction happens when electromagnetic radiation passes *through* a substance with a different density, at an angle. A medium such as water is more dense than air. As light enters, it slows down. But the light doesn't change energy; you've all seen that light doesn't change color just because it passes through water or clear glass. What *does* change is the distance between the wavefronts. Let's return to our analogy of the boat on the ocean. Those original slow, mild waves get closer together, but move proportionally slower, so your boat is still only experiencing *one* rise and fall every minute. It's steeper, but the total energy of the light waves hasn't changed."

The illusion morphed to show a series of waves hitting a glass block straight-on. As they passed through it, they grew much closer together, stretching out again as they exited. The block slowly rotated, and the waves within angled with it, straightening out again as they exited the block on the other side—but now slightly lower down.

"Imagine a sheet of metal is passing through the air toward you. It's too stiff to bend. You press your finger against one side of it and apply a little resistance. The part you pressed on is suddenly moving slower, and so the whole sheet of metal pivots toward that side, and is now moving at an angle. The light has just entered a substance with a different density. Now, say someone else is behind you, and when the metal sheet reaches them, they poke the other side and straighten the metal sheet out again, sending it off in the same direction but at a slightly different location than its original trajectory would have caused. The light has just exited the substance. Refraction works kind of like that, and it's why you'll only see refraction when light enters or exits a substance *at an angle*. The really interesting thing is, that angle doesn't need to be a straight line. It can be curved. This is the concept that optical lenses are based on, allowing the creation of eyeglasses, telescopes, and even your own eyeballs."

Instead of undulating waves, the light changed to be depicted by flat sheets passing through the block of glass.

Sebastien had reached out to the block, moving slowly and telegraphing her intention for Professor Lacer's benefit. She adjusted its angle and watched as the representation of refracted light moved with it, forced to turn as it passed through, and then allowed to straighten as it exited.

The students around her gasped. For once, she agreed with the general sentiment. *'This is amazing!'*

Gnorrish continued as some of the other groups started to pick up on the true nature of this lecture and the utility of the simulation chamber. "Now, when the substance is too dense for light to propagate within, instead of refracting, it *reflects*. Glass, water, and other semi-transparent substances are only reflecting a small percentage of the overall light that hits them, but when their surfaces are smooth enough, it allows a mirror-like reflection. In fact, if any substance was smooth enough, you would get that same mirror-image reflection, because there's no natural substance with complete transparency." The lecture had continued after that, moving on to their experimentation with lenses while Professor Lacer controlled their group's illusion.

Siobhan held all the relevant information in her mind simultaneously, like water in a glass, as she skidded to a stop at the edge of the flat-topped roof. Around her, the others were hurriedly setting up the portable battlements they'd stashed for just such an attack. The largest sheet of seaweed paper she had was already in her hand, and rather than carefully unfold it, she shook it wildly, letting its edges catch the wind and rip it open. "Help me stabilize it!" she snapped to the nearby enforcers. "One at each corner!"

They hurried to place hands or weighted objects down over the paper.

This sheet, and the blank Circle already drawn on it, were big enough to cover an entire person. She hadn't known what she might need it for, but it was one of the many emergency preparations she'd been slowly building up.

More thankful than ever for all the practice she'd been getting with minimalist spell arrays and working with light, she scrambled atop the paper to draw out the glyphs and central numerological symbol as quickly as possible. Then, she added the output-adjusting parameters for height, to take the half-sphere of invisibility down to street level.

She hadn't practiced moving the output while casting with Professor Lacer, but she had no trouble doing so with her shadow-familiar, and believed the mental tether that he had called a crutch could handle such a maneuver.

She peeked over the edge of the battlement to see Gerard already running down the street toward the fighting, the moonlight sizzle smeared on his back a beacon against the night. He obviously had no plans to wait for or rely on her, but without some kind of protection, not only was it unlikely he would make it out alive, he might not even manage to take down the enemy thaumaturge.

Siobhan allowed herself a single blink to finalize the operation of the spell in her mind. All she needed to do was capture the light in the half-dome behind Gerard, route it around his body to the exact same equivalent location, and release it again. To do that, the magic would need to create the equivalent of a denser medium around him, angled in such a way as to refract the light in an arc. She held the idea of this invisible sphere around the man so tightly in her mind that she could almost feel it. And then, she created a tether between them, reaching out from the edges of the spell array, down to the street, and latching on to him, as if her shadow had stretched out and combined with his, becoming a single entity.

Siobhan opened her eyes and cast.

It took only a second for her Will to climb over the mental hurdle that allowed her to distance the output location, reaching out and grabbing the beacon of his light, gobbling him up inside her sphere of control.

For a moment, she felt like Myrddin.

Sure, with the lack of moon and all the distraction of the fighting, her spell had to redirect so little light that she could still handle it even with the increased strain of this long a distance, much farther than she had ever achieved in practice. And even though she could tell pieces of the refraction dome occasionally faltered, most likely creating mirage-like distortions or making Gerard seem like a chameleon moving just out of sync with the background, those same environmental conditions meant that it would be hard for anyone to notice.

But she felt powerful. Her knowledge and her Will could reorder the natural laws. Even if Professor Lacer had been unimpressed by her lazy work-around, and she wasn't even strong enough to get all the way through his tests, she could do *this*.

That sense of triumph lasted for only a few seconds before the strain of continuing to move the output Circle along with Gerard made itself known.

Some tiny portion of her mind caught Oliver's mussed hair rising again next to one of the crippled wagons, and any peripheral attention she had left focused on him without her conscious direction.

He had climbed up the side of the wagon and was…killing the prisoners?

Gerard had made it to the enemy. Hunching down to seem a little smaller, he cut diagonally across the street, right toward the man in the middle, whose arms were raised dramatically.

The enemy thaumaturge made a violent motion with his fist, and even from this distance, Siobhan could feel the power of it channel through to the world.

The sounds of the battle returned.

A huge, faint ripple tore through the air between the two groups, moving down toward Oliver. It ploughed through the bodies of the prisoners he had been executing and crashed into the wagon he'd been clinging to. The whole mass exploded outward in splintered wood and splattered viscera.

Siobhan's vision flickered as something in her tried to pull her concentration away from Gerard and the spell to better see what had just happened.

She didn't know how Oliver could have survived that attack.

The realization sent a wave of static numbness through her mind, and her concentration on the spell wavered once more.

She couldn't spare a glimpse for Oliver's remains. Without her, Gerard would die, too, and the enemy would roll forward over all of them. She threw her desperation and worry into the spell, letting it buoy her fatiguing Will. No matter what happened to Oliver, she would continue on. She would live. And for her to live, the enemy had to die.

The sheer violence of the attack had stunned everyone, and the friendly spell-fire that had threatened Gerard temporarily petered off. Probably, people were hiding from a potential follow up, or trying to regain their breath now that the enemy thaumaturge had released his suffocating grip.

The man swayed from the effort of that great blow. Perhaps he had reached his limit, or maybe he was only collecting himself before exerting his control over the battlefield once more, single-handedly carrying the fight for his side.

Siobhan wouldn't learn which it was, because at that moment, Gerard threw himself forward.

The tip of his machete reached beyond the range of Siobhan's spell, catching some reflected light for a flashing instant.

The thaumaturge looked up, but Gerard was already bringing the blade down at an angle, the force of his whole body behind the swing.

The machete hit the thaumaturge's jaw, met the resistance of a ward that flared grey, and instantly overpowered it. The blade continued through, angling down through the jaw, and then the neck, stopping only when it met the thaumaturge's opposite collarbone.

The man's head flew off, launched by a geyser of blood.

Gerard stumbled as the full-body commitment to his blow pulled him off balance.

The two closest attackers stood stunned, not immediately able to comprehend what had happened, but Siobhan could feel her grip on the spell slipping. Gerard was too far, and she was too unpracticed. But she mentally dug in her claws and wrapped the weight of her Will around the spell. Her clarity might falter, but her determination remained.

Instead of immediately running away, Gerard swung again, this time cutting off the wand of the closest attacker, along with the hand that had been gripping it.

Gerard took two more steps. As he shoved the gently curved blade of his machete all the way through the chest of a third enemy, the blood spraying out and hitting a fourth in the face, Siobhan lost her grip on his concealment.

She slumped down, fighting back dizziness as she tried to ground herself in the sensation of rough gravel against her cheek and hand, one arm crushed awkwardly beneath her. She hadn't strained her Will, hadn't lost control or broken, she'd just given out. She had burned through her mental energy like a wick with no remaining candle, and her mind felt bruised. If she wanted to be safe, she wouldn't be of much use for the remainder of the evening.

She couldn't even lift her head to see over the battlements and search for Oliver's body.

4 3

———

ARMAGEDDON GAME

Oliver

Month 3, Day 13, Saturday 1:45 a.m.

HUNTLEY CRAWLED OFF OF OLIVER, the bigger man's knees digging painfully into Oliver's thigh as Huntley dragged himself to the side. The single-use emergency ward Huntley had activated flickered against the dust and debris, then died.

Huntley coughed, rising to his hands and knees to turn a baleful scowl onto Oliver's prone form. "What were you thinking, you imbecile!? You were standing there in clear view of the enemy! Did you think none of them would try to take advantage of that? You can't expect to use the prisoners as a shield if you're actively slaughtering them!"

Oliver groaned, feeling as if his body were a scrambled egg. He had been thinking that Elmira was crippled and dying, and that they were all being suffocated into debility. He had been thinking that the situation was desperate, and that killing the prisoners might give them some leeway. They would do too much damage if they were allowed to go free, anyway.

In a way, his plan had worked.

Oliver rolled onto his side, coughing out a fine spray of blood onto the filthy cobblestones. He stared at it in surprise for a couple of seconds, then climbed unsteadily to his feet. His battle wand was gone, and when he took a step, he stumbled and would have fallen if not for Huntley's stabilizing grip. Long wooden splinters had impaled Oliver's leg in several places. He reached down and tugged at the largest, but his fingers slipped off the bloody surface, and the movement sent another dizzying explosion of pain throughout his chest and back.

He straightened, fumbling for the emergency healing potion he kept within a metal-plated pocket of his jacket. The reinforced crystal of the vial was thankfully still intact. Oliver downed it in a single searing gulp, his eyes closed against the light of its glow, and Huntley surprised him by yanking a piece of wood as long and thick as his forefinger from Oliver's leg. The rest, he left in, simply wrapping the whole mess in a large green handkerchief.

The healing potion spread its magic throughout Oliver's chest, but, despite its potency and commensurate price, he could feel it petering out against his natural resistance before it made it much further. One of the many curses of his bloodline.

Huntley helped him to stand and move away a little, sending a spray of fire over the ground where Oliver had fallen, hot enough to render any bits of flesh or splatters of blood unusable.

Coughing again, Oliver looked out over the battlefield. While he was still insensate after the attack, someone had taken down the air witch and a couple of the others, but the remaining enemy forces hadn't lost their determination, even though there were only a handful left. That didn't bode well. A couple were crouched down behind liquid stone barriers, but some moved to run off to the side. They didn't appear to be fleeing in panic.

A masked person stepped out of the darkness around the corner and shot a stunning spell at one of the withdrawing attackers, hitting them in the back and sending them into a comical, painful-looking sprawl. The masked person, whose only distinguishing feature was their chin-length blonde hair, nodded at Oliver and returned to the darkness. His first thought was that one of his people had been clever enough to disguise themselves and infiltrate the enemy, but he didn't recognize that mask, and all of the spells that had been tossed around so casually tonight had been lethal, not safely incapacitating. It seemed the enemy had a traitor in their midst.

Oliver drew a deep breath to shout again for their people to retreat into Knave Knoll, throwing himself into a coughing fit. They needed to hurry, because he was worried about the enemy circling around to come at them from the sides, or even try to cut them off entirely. But Huntley understood this as well, and it was he who shouted the order, saving Oliver the pain.

His men moved as quickly as their battered bodies could manage, using the wagons and some hastily poured liquid stone in the gaps and even over the wood itself to create a barrier between themselves and the few remaining enemies on the main street. They used what horses still lived to carry bound prisoners like sacks of grain. As people passed over the canal bridge to the front of Knave Knoll, Oliver looked for Elmira. She had been downed by that first blow that knocked him off his feet, one of her legs shattered near the hoof, but still alive, lying on the ground beside the wagon.

At first he found only chunks of meat, wood, and broken cobblestone whose specific origin he couldn't distinguish. There had been eight prisoners in that single wagon, and at least half of them had been caught by the witch's vindictive final attack. Then he found Elmira's head. It lay a few meters away from where she'd fallen, blown away from her body. He had hoped that perhaps she could still have been saved. With enough money and the right magic, even a pulverized leg was not a death sentence for an erythrean. No such hope remained in him, and he turned away.

Together, he and his remaining men moved over the canal, every step sending a spike of knee-trembling pain up through his leg. The front doors of Knave Knoll opened, waiting for them to reach it.

Oliver instinctively glanced back at the sound of splashing water behind them. When he saw the group of battle-ready fighters arriving, shooting along the waters of the canal itself at the speed of a galloping horse, for just a moment he thought that the reinforcements he'd called for had come up with some strange and innovative new method of travel.

That moment was over faster than the blink of an eye, as he immediately realized they weren't his reinforcements at all. They were the enemy's.

Stopping before the bridge, a huge water elemental clambered out of the canal. Elementally imbued liquid made up the body of a great sea turtle, swirling a serene, crystalline blue with streaks of rust red concentrating around its shell.

Eight more enemies sat upon its transparent back. Its witch rode in a strange saddle at the base of its neck, while the others clung on wherever they could find a grip.

The sea turtle's paddle-like flippers were poorly suited to walking on land, but as its human cargo hopped off, it rose into the air, floating as if it were in the water. On the mundane plane, such a stunt must take quite a lot of energy to maintain.

Oliver's people responded quickly to the new threat, some attacking the turtle and its former riders while others hurried to move their prisoners and injured into Knave Knoll.

From the battlements above, spells rained down, and Oliver caught a glimpse of Siobhan, looking like the bright-eyed school mistress everyone had been terrified of as a child. Her grey-streaked hair was pulled back in a severe bun, her artificially blue eyes seemed to glow against the backdrop of the darkness, and her expressionless face promised punishment.

She pulled a bright green potion out of her bag, stood, and hurled it in a full body motion toward the rear of their position, where one of their enemies had been trying to circle around them.

The potion vial broke on impact, spilling across the man's chest and activating with a screeching sizzle. The man screamed with matching shrillness as his clothes and skin melted away with a burst of steam.

The turtle turned sideways so that its shell was facing his people, swimming quickly between them and its crew. It caught the majority of their spell attacks on its rust-swirled shell, which took far less damage than it should have, only to quickly begin to repair itself.

Siobhan stood up again, hurling another of her green vials. It seemed to agitate the elemental, drawing a warbling scream from its throat. Its waters swirled more quickly, and then some green-tinged drops rained down, expelling the potion along with some of its mass. This seemed only to make it angry, however, and it swam faster through the air as the water witch glared murderously at Siobhan.

A bruise-purple spell shot toward Siobhan. Without any change in her alert, focused expression, she lazily sidestepped it, her battle wand flicking out from some hidden spot and shooting two bright red stunning spells toward the enemy who had attacked her, one just over his left shoulder, to draw his attention, and the second right behind it, aimed for the spot he stepped into as he attempted to dodge. She barely even watched to make sure the man went down.

Protected by Huntley, Oliver was one of the last to make it past Knave Knoll's entryway. As the doors closed behind him, he caught sight of a large group of uniformed coppers arriving from the south, moving in an alert formation and armed for battle.

One of the guards by the door looked them over. "Healer Nidson is set up in the infirmary for anyone who needs help."

Huntley turned immediately to Oliver, wearing a half-expectant, half-demanding expression. "Let's go."

Oliver waved him off. "I already took a healing potion. There are more important things for me to do at the moment, and people who need help more than me." Doing his best to disguise the agony it caused, he made his way up the stairs to the office on the second floor, where the security measures were controlled, and where he hoped to find Mr. Gerard waiting with some good news.

Instead, he found that Gerard had gone out on a suicide mission, leaving one of the lower-level enforcers in charge.

Three of their five prisoner convoys, he learned, had made it to their destination without issue, but the reinforcements Oliver had called for had never arrived. Those who came from Knave Knoll to help were some of the enforcers who had been meant to escort the final convoy.

Outside, the coppers were hurriedly setting up a barricade. They had activated spotlights that shined down on the attacks, similar to what had been done to the convoy. Using a voice-amplifying artifact, one of them called for those fighting both down below and on the roof to stand down or be met with force.

The turtle turned toward them and spewed out a concentrated stream of water, not at any of the people, but at the liquid stone barriers they were trying to establish. The expanding potion was washed away even as it was being poured, before it could solidify, and those coppers that were clipped by the stream of water were knocked off their feet.

Knave Knoll was burnt. After the original conspicuous battle to take down the Morrows, the coppers couldn't afford to keep letting incidents like this happen. It made them look ineffectual. With Knave Knoll's location and purpose known, it was useless.

The coppers needed a win, and Oliver only hoped he could take advantage of that to redirect some of the following antagonism away from his people. Despite the fighting, he and Lynwood were effectively delivering over a hundred criminals to pump up the arrest numbers, and if the coppers could overcome those attacking the building, they could claim victory in a huge battle.

At least if it had to happen, it had happened here, Oliver acknowledged. Knave Knoll was located in a more industrial area, so there weren't as many people out on the streets. There were few homes in the area, and any homeless that could have become collateral damage during the battle had the opportunity to run away. The surrounding buildings had not been the focus of any attacks, leaving the innocent mostly unscathed.

But as Oliver turned to the messages hanging from the distagram on a curling strip of paper, his attention slipped away from the fighting and any plans to manage the fallout.

The reinforcements he'd called for hadn't come because they were needed elsewhere. At nearly the same time their convoy had been ambushed, two of their major storehouses and the Verdant Stag—their home base—had also triggered emergency alarms.

Was someone trying to loot their supplies while they were too busy elsewhere to respond?

But then, even as he watched, the distagram printed a third, simple code of letters and numbers. The alarm for the Verdant Stag's underground vault had been triggered. The vault that so few people knew about, where he kept only the most important items. Katerin couldn't have revealed its location, not even under torture.

This, more than anything, cemented his surety that the Architects of Khronos had been behind the attack, despite how much he'd been hoping for an alternative explanation. He knew this, because that was the same hidden, secure vault where he kept the censer they had given as a tribute to the Raven Queen, while waiting to sell it.

It was also, however, where he kept the book. The one that he'd paid well to have stolen from the University's archaeological expedition. The *real* book, replaced without anyone's knowledge with one that looked similar from another box, well before anyone had a chance to catalogue Myrddin's journals.

It was this replacement book, of course, that Siobhan had been so unfortunate as to steal, and before the University could even discover the duplicity. Now, somehow, the spiral of events leading out from that single action had brought them here.

Oliver had to get back to the Verdant Stag.

4 4

EMBERS OF A DEAD STAR

Siobhan
   Month 3, Day 13, Saturday 1:50 a.m.

Siobhan's warding medallion had activated several times, helping to protect her against multiple attack spells and even some shrapnel, and its unpleasant cold against the skin of her chest was a constant reminder of the danger she had stepped into. Believing that they'd killed Oliver, she'd been vengeful and had recklessly joined in attacking the enemy along with the guards on the roof around her.

But somehow Oliver had survived. She'd watched as he made it through the doors to Knave Knoll, covering his retreat as best she could when the Architects of Khronos sent even more powerful enemies to try and stop them.

'*I should probably go back down and assist Healer Nidson. I saw a lot of injured men and women,*' she thought. She was running low on stunning spells and battle philtres, anyway. Before she could retreat into the safety of the building, however, she was distracted by an alarming sight.

At the rear of the enemy reinforcements, near the bridge behind the sea turtle, an old man who looked half-desiccated, with thin, mottled skin that clung tightly to his bones, was crouched on the ground beside a chest of supplies, setting up a spell array of wrought iron with a diameter wider than he was tall. She'd heard that soldiers sometimes used huge metal war arrays with modular pieces for powerful attacks.

The thaumaturge slid a metal glyph the size of his palm into place within this portable war-Circle.

"That man in the back is the highest priority target," she called out, pointing down at him. "Take him out with prejudice, before he can finish whatever he's preparing."

Several of her allies attempted to do so, but the water elemental protected him from all their attacks, and he didn't even bother to lift his head from his work, so assured was he of his safety.

"It could be an artillery spell," Siobhan warned, turning back to the trap door in the center of the roof. *'I'm not sure if the wards can stand up to something like that,'* she worried silently. *'I'll tell whoever's in charge below, someone who might actually be able to do something about it, and then I'll go help Healer Nidson. I'm useless in the fight at this point, and this isn't exactly a safe location.'*

Before she could step down, Oliver's head poked out of the trap door's entrance. "Are you sure you don't have a taste for danger? At the most, I expected you to be safely assisting Healer Nidson, not battling like a valkyrie up here." The grin hidden by his mask was clear in his voice.

Siobhan scowled at him, ignoring his teasing. "I think we're still in danger." She explained quickly, and his expression sobered.

"Everyone should come inside. As soon as we activate the final lockdown wards, not much should be able to get past them. Let the coppers deal with these mercenaries; we have more important things to worry about. The Verdant Stag is being attacked. I need ten men to resupply and come with me to assist the home base, urgently."

Siobhan didn't understand why he would be willing to leave Knave Knoll in such a precarious situation. The Verdant Stag had their own enforcers, after all. But then she shook herself. The Verdant Stag also housed Katerin, and *Theo*. His life was more important than the remaining prisoners, and the guards and enforcers here were as safe as they could be considering the circumstances.

"You stay with Nidson. The others will need your help to evacuate," Oliver said to Siobhan, already lowering himself back down.

"What about the coppers?" she asked, moving to follow him.

"We'll be leaving the Morrows to them. Anyone who's still in this building when the coppers enter is going to be arrested. It's a shame to lose the investment, but it was too late as soon as the fighting drew attention here. It was only ever viable as a secret."

She hoped the circumstances wouldn't somehow allow the Morrows here to go free but knew that was out of her hands. "How long do we have?" she asked, stepping away from the flimsy, unfolded stairs so those following her could descend.

Before Oliver could answer, something changed above her, making the hairs on the back of her neck stand up like the moment before a lightning strike.

She threw herself to the ground. "Take cover!" she yelled. The decrepit thaumaturge had moved so much faster than she had thought possible.

Those still on the stairs scrambled down in a reckless mass of limbs. One of the people stuck on the roof let off a scream of despair. Some scrambled toward the edge of the roof furthest from the fighting, while others hunkered down and activated shielding artifacts if they had them.

The effects of the spell didn't come as she had feared, and after a few seconds she lowered her arms from around her head and tentatively peeked upward.

In the air a dozen meters above Knave Knoll, a wispy glow of light undulated, reminding Siobhan of a rare aurora she'd seen once as a child on an island far to the north. From its billowing, ethereal sheets of color, a mottled, pockmarked boulder grew from nothing.

The dark rock reminded her of a piece of coal, somehow grown to the size of a whale. It looked like she imagined a meteor might. It even began to twinkle with little embers of light, but those glitters looked not like the orange smolders of coal, but like the yellow-white embers of a dead star.

As she watched in stunned silence, those twinkling sparkles of gold grew brighter and brighter. The floating meteor trembled, the gold pulsed, and glowing dust began to fall from it.

Siobhan scrambled back from the trap door's opening, until her back pressed against the hallway wall. "Don't let it touch you!" she called out. There was no way this was harmless, or their attackers wouldn't be waiting patiently outside.

"What is it?" asked one of the men beside her, shield spell stretched out from the tip of his trembling wand.

"Help! Help!" a woman above screamed. "We're still here, don't leave us!"

"They're going to drop a giant rock on us!" one guard yelled, turning to run away.

This only caused more panic, but the glowing dust came down surprisingly slowly, wafting back and forth on every small current of the air, as if each piece were made of feathers rather than stone.

Siobhan grew even more worried as that dust fell right *through* the ceiling, completely unaffected by the physical barrier.

The guard beside her lifted his wand so the domed shield faced upward, but it, too, did nothing to slow the dust. Siobhan's heart went cold with dread. She looked down the hallways that stretched out from this central area in all four directions. The gold dust was sprinkling down in every direction that she could see, seemingly unaffected by distance. *'But the wind is blowing outside,'* she remembered. *'If this was anything like real dust, the direction the wind is blowing from would be less saturated, because the particles would have been swept away.'*

The twinkling of the bizarre meteor above them brightened as she fumbled for the paper spell array she'd drawn Grubb's barrier spell on. It might be the lowest-powered barrier spell she'd been able to find in the University library, but it was supposed to protect against weak physical projectiles.

Since it didn't matter where she stood, she moved closer to the trap door so that she could see what was happening above more clearly.

One of the guards stuck on the roof stepped closer, his wand lifted in a trembling, white-knuckled grip. He released a fireball spell right at the meteor. Past the *woof* of impact and the hungry roar of the flames, myriad tiny fire-cracker-like pops were audible. The flames seemed to burn away some of the rock on the pockmarked surface above, though even the full impact of the spell barely caused its looming mass to tremble.

"Why would you do that?" another guard screamed at him. "You have no idea if that would have worked. It could have exploded the whole thing and brought it down on us!"

"I've never seen a problem that enough fire can't kill," the first man spat back, lowering his wand. "But I'm out of charges. I think it helped a little?"

More gold sparkles had been revealed, glowing even brighter. The dust sprinkled down more thickly, though it still floated extremely slowly, catching each eddy in the air and swirling under the golden light like dust motes in a late afternoon sunbeam through a window. *'It didn't help at all. If anything, it worsened our situation,'* Siobhan thought. *'But the fire did seem to affect the dust.'*

"This has to be some sort of poison," one of the men babbled loudly over the frightened murmurs of his companions. "We can't just sit here and let it get us! I say we all make a run for it a-all…" He swallowed and seemed to lose concentration for a moment. "All at once. Before we can't."

Oliver agreed. "Come down!" he called. "Single file, no shoving."

As the guards tentatively followed his orders, fearful to move directly underneath the mysterious meteor, Siobhan went into the nearest hallway, holding Grubb's barrier spell up above her head. Clutching her Conduit and the second beast core she'd splurged on, she cast the spell. It, too, did nothing.

She watched the dust sprinkle down around her, noting that her warding medallion didn't seem to recognize it as a threat. Whatever wards the building contained were similarly unresponsive.

Dropping the spell as she reached the end of the hallway, she looked out and to the left to catch a glimpse of the ongoing battle outside. *'Shouldn't the coppers be* doing something *about this?'* She snorted at her own naivety. When had she ever been able to rely on the coppers to save her? The enemy thaumaturges were still at the edge of the canal in front of Knave Knoll, and the coppers were still in their barricaded station on the street beyond. Though she caught the light of a few spells flying in various directions, it was obvious they weren't particularly effective.

The glowing dust was floating down to the floor now, and where it touched her, it passed through her clothes and flesh without sensation, seeming completely harmless.

But as she watched, one piece of dust right in front of her face lost its glow, and was caught in the soft wind of her exhale, swirling forward into the window. Where it touched, a little pointy black bulb grew on the glass, and in between one second and the next, the glass in front of her face turned into the same mottled substance as the meteor above. Siobhan stumbled back in horror, but couldn't tear her gaze away from the spot, which continued to grow as tiny gold motes of light bloomed in it, too.

She pressed a fist to her mouth, biting down on the knuckles to keep herself from screaming as she spun around, her eyes searching for more signs of the spell's effects.

"What is it?" a woman asked. Siobhan was surprised to see the hallway before her filled with most of those she'd been fighting with on the roof above. They had followed her, as if she must know what she was doing.

Siobhan ignored her, spotting several sections of the ceiling that were becoming dark, pockmarked stone, some already meeting and melding together into a single mass that released even more dust. She shared a look with Oliver, and they seemed to come to the same conclusion simultaneously.

"We have to get out of here, *right now*," Oliver said. "Split up, one group for each wing. Get everyone. I don't care how injured or busy they are. Carry them with you if they can't walk. We'll meet by the emergency back exit. If you're not there in two minutes, expect to be left behind."

Siobhan began running even before Oliver had finished speaking, more grateful than ever for Fekten's lessons that had kept her in the best physical condition of her life. One of the men who had chosen the same direction as her nodded jerkily as he ran, his head flopping a little too far up and down in a way that looked uncomfortable. "Small groups," the man said. "Be-because..." His eyes lost focus for a moment, and he shook his head as if to clear it. "It's easier to hide when you're small. Easier to... We could hide under the bed, maybe? Or if it gets really bad, in the c-c-closeeeeet?" It was obvious that something was very wrong with him.

Quickly, the cause became apparent.

"He's got black spots on his skin," the woman nearest him announced, flinching back. "Little bumps. They're growing!"

He twitched, his lips pursing and retracting wetly. "But I'll need, my, my" —he searched for the word—"blanket-t-t." He continued to make tapping sounds with the tip of his tongue.

It was true. Some of the dust that had stopped glowing must have landed on him, and just like the window glass, he was being consumed.

"Cut them out!" Siobhan screamed, almost tripping over her own feet as she reached down to pull the long, thin dagger from its place between her shin and her boot. She grabbed the man, yanking him about so that she could see the black spots more clearly. Some of the others stopped and helped her hold him still as he jerked against her grip, but others left them and ran ahead with clear terror.

Siobhan found a couple of black bumps on his neck, and one on his bare forearm, and dark vein-like tendrils were starting to spread from them. She peered at the growing masses for a moment before pressing in near the edge of one with the tip of her dagger.

To everyone's surprise and horror, the spot pried out easily enough with a knife, though the dark tendrils seemed to resist extraction. It was *wriggling*. Siobhan held it up to the light, displaying a small, squid-like form with thin, barbed tentacles. She tried to crush it between the ground and her blade, but despite the pressure she applied, it wouldn't die. To the contrary, its tendrils seemed to reach greedily for the exposed flesh of her hand.

She felt her skin ripple as her whole body shuddered with a wash of visceral disgust. "The dust, it's actually spores, or eggs, or tiny little bugs," she deduced aloud. "If it touches you, it latches on and affects your mind, and maybe it'll slowly turn you into stone, too."

Everyone else quickly began to check themselves for similar black spots, some discovering them and prying them out. One of the men discovered a black spot on the back of his companion's neck, and in his haste to remove it, cut the other man quite badly.

Siobhan turned to run again, doing her best to examine herself visually while also avoiding any dimmed motes of magical dust—tiny parasites. She wished she had a strong beam of light, as that would make seeing their inconspicuous forms floating in the air much easier. When she passed a couple of guards stationed at the outer windows to watch for danger from other directions, she screamed for them to follow.

They were alarmed enough at the phenomenon with no apparent source that they followed without question.

One of the Nightmare Pack men had a physical shield, wood reinforced by bands of metal. He held it up over himself and a couple of others that huddled together under it like an umbrella. It did nothing for the glowing dust motes, but Siobhan noticed it push away some that had dimmed, though they were so light they just hung in the air and swirled around in the wake of their passing, wafting after them as if reaching for their skin.

As her group skidded and stumbled to a stop in front of the door that led to the stairwell, Siobhan clenched her jaw. The door was a quarter converted into dark stone already, and the corruption was spreading toward the ground. The door wasn't locked and the handle was still clean, but it wouldn't open. The door and wall were melded together into a single entity where they'd been converted to stone.

She stepped back sharply and gestured to her companions. "Break it down!"

They got to work immediately, clearing the space a few meters in front of the door while a couple of women with concussive blast charges in their wands attacked the bottom half of the door. It was sturdy, reinforced specifically to stand up to attacks, and the glowing ripple that ran over its surface under the blows revealed it was magically reinforced, too.

The rest of the group tried to huddle under any physical barriers they could manage, but while the glowing motes of dust passed through everything, their dimmed counterparts were not constrained only to traveling on the currents of the air. Though the man with the wood and metal shield continued to hold it up, the dust that fell atop it somehow rolled over the bands of metal that should have acted as a barrier, tumbling off the sides and then floating inward again.

As one crossed in front of Siobhan's face, she saw the almost invisibly thin tentacles that would grow if allowed to plant themselves in flesh. It was using them to grasp the air, sailing through the currents like a boat through the ocean.

She thought back to the meteor floating in the air above them. '*What the hell is this spell? It seems ridiculous—impossible. It's so excessive—that rock isn't an illusion, it's a physical mass. Where did the energy for that come from? And so complex, creating the semblance of life to disseminate its effect. Are we fighting against a Grandmaster, or even an Archmage? But even so, why not just some widespread hex or curse? All this extra effort seems…prohibitive.*'

People were scrambling like they had ants under their clothing, letting out a little burst of panicked activity every time they found a parasite latching on, often slicing into themselves as they fumbled in their attempts to cut them out.

Another group of escaping guards joined them at the door, and soon enough they had it blown open. They all scrambled down the stairs with so much stumbling, shoving panic that Siobhan felt like they were on the edge of turning against each other.

Once on the ground floor, they sprinted toward the back exit, those with injured companions either dragging them or outright carrying them if they had the strength. The glowing motes were already down here, having passed right through the floor above.

Oliver's group, much larger and coming from the other direction, had arrived before Siobhan's, and were already trying to break down the door. But several of his people were yelling as they attacked it, and those on the edge were staring with numb defeat. Many others were displaying strange tics or vacant stares that indicated they'd been infected. Perhaps some of them didn't even know what to watch out for.

Siobhan knew, without even needing to push through the crowd of panicked and injured, that they were too late. She looked around, noting how much of the structure was pocked black rock, and how thick the glowing motes in the air had grown.

They were trapped within Knave Knoll, and even the walls had turned against them.

4 5

———

EXPLOSIVES SOLVE EVERYTHING

Siobhan
Month 3, Day 13, Saturday 1:55 a.m.

"We need to find the most wide-open area, farthest from the ceiling or any walls," Siobhan called out, pitching her voice to be heard over the increasingly loud panicking crowd. "If you have any black dots, use the edge of a knife to pry them out before they poison you."

Oliver and some of the others who hadn't lost their senses to panic or the effects of the parasites moved to guide the group toward the center of the ground floor, a common area with cells surrounding them on all sides.

Some of the scattered prisoners that remained were panicking, pleading for help or to be set free, but at least half of them were drooling, twitching messes collapsed on the floor of their cells.

Oliver moved to her side, murmuring just loud enough to be heard. "It affects everyone indiscriminately. That might actually be a good thing. The Architects of Khronos seemed pretty determined to take the prisoners *alive*."

Siobhan ran her tongue over the back of her teeth. If that was true, the spell would have to end at some point so they could get into the building. Likely, by that point, everyone within would have collapsed into gibbering messes. "So we just need to wait it out?" she murmured, feeling skeptical. *'How long can that decrepit thaumaturge keep this up?'*

But she knew it was a mistake to underestimate the man. If they hadn't stagnated, all old thaumaturges were powerful, having had the time to grow their Will with thousands of hours of practice. They really might be facing off against someone with Archmage-level power.

A nearby woman fumbled out a small cylindrical artifact, and, with a flick of the switch on its side, created a candle-sized flame. She waved it through the air, catching a couple flecks of dimmed dust. They let off sharp popping noises and disintegrated. The flame did nothing to the still-glowing motes, but after Siobhan pried a growing parasite out of the skin of her wrist before it could dig too deep, she held it out to the fire. It sizzled and, after a few moments, popped like its smaller brethren.

Others followed Siobhan's example, one man laughing humorlessly. "I never thought I'd be grateful for your disgusting etherwood-smoking habit, Sarah," he said, "but now I wish I had a flame of my own."

"The benches!" another man pointed out, already moving to try and break one apart. The seat was made of wood. "We can light a fire!" With a roar, one woman snapped one of the benches in half with a single, dramatic punch. After this example, several more joined in trying to create shattered pieces of firewood, and others even removed their clothes to act as tinder.

Anyone with the ability to create even a small flame suddenly became incredibly popular, and sporadic popping of the little squid-like parasites grew to a comforting staccato.

One of the Nightmare Pack men fumbled in his pockets, triumphantly producing a small stone, which he held aloft. "I use it to heat my soup at lunch. It's not fire, but it gets quite hot."

Using the heat stone, they were able to burn out several infected areas difficult or unsafe to reach with a knife's blade. While cackling evilly even as his own fingers sizzled and smoked under the heat of the stone, the man said, "Make them uncomfortable enough, and they'll detach on their own. It's just like sizzling the ass off a tick!"

That first man who had started to show side effects while they ran down the hallway was curled up on the ground. He had stopped tapping his tongue but was still silent and a little vague. She could only hope the effects weren't permanent.

"We need a shield of fire," Oliver called. "Can anyone produce something like that?"

They all looked around at each other. Enforcer Huntley pointed to an unconscious man who had been injured much earlier in the fighting, and who now had a large lump under one side of his shirt. "He's a fire witch, but he only has a drake familiar, and the creature's on the brink of death."

Healer Nidson pushed through the crowd, looking harried and mussed, his clothes smeared with blood and ash, and a bruise growing quickly around the flesh of one eye. He took a few moments to examine the unconscious man and his familiar. "I might be able to wake them up," Nidson said, shaking his head, "but there's no chance of them managing a spell in their condition."

"Get working on it anyway," Oliver ordered. "We need everyone in the best possible condition for our escape."

Siobhan noticed a black spot growing just under her collarbone. It was almost out of her line of sight, and she'd missed its initial attachment, giving it time to grow. Moving as quickly as she could under the sudden renewal of horrified adrenaline, she covered her free hand with a fold of her skirt, then pinched the exposed nugget of bug between a finger and her knife, slowly and firmly pulling it out. Its tentacles resisted, and she applied slow force, shuddering at the thought of one of them breaking off inside her and festering under her skin.

The dim motes were sprinkling down on them in ever-increasing numbers.

She tossed the bug-squid into the nearest fire, which had grown smoky with the addition of more lacquered wood and what looked to be a piece of mattress from one of the prisoners' cells. The raw hole left behind in her skin wasn't bleeding, and it didn't even particularly hurt. A horrifying idea had her examining it for signs of eggs laid within, but there didn't seem to be any.

She tried Grubb's barrier spell again, now that so many more glowing motes had dimmed into their parasite forms. Again, it did nothing, which left her surprised and frustrated.

'What are these? This spell should work against physical matter. I'm pretty sure it doesn't discriminate between living or non-living, so that shouldn't be the problem. One of its most common uses is as an umbrella against rain. But it doesn't block air. Perhaps the parasites are too small and pollen-like to be blocked. Or perhaps they have some other property that allows them to bypass the spell, like partial incorporeality. Nothing but fire seems to work against them, and that's strange.'

'But...they can ride the wind. They're tangible enough for air to affect them.' She quickly ripped into her satchel for another piece of seaweed paper containing only a single ink Circle, this one much smaller than the one she'd used to give Enforcer Gerard partial invisibility.

With strokes of wax crayon, she improvised a spell that was a combination of the air-compression sphere, the air-based slicing spell, and Grubb's barrier. She didn't have time to make it detailed and perfect, but it had to be good enough that the magic, which was likely to be wild, remained controllable and containable. Her tired Will had to handle it.

She palmed her Conduit and beast core and applied her Will. A dome of air, tightly controlled but almost invisible, grew from the Circle. She held the page up to a few motes of the falling dust, watching as they were caught in the barrier and flushed to one side. More layers of the barrier continued to pulse out from the center, ready to catch any parasites that had dimmed after floating through the edges.

A smile of triumph stretched across her face. It didn't block the parasites exactly, but it allowed her to guide their trajectory. With the right output parameters—which she didn't know—or a large enough spell array, which was possible, she could protect their entire group.

"Are there any other sorcerers?" she asked, shuffling along in her crouching position as she hurried to draw a Circle large enough to contain everyone around the remnants of the benches. "Anyone who can cast a gust spell, or a fire spell? We can burn them or blow them away. I just need you to buy me enough time to set up a barrier spell that will work against them."

One man raised his hand tentatively, and she handed him the spell array page with the gust spell. Her improvised barrier was too dangerous to trust to someone unsure of his own skill. The man had his own small Conduit, but had to use a piece of burning wood held over the seaweed paper page as a power source. The gust of wind he produced was rather weak, but it was enough to catch the parasitic bugs and waft them away as he swept the paper back and forth in slow, wide swaths.

Healer Nidson probably could have been quite helpful, but he was needed to keep some of those with the worst injuries alive. There were a couple of other people with very limited spellcasting experience, and they focused themselves on fire spells, one of the earliest magical applications most thaumaturges learned.

As Siobhan worked, the others kept prying out more of the little bugs from themselves and others, huddling as close together as possible. If the parasites were removed quickly, it seemed to help mitigate their lingering effects. Someone else discovered the parasites could even be caught in wetted cloth waved gently through the air, though they would still try to crawl toward the hand holding the cloth, and the whole thing would have to be discarded into the flames after a few passes.

The Morrows in the cells around them did not have such luxury, and were completely incoherent by this point. Siobhan had no love for them, but this kind of torture, to lose one's mind, seemed too cruel a fate for anyone to be forced to endure. Still, no one had yet died under the effects of the squid-like parasites, and no one had turned to stone either, but Siobhan could see black tentacles twitching visibly beneath the skin of the afflicted prisoners.

Even with their precautions, many enforcers began to show signs of confusion and disorientation, taking longer to speak, looking or pointing in the wrong direction, and jostling into each other as if drunk.

Soon, Siobhan was finished. They all huddled in together, and she cast the air-based barrier spell in much larger form. The spell array came to life with a glow to match the yellow-white light of the motes and sweat beaded on her forehead as she struggled to contain and guide the energy surging within the spell array around their feet. She controlled the air in a dome shape above and around them, hardening it in pulsing waves of movement that caught dimmed parasites and funneled them toward the fire contained within a secondary Circle on the far side. The pops and cracks reminded her of festive fireworks on a cold night.

With the leeway of her shield, Oliver and the others grew busy planning their escape, but she was too focused on keeping the spell up, stable, and working efficiently against the parasites to listen in.

If they didn't make it into the fire and die, the parasites she pushed away would come back for them, skittering on their tiny tentacles with a preternatural hunger for living flesh, but it took them much longer, and they still had to get past the base of her barrier.

Eventually, all the walls and furniture outside of her barrier were fully converted into the black, glittering stone, and dust and glowing motes filled the air so thickly it was hard to see the opposite wall. Inside the barrier, they were all illuminated with the brightness of a sunny day, which in other circumstances would have been pleasant, but here was terrifying.

She knew it could only have been a few more minutes, fifteen at most, when the ancient thaumaturge outside finally dropped the spell, but it seemed like much longer.

The motes of light melted away first, and then the air cleared of dust. Better even than that was how the spell-created parasites within people's flesh disappeared, leaving raw, pink holes in the skin. Her group had fallen silent to mimic the insensate prisoners, the last of the preparations to escape when the enemy came for them being planned in whispers. Teams had been established, those with injuries were patched up, and the remaining supplies had been redistributed to give everyone a fair chance.

Everything she and Oliver had prepared, and it hadn't been nearly enough against a few powerful thaumaturges.

But what followed surprised Siobhan. With the same colorful, aurora-like glow that had heralded the appearance of the floating meteor above, the walls around them were unmade, layer by layer. The building, the furniture, and even the floor.

Those few people who had been stuck on the floor above fell through as it melted away, and the building's wards let off strange explosions that were quickly absorbed by that same light as they were destabilized and their energy released.

Siobhan released her barrier spell, worried that some part of the floor would disintegrate and take a piece of her spell array with it, which would be disastrous.

"We don't need to wait," Oliver said, elation cutting through the group's awed silence as they watched the magical unmaking. "We can leave right now. Through the walls, even, no need to wait for a door." Siobhan's thoughts felt muted under her fatigue, but she allowed herself to be carried along with the others easily enough.

They did indeed break right through the melting wall, exiting from the end of Knave Knoll farthest from the front and possible observation. Those who couldn't move on their own were carried by others, and Siobhan caught a glimpse of the cursemaster, thrown over someone's shoulder, still alive but mindlessly drooling everywhere. Her lips twitched with amusement.

Outside, Siobhan couldn't help but turn to watch the end of Knave Knoll. The meteor above had disappeared in the aurora, too. Soon, all that would mark the spot would be a shallow, rough pit in the land. *'How is this possible?'* she wondered. *'I wouldn't believe it if someone told me they'd encountered such fantastical spell effects. Not because it should be impossible, but because it's so…wasteful. Stuff like this is the purview of tall tales and Aberrants, but that old man was definitely human. Right?'* He had not been a slavering monster, and though decrepit, he had seemed coherent. Above all, he'd been using a spell array. Aberrants couldn't use spell arrays. They cast through their bodies, and only had access to their single anomalous effect.

"Arise, and come to me!" cried a brittle voice. Siobhan had never heard a less compelling offer.

Oliver and Siobhan shared a look as the Morrows left behind in the disappearing building struggled to comply against their bindings, grunting and moaning futilely.

A few of their own people even seemed enticed by the order, but they were held back by their companions.

"Kneel at my feet, my servants, and sleep. When you awaken, all will be well," the thaumaturge continued.

Siobhan's skin prickled, and she turned her head slowly to the side, toward the canal. Maybe it was just a trick of reflected sound, but the old man's voice seemed entirely too close. Like something out of a nightmare, the head of the elemental turtle passed the disintegrating edge of Knave Knoll. The riders were atop it once more, floating through the canal alongside Knave Knoll instead of waiting by the front door.

And so, suddenly, the enemy had a clear view of their escaping group.

There was a single moment of silence as both sides were taken aback, and then, by universal consensus, Siobhan and the others began to run.

She wasn't sure what their enemies' plan had been, as the Morrow prisoners were shuffling toward them. Did they plan to drown the Verdant Stag and Nightmare Pack enforcers, and somehow use the water witch's abilities to tow the Morrows along the canal to safety? There was not enough space atop the elemental turtle's back to carry anyone else. Perhaps they planned to capture them all. Hostages might be of use, after all.

The old, liver-spotted thaumaturge stood atop the elemental's broad back, his face twisting in a rictus of rage.

"Scatter!" Oliver screamed, tossing out a vial that exploded into burning, noxious clouds. With the air witch controlling the earlier battle, their people hadn't had a chance to use many of the battle philtres they had prepared, and had enough left over to be useful now.

Siobhan threw her own philtre of smoke with one hand, shooting one of her few remaining stunning spells with the wand in her other, even as a young man with a hastily splinted broken leg used the last concussive blast spell in his own artifact on the cobblestone edge of the canal, smashing the Architects of Khronos with debris.

Siobhan fired her last two stunning spells blindly over her shoulder as she turned to run, hoping to add to the confusion more than anything.

The young man with the broken leg struggled to hobble away, and she quickly outpaced him. She hesitated, wondering if she should try to help, but a Nightmare Pack enforcer picked him up like a sack of flour and ran away, shouting, "We'll meet the dawn free and whole, you cowards. And don't think I'll forget your faces!"

Perhaps because of this, or just that there happened to be a break in the smoke between Siobhan and the decrepit thaumaturge at that moment, allowing him to pinpoint her location, the liver-spotted man's expression hardened with sadistic determination. He crouched beside his chest of supplies and began to prepare a spell.

Siobhan raced toward the cross street a few dozen meters away that would put the corner of a building between the two of them, cutting off his line of sight and improving her chances at freedom. As she turned the corner, she paused to make sure no one was left behind.

A few stragglers were hurrying in her wake, led by a woman wielding the lid of a barrel as a makeshift shield to protect some of the more heavily injured. Siobhan tossed a revivifying potion toward a man who was pale to the point of greenness, then turned to continue on, mentally running through the most efficient route back to the Verdant Stag.

She took one long step, and then was wrenched off her feet by the strap of the satchel around her chest.

Her feet slipped upward as her torso was pulled backward, and she slammed into the ground, wheezing out most of the air in her lungs and cracking her tailbone against the cobblestones.

She wasted no time on being stunned, struggling against her attacker before she could fully comprehend what was happening. As she was dragged back along the ground toward the corner of the building she'd just passed, frantically scrabbling, her fingers caught on a length of rope, which twisted and contracted like a snake. It had her satchel and was pulling with some of its bunched-up coils while the head stretched out to get a better grip on the rest of her.

"You cannot escape," the hoarse voice of the old thaumaturge called, sing-songy and unconcerned by the commotion around him. He wasn't particularly loud, but she could still hear his voice clearly.

Siobhan scrambled to get her feet under her. She turned, wrenching away from the grip of the prehensile rope with all her weight, but it had already coiled itself well around her bag. *I have to let it go.*

In the moment of hesitation that followed, a masked figure stepped out from an alley diagonally across from Siobhan and shot an indistinct spell at the rope. It missed, and when the figure steadied their arm and tried to shoot again, a crack of water slapped through the smoky air and knocked them off their feet hard enough that they bounced off the brick wall behind them.

Siobhan blinked, only then realizing she had seen the mask before. It was the same one Tanya Canelo had worn to the secret thaumaturge meetings.

Spurred back into motion by Tanya's failure, Siobhan tore the strap off over her head, careful only to avoid ripping out any of her hair, then yanked her wrist away from the searching head of the rope before it could tighten around her. Without the opposing force, she stumbled backward, almost falling over again.

Under the force that had been enough to yank her off her feet, her satchel flew toward the decrepit, vindictive thaumaturge. Siobhan stepped back to the corner, her eyes seeking out the enemy.

Behind Siobhan, a couple of the enforcers had doubled back, perhaps on Oliver's orders when he realized she wasn't with them. But there was nothing they could do to help her against enemies like this.

The corpse-like man's expression of triumph soured as his bounty arrived at his feet inside coils of rope. As if drawn to her like a magnet, he noticed Siobhan peeking around the corner immediately. His eyes narrowed and his lips stretched wide in a smile. He reached a hand toward her.

She lifted her own hand to the side of her abdomen, finding the spot on the holster she wore where she had housed the button of the disintegration mine. She pressed three times in quick succession, then waited, ready to throw herself out of the path of an attack. One second passed, then two…and then the disintegration mine hidden in the bottom of her satchel activated.

The reaction was much more spectacular than she had ever anticipated. Perhaps the mine was faulty. Or perhaps it was just a result of the sudden mix of volatile potions, magical components, and space-bending spells as the disintegration effect worked its way outward. Light and color bloomed in strange, flower-like shapes, one layered atop the other in an organic expression of magic as the very air screamed and popped and twisted.

Siobhan's eyes were still in the process of widening with surprise when the backlash from the magic-laden explosion hit her, catching her cloak and hair in a wind so strong her eyes were forced to close, throwing her backward until she hit the ground again a couple of meters back.

She curled up, flinching with an instinctive fear of being hit with debris, trying to clear the dark spot in the middle of her vision where she had been staring at the thaumaturge. After a moment, she crawled back to her feet, ears ringing, and carefully glanced around the corner, looking for the thaumaturge out of the corner of her eye rather than straight on. Her peripheral vision found nothing but a crater at the edge of the canal where the elemental had been carrying them along, but the sight made the hair on the back of her neck rise with instinctive fear. The air still swirled with colored mists and made strange sounds, and the water moved strangely at the effect's edge, as if afraid to touch its borders, preferring to flow around.

Her satchel and all its contents were gone.

More importantly, however, the thaumaturge was definitely dead. And not just him. A ring of mutilated body parts surrounded the crater's edge, just beyond the radius of the explosion, apparently all that remained of their attackers.

4 6

———

THE DEVIL IN THE DETAILS

Siobhan
   Month 3, Day 13, Saturday 2:10 a.m.

THE ENFORCERS who had come back for her looked from the lingering effects of the magical explosion, to her, and back again silently. There was a long pause.

Then one of them cleared his throat and stepped forward. "Excuse me, my lady. It seems you have no need of our help, but we would be pleased to escort you to a calmer location."

Siobhan nodded wordlessly, but as they moved to walk away, she remembered Tanya's strange and unexpected appearance. "Grab her, too," Siobhan ordered, motioning to the alley where Tanya had been thrown as she attempted to save Siobhan.

She moved to adjust her fake glasses, but discovered that she must have lost them during the night. Her hair was coming out of its bun, and her prosthetic nose felt like it might be a little lopsided.

While no one was looking, she quickly took it off, stuffing it in a pocket and rubbing at any remnants of glue on her skin. It was dark enough that no one would probably notice, but it was more conspicuous to be obviously wearing a disguise than for the nose of someone you barely knew to look slightly smaller than you remembered.

She carefully tightened her bun, making sure that no loose strands of hair escaped. Just in case.

Tanya had a dislocated shoulder and likely a few broken ribs, but she could walk, and so their smaller group shuffled through the streets. They caught up with the main group after a few minutes, and even though she couldn't see Oliver's face through his mask, she watched as some of the worry in his shoulders dropped away when he caught sight of her.

They shared a silent nod, and then his attention turned to Tanya. "I was… surprised by your actions this evening. Is this your way of declaring your allegiances?"

Tanya frowned in confusion, peeking for just a moment at Siobhan, then looking back at Oliver.

He waved her forward to come stand beside him.

She complied, but not without another look over her shoulder at Siobhan, uncertainty and fear mixing behind her eyes.

Siobhan wasn't the best with people, but even she, in her exhausted state, could recognize the conclusion Tanya was coming to. The blue eyes and the grey streak in her bun, along with the lack of feathers, didn't seem to be enough for someone who had interacted with her directly before. Perhaps Siobhan should have left her prosthetic nose on, after all. But, small mercies, at least Tanya had previously shown a marked lack of aggression toward the Raven Queen.

"I was sent to warn you of the attack," Tanya murmured, just loudly enough that Siobhan could hear. "I arrived too late, but I did my best to help."

Siobhan could imagine Oliver's eyebrows rising underneath his mask. Tanya didn't seem to be lying, but if that was the case, how had Kiernan known the location of Knave Knoll to send Tanya to them? And who had been behind the attack, if not the Architects of Khronos?

She tried to keep her own expression contained as the two continued to talk, in lower tones that she couldn't make out. Silvia Nakai really shouldn't have much of an opinion about these things. At that thought, she looked around for Healer Nidson and moved to walk beside him. "I'm sorry I wasn't able to help more. I got caught up in everything happening, and then… Well, you know."

Nidson gave her a long look. "Healing is not the only method of preserving lives. I would say you did quite a lot. Though I was rather miffed to suddenly be without an assistant. If you still have some life in you, I am sure there will be plenty more to do before the night is over."

Siobhan's heart clenched tightly at the reminder that the Verdant Stag had been under attack as well, and people there, like Katerin and Theo and even the patronizing shop attendant Alice, might be injured or dead.

When they finally arrived at the Verdant Stag, the signs of the battle were conspicuous, but the active violence seemed to have passed. The fighting had been fierce, and she even noticed a couple of bloodstains frozen on the street.

The Verdant Stag itself was still standing, but barely. A section near the kitchen and bar was completely blown away, leaving a gaping wound in the side of the building. Part of the floor had collapsed into the cellar, and a charred wall and support beams showed where a fire had been put out in time to save the whole building from conflagration.

People swarmed over and around the building like ants, and the performance stage, which was in the still-intact part of the building, had been set up as an emergency healer's station, with the injured lying on rows of cots. Healer Nidson made a beeline in that direction, and she followed.

Those who had been badly affected by the magical parasites took some time to recover, but there seemed to be no long term side effects, and the holes the parasites left in the skin were mitigated with some potions and salves. The cursemaster regained coherence after a few hours of care, and went into a shrill screaming fit, declaring that he held them all at fault for the ordeal he had experienced. He quieted quickly when Katerin marched over and dragged him off by the arm, grim-faced.

Most of the night was a blur, and it wasn't until the sun began to rise that Siobhan had a moment to sit, which immediately led to her finding an intact room off to the side and collapsing backward against the wall like a puppet with cut strings. She blinked sleepily, watching the busy people outside through the open doorway.

Oliver had been supervising a team that seemed to be trying to excavate the cellar. She'd known the Verdant Stag was probably some rich person's mansion before it went into disrepair and Oliver bought it, and the wine cellar was proof of that, because the water table was too high in Gilbratha for such a building feature to be common.

Katerin was milling about, but Theo was nowhere to be seen. Siobhan assumed that he was safe, because, while weary, frustrated, and covered in streaks of dirt and blood, Katerin did not appear devastated.

Siobhan was positioned so that the light of the slow sunrise washed over her through the doorway as the sun began to peek over the white cliffs, painting her in shades that felt slightly less exhausted. One of Healer Nidson's other commandeered assistants bustled over and handed her a mug with the distinct smell of a nourishing draught. She downed the entire pint in a single breath.

The workers had cleared the stairway into the cellar, and Oliver hurried down into the pit. 'Perhaps he had supplies down there,' she thought. 'Though the storehouses must have held most of the goods, it would have been smart to keep the highest-priced items in a more secure location. The vaults in his and Katerin's office are clear for the world to see. The University must have wanted to retrieve those confessions and vows Oliver made all the Morrows give. It's probably where he kept the censer. If they got that, they might have taken a lot of other important things, too.' Perhaps her own blood-print vows with Katerin had even been housed down in the secret cellar vault. The thought sent a jolt of alarm through her, because despite the tamper-proofing on the spell, it wouldn't be safe in the hands of an expert with a delicate touch. If more than one enemy group had a piece of her, her problems grew even more complicated. And others might not be so lawful in how they used it.

She let her eyes fall almost closed as she waited for the nourishing draught to be absorbed, but she couldn't entirely relax, half out in the open like this. Before she returned to the University, she would need some bruise paste, and maybe a skin-knitter to get rid of the obvious signs of being in an altercation.

All of her supplies, all the components and artifacts that she'd kept in her bag, her seaweed paper spells—all of it—was gone. She only had the things she'd put in stashes around the city, and the supplies left at the University itself. She would need to rebuild her thaumaturge bag from scratch. *'How much coin will that take?'* she wondered, tears pricking at the back of her closed eyelids even though she didn't particularly *want* to start crying. She didn't even feel sad, really, just…overwhelmed.

Even though Siobhan's eyes were almost closed, Katerin's blood-red hair caught her attention as the other woman came down the stairs from above. Katerin's gaze swept the room, sliding over Siobhan and then catching and returning to her. She started making her way over, but was stopped several times by Verdant Stag members giving reports or asking for instructions.

What should have taken thirty seconds ended up taking several minutes, and before Katerin could make it to Siobhan, Oliver had completed his inspection of the cellar and whatever else was down there, and climbed back up. Pale dust had created a film over his dark hair, but his shoulders had lost their tightness, and she suspected that, under the mask, he was smiling.

He hurried toward Katerin, too, stopping her a few meters from the room Siobhan had collapsed in. He looked Siobhan over, perhaps not catching the fact that she was still awake because her eyes were so narrowly slitted. He spoke in a soft voice, leaning in to Katerin. "They got the decoy vault," he reported. "It's entirely gone, ripped up by the roots and carried away, but they didn't manage to find the folded space. None of the contracts, or—or the other thing. You cannot crack or steal a safe that you do not know is there. That particular investment has proven its worth ten times over."

Katerin hugged herself, her hands gripping her elbows with a kind of half-suppressed vulnerability that seemed out of place on the normally confident woman. "Good, that's good. They got the gold vault in my office, but not the one hidden behind the wall. I don't think that's what they were going for, anyway."

"No. They knew exactly what they wanted. Unfortunately for them, the *true* treasure remains safe," he said, venomous glee clear in his voice. "If only they knew how futile all their efforts have been."

They both turned to Siobhan then, and she opened her eyes fully as Oliver closed the door behind himself and Katerin and took off his mask, then sat down gently beside her.

"I'm fine," she reported before either of them could ask. "I'll need some rest, but I've got the weekend to recover. What of my blood print vow? Did they get that?"

"No, it is safe," Katerin answered. "I take the security of the vows I make seriously. After all, my blood is on them, too. They found naught but some gold and other valuables, along with some decoy documents that have little importance, or are entirely fabricated."

"You were prepared," Siobhan said.

"Not as well as we should have been, obviously," Oliver said, taking her hand and holding it between both of his own. "I do have some bad news to report." His expression had sobered completely. "I have to apologize, because at least part of tonight's fracas was my fault. That censer that the Architects of Khronos offered as tribute, I had it checked for tracking spells, and they found one in the packaging. Which was discarded, of course. But I didn't consider the fact that the piece itself might be inherently trackable. One of a matched pair, made from the same batch of metal. They must have traced it back to the Verdant Stag, and were probably hoping the Raven Queen was keeping it in the same place she kept the stolen book. They never intended to deal fairly with either of us. Tonight's attack on Knave Knoll served dual purposes, as they used it as a distraction to try to find the book. Of course, it wasn't there, but they did manage to retrieve their censer. I will still compensate you for seventy percent of its approximate value. And hazard pay, for your actions tonight."

"I need you to cover the cost of restocking my supplies, too," she urged, tensing up a little. "I had to blow up my bag and everything in it to kill that old sorcerer. It should be considered an operational expense."

"Okay."

She relaxed. That had been easier than she expected. "What does this mean, for all of us? I warn you, I am *done* accepting missions like this for you. Never again, Oliver."

"I understand. Things are going to become…contentious, I imagine. Even after all their attempts to stymie our delivery of the prisoners, I believe they will all have been arrested by now, though it is possible that some managed to avoid being poisoned by those glowing bugs and slipped away from the remains of Knave Knoll before the coppers were able to round them all up. Luckily, we got the simulacrums anchoring the curse seals out safely. I will still be stretched thin doing damage control over the next few days. It may not be possible, but it would be ideal if we could avoid local law enforcement deciding that the Stags were at fault for making the city seem so unsafe. Luckily, I have a few more connections than I did the last time we faced something like this, and very few civilians have been impacted. On the other hand, the kind of destruction that was caused tonight is very visibly...frightening."

Oliver rubbed his bloodshot eyes, pressing a little too hard. "Unless you wish to get more directly involved in our efforts to rebuild and maintain the right kind of influence, you should keep your head down for the moment. Don't give Kiernan or his people any reason to look twice at Sebastien Siverling. I will give you an update when I have a more complete understanding of our situation going forward, or if there are any emergencies that could affect you." He fell silent, sagging with discouragement for a moment, and then one side of his mouth quirked up. "Also, that textile sub-commission would be a really nice break right about now, if you could swing it." He gave her a pointed wink.

"Soon," she promised, though at that very moment she was too drained to be excited about the prospect. "Is it safe for you to be hanging around like this? As Lord Stag, I mean. The coppers might drop by at any time."

Katerin crossed her arms. "Hah! I'd like to see any of those fools actually manage to reach this building without our knowledge."

"We have already sent the coppers a few Stags to make a statement about what happened from our point of view. I imagine they're quite busy elsewhere, but when they do make their way here, anyone who lives or works nearby knows there's a small reward for advance notice of such things, and we have a couple of reliable informants placed around the area, too. If the coppers still managed to surprise us, I would just change clothes and slip out of the secret tunnel exit I had built last month." Oliver winked. "Oliver Dryden has made several public appearances around members of the Crowns and prominent businessmen at the same time that Lord Stag has been sighted elsewhere. They might suspect me of *something*, but not of being Lord Stag. The ruse probably won't hold forever, but it is hard to overcome the assumptions that such 'knowledge' creates."

"A body double?" Siobhan mused. "That's pretty clever."

When Siobhan felt well enough to move, she left, but not before borrowing a self-defense artifact from the Verdant Stag's dwindling stores, just in case. The battle wand she got was quite nice, containing a set of stunning, shielding, and concussive blast spells.

Instead of going to the Silk Door from there, she borrowed some ill-fitting clothes and went to another nearby inn, where she changed back into Sebastien's form and did some basic washing up to make herself look presentable. Then, hidden inside a cloak with a deep hood, she hired a carriage to take her to Dryden Manor, where she kept a better-fitting set of clothes. She had been coming and going from the Silk Door quite a lot lately, and wanted to avoid drawing attention to it, just in case someone from the University was watching everyone who came to or from the Verdant Stag.

As she arrived back at Dryden Manor, where the servants rushed around to get her fed, watered, and into bed under Sharon's command, Sebastien thought back over the events of that night, specifically the Architects' attack on the Stags' home base.

The vault in the cellar, or perhaps connected to the cellar through some hidden passage, had captured Sebastien's imagination. She'd always loved hidden compartments and secret rooms. The hidden dagger in her boot had even come in handy earlier that day, not to mention the effects of the concealed disintegration mine during the battle.

But something was niggling at the back of her mind. The Architects of Khronos had taken an entire vault—and apparently her censer—but didn't get what they were looking for. Which made sense, if they thought the censer would be with the stolen book. But the way Oliver had told Katerin, so confidently, so vindictively…

'*I'm confused,*' she realized. '*I notice that I am confused,*' she repeated, grasping onto the notion like Professor Lacer had been so adamant was necessary for any great thaumaturge. But despite realizing that, and mulling the matter over in her mind for a few minutes as she rubbed in bruise balm and skin-knitting salve and set up her dreamless sleep spell, she came to no further conclusions. '*I'll ask Oliver about it when I see him again,*' she resolved, letting her exhausted and much-abused brain slip into unconsciousness.

47

———

BLITZKRIEG

Damien
Month 3, Day 13, Saturday 7:00pm

Damien fidgeted impatiently, checking his pocket watch, and then looking out of Ana's carriage window for the dozenth time in the last fifteen minutes, searching for signs of Sebastien. He was worried, both because Sebastien was late for the final phase of Operation Defenestration and because there had been more fighting in the city the night before, and Damien suspected that Sebastien had never returned to the dorm after leaving early Friday evening. Sebastien might have been involved in it somehow, and it was possible that he had not returned because he was injured or even dead.

But no, that couldn't be. Sebastien was so terribly competent. He wouldn't die. Especially not without any warning, leaving Damien so oblivious to his fate. It wouldn't be like what happened with Newton. Damien ran his hand over the bracelets hidden under his sleeve surreptitiously. None of their pewter beads had grown cold with alarm. Surely, if something were wrong, Sebastien would have alerted him?

A hired carriage approached down the well-lit street, its single old horse and lack of livery or lacquered polish standing out in this neighborhood. Of course, Sebastien climbed out of it, carrying a heavy box. "I apologize for my tardiness. I was on a shopping excursion and lost track of time, and then security had to stop and check my carriage before they let me into the Lilies." There was something darkly amused about his tone.

"You are forgiven, I suppose," Ana said, smoothing out the pleats in her high-collared blouse. She'd been fidgeting from nervousness almost as much as Damien, but now seemed calm and collected, except for that small tell. "We will need to proceed quickly. I sent the runners with the messages to the coppers and my father already, so the timing is tight. If all goes well, both parties will arrive at approximately the same time, and it will be much too late to recover the situation."

"You're prepared to improvise if need be, though, right?" Sebastien asked. "We don't know exactly how Malcolm might respond, and things could change wildly depending on whether your father or the coppers arrive first. We have to strike a killing blow tonight—metaphorically—or we face possible retaliation."

Damien thought that if it were possible, and he weren't worried for Ana's safety, Sebastien might have avoided being present tonight at all. For someone so competent, who cared enough about proactively improving the world that he joined a secret organization to do so, Sebastien could be very averse to risk.

"I am extremely prepared," Ana said. "And if need be, improvisation has never been a weakness of mine."

They arrived at the front door shortly, and Ana took the lead, stepping forward to loudly tap the knocker while Sebastien and Damien stood silently a few feet behind her. This was her show. They were there only as backup.

As soon as the doorman opened the way, the three of them pushed past the confused, older servant. "Where is Uncle Malcolm?" Ana demanded, looking around imperiously.

"Err, Master Gervin is currently retired to his quarters, preparing for a visit to a friend this evening. May I take your coat, my lady? I will tell him you have arrived, though, if I may ask, what is the purpose of your visit? Did you and your friends wish to take dinner here? Or is there some emergency?"

Ana tugged off her gloves, but waved off the man's attempt to take her jacket. "Tell Malcolm that I am here and that I need to speak with him urgently. If he does not arrive within sixty seconds, I will start expressing my displeasure on the surroundings."

The servant paled, obviously remembering the last time Ana had visited. "Won't you go into the drawing room? I will fetch Master Gervin immediately."

"I will wait here while you fetch *Mister* Gervin. Tarry further and face my wrath." Ana loosened her fingers one by one, allowing her gloves to drop dramatically to the floor.

The man paled further, if that was possible, and walked off with indecorous urgency, on the very edge of breaking into a run. He passed another servant on the way, snapping at them as he did so to watch over Lady Anastasia and her companions.

Damien's heart was beating hard enough to flush his cheeks and leave his armpits and the palms of his hands damp.

While Ana's expression was confident to the point of arrogance, her eyes roving around the entranceway with judgmental disdain, the signs of anxiety were clear in the way she held her hands still to keep them from fidgeting with her clothing.

Only Sebastien seemed unfazed, his eyes dark and intent, obviously aware of every movement of the servant and the details of their surroundings, his back to the wall and ready for danger. But not even a hint of fear showed in his expression or body language. If Damien didn't know better, he would say Sebastien was *bored*. But that was impossible, right? Sebastien was such a worrywart that he demanded two dozen backup plans for anything that could possibly go wrong. He had more experience with dangerous situations than Damien, probably, but not so much that a situation like this was commonplace, surely? Maybe he just felt that with all their planning and his own prowess, the entire situation was within his grasp, under his control.

That...made sense. Suddenly, it felt a little surreal, to realize that Damien and two of his friends, barely into adulthood and with nothing but their own limited power and a bit of ingenuity, were going to take down a pair of unworthy Crown Family members. A ragtag trio of friends, acting in the shadows to control the politics of the most powerful country in the West... He shuddered, not with fear or disgust, but with an embarrassingly visceral pleasure. Trying to control his expression, he surreptitiously wiped off his sweaty hands before checking his pocket watch. "Time's up," Damien announced.

Ana turned to a vase standing on a pedestal against the wall. The delicate porcelain was as tall as her torso, painted with exquisite designs from the East, hundreds of years old, and probably worth at least a few hundred gold. She picked it up, and then, with a heave, hurled it across the room to shatter against the wall.

The servant who had been fluttering around nervously at the behest of the doorman, asking if they wanted tea or some such nonsense, gasped aloud, the sound long and drawn out, clear in the ensuing silence.

"Cease your tantrums immediately!" Malcolm Gervin roared from the hallway at the top of the double staircase, his cane tapping against the floor in rhythm with his footsteps as he strode angrily toward them.

Ana turned to watch the man come down the stairs, her chin raised with a defiant contempt that reminded Damien of Sebastien. "What right do you have to chastise me, Uncle, when your own hands are so terribly filthy?" she asked coldly, her voice carrying over the marble floors, loud enough to reach, loud enough for the servants to hear and do what servants did best—gossip.

Sebastien hadn't moved, but was watching Malcolm Gervin with hawk-like focus, ready to react to a foolish move on the man's part. One hand rested in his jacket pocket, casually threatening.

"What nonsense are you yapping about, girl?" Malcolm asked, his eyes roving over the three of them, and then settling angrily on the shards of porcelain scattered across the floor near the stairs.

"Collusion with the Raven Queen," Ana announced, wasting no time at getting to the point. "*Treason.*"

Several quickly muted gasps came from the surrounding rooms.

The accusation drew Malcolm's attention away from the shattered vase and back to Ana. "Are you daft? I would never do something so foolish."

"I should be asking you that. Are you daft?" Ana sighed deeply, crossing her arms over her chest and turning her back to Malcolm. She took a few steps toward Sebastien, whose eyes never left the man, ready to protect Ana from any sudden movement. "I noticed that you were acting...strangely, Uncle. There were some rumors that you had gotten yourself in trouble with one of the businesses. I thought maybe gambling, unlikely though it might seem. So I had you followed. I hired a private investigator." She spun on her heel, turning back to Malcolm and walking again in his direction.

He was no fool, and had realized something was wrong. "What is this?" he asked, but his voice was quieter—less bluster and more suspicion.

"Imagine my surprise when my private investigator found you meeting with the Raven Queen herself, attempting to make a trade with her. Did you know, Uncle, that the Raven Queen's father agreed to a marriage between her and one of the sons of the *Gervin branch line?*"

Malcolm drew himself up imperiously. "You know not of what you speak, girl. That agreement was made merely in an attempt to capture her. If we had been successful in luring her, we would have obviously turned her in to the authorities at once."

Ana crossed her arms, —dipping her head in acknowledgment. "Perhaps. But then, it seems strange that you went to meet with her in person to make a very valuable trade, *without* alerting the coppers or any other authorities. You were seen, Uncle. You were recognized."

Malcolm swallowed, the grip around his cane tightening. "It is a misunderstanding. We were contacted and told to come alone, but we—we hired backup and attempted to catch her. We were not colluding with her, simply taking advantage of an opportunity to bring honor to our family and safety to the city. She offered the stolen book in exchange for her father's ring. If we could successfully pull off the capture, we would get both. Even if we failed, if the trade went well, we would have the book. Through no fault of our own, we were unsuccessful, but it was not collusion, nor 'treason.'" He tried to scoff, but he was too tense to seem believable.

Ana reached into the wide inner pocket of her long jacket, pulling out a folder. "That is an interesting rendition of events. Interesting, as well, that my private investigator was able to find information suggesting that the attackers were not, in fact, affiliated with you at all, but a third party who wished to capture the Raven Queen for themselves when they got word of your meeting due to your frankly *incompetent* security and lackluster secrecy measures."

Damien glanced to Sebastien, whose expression didn't waver at this. The private investigator had found no such thing, but Sebastien had assured them that such testimony could be provided from hearsay, second and third-hand statements from those who supposedly knew the attackers. Attackers who, Damien was almost entirely sure, were other members of their secret order.

Malcolm remained silent, perhaps wisely.

Ana opened the folder, revealing the photographs. Damien didn't look, taking his cue from Sebastien and remaining alert for danger. He knew what they depicted. The photographs were taken from above, a little grainy, but from close enough to make out what was happening. A shot of Malcolm and Randolph being searched by a masked figure, their faces clear. A shot of them meeting in the middle of that condemned building, clearly reaching out to trade something with an imposing creature of dark clouds and black feathers that could only be the Raven Queen, and finally, the meeting breaking up under spell-fire, with the two brothers escaping most pitifully.

Malcolm's pallor began to redden with anger.

"What do you think, Uncle? Quite incriminating, is it not? Especially because you didn't come forward when the coppers were investigating this incident. And because, I believe, you have the ring that the Raven Queen so desires up in your vault. I did some more digging after that, to figure out why you would be so desperate as to make such a risky trade." She flipped the pages, displaying a short list of business names next to monetary figures. "This is what you and Randolph have been embezzling from the Family coffers, funds that rightfully belong to my Lord Father. And I have several reports of other crimes, including eyewitness accounts. So I must ask, *Uncle*. Did the Raven Queen bribe you into that meeting, or blackmail you?"

Malcolm's face grew even redder, a vein throbbing visibly at his temple. "What do you think you are doing, you child? Why did you and your little friends come here tonight? Do you think you will blackmail me with this? Do you think that I would ever let myself be crushed under your heel?"

Ana closed the folder and took a step back, ignoring the way Malcolm's hand twitched toward it as it was drawn away. "No, Malcolm," she said with false kindness. "I have no intention of blackmailing you. It is much too late for that."

And for the first time, Malcolm realized the gravity of what he was dealing with. How he had taken so long to guess it, Damien did not know. "What have you done, Anastasia?" Malcolm whispered.

"I have sent a copy of all the information my private investigator collected to the coppers...and to Father. They will be here shortly, and I'm sure they will find all the further evidence they need within your vault. I've heard that you made some security upgrades recently? But don't worry, I doubt that will stymie the coppers for long. Not with this case being linked to the Raven Queen. If you're lucky, and pay a lot of people off, you might be able to keep the scandal out of the papers. But probably not."

A heavy second of silence passed, and then another, and another.

Ana was the one to break it, wearing her gentle, ladylike, fake smile. "Even if you could weather the scandal, Father does so hate incompetence. Better to have committed a crime and gotten away with it, than to have been *caught*."

Malcolm raised his hand to hit Ana, and both Damien and Sebastien surged forward, wands out and pointed threateningly at the man.

Malcolm's hand stopped in mid-air, glaring at all three of them with such bile that they might have been burned by it if he were a free-caster. "Get out," he said bitingly. Turning to one of the doors, through which the doorman had disappeared, he yelled, "Remove these traitorous cretins from my house at once! Feel free to use force, if necessary." With that, he backed up a few steps, his cane held up as if to ward them off, then turned and hurried back up the stairs toward his office.

A few of the servants approached to try and get Damien and his companions to leave.

"I would advise you all to think twice," Ana said, eyeing each of the approaching servants. "By this time tomorrow night, Malcolm Gervin may no longer have a place in the fourth Crown Family. Of which, might I remind you, I am the heir. To make it exceedingly clear, your jobs are on the line."

A couple of the servants hesitated, which caused a cascading effect of further hesitation.

"The coppers and my father will be here within minutes," Ana said. "Please gather all household staff in the ballroom and prepare for questioning. If you are open and honest, it may improve your chances of retaining your position." She didn't give them the opportunity to consider further, pushing through and past them to follow Malcolm up the stairs. Every movement of her body and nuance of her expression indicated she had no doubt she would be obeyed.

That, more than anything, caused them to part for her, though Sebastien eyed them all grimly as they passed in Ana's wake, ready to strike.

Malcolm had locked the door to his office and no doubt activated the emergency wards, but the room wasn't designed to be protected from enemies already inside the house. He had made the oversight of believing the wards around the manor wall would protect against such things. Within, he was making quite a bit of frantic noise, tossing things about.

"Can you unlock it?" Ana asked.

"Step back," Sebastien ordered. "Quicker just to take the whole thing down." The first concussive blast cracked the door and ripped some of the reinforcements from the walls on either side.

It also blew Damien's hair back and peppered him with chunks of wood and plaster. He stepped away, smoothing his hair and shaking debris from his clothing as Sebastien loosed the second blast.

The door fell inward in a cloud of dust, hitting the floor with a heavy *thud*.

Sebastien walked into the room, stepping atop the fallen door with his wand out. "Stop."

Malcolm froze, one hand holding a folder of papers outstretched toward the fireplace, where other folders and a ledger were already burning.

Ana hurried past Sebastien toward the drink table against the wall, which held not only an assortment of alcohol, but water and fresh ice.

Malcolm unfroze, tossing the folder into the fire even as his other hand lifted his cane at them, which shot out a foggy, quickly-expanding spell.

48

THE FINAL FIASCO

Damien
Month 3, Day 13, Saturday 7:10pm

Ana screamed as the spell approached, jerking the decanter of water up in front of her head as if that would save her, but instead just splashing herself in the face.

Damien whipped his wand forward, but Sebastien was in front of him, between Damien and Malcolm. The stunning spell he almost released would have hit Sebastien in the back.

Sebastien stepped *forward* into the foggy spell, his own wand producing a shimmering shield about a meter in diameter, held at such an angle as to deflect the hostile spell just enough to send it blasting into the wall rather than himself or Damien behind him.

The force of the concussive blast pushed Sebastien's arm aside and drove him back a step. Malcolm had actually attacked to kill! For some reason, Damien had expected the man to use a more acceptable stunning spell, or maybe a binding spell. Ana was his *niece*.

Without the slightest change in expression, Sebastien's fingers twitched over his wand, switching its output, and then shot a bright red, crackling stunning spell.

Malcolm dodged the spell almost contemptuously, the dueling training that all respectable Crown Family members went through on full display in the way he held his cane—more suitable for a wand than such a large artifact

—and his nimble footwork. He returned another concussive blast. But Damien had confiscated his normal cane during their meeting with the fake Raven Queen, and Malcolm's temporary replacement was heavier and more unwieldy. His aim was imperfect, and the spell went wide.

Sebastien didn't even bother to dodge it, walking forward calmly. "Ana, the fire!" he snapped, still expressionless.

She let out a small, dismayed chirp, and Damien hurried forward to escort Ana across the room so she could douse the fire, putting himself between her and the two fighting men.

Sebastien put up another shield against a concussive blast, this time bracing himself against the magical blow head-on, his platinum hair fluttering back in the wind caused by the magical impact. His free hand slipped into his pocket and whipped out a familiar, slim disk, which he pointed toward Malcolm. Another stunning spell from the wand followed, pointed toward Malcolm's right foot. Half a second behind, the thirteen-pointed star went black, and then a bright blue spell shot out of it.

Malcolm dodged to his left to avoid the stunning spell, but his eyes widened as he saw he had moved into the path of the mysterious blue follow-up spell. But, alas, he twisted around with impressive alacrity, catching the spell on the metal side of his cane, which flared with its own magic and allowed him to deflect the blue light into the wall behind him, where it disappeared without a trace.

But Sebastien was already following that spell up with another from the disk. This one was purple, and the one that followed a bright, alarming green.

Damien hadn't even seen him adjust the output, though it might be possible that the different spells were stored in a particular, static order, and Sebastien had no choice of which came next. He'd heard of such "dueling-chains" before.

Malcolm exerted himself to the limit to dodge the consecutive spells, but the next one, a cheery pink, managed to clip his leg as he was still recovering from an impressive spin move. Malcolm's features contorted into a horrified grimace, but then his face slackened in surprise.

Sebastien had already fired a concussive blast spell from his wand, but whatever had been done to Malcolm's leg wasn't enough to stop him from meeting the blast with his own.

The air rumbled like distant thunder under the force of the colliding spells, and wind blasted out in every direction, so powerfully that Damien had to brace lest he be pushed backward into Ana.

Malcolm threw back his head and laughed. "Did you think I wouldn't notice, boy? That is nothing but a bauble, shooting pretty lights."

Sebastien grimaced but continued to attack, his hand snapping out to grab a decorative pillow off the back of an armchair and whip it toward Malcolm.

Then, moving so quickly Damien could barely keep up, Sebastien shot another stunning spell in the pillow's path, followed by almost simultaneous releases of a dark blue spell from the light crystal artifact and another stunning spell, with the stunning spell following so closely behind the dark blue spell that they almost overlapped. Then, lowering his wand back to his hip, he switched the output and shot a concussive blast to cap it all off.

Sebastien's footwork was anything but polished, and he kept his wand held close to his torso and stable rather than outstretched and flashy, but there was something about him that was simply inexorable, each movement bringing him closer and closer to Malcolm.

The first stunning spell caught up with the pillow, exploding it into a cloud of smoking, electrocuted feathers and fine dust. Malcolm sneered at the blue spell, noticing the red crackle hiding at its rear almost too late. He lunged to one side, his knee twisting under him as a low table got in the way of his movement. The stunning spell didn't hit him, but some of its expanding edges caught the arm that held his cane, sending it into twitching spasms and forcing him to switch the weapon into the other hand. "You're a clod-heeled fool—" he began to snarl, but was shut up by the arrival of the slightly slower concussive blast, thrusting the smoking feathers toward Malcolm in a wave.

Malcolm slammed his cane against the ground to give himself leverage, but his starting position was too awkward, and the blast took him in the side, throwing him through the air and into a chair near the wall, which tumbled over backward with him in it. He tumbled to his feet, disheveled and wild, his cane rising quite impressively with the momentum to point at Sebastien again. His mouth stretched in a feral grimace, his intent to kill clear and frightening.

But Sebastien was, somehow, only a couple of steps away already. He crouched out of the path of the cane and lunged forward. The light crystal artifact had returned to its place in his pocket, where its light peeked through.

Malcolm tried to drop the cane's tip, but ended up only hitting Sebastien's guarding forearm, shooting another concussive blast over Sebastien's head and into the floor behind him.

Sebastien's wrist twisted around, his fingers gripping the shaft of the cane and then continuing to twist, even as he head-butted Malcolm right in the abdomen.

The cane was ripped out of Malcolm's grip just as his breath was driven from his lungs. Malcolm stumbled back, the knee he had twisted earlier almost giving out on him. Still maintaining his sneer, his hand reached into his suit's inner pocket for a backup weapon.

But Sebastien swung the cane by its end, taking Malcolm across the jaw with the ornate handle hard enough to produce a sickening *crack* and snap the man's head to the side.

Malcolm's knees collapsed from under him.

Sebastien adjusted his grip on the end of the cane, and then struck Malcolm again, this time in the shoulder.

Malcolm screamed then, his jaw hanging strangely.

Sebastien stilled, finally, his wand pointed directly at Malcolm's face from only a few inches away. He was panting as if he'd just finished one of Professor Fekten's grueling classes.

Despite his injuries, Malcolm still glared up at him defiantly, his gaze moving from Sebastien's own to the tip of the wand trained on him.

"I only have concussive blast spells left," Sebastien said. "Try anything, and I'm sure I can press the trigger before you can get out of the way."

Malcolm remained still, his eyes moving instead toward Damien and Ana.

Damien let out a shaky breath, realizing his hand was trembling around his outstretched wand.

Behind him, Ana had managed to douse most of the flames and pull the half-charred, partially soaked documents from the fireplace. She had remained crouched on the floor, watching the fight just like Damien. "The coppers will be able to reconstruct the information, surely," she said, her voice cracking. Her hands were shaking, too, which was somehow a relief, since it meant Damien wasn't alone. He had thought this would be exciting, but the rush of terror, both for himself and for his friends, was anything but exhilarating.

Damien lowered his wand but kept it clenched tightly in his sweaty palm, feeling slightly sick from the rush of anxiety.

"Damien, help me tie him up and search him," Sebastien ordered, his eyes never leaving Malcolm. He stepped back a few feet, his wand steady.

Outside, the sound of multiple approaching carriages, some stopping at the front, while some horses clopped around the edge of the mansion toward the side and back entrances, signaled the arrival of the coppers. There was too much commotion for it to have been Lord Gervin alone.

Damien did as Sebastien had ordered, feeling a little safer with each artifact and piece of clothing he stripped off of Malcolm.

They left the man in his underclothes, tied up by his own torn up shirt. His jaw was broken, but Damien still wrapped a sleeve around his mouth to muzzle any attempts at speech.

"The journal?" Sebastien asked urgently.

Ana pulled it out of her pocket, unwrapped it from the wax paper protecting it, and, after a moment's hesitation, held one end over the small flames toward the back of the fireplace that had survived her dousing. The edges blackened and smoked, and when the pages caught, she quickly snatched it back and used the wax paper to pat out the fire. Then, she stood and walked over to Malcolm, holding the little journal.

She reached out to the older man as he glared up at her spitefully, running her fingers through his hair like a mother might to her child. Then, her fingers clenched into a fist and she yanked.

Malcolm let out a muffled grunt of pain, and she pulled back a dozen or so plucked hairs. Letting the journal, filled with achingly precise handwriting, fall open, she carefully placed a couple of the hairs between the pages. Then she shoved the journal into his face, rubbing its leather surface against his cheek, grinding against his skin and the saliva-soaked gag. She opened the book and rubbed some of the pages against his other cheek. Finally, she walked around behind him, forced his clenched fists open, and pressed his fingers into the surface. "This is overkill, in my opinion," she said conversationally. "This journal isn't going to the coppers, after all, and I doubt Father will be so thorough as to have a divination cast on a journal filled with what is obviously your handwriting and a ton of evidence that is independently corroborated elsewhere...but I promised I would follow all the safety measures."

The coppers were inside now, some of them shouting. Ana stood back up, slipping the journal into her pocket and moving to stare down into her uncle's face. "You will never belittle, undermine, or spew your cruelty to Natalia or me ever again. You will not make my mother feel somehow inadequate. You will not make my sister cry, or encourage others to do so. You will not scar Alec, physically or emotionally. You will not keep tearing at him until he becomes more and more like you. You will lose the respect and trust you have so meticulously cultivated in my father, and when this is over, I am sure even that idiot Randolph will not stand by your side."

Multiple sets of loud footsteps spread into the rooms below and started pounding up the stairs.

Ana leaned down to whisper to Malcolm. "Everything that is about to happen to you, all that you will lose, all the indignities and pain you will face, know that it was because of me. And know that there is nothing you can do. If I have any reason to believe this punishment was not sufficient for you to learn your lesson, I will take care of the matter more...permanently."

The meaning of that threat was obvious, like something an international villain or heinous gang lord would say, but somehow sounded so thrilling coming out of her mouth.

Ana stepped away, the confidence slipping from her shoulders even as huge tears welled up in her eyes and slipped down her cheeks. She reached for Damien and tucked her head into his shoulder, sobbing loudly just as the coppers pressed into the room, their own wands out and sweeping over the four of them.

Sebastien, who had tucked away his wand just in time, stepped back from Malcolm, raising his empty hands to the coppers. He looked to Ana, but she was too busy crying to talk.

"How could you take so long to arrive!?" Damien complained. "Is this the kind of response time the Crown Families can expect?"

The coppers shared several awkward, confused glances, and then a man Damien recognized as Investigator Kuchen, who had been working with Titus on the Raven Queen's case, stepped forward. "Apologies, my lord. Can you tell us what's happened here?"

"We've apprehended the criminal ourselves," Damien said, patting Ana on the back as she continued to cry. "Heiress Gervin didn't want to believe that her uncle could do something so heinous and insisted on confronting him to hear the truth from his own mouth. But when he learned he'd been discovered, he set about trying to destroy the evidence, and then attacked us when we tried to stop him. My friend Sebastien Siverling defeated him in a duel. So, as you can see, we have done your jobs for you, and the criminal is subdued and ready for arrest. Much of the evidence is on the floor in front of the fire, I imagine, half-burned and rather waterlogged. If you show any measure of the competence I know Gilbrathan coppers are capable of, I am sure you will be able to recover any relevant information from it."

They had more questions, of course, and when Lord Gervin burst in only a few minutes later, pushing forcibly past a couple of the coppers who tried to stall him, the whole explanation had to start from the beginning.

Ana had stopped crying by then, making a show of composing herself again, smoothing down her blouse and tugging at the seams of her trousers.

Lord Gervin was quickly caught up on the situation, his expression darkening with anger and disgust as his younger brother was hauled out of the room.

"We'll see that he gets the medical attention he requires," Investigator Kuchen assured Lord Gervin. "The investigation will be thorough and unbiased."

It was unclear whether this was meant to be a reassurance or a threat, but Lord Gervin nodded. "No less than I would expect."

The night stretched on for quite a while longer as they were moved into another room and questioned while the coppers searched Malcolm's office and the rest of the house for evidence. With the adrenaline wearing off, Damien realized how tired the whole thing had made him, but he didn't deviate from the story they had set up ahead of time, and he was sure Sebastien and Ana were sticking to the story just as closely. They had even practiced this part, after all, with Ana giving them tips about how to seem most believable while Sebastien did his best to trip them up.

Finally, as the hour grew late, Ana's father stepped in and put an end to the questioning. "My daughter needs rest, and her friends as well, after such a harrowing event. We will comply fully with the investigation into these deeply surprising and saddening crimes carried out by my brothers, but any further questions can be answered later. Please make an appointment beforehand."

He waited until all of the coppers had filed out of the room, then eyed the three of them silently. "What is this?" he asked, inadvertently repeating the words of his younger brother from earlier that night.

Ana stood up confidently, reaching into her pocket and pulling out the slightly burnt journal. "I pulled this from the fire," she said, offering it to her father.

"You kept this from the coppers?" Lord Gervin asked, accepting it slowly.

"I flipped through it before they arrived. There are some...sensitive entries. Things I thought you might not want getting out. Specifically, some interesting ideas about the Gervin Family line of succession in the case of your unexpected and early demise."

Lord Gervin stared at her for a few moments, then down at the journal in his hand.

Out of everything they had done for Operation Defenestration, the journal had taken the longest hours and some of the most meticulous work. It had been written in a hand indistinguishable from Malcolm Gervin's own, using the sample photographs of the documents from the vault to ensure fidelity. Ana hadn't touched it with her bare hands until just that night. She had used ink from Malcolm Gervin's supplier, and the exact same model as his favorite pen. It had a couple of Malcolm's hairs in it, his fingerprints, and even probably some of his saliva.

Much of the information would be corroborated by the other documents the man had tried to destroy, and from the work the private investigator had done. She had only needed to add a few pieces of false information, hidden among the rest.

"You kept this from the coppers, but not your young friends?" Lord Gervin asked, his eyes resting longer on Sebastien than Damien. "I do not recognize this young man."

Ana gestured smoothly to Sebastien. "This is Sebastien Siverling, Professor Thaddeus Lacer's apprentice."

Sebastien bowed slightly, seeming rather bored, as if he met Crown Family heads all the time. "Well met."

The man narrowed his eyes. "Hmm. You were the one who assisted the Red Guard in taking down an Aberrant earlier this year? I read about you in the paper," he said with grudging acceptance. "Always playing the hero, I see," he added sourly.

Ana ignored that comment. "Damien and Sebastien are both my allies, Father. I had no intention of confronting Uncle Malcolm by myself. I needed *trustworthy* backup."

Her father's eyes narrowed. "I could comment on your choice to confront him at all, daughter. It all seems rather…orchestrated, does it not? If you truly wanted to keep this within the Family, why alert the coppers?"

She returned his gaze unflinchingly. "The private investigator was becoming…unmanageable. He was frightened, both by the evidence of treason, which he was legally obligated to report, and by the involvement of the Raven Queen. He believes she saw his face. I tried to pay him off, enough to leave Gilbratha and live in another city for the rest of his life, but…fear makes people irrational. By the time I learned of what he'd done, alerting the coppers, all I could do was send the message to you and rush here. As for keeping this matter within the Family, as I mentioned, these are my *allies*, Father." The emphasis gave the word a different, more political meaning, and Damien saw it when the understanding and suspicion crystallized within Lord Gervin's eyes.

Ana noticed, too, her voice hardening and tone growing colder. "Besides, Malcolm and Randolph are only branch Family members, and surely soon to be denounced. *I* am the heir, and I don't consider myself associated with them. Neither will those who really matter associate me with them. Especially not after tonight, when Malcolm tried to kill me as I confronted him. I'm sure the news will spread."

Lord Gervin's hand pressed against the pocket containing the journal. "Rather vicious of you, daughter," he said, but his tone was approving, a contemplative smile growing on his face. "I see you do not wear those trousers just for show. You have taken down an opponent without leaving any leeway for feminine kindness. Perhaps you are not as weak as your mother."

Ana gave him one of her sweetest smiles. "I may have a velvet exterior, but I assure you, it hides a core of steel."

"You are my daughter indeed," Lord Gervin said, the smile growing larger.

The man was very stupid and extremely blind, Damien thought, for it to have taken something like this for him to realize Ana's worth. But even as Damien was somewhat disgusted, he couldn't help but feel a pang in his chest. He doubted there was anything he could do to get his own father to approve of him like that.

He looked to Sebastien, and the other young man slipped him a secretive, wry smile, and the barest hint of a nod.

Damien smoothed back his hair, and then suppressed a smile as he slipped his hand into his pocket. He realized with giddiness that it was done. They had succeeded. He ran his fingers over the smooth crystal of the thirteen-pointed star symbol within. He was part of something larger than himself, doing something as meaningful as it was sometimes difficult. Here, his efforts actually mattered.

4 9

PIXIES AND RAVENS

Sebastien
Month 3, Day 13, Saturday 11:30pm

As Lord Gervin escorted the three young people who had caused him so much trouble that night into Ana's carriage, which would take them back to the University, he extended his hand for Sebastien to shake.

She did her best to stifle the lingering tremors in her hands. The terror of fighting Malcolm Gervin had been almost as bad, if in a different way, as surviving the attack on Knave Knoll. Her face still felt stiff and bloodless, but she did her best to smile pleasantly.

"If you are in town this fall, I would like to invite you to attend my Family's annual soiree, Mr. Siverling. It will be a good opportunity for you to network."

"He will be there," Ana replied on Sebastien's behalf, pulling her into the carriage.

Once they were settled inside and safely on their way, Ana threw her head back and let out a cackle.

They all shared triumphant smiles, and then Damien finally exploded. "Myrddin's bushy black beard, Sebastien! That battle was amazing! Why don't you perform at that level in Fekten's class?"

Sebastien leaned her head against the seat's plush back, closing her eyes. "I cheated, you might say, in the fight against Malcolm. Fekten's class requires actual skill with the mechanics."

"Speaking of, why didn't you tell me the, um, your artifact can shoot spells? I thought it was only a light!" Damien, impressively, did not look guiltily toward Ana, who had no idea about the significance of the modified drink coasters that both Sebastien and Damien had.

Sebastien pulled it out from her pocket, showing Damien the back, where she had carefully painted a spell array in a color that almost matched the stone. "It is just a light crystal. I was using this spell to Sacrifice the produced light and then shoot it. Malcolm was right, it's just a harmless visual effect, but it ended up being quite useful."

Damien leaned closer to stare at the spell array, his brows climbing up his forehead. "But the spell spheres were coming out all different colors."

Sebastien tucked away the thirteen-pointed star. "That part wasn't too difficult. Shorter electromagnetic wavelengths have more energy, while longer wavelengths have less. I had to do some practicing to get my control fine enough to reliably hit specific colors, but I wanted to be sure that my Will's clarity was high enough to differentiate my control over the particular effects of *my* spell array while maintaining the light crystal's internal integrity."

Damien sat back, staring into the distance with cloudy eyes. "Right. We learned about that in class." His voice grew softer and softer as he continued. "So I suppose, if you're ingenious enough, this little stuff really can come in handy…"

He recovered after a few minutes, turning to Ana, who was still grinning and letting out sporadic malevolent laughs. "How is Alec going to take this?" he asked.

"Alec will be fine. After all, he is going to become the head of the Gervin Family's closest branch line, once Malcolm and Randolph are officially disowned," she said.

Sebastien knew it wouldn't be quite that easy. But at least, when the gossip grew rampant, Alec would be able to rely on his friends, the clout of his station, and his personal fortune.

When they finally arrived at the University, it was past curfew and the lights were out, so they snuck into the dorms as silently as possible. It was all Sebastien could do to cast her dreamless sleep spell before passing out.

She struggled to wake and clear her fuzzy mind enough to recast it halfway through the night, and didn't even bother with the usual hour of homework she got in around that time. Some inconsiderate idiot's playful shout woke her in the morning, and she just laid in bed for a few minutes afterward, watching the light come in through the window to her right.

When she finally crawled out of bed, she saw all the replacement supplies she'd purchased the day before sitting on the ground, waiting for her to organize and store them. She hadn't replaced her artifacts, but had managed to find most of her components and a few emergency potions that she either didn't have the time or the expertise to brew herself. All in all, it had been an expensive affair, as the prices had climbed even higher than usual. She tossed her blanket off, exposing herself to the chill air and cold stone of the floor, and began to rifle through the drawer of her bedside table.

She pulled out the almost-empty vial of beamshell tincture, saved from destruction by virtue of being left out of her bag. Her fingers trembled as she unsealed it and caught the acrid scent of the gritty sludge within.

She stopped, holding out the vial to the light. Setting it on the windowsill, she stared at it, reflecting on what she'd just done. The automatic way she'd searched it out, the way her body reacted to the unpleasant scent, but most importantly, the visceral memory of electrifying energy that was urging her on so subtly from the back of her mind.

She rifled through the drawer again until she found the information card originally tied around the vial's neck. Though she knew what it said, she read it again. Beamshell tincture was addictive, of course, but it also caused trouble sleeping, energy debts, and most importantly, could impair the memory.

Sebastien stepped back, pressing her lips together and folding her arms over her chest in a hug. She prided herself on her mental strength, and that included the absolute grasp of her memory, but she couldn't help but think about the small slips, the little failures of recall she'd been having lately. Times when thinking or casting magic had felt dizzying. She had ignored them, or made excuses.

For a moment, she imagined taking just a half-dose, just enough to help her get through the day. '*Oh*,' she thought. With shaking hands, she picked up the vial, slid it into her pocket, and hurried to the bathroom, where she didn't even bother to avoid the other students as she poured the remaining contents down the sink, running the water until the glass container was empty and clear. '*I don't need it. I'll just steal some of Damien's coffee,*' she assured herself. '*I'm fine. I don't need it.*'

She did her best to put it out of her mind. '*The sleep-proxy spell will do a better job with what I really need, anyway,*' she thought, trying to be optimistic.

But then, with a sudden rush of horror, she remembered that Professor Lacer had invited her to practice detaching the output of her spells again on Saturday…and that, between the battle and Operation Defenestration, she had completely blown past the entire day without a second's thought of Lacer or schoolwork.

She dressed in a flurry and hurried across the grounds to Professor Lacer's office, only to find a note on the door stating that he had cancelled his weekend office hours. '*Because of the fighting. He's probably helping with the investigation,*' she realized. '*He wasn't here, so he has no idea I completely forgot.*' She sagged with relief.

"No need to be so disappointed. I am here now," Professor Lacer said, speaking directly behind her.

Sebastien jumped a full foot in the air, then spun to face him while clutching the fabric of her jacket over her hammering heartbeat, scowling fiercely.

He seemed to find her reaction amusing, raising a steaming coffee mug to cover his smile. His eyes were bloodshot, and his hair was starting to come loose from where he had tied it at the base of his neck. "I heard about what happened yesterday evening. Are you well?"

"With Malcolm Gervin? I'm fine."

He moved past her, unlocking his office door. "You took a big risk. Do not imagine I am blind to the political motives behind ruining such a powerful man. Do you realize how high the stakes were? That man attempted to murder you and your companions. It is good to make powerful friends, but you must be sure that they are worth the effort."

"I was prepared," she said.

Professor Lacer raised a dubious eyebrow, but said, "I suppose you did escape unscathed, though that does not mean you were wise. Risking your safety to increase the weight of a scandal? If not for some connections in high places, you may have been charged with illegal possession of a battle wand, despite the upstanding way in which you used it."

Her mouth opened, but no sound came forth. She knew a license was required to carry a battle wand, but she had been carrying one for some time now, and used one more than once without ever needing to consider the legality. Damien had his own…but no doubt did so legally.

Professor Lacer sighed deeply, seeming to read her thoughts from her expression. "Indeed. You are no end of trouble to me." He pulled an envelope from his jacket's inner pocket and tossed it to her.

With trepidation, she opened it, only to discover a license for a battle wand of "reasonable offensive and defensive power" within. It was dated the day prior, and her name was written as the recipient. Someone had pulled some strings for her. "I don't know what to say," she admitted.

"You may thank me."

She cleared her throat past the lump that had suddenly formed in it. "Thank you. Truly."

He waved away her words with an absent motion of his hand, but the harsh lines at the edges of his eyes and mouth softened somewhat. "There will be no output detachment practice today. You have just been through an ordeal and were no doubt up until the wee hours testifying to the coppers, and I have other pressing work."

Sebastien hesitated before leaving. "What happened on Friday night… Did that have anything to do with the Raven Queen?"

"The investigation is still ongoing, but I suspect she did respond to the attack, and managed to kill the perpetrator. Identification of the remains will be…complicated. This time, the coppers should be grateful to her. The man would likely have gone free if not for her, and was undoubtedly a danger to more than just a small-time gang."

Sebastien wanted to ask more, but Professor Lacer shooed her away with another absent wave of his hand, already focused on a stack of homework papers from one of his upper-term classes. She closed the door behind her as she left, wondering if the prisoner transport going so wrong would in turn make things even harder for her. At least, with her debt soon to be wiped out, she wouldn't need to keep putting herself in danger for the Verdant Stag.

She headed south, toward the transport tubes. The University grounds were abuzz, contractors milling about under the supervision of professors and other faculty members as they decorated and set up facilities for the end of term exhibitions. From the look of things, they were expecting a large influx of people.

In the city below, it seemed everyone had a newspaper to read about the recent slew of exciting events, and Siobhan even noticed several copies of Oliver's publication, *The People's Voice*, which was now slightly larger than the average pamphlet.

Liza opened the door after only one use of the lion's-head door knocker, seeming excited—even energized—for once. "About time you arrived," the woman said, grabbing Siobhan's arm and pulling her inside. "I've been waiting for you since five this morning."

Siobhan let Liza pull her through the door, deciding not to mention Liza's grumpy complaints the last time she'd come over early in the morning.

"I bought another batch of animals to do the third round of testing on," Liza continued, barely looking at Siobhan. "More mice, plus some of the new batch of raven chicks, and a set of raccoons. Your notes were right about them; both have better brains than mice. For thoroughness, we should test some magical creatures as well, so I got a set of pixies, too. I wanted monkeys—they have brains most similar to a human's, without needing to break the harsher laws—but my usual supplier is having issues getting stock into the city after that whole fiasco with your friend Oliver and those red-clad thugs."

Liza's excitement was contagious. "The test results are still good, then?" Siobhan asked, grinning.

Liza wound her mane of springy curls into a bun, which she stabbed through with a wand to keep in place. "No deaths. One month in, and no signs of lingering trauma! Our sleepers are down pretty much constantly, and the second round of waking mice are showing signs of fatigue, but are still healthy overall."

"That's amazing! A one-hundred percent success rate is pretty impressive, even if our sample size isn't that large. Liza, we are geniuses!"

Liza's lips pursed at first, but she couldn't keep them from spreading into a smile. "So it seems." She pushed a cup of steaming tea into Siobhan's hands, then ushered her into the adjacent hidden apartment through the false back of the bedroom closet. The room smelled faintly of plants, dirt, and animal musk, and was filled with the muffled chirps, squawks, and growls of various creatures. It probably would have been much louder and smellier if not for the convenience of magic. "However, there is one side effect," Liza added. "It seems our waking mice cannot sleep with the spell active. That ability seems to have been Sacrificed. I wasn't sure if that would happen or not, but I think it's safe to say their fatigue has grown great enough that they would be sleeping if they could."

Siobhan frowned. "Is that going to be a problem, do you think?"

"Binding magic works with active, ongoing trades. The ability to sleep returns once the spell is ended, and as I said, there is no long-term infirmity. Once we break their connection, both mice return to normal, though of course the sleeper mice are permanently more robust."

"And the sleepers aren't being damaged?"

"Well, they probably are, but the increased healing factor of the spell is balancing that out for now. I've been trying to keep them hydrated with a nutrient draught while they're unconscious, but I imagine if we were to continue the spell for longer than a couple of weeks at a time, they would all die."

Siobhan hesitated, but eventually voiced her thoughts out loud. "We should keep the spell running until they do die. For the data." It felt cruel, but nothing worthwhile came without a cost. They needed to know what would happen. After all, a raven was more likely to die under the strain of a human's mind, and if that caused some catastrophic backlash, she would much rather learn about it now.

Liza nodded absently. "Of course. We'll want to have as much information as possible before we start human testing. That's going to be the hard part." She waved Siobhan over to the logbook where she had diligently recorded the daily status of their mice. "Go ahead and review everything. I had a couple of ideas for minor improvements to the spell, which I've noted. While you familiarize yourself with that, I will make the final preparations for the third round of experiments. Meet me down below as soon as you are ready." She grabbed two of the cages along the wall, heaving one under each arm and ignoring the alarmed whines of the fat raccoons within.

Siobhan turned her attention to the logs and notes, which Liza had put her customary great care into. The sleeping mice actually started out healthier than the waking ones, likely because of the blood magic they'd done to boost their vitality and brain function, along with the continuous healing provided by the sempervivum apricus while the spell was ongoing. The equilibrium shifted after about ten days, by which time most of the sleeper mice were unconscious the majority of the time, with a few of them only waking long enough to eat, drink, and defecate. By this point, fourteen days into the second round of testing, the sleeper mice were no longer waking at all, and the diagnostic testing showed their health declining precipitously despite Liza's attempts to keep them alive.

When Siobhan had gone over the logs as well as thoroughly internalized Liza's improvements to the spell, which required her to read a few book-marked passages from some medical reference texts, she joined the older woman in the casting rooms down below.

Liza had filled up two more rooms with the expansive sleep-proxy spell array, and apparently bought her own supplies, including more mandrakes and sempervivum apricus. They were all larger—and therefore more expensive—than the ones Siobhan had supplied. The whole lower level was filled with various terrariums of mice going through different stages of the spell, and their body heat alone kept the place warm.

Siobhan looked around with admiration. Liza had been working on this constantly, it seemed, whether or not Siobhan was available. She felt a warm spike of gratitude, before she remembered that the older woman was getting as much out of this as Siobhan.

Siobhan almost expected Liza to try and hand her a bill for half of the additional creatures and supplies, and was already planning how she could argue her way out of it, but Liza didn't mention anything, and Siobhan wisely kept her mouth shut. After all, what was this if not Liza's way of helping develop and test the spell, which was part of their contract? Siobhan mentally patted herself on the back for the foresight to bring the other woman in on the project.

"Are you ready?" Liza asked.

"I am." With that, they began a full day of strenuous spellcasting. They started with a couple more sets of mice, then a set of raccoons, then the ravens, before breaking for lunch. The raccoons and ravens were both more difficult than the mice, and Siobhan wondered what it would be like to try and cast the spell on a human. She had calculated an extended casting time, but without Liza it probably would have taken Siobhan at least three hours, even on a mouse. Casting for such an extended time was a danger on its own, as most minds had trouble maintaining such extreme concentration for long periods of time.

When they broke for lunch, Siobhan discovered that Liza had only a moldy heel of bread, some pickled plums, and a bit of jam in her kitchen. Neither of them felt like shopping for ingredients and trying to prepare anything, so they ate at a nearby bar, where the proprietress provided fresh fruit at Liza's request—with a little extra coin slid across the counter—despite the fact that it was still winter.

"I really think it's going to work," Siobhan said as they ate.

Liza smiled, wiping some clotted cream from her dark lips. "I think so too, girl. What are you going to do with an extra eight hours every day?"

"Everything," Siobhan responded immediately, her voice dreamy. Liza snorted, and Siobhan flushed, hurrying to correct herself. "Well, I'll study things I'm interested in, work on some projects I never seem to have time for, and maybe even do some work to bring in extra coin. Do you think it will improve our Will's recovery time? That's one of the main functions of sleep. If it does...I could cast for an extra three hours a day, maybe, without needing to worry about strain."

"Three hours out of eight? Do you spend six hours a day casting now?" Liza asked, one arched eyebrow raised.

Siobhan hummed noncommittally. "Not every day. Sometimes I spend more, generally on the weekends. I think it averages out to about six hours a day, though."

Liza nodded approvingly. "No wonder your Will is improving so quickly. Most serious thaumaturges don't average over four hours a day. What do you do that takes so much time?"

Siobhan hesitated.

"If that is too invasive a question, feel free to change the subject," Liza said, pointedly looking away to give Siobhan a semblance of privacy.

"Well, no, it's not. I brew for the Verdant Stag and sometimes do other projects for them, but the majority of my casting time is spent practicing basic spells, pushing myself to tweak their outputs while still using the basic spell array, that kind of thing." She paused, adding cream to her second cup of tea. "I want to be a free-caster," she admitted.

"Ambitious." Liza eyed her for a moment, taking another bite of food. "Not impossible, though. Free-casting was never my own focus. It requires too much instant mental flexibility. I prefer to sit down and slowly work through a problem, layering new revelations and improvements into my work. Artificery is much less dangerous, as well."

"What will you do with your extra eight hours?" Siobhan asked.

Liza looked down at her plate, now almost empty, for a few seconds. "Research," she finally replied.

"Research about what?"

"That is too invasive a question." Liza met Siobhan's gaze unflinchingly, but didn't sound angry.

Siobhan nodded easily. "Okay. Shall we get back to work, then?"

"Let's."

Siobhan's excitement hadn't waned, despite their large lunch trying to draw blood away from her brain for digestion. However, when she got a good look at their next test subjects, some of the feeling soured.

The pixies watched with big, frightened eyes as Liza and Siobhan prepared the spell array for them. They were less than eighteen inches tall, their small fingers wrapped around the bars of their cage, their multi-petaled flesh wings trembling enough to shake off flakes and peels of ever-regenerating dandruff—more commonly known as pixie dust, a useful magical component and the main reason the creatures were often kept as pets.

They made nasty faces and gestures, and one of them even knew a few curse words, which it threw out with little artifice or understanding. Like parrots, they could memorize and reproduce sounds and words, and even understand a few of particular importance, but couldn't hold a coherent conversation.

The little creatures fought back viciously when Liza took them out of the cages, scratching and biting and shrieking until the woman subdued them all with her docility spell.

Siobhan wondered if they understood what was about to happen to them. She found herself sweating a bit as they took away the creatures' fear and ability to feel pain with a couple drops of a potent numbing potion.

Transferring the vitality and brain function of the Sacrifice was harder than with the mice, and even harder than the raccoons, about on par with the ravens. The pixie they were drawing from didn't try to escape, and she assured herself that it wasn't frightened or feeling pain, but at the last minute, as the connection took hold and wrenched, its dark eyes met hers. One second it was alive, and the next it wasn't. Its eyes were still wet and glassy, still looking at her, but empty. Its fingers twitched once, and a mix of blood and clear liquid ran from its snub nose.

Siobhan took a clumsy step backward.

'*This feels wrong. This is* wrong.' The thought filled her mind, unbidden but undeniable. The pixie's body was limp, flaking wings still, half crushed beneath its body, senseless little fingers and sightless staring eyes—

Bile suddenly rose up in Siobhan's throat, and she took another step away, turning to rest her forehead against the cool stone of the wall, her back to what they had just done—what she had just done. She closed her eyes, breathing deeply until her stomach stopped trying to surge up into her throat. Her back tingled with a cold sweat as she straightened her shoulders and turned around.

Liza was watching her silently, her expression inscrutable.

Siobhan swallowed, keeping herself from looking back at the dead creature as she met Liza's gaze. "I don't want to do that again. They're so—they're too intelligent. No monkeys, either. Pixies, monkeys, anything intelligent shouldn't have to die for our experiments. We can test on them, but I don't want to kill them just to boost our sleeper."

Liza looked down at the dead pixie. "Pixies and monkeys do look very human, don't they? But magic comes at a cost, girl. Always. Great magic comes at great cost. If you cannot bear to pay it, perhaps you are not suited to this life."

Siobhan flinched as if she'd been slapped, but clenched her fists. "There is a reason blood magic is illegal."

Liza scoffed derisively, contempt clear in her voice. "Please tell me you do not believe that shite about evil magics corrupting the Will. *Weakness* corrupts the Will. Hesitation. Indecision. Any other tales are just pretty words to keep the masses from realizing the truth." She pressed her lips together firmly, and when she spoke again her tone was kinder. "What makes one animal more important than another? You eat them, you use their pieces in your magic, you even wear their skin," she said, waving to Siobhan's leather boots. "The pixie looks so much like us, and suddenly you grow a conscience, but you must realize, your hesitation is not based on some inherent 'rightness' or 'wrongness.' Ravens are at least as intelligent as these creatures, whether magical or not. Some believe them to be sapient, you know, able to communicate with each other, make plans for the future, and solve complex problems. They, too, can learn to speak some of our words. And yet, you have been okay with killing quite a few of them."

"Is that true?" Siobhan asked, though she really didn't think Liza was lying to her. She remembered the feeling of using the Lino-Wharton messenger spell to control a raven's body, speak with its tongue, and see with its eyes. All that was possible, of course, because the ravens were strong and smart enough to handle the strain of her human mind, if only for a short time. "They're as smart as pixies?"

"Ravens are social creatures full of curiosity. They can solve puzzles and problems, learn new behavior to obtain desired results, and innovate solutions. They use improvised tools to obtain food and defend their territory. Some pairs even mate for life. In my opinion, if the only criteria is intelligence, they far surpass the pixie."

A sickening mix of chemicals rushed through Siobhan's bloodstream, making her heart clench a little too hard and her veins burn. She was too aware of her skin, and every touch of fabric or air against it was an irritant. She wanted to move, but she forced herself to stay still, letting this new perspective sink in.

Liza scoffed. "I should have known you were too soft when you wanted to give the mice a pain potion," she muttered. Louder, she said, "Take a good look inside yourself, girl, and question *why* you are hesitating *now*."

Siobhan looked back at the dead pixie, letting out a slow breath through pursed lips, just on the edge of a whistle. If the pixie had looked like a giant cockroach instead of having fingers and pink flesh, even if someone had told her the cockroach was just as intelligent, it wouldn't have *felt* so wrong.

'*Be honest. Twist the knife,*' Siobhan ordered herself. She cared *more* because of the way it looked. It hurt to admit that to herself, but it was the truth. She twisted the knife of introspection further, as Professor Lacer had taught her. '*If it is wrong to kill a pixie, then it is wrong to kill a raven. And perhaps it was. Was it also wrong to kill a mouse? Where is the line between an acceptable Sacrifice and excessive cruelty?*' No matter the creature, it was legally blood magic to use a living creature not just as a component but as a Sacrifice.

"Perhaps it would ease your mind to know that the Sacrifice of their life is well worth the gain," Liza said after Siobhan's silence dragged on. "I am not wasteful nor disrespectful of their lives, child. When we are finished here, each piece of them will be saved for use as components in other magic. These creatures are not afraid or in pain, as we ensured. Their lives were ended as gently as possible, and their Sacrifice will go toward a remarkable, significant advance in magic."

Siobhan still didn't respond. Using a creature in magic was not so different from slaughtering a creature to eat. In fact, it might be better, because many spells would not use up all the matter of a Sacrificed creature, allowing the remains to be used for food, tools, or even other spells afterward. She didn't feel guilt when she ate meat. But she usually didn't eat sapient creatures, either.

Would she have had such a reaction if someone else had done the butchering for her? Most likely not. This realization shamed her, because that kind of dissociation from reality, allowing someone else to take the blame and the responsibility, was a betrayal of herself. '*If I am in control, then everything within my control is my responsibility. Just like it was my fault that Jameson died, like it is my responsibility to prepare for the future, I am accountable for the weight and consequence of my actions. A living creature that can have hopes for the future, that can make plans to solve its problems and carry them out, that can understand and think and feel… That's a person. Not a human, but I never want to make the mistake of believing only those who look and act like me are people. And to kill a person… That is murder.*'

She felt another rush, a visceral response as her stomach churned and goosebumps rippled in a wave across her skin. For the first time, she longed for the transformation contained in the amulet around her neck, if only to *get out* of her own body. "Would it be possible to use mice, or some other less intelligent creature, to boost a pixie, or a raven?" Siobhan asked. It wasn't *right* to kill mice, either, perhaps, but it was a sin she felt she could still bear, for a worthy purpose.

"It is not so simple, for the same reason one should not attempt to Sacrifice the mind of a pixie to increase your own intelligence. They are too weak, and incompatible besides. If we were willing to risk failure and its consequences, we might Sacrifice the pixie to boost the mouse, but not the other way around."

When Siobhan remained silent once more, Liza continued. "There are other alternatives, but I believe you will find them even more distasteful. We could cast this spell, now, with unboosted creatures, but if you try to do that later, you will find that you kill raven after raven with the strain of taking your sleep. This doesn't solve your problem with causing a death, and it might prove dangerous to you, as well. We do not yet know what happens when the sleeper dies under the strain of the spell."

That option was, in effect, giving up on the spell—something Siobhan couldn't bring herself to do, despite her guilt. "And the other option?" Siobhan asked.

"Use a human instead. They would not be in danger with spell periods of a week or so at a stretch, if the notes you've given me about the source of this spell are correct. However, that option comes with dangers and difficulties of its own."

Siobhan flexed her fingers, spreading them wide to avoid digging her fingernails into her palms until they bled. "Even if we could find someone willing to give up their waking hours, there's still the ethical dilemma of testing something potentially dangerous on a human. Also, the extreme illegality makes it perilous. If word got out…"

Liza nodded. "I can tell you now, I will not be developing the spell with human sleepers. Too many things could go wrong, and the consequences are much too severe, especially when we have a perfectly viable alternative right here. If you take that path, you will be on your own. So, girl, I believe you need to make a choice about what is more important to you. An extra eight hours a day for the remainder of your life, and all that such an opportunity could bring you, or the lives of these small creatures. I do not deny that their lives hold obvious value, at least in the eyes of magic, but their continued existence will not bring any value to you, nor to the world as a whole. I think the greater good is obvious." Her eyes roved over Siobhan's face for a few seconds, and something about what she saw softened her expression. "I think you know it too, child."

Siobhan hesitated. It wasn't just the extra time that this spell would give her, but an escape from sleep and all that it entailed. But she wanted to stop regretting her choices, and this seemed like the kind of festering, small wound that would poison her over time. She didn't want to stop caring about people who were different than her, who couldn't defend themselves against her. Her forehead and back prickled with cold sweat under Liza's impatient gaze. "I need some time to think about this," Siobhan said finally. "Maybe, in the meantime, we could finish off the rest of today's tests with some different variations? Mice sleeping for some of the more complex creatures, to test what happens with inherently uneven binding spells? It could give us some good data about what will happen when it's a human on the waking side." That it would also save the lives of those more intelligent creatures went unspoken between the two of them.

With a displeased grimace, Liza agreed, and they returned to work, though the ruined mood between them made the ensuing hours uncomfortable and silent.

Liza apparently hadn't forgotten about the cost of the extra supplies she bought, because she informed Siobhan as she was leaving that she could either provide half their value in gold or Liza would take those funds out of Siobhan's cut of any coin she earned from the knowledge in the long term.

Dejected, Siobhan agreed. At least she didn't have to pay from her own meager funds.

That evening, she had to use Newton's self-calming spell to force her body to relax enough for sleep, as her thoughts kept returning to a small, snub-nosed face with blood and brain matter running from the nostrils, and the final twitch of dirty little fingers. *'I am a blood magic user, and not just by legal inter-pretation. I have used the life of a still-living being as a Sacrifice, and I cannot deny that it is a loathsome, monstrous thing. Whether morality is objective or subjective, killing a sapient being when I do not need to for my own survival still fills me with shame all the same. And yet, I am so greedy, I want to find some way to justify it, to rationalize it, so that I can continue to gain the benefits. But I cannot do that. It would be lying to myself. If I move forward with these experiments, I must do so with my eyes open to my own char-acter. If I continue, it will be because I have decided that my own happiness, comfort, and curiosity are worth more than the life of another who does not deserve death, but is too weak to stop me.'*

Having admitted this to herself, Sebastien was able to find some peace. Whatever her decision, she would face the truth of it directly. And if she was honest with herself, which she was trying to be, she knew that she might very well decide to continue.

50

SWORD OF DAMOCLES

Sebastien
   Month 3, Day 15, Monday 6:00pm

After spending a few hours catching up on schoolwork, Sebastien retrieved her borrowed books about Myrddin, settling in for some light reading to pass the evening hours. She was both antsy and tired, and had been having trouble concentrating. Though it almost physically pained her to admit, she knew it was because she was craving the beamshell tincture.

She ground her teeth together with futile anger. '*I can't believe it's so easy to almost destroy your own future. But at least I realized now, before things got worse. My Will is still strong enough to get back on track. I control my mind. I control my body. They do not control me.*'

Hoping to distract herself, she bundled herself up in her bed, still wearing her jacket for warmth. Resting *Myrddin: An Investigative Chronicle of the Legend* on her knees, she flipped toward a section nearer the middle.

Several accounts corroborated the fact that Myrddin had, at some point after rising to fame, replaced his more traditional jewelry-style Conduits with a huge sphere of celerium mounted atop a staff. Accounts of the staff itself varied, and even during his life didn't seem to have a common consensus.

Some said Myrddin had taken it from a twisted branch broken from the heart of a lightning-struck tree—a tree that had grown alone at the top of a mountain, constantly buffeted by storms. Other accounts said the staff was smooth dark stone, inlaid with symbols and lines of gold. Still others said that it was white and slightly porous, carved from the finger bone of a long-dead Titan.

What remained relatively consistent were reports of the Conduit itself, a sphere of polished crystal, as clear and bright as fresh spring water. Its size had been compared to both of a man's fists together or a pomelo fruit. If true, the book estimated it would have been one of the largest celerium Conduits known to history, at approximately eight to ten inches in diameter.

Its true clarity was somewhat controversial, as one of Myrddin's contemporaries had written a letter in which he claimed to have examined the Conduit and found a black speck at the very center, about the size of a peppercorn. But even with a small imperfection, such a Conduit could theoretically channel hundreds of thousands of thaums.

Sebastien lifted her gaze from the page, staring into the middle distance as she imagined what it would mean, to need a Conduit that robust. Even Archmage Zard, capable of amazing feats, having been witnessed putting out forest fires and capturing a whale as big as the ship he rode upon by simply lifting it out of the water and holding it there, was only estimated to have a capacity of seventy to ninety thousand thaums.

She thought back to the theory that Myrddin himself had created the white cliffs that surrounded Gilbratha. Suddenly, it didn't seem quite so unrealistic, though the real question was how a human could grow their Will to that level before simply dying of old age. Thaumaturges lived longer, of course, but generally not more than one hundred twenty years, even for the most dedicated and accomplished. Myrddin had lived longer than that, between two hundred and three hundred years. For a long time after his final disappearance, people had refused to believe he was truly dead.

'*What must it be like, to walk through the world like that, knowing that with a single thought you can end storms, level mountains, and erase anyone or anything that angers you from existence?*' Siobhan wondered. She imagined the weight of a Will that powerful. It would feel like fate itself was drawn toward her, like she was a star in the midst of the sidereal void, her gravity the only thing that mattered.

Sebastien was so lost in her thoughts she didn't recognize the cold prickling in her back at first. It was the sense of prying violation, fingers grasping for her body, eyes roving over her secrets, that had her shooting upright so quickly the book tumbled to the floor.

She fell to her hands and knees, stumbling over her blanket and almost tearing the fabric as she tried to free herself. She fumbled out her Conduit so that she could boost her divination-diverting ward's power.

As the five disks under the skin of her back drew more blood, the deflecting shield pushing the prying divination tendrils away with more power and giving her the pseudo-sensation of more space, she took a deep, relieved breath. '*My blood must not have been destroyed in the Eagle Tower explosion, like I hoped,'* she realized. *'Either that, or they have something new from me.'* She had known the Eagle Tower repair was almost finished, but foolishly hadn't been on guard for a surprise attack.

One hand reaching for her satchel, she swung the strap over her shoulder, picked up the fallen book, and cautiously peeked around the dividing curtain between her and the rest of the dorm. Several students were sitting in the hallway between male and female cubicles, playing a game that involved cards and dice. But they didn't seem to have noticed her sudden panic.

Moving as quickly as possible, she settled back down and prepared to cast a disintegration curse on her blood, targeted precisely through the reverse-scrying spell she'd previously used to pinpoint the diviners' location at Eagle Tower.

Despite the unpleasant pseudo-sensations and fear that always accompanied a divination attempt on her, she grinned. Finally, she would be free of the threat hanging over her head like a sword waiting to drop.

Keeping a small part of her concentration on empowering the divination-diverting ward, Sebastien used the majority of her Will to cast the curse.

She waited for the divination to drop as the blood was destroyed, but nothing happened. She pushed harder, feeding more power into the spell and scowling with the force of her concentration.

Still nothing changed, except that the strength of the divination slowly increased.

She kept trying for a minute longer, but with each second that ticked by, her hope faded. More and more of her concentration was required to empower the ward as the divination grew stronger, leaving less to cast her curse. Finally, there was no choice but to admit that she had failed. And worse yet, this divination was already as strong as any she had faced before, and was growing only stronger.

'They're going to put everything they have into this.' Sebastien felt her shoulders tightening with anxiety and straightened, rolling them backward to release some of the tension. *'What do I do?'*

She knew from experience that she couldn't stand up to their best efforts. Surely the pressure would only get worse. If Liza were here, the woman could probably throw up a quick ward to help, but she wasn't.

'Liza's wards can still protect me. I just need to get inside her house.' Cautiously, she slipped from the room and walked down to the end of the hallway, trying not to draw any extra attention to herself that would cause someone to notice the spillover effects of the ward. She clung to the less used pathways to the University entrance, slipping down in one of the tubes while the guards were distracted by a group of drunk students returning from their weekend revelries. Below, she traveled through side streets and alleyways, keeping her cloak pulled up to hide her features as she hurried.

Some part of her had hoped that the divination attempt would give out after a few minutes, and then a few tens of minutes, but instead the pressure only increased, until she could feel her heartbeat pushing against the inside of her skull. She didn't have the luxury of time to stop by the Silk Door, but she'd had the foresight to put a pair of clothes for either form in each of her emergency stashes. She retrieved one from a hole under a particularly large cobblestone in a fenced-off alley, changing her form and her outfit right there in the cold twilight.

The dress was frilly and pastel, nothing like what she would normally wear. With a small hand mirror, she added her prosthetic nose as well, but passed over the blue contact lenses. They were memorable, and she did not want to be noticed. She shoved the emergency bag inside of her school satchel, which she had no intention of abandoning even if it was a clue.

She was grateful for the half-light of the setting sun as she scurried up the metal staircase to Liza's door, frantically clacking the door-knocker.

Siobhan waited, shifting from foot to foot and biting her lip impatiently. She knocked again.

No response.

She turned to grip the railing, squeezing the cold, hard-edged metal until it dug into the skin of her palms. *'I have to leave,'* she realized. *'I cannot hold it off, and so I must escape. If I cannot get far enough in time to weaken the divination's power, I may have to leave the city for good, giving up my life here—everything I have come so close to accomplishing—entirely. And every moment I waste makes that increasingly likely.'*

Siobhan threw herself down the stairs and began to run south. If the coppers were in Eagle Tower, the direction opposite them was the most direct method of escape. If they were in Harrow Hill Penitentiary, she would be better served by going across the Charybdis Gulf to the east, but that would more likely slow her down than anything, especially since she still needed to go south to exit the encirclement of the white cliffs.

She flagged down the first carriage she could find, a nice vehicle with two healthy looking horses and shock absorbers attached to the wheels. She hurled herself inside, urging the driver to continue on her way.

With the increased speed of the carriage, she felt some incremental relief, though the pressure was not receding quite as quickly as it had originally built. Even as she was moving away, they were pouring on the power like syrup over pancakes. Still, at least the balance was moving in the right direction.

The carriage driver grew uncertain as they moved farther into the Mires, but she urged him on. He asked again for a particular destination when they crossed the demarcation line of the white cliffs, which was surrounded by a shanty town that had spilled beyond the once-perfect circle of the city.

When they left the sprawling, improvised housing behind, the countryside opening up to rocky, brush-filled stretches of land on either side of the pitted road, the driver finally stopped the carriage. "I'm not taking you any further without payment."

Siobhan huffed at him, dug in her purse, and tossed up a handful of silver coins. "My sister is giving birth in the nearest village." She searched her memory of the maps she'd studied in Oliver's office. "Umm, Tidewater, I believe it's called. Hurry."

The man gave her a dubious look, but weighed the coin in his hand, tucked it in a pocket, and urged the horses on.

Slowly, the strain receded, and finally, an hour after it had started, the divination dropped entirely. Siobhan sagged with relief. They hadn't broken through. She was safe and could return to the city.

The only problem was, she couldn't very well tell the driver that she no longer cared about attending her niece or nephew's birth, and that he should just turn around.

It took them another half hour to arrive at the little village that she hoped was named Tidewater, and she had to give the driver even more coin before he left. By then, it was already quite dark, and of course such a small town had no carriages waiting to be hired. If it were day, she might have bummed a ride on the back of a north-bound wagon, but for the remainder of the evening, it appeared she was out of luck.

She could probably get a ride in the morning, but she needed to be back at the University in time for her classes, shortly after the sun rose. She searched her coin purse, judging what remained after replenishing most of her stock over the last couple of days and her impromptu carriage ride. She somehow had enough coin left after her shopping excursion to buy a donkey, or even a horse, if one were available for sale, but such an urgent purchase would be suspicious. Oliver had been generous, with both the hazard pay and the funds to reimburse her for what she had lost.

A search of her memory and some quick calculation of the time she had traveled told her she was about fifteen kilometers outside of Gilbratha. *'That's not much,'* she reassured herself. *'I can walk that in just a few hours, and be back at the University and in my bed before curfew.'*

And so she set off, following the distant carriage back down the road they'd come from. It soon became clear to her that, while her overloaded school satchel was wonderful for storing components and books, it was less ideal for hiking. She had also unfortunately failed to replenish her customary bottle of moonlight sizzle, and her normal lantern had been disintegrated. She searched for the light crystal coaster that had come in so handy recently, only to remember that she'd carelessly left it in her bedside drawer the evening after using it in the fight against Malcolm Gervin.

The weight of the satchel's strap seemed to dig into her shoulders and hurt her ribs with its increasingly cumbersome weight. She quickly drank through her entire canteen of water, but without a convenient source of light, couldn't stop and set up a spell array to gather more. Her mouth grew dry, and then a headache bloomed. The potions in her bag began to seem appealing more for their liquid content than their magical properties.

The night was so dark that she could barely see the road beneath her feet. But she could hear the ocean, and the occasional yips, howls, and hoots of animals, their cries carrying far on the still night air and leaving her on edge and jumpy.

Shivering and stumbling in the dark, she finally had an idea. She stopped in what she thought was the middle of the road, pulled off one of her boots, and retrieved a paper spell array from her emergency bag. With fingers numb from the cold, she managed to pry open the heel of her boot, then used the finger-knife sheathed within against the flint to create a spark. It lasted only a moment, but by doing this repeatedly, she hoped to read the spell array's purpose. She might be able to cast in the dark if she already knew with total surety what spell it was, but accidentally mis-matching her Will to the Word could have disastrous consequences.

The sparks revealed that the paper held Grubb's barrier spell, which she then funneled power through in the most inefficient way possible, allowing the lines of the spell array to glow and heat. With one half of her mind focused on the light from that, she was able to set up a spell to gather water from the air, which she switched over to until her canteen was full. She emptied the bottle, grimacing at the slightly strange taste of the water, and then repeated the process. '*It would be a good idea to carve the water-gathering spell array into the base of the canteen,*' she realized.

This emergency bag didn't have any light-based spells in it, but it did have a few blank sheets of paper, and she was still wearing her holster with the beast core. After once again switching to the inefficient barrier spell to create a glow, she drew out a standard glow spell with a directed beam.

Finally, she slipped her boot back on and continued, holding the sheet of shining paper out before her.

She shuffled and limped her way north for hours. Tanya had created an extended reprieve for Siobhan when she blew up Eagle Tower. It had allowed Siobhan to grow complacent. Sure, she'd been trying to prepare for every eventuality, but this problem had begun to seem less urgent. '*It's like the sword of Damocles, constantly hanging over me like a guillotine,*' she thought wearily.

When she finally made it into sight of the Mires, she dropped her glow spell to be less conspicuous. She wasn't alone in the streets, despite the late hour, and some of those who noticed her passing eyed her with predatory contemplation. '*Stumbling through the southern Mires so obviously alone—and wealthy, in this dress—is a great way to get stabbed and stripped naked, left to die in some unnamed alley.'*

She crouched down to retrieve the thin, hook-edged dagger from the calf of her boot, rolling her tired shoulders back and meeting the eyes of anyone who stared too long. This late at night, in this part of the city, there were no carriages she could flag down. She was so tired, and every joint in her body ached.

She tried to run coherently through her options. The safest place would be Liza's, but there was no guarantee the woman would be home this time, either. She could go to the Verdant Stag, but it was still a couple of kilometers away, and Siobhan didn't feel like she could manage even a few hundred more meters.

'*A safe house,*' she thought. Latching onto the idea, she combed through her memories and tried to place herself on the dense map of the city. There was a place close by.

She was still trying in vain to remember the password when she arrived fifteen or so minutes later, but when she saw the building, she remembered this location was unoccupied. She counted the bricks on the wall from the back door, seven over, six down, then pried off the facade, pulling out the rugged iron key and using it to let herself in.

After closing and locking the door behind herself, she dropped her satchel, leaned back, and slid down the door until she sat on the floor. She drew her cloak closer, hugging herself as she shivered from a combination of cold and bone-deep exhaustion. "I made it," she murmured. "Everything is still fine. Just a bit of extra exercise. Fekten would be so proud if he knew."

She planned to rest for a while and then continue on, thinking somewhere in the back of her mind that she would rise when dawn came and hurry back to the University before anyone important noticed that she had been gone.

Instead, crouched against the wood wall of an abandoned house, Siobhan fell asleep. Without the dreamless sleep spell to stop it, she dreamt.

Siobhan found herself in a diaphanous nightgown, her small brown feet peeking out under the hem, her toes dirty and soles calloused. She looked at her hands, noting their equally small—childlike—size, and the fact that she was having trouble counting exactly how many fingers she had. "Oh no," she muttered. Or maybe just thought. She couldn't quite be sure because her lips hadn't moved.

She was in her childhood house where she had stayed with Grandfather, in front of the tower room with the lead door. Her hand reached toward the doorknob and twisted, then pushed the heavy door open.

Siobhan kept her eyes down, her long dark hair falling forward to obscure her vision at the peripherals. Her bare feet passed over the sticky, red, fungus-like tendrils that had crept their way over the stone floor. They pulsed gently under her, warm and alive compared to the cool stone.

Though she tried to stop, or at least to slow herself, she walked to the center of the room, catching the edge of a mirror frame in her vision. She tried not to look, but she wasn't in control. The mirror, a rectangle taller than it was wide, was framed in smoldering brimstone, carved in the shape of twisted and elongated limbs, with disjointed fingers poking out here, a knee bent backwards there at the corner, and horribly mangled human feet at the bottom, as if they had been crushed under the monstrous weight of the mirror.

Siobhan's heart began to beat rapidly, dizzying her and leaving the edges of her vision blurry and dreamlike. Her eyes dragged themselves up to the reflection, which showed not her, but a window looking out over a surreal landscape that had been painted in muted earth tones and fog.

In the distance, hunched forms shuffled. As she stared, they became more defined.

"No, no," she pleaded, trying to wrench her focus away.

As if in answer to her desperate prayer, her eyes began to move again. But not away. Up—toward the top of the frame—and she couldn't stop them and she couldn't look away, but she knew that whatever she saw was going to be horrible, going to break her heart and wrench open her mind. She tried to scream, but what came out were just muted whimpers and whines, like a wounded animal.

Finally, the smoldering brimstone face at the top of the mirror came into view, bound into the frame.

Siobhan tried not to recognize it.

She reached up, ready to claw at her own eyes to stop herself from seeing. Just as her fingertips dug into their slimy wetness, she woke.

She was keening, low and strained, her cheek pressed against the wood panels of the floor. She jerked her head back and scrambled backward like a crab, slamming her head into the wall, her eyes still clenched shut. A few more keening moans slipped out of her before she had the wherewithal to clamp a hand over her mouth.

She flipped over onto her knees, pointing her feet so that she could fold forward over her legs until the top of her forehead made contact with the wooden floor again. She felt like she couldn't breathe, like she was suffocating, her heart pounding so hard, pumping so much blood that she started slipping around at the edge of consciousness, black and red washes spilling across the backs of her eyelids. *This is a panic attack,* she told herself. *Get control. Breathe. Count and hold.*

Slowly, much too slowly, she regained control of her body, calming enough to function, the involuntary reactions to panic ebbing away like a lazy tide, breath by breath. It could have been seconds or minutes, she couldn't tell.

'*I need the sleep-proxy spell,*' she told herself. '*It doesn't matter what I have to do. Development has to move forward.*'

She changed forms in the dark, fumbling with her clothing.

Climbing up to stand on trembling legs, she stumbled to the window shutter and opened it, letting in light and fresh air through the glassless frame. Some detached part of her noted the paleness and largeness of her hands. In some small way, it was a comfort, this sharp divide between reality and the dream. '*I'm Sebastien now,*' she thought with the smallest twitch of a humorless smile.

She had to admit to herself that she had probably always been going to give in to Liza, to set aside her qualms and whatever worth the life of a raven or a pixie or a monkey held. She had just been looking for a way to keep going past her own guilt and shame. Otherwise she wouldn't have only asked for time away to think, she would have made concrete promises about the lines she was not willing to cross.

'*If there was any other option, I would take it,*' Sebastien thought.

Tears welled up in her eyes and flowed down her cheeks, accompanied by a sharp, aching pain in her chest that made her want to wail and devolve into body-convulsing sobs at the unfairness of her life.

Instead, she kept breathing smoothly, pushing that feeling down until it reluctantly ebbed away. The tears didn't stop for a while, nor did the shivering.

51

FAUST

Sebastien
  Month 3, Day 16, Tuesday 5:00am

Sebastien hobbled out of the safe house, carefully locking the door behind herself and re-hiding the key. She walked slowly, allowing her stiff joints to ease as they warmed up. Despite her fatigue, she felt more comfortable out in the open than she had the night before. Most of those she passed now were laborers just starting their day, with the disquieting midnight crowd having slinked away at the earliest perceptible lightening of the sky. She didn't make it far before she smelled food, and her focus was drawn to a stall down the street, which was selling meat pies. Her stomach gurgled, and she felt another wave of nausea. *'I haven't eaten since yesterday afternoon,'* she realized. *'Perhaps some of my condition is simply due to requiring nourishment.'* She knew she could return to the University cafeteria and eat there, but the meat pies smelled so good.

'I still have plenty,' she remembered, taking a quick peek at the coins filling the bottom of the purse with a strange emotion. *'And there is more to come from the Gervin textile sub-commission.'* It was somehow difficult to reconcile, hard to believe, that she need not scrabble to save every copper. But the evidence was clear.

So she bought herself *two* meat pies, then savored them as she took a carriage to the northern transport tubes, which accepted her student token and sent her shooting up to the edge of the white cliffs.

Damien had noticed her absence from the dorms and been worried, but she explained that she'd been asked to run a small errand for their secret organization and then got stuck without transportation.

"Are you sure that's it?" he asked, tilting his head to the side. "You look... worn. Worried? It's nothing to do with Malcolm Gervin, is it?"

"No, nothing like that. I...well, you know I have trouble sleeping. It was a rough night." That was close enough to the truth that she didn't feel so bad lying in the face of his genuine concern.

Damien placed his hand on her shoulder. "I won't pry, but just know that if you ever want to talk about...anything, you can come to me." Without waiting for her response, he returned to his own cubicle.

Against all odds and sense, Sebastien made her way through the day's classes, then forced herself to catch up on sleep that evening. Her fatigue seemed to be a trigger for the beamshell cravings, and for the first time, she realized that sometimes Will alone might not be enough to persevere when everything inside you wanted to make a bad long-term choice for the benefit of temporary relief. Thankfully, she had thrown the beamshell tincture out, and trying to get more would require a complicated scheme involving forging a healer's prescription. Perhaps sensing her mood, Damien and Ana left her to her own devices.

After classes, she stopped by Liza's to tell her that she would continue to help with the sleep-proxy spell. Liza was...sympathetic, perhaps sensing how much Siobhan hated herself for this decision. But Siobhan didn't allow herself to take any comfort in Liza's affirmation that she was making the smart choice. Siobhan was willing to do whatever it took to achieve this goal, but that didn't make it right.

When Siobhan belatedly mentioned her failed attempt to destroy the coppers' blood sample, Liza snorted.

"Of course that didn't work, girl. You're slightly clever, not a trained expert. Did you expect that they would have no recourse against counter-divination methods developed during the Haze War?"

Siobhan flushed. *It does make sense that a method I got out of the first level University library would be deprecated. The coppers should be working with the most recent advancements and the best contracted casters.* It had been hubris to assume she could best them after less than a single term at the University.

"As I've mentioned before, I could solve this problem for you, for a fee. Your idea to target them while they are scrying for you was a good one, and with the right implementation, could make things much easier. There would be some problems to solve, such as ensuring your safety under wards while I handled their blood sample, and the fact that I cannot guarantee the destruction of all samples, only the one they are using. If they left some under the protective wards of Harrow Hill's evidence storage, your problem would remain unsolved."

Siobhan narrowed her eyes. "You quoted me eight hundred gold before. If I could tell you when they are scrying me—and *where* they are doing it from—would that make it easier... Enough, perhaps, to reduce the price to something reasonable?"

Liza rolled her eyes, took a moment to reluctantly consider it, and finally said, "Perhaps. No less than five hundred gold."

Siobhan hummed. "I'll think about that. Maybe there's a way to make it even easier. What if I lent you a sample to work with, too?" She wouldn't have considered such a thing normally, but Liza had no need of extra tricks if she wanted to harm Siobhan. She hadn't so far, after all, despite the bounty on the Raven Queen.

"We can talk about this again when you have the coin. *Five hundred,*" Liza repeated.

The possibility of purchasing help couldn't dispel Siobhan's dark mood, but the spark of an idea was growing.

As she left, she wondered, '*What do I do now?*' The answer that came to her had little to do with her current dilemma, but was instead a task that had been lingering in the back of her mind for months now, actively avoided with almost the same fervor that she avoided her dreams. She pulled out a tattered envelope from her bag. It contained only a simple address, one she'd long ago memorized.

That was how, after returning once more to the Silk Door, Sebastien found herself looking up at a building in Oliver's territory that had, only a couple of months before, been a brothel. It was nothing like the Silk Door. This building was a squat, run-down rectangle with only a few grungy windows.

The last couple of days had been warmer, and the stench of rot and waste was stronger in this area of the Mires. Oliver's vaunted cleaning crews hadn't made it here yet. When she opened her mouth to try and escape it, it coated the back of her mouth and throat instead, which was no better.

Steeling herself, Sebastien walked in the front door. The interior was packed with people, apparently gathering for dinner. Those without bowls of hearty seafood porridge stood in a haphazard line stretching toward the kitchen. The people were dirty, tired-looking, and distrustful, but at least not starving or freezing to death, and there was a single Stag enforcer to keep the peace between those both too desperate and packed too closely together for amity.

Sebastien managed to find someone who knew the Moore family after only a few attempts, which left her more disappointed than relieved. She had hoped they might have left for somewhere better, using the funds they got for allowing the investigation report to malign Newton to start a new life.

Both for their own sake and so that she might have an excuse not to face them.

Newton's mother, pointed out to Sebastien by her guide, was in the kitchen, ladling up soup for those in line. The woman looked haggard, and the rolled-back sleeves of her shirt openly displayed her burn-scarred forearms. She eyed Sebastien suspiciously. "How can I help you, my lord?"

Sebastien cleared her throat awkwardly. Her knees trembled a bit, and she stepped forward to disguise it. "Hello. Er, my name is Sebastien. I was a friend of Newton's."

The woman deflated immediately, though her expression didn't change at first, as if she was too tired to emote. She seemed to shake herself awake, standing straighter and setting the ladle down for one of the other kitchen helpers to take over before turning to Sebastien, her brows furrowed and jaw clenched. "A little late for this kind of thing, isn't it?" she asked.

Sebastien flushed bright red, her eyes fluttering closed in shame. "I know. I should have come earlier. I—I'm sorry. We did—a couple of my friends and I, we sent letters and a care package, when it first...when he first died. You did get it, didn't you?"

Newton's mother considered Sebastien for a moment, then softened. "I did. I suppose you'd better come on back, son. We can talk in my family's rooms."

The Moore family's quarters weren't as bad as Sebastien had feared, two rooms behind the kitchen that stayed a little warmer than the rest of the building, and with an actual lock on the hallway-facing door.

It seemed the whole family was packed together into those two rooms—a little cramped, but not worse than many of the rural farm homes she had seen in her time. Only here, there was no open space just outside the door, no fresh air or freedom. They were using a dying bottle of moonlight sizzle for light, because there was no window.

In the blue-tinted gloom within, an old woman huddled in the corner, staring at nothing—Newton's "Grams."

A man lay on the bottom bunk of two beds, asleep. The table beside him was filled with an array of potion vials, some empty. *'Newton's father. At least they have the means to afford healing for him.'*

Two younger girls looked up from practicing sums with an abacus in the corner.

Newton's mother stepped forward, snatching up the moonlight sizzle and shaking it harshly to try and eke out a bit more light from the bubbling bottle. "It's no mansion, but we can afford it while our house is being rebuilt, and I've got a job in the kitchens that pays a little extra."

"You did get enough...funds, then?" Sebastien asked hesitantly. "From the investigators."

"Well, *enough*," the woman agreed. "Both girls have been accepted into a school up on Lette Street, and the first year is already paid for, with enough left over for the house and the healer. My husband's had a bit of flare-up with the continued cold weather. His lungs have some scarring that settled before we were able to get him treatment, but it's nothing compared to the prognosis we were originally facing. It was actually your letter that did the most for us, though. Coal in the snowstorm, as they say, just enough to get by when we really needed it the most."

Sebastien swallowed, her eyes prickling with humiliation. That had been Alec and Damien's idea, really. She just contributed, and the letter she had written wasn't even the truth.

"Sebastien, was it? Terrible business, really, I—" The woman's voice broke, and she cleared her throat wetly. "Were you one of his classmates, then?"

"Yes. I—I just wanted to give my condolences," Sebastien said, knowing even as the words came out of her mouth that banalities like that never really helped, especially from strangers. She wasn't even quite sure they were *true*. '*Is that why I'm here? To say that I'm sorry?*' Since the moment when she crawled up off the furniture shop's floor and realized what had happened to Newton, she hadn't let herself sink into really thinking about it. It was impossible to avoid, now, looking at the people he'd left behind. Apologizing was rather useless, just sentiment. What was really important was the resolution to do better.

She could console herself with the fact that she had never lied to Newton or tried to coerce him into doing anything dangerous. He had known going with Tanya would be a risk, and he had known there could be greater reward in it, too. Perhaps he hadn't truly understood what he was getting himself into. Or perhaps he had just been too desperate to decline. If she hadn't pulled him into this whole thing in the first place, he would undoubtedly be alive. Hells, if she hadn't gotten caught and allowed that whole fiasco with the Morrows, if she hadn't frightened him to death with her shadow-familiar spell…

Sebastien had known since she was young that anything she cared about, she had to take responsibility for. There was no use in blaming anyone else when things went wrong, just as she couldn't depend on anyone else to make things go right. *She* was the only thing she controlled. Her, and her magic.

If she could have done something differently to change the outcome, and she didn't, then it was her fault. Pretending the weight of responsibility didn't land on her just because she was too tired to admit it, to accept it, was weakness. It was a deflection. Newton coming to harm wasn't unforeseeable. She'd chosen to involve him anyway. Other people, even he himself, had chosen to go along with it. But no one else's culpability lessened her own.

She swallowed hard past the lump in her throat. She had facilitated

Newton's break, his death. And maybe there were things she could have done to better prepare him. Ways she could have mitigated the danger. She would keep this failure in mind for the future. But she couldn't pretend that she would never place someone else in harm's way again. The world was dangerous. She wasn't powerful enough to control everything. And sometimes things spiraled out of her control and people got hurt. She was responsible, but she wasn't *to blame*. She wouldn't put this, at least, on herself. Not all of it.

"I am sorry," she said. "For your loss. Newton didn't deserve what happened to him." And it was true.

"Oh, thank you child." His mother pulled over the room's single small stool and waved for Sebastien to take it, perching herself on the edge of her husband's bed instead. "It was a horrible shock. I mean, I noticed he was getting a little too interested in magics better left alone, but I never thought —" She pressed her fingers to her lips, shaking her head as her eyes grew glassy.

Sebastien frowned.

"He fell in with a bad crowd," the grandmother said from the corner, still staring into the air.

"Yes," his mother said, "but we never expected him to dabble in whatever corrupted magic transformed him into a creature of evil—one of those Aberrants."

In the corner, one of the girls began crying softly. "It wasn't his fault. I know it!" she said.

The mother shook her head sadly. "He did what he did, Beshi. Sometimes you don't know people as well as you think. Maybe it was our situation that pushed him to it in desperation."

Sebastien opened her mouth, closed it, then shook her head. "Umm…well, I don't think that's exactly true."

The father had woken at some point and struggled to sit up. Newton's mother hurried to help him. "What do you mean?" he asked.

"Newton did get caught up in things that were too much for him to handle," Sebastien said, "but he wasn't doing anything…*depraved*. It was the circumstances that caused his break, not a corrupted Will."

The man shook his head, but started coughing. After that, he seemed too blearily exhausted to continue contributing to the conversation.

His mother frowned at Sebastien. "He was dabbling in magics better left alone."

"No. He was casting a completely harmless self-calming spell when it happened. He taught it to me at school, and I've cast it myself several times. He said his grandmother taught it to him." She looked to the woman in the corner, who seemed to focus for the first time, meeting Sebastien's eyes. This was information that she shouldn't have, perhaps, but she couldn't let them go on believing a lie about their dead son.

"He wasn't, and then suddenly he was," the decrepit woman said. "He wasn't, and then he was, like a sick wind."

Sebastien's hand had fallen to the pocket where she normally kept her Conduit, and she forced herself to settle both hands in her lap, not wanting to be rude. She felt uneasy, as if she were standing at the edge of the white cliffs above the sea, and the wind was a little too strong for safety.

"I don't think that's true at all. He got involved with something over his head, and it was too much for him and he broke, but he wasn't doing anything nefarious. He was captured, along with some other University students, and threatened by the Morrows." She swallowed hard to push past her tightening throat as the vow she'd given to the Red Guard tried to restrict her. "There was fighting. He wasn't even involved. Just an innocent casualty," she finished quickly, before it could stop her.

"I knew it!" the crying girl said. "I knew he wouldn't!"

His father frowned severely. "Are you sure? But that can't be—" He was cut off by another coughing fit, wet and painful-sounding.

"That—" His mother was shaking her head, over and over, touching her ear as if she'd gotten water trapped inside it. "That can't be. Newton—my son, my son was dabbling in magics better left alone. He was dabbling."

Sebastien's back muscles were tightening almost painfully with how straight she was sitting. Looking around the windowless room, she suddenly felt claustrophobic.

The father's coughing fit went on and on until he was red-faced and teary-eyed, struggling to draw breath.

His wife hurried to uncork one of the potions on his bedside table and help him drink it, calming his coughs but also drawing his eyelids down into heavy, sleepy blinks.

"The scarring is treatable, but it's a painful, expensive process. We're hoping things will get better once it warms up around here," she explained, as if fearful of judgment.

Sebastien shifted uncomfortably. "Why do you think that Newton was dabbling in corrupted magics? Did he ever mention something like that to you?"

"No, of course not!" the woman snapped. "But he was. I *know* it."

Sebastien swallowed. "*How* do you know it?"

The woman pressed her hand over her mouth again, shaking her head rapidly while looking toward the ground.

Sebastien looked between the father and the grandmother. "Is there any actual evidence that he was doing something nefarious? Did the coppers tell you that?"

The grandmother spoke up again. "He was innocent, and then, suddenly, he wasn't. And we knew it."

Sebastien went cold. "When did you know?" she asked, her lips numb as the words passed over them.

"Few weeks ago. Maybe a couple months."

"And around the time when you suddenly *knew*, did someone visit you? Someone who asked questions about Newton? Any thaumaturges?" Sebastien's voice grew unconsciously softer, as if she were afraid of someone overhearing her. She looked around to all the family members packed into the small room.

They looked confused, shaking their heads, except for the grandmother. "I definitely did not meet anyone who wanted to change my mind about little Newt. Definitely."

That was a little too specific, and a little too sure.

Sebastien supposed if someone had put a geas or similar magic on her, forcing her to believe something, then forced her to forget about that, too, she might be able to suss out what had changed. She would need to be able to recognize that what she believed now was suddenly and inexplicably different than what she'd believed before, without any new evidence to create the shift.

She would ask herself who had done this to Grams, or when it had been done, and find an answer that she was strangely, absurdly sure *wasn't* correct. This belief would have no corroborating evidence. And so, the one that felt least likely was, conversely, most likely to be the answer.

It's what Newton's Grams had been hinting at from the beginning. Sebastien supposed that, being a thaumaturge, even a weak one, Grams' mind was more resistant to whatever had been done to them. At least whoever had tinkered with their brains had spared the two children, though she didn't know if that was because they had a sense of ethics or if they just thought it didn't matter because no one would believe a child, anyway.

"Has anyone suspicious been hanging around? Or anyone who definitely *isn't* suspicious?"

None of the Moores remembered anything, though Sebastien was sure she couldn't trust their judgment on the matter. Sebastien attempted to keep digging, asking increasingly specific questions in an attempt to reverse-engineer the answers, but within minutes Newton's mother and both sisters had collapsed into frustrated, confused tears, and the grandmother had begun to bang the back of her head against the wall, staring at nothing as she repeated, "I know it, I know it," over and over.

Knowing that her absence would likely do more to calm them than anything else she might attempt, Sebastien retreated, feeling like she was escaping as she stepped into the light outside. She couldn't help looking around suspiciously, paranoid that whoever had done this to the Moores was watching. *'Is there anything that's suddenly changed about my own beliefs? Anything that I'm strangely sure of?'* She tried to rifle through her thoughts in search of concerning signs but found nothing. She didn't know if that meant she was fine, or just really bad at noticing whatever geas had been placed on her.

'Could this have anything to do with the investigation into the Raven Queen? But that doesn't make sense. How would doing this help the investigation? And if they got to his family, who else?'

She hailed the first carriage and took it straight back to the University. Professor Lacer wasn't in his office, but she remembered where his cottage was. She hurried east across the grounds, and, when she found it, pounded on the door.

Professor Lacer opened it with a thunderous scowl. "What is the meaning of this?" he snapped.

"I need to speak with you."

He looked her over, his concern both obvious and somewhat surprising. "Is this about what happened over the weekend? Did the Raven Queen contact you?"

"What? No! I need to speak with you," she repeated. "Privately."

His gaze swept over the grounds behind her, but he stepped back and let her in. "What is the matter?"

"Do you remember the night that Newton Moore broke? *All* of it?"

He leaned forward, his gaze piercing. "I do. Have you remembered something relevant about the incident?"

"No. This is about... I went to visit his family." She took a deep breath, watching him carefully as she said, "I believe Newton broke while casting a simple self-calming spell. Esoteric, vibration-based. Not corrupted in nature. It was an unfortunate accident. Do you agree?"

"I do."

She sagged with relief. "Oh, thank the stars above."

"What are you getting at?"

"Someone has tampered with the minds of Newton Moore's family. Poorly. They now believe he was involved in some sort of blood magic, and that's what caused his break. I worry the same might have been done to some of the students in his term. The ones who gave those statements about him."

Professor Lacer leaned back. "Is that all?"

"Well...yes." She rocked back on her heels. *'Isn't that enough?'*

"I thought it would be something much more dramatic, with how anxious you were. Still, you did the right thing in making me aware. Sloppy work, to make it so obvious. I will send them back to do a better job."

"Who?" she asked, her voice barely a whisper.

"The Red Guard, of course. Sometimes memetic spells, when cast incorrectly, will start to fray and show their holes over time as the brain picks at their edges."

Sebastien had gone cold inside. She felt suddenly, starkly unsafe. "And why did the Red Guard do this?"

"To control public perception, of course." He raised a hand to stop her, as if she had been going to protest. "I know that is not the answer you seek, but if you wish to dig deeper, you should do so on your own. Some answers are best discovered yourself, if you wish to ever truly understand them. But...be cautious. You do not want to draw so much negative attention that you receive a visit yourself."

Sebastien hadn't known it before, but there had been some sense of security granted by the structure of society, the supposed duties of the Crowns and the Red Guard toward the citizens. She had thought her own model of the way the world worked to be correct. And despite his caustic nature, she had believed in the bulwark of her professor, Thaddeus Lacer, against danger.

And in a handful of sentences, that naivety had been stripped from her.

52

POST MORTEM

Sebastien
Month 3, Day 16, Tuesday 7:00pm

After receiving some more cutting commentary about her involvement with Ana's dangerous scheme, Sebastien left Professor Lacer's house, trying to offer as little indication as possible about just how shaken she was. She moved mindlessly, and found her feet had taken her back to the dorms without her conscious input.

In the cubicle across from her, Ana threw open the curtain and gave Sebastien a bright smile, holding up an extra-large envelope thick with paper. "Signed and sealed," she said with a dramatic wink, handing the envelope to Sebastien. "I thought you could deliver it to Lord Dryden yourself."

Sebastien took it numbly. "Thank you."

Ana's excitement fell away. "Is something wrong?"

Sebastien looked around, noting the surreptitious glances of the nearby students. She had no intention of speaking about what she'd learned of the Red Guard, and by association, Professor Lacer, lest she too be subjected to invasive fingers tampering with her thoughts and memories. Even the notion sent a cold shudder rippling up her spine until her scalp tingled. Her heartbeat was too loud, and her armpits and palms were damp with sweat.

The pause after Ana's question had drawn on too long, and the other young woman took her by the arm and dragged her into the cubicle. Ana drew the curtain closed, ignoring the sudden explosion of scandalized murmuring around them.

Sebastien rolled her eyes. "You've taken me into your boudoir, Ana. We must be having a salacious affair."

Normally this would have amused Ana, but she waved her hand in irritation as she activated a privacy artifact that ran around the length of the cubicle's walls. "What happened?" she asked soberly.

Sebastien considered trying to lie, but she knew that Ana was much better at reading people than Sebastien was at lying. If Ana was already asking, it was too late to seem normal. Instead, after a moment of hesitation, Sebastien said, "Something disturbing happened. I...learned something I wish weren't true. And I don't want to talk about it."

Ana stared at her for a moment, searching Sebastien's eyes, and then simply nodded. "Alright then." Pulling a box of expensive candies from her bedside drawer, she handed one to Sebastien. "So, did you hear about the feud going on between Mischner and Letty? Mischner got caught trying to spike Letty's food, and it's probably because Mischner's worried about being in the bottom ten percent of the class. Mischner got a demerit, but Letty wasn't satisfied because she felt that such a light punishment was blatant favoritism, so she wrote to Mischner's father..."

'*I have good friends,*' Sebastien realized, swallowing down the lump in her throat. For once, she was grateful for Ana's tendency to gossip, and tried to genuinely listen and remember who the people were, sinking into this alternate reality where the latest scandal was actually important.

Sebastien went through the next day feeling like she was being watched. Unfortunately, this was true, as the rumor mill had begun to churn with interest in her and her friends again. The whole Gervin Family debacle was blowing up. Even Ana, who said that this publicity was good for her future prospects and would allow her to more easily forge her own path once she took over the lordship, found it wearying, her smiles growing more and more perfect as their fellow students began to grate on her.

Damien and the rest of the group didn't even bother to smile, circling up around their more vulnerable members like a group of wagoners defending against wolves.

During Practical Casting, Sebastien examined Professor Lacer for any hint of the outcome with the Moore family's mind control, but he seemed the same as ever. She considered just asking him about it, but decided against it. She had been growing comfortable with him, but that was gone.

Finding herself antsy but at a loss as to what to actually *do*, she decided to take the textile sub-commission down to Oliver at the Verdant Stag. As the saying went, "Money doesn't solve all problems, but it at least solves money problems." And really, with the right attitude, quite a lot of things could be "money problems."

On a sudden whim, she stopped by a licensed apothecary and bought herself a mild detoxifying potion that was safe to take even without healer supervision. She could have bought one at the Verdant Stag apothecary, but chose not to for two simple reasons. First, she didn't know if the little shop was still up and running after the attack. But mostly, she didn't want anyone to know that she needed it. The potion was unreasonably expensive, but it was worth it to help heal whatever subtle damage she'd done to herself, with the added benefit of smoothing over the cravings she was *still* having.

She disguised herself fully once more, but still wore her hood up to conceal her features in case the coppers were tracking who came and went from the Verdant Stag. Siobhan had fake identification papers, but didn't know how well they would hold up if the coppers wanted to question or arrest her. If they didn't cast any divinations, she would probably get through it safely, but she couldn't count on that.

The Verdant Stag's repairs were already well under way. The newly constructed sections of the building looked even nicer—and much sturdier—than they originally had. Workers with supplies both magical and mundane scurried everywhere, and the noise required one to shout to be heard.

Katerin was there amongst the hubbub, looming over Theo with one arm pointed imperiously up the stairs to her office.

The boy crawled out from underneath the floorboards, which were being replaced with a thick stone tile, his head and shoulders drooping with comical dejection as he shuffled away. As soon as he caught sight of Siobhan, he perked up, totally rejuvenated.

Katerin followed his gaze to Siobhan, then sighed and waved her over, moving to follow Theo.

They met at the bottom of the stairs.

"I only have a couple weeks to go until I've earned enough for my utility wand!" Theo quickly announced, beaming.

Katerin eyed him dourly. "You forgot that you'll be fined for escaping Mr. Mawson's lessons both yesterday and today."

Theo deflated again. "But how am I supposed to concentrate with everything going on? It's so loud, and everything down here is so much more interesting than doing fractions and writing essays about the government. It's not fair! If you really want me to learn, one would *think* you'd get me a more interesting tutor." He looked to Siobhan expectantly. "You think so too, right?"

"It is important to make learning fun," she agreed. "But most children need external motivation because they can't maintain interest in the whole spectrum of required subjects."

"External motivation, like being paid to save up for a battle wand," Katerin said pointedly.

"Perhaps extra credit, for intellectual work that Theo finds interesting?" Siobhan offered.

This devolved into Theo throwing out ideas about essays he could write, ranging from "the Raven Queen's true powers," to "best practices for solo-hunting magical beasts."

Katerin promised only that she would consider it, then sent Theo off to her office alone while the two women continued up the stairs. "It's been a bit busy, but I think we should sit down and talk with Oliver. There have been some…interesting developments. As an aside, you might be interested to know that Enforcer Gerard survived, thanks to a powerful healing potion that cost about three months of his wages and which he has submitted a reimbursement request for. His legs will require rehabilitation, and he's made some inquisitive comments about possibly owing a debt to the Raven Queen." Seeing Siobhan's face, Katerin laughed. "Do not worry so much, girl. He doesn't buy into *all* the stories. He was around to watch you from the beginning, after all. I think he just wants to thank you for your help. As do I."

Siobhan looked away awkwardly. "Um. You're welcome."

Katerin nodded solemnly. "I will pass that along."

They had to wait outside Oliver's office, as one of the higher-level enforcers was giving him a report, and two other people were already waiting for a moment of Oliver's time. Katerin sat and immediately focused on a folder full of her own reports, ignoring the world. '*If his Verdant Stag office is going to be this busy, Oliver should get a secretary and put in a little waiting area with chairs,*' Siobhan mused, trying to keep her thoughts from turning back to the Moore family.

When they finally entered, Katerin closed the door behind them, suddenly and obviously dampening the cacophony of shouting and hammering that filled the rest of the building. But the chaos had made its way inside anyway, in the scattered papers over Oliver's desk and some of the chairs, the stubble on his jaw, and the dark circles under his bloodshot eyes. But despite all this, his shoulders were squared, his eyes quick and alert, and his mouth was set in a grim, determined line. No hint of defeat hung about him.

As they sat in the plush chairs before Oliver's desk, he moved to the front and leaned against it, ankles crossed and hands in his pockets. He stared at the floor for a few moments before lifting his head. "First, let me say that I believe the Architects of Khronos were behind the attack on Knave Knoll."

Siobhan blinked. "Okay…? Was that ever in question?" She looked to Katerin to share her confusion.

The woman snorted, playing with the tip of her single, blood-red braid. "Exactly."

Siobhan looked back at Oliver. "Does this have anything to do with what Tanya was talking about?"

"It does," Oliver said. "Shortly after the attack and its…spectacular failure, costing numerous enemy lives while freeing none of the Morrows, Grandmaster Kiernan reached out to me to affirm that the whole thing was a surprise to him as well."

"But you don't actually *believe* that," Siobhan blurted.

Oliver just smiled. "Supposedly, Kiernan had recently been contacted by a powerful man with some sort of allegiance to the Morrows. He tried to blackmail Kiernan into helping free them, under threat of releasing information about the activities of the Architects of Khronos to concerned parties in the Thirteen Crown Families. Kiernan maintains that he denied him, but when the man somehow found out about the prisoner transport, he went to Kiernan with an ultimatum. Work together on the attack, or all the information would be released. Instead, Kiernan killed him and sent Miss Canelo to warn us, but everything was already in motion, and she was too late to help.

"And Miss Canelo corroborates this story. As far as I know, she even put herself in danger multiple times during the battle in attempts to help our side. Personally, she expressed relief to me that Kiernan and his people had finally seen reason after their previous stubborn antagonism."

Siobhan's eyes narrowed. "It's very *convenient* that the supposed blackmailer both cannot blackmail any more, and also cannot speak about Kiernan's involvement."

Katerin snapped her fingers and pointed at Siobhan. "Again, exactly. Even more convenient that this Kiernan supposedly knew where Knave Knoll was all along, but didn't do anything with that information until it was necessary to 'help us.' He would have done better to claim that his blackmailer told him the location at the last minute."

Oliver shrugged. "Well, Kiernan was acting under pressure. To clarify, I believe this Morrow ally was real, because upon his death, he had multiple failsafes in place that really did attempt to release damning information about the Architects of Khronos. Those attempts were quickly quashed by the Architects, of course. However, contrary to what Kiernan claims, I believe he went along with this man's demands from the beginning, and was likely even the driving force behind the decision to attack the Verdant Stag. Freeing the prisoners wasn't his main goal; that was simply a convenient distraction for his attempt on the book. Tanya was sent to warn us, but he never expected her to succeed. More likely, he was sending her to die while creating some insurance for himself in case things went wrong. Which they did. And so, when he got word of how disastrously the entire plan failed—"

Katerin snickered, interjecting, "Particularly, the rumors that a woman who looks suspiciously like the Raven Queen appeared out of the darkness behind our fleeing people and called down a magical attack from the heavens that was so powerful and twisted that it left remnants behind for hours, like the Black Wastes themselves had manifested in the middle of Gilbratha…" Her bright white smile stood out sharply against her red lips, and there was a dark rage there that Siobhan had never seen in it before. Katerin did not take kindly to being attacked, it seemed.

Siobhan groaned. "So, I really was recognized?"

Oliver rocked one hand side to side. "I wouldn't say that, exactly. Maybe some of our people have suspicions, but no one has been throwing around any civilian names. You have to realize how big this little folk legend of the Raven Queen has grown. When spectacular things happen, her name is easily attached. Especially because she has been known to protect the Stags before, in equally fantastical ways. In any case, when he heard the news, Kiernan quickly pivoted to try to avoid blame and retaliation."

Siobhan leaned back in her chair, toying with her Conduit. "Does he really think we're so stupid?"

Katerin barked out a laugh.

"Kiernan isn't so foolish. But at this point, when antagonism has failed so spectacularly and danger comes from multiple directions, he has little other choice. It's a gamble without downsides. But in a way, this works out best for us. As I mentioned, Kiernan's blackmailer had a deadman's switch to send out damning information on their activities, which was very useful in drawing the coppers' attention toward them, and off of us."

"What were their activities?" Siobhan asked.

Katerin answered. "They seem to be preparing for a power struggle against the Crowns. Whether that should come from direct warfare or through political and commercial pressure, we're not sure. But the Crowns hold certain powers over the University that restrict their freedom, and it seems these restrictions have chafed some beyond their tolerance. The Architects of Khronos pull members from more than just a disgruntled faculty, I am sure, but we are still trying to uncover more."

Oliver pushed himself off the desk, moving to one of the shelves along the wall, where a small box sat. He opened it and removed a small vial of clear liquid from within, using the attached pipette to place a single drop in each of his bloodshot eyes. He let out a breath of relief. "I have spent the majority of my time these last few days mobilizing every resource at my disposal to turn the massive beast that is Gilbrathan law enforcement toward the Architects of Khronos. What happened at Knave Knoll was far beyond gang action. People are going to look at the gigantic hole in the warehouse district where a building used to be, and hear about the lingering magical effects on the canal, and they're going to see a terrorist attack."

The words chilled Siobhan. Some time ago, a group of thaumaturges deliberately turned an Aberrant loose in the heart of a city, earning the wrath of both the public and the authorities. They'd been convicted of terrorism and publicly executed—by being dragged through the streets while people lobbed balls of burning pitch at them. Such attacks were *not* treated lightly. "It's going to have serious repercussions." She had known that, but this put things in a different perspective.

Even Katerin's vindictive amusement had sobered. "That is why it doesn't matter how friendly this Kiernan tries to be, after his betrayal. Even if he were to work with us in good faith from now on, it is too late. The Verdant Stag cannot bear the weight of responsibility for this."

Oliver took out a pouch of dried berries and meat and shoved a handful into his mouth. He chewed for a moment, then swallowed and continued talking. "I wanted to work together with the Architects. If not directly against the Thirteen Crowns, then at least supporting each other's defiance out of convenience. But instead, it is going to be each beast fighting alone. I hope to put enough emphasis on the Architects and their potential threat that we seem like a small catch in comparison. And while they fight with the Thirteen Crowns, the Verdant Stag can dig itself in and continue to grow."

"How likely do you think that is to work?" Siobhan asked.

"Very. The coppers will have released their report about the forces behind the attack a few hours ago. You should see emergency extras coming from the newspapers by this evening. While the upheaval and conflict this will cause is not ideal, I felt there was little other option. However, this method also comes with risks. Attempting to influence the coppers necessarily allows them some influence on me in turn. They've already begun trying to pressure me to help them retrieve the stolen book through my obvious connection with the Raven Queen."

Siobhan tensed.

He noticed, waving his hand to stop her from jumping to any conclusions. "So, I would suggest the Raven Queen stay out of the public eye, indefinitely. Perhaps even Silvia Nakai should cease her activities, as things seem to go so easily wrong around you."

'*Things go wrong when I work with* you!' she protested mentally, but, though she was sure it was clear on her face, she didn't say anything out loud.

He took another bite of the dried food. "The Verdant Stag's resources are expanding to the point that we have many options to deal with various difficulties without you, so settling down as Sebastien Siverling shouldn't be a problem."

Siobhan peered into the depths of her Conduit while she thought about this, unable to quell a sense of foreboding at being cast aside, even though this was what she'd wanted. '*I'll be safe,*' she reassured herself. '*I have no need of the coin, and I'm not so altruistic as to sacrifice my well-being or my life for Oliver's ideals.'* And to make this thought a reality, she reached into her bag, which had undergone a quick color-change along with the rest of her transformation as a stopgap until she could buy a replacement.

She pulled out the envelope that contained Oliver's sub-commission to produce textiles in the name of the Gervin Family, Fourth Crown of Lenore. "That seems reasonable, especially since I have some good news, which will bring me the funds I need to focus solely on learning."

Oliver stared intently at the envelope, then broke the seal and took out the contract from within, skimming over it until his eyes rested on Lord Gervin's signature and stamp at the end, right above Oliver's own. "The terms are even better than what I initially negotiated with him," he murmured. He threw back his head and laughed, loud and joyful, then reached out and yanked Siobhan to her feet, pulling her into his embrace as he half-leaned, half-danced from side to side.

Siobhan was horribly startled and embarrassed, peeking around to look at Katerin, but the older woman was smiling indulgently, and Siobhan couldn't help but smile, too.

Oliver drew back, holding her shoulders, his smile so wide his eyes crinkled almost all the way closed. "You've done it! Oh, Siobhan, you have no idea the difference this is going to make. Our cloth is going to spread across the entire continent. We will employ thousands and clothe hundreds of thousands. And that is just the first step. In a few years, the Verdant Stag will have grown larger than any Crown Family, with the power of the common people behind us, feeding us even as we feed them in an endless cycle. I am going to take over Gilbratha, and then Lenore." He threw back his head to crow at the sky. "I am going to take over the *world!*"

She laughed. "The entire world?"

Oliver waved a hand nonchalantly, releasing her and moving back around his desk to place the contract carefully in the center, like a babe in its cradle. "Well, that may be a bit of an exaggeration. At the very least, Lenore will become the hub of power for the entire continent, and a refuge of freedom and opportunity for those who feel persecuted in their homelands." He smiled at her once more, softer this time. "I made a good move saving you from the coppers all those months ago. In some ways, it feels like so long has passed since then, and so much has happened. But in other ways, I feel as if I met you just yesterday. Do you know how startled I was when you suddenly turned into a strange young man? I was actually quite worried about the extremely powerful sorcerer I seemed to have gotten myself involved with, though I tried to put on a confident front."

Siobhan smirked wryly. "I assure you, no matter how worried you were, I was much more terrified and in over my head." She fidgeted then, her smirk falling away as she remembered that Oliver didn't know about the latest scrying attempt on her.

She was loath to dampen the wonderful mood, but this wasn't something she could put off mentioning.

Oliver sat back down, sobering slowly as she spoke.

Katerin groaned and rubbed her temples, glaring at Siobhan with exasperation, as if this was somehow *her* fault.

Siobhan glared back, suddenly remembering that this was the woman who had fooled her into accepting a loan with fifty percent interest. Repaying said loan was what had led to this escalation in the first place. If not for that, she could have disappeared into Sebastien Siverling almost completely.

Oliver tapped an agitated finger against the side of his desk. "You couldn't have left some other piece of yourself behind during the fighting, could you?"

"It's possible, of course, but I was cautious about that possibility. And there were so many people losing blood, it seems unlikely they would have collected all the samples and then performed a scrying spell of such overwhelming power on each."

He steepled his fingers together, pressing them against his mouth for a few long moments. "I think you need to approach this problem from a different angle," he finally said, seeming self-satisfied about whatever idea he'd had and basking in her undivided attention. "Rather than simply defend against attacks in the hope that someday you might be able to take away their leverage, why not create a scapegoat? You could make them believe they've succeeded in finding the Raven Queen in a way that separates you from their investigation. Or, and this is my preferred method, you send them off after a decoy. One they also can't catch, but that will keep them occupied and distract them from realizing they should look in your direction."

He kept talking, offering some vague ideas for how she might go about this, but Siobhan could no longer parse his words into anything coherent.

She looked from his bright eyes, to his expressive mouth, to his long fingers, and back again, searching for meaning. There was something, some hint of his body language or smugness in his tone, that tugged on the memory of him talking with Katerin after the attack, so pleased that the Architects of Khronos hadn't found what they were looking for.

Perhaps it was just intuition, or inspiration, but she realized with a sickening shift as the world ripped itself out from underneath her feet, that maybe Oliver had carried out this exact idea already. With Myrddin's book. The same book she had accidentally assisted in stealing, and which the coppers and the University had been coming after her for all along.

They couldn't catch her, but they were occupied, and looking in the wrong direction.

53

—————

EPIPHANY

SIOBHAN
  Month 3, Day 17, Wednesday 6:00pm

SOMEHOW, Siobhan was able to hold her tongue.

In a way, it was one of the hardest things she had ever done. She wanted to ask Oliver what he had that the University hadn't found. She wanted to confirm her suspicions. She also wanted to flip over his desk, pin him to the wall with her forearm, and scream for him to tell her the truth.

In another way, however, the enormity of this suspicion, this revelation, went beyond any pain her tongue could inflict in return. Words felt too inadequate a response, and that helped her suppress them entirely.

So instead, Siobhan thanked Oliver and Katerin, made some flimsy excuse, and left with her gold, the papers proving that Sebastien Siverling was a four percent shareholder in Oliver's textile company. She stayed only long enough to make sure both copies of the blood print vow she'd made with Katerin were ash.

She lost time to the swirling maelstrom of her thoughts, her focus returning first at the Silk Door, as she checked in the mirror to make sure she had returned to Sebastien's form properly, and then again when she stepped from the clear transport tube onto the edge of the white cliffs.

The sight of the Citadel in the distance, partially concealed by the trees growing between her and the building, calmed something in her. '*No matter what, I am a student here. I made it in, and I am learning to be a free-caster.*' But that only reminded her of what she had recently learned about Thaddeus Lacer. In the space of a single day, the foundation of trust and security she had slowly begun to rely on had been ripped out from under her. Feeling physically off-kilter, she paused for a moment, pressing her hand against a tree trunk for support. She focused on the sensation of rough bark against her skin, taking in the scent of wood and earth and the ozone of a coming storm, allowing the physical input to ground her mind.

Instead of returning to the dorms or the library, she walked east along the edge of the cliff. After a few minutes, she found a secluded spot beyond the transport tubes and out of sight of the buildings. Clustered behind her, stoic evergreens mingled with trees budding green from their skeletal branches. The cold wind rattled through the winter-bare branches and scraped against the cliffside, causing a disorienting echo all around her. The sensation was only made more uncomfortable by the wind's grasping fingers in her clothes and hair as it shoved against her back, almost as if to drive her over the edge.

In the west, the sun was setting, spilling its red-orange rays like blood across the city that stretched out below, but above them both, the dark clouds of a storm were brewing.

Sebastien did not move. A fire in her chest warmed her from the inside, flushing her cheeks, lending strength to her legs and steel to her spine. She would not yield.

She turned her mind to the evidence. She'd made an intuitive leap, but she needed to sit down and rationally consider the information that her subconscious mind had collected. Perhaps she was simply jumping to conclusions because she was so unused to trusting people.

The first piece of evidence that she considered was the conversation Oliver had with Katerin after returning to the Verdant Stag, which he probably had not thought Siobhan awake to overhear. He had something valuable in a hidden vault inside a folded space. Something more valuable than the censer, estimated at a thousand gold.

He had deduced that the Architects of Khronos had attacked Knave Knoll partially as a distraction while they sent another group to the Verdant Stag in search of the book. Which made sense. But the real book was hidden at Dryden Manor. His house had wards, but nothing like this secret vault, and he had never seemed particularly interested in where she was keeping the book, nor suggested that she should move it to this extremely secure location.

'*Would I have agreed to let it out of my control like that, if he had offered?*' she wondered. But no, that wasn't the point. He had never seemed interested in her book at all. Not even just to take a look at it. To her knowledge, the book had been safe and untouched by any other the entire time. Even if he didn't want it or the knowledge it contained for himself, he could have turned it in to the University or the Crowns for a huge negotiated payment. He could have said that he tracked down and killed the thief for the reward, thus absolving her of any suspicion while keeping himself relatively clear of the fallout.

He had even discouraged her from turning it in herself, for reasons that might have been valid but could also just be an excuse.

She remembered the secretive, smug tone of Oliver's voice when he had been discussing the Architects' failure with Katerin. The two of them shared a secret. Sebastien knew Oliver wasn't obligated to share all his secrets with her, but this felt important. He had said "*all* their efforts" were futile, not just that night's attack.

What if Oliver had taken something else from the same archaeological haul? An artifact, or Myrddin's famous Conduit, or a different book. What better decoy for a missing book than another book, after all? But all the evidence pointed to her book being Myrddin's real journal, as well as the item everyone was searching for. She didn't think someone else could have created the transformation amulet, and Damien had mentioned to her that as far as the coppers knew, even the History department was having trouble decrypting the other texts they had retrieved.

'*But how likely is it that two things could go missing, and they only notice one? If they were looking for something besides my book, wouldn't someone have mentioned it at some point?*' But then, if the gossip was to be believed, most of the members of the original expedition had died, and the three who remained had all been admitted to an asylum or some such place.

Any theft other than her book had to have been completed before the items were delivered to the University, and if everyone who was there in the Black Wastes to see exactly what they retrieved was either dead or insane…

Sebastien shuddered. She had previously dismissed the idea that Ennis was compelled to steal the book, when the alternative explanation was so simple. But what if it wasn't so outlandish a claim? Had someone sent Ennis to jail for a crime not entirely of his own choice?

She wanted to believe that Oliver had never meant to set her, or anyone else, up for a decoy theft. Even if he had stolen something from the expedition, perhaps he had meant for its absence to go unnoticed, or to remain a mysterious disappearance.

She wanted to believe that he had been genuinely acting to help her all along. Because, really, she had needed him, provider of coin and connections, so much more than he needed her, an inexperienced and weak sorcerer with a huge target on her back. He had genuinely seemed to care for her wellbeing.

'*The first night I met Oliver, when he came to rescue me from the coppers, why did he do that?*' He had gone out of his way to offer his help, and on rather short notice, at that. She closed her eyes and searched her memory for detail. '*He asked about the book, and specifically my ability to decrypt it. He was looking for a powerful sorcerer who would have had reason to steal it—exactly what everyone thought*

I was. And when I later asked him why he was doing so much to help me... He seemed irritated. He turned the question around on me, telling me not to be so self-absorbed. And he specifically mentioned that I was not special to him for some nefarious hidden reason. That he was helping me simply because he felt like doing so.'

Sebastien rubbed at her breastbone, as if pressure could take away some of the ache beneath it. *'Why would he word it like that? What if the real reason isn't so innocent?'* She had previously speculated that the book held some important knowledge lost to time, such as advanced self-charging artifacts. If Oliver had something similar, perhaps he had been looking for her, or a potential employer behind her, because he hoped to collaborate on reverse-engineering some artifact, or decrypting some text of his own. Otherwise, why would that have been his first question? And why would he have kept her around when she couldn't satisfy his hopes? Perhaps he had been secretly trying to decrypt Myrddin's journal when she wasn't around.

'On the other hand, if he did steal something, and I am just a decoy, wouldn't it make sense to distance himself from me rather than associate so closely, and with both *my iden-tities? All three, if you count Silvia.'* After all, association with her was what got the Verdant Stag raided and how he almost lost whatever was kept in the ultra-secure folded-space vault.

But maybe he felt guilty when he learned her situation, and that was why he decided to involve himself. Maybe he never planned on things working out as they had. *'After all, it's only now, when his interests and his secrets have been threat-ened, with his enemies drawing a little too close for comfort, that he suggested a way to create a third degree of separation.'*

Sebastien tried to calm herself down. There wasn't enough evidence to be sure of anything. This could all be coincidence and her jumping to conclu-sions. But she had been confused. She was still confused, and the sick weight of loss in her stomach suggested that something irreparable was broken.

All these little suspicious events didn't prove anything. But she could not easily dismiss them, either. She didn't consider herself an intuitive person, but something about the look in his eyes and the set of his mouth as he talked about creating decoys had created an undeniable shift in her understanding of him. *'So where does that leave me?'* she wondered. *'I suspect that Oliver got his hands on something sensitive and valuable that people would go after him for. Where he got it from, or what it is, I do not know. Perhaps it could be something entirely unrelated to my book, or to Myrddin. Maybe there have been rumors about some other powerful item being found or going missing that I haven't heard. Secondly, I suspect that my circumstance was at least taken advantage of, if not engineered directly. At the moment, that is all I have. Suspicions and strange coincidences.'*

Oliver was good with people. With manipulation. She was afraid that if she simply asked him, he would lie to her.

And she wasn't sure if it would be worse if she believed whatever explanation he gave or if she didn't.

Even if he did have something that her own book had become a decoy for, knowing the truth wouldn't have changed much for her. The knowledge would only have made her even more of a liability to him. And though she didn't want to think that idealistic, philanthropic Oliver would act to harm her, Sebastien also remembered the way Oliver had bound her to him with a huge debt. How he had forced the Morrow prisoners to accept a curse seal, and then, when it seemed like they might be rescued, had *killed* them. If he had something as valuable as her book, she could use that for leverage, either against him or to buy her own freedom. What if he decided she was a liability?

She needed another, external, way to confirm or deny her suspicions.

'*I am going to find out,*' she resolved. Whatever had snapped inside her, causing the sudden and overwhelming suspicion she felt toward Oliver, now buoyed her up with strength, a cold-burning source of power that would never run out until her goal was achieved. She took a deep breath of the oncoming storm, tasting the ozone in the air. She felt anything but defeated, or weak, or tired.

'*And while I am at it, I might as well solve my other problems, too. I am going to take control of my life, and become the master of my own fate in truth.*' She bared her teeth to the city, letting out a laugh that was all humor and no joy. She spoke, enunciating every word clearly and calmly. "The world will bend to my Will in this, just as it does in magic."

54

CASTLING QUEENSIDE

Thaddeus
Month 3, Day 17, Wednesday 8:00 pm

It was quite simple for Thaddeus to find a Verdant Stag enforcer and free-cast a compulsion spell on the woman to get information about Lord Stag's whereabouts. It was somewhat of an anticlimax to find that, with the right timing, he could simply walk into the Verdant Stag's inn-cum-entertainment hall and request a meeting with the man.

He flagged down a carriage to take him there. Discarded within lay a recent issue of *The Daily Sun*, a rather gossipy rag. However, with little better to do in the meantime, he picked it up. The headlining article was about the recent mess with the Gervins.

Dear Reader, you may have heard rumors about the arrest of two Crown Family members, Misters Malcolm and Randolph Gervin, both younger, non-inheriting brothers to the current lord of the Fourth Crown Family.

While Harrow Hill has not yet released an official statement, this reporter was shocked to learn that the true reason for their arrest was even more scandalous than some of the rumors.

Sources close to the Family say that the brothers were acting strangely for some time before the incident. Because of this and her concern for her cousin Alec Gervin, heiress Anastasia, currently a first-term University student, set out to uncover just what was going on with the help of an anonymous private investigator.

"I don't think she expected something like this at all," one anonymous source said. "But once she found out they were dabbling in treason, trying to make secret deals with the Raven Queen, she couldn't stand idle. And then Lord Malcolm tried to kill her to keep her mouth shut while he destroyed all the evidence. I heard the fighting, spells flying everywhere, and afterward the room was completely destroyed."

Truly, if young Anastasia had not brought along her two best friends for moral support while she confronted her uncle, Damien Westbay and one Sebastien Siverling (see our March 1st article for further heroic exploits), she likely would have been killed.

Usually, in an article like this, the anonymous "sources" were either servants, employees of businesses the nobles had visited, or common business associates with a grudge. Here, he guessed servants.

The article went on in a similar thespian manner, focusing on the heroism of Thaddeus's apprentice, who fought the older man to a standstill with the help of his two friends before the coppers could arrive. They even provided a drawing, done by a "source close to the trio," of Siverling sitting in a window seat, looking into the distance as the light from outside spilled over him. Thaddeus thought the artist's rendition made the boy look rather more handsome than he actually was, though the expression of focused determination was accurate.

Of course, the details about the Gervin brothers' treasonous collusion with the Raven Queen were half-speculation and inaccurate even beyond that, but Thaddeus couldn't be sure whether that was because of shoddy journalism or the fact that the investigators on her case were so eager to be gathering evidence about her movements that they set logic aside.

In any case, it was true that the brothers had thought they were meeting with the Raven Queen, and not to further the High Crown's interests.

Thaddeus skimmed through the rest of the paper to ensure that it held nothing of interest or substance, then refolded and rolled it up into a tube for disposal in the nearest fireplace.

As he disembarked in front of the building that bore the green antlers so proudly, Thaddeus smiled in anticipation. The establishment was already mostly rebuilt, though the seams where new met old were obvious.

He stepped through the front door, allowing his Will to sweep out with just enough grasp on reality to make his presence felt by those who mattered.

He turned to the closest enforcer and announced, "I am Grandmaster Thaddeus Lacer, and I am here to meet with Lord Stag."

The man looked from side to side as if hoping Thaddeus had been talking to anyone but him. When everyone else pointedly refused to meet his gaze, he swallowed audibly and stepped forward. "Err, can I ask what this is about?"

"A personal matter."

The man shifted uncomfortably. "Nothing official, then? I heard you were working as a part-time consultant for the coppers…"

"I am not here in any official capacity, and even if I were, I am not employed by Harrow Hill and thus have no authority to make arrests on their behalf," Thaddeus said, guessing at what had the man so worried. He did not bother to say that if he really wanted to arrest someone, there was little that could stand in his way, official remit from Harrow Hill or not. After all, he was still a special agent of the Red Guard.

The enforcer cleared his throat, gave Thaddeus a bow, and said, "I will pass along your request. Please wait here," before hurrying off toward a side door with surprising self-control.

Thaddeus took a seat at the bar on the left side of the room and ordered a surprisingly nice beer, dark as coffee and twice as bitter.

When the bartender delivered it, she tossed a paper down beside it. "Hot off the press. Something better than that drivel," she said, nodding to *The Daily Sun* still in his hand.

"How much?"

She waved him off. "Free with every purchase."

Thaddeus raised an eyebrow, intrigued by the rather thin paper titled *The People's Voice*.

Before he could get far into either the news or his beer, the enforcer from before returned. "Please follow me, sir." He led Thaddeus to an open antechamber in front of a dark wooden door on the third floor.

Seeing that several others were already waiting, Thaddeus settled into one of the chairs with the beer that no one had dared tell him to leave behind, and returned to his reading.

Terrorists Attack Gilbratha to Free Criminals

Lord Stag, leader of the Verdant Stags, is quoted as saying, "I believe justice is the responsibility of all those who find themselves with power." However, his organization has made it clear they have no intention to take dispensation of that justice from the hands of the Crowns.

As you know, many of the members of the former Morrow gang were defeated and captured by an alliance between the Verdant Stag and the Nightmare Pack, determined to improve the lives of people in their territory. After compiling their crimes and affording some measure of restitution to those who were harmed, the Verdant Stag, with the help of the Nightmare Pack, went about transferring those heinous criminals who once walked the streets with impunity to Harrow Hill for official sentencing and punishment. Unfortunately, some parties felt removing these tyrants went against their interests.

Hidden individuals with wealth and power had been preparing to strike against Gilbratha for some time, gathering resources for battle and hiring powerful mercenaries who had lost all sense of virtue. In the wee hours of Saturday morning, they struck out in an attempt to free the criminals and sow fear into the heart of Gilbratha with a display of magical power in our vulnerable midst.

Verdant Stag and Nightmare Pack enforcers fought against these terrorists on one side while the coppers approached from the other, allies by chance. Eventually, they managed to overcome the villains, leaving over a dozen mercenaries and their masters dead, and some of the land in west Gilbratha scarred.

THE ARTICLE WENT on to cover some of the details of the battle and the impressive might of the enemy in clear, concise detail that drew Thaddeus's attention. Particularly, the description of an elderly thaumaturge who used a war array to great effect. He matched the physical description and particular magical capability of an ex-Red Guard member. A defector who had managed to escape retaliation, until now. Thaddeus would ask for confirmation, though he was unsure if his current clearance levels would allow him access.

No civilians were killed, though several enforcers working for the Verdant Stag and Nightmare Pack fell casualty to the terrorist attack, and a handful of coppers sustained injuries. *See the end of this article for names.

Despite all the efforts made to the contrary, over one hundred Morrow criminals were apprehended and are soon to face sentencing.

Little is known about the powers behind this attack, but it is likely they still walk free, plotting to strike once more.

As always at The People's Voice, we asked for commentary from those involved in and affected by this event, with allowance for responses to previous statements.

Mary Crafford from Bett Street: "I'm not sure why no one is talking about how the Raven Queen stepped in and kept a whole section of coppers from being annihilated. She created an eldritch maw of darkness that reached straight out of the ground and swallowed a whole squad of those [terrorists] all up before they could do any more damage. She might be mischievous and whimsical, but she gets serious when it matters."

Terrence Filibun from Madders Row, in reply to Mary Crafford: "Everyone knows the Raven Queen is territorial. Not with land, but with her people. My uncle Dominic was there, and he told me that he was just about to be hit by a spell when she acted, probably to protect him. He has a whole nest of ravens in his backyard that he keeps fed, which everyone agrees is why she likes him so much. He's making offerings every single day."

Bob from Brewer Avenue: "What I want to know is, how did some group of anti-Lenore radicalists manage to hire mercenaries and infiltrate Gilbratha without the coppers getting any wind of it? Don't we have any people assigned to protect our interests from the shadows?"

Hamish Cordwain from Worlow Apartments, in reply to Bob: "If you're wondering how something like this could happen, why anyone would want this, just follow the gold. I'd bet anything some of the Crowns are involved, and I don't need to be anonymous to say it. Who else has access to that kind of firepower? I went down there personally and saw the clay shards of army-issue battle philtres, just the same as we had when I was a soldier."

Grom from Calcifer Crescent: "My niece and I watched the edges of the battle from our roof a few blocks away. We saw that huge glowing rock in the sky that disappeared a whole building, and now she's afraid to go outside. Does anyone know the details of making an offering to the Raven Queen? I think it might give my niece some reassurance."

THADDEUS'S BROWS slowly rose higher as he continued through the civilian commentary, which was a mix of ridiculous, myopic, and insightful, but altogether quite amusing. Creating a curated forum for discussion through a free newspaper was an interesting approach. If Lord Stag was behind it, as seemed likely, the man was more clever than Thaddeus had given him credit for. He would be one to watch.

As the next person left the room beyond, Thaddeus stood and entered, heedless of whether he was technically the next in line or not.

The room was slightly ostentatious, but simple enough. The office of the one man in Gilbratha with an obvious connection to the Raven Queen, who, if the rumors were to be believed, could facilitate a meeting with her, for the right price. "I am Grandmaster Thaddeus Lacer. I wish to meet with the Raven Queen, and understand you may be able to facilitate this," he said, not bothering with time-wasting pleasantries.

The man behind the desk, a featureless mask obscuring his expression, stared at Thaddeus through artificially shadowed eye holes. "You understand the need to prepare a worthy tribute?"

"Yes. That will not be a problem."

"Even if the Raven Queen accepts, she may not meet you in person, as she has been known to send raven messengers in her place."

Thaddeus did not smirk, because that would be obnoxious. "I believe she will meet me in person," he said simply.

Lord Stag stared at him silently once more. Finally, he said, "Very well. I will inform her when she deigns to grace me with her presence. I cannot guarantee any sort of timeline, and if she accepts, she will choose the location."

"That is acceptable." With that, Thaddeus left, pleased that the whole thing had been much less trouble than he expected. When he returned to his cottage, he made himself a cup of coffee, using the more luxurious, slow-roasted, low-acid beans with pine nuts for flavor that he saved for when he wanted to savor the experience rather than knock back a bitter cup of energy-infused liquid. Swirling the cup gently as steam wafted from it, he looked over the papers and personal research stacked neatly across his desk.

His research was making progress, despite the time he was forced to spend in classes or grading inane homework, and the more recent distraction of the Raven Queen. It had been worth it, to take the Red Guard liaison position at the University.

But his thoughts strayed from translating pre-Cataclysm textual relics and toward the mysterious woman who they called the Raven Queen. He made his way to the room at the back of his cottage, setting down his mug of coffee atop the warded vault before moving to his bedside table, where he had personally warded a secret compartment.

He opened it, pulling out a small lead box.

Within, nestled snugly in velvet, lay an old ring. Clear celerium made up the stone, while the silver ring itself was a simple artifact, which could be activated to create a small anti-awareness field along with a minor chameleon effect. He had stolen the ring on a gamble, slightly surprised at the time that she had not already done so herself. Of course, it was possible he had taken only a competent replica, much like the one he had left behind in that idiot Gervin's vault.

But if the ring was real, as Thaddeus believed, he was sure the Raven Queen had discovered his forgery and replacement by now. The original heirloom would be a fitting tribute to request a meeting with her, and to express his lack of hostility.

As he stared into the celerium depths, which held only a tiny flaw, a warm and visceral excitement shuddered through him. He could not wait to meet her.

. . .

THE STORY CONTINUES in *A Practical Guide to Sorcery Book IV: A Foreboding of Woe*

Get it now: https://geni.us/FOWEBWide

IF YOU WOULD LIKE access to:

- Illustrated excerpts from Siobhan's grimoire and portraits of the characters
- Exclusive short stories/bonus chapters/deleted scenes not available elsewhere
- The chance to read the latest pre-release chapters of the upcoming book as I finish them
- And other story-related goodies and opportunities…

Consider supporting me on Patreon:
https://www.patreon.com/AzaleaEllis

GLOSSARY OF MAGICAL TERMS

Aberrant

Thaumaturges who have lost control of the magic they channel, but instead of dying, have been changed. They are usually much more magically powerful than they were in life, and almost always have physical mutations. Some Aberrants merely mutate into a dangerous beast-like being, rabid for death and destruction. Some mutate into grotesque or phantasmagorical forms, and have esoteric magical effects. Some mutations remain minor, while the mind and powers are twisted insidiously.

Uniformly, an Aberrant is no longer human, having lost their previous thoughts and desires. Almost all Aberrants are malicious, even those with seemingly benign effects. It is believed one is more likely to break and become an Aberrant with a corrupted Will from casting immoral magics.

Adder stone

A stone with a hole worn through the middle by natural means, it is said that adder stones impart clarity of mind and vision, and one can look through the hole to reveal illusions. Useful on their own, or as a component in spells.

Adhel juice

Mixed with honey, it creates a strong sticky substance. It can be cleared through applying oil.

Adze

A magical insectoid creature most prevalent in the few areas of the Tataroc Desert with year-round water—and static communities—the adze is a nocturnal bloodsucker. Upon its hatching, the first person with an eligible disease that the adze drinks from will be cured, as the adze absorbs it, but after that all other victims will instead be infected by its bite. Each time a disease is absorbed, it is added to the adze's collection and passed on along with the others. This can lead quickly to the annihilation of entire communities, making the adze one of the most feared magical beasts. Anyone who hatches one is to be put to death, along with all those who knew and did not stop them.

Alchemy

A ritual form of spellcasting that uses organic and inorganic components to create magical concoctions. The most common method of performing alchemy is through the use of a cauldron to create potions, philtres, draughts, and tinctures. It is the least expensive way to save a particular magic for instant use at a later time, but not the most efficient way. As with all ritual spells, the magic woven into alchemical concoctions is semi-permanent.

All-purpose antidote potion

A mild antidote to common poisons and venoms, the all-purpose antidote is best used on mild irritants, or to buy time for a more thorough solution to serious toxins. It can be used in lieu of a sobering potion to diminish the effects of alcohol.

Animation spell

Animation spells give temporary and false life to an inanimate object, such as in the case of the Glasshopper's eponymous confections.

Anti-anxiety Potion

Also known as a calming potion, this is a weaker and less addictive version of the elixir of peace. The University infirmary keeps a large amount on hand for students struggling with stress.

Anti-coughing philtre

Suppresses the urge to cough. As coughing is often useful to clear liquid from the lungs, this philtre is used when there are extenuating circumstances, like broken ribs, that may cause more damage.

Arcanum

A magical institution, teaching "secrets" of magic and the arcane.

Artificery

A craft of magic that embeds a pre-cast spell in an object for later release, or enchantment—changing the object's state. Battle wands, light crystals, and self-cleaning chamber pots are examples of artifacts. Enchantments and Wards are a sub-set of Artificery.

Auger

A drilling artifact created in Osham. Though meant for mining and construction, it can also be utilized to brute-force wardbreak.

Avery Park

An area of greenery around southwest Gilbratha.

Ball of light spell

Causes a spherical section of the air to glow with the illusion of a ball of light. Brightness, color, size, and location can be controlled.

Banshee

A humanoid magical creature that is dangerous to humans, and attacks with their voice through incapacitating screams and songs with a soporific effect.

Bark skin potion

Grows a protective layer of bark over the skin of the drinker, while still allowing them most of their range of motion. While not as strong as plate mail armor, it is much lighter, and more effective than chainmail against atmospheric attacks. When damaged, chunks of bark will fall off, which can be useful against spreading attacks like rotting curses or acid.

Battle wand

A wand-shaped artifact charged with offensive spells. For law enforcement, this is most commonly a stunning spell.

BCE

Before the Current Era.

Beamshell tincture

A highly addictive magical potion that infuses the user with energy, often used to treat narcolepsy or insomnia. Beamshell creates an energy debt, and addicts frequently push through it until they collapse, starving and dehydrated. It's even riskier for thaumaturges, with high chances of Will-strain.

Beast core

Beast cores, which resemble raw gems, are harvested from dead magical beasts, and can be used to power spells in place of other sources of energy. They come in many different colors, though the color itself is not as important as the brightness and clarity, with brighter and clearer cores being easier to drawn energy from.

Beast cores contain a total energy value of thousands of thaums, up to millions of thaums, and are generally rated either by their total energy value, or their per-second capacity if they were drained completely over the course of an hour.

When drained, beast cores will shatter and crumble, and cannot be recharged. Due to this, they are a rather expensive source of power, and are most commonly used for emergencies, for high-power spells that make it inconvenient to use lesser sources of power, or by those who have the coin to spend in exchange for convenience.

Beast cores become exponentially more expensive as their quality increases, similar to celerium.

Beast king

A figure shrouded in mystery and fear, the beast king is sleeping in Silva Erde, deep below the ground. While details about him are vague, diviners consistently find that if he wakes from his long sleep, calamity will follow.

Bewitchment hex

Draws the attention and interest of the victim.

Bini frog

A magical amphibian often found in northern peat bogs, when under duress or unable to find others of their species, the bini frog will change sexes, allowing themselves to lay eggs as a female and then fertilize them as a male. Notably, their male form has corrosive skin, a defensive which may have led to an initial imbalance of sexes and required this adaptation.

Black star sapphire

A gem that can be used (as can many gems) as a Conduit. It is not as robust as celerium. As components, star sapphires can be used in space-bending spells, and it is said that a black star sapphire was used in a spell to travel within and through shadows faster than any mortal could otherwise move.

Blight-type Aberrant

These Aberrants spread their anomalous effect, physically or otherwise, expanding their area of influence. If allowed to get out of control, they can cause true devastation. The first priority for this type of Aberrant is containment.

Blood clotting potion

Poured on a wound, clots blood and can stop excessive blood loss. It can allow someone to wait till medical attention arrives when otherwise they might bleed out. Not typically considered a battle potion, because it does not have offensive effects.

Blood Emperor

The Blood Emperor was the leader of the Third Empire, also known as the Blood Empire. His invading forces, from an unknown land beyond the northern ice oceans, conquered the continent about three hundred years ago. His empire was eventually overthrown, but his policies shaped much of modern society even after the Third Empire's downfall. However, atrocities committed in the name of learning and power caused a severe backlash against all forms of blood magic and its practitioners.

Blood print vow

A spell that binds two or more parties to an agreement spoken while casting, bound by a thumbprint of blood. If at least one of the vowers cannot cast magic, a third party binder must be present to do so.

Blood-regeneration potion

Boosts blood regeneration, but takes time and places strain on the body.

Bogles

Known for disguising themselves as scarecrows or other inanimate objects when spotted, bogles may cause mischief to human homes and settlements, but rarely serious harm.

Brillig

A powerful race with strong affinity to magic, now extinct, or close to it.

Caidan's Theorem

If distance is measured in meters, a divination spell with the base cost B will require B x distance/100 ^ (B/100) thaums to cast.

Calming spell

Forces calm and docility on the target.

Carnagore

Myrddin's most famous self-charging artifact, a horse made of white metal, who he rode into battle. The name Carnagore has roots in the words "hooves of dawn."

Cat's cough

An herb. Commonly smoked, it is addictive and gives a raspy, deep voice over time.

Cataclysm

An apocalyptic event that destroyed civilization over ten thousand years ago, and which is still shrouded in mystery.

Chameleon spell

Allows a non-living object to partially blend in with its surroundings.

Charybdis Gulf

The sea inlet that bisects the main area of Gilbratha from the Lilies—the rich area where many of the nobles and socialites live—to the east. The Charybdis Gulf is dangerous, containing magical water beasts that will drown a swimmer and even capsize small fishing boats, yet despite this remains a large source of income and food, especially for the poorer citizens.

Cinder Stag

A powerful Aberrant that is contained within a sundered zone, the Cinder Stag still manages to affect the world outside the sundered zone with karmic flames of retribution that can follow a chain of cause-and-effect back to its source.

Circle

Facilitates the three main elements of magic. It places a physical boundary around a spherical domain controlled by the thaumaturge, signifying that the things within are theirs to trade away and change as they wish.

Cockatrice

Two-legged dragon-like creature with a rooster's head. (And more or less the shape of a chicken.) Weasels are their natural enemy. Can be the familiar of a witch.

Cold box artifact

Sometimes referred to as an ice box, this is an artifact which keeps the contents placed within it chilled or frozen by siphoning out their heat.

Compass divination spell

Uses two halves of a spelled, linked bone disk as a sympathetic beacon and a stick with one burnt end. Using one half of the bone, the burnt end of the stick will point toward the other half, like a compass.

Comprehensive Compendium of Components

A restricted book that contains its namesake, including components that are illegal and unethical.

Concussion-modified fireball spell

Adds a force effect to the fireball spell, similar to an explosion.

Concussive blast spell

Shoots ball of force which expands and weakens with distance, but can cause severe damage to a human (particularly their internal organs) or even break through walls at close range. It is often visible as a waver or fogginess in the air, but much less conspicuous than a fireball or stunning spell.

Conduit

Channels the thaumaturgic energy being converted as a spell is cast. For most sorcerers, this is a celerium crystal, which is resistant to the destructive effects of channeling magic. Witches may use their familiars as Conduits, and those sorcerers who cannot afford celerium may use lesser gems, such as diamonds or sapphires.

Contact stunning spell

Set into a ring artifact, releases the spell on firm, sudden contact, like a punch.

Continue-motion spell

A complex, finicky spell that allows the caster to demonstrate an action as one of the inputs of the spell. The spell will continue this action, *exactly*, for as long as it is empowered. It is good for things like stirring a pot continuously, spinning thread, or weaving cloth, which require relatively simple, repetitive movements.

Coppers

Law enforcement, named for the copper nails in the soles of their boots, the distinctive sound of which announces their approach wherever they go.

Craft

Specific path of magic: Sorcerer, Artificer, Witch, Magician, Shaman, Animist, Gestura, etc.

Deafening hex

Causes deafness, usually temporary, though some variations will persist for a period of time after the caster stops focusing on the hex. Some variations can be used to some effect against a banshee in place of a vibration-canceler.

Devil

They possess living beings.

Dingleberry bushes

Dingleberry bushes are named for their small, hard brown fruits that smell like feces and rot even before they fall to the ground.

Dissolving tincture

A concentrated alchemical concoction that will dissolve other substances it comes into contact with, the dissolving tincture has many variants that can be adapted to the type of material the alchemist wishes to dissolve. Similar to a strong acid, but more versatile.

Distagram

A long-distance messaging artifact recently created by a University graduate that operates by using different frequency bands.

Diviner's sight

Special magical sight of the divination realm, which reveals that which might not be seen with the normal eye. It is a catch-all term that includes any ocular enhancements, such as the ability to see in the dark.

Doorjamb alarm ward

A small ward spell, carved into the underside of a door, will alert the caster when the door is opened.

Dorienne invisibility spell

A spell that uses the self-camouflaging dorienne fish to create true invisibility through which light can pass. The dorienne fish itself sees through its skin and adjusts its pigment on one side of its body to what it sees on the other to appear invisible.

Dragon scales

A magical component.

Drake

A miniature dragon creature. Not as intelligent or powerful. Can be the familiar of a witch.

Draught of borrowed gills

This concoction allows someone to breath underwater by dropping a small, living fish into a mucousy concoction and then gulping the whole thing down whole. The fish is kept alive within a bubble of potion within the stomach for a few minutes, during which time the fish's ability to filter oxygen from water is transferred to the drinker's lungs.

When the fish dies and the draught's effect wears off, the drinker must expel the water from their lungs quickly to avoid drowning. Often, use of this potion in dirty water can lead to complications and long-term side effects, so it should not be used recreationally.

Dream-walking

Often practiced by shamans, it is a form of divination that sends their consciousness into the dream of another, most often for exploration or healing purposes.

Dreamless sleep spell

Keeps one from dreaming, using crystal and eagle feathers as components, and cast on the pillow Siobhan uses, or anywhere under her head. Uses alcohol and herb tincture as the Circle, which evaporates quickly and isn't uncomfortable to sleep on.

Dryad

A creature of living wood, shaped like a humanoid woman. They come in different sub-species of trees, and can be very small when young. Sometimes they disguise themselves as trees before the unwary or unobservant, and short bursts of activity are often followed by long periods of "sleep."

Dueling board

A game where the pieces shoot fake spells at each other and dodge attacks under the control of the players.

Dysentery sustaining potion

Diluted in large amounts of water, will keep a patient with diarrhea or dysentery hydrated with a small amount of calories and the immediately necessary electrolytes and minerals, and slightly slows the rate of expulsion, allowing absorption.

Earth disintegration and stone creation spell

One of Professor Lacer's practice exercises. Dirt or stone can be turned to sand and back again to stone using either transmutation, which creates the effect through natural processes, or through duplicative transmogrification, which copies the properties of existing material.

Earth-aspected weta

Magical beast with a very tough hide.

Elcan irises

A deadly, flesh-eating plant with purple-streaked flowers whose long, tapered petals open and turn to follow prey as it passes, releasing sweet-smelling pollen into the air. They lure their prey with their beauty and the soporific properties of their pollen.

Elemental Planes

The five known Elemental Planes are accessible through planar portal spells from the mundane plane, where humans and other mundane races live. Each Elemental Plane corresponds to an element: Radiance, Fire, Air, Water, and Earth. Creatures, plants, and even the water and soil from the Elemental Planes will be imbued with the energy of their plane, and are powerful spell-casting components. Each Elemental Plane has sapient creatures, some of which are humanoid and can even cross breed with humans.

Elementals

Beings from the Elemental Planes. On the mundane plane (Earth), they are most often encountered as the familiars of witches, who use them as a Conduit to channel magic. When sapient and humanoid, they have specific labels.

Radiance—Angels

Fire—Demons

Air—Sylphides

Water—Undine

Earth—Erdgeist

Elixir of Euphoria

An alchemical concoction which, in low doses, combats depression, but is more often sold recreationally for the eponymous euphoria.

Elixir of peace

Imparts a sense of well-being, and can be used in small doses to combat depression and anxiety, or for its recreational effects in larger doses. It is used in war to give soldiers who are dying some peace in their last moments.

Enenra

Magical beasts native to the East, enenra are creatures that seem to be made from smoke and tattered cloth, said to be born from bonfires and visible only to those of pure heart and mind.

Energy-reflecting spell

A general-purpose ward. A more expensive and inefficient defense than setting wards against more specific spells or incidents.

Enkennad's draught of shadowed concealment

A powerful potion that allows the user to disappear from view, blending subtly with the shadows.

Erlkings

Their name coming from the words "alder king" the erlkings are a magical creature found in woodland areas, sometimes conflated with the fey by the ignorant. They are known to secrete poisonous substances from their hands, the most potent of which allows them to kill with a simple touch, and to enjoy chasing children and lost travelers who have intruded on their domain.

Erythrean horse

Horse with partial magical lineage. They are extremely expensive, but don't look much different from a normal horse.

Etherwood leaves

A luxury leaf for smoking. They are dark blue. The smoke is smooth and calming, great for blowing smoke rings, but nonaddictive.

Ever-inking pen artifact

Comes as a set with an inkwell. Spelled to automatically refill the ink cartridge of the pen with ink from the inkwell whenever not in use. More expensive ones refill based on the rate of expenditure, and some very expensive ones maintain a folded space within the pen's ink cartridge, so the user never needs worry about their inkwell running dry.

Fabric cutting spell

This spell creates a short-range slicing blade of air that extends outward in an arc, the shape of which can be controlled to some degree by the caster's Will. Unlike many similar spells, it doesn't require the target to be within the Circle, as it uses compressed air as the cutting edge.

At longer distances the cutting edge, visible as a faintly glowing shimmer in the air, degrades severely.

With practice and enough power, it can be used to overcome the inherent magical barrier that living creatures possess, and injure a human or animal.

Fever Reducing potion/balm

Cools the head, with some cooling to the body as well, along with pain relief. Encourages comfort, allows sleep, and should be given in conjunction with a sustaining draught.

Fey

A powerful race with strong affinity to magic, now close to extinction. They were supposedly so agile they could dance between raindrops without ever being hit.

Fey Flowers

A fluorescent flower prized as a component for its rarity and power.

Finger bone divination

Human finger bones can be used in (illegal) divination, after being processed and etched with symbols and glyphs. The diviner will shake them while casting the divination, throw them, and then read the spell's output in the way they have fallen, with certain glyphs in certain positions or crossing others. Depending on the amount of bones and what output options have been etched into them, this type of divination can have nuance and impart a greater amount of information than similar methods like dice-throwing or card reading.

Fireball spell

Shoots a ball of fire at about 12 meters per second.

Fleetfoot potion

Fractionally increases movement speed, but not reaction speed.

Flesh-fusing potion

A more powerful version of the skin-knitting salve, this potion is meant to seal larger wounds, ideally after the use of the blood-clotting potion.

Flicker-feather bird

Small birds that blink in and out of visibility with every flap of their wings.

Forest of Nod

The mythical forest that is said to be the center of the world, if it ever existed, the Forest of Nod's location has been lost to time. Some suggest that it still exists, beyond the known lands civilization was able to reclaim after the Cataclysm, and some insist that it is, in fact, one of any number of forests that now go by a different name.

Fortner's

A high class, bespoke clothing shop.

Free-casting

Casting magic at will, without the stabilizing external Word of a physical spell array, a ritual, or special movements. The Word, and sometimes the Circle as well, is instead held solely in the mind. This feat is extremely difficult, and only a few are proficient in it.

Garden of wonders

An element of a children's tale, which the University Menagerie seems to exemplify.

Gasping-tentacles spell

A spell which creates temporary tentacles growing from a solid, nonliving surface. Used to bind or obstruct movement from a distance, and often employed as a nonlethal method of detainment. Gone wrong, can strangle a victim to death.

Glow Slime

A phosphorescent magical slime that slowly releases the light it absorbs during the daytime or from decaying plants with an eerie glow through the night.

Glow spell

Perhaps the most rudimentary light output spell possible, can cause an object to let off a diffuse glow.

Gold duplication spell

A duplicative transmogrification spell that copies a source of matter. As with most attempts to create matter through magic, only the most skilled thaumaturges can create a truly perfect copy that will have the same magical properties as the original, and thus duplicated gold or other substances are often worth less than the authentic originals.

Golden apple
Fruit from a magical tree that closely resembles a gold-skinned apple, and are said to improve organ function and thus increase a person's lifespan.

Gregorian snail
Magical animal. Mucus can be used as a thickening agent in most salves and lotions, especially those meant for the face.

Gremian
A small, humanoid stick creature that desperately wishes to fly once again, and goes so far as to nest in the trees and crack eggs on their bark-like skin to feel closer to birds. They are an excellent familiar for a beginner witch to practice a binding contract with.

Gremlin
Small humanoid creatures with spiky backs, large, strange eyes, and small razor-sharp claws. They seem to have a great desire to fly, and collect feathers, steal eggs, and other futile attempts to reach the skies. They are sentient and somewhat trainable, but not considered sapient.

Group proprioception potion
Lets everyone who drank from the same batch instinctively know where the others were for a period of time. Its main component is a magical sea lichen that connects and disconnects any singular part of itself at will, still somehow communicating with the greater whole to capture prey and then confine it until it starved to death.

Grubb's barrier spell
A weak barrier spell that only protects against physical projectiles, with a minimum requirement of under 200 thaums to cast.

Gryphon
Creature with the head and wings of an eagle, with the body, legs, and tail of a lion. Can be domesticated and flown.

Guld fish
Minnow-sized fish that glint as if they are made of precious metals polished to a high sheen.

Gust spell
Creates a simple gust of wind, with the size and speed depending on the size of the Circle and the amount of power fed to it.

Hag
A magical humanoid. They have a natural predilection to the dark, and good night vision. They have some facility with hexagon/hexagram spells, dealing with balance. Hags who integrate with society may sell good luck talismans (or cursed objects.)

Hangover-relief draught
Taken in doses of a liter or more, this draught rehydrates, replenishes electrolytes, and mitigates the pain of a hangover. The University infirmary stocks many doses.

Harrow Hill Penitentiary
Gilbratha's jail, a stout stone building in the shape of a cross, within a circular wall that encloses the grounds.

Headache-relieving salve
Minty. An alchemical concoction that relieves headache pain and helps to rejuvenate the senses.

Healing potion
Generalized healing potions, of which there are many different variations of different strengths and capabilities, are an extremely effective method to preserve an injured or ill patient's life. They can be used for most types of wounds or illnesses, and are both convenient and practical. However, due to the price of components—many of which are from the Plane of Light—and the abundance of magical energy packed into these potions, they are expensive.

Hellfire
Is sometimes bright neon green.

Hemorrhaging curse
This curse causes the target's blood vessels to rupture and encourages excessive, forceful blood loss. It can sometimes be recognized by the shape of its glowing force as it travels.

Henrik-Thompson
A measure of scale for maximum Will capacity. It is measured by a crystal ball in an array that filters incoming energy and outputs a portion of it as light through the glowing crystal. It's the most widely-used metric, likely due to the fact that Will-capacity is the easiest to test, and often shows correlation to the overall caliber of a thaumaturge's Will. The brighter the light, the more power (thaums) is being channeled per second.

Homunculus
Very small people, who outwardly seem indistinguishable from humans, but are argued to be a different species due to their facility with certain magics.

Human fingernails
A component in some spells, human fingernails are illegal due to the restrictions against blood magic.

Humphries' adapting solution
An alchemical concoction that can be spelled directly into the veins to take the place of blood in a blood-loss emergency. Expensive, and the shelf-life isn't super long, so it may not always be on hand. Can also be used to keep creatures from the Plane of Water alive on the mundane plane, which was its original purpose.

Hydra
Multi-headed snake. The number of heads ranges from two to nine, with more heads generally indicating a more powerful, intelligent creature, as information processing and bodily processes are divided among the heads based on their individual priorities and specialties.

Ice lion
A predatory, large, shaggy cat that lives near the northern ice oceans.

Ignore pain spell
Muffles pain slightly, allows mind to detach from the focus pain draws, effects wear off quickly once spell is released, but it can allow someone to prepare to heal themselves. Recommended strongly against using this to do things like set bones or put sockets back into place, in case the sudden shock of pain causes the caster to lose control of the spell. Muffles pain by about 15%, so of moderate usefulness. May be good for exercise pain. Esoteric magic.

Impotence curse
A curse that removes the victim's ability to successfully complete intercourse, either through removing their libido, or suppressing their physical ability to copulate.

Improved hearing spell
An esoteric spell that uses hands cupped behind the ears to gather and direct amplified sound, and thus improve selective hearing.

Injury-protection ward
Makes physical damage less likely over a set diameter. Very expensive, but nebulous and thus not very powerful. Still can make a difference, either over time, or in dangerous circumstances.

Jentil
Giants, who are known for building megalithic monuments.

Kitsune
A sometimes fox, sometimes woman. In human form, the kitsune will still have her tails, more depending on how old and powerful she is, up to nine. They often use their tails to cover their bodies, wrapping around it in place of clothing, and are considered seductively attractive, though they do not appear often in Siobhan's part of the world.

Kreidae spider
A magical creature known for stealth and ambushes. Its silk is highly coveted for its transparency and use in camouflage or invisibility cloaks.

Kuthian frog
Has sedative saliva, which is dried, powdered, and used as a component in stunning spells. Upon

release from the spell, the treated saliva quickly degrades and becomes inert.

Landrum's nourishing draught

As with many spells, there are multiple variations of the nourishing draught.

Should be diluted in large amounts of water, which will thicken with the concoction. It contains vitamins, minerals, and electrolytes, as well as some complex sugars/starches. When given frequently, will keep the patient hydrated and with the resources their body needs to continue fighting. The nourishing draught should be created over low heat, to avoid killing the vitamins. Sometimes, it is then dehydrated for long-term storage.

Some versions also induce repeated swallowing, for patients who are insensate and cannot wake to drink. For those with extended nausea, some versions can also help them keep something down, though not stop diarrhea.

Laughing poppy

A component in a sedative potion which is known to cause allergic reactions, preferred for its ability to tranquilize without causing depression.

Light crystal

A non-celerium crystal made into an artifact spelled to release light on command. The rich use them in place of candles or lamps, as they are much brighter and require less maintenance. But, though they also last longer than a candle or lamp, they are expensive enough that the common person cannot afford to buy one, even if it would save them money in the long run.

Light Sacrifice

Light can be used as a source of magical power just like heat, matter, and kinetic force. Converting light within an area to magical power will create an area of darkness, as the light is absorbed before it can pass through or be reflected.

Light-show spell

Cast on an object, this spell creates many pulsing lights of different colors, and is meant to draw the eye and be visually enchanting. Good for traveling performers, distracting wildlife, or to cast on the harlequin above a baby's crib

Lineage test spell

A divination spell that uses a piece of the target to confirm the existence of other members of their bloodline over several weeks. It is known to give unreliable results, and does not by itself allow one to track down the supposed offspring.

Lino-Wharton messenger spell

A power spell with several pre-requisites. It binds a raven to a controller, allowing the controller to speak through the raven at a distance to transmit messages, or to complete simple tasks.

Liquid fire potion

When exposed to air, this potion catches fire.

Liquid stone potion

Expands like an aerosol foam and hardens quickly upon contact with air. Can be used as a barrier or a splint for broken bones, among other things. Not permeable to air, or malleable once hardened, so it can suffocate if it lands on the face. Liquid stone's expansion is purposefully inhibited when in contact with living flesh so that those who carry it do not accidentally entomb themselves if a vial breaks accidentally.

It is softer than normal stone, similar with a similar durability as sandstone.

Loomis anti-awareness field

A spell, in artifact form on Siobhan's heirloom Conduit ring, that dissuades people from noticing or remembering a small object.

Lore-master

A scholar who focuses on the stories of old, on the little-known or forgotten facets of magic and the creatures who use it.

Lotus flowers/bulbs

These flowers grow in the mud. Each night, they return to the mud, and then miraculously re-bloom in the morning. In transmogrification, they signify rebirth, self-regeneration, cleansing, and enlightenment.

Lugubrious
A powerful Aberrant.

Lung-sealing philtre
When breathed in, this philtre creates a sealed bubble inside the lung, which can apply internal pressure to a puncture wound and keep someone from drowning in their own blood.

Lycanthrope
A type of skin-walker, lycanthropes take on and off the skin of a wolf, transforming into the animal at will. Divested of their wolf skins, they lose the ability to transform. A Lycanthrope's animal skin can be used to give a thaumaturge a lesser version of the animal-transformation skill practiced by the skinwalkers themselves, or as a component in taming and binding spells.

Magician
A person who uses magical artifacts rather than cast spells themselves. Often derided as scammers, charlatans, and unworthy by "true" thaumaturges. An artificer who uses their own artifacts is not considered a magician.

Malediction
A curse spoken with a wronged person's dying breath with brings long-term misfortune to the cursed party. These are considered baseless superstitions by most.

Mandrake root
A root plant whose tuber takes the shape of a humanoid being, and which can incapacitate and even kill with their cry if pulled from the muffling earth. They grow more expensive with age, and can be difficult to keep alive. They enjoy being sung to, and may die if not given enough personal attention even if conditions are otherwise optimal. The mandrake root's similarities to the human form make it valuable for spells that would otherwise need a human, such as simulacrum or surrogate spells, and they are most well known for their ability to receive, as a surrogate, a curse transferred from a human victim. They are also used in hallucinogenic spells and concoctions.

Map-based location divining spell
A divination spell that guides a drop of spelled mercury over a place-anchored map to find a location based on a sympathetic connection.

Mending spell
Repairs mundane objects, but requires all the pieces as well as components that would otherwise be required to mend the objects by hand. The mending spell is able to achieve somewhat finer control and dexterity than one might with their hands and fingers.

Mermaid
Mermaids are a magical cephalopod. They lure prey by sticking tentacles above water and making them look like a human woman, who asks for help. When the victim gets too close, the "mermaid" suddenly comes apart into a mass of tentacles that grab them and drag them into the water to be eaten.

Metanite
A powerful Aberrant that the Red Guard has been unable to destroy or contain. It is a void-black form, which destroys everything it touches, but moves very slowly. The Red Guard uses space magic to adjust its path and evacuation to keep people safe from it.

Mimeo-motion spell
A more complex version of the continue-motion spell, the mimeo-motion spell allows duplication of the copied motion in multiple places. It is used most commonly for mass-producing books.

Mind-muddling jinx
Causes the victim trouble reading, comprehending, and focusing. As with all harmful spells classified as jinxes, it is not permanent, and cast lightly, the victim may not realize they have been affected.

Mirrored healing spell/Flesh-mirroring spell
Using blood of the injured person as a Sacrifice, this spell can mold flesh and bone to match the mirrored side of the body, and thus heal injuries without the need for rare and expensive components.
Uses glyphs "blood," "mirror," and then the physical part in need of mirrored healing, like "tooth."

One large Circle around the whole area, and then two inner Circles, meeting in the middle, one which has the good side and one the injured side. Uses a pentagram inside a pentagon, for the combination of transmutation and transmogrification this spell requires. Relies more on the Will and Sacrifice than the clarity or complexity of the written Word. Requires a detailed, focused image of what the caster wants to happen. Using the wounded person's own blood is especially efficient.

Mnemonic-link tracking spell
Creates a sympathetic link between an object and the target, but depends on the caster's extreme familiarity with the target, and best augmented by an item that has a direct connection to the target.

Moonbeams & fairy wings
Moonbeams and fairy wings, harvested (from the Menagerie) at night, have mind-altering (recreational drug) effects.

Moondew Drosera
This carnivorous magical plant is bioluminescent, and preys primarily on insects and other small creatures. It resembles a succulent during the day, and at night, its spines drip with glowing mucous that lures creatures into its sticky grasp.

Moonseeds
Commonly used in their dried form, similar to pepper, moonseeds are berries from a twining vine. The moonseed vine is nocturnal, growing off-white berries that resemble the pitted moon once dehydrated.

Myrddin
An extraordinarily powerful sorcerer who lived over a thousand years before. He has many incredible feats to his name, some based in reality and others in fiction, and has become enough of a household name that he's occasionally used in curses, E.G. "Myrddin's crusty black butthole."

Nightmare-type Aberrant
This type of Aberrant is the most difficult to deal with, as they use stealth, memetic control, or subversion.

Okora's instant cottage
A spell that raises material from the ground to create a small cottage in the shape of a small model cottage used as a component. Size is dependent on power input and spell array parameters. It is easiest to cast with loose material that can be compacted together, such as snow or mud.

Orbs and Amulets
The Conduit shop at the north end of Waterside market

Osher tree
Young sapling that can uproot itself and move short distances. Sometimes confused for a dryad, but an osher has no humanoid form and is not considered to be intelligent.

Paired Movement Ward
When the ring holding a banner to the base of the spell is ripped away, the sympathetically linked counterpart held elsewhere also detaches. Spell must be cast ahead of time, with both halves of the pair together.

Paper bird spell
Used to send letters or messages. The paper birds are spelled to take flight and deliver themselves to set destination or recipients. Unsuitable to fly in heavy winds or rain. They are created from special ingredients that make Siobhan feel they are not as practical as she suspected.
The special paper used to make them requires flicker-feathers from the sparrow-like bird of the same name, which the University cultivates in the Menagerie.

Password puzzle artifact
In the Night Market, inside a component shop, a stone puzzle disk that must be solved with magic to make the center rise up, allowing access to the warehouse in back and the half-troll, Harvester.

Pendragon Palace
The home of the High Crown, the head of the Thirteen Crown Families and leader of the country of Lenore. It is built atop the white cliffs, to the northeast of Gilbratha.

Perimeter alarm ward
Alerts the caster within when a perimeter has been breached.
Philtre of darkness
After brewing, when this concoction is suddenly exposed to air (e.g. when the bottle is smashed) the
    roiling liquid within bursts into clouds of magical darkness, which not even powerful night-
    vision can penetrate.
Phoenix ashes
An incredibly rare spell component, the ashes of a phoenix that has reached the end of one of its
    many life cycles are used to incubate the phoenix's egg as it rebirths itself. They are used in
    powerful healing and fire spells, and even supposedly spells that can affect one's destiny. Most
    famously, they were said to have been used by Myrddin to resurrect his recently-deceased lover.
    They sell for about a hundred gold crowns per gram.
Piercing spell
A shaped spell that, unlike the area-effect concussive blast spell, is focused on penetrative power,
    and can gouge out a few inches of stone in a narrow diameter.
Pixie
Humanoid creatures with very delicate, multi-petaled flesh wings that constantly regenerate, drop-
    ping dandruff and little peels of dry skin. This "pixie dust" is an expensive magical component,
    and many humans keep them to harvest it. They are intelligent and mischievous, even sometimes
    malicious, prone to irritation and insults.
Planar divination-diverting ward
Protects against divination. The recipient will feel pressure under any type of divination/scrying
    attempt, and can add their Will to the artifact's inherent shielding capabilities to divert stronger
    and more determined attempts. The ward does not directly oppose a scrying spell, but turns
    aside, deflects, and hides instead, using its connection to the five Elemental Planes. The effects
    may also spill into the physical world, making it harder for people to notice and focus on the
    user.
When actively diverting, the disks may be painful as they consume the user's blood for power.
Planar portal
A portal to one of the other Planes.
Plane of Darkness
The undiscovered sixth Elemental Plane, the Plane of Darkness, is a hypothetical plane that has long
    been hypothesized to balance the Plane of Radiance, creating an Elemental hexagram. However,
    despite innumerable attempts to access the plane, it remains entirely theoretical.
Plane of Radiance
One of the five known Elemental Planes, the Plane of Radiance hosts the element of Light in its
    many forms *and connotations*. Creatures and plants of the radiant element are very valuable spell
    components, and the most powerful, sentient Elementals from the Plane of Radiance are often
    called angels. The Plane of Radiance has sympathetic connections to the ideas of light, cleanli-
    ness, knowledge, strict justice, and healing.
Planes-damned
A curse word, referring to the Elemental Planes.
Portable office
A wooden block that unfolds into a chair and desk made out of hundreds of smaller segments,
    created by Liza. She sells them for ninety gold.
Potion of feather-fall
It uses a (preferably white) feather as a main component, and seems to reduce the effects of gravity
    on the imbiber, allowing them to jump from a high place without injury.
Potion of moonlight sizzle
A potion that lets off a soft blue, bright glow that mimics the light of a full moon from its sizzling
    bubbles when the bottle is shaken. It's powerful enough to illuminate a small room on its own,
    and when sold at a reasonable price, much more affordable than light crystals or candles.
Potion of night vision

Allows one to see more clearly in the dark, in monochrome.

Prognos

Skilled in divination, have a single large eye in the middle of their head. It's said the best prognos diviners can see into the past to discover the identity of a criminal, but that's a myth. They are simply perceptive. They mature slowly and have longer lives than most humans.

Purple lobster

A luxury food.

Puzzle band rings

A wedding ring, historically used to keep women from cheating on their husbands, with the thought that they would be unable take the ring off for their infidelities and then fit the ring back together in time to keep their misdeeds secret.

Quintessence of quicksilver

The powder of a potion boiled down into a solid and then crushed. It temporarily frenzies the mind, making you smarter and granting a liquid creativity. Gives the illusion of power and lowers inhibitions. The effects of a single dose last about six hours on those who haven't built up a tolerance, and the come-down crash lasts a day or two. Long-term users lose their ability to focus and display various memory problems, becoming dependent on quintessence of quicksilver to function normally.

Radiant Maiden

The progenitor of the Order of the Radiant Maiden. She is a powerful Elemental from the Plane of Radiance. These humanoid, often-winged beings have been referred to as angels.

Raven summoning spell

A spell originally designed to summon the Raven Queen, which, instead appears to be a mild area-effect compulsion that summons nearby corvids.

Red Sage

A powerful Aberrant that is contained within a sundered zone, but still manages to meet people. It has three eyes, each of which are said to see the future. All prophecies that it gives come true, but it seems that the Red Sage can either choose who it meets through a sort of subtle summoning (and thus control the prophecies it gives) or it chooses what to prophecy—it can be bribed to give a better fortune. However, in coming true *all* prophecies cause great suffering and destruction, if not to the recipient, then to the people and world around the recipient. Two of its prophecies—and eyes—are in constant use, and ensure its continued existence and ability to affect the world. The Red Guard facilitates the prophecies from its third eye coming true to try and mitigate the damage, and attempts to control who can meet the Red Sage.

Regeneration-boosting potion

This potion boosts the body's natural immune response, lending some of its power to boost the healing effect and taking the rest from the stored energy and nutrients of the injured person's body. It will struggle to fix anything larger than a small dagger wound, a bone fracture, or a hand-size burn. It takes time to work and is uncomfortable, and cannot be used in quick succession, but is much cheaper than a real healing potion.

Revealing spell

Uncovers non-physical illusions and can see through non-magical darkness. Usually cast via a wand, issued to some coppers. A revealing spell shoots vibrational and magic waves, which penetrate and bounce back to the wand.

Reverse-scrying spell

A divination spell with the base of a map-based sympathetic divination, but which targets instead the other sympathetic end of the connection which is being used to scry. Used to find the finder, historically most often in warfare.

Revivifying potion

Boosts organ function and energy levels. Can be used for many different illnesses, but is expensive due to its high magical load.

Rune-inscribed basin

A basin for far-viewing, a type of divination that uses water to see distant places, generally from the point of view of another surface of water. The basin can be used to contact other powerful diviners if they cast at the same time, with the same intent. Far-viewing in this manner does not transmit sound.

Sacrifice

What you give up for the effect of a spell. It can be an object, like a blob of mud used to create a brick, or energy, like the heat from a flame. Components can have either a natural or a sympathetic link to the effects of the spell.

Selby-Forman binding

A variation on conjuration/elemental binding used in the Second Empire.

Self-charging artifacts

Artifacts that contain the parameters to not only cast a spell, but to gather and transform the energy for that spell as part of their activation and release process. Creating a self-powered, or self-charging, artifact is a Grandmaster-level feat said to be pioneered by Myrddin, who supposedly came up with several methods, some of which have now been lost.

Self-powered artifacts cannot cast truly endless spells, as eventually the spell array breaks down—and more quickly with heavy use, but they are still widely coveted.

Self-cleaning chamber pot artifact

Cleans and dries the nether regions, then processes the waste, removing the liquid from fecal matter and dehydrating urine into a thick paste, which it stores in a sealed container for later removal. An auxiliary spell keeps the smell from filtering out away from the chamber pot.

Sempervivum apricus

A low-growing succulent plant from the Plane of Radiance. Its juicy leaves grow in complex rosettes, glimmering with tiny motes of light that travel beneath the semi-transparent skin along with the water and nutrients. It is technically a "low-light" plant in the Plane of Radiance, and thus is able to survive on the mundane plane in areas with bright sunlight and long days, or with the help of artificial sunlight sources. They propagate by sending out root offshoots that grow into new baby plants.

Shade (dust)

Shades are predatory creatures that take humanoid forms and live in barren, arid areas such as deserts, where they will prey on the sleeping or stalk the lost traveler until they collapse from exhaustion. They are made of a fine powder which can be gathered and used as an expensive magical component.

Shadow-familiar

An esoteric ritual spell that gives the user control of their own shadow, allowing it to move, stretch, and take unnatural shapes. "Life's breath, shadow mine. In darkness we were born. In darkness do we feast. Devour, and arise."

Shaman

A thaumaturge who specializes in contacting the spirit realm for the purpose of divination, as well as certain types of mental healing and wards. They often use mind-altering or hallucinogenic substances to facilitate contact.

Shaman-king Deon

He ruled in Qusnia, a country that exited to the southeast of current Lenore in the distant past.

Shipp Evidence box

Metal cube meant to put evidence in stasis. Has a transparent setting to allow examination of the contents within.

Silk Door

An upscale brothel known for its cleanliness and discretion, and frequently used by Siobhan under the assumed name of Silvia Nakai to conceal her whereabouts.

Silva Erde

A neighboring country that Lenore frequently trades with, known for its celerium mines. The Beast King is rumored to be buried deep beneath its forests.

Simple locking spell

Learned from one of the warding books Katerin bought Siobhan, this spell locks a container that can be opened and closed, without need of a key or even a physical locking apparatus. Does not stop one from breaking in physically or magically, but will require some extra effort.

Simple unlocking spell

Used to bypass either mundane locks, or negate the simple locking spell. Cannot unlock a locking spell cast with greater power.

Sinus-clearing spell

A variation on the water falling spell, used to draw off liquid and thus clear the airways. Esoteric magic taught to Siobhan by a hedge-witch.

Siren

Sometimes confused for mermaids, sirens are not in fact associated with aquatic animals, but with avians. Sirens have brightly colored feathers that sprout from the scalp and sides of their face where ears and hair would be on a human. They are best known for their mesmerizing voices, which are said to cause sailors to steer their ships into submerged rocks or even directly into cliff-sides in an attempt to get closer to the enchanting sound of the siren song.

Largely carnivorous, sirens are intelligent beings and those who are willing to integrate into human society are rare and coveted for their abilities.

Skin-knitting salve

An alchemical concoction that mends small cuts over the course of about an hour. It can heal a deep scratch, cut, or a second-degree burn, but not a serious wound, and most (less expensive) versions will leave minor scarring.

Skinjacker

A creature used in cautionary tales to children, which can take over a person's form and replace them.

Skolex worm

Magical worm-like beasts that can grow hundreds of meters long, the skolex has no eyes, and hunts through vibration alone. When devouring its prey, the skolex's mouthparts one up in four directions simultaneously, revealing multiple inward-facing rows of serrated and hooked teeth which ring the entire mouth opening. The teeth are coveted for their piercing ability and how difficult wounds formed with them are to heal.

Sleep-proxy spell

Using the principles of binding magic, one can allow a magically boosted creature to sleep in the place of another being.

Slingshot spell

Created by Siobhan based on a Practical Casting exercise, it uses the glyphs "line," "movement," and "circle" to send a projectile revolving around a central axis. When it is released, the projectile shoots out, similar to a stone out of a shepherd's slingshot.

Smoke cloud philtre

A battle philtre that creates a sudden and thick smoke cloud when released from its container. Considered a battle potion.

Sobering potion

This potion speeds up the process of filtering alcohol from the body, but can cause an overwhelming need to urinate and, if overused, lead to dehydration.

Sound muffling spell

Creates a bubble of stilled air that suppressed the ability of vibrations to travel through it, and thus muffles sound.

Space-bending spells

This type of magic can bend, and even fold space. They are extremely difficult and expensive. If a smaller area is filled with more space than it could normally hold, that space must come from somewhere, which will in turn be smaller than it normally is. There are usually visually-disorienting signs of the spell when you try to gain perspective or mentally measure the space.

Spark-shooting wand

Artifacts charged with firework-like sparks of light. Can start a fire, with the right tinder, be used as a distraction, a signal, or a threat, though the spark-shooting spell is a non-combat spell.

Speer's philtre of stench
A powerful, physically painful stench that causes tears, mucus buildup, and vomiting, like a combination of a stink bomb and pepper spray. Used as crowd control to non-lethally incapacitate a large number of people. It has magical as well as physical properties.

Spirit
Ephemeral, small and often harmless beings, it is argued whether spirits are technically "alive" or merely accumulations of a concentrated type of magical energy over time, or perhaps imprinted residue from once-living beings. They may be summoned and contracted, but often have little ability to exert influence on the mundane world. Shamans often communicate with spirits to gain information through their particular brand of divination.

Spirit-trapping spell
Useful for trapping spirits for communication or contracting. There are many variations on this type of Circle.

Sprites
Tiny, insect-winged humanoids. They have some measure of intelligence, but are not considered sapient "people," rather more akin to interesting bugs.

Star-maple wood
A wood with properties from the Plane of Radiance, it can be used in regenerative and healing spells, as well as other spells using the Radiant attribute, or for its beauty. As it can be molded into an accessory while still living, it is rather valuable. As an accessory, sometimes is used to enhance beauty through improving health.

Stunning spell
Red projectile spell. When high-powered, can leave scorch marks and a little steam or smoke at the point of impact. Uses a combination of low-current electricity and sedative material (the powdered saliva from a Kuthian frog), contained within a field of force, to incapacitate the target.

Summoning ritual
Summoning is said to slightly skew fate to cause a being that meets your requirements to come into contact with you. It has inconsistent results, and clarity of wording and intention is very important. One can summon spirits, animals, or even another person who has the capability to help you with a certain problem. Once summoned, you may come into contact with a being that meets your requirements as if through coincidence after some time has passed, or more directly and immediately. Some question the efficacy, hypothesizing that the vagueness of most types of summoning rituals leads to false interpretations of fulfillment.

Sundered zone
The strongest barrier spell known to man. From the outside, it looks like a perfect white dome, with all light reflected. They are used to quarantine Aberrants that cannot be killed. The sundered zones cannot be exited by the thing they were created to contain or anything tainted by them, but can technically be entered by sapient creatures who are able to give their informed consent.

Sylphide
Powerful, humanoid elementals from the Plane of Air, given to song, laughter, and knowledge carried on the wind.

Tataroc Desert
Known for its dryness, a line of standing stones through this desert signifies Lenore's border to the east.

The Bitter Phoenix
A tavern with a private back area where people partake of the illegal quintessence of quicksilver, and a powerful diviner will sell you information or make connections for the right price.

The Black Wastes
An area where dangerous magic has infected the land itself. The environment shifts rapidly, with deadly and mutated land, flora, fauna. Time spent in the Black Wastes causes paranoia, hallucinations, and makes it difficult to find your way.

The Charmed Highlands
An area where celerium is mined.

The Citadel
The main University building, where the classes are held, and which also contains the supervised casting rooms. It looks like a coliseum made of white stone, with shimmering spelled windows and tall columns. It is huge and towering, and laid out in rings, like a cross-cut of a tree stump.

The Dawn Troupe
A powerful Aberrant which is not contained within a sundered zone. It manifests as a group of wealthy, attractive horse-riders with weapons and musical instruments. This Aberrant appreciates intelligence and talent, and will give boons to those who meet it and impress it. The Dawn Troupe can be bargained with, and never breaks its promises. The Red Guard has agreed not to attempt to contain it, and as long as it receives a certain amount of people interacting with it—usually to attempt to gain one of its boons—it does not leave a certain area to go on a hunt. The Red Guard allows people to know about the boons so they will risk their lives to try for one.

The Elementary
A shop in the Night Market which secretly sells, in the back room, items from the Elemental Planes. Their supplier, Harvester, is a half-troll.

The Gervin Family
The Fourth Crown Family. They control much of the textile industry, as well as the high-end fashion industry.

The Mires
Gilbratha's slums, which get worse further toward the south of the city. The Mires are named for the sticky, stinking waste that lines the streets and wafts from the canals. They spread beyond the bounds of the white cliffs, which have been sunk, broken, or taken apart for use as building materials on that side of the city.

The Nightmare Pack
A gang consisting mostly of non-humans, which holds territory that houses a large percentage of non-humans. They are led by Lord Lynwood, a lycanthrope, and his adopted prognos sister, Gera.

The Red Guard
A special, semi-autonomous branch of law enforcement which handles rogue magic beyond the abilities of the normal coppers. Their operations are confidential.

The Surior Mountains
An area where celerium is mined.

The Thaumaturgic University of Lenore
The most prominent and prestigious arcanum in the country, and the only one that can give a Mastery certification. It is matched in status only by Pendragon Palace, and looks down upon the city from atop the northern side of the white cliffs. Its grounds are extensive, and its structures include areas dug into the white cliffs themselves.
Every year, thousands of students, both new to magic and who have come from other arcanums to achieve their Mastery certification, take the entrance exam.

The Westbay Family
The Second Crown Family. They control the Gilbrathan coppers, and often have influence in the army as high-ranking commanders.

Timed alarm spell
Cast on a time-keeper such as a pocket watch, goes off at a set time to alert anyone nearby to the conditions of the spell being reached.

Titan
A gargantuan, powerful, humanoid being prevalent in the early days of recorded human history, who survived the Cataclysm. A Titan might simply walk by and decide to crush half a human city like a child kicking an anthill. They had enormous appetites and were entirely omnivorous, in the true meaning of the word. Extremely magically powerful. Now extinct.

Tome
A large, expensive book created with high-quality material meant for channeling magic. It has very thick pages, with a spell array drawn on each page. This allows the holder to carry portable spell

arrays, open to any particular page, and cast the spell as quickly as they can place any necessary components and/or Sacrifices. Each tome usually carries between 12-20 spell pages.

Turtle creation spell

Uses a turtle egg and duplicative transmogrification to create an anatomically-correct, edible, dead turtle.

Under-bed dust bunnies

A magical creature that is spontaneously generated from the fluffy dust under a bed in a magical environment. Supposedly.

Unicorn/Pegasus

A magical, horse-like beast with a valuable horn on its head. The pegasus is the progressed form of a unicorn, the wings growing after an intense accumulation of magic.

Unnamed subtle curses

Uses sea spray gathered on a moonless night. "I swam through an ocean of uncertainty."

Scourge-type Aberrant

The most common classification of Aberrant, Scourge-types have a short to mid-range effect whose anomalous effect is clear, allowing quantification and elimination or containment.

Utility wand

A wand artifact with multi-purpose spells meant to be widely useful for a variety of emergency situations, not simply battle.

Vampire

Sentient, magical, humanoid beings, who often prey on humans for their blood. They often have blood-red hair, pale skin, and a mouth full of canine teeth. They are weak to things from the Plane of Radiance, and a common weapon against them is water imbued with energy from the Plane of Radiance. They have a natural predilection to the dark, and good night vision.

Vibrational self-calming spell

Esoteric, rather than using a written spell array, it uses the hands over the chest to form the Circle, and the vibration of the voice as a sympathetic component for forcibly calming the body. The longer you draw out the hum, the further it "stretches" your body into a calm state. Repeat ad nauseam.

Wakefulness brew

A pseudo-alchemical concoction, but more commonly classified as "kitchen magic," this spell marginally boosts the rejuvenating effects of caffeinated beverages. Better quality base materials take the wakefulness magic more smoothly, just as in standard alchemy.

Ward against untruth

The strongest legal wards against lies create a moderate vague compulsion, and are thus utterly useless against a strong thaumaturge who can imbue their lies with their Will. Illegal wards create stronger compulsions, but are considered blood magic as they take away the free will of a human.

Wardbreaker

A specialist in diverting, subverting, and breaking wards.

Waterside Market

A sprawling market within Gilbratha proper that has a lot of shops in the streets around. People of all ages and races can be seen, as well as thaumaturges who practice many different crafts, a testament to Gilbratha's diversity. Sells everything from food to magical animals. There are stalls as well as shops, with stalls being cheaper, but shops having a better selection.

Whiskerton's Whiskey of Well-being

An expensive magical whiskey guaranteed to impart an additional sense of warmth and wellbeing by the shot, in addition to the standard effects of liquor.

White cliffs

Gilbratha is built within a gargantuan circle of white stone cliffs that have been drawn up from the ground in what is undoubtedly a legendary feat of magic. These cliffs are intact to the north, but have sunk, crumbled, and been demolished for other purposes toward the poorer south.

The Thaumaturgic University of Lenore as well as many Crown Family houses have been built into and atop the cliffs, and nearer the bottom are many buildings placed on the staggered plateaus. Tubes run down from the University to transport people and goods, powered by magic.

Will

The Will makes magic possible. The stronger a thaumaturge's Will, the more power they can channel, the less defined the Word needs to be, and the less power will be lost in conversion from input to effect. There are different facets to a strong Will.

Will-strain

Caused by over-exertion when casting magic. It starts with headaches, dizziness, and inability to concentrate. With more moderate strain, judgment is impaired. Sometimes thaumaturges display difficulty modulating emotions, with rapid swings from one to the other. Then hallucinations, with the more severe ones resulting in paranoia and even accidental harm to oneself or others. Beyond this, Will-strain damage is irreversible, and results in complete insanity and at times, the loss of higher brain functions. In extreme circumstances, loss of control while casting will lead directly to a "break" and the creation of an Aberrant.

Wit-sharpening potion

While it doesn't actually increase intelligence, it will temporarily make the drinker more aware and improve performance in situations that require multitasking. In too high a dose, it can cause overstimulation through increased sensory input. It is somewhat addictive.

Witch

A thaumaturge who uses a summoned contracted creature, often from one of the Elemental Planes, to cast spells, rather than using an inanimate Conduit like sorcerer.

Word

The Word guides the transformation of energy or matter, steering the effects of a spell. It can be any type of instruction, though with sorcery it is most often written into the Circle as an array of glyphs and numerically-significant symbols. These are often supplemented with speech or written instructions, especially for complex effects.

Wortcunning

Magical herbalism, the study of plants and herbs, specifically for their healing and magical properties.

Wound cleansing potion

There are many different versions of this potion, and they come in different strengths and act in different ways. Uniformly, however, they work to clear the wound of dirt and debris, as well as kill any infectious agents such as viruses or bacteria. Formerly, this was understood to be overwhelming the "bad humors," and so, wound-cleansing potions often have strong scents due to components like distilled alcohol and herbal oil extracts.

Yak urine

Used to help dyes stay color-fast.

ALSO BY AZALEA ELLIS

Did you know I have my own little online shop? You can support me directly and get my latest book **earlier than it releases anywhere else**, along with special Inner Circle and full-series discounts.

You can also get extra story content that's not available on retailers, like bonus chapters and novelettes. My books are available in ebook, paperback, and audiobook format.

To buy from me directly go to: books.azaleaellis.com

Seeds of Chaos Series (Complete)

Book I: Gods of Blood and Bone

Book II: Gods of Rust and Ruin

Book III: Gods of Myth and Midnight

Book IV: Gods of Smoke and Stars—A Seeds of Chaos Adventure

Book V: Gods of Ash and Amber

A Practical Guide to Sorcery Series

Book I: A Conjuring of Ravens

Book II: A Binding of Blood

Book III: A Sacrifice of Light

Book IV: A Foreboding of Woe

Book V: A Cauldron of Bitterness

Book VI: A Builder of Dreams

<u>A Practical Guide to Sorcery Additional Stories (Available Exclusively from Azalea</u>

Book 2.1: Codename: Moonsable (Short Story)

Book 3.1: Good Advice (Bonus Chapter)

Book 3.2: Preventative Measures (Bonus Chapter)

Book 3.3: The Honeymoon Suite (Novelette)

Book 4.1: Harry Harold Had no Hands (Rhyme)

Book 4.2: Immovable Objects (Bonus Chapter)

Book 4.3: Recruitment Drive (Deleted Blooper Scene)

The Catastrophe Collector: A Practical Guide to Sorcery Spinoff Series

Book I: Larva

Book II: Bloom

More books may have been published since you purchased this copy. Find a complete list on AzaleaEllis.com

Here's a Quick Link to All my Books

www.azaleaellis.com/the-books/

ABOUT THE AUTHOR

I'm the type of person that often has a wacky, shocking, or silly–but totally *true*–story to tell about my life.

(Like the time my brother and I were chased through a secluded strip of woods in the middle of the city, for over a mile, by a naked man with an erection.)

(Or the time a trucker threw an open bottle of pee out his passenger side window without looking right as I was walking by. You can guess what I got splashed with.)

I've got an active imagination that tends toward the outrageous and the macabre, which led to me being voted "most likely to borrow someone else's car to transport a dead body."

I write books about things that interest and excite me. I'm always in the middle of teaching myself something new, and if I'm not overwhelmingly busy I tend to get antsy. I believe that the impossible is only so if we believe it to be so. Therefore, nothing is impossible.

If you'd like to get updates from me, both about my books and about what I'm up to from time to time, the newsletter is the place to be, as I tend to be very scarce on other social media.

https://www.azaleaellis.com/newsletter

For more information:
www.azaleaellis.com
author@azaleaellis.com